ER CRIMES

THE STEELE FILES, BOOKS 1-3

RADA JONES MD

APOLODOR PUBLISHING

OVERDOSE, MERCY and POISON were first published in 2019

This combined edition was published in 2021

ISBN: 978-1-955949-00-2

APOLODOR PUBLISHING

Cover design: GermanCreative@Fiverr

ALSO BY RADA JONES

STAY AWAY FROM MY ER, and Other Fun Bits of Wisdom

Wobbling Between Humor and Heartbreak

BECOMING K-9: A Bomb Dog's Memoir

(K-9 Heroes: Book 1)

BIONIC BUTTER: A Three-Pawed K-9 Hero

(K-9 Heroes: Book 2)

K-9 VIPER: A Veteran's Story

(K-9 Heroes: Book 3)

K-9 LOVELY: A Prison Puppy

(K-9 Heroes: Book 4)

ABOUT THE AUTHOR

About the author

Rada Jones was born in Transylvania, ten miles away from Dracula's Castle. Growing up amongst vampires taught her that while humans can be fickle, you can always trust books and dogs. So, she read every book she could get, including the phone book (too many characters, not enough action), and took home every stray she found, from dogs to frogs.

After immigrating to the US to join her husband, she spent years getting her medical education and working in the ER, but she still speaks like Dracula's cousin.

Rada, her husband Steve, and their German Shepherd Guinness live in a cozy Adirondack cabin supervised by a deaf cat named Paxil. They enjoy writing and hiking, and Paxil loves hiding in boxes.

To sign for updates and freebies or to get in touch, check out RadaJones.com.

OVERDOSE

AN ER PSYCHOLOGICAL THRILLER

PROLOGUE

Twenty-four-year-old Eric Weiss wasn't planning to die. He wasn't even looking for a high. He was just trying to sleep.

He died anyhow.

1

D r. Emma Steele was late. Only twenty minutes to the start of her shift. She pushed the pedal to the metal.

She could make it past the old sedan. *I can't stop. I've got only five more minutes to get there and save lives.*

She stopped anyhow.

She knocked at the window, shivering in her faded scrubs.

"Can I help?"

An old lady. Crying.

"I'm stuck."

"Start when I tell you. Go really slow."

She shoved her floor mat under the spinning wheel.

"Go now!"

She pushed. The crocs slid back.

Darn. Where's a man when you need one?

She took off her crocs and pushed again.

The car crawled forward, then accelerated, spitting snow in her face. *Gone.*

Emma shook off the snow and sloshed to her car in her red socks.

I'm frozen. I'm late. Ann's going to bitch again. Twelve hours to go.

Stupid.

She'd barely made it through the doors when the shit storm started.

"Code 99, Room 3, Emergency Department," roared the overhead speakers.

The scrubs streamed toward Room 3.

Wailing sirens pierced the air, then choked. The flashing lights went dark as the ambulance pulled in.

Emma hit the silver-plated door opener with the back of her fist and walked sideways into the sharp cold outside. Suzy, the EMT, glanced at her as she opened the ambulance door. Her dark-chocolate skin shone with sweat. *Good, deep chest compressions,* Emma thought. Their eyes met. Suzy's shoulders softened, but she continued compressions. Joe, her partner, unlocked the stretcher. They slid it off the ambulance with a bump and headed to Room 3. Suzy kept on the chest compressions while giving report.

"Found down... no known downtime... roommate started CPR... we arrived nine minutes later... no pulse, agonal breathing... couldn't establish an IV... got an IO in the left tibia... gave epi x 3..." Her voice came in bursts as she continued pushing down on the breathless chest while walking sideways.

The air smelled like sweat and dread. Joe kept bagging, but little air went in. *He's bagging too fast, and the mask seal is bad.*

"How long have you been doing CPR?"

"Nineteen minutes. We gave Narcan IO, 2 mg, with no result."

"Where was he?"

"In his bedroom downtown. In his bed."

"Any history?"

"No."

"Anything at the scene?"

"An empty bottle of Scotch. A pill bottle in somebody else's name. The other rig has it."

"How old is he?"

"Twenty-four."

"We have an ID?"

"Eric. Eric Weiss."

"Did you ever get a pulse?"

"No."

He looked asleep. There was no livor mortis, the dark patches of death, on his skin. Emma touched his neck, feeling for a pulse. None. His blond hair, darkened by sweat, covered his eyes. She brushed it away softly with her gloved hand. She gently parted his eyelid between her fingers. The iris was glazed, the black pupil a tiny peppercorn. *Opiates.*

"We're going to take care of you, Eric," she promised, though she knew he couldn't hear. It didn't matter. She said it for the team as much as she said it for him.

"Narcan, 2 mg." *Heroin, morphine, oxycodone, even methadone—all opioids relieve pain. They also give users a high. That's what gets them addicted. Enough opioid will put them to sleep. More than that will stop their breathing and kill them. Narcan is the only antidote that can reverse opioids. If that's what this is.*

"IV access?"

"Working on it," Judy said, without looking up. She knelt near his right elbow. *She's a whiz with IVs. If she can't get it in, nobody can.*

"IO drill." Brenda went after it.

The kid lay on the ER stretcher, his chest rising and falling about two inches with every compression. Suzy stood back at the end of the line waiting for her turn to perform CPR again. She had delivered him, but she couldn't leave him. Still no blood pressure. For the lack of a heartbeat, the shattered line of the EKG danced with the rhythm of the compressions. Tom, the RT, respiratory therapist, took over the airway. His left hand pulled the livid face into the mask while his right squeezed the airbag. The escaping air made obnoxious farting sounds. *Poor mask seal.*

"How's he bagging?" Emma asked.

"Not great."

"Epi, then bicarb, then another 2 of Narcan." Emma looked at Sal, the ER pharmacist. "Let's get ready to intubate."

"What do you want for intubation?"

"Sux maybe, no sedation. He's out already."

"Succinylcholine," he confirmed. "How much?"

Emma looked the kid up and down. Skinny and not too tall. Seventy kilos maybe? "One hundred twenty."

"Epi given."

Emma moved to the head of the bed to assess the airway. *The neck is mobile and slender. No scars. Good strong chin—three fingers to Adam's apple. I should have enough room to get the tongue out of the way to expose the airway.* She lubricated, then loaded the metal stylet curved as a question mark into the soft plastic ET tube. She checked the suction. The oxygen saturation didn't read at all. *It doesn't matter now, does it? He doesn't bag well. He needs an airway. Simple as that.*

"Second 2 mg of Narcan given."

"Prepare a third, and one more of epi in 5."

"That's 6 of Narcan, yes?" Sal asked. Two mg of Narcan was a full dose. Six was a lot.

"It won't hurt him any," she said. Narcan didn't do much to the body, except for throwing it into acute withdrawal. "Better in withdrawal than dead."

Sal nodded.

"I'm ready," Emma said.

She lifted the blade of the video laryngoscope and held it gently in her left hand with the tips of her fingers. The RT removed the mask covering the mouth. Emma pried the kid's teeth open with her right hand, then slid the plastic blade around the tongue until the blade tip came into full view on the screen. Secretions, a mass of white foam, blocked her view of the airway. *Opiates, of course, probably pulmonary edema. That's why he wouldn't bag.* She slid the blade forward another half-inch, then lifted the tongue with it until the epiglottis, the pink stalactite of tissue protecting the airway, fell into full view in the middle upper part of the screen, where it belonged. *Textbook, but for the damn secretions,* she thought, her eyes glued to the airway.

"Suction."

The RT slapped the Yankauer, the plastic cylinder attached to the suction tube in her right hand. She slid it through the open mouth, suctioning secretions and moving the tongue away to uncover the vocal cords. She removed the Yankauer and placed it on the stretcher, under the kid's shoulder, to free up her right hand.

"Tube."

The tube landed in her open right hand. She slid it in past the tongue and the blade. She looked inside the mouth until the tip went out of view, and then returned her gaze to the video screen.

"Hold CPR and check for a pulse."

She slid the tube further in, aiming for the white triangle between the vocal cords, the gateway to the trachea, the windpipe. The slanted tip of the tube got caught in one of the arytenoids, the curly little cartilages sheltering the cords. She pulled it back a quarter of an inch and then pushed it forward, only to have it catch again. *We're running out of time.* She pulled the tube out once more and gently twisted it left less than a quarter turn, then pushed it forward again. This time it appeared just between the arytenoids. Another half-inch forward and the tube slid into the trachea, where it belonged.

"Stylet."

The RT pulled out the rigid stylet. That allowed the soft ET tube to take the sharp turn into the airway. Emma pushed it in until the balloon went out of sight.

"Balloon."

The RT pushed in the air from the 10 cc syringe attached to the balloon. The balloon filled with air and sealed the airway. The RT secured the tube. The airway was safe.

"Restart CPR."

"Bilateral lung sounds. Nothing over the stomach."

"Oxygen sat?"

"Can't get it. No waveform."

"No pulse."

"We have a twenty in the right AC," Judy said.

"One more dose of Narcan. Then bicarb."

The RT took over the tube. "Twenty-four at the lip," he said, and the nurse recorder wrote it down.

"Fourth dose of Narcan in."

The RT suctioned the bloody foam inside the tube. Then again.

More CPR. Each tired provider took his place at the back of the line to rest and start over.

"Bicarb given."

"How long have we been doing this?" Emma asked.

"Thirty-four minutes," the recorder answered.

"So we have unknown downtime, then bystander CPR for ten minutes, then EMT CPR, and Narcan x 1 and epi x 3 via IO, then CPR x 34 minutes and Narcan x 3 and epi x 2.

"And bicarb x 1," Sal said.

"Let's give one more. And one more of Narcan."

"That's 10 mg of Narcan altogether."

"Yes." Emma looked at the dead body on the stretcher. *He's somebody's son. Somebody's lover. Somebody's life will never be the same again after today.* "How's he bagging?"

"Better," the RT said.

"Narcan 2 mg dose 5 given."

Emma looked at her team. "Anybody have any more ideas?" *They need to have a chance to air out any issues before it's too late. This one's going to be hard for all of us.*

Silence. They had done all they could.

The beeps of the monitors and the whoosh of air flowing in and out of the bony chest made the silence feel even more deadly.

"If there are no more ideas…"

ITSY BITSY SPIDER

I gots the shakes. Bad.
I need a fix.
"Look in the ambulance bay," he said.
I look.
I find it. A red bag with a skull on it.
I open it. It's my fix.
A foot-long brown paper parcel, slim. Heavy.
A picture. Car number on the back.
"That's the ticket to your next fix," he said.
"How do I tell you I'm done?"
He laughs.
That laugh.
It gives me goose bumps.
"I'll know."
I shiver.
I go looking for the car.

2

———

Emma looked around the room one more time.

"If there are no more ideas…"

"The CO_2 is up!" The RT's voice, high-pitched with excitement, shattered the silence.

It's up indeed. Up to 35. The first sign of success. Pulse, maybe?

"Stop CPR."

In the silence of the room, the monitor held the beat like a metronome—125 beats/minute, his own. The heart was back.

"Blood pressure?

"Checking."

"Start an epi drip. Whatever pressure we have, it's going to fall as soon as the epi wears off. Let's get a Narcan drip. Get me the intensivist."

"You want an EKG?"

"Yes, please."

The heart is back. But after so long without a pulse, is the brain dead? She looked into the frozen blue eyes. The pupils were still pinpoints. *At least they're not fixed and dilated. He's got a chance. We did the best we could.*

The pressure was good. The pulse was holding.

"Oxygen sat 100 percent."

"Let's go down on the oxygen. Chest X-ray, please, OG tube, Foley. The whole nine yards. You all know the drill." She looked each of them in the eye. "Good job, team. You did well."

They smiled at her. "You too, Dr. Steele."

She smiled back.

With a well-practiced move, she took off her soiled gloves and dropped them in the trash. *No bad news today.* Speaking to the family was harder than running the code, especially if the patient was young, or even worse, a child. *It's hard even when they're one hundred years old and demented. They're all some-body's—mother, wife, child. Emotions run deep—grief, despair, guilt. Facing them is hard. It's easier to channel them into anger and lash out at the ER staff.*

"You know him?" Brenda asked.

"No."

"He's Joey's grandson. He's a nurse in the ICU."

Emma shuddered. That was awful news. Joey, their elderly clerk, had retired last year. He was an old friend and a good man. The kid being one of their own nurses didn't help either. Emma hoped she was wrong. *Maybe it's not an overdose,* she thought, but she knew better.

She went to the bathroom to steal a private moment. She washed her hands and face in cold water, rinsing away the sweat and the sting in her eyes. She looked in the mirror at the tired woman looking back. *Pale as a ghost.* She took her lipstick from her coat pocket and put on some, trying to look less dead.

I may not look any better, but I feel better. It's like donning a shield. They don't need to know how weary I am. She straightened her back, took a deep breath, and went back to work.

3

———————

Back at her desk, Emma logged on to check the board. Nobody new, just the same headache in Room 11 and the fever in Room 5. She checked her iPhone. *Nothing from Taylor. Should have been home hours ago. She must be in another funk.* She texted another question mark.

Her neck ached. She rubbed it hard, her fingers digging into the achy knot just right of her spine. *I wish I could cut it out.* She grabbed her stethoscope and threw it over her right shoulder, heading to the headache in 11. Room 11 was one of the few double rooms they had left. Her colleague, Dr. Crump, Kurt to his friends of which she was no longer one, was already there. He was over-dressed, as usual, in a well-cut suit and silk tie. He looked polished and expensive as he talked to the other patient in the double room, a heavy young woman with stringy purple hair falling over her tattoos. He sat on the corner of her bed. *He really shouldn't be doing that, not in this climate of sexual aggression and hyper-alertness to anything looking like it. Not with this patient. Her looks scream borderline personality disorder. They're as reliable as ticking bombs.*

His voice was soothing and low as he touched her hand. Emma considered letting him have the room to finish. She could go see the fever in Room 5 instead, rather than interfere with his patient encounter. The headache was texting and eating chips. She'd be fine for a few more minutes.

Kurt looked up. Their eyes met. His softness vanished. His left masseter, the little muscle at the bottom of his clenched jaw, twitched. *He's still angry. After all this time, he's still angry.*

They got along well in the beginning. He helped her learn the ropes. He'd taught her who to trust and who not to, where to go when she needed things done, and who to avoid. He'd been invaluable to her in her first weeks after residency. This rural ED in the middle of nowhere was nothing like the trauma center she'd trained at. Here, resources were scarce. She had to learn to do without. Specialties that she'd taken for granted were not available. The best way to care for the sickest patients was to transfer them. They had to go by ambulance, via ferry, over the lake to the regional trauma center. The ones who needed to go were always those fixing to die—septic babies, crashing traumas, bad strokes, risky deliveries.

Ambulance was king. Kurt was the EMS medical director. He provided education and oversight to the EMTs and paramedics. He loved it. They loved him. Until the day when things went bad.

All the ambulances came straight to the ED to offload their patients. It didn't matter if there were sicker patients who'd been waiting for hours and the ambulance was bringing over a hangnail. The ambulance got the available bed.

That made no sense to Emma. *They should get triaged like everybody else. The whole point of triage is to decide who's the sickest and needs to be seen first.* She talked to Kurt and tried to change the protocols. The change would also curb ambulance overuse by the "frequent flyers," the regulars who knew the rules and took advantage of them.

Kurt disagreed. He wanted his ambulances free as soon as possible. The EMTs had to offload immediately and head back out. "They don't have time to sit around waiting for the triage nurse. Drop them off and go; that's the way."

"They still have to wait to give report to a nurse. The triage nurse will see them faster."

Kurt didn't buy it. He shook his head, clenched his fists in his tight pants, and scowled. "Getting the stretcher into the triage area is complicated. It's difficult, and it takes time."

"The triage nurse can meet them in the ambulance bay. That's going to save time."

"That makes no sense."

She insisted. He got angry. He'd been there longer; he had administrative experience; he was a man.

He may not say it, but she knew damn well that she was only a woman in a man's world. From the patients who called her "Nurse," after she'd just introduced herself as Dr. Steele, to the CEO who called her "Honey" instead of Doctor, and to Kurt here, they all made sure she wouldn't forget that she was just a woman.

She couldn't talk him into it. She couldn't convince Dr. Kenneth Leep, the ED director, either. Maybe because he was Kurt's friend and mentor. Maybe because he just didn't see the point. Maybe because she was wrong, even though she'd seen this work at one of Boston's best-known hospitals. She failed.

Status quo. The ambulances continued to drop their patients in the ED stretchers no matter what else was going on in the department. Nothing changed. Until one day.

That day, Mrs. Gail Rose, who suffered from anxiety, fibromyalgia, chronic pain, and depression, felt lonely. She needed Dilaudid, her drug of choice. She was one of the regulars. She may have been drug seeking, or maybe not. Nobody but her knew for sure. She was distressed and disturbed, and she knew better than to drive herself to the ED to wait for hours. She called 911 and got an ambulance, her much-needed Dilaudid, and the last open bed.

In the meantime, Mr. Tom Curtis sat patiently in the waiting room. He was sixty-nine and healthy. He was there for indigestion. It had started earlier in the day, as he dug a hole to bury Mocha, his beloved eleven-year-old chocolate Lab.

Mr. Curtis had been waiting for five hours when he suddenly fell to the ground. Joann, his high school sweetheart and his wife of fifty-one years, screamed. The triage nurse called the charge nurse, who pulled Mrs. Rose's stretcher out to make room for Mr. Curtis. They coded him for forty-five minutes, but he stayed as dead as his beloved Mocha. He went to the morgue in a covered stretcher, allowing Mrs. Rose back to her room. Then the questions started. Why? Who? How?

That unfortunate incident, as Kurt called it, caused a lot of discussion about triage protocols—and other things. Somebody remembered Emma trying to change the system and Kurt and Ken disagreeing. That person reminded Kurt about it and also told Administration.

That was not good news.

Mr. Curtis's family sued the hospital for five million dollars for their losses, including lost work and income opportunities for Mr. Curtis, loss of emotional support for his children and grandchildren, and loss of consortium for his wife. Whether Mrs. Curtis's sex life was worth five million dollars or not was debatable. The hospital had to settle for an undisclosed sum of money, and the administration was not pleased. Neither were Ken and Kurt.

Kurt, as always, talked his way out of it, but he resigned the EMS director position and he never forgot. Since that day he had only spoken to Emma when he had to. That was unfortunate, but there was nothing more she could do.

That had been years ago. She wished he'd forget it. He didn't. She wanted to walk out and leave him the room, but she couldn't. It would look like she was afraid of him. *No can do.* She gave him a big smile, then pulled the silly beige curtain between the beds. It was meant to give the patients some privacy, but it did nothing to stop the sound. Unless they needed hearing aids, everybody could hear clearly whatever everybody else said. That made for a good time when people described their sex lives, their discharges, and their bowel movements.

There were no chairs, so Emma pulled out the red hazard disposal bin and sat on it. That made the patients more comfortable and gave her back a little rest.

Kurt glared at her and left. Emma smiled, introduced herself, and started asking questions while proceeding with her evaluation. *She looks comfortable; there's no facial droop; she's moving all extremities; no slurred speech, no increased work of breathing, no fever, no confusion, good eye contact.*

"What were you doing when the headache started? Did it come on suddenly, or did it start gradually and then get worse?" Emma asked, trying to rule out the dangerous headache diagnoses—stroke, meningitis, glaucoma, bleeds.

"I was watching *Jeopardy*. It's just a migraine. I've had migraines for years, and this one is no different." The woman rubbed her right temple with her thumb, massaging away the pain.

That was good news. As Emma proceeded to the neuro exam, her phone vibrated in her pocket. She hoped it was Taylor. Her daughter had been having a hard time since she'd broken up with her boyfriend, Tom, a few months ago. Taylor had come home one day and said, "No more Tom. I don't want to hear his name anymore."

She refused to answer any questions. Emma had wondered if he'd ditched her and Taylor was too proud to admit it. *She hates appearing vulnerable and would rather drown than ask for help.* Her grades started falling, and she became even moodier. She was barely, if ever, home. Emma tried to speak to her again and again, but Taylor would have none of it—she seldom bothered to take her eyes off her phone.

Minerva, Emma's old friend and Taylor's pediatrician, wasn't worried. "That's what happened to Mai. She'd been a wonderful child. We got along great until she turned thirteen and became a monster. Five years of dealing with her felt like fifty. When she turned eighteen, the monster disappeared and Mai came back. It's the raging hormones. It's going to be the same with Taylor."

Minerva is wrong. Emma and Taylor had never gotten along, not even when Taylor was a baby. She'd always preferred her father. When Emma and Victor divorced, Taylor broke up with Emma for good. She didn't speak to her for months. Even now, years later, when the bygones were bygones and Victor and Emma were good friends, Taylor avoided her and ignored her. Something was missing in their relationship. It always had been. Moreover, Taylor was in trouble. Emma didn't know why, but she knew that something was wrong. *Really wrong.*

She shrugged and got back to the present. The headache looked fine. Her neuro exam was on point. Her story was reassuring. Emma decided to skip any further testing. *I'll treat her and street her.*

SPIDER

I'm cold. Been looking for hours.
I find the car in the far parking lot.
A nice one.
I look inside.
A jacket. Books. Not much.
I try the door. It opens.
Stupid!
I slide inside. I open the glove compartment.
Registration?
Yep.
Got his name.
Doing good.

4

Emma stretched her back. It hurt. She wished she had taken her Motrin. She sighed. The smell of freshly ground coffee hit her, immediately followed by the foul smell of human feces. Code Brown. Somebody didn't make it to the bathroom. *They say ground coffee absorbs the smell. Not really; you just get coffee that smells like shit. Or the other way 'round.* She held her breath until she reached her desk.

An EKG, somebody's heart tracing, sat on the keyboard. She frowned. *The EKG shouldn't be here; they should have brought it to me to read.* It looked OK. The patient was young, only 35. It made a heart attack less likely. They'd call her if he was sick. She signed it and forgot it.

She logged in again, going through the multiple obligatory steps of swiping her ID, putting in her password, her ID number, her PIN, her mother's maiden name, her shoe and bra size, and God only knows what else before she was finally able to place orders for the migraine she'd just seen.

She took a phone call—a referral from the Urgent Care down the road. They were sending a patient over. *What are these urgent care places good for if they can't even deal with a young healthy urinary tract infection? I hope they'll at least send the lab results with her so we don't have to repeat them and charge her again.* She re-paged the intensivist for the kid with the OD, then checked the labs for the sepsis in Room 2. *He's old and sick. He needs antibiotics. Now.* She stood up and unbent, then walked to Sal's desk.

Sal sat with his back extra-straight, as if he were playing the piano. He was the son of musicians. His father played the cello; his mother the violin. He was supposed to become a musician but somehow ended up being a pharmacist. He was smart, pleasant, and single. *I wonder if he's gay.* His long slim fingers danced on the keyboard in a graceful fury, as if he were playing Rachmaninoff, but instead of a concerto he produced the med list for the demented patient in Room 5.

"Sal, could you put in antibiotics for Room 2, for sepsis, please?"

"Sure. Do we know the source?"

"I'm thinking pneumonia, his sats are low. He was in the hospital last month with the same."

"Of course. Dr. Steele, do you have a moment?"

She didn't, not really, but if Sal needed her, she would. She drew up a chair.

"What's up?"

"That code, earlier today… the overdose…"

She looked at him, waiting.

"He got a lot of Narcan."

So that's what's bothering him. It's bothering me too.

"He did."

"I've never given that much Narcan to one patient at one time."

"Neither have I."

"He did look like he responded to it in the end."

"Either that or we were lucky. But I agree, it looks as if it was the Narcan."

"Why?"

"I'm not sure. I read an article about a slew of poorly responsive overdoses in New Hampshire. They thought it was a batch of heroine mixed with fentanyl. Then there was another one, apparently carfentanyl, in Ohio. In some cases, they needed up to twenty-five milligrams to respond."

"That's exactly what I was thinking," Sal said, his face lightening. They were on the same page. "Fentanyl is one hundred times more potent than morphine. It binds tighter to the receptors, so you need more Narcan to make it work."

"That makes sense."

"This isn't the first case like this. There was another one a couple of days ago."

"Who was the doc?"

"Dr. Umber."

Dr. Richard Umber, a slightly older and taller replica of Tom Cruise, stopped by. "Are you taking my name in vain?" he asked smiling, showing his left dimple.

"I was telling Dr. Steele about the overdose you had the other day."

"Which one? They're dropping like flies up here."

Dr. Umber was new to the area. He was a *locum tenens*, a traveling physician working a few shifts here, a few shifts there, as needed. He'd only been with them for a few months, on and off, but he was pleasant, competent, and terribly good-looking.

"The elderly woman in Room 2, the one you gave multiple doses of Narcan before she came through."

"That wasn't an overdose. It was a heart attack," Umber said. "I gave the Narcan just in case—you never know—but it didn't do anything."

"But she did get a pulse after the third dose?"

Dr. Umber dismissed the idea with a flick of his right hand. The red stone of his school ring gleamed like a drop of blood. "Yeah, but that was also after the fourth dose of epi and the second dose of bicarb and the calcium and the magnesium and the CPR. You don't know that it was the Narcan. It could have been any or all of the others. It probably was."

Sal shrugged. Dr. Umber was right; it could have been anything. It could have been just her luck.

"Did you send a drug screen?" Emma asked.

Umber shook his head. "We never even got a urine. She didn't make it through the code. What's the point? Dead is dead." He shrugged and walked away with the smooth, low walk of a big cat.

"It sure looked like an OD though," Sal said.

Emma didn't know what to think. *Sal is awesome, but he's only a pharmacist. Umber is an experienced emergency doc with lots of clinical experience. He must have coded hundreds.*

"Maybe her heart couldn't take the stress," she said. "Or maybe it was an overdose. The one today surely looked like one. We could have a bad batch here, Fentanyl mixed into whatever they're using."

"It makes sense, doesn't it? I read that they make it cheaply in China, and it's easy to bring over since it's so potent that a little goes a long way. They mix it with all sorts of adulterants to sell it. Maybe they put in a little too much, or maybe our folks aren't used to it and they don't know how much to use and then end up with unintentional overdoses."

"It makes sense. I'll send his urine for a drug screen and see what shows up."

"I'll make sure we get some extra Narcan in here," Sal said. "I had to run down to pharmacy for the last two doses. We shouldn't need to do that on top of everything else."

"Thanks, Sal. I'll run that drug screen, and I'll let you know."

"I'll call the Poison Control Center. I have a friend working there; I'll have a chat with her."

Emma stood up and straightened. *It hurts. I wish this shift was over so I could go home and find out about Taylor. And rest. And have a drink. Four more hours.*

She looked at Sal staring at his screen, his back straight, his slim hands flying over the keyboard.

"Sal, why did you quit the piano?"

His eyes widened in surprise. "I didn't quit. I still play."

"But you dropped it as a career when you decided to be a pharmacist rather than a musician. Why?"

Sal looked at his hands, then back at her. "I wanted to make the world a better place. I thought that as a pharmacist I could help people."

"Musicians help people too. They bring beauty and solace to the world."

"Yes. But people have to first be healthy and free of pain to enjoy music and beauty."

Emma nodded.

Sal asked, "Isn't that why you chose to be a doctor? To help people?"

She laughed. "No, not me. That's what they all say to get into medical school, but that's bullshit. If I weren't here to care for these patients, somebody else would. Somebody faster and better than me. Nobody is irreplaceable; I sure am not."

"It's hard to believe."

"Thank you. That's nice to hear. I became a doctor for the challenge. I enjoy the thrill of finding the answers, the search for a diagnosis. Like a detective looking for the killer, I love the chase. I also love the procedures. I didn't do it for them," she said, nodding toward the hallways packed with stretchers after all the rooms had been filled. "I did it for me."

"Well, lucky them, anyhow. And lucky us."

"Thank you." Emma smiled. *I can use a little love.*

SPIDER

I'm sitting on the bench by the door.
Waiting.
People go in. People come out. None of them is him.
I'm cold. I can't feel my toes. Gone for half an hour now.
My fingers too.
I tighten my fists in my pockets.
My coat's wet. Not warm. Nothing's warm.
I shiver.
It's been an hour now.
"He'll be done in half an hour," they said an hour ago.
"I wanna thank him," I said. "I wanna thank him properly for what he did for me."
I show them my package. Long, white, spruced with a golden bow.
It's a gift.
They don't know what's inside. I do.
The fat one with the bad teeth smiles.
"He'll be out soon. I'll tell him you're waiting."
"No, no, don't. I wanna surprise him."
"I see."
She doesn't.
I wait until my fists can't open anymore.
I'm so frozen I couldn't open the box to get the knife.
Tonight's not gonna work.
I head out.
I'll be back tomorrow.

5

———————

Emma got home past midnight. She was frozen and tired. Her neck was killing her. Her bag was heavy with her uneaten lunch and her never-without essentials: scalpel, rubber gloves, flashlight, an alligator forceps to remove tiny things from narrow spaces, a tourniquet to stop bleeding, a few other bits and pieces, and a couple of her favorite medical books. She dropped the bag on the corner chair that used to be Victor's.

She straightened her back, grateful for the warmth embracing her. She'd been cold ever since she left home in the morning. The air-conditioning in the ED was the only thing that never stopped working, summer or winter.

She looked at the pile of dirty dishes in the sink. She didn't know if she was mad or happy. *The kid is home and safe. The sloth could have cleaned the kitchen after herself. I should wake her up to deal with her mess... but do I really want to argue with her now?*

She looked at the wine rack. This was the best moment of her day, choosing her wine and enjoying it. Waking Taylor would be a fight. She had no more fight left in her tonight. She shrugged. It wasn't worth it.

She went to the rack to choose a bottle. *Chianti? Too rough. Pinot noir? Too weak. Sancerre? Too cold. Malbec? Perfect. It's going to be a Malbec night. That will warm me up nicely.* Yesterday's bottle of Shiraz was in the trash.

She took a long sip, then another. The wine was dry and smooth. It did smell like dry cherries, just like the label said, but she didn't taste any leather. *Just as well. I don't care much for leather in my wine, only in my shoes.* It warmed her inside as she finished the glass. The tension in her shoulders eased.

She started running a scalding hot bath, poured herself another glass, and then turned on the news for company. She checked her email. Work related mostly, a few beautiful Russian brides, an amazing male enhancement cream, a Nigerian philanthropist offering her money. Somebody asking her to save the planet.

I'd love to help, especially with the polar bears, but saving the planet is too tall an order for me the way I'm feeling these days. I'm lucky if I can help Taylor.

She refilled her glass and walked to Taylor's room. Syncopated hip-hop music was coming through the door, the bass loud enough to make her insides shake. She knocked. No answer. She knocked again, then opened the door. Taylor was asleep, her dark hair falling over her face, a heavy book resting on her stomach. Emma picked it up—it was the second Harry Potter, the book that Taylor kept returning to whenever she was upset.

She sat on the chair by the bed and watched her strange, awful, beautiful daughter's slow and steady breathing, her heart torn between love and pain. *She's home, in her bed, safe, at least for tonight.* She remembered the kid she'd coded earlier today—no, it was yesterday by now; it felt like an eternity ago.

His urine had tested positive for fentanyl. Sal had called poison control. They agreed that the fentanyl was a possibility, but had nothing else to offer. Emma hoped the police would do better.

A detective had come to the ED to speak to her. He showed her the pill bottle they had collected at his home. *That would explain why there were no track marks. He wasn't injecting, he was using pills.* The bottle was under his roommate's name, and it was empty.

He'd made it to the ICU. *Is he going to pull through? Who knows? His brain was starved of oxygen for God knows how long after his heart stopped. At least he could be an organ donor,* Emma thought, with the pragmatic ruthlessness that working in the ED teaches you.

She felt sorry for him and his family. There were so many that she felt sorry for every day, so many who could use his kidneys, his liver, his heart, his lungs, his corneas, his skin, and even bones, and live a better life.

She still hoped he was going to pull through. She was invested in him after that code. She had a daughter who could have been in his place. Fortunately, she wasn't. Not yet.

She turned off the lights, turned down the music, closed the door gently, and went back to the sofa where her friend, the Malbec, was waiting.

She remembered the bath.

Too late.

6

Dr. Kurt Crump hadn't had a good day. As a matter of fact, he hadn't had a good day in a while. Working alongside Emma Steele, that know-it-all, didn't help any. Seeing the nurses swoon over her drove him nuts. "Dr. Steele said… Dr. Steele did… Dr. Steele doesn't think…" Who the hell cared what Dr. Steele thought?

The whole day had sucked, from the drug seekers lying to him, to the demented patient the family wanted resuscitated at any cost. They'd worked on him for an hour before sending him to the ICU to die. Then this Umber guy giving him lip for the sign-out, after he'd stayed two hours over, just because he signed out that non-ambulatory back pain that he couldn't send home.

He walked to the far end of the parking lot where he'd parked his red Audi A7 and unlocked the door. The sight of the beautiful, cream-colored, soft leather seats and the new-car smell should have made him feel better. They didn't.

The radio was on. Madonna's "Material Girl" startled him. He turned her off. He wasn't in the mood for music. He didn't care about the news, either. He really didn't want to hear anything. After fourteen hours spent in the ER chaos, his ears rang with the beeps of the monitors, the screaming patients, the crackling speakers summoning him somewhere. He could do with some silence for a change.

There wasn't going to be any peace at home. He thought about going else-where, anywhere. Sheila had been in a foul mood lately; she wasn't going to be any better tonight when he got home three hours late. He hadn't called from work. He didn't have another fight in him. He didn't want to hear her endless questions: "Where are you? Who are you with? Why are you late? When are you leaving? Are you coming directly home?"

He'd texted her: "Leaving now," then turned off the phone. He didn't expect a pleasant reception.

He was right. She'd been crying; he knew it the moment he opened the door and saw her, eyes red and swollen, the smudged mascara making her look like the Joker. She gave him a death stare.

"Where have you been?"

"Where do I look like I've been?" He pointed to his clothes, fresh this morning, now crumpled and stained from a long day of wear. There was some vomit on the trousers and maybe blood on the left sleeve. What else? He didn't want to know.

"Your shift was over three hours ago."

"Tell that to the patients, will you?" he snapped, slamming the bathroom door behind him.

He dropped his shirt in the laundry basket, did the same with his pants and his underwear and everything else he wore except for the tie. It was his favorite Armani tie. The deep blue of the peacock feathers brought out the blue of his eyes, Kayla said.

He looked at it, smelled it, and dropped it in the garbage bin. He took a long, hot shower to wash away the misery, the pain, the dirt, and the rest of this trying day, one of many. The scalding hot water felt good and clean. Liberating. He forced himself to turn off the shower. He dried himself with an old blue towel, put on his well-worn navy flannel pajamas, and resigned himself to facing his fate.

She was still seething.

"Why did you have to stay three hours past your shift?"

"Because I had to finish seeing and dispoeing my patients." He poured himself a glass of Redbreast Irish Whiskey, no water, no ice. The smooth burn of the Single Pot Still in his mouth helped him feel better.

"Why didn't you sign them out?"

"I did, but I had to see them first. They'd been there for hours."

"I don't believe you."

She choked with sobs, her mouth fish-ugly as it curved down. He looked past her at their wedding picture, a long-lost time when she was pretty and smiling.

They were happy.

That was long ago.

"You went to see her," she wailed, hugging her knees. Her brown hair with dirty white roots fell over her face.

She looks like an old witch, he thought, and took another sip.

"I didn't. I'm coming from work."

"Then you saw her there!" she wailed again. "Stop lying and at least admit it. Be a man!"

He wondered what he could say to make this stop.

Nothing, probably. She'd go on and on until she ran out of steam.

After her second miscarriage, she had become pathologically jealous. She felt that she was worthless if she couldn't bear his children. She thought that any other woman could replace her. She became more and more demanding. She called him at work when she knew damn well that he didn't have time for this. She sat at the same side of the table with him at restaurants to see who he was looking at. She drove to the hospital to see if his car was still in the parking lot.

He'd tried to reassure her. He had put up with her demands, hoping she'd finally understand that he wasn't cheating on her. He wasn't interested in other women.

It didn't help.

Then he met Kayla.

Kayla was young and pretty. Kayla was funny, and she never cried. She had lustrous chestnut hair falling to her waist and the figure of a runway model.

Kayla liked him back. She never asked for anything. She was happy with what he could give her, which, between work and Sheila, wasn't much. Kayla made him smile. With her, he felt like a man still worth looking at.

Kayla was everything that Sheila no longer was. His heart soared at the thought of her. But she was far away, and Sheila was here.

He took the last sip of whiskey and held it on his tongue to let the heat seep in. He swallowed and took a deep breath. He sat on the couch beside Sheila and forced himself to put his arms around her. He held her quietly.

He thought about her, about Kayla, about Emma. He thought about his old patient who had died earlier, demented and alone.

He held her shaking body until the sobs stopped.

"Let's go to bed."

He lay awake for a long time, thinking about the mess their lives had become. This wasn't what they planned. She had been young and pretty and full of hope.

They had met at an art exhibition. He showed his spring watercolors. She displayed pottery, in curious, inexplicable shapes. He gathered his courage and asked her what the penis-looking thing was.

"Why, a cup of course!"

Her laughter had gone straight to his heart. He'd taken her to dinner, then to bed. They had never looked back.

Is it too late for us?

SPIDER

"He's not on."

They're lying. "He told me to come back tonight. He said he'll be on after 3," I say, smiling like I like them.

Fuck them. Fuck them all.

"He's not," says the fat one with the droopy mouth. She rechecks the papers.

"No, not tonight. You've got it wrong."

I shrink under her gaze. I take out the package. I show it to her.

"I got this for him."

The package is tired. I've been carrying it around. I got it squished under my arm so many times it's shaped like my armpit. It's still white-like, but the bow's about to fall off.

It looks secondhand. It is. I found it in a garbage bin. It smells it too, like smoke and booze and sweat.

Never mind, the knife inside it is sharp. I checked. I sliced through a tree branch with a flick of the wrist. It's an old hunting knife shaped like a fish, its scaly handle growing into a long, smooth, solid blade thick enough to cut through ribs.

I'm the hunter. I'm gonna get my kill.

Tonight or tomorrow, I'm gonna get him.

I make myself small. They like it when you're small. Makes them feel big and strong. I bend my good right knee a bit more and slump my shoulders.

"Got it wrong then. Sorry. When's he on?"

She looks at me, her sharp eyes getting soft. I don't matter; I'm nothing to worry about. I'm small and old and dirty. She's sorry for me.

"I can't tell you," she says. "It's against the rules."

I rub my left eye, the one with the infection. It tears. "I just wanna thank him," I say. "He helped my son; he's a great doctor." I look down and make myself smaller. "I have a gift for him."

I show her the box again.

She breaks. She looks at the papers and says, "Tomorrow. Tomorrow at 9. He'll be here."

I rub my eye and thank her. I leave slowly, limping on the left like I always do.

I don't rush until I'm out in the dark and I know she can't see me. They can't see me. Tomorrow at nine.

7

———————

Emma scrutinized the X-ray, sliding the magnifier over the lungs, looking for the markings to go all the way to the edge. They did.

The screams came first. "You motherfuckers! I'll have my lawyer arrest you all!"

Then came the stretcher. The man handcuffed to it was squirming and spitting. Two policemen and two sweating EMTs were struggling to hold him down. The uniformed security guards by Room 8 were ready, gloves on, Tasers on their hips.

Emma looked up to see Judy following the stretcher, soft restraints under one arm, blue paper scrubs under the other.

"Mine?" Emma asked.

"Yes."

Emma followed.

"Let me go, you assholes!" the man shouted. His navy sweater was torn. His bruised left elbow peeked out. His heavy, off-black pants were unzipped. The crotch was wet. No underwear. Boots, no socks. Not enough clothes for the sharp cold.

His purple left eye was swollen shut. The blood around his mouth had dried, but more bloody spit sprayed out with every curse.

"Let's get him a mask. What's his story?"

The black officer holding down his right leg used to be one of their EMTs.

"Good to see you, Dr. Steele. We found him asleep in the doorway at the dollar store. He smells like he's had a few drinks and he looks like he's been in a fight, but he won't answer our questions. Tried to bite us on the way. He spat at the EMTs. Didn't get them though."

"Do we know him? Any history?"

"I'm getting it," Judy said. "He's been here before." She bent over to cover his mouth with the mask. He tried to bite her. She pulled back. He missed.

He launched into another stream of slurred obscenities, struggling to break free. The EMTs held him down. A dozen gloved hands lifted him to drop him on the ER stretcher.

"Five and 2?" Judy asked.

"Great idea," Emma said, "and 25 of Benadryl."

Judy nodded and went to get it. The "5 and 2," the classic "agitation cocktail," 5 mg of Haldol, an antipsychotic, and 2 mg of Ativan, a sedative, could be given in one smooth shot, through the clothes if need be, to sedate agitated patients and keep them, and the staff, safe. *I don't know many things that work better than Haldol, thank God and whoever invented it, and the Ativan is a nice touch. They should make this guy feel much better. Me too.*

"You need help?"

Emma looked up into the smiling, water-colored eyes of Dr. Dick Umber. His blinding-white coat and his perfect steel-gray hair showing off his Caribbean tan made Emma feel like a shabby mess. *How on earth does he do that? It's like nobody ever spits at him! That's unreal!* She swallowed her envy and smiled back.

"I'm good, thank you." He was handsome, helpful, and smelled bitter-green, like wild carnations. He was the best-looking thing she'd seen all day.

"You'll have to scan him, you know. He looks like he's gotten into some trauma."

"Yes, I know." She was irked at being treated like an intern, but he was right, of course. The guy was drunk, belligerent, and hard to evaluate. Putting him through the scanner was going to be a challenge, but she didn't need him to tell her that.

"I had a guy like that in Colorado Springs. He'd hit a tree skiing. No helmet. We all thought he was drunk. He was acting so drunk that he could barely speak. His blood alcohol was zero, but he had a head bleed the size of an orange in his frontal lobe. He was so altered that we had to tube him to get him in the scanner."

Emma wasn't looking forward to that, but she might have to do it if the Haldol didn't work. The patient needed to be perfectly still for a couple of minutes to get the scan. Not likely.

"I may have to do that. Let's see how this works."

"What would you use?"

"Ketamine, probably."

"For a head injury?"

So he's old school and not up to date. Who'd have thunk? Ketamine, also known as Special K or K-hole by its many fans, was often used to sedate horses—and people. A cousin to PCP, maligned for decades and forbidden in people with head injuries for fear that it would increase the intracranial pressure and squish the brain out. Not true. Newer research showed that Ketamine actually helped in brain injury. The old-timers didn't know it though, unless they kept abreast of the news.

She wouldn't have thought him an old-timer, but he must have been in his late forties, so maybe twenty years out of medical school? He was quite the show-off, she'd heard. The nurses liked him, and he liked them back, especially the young and pretty ones. They liked his stories about sailing around the world and escaping sharks and climbing down mountains on broken legs. Quite an adventurer, Dr. Umber, but not so keen on the latest in medicine.

"Yes. Haven't you heard? Ketamine is the cat's ass now. They use it in head injuries and for sedation in psychotics and even for seizures and depression. Ketamine is the new black." She smiled and turned back to her patient.

"Hey, Emma, what are you doing tonight? Wanna go for a drink after work?"

Is this a date? Or just a friendly "Let's chill together after work" thing? She hadn't been on a date since… last summer? Or maybe the one before that? And no matter what it was, should she go drinking and then drive home? But then he was funny and handsome and smelled good, and she hadn't been out in ages. She could take a taxi… or maybe he'd give her a ride.

She smiled at him with new warmth. "Why not?"

"A few nurses and I will be at The Apple at six. Come chill with us."

Not a date, after all. Getting involved with a colleague was a bad idea, but she hadn't felt attractive in so long she could have used a boost. She was a doctor, a mother, a housekeeper, in that order. Being a woman was not on the list.

"Thanks, I'll see how things line up."

8

The first "5 and 2" didn't do much, but the second shot put him to sleep. They rushed him through the scanner. No bleed. Emma checked him out thoroughly. No badness beyond the bruises. Relieved, she left him sleeping and went back to her desk.

Ken, the ED director, was waiting for her. No white coat. *Office work for him today. It must be nice.*

"How is he?"

"He's fine; he just needs to sleep it off. How are you?"

"I'm OK. Busy today?"

"As usual. We're full here. Seven more in triage."

"Can you stop by for a moment?" She looked at the line of stretchers in the hallways, all full, and then looked back at him. He waited. *It must be important.*

"I'll be there."

She sat in the guest chair in Ken's office, staring at the open door behind him. *How can he sit with his back to an open door? Anybody passing by can look at him and at his computer screen without him even knowing. That's crazy! I walk out of restaurants when I can't sit with my back against the wall! I'm paranoid, but he's not paranoid enough!*

She looked at his kind, tired face. For once he wasn't smiling. Something was wrong.

"What did I do this time?" she joked.

"They didn't tell me yet." He stood up and closed the door. "This is a private conversation."

Emma nodded.

"It's about Kurt. I need your help."

That's odd. Kurt is no friend of mine, and Ken knows it.

"Sheila, his wife, thinks that Kurt is having an affair with Kayla and that he's getting ready to leave her. She says Kurt bought Kayla a new car."

Emma pulled her feet under her chair, hoping it was going to be over soon.

"If that's true, it's not only a tragedy for them but an administrative problem. Kurt is Kayla's superior. In these #MeToo times, when even an innocent joke can be perceived as sexual harassment, this is a ticking bomb. This will reflect poorly not only on him but on the whole ED. I thought about talking to him, but it's difficult. We have years of friendship that I don't want to jeopardize. Would you speak to Kayla? She likes you and trusts you."

That's weird. "I have no authority to ask Kayla anything about her personal life. We aren't close friends. You want me to ask her if she's sleeping with Kurt?"

"You can do better than that. As for authority, I recommended you for the position of ED assistant director."

"Assistant director? How about Kurt?"

"Kurt will continue to be an ED attending."

"But nothing's been proven yet! How about due process?"

"Kurt has had previous issues. Administration had already considered replacing him. This is just the last straw."

"What did he do?"

"I can't tell you."

"He won't like this."

"I know. There's nothing I can do. As a matter of fact, my days on the job are numbered. I expect to be fired any day. I'm just trying to clear up this mess before they throw me out."

"I'm so sorry."

"Me too. For the last twenty-five years I've given my life to this place. I didn't expect it to end up like this. This place has no soul." He started shuffling papers on his desk, avoiding her eyes. His hunched shoulders spelled defeat, and his large, knotty hands trembled.

"What are you going to do?"

"I'll retire. I've been thinking about that for a while, but I couldn't bring myself to do it. They've made it easy. I'll finally have enough time to go fishing and hiking. I'll read the books I've been putting off for years. I'll spend more time with my wife. I'm almost looking forward to it." He looked her in the eye and asked, "The real question is: What are *you* going to do?"

"I need to think." *This is the opportunity I've been waiting for. This would boost my career and set me up for further promotions. But there's Taylor. I don't have much time for Taylor as it is; on the other hand, Taylor is turning eighteen and she'll be leaving for college.*

"I think I'll take the job. What do you think?"

There was kindness and pity in Ken's eyes. When he spoke, his words came out like splinters.

"Emma, I've known you for years. You're bright, tough, and hardworking. I wish I had more docs like you. You're ambitious and dedicated. That's why I floated your name. I know you'll do a great job. I just hope you won't get crushed in the process.

"Kurt will hate you even more than he does. The others too. Their friends in the department will make your life miserable. They'll get rid of me, and that will make things even worse. You'll be the scapegoat for everything that doesn't work. You'll be the punching bag for the doctors when they don't like the schedule or the support services fail or the computer system goes down, and the punching bag for the administration whenever there's a complaint. Whatever goes wrong will be your fault."

"You sure know how to talk me into it." Emma tried to lighten the mood.

"Whatever they tell you, this is a full-time job and then some. 24/7 on call. Whatever happens, whenever it happens, it's your problem. They'll call you if things get bad, if somebody gets sick or forgets to show up for work—whatever happens, it's all you. I'm an old man with not much of a life. You're a woman and a mother. Shouldn't you spend more time with Taylor instead?"

Emma hung her head. She was about to put her career ahead of her daughter. Again.

"Thank you, Ken. You're right. I'll think about it."

She went back to the ED.

They were waiting.

9

───────

Emma was late to the Apple. She had met with Victor and Taylor's counselor.

Taylor was skipping classes. She was moody and difficult. She was giving her teachers a rough time. She was failing classes. She'd failed to even turn in her English homework, she, the best writer in her class.

"She's hanging out with the wrong crowd," Ms. Perkins said, looking at them over her round glasses. Paired with her stringy gray hair, they made her look like the wicked witch of the West.

Emma shrunk, raised her shoulders, and drew her feet under her chair, assuming her guilty posture. She'd done it as a child whenever her mother blew up. She was still doing it, thirty years later.

"She'll grow out of it." Victor shrugged. "She's just a kid."

He was annoyed that he had to carve time out of his busy day for this. Rocking in his chair, he looked like a kid himself, with his unruly curly hair, his pout, and his muddy boots.

"She's seventeen. She's no longer a kid," Emma said.

Victor had always been too lenient with Taylor. *He's her best friend more than he's her father. That leaves me to be the bad guy, the only one to ever say no. No wonder Taylor wants to leave home and move in with him.*

43

That worried her. Between Victor's schedule—on call every fourth night and every fourth weekend—and his lenience, Taylor would go completely unsupervised. *Sure, Amber's there, but Amber is barely older than Taylor—what is she, 29?—and she's busy taking care of her own kids. Not to mention the hairdresser, pedicures, and shopping. I bet Victor isn't helping much. He likes playing with his kids, but disciplining them? No.*

"She'll be of age in one year."

"She's exactly as I was at her age. She's got to have some fun. If not now, then when?"

"You got straight A's when you were her age. You were polite and loving to your parents, no matter what else you did. She's failing three subjects. She's a pain to deal with at home. Take my word for it."

"She just needs a little time. She never got over that business with Tom."

"Did she tell you about Mike?" Ms. Perkins asked.

"Who's Mike?" Victor asked, checking his watch.

"Mike was one of Taylor's friends. Nice kid. Troubled. He died last week."

"Died? How?" asked Emma.

"Drug overdose, apparently."

Emma and Victor looked at each other.

That was beyond skipping classes and acting like a teenager. If her friends were doing drugs, Taylor may be too. That would explain her sudden change, her rotten mood, and her poor school performance.

"Did you know about this?" Victor asked Emma.

"Of course not. She never speaks to me, as you are well aware. Did *you* know?"

"No, I didn't."

His body slumped. The chair rocked forward, resting on all its feet. The carefree kid disappeared. A worried father took his place.

Emma wished she could feel sorry for him, but she was too angry. *It's his fault that Taylor is unmanageable.*

"We don't know that she's using, though," he said. "We shouldn't jump to conclusions. For all that we know, this has nothing to do with her."

"So what do you suggest? Wait and see if we find her dead?"

Victor looked her in the eye.

"You didn't really mean that; you're just upset. I am too, but there is no point in ripping into each other. We need to work together."

He was right, of course, but she was too mad to think. She took a long deep breath, opened her mouth to speak, and then closed it tight enough for her jaw to hurt.

"I'll speak to her," he said.

"What are you going to tell her?"

"I don't know." He took off his glasses to wipe them clean with slow circular motions using the bottom of his shirt, like he always did when he had to make a difficult decision.

She remembered him proposing to her, eons ago. Then too, he'd taken off his glasses. He'd wiped them clean with the bottom of his short white coat that all medical students wore. *He used to be young and handsome, his jet-black hair curling around his ears, his smiling eyes ocean blue. We were both medical students. We were ready to take on the world. Invincible. Now? We're old, our marriage is dead, and we're about to fail our only child.* Her heart ached for all the things they'd lost: youth, love, marriage.

"You want to talk to her together?"

"Good idea," Ms. Perkins said. "Show a united front."

She thinks Victor won't push Taylor, but she knows that I will.

They walked out together and stopped near Emma's red Hyundai.

"How about tomorrow?" Emma asked. She opened the door and dropped her bag on top of the green jacket Taylor had left on the passenger seat.

"Not tomorrow. Sunday? I can be there by nine, before she wakes up and takes off."

Emma nodded. He turned to leave.

He took two steps and turned around, his fists tight in the pockets of his old jeans.

"Should we have her tested?" he asked, staring at his muddy boots.

"How would that help?"

"At least we'd know for sure whether she's using or not."

"We wouldn't. We don't even know what to test her for. A lot of drugs won't show in the usual drug tests. Plus there's so much cross-reactivity that she could test positive even if she didn't use anything—like testing positive for amphetamines after taking decongestants." This was her field. She knew it inside-out, just like he knew his cardiology stuff.

"Why don't we ask her first?"

He nodded and walked away.

Emma started her car. She sat, watching his tail lights fade.

He's going home to Amber and the girls. He'll get dinner, company, and love. He's even got the dogs. I'm going home to nothing. Unless Taylor's home. Then it's even worse. Like the night he told me.

It was years ago, but she still remembered every sound, every taste, every shadow.

10

———————

The only light was in the kitchen. Emma wondered why. It was late, past Taylor's bedtime, and Victor barely knew where to find the kitchen.

Is she sick?

She pulled in. She parked too close to Victor's Subaru, but she was too tired to care. Her nine-hour shift had turned into twelve. She had nothing left inside.

The cold had gotten into her bones. *I hate the air-conditioning. They must be doing it on purpose, so that the living don't get too comfortable and the dead don't rot.* She shivered, looking forward to a hot bath to wash off the grime and the misery of her many patients since this morning. Yesterday morning now.

She walked to the kitchen.

Victor read at the kitchen table, empty but for a bouquet of roses and an open bottle of red wine. The roses made the kitchen look both festive and foreign.

"You're late," he said, pouring wine into a pair of long-stem glasses and handing her one.

Emma did a mental check. Anniversary? Birthday? Mother's Day?

She lifted her glass and watched the light struggling to flow through its dark redness. *It's thick as blood.* She sniffed it, then swirled it for a second nose. The darkness was there too, the bitter cherry flavor and licorice and maybe violets, a rich bouquet of wildflowers and dark fruit, spelling money.

She took a sip. She let it flow under her tongue, then behind her teeth, striking the remotest taste buds. The acid, the tannins, and the floral bitterness made them sing.

"Nice wine," she said. She sat, pulling her jacket around her.

She eyed the flowers. A dozen red roses with baby's breath and greens, spilling out from their only vase. Their glamour clashed with the peeling cabinets and the chipped sink. The kitchen was empty. Everything was put away. That never happened—neither she nor Victor were the housekeeping type—and as for Taylor, she was the child goddess of entropy.

Sports jacket past midnight. He's looking tired. Even his curls look flat. His periwinkle eyes, red-rimmed behind his glasses, didn't meet hers. Her heart skipped. She opened her mouth to ask.

She didn't.

She took another sip of wine instead.

Victor sat his glass on the table, took off his glasses, and started cleaning them with his shirt, like he always did when collecting his thoughts. He blew on the lenses and wiped them with slow circular movements, without looking up.

It's not Taylor. It's something else, and it's bad.

"Emma, you know how important you are to me."

It's worse than bad. Emma finished her glass and poured herself another. She picked up the bottle and checked the label. Chateau Pavie, St. Emilion, 1999. Good vintage. Excellent in fact.

"Taylor too."

Her brain splintered and burned. *Divorce. That's what's happening. I didn't see it coming.*

She thought back about the last few months. He'd been away a lot. She'd been busy herself, between the ED shifts, the house, and Taylor. This was the first time they were sharing a bottle of wine this year. As for the flowers...

"Nice flowers."

He blushed.

She looked into the living room for clues. Nothing there. She recalled the vague shape of boxes in his car.

More wine.

"I'm leaving."

"Where to?"

"I'm leaving you."

Emma nodded.

"You're not making it easy!"

Emma laughed. "Where are you going?"

"Where? Don't you want to know why?"

"I imagine you found a better option."

"I'm expecting a baby."

"Congratulations! You may get a Nobel prize for that!"

Victor's eyes finally connected. "I'm sorry, Emma."

"That's too bad. You should be excited."

"I'm sorry about doing this to you."

"How about Taylor?"

"I'm very sorry about Taylor too!"

"Me too. You're taking her."

"Taking her? Taking her where?"

"With you."

The shock on Victor's face was fun to watch. *Almost.*

"I can't take her with me!"

"Why not? She's your daughter, just like this child you're expecting."

"But…"

"But what?"

"You're her mother!"

"I couldn't help but notice. And you're her father."

"She needs to be with you!"

"Did you ask her?"

"No."

"You should. She'd rather be with you."

"But she's only eight! She doesn't know what's best for her!"

"And you do?"

"Don't you want her?"

"No."

"Why not?"

"Like you, I have better things to do."

"But she's your daughter!"

Emma laughed. "She's yours too, remember?"

"You're kidding, aren't you?"

"Not at all."

"But I'm busy! I have my work and my patients and…"

Emma waited.

"And Amber's pregnant!"

Emma remembered Amber. *Young, pretty, girly. Giggled a lot. She rotated through the ED in nursing school, then she got a job in Cardiology. The rest is history.* Emma tried to not be bitter. She failed. *Giggly, girly Amber, twelve years younger, took Victor and destroyed my marriage.*

"It's going to be good practice for her to take care of a child. At least this one is potty-trained. As for busy, I'm just as busy as you are. I have my shifts and my patients. I'm in no better shape to take care of Taylor than you are. I'll keep the dogs."

Victor's mouth narrowed into a thin line.

"Listen, Emma, if this is your way of taking revenge…"

"Where are we going, Daddy?" Taylor asked. She stood in the open door with Dora, her rag doll, under her arm. Her faded pink blanket dragged behind her, like it had been since she'd started walking. She had Victor's dark curls falling over her fierce eyes. She was packed and ready to go.

"To bed, sweetheart. We're going to bed now." Victor picked her up—Dora, blanket, and all—and took her to her bedroom.

Emma sat in the empty kitchen. She focused on the wine, on its red glow in the crystal glass, on its full-bodied flavor, on the smoothness of the stem. She pushed aside the emptiness, the murmur of the bedside story in Taylor's room, the guilt in Victor's eyes.

Tomorrow.

She kept pressure on the thought of tomorrow like she'd keep pressure on a bleeding wound.

For tonight, she'd just stay alive.

Tomorrow.

Nine years ago and it still hurts.

They didn't tell Taylor until weeks later, when they returned from their last family vacation. Victor had taken the dogs, of course, and Emma ended up with Taylor. *What a deal!* She shook her head and headed home. Two minutes later she changed her mind. She turned around in the hospital parking lot to drive to The Apple.

SPIDER

It's getting dark.
He's coming. Heading to the car.
I follow like the whisper of a shadow.
Going to the far parking lot. Good.
The farther the better.
I close in, right hand in my pocket, making love to the handle.
I love this knife. She loves me.
He's by the car. I step forward to grab him.
The lights hit him. A car. It stops next to him.
The window opens.
A woman.
Brown-haired, white coat, scrubs. Smiling.
"Emma!" he says.
She looks at me sharply.
One step and I melt in the dark.
I move on.
I'll be back.

11

———————

They were still there. After a few drinks, they were laughing and speaking all over each other in the private back room.

Umber was whispering in Kayla's ear, his golden tan set off by his sweater in the color of deep water. Judy, still in scrubs, was laughing with George, who looked like a satyr with flushed olive skin. Kelly was chatting with Nora, the new, pretty CNA who looked a little out of place sitting on the other side of Dick.

Their cheerful welcome filled her heart. It felt good to be wanted. These were her people, more than her own family. With them, she belonged.

Sal moved aside to make room for her. She sat between him and Kelly.

"I'm glad you made it," Dick said, pouring her a generous glass of wine. "To good friends!"

Emma raised her glass and took a sip. The wine was good, dry, robust, and a little rough, like most Chiantis are. She thanked him, but she didn't fail to notice that he'd poured her wine without asking.

Mr. Macho Man had decided for her.

"Good to see you, Dr. Steele," Kayla said, prettier than ever with her wine-flushed cheeks and sparkling eyes.

"Good to see you, Kayla."

Emma liked her easy smile and outgoing personality almost as much as she appreciated her competency. She was an ED clerk, the hub of communication with the other departments. She made things happen with a smile, even when she had to deal with grumpy surgeons and irate family members. She was a gem.

I hope the rumors about Kurt and her are false. She deserves better.

Dick refilled Kayla's glass, though it didn't need it. "This wine's not bad, but it's not as good as mine. Did I tell you about my vineyard in Languedoc? Great terroir. We make a nice dry red."

"Really? You own a winery? In France?"

"A small one. Just one thousand bottles per year."

"Who looks after it?" Emma asked.

"The old Frenchman I bought it from. His wife died, and he had to sell. I offered to let him live there in exchange for managing the place and a little cash. It's been one of the best deals I've ever made.

Dick took another sip of wine and rested his arm on the back of Kayla's chair. "Too bad that I don't get to spend much time there between my work and my boat."

"You have a boat too?" Kayla asked.

"I bought this Sun Odyssey 49. I'm keeping it in a marina in Mazatlán to get it refurbished. I'll have to take you sailing some day. It should be ready by June."

"You sail it yourself? Where?"

"Looking at transatlantic crossings. Thinking about starting a business of themed sailing vacations. I'll get an Iron Chef to give cooking lessons, or a yogini to lead a meditation cruise, or a yoga retreat, something like that."

Kayla looked at him in awe.

Kelly elbowed Emma and rolled her eyes. "Wait until he gets around to saving the Dalai Lama's life," she whispered, loud enough for him to hear.

Emma choked. "How do you manage to do all this and still work?"

"I delegate. I have people who do it for me. I'm flying to Mexico in a couple of weeks to check on the boat progress. Wanna come?" he asked Kayla.

She smiled.

Emma hoped she wasn't taking him seriously. He had shifty eyes. No wonder Ken was thinking about getting rid of him. "He's too much trouble. He can't see a girl without going after her." Emma had tried to talk him out of it, but Ken had had it. "Yeah, I know he's a good doctor when he's not in bed with one of the nurses. I warned him twice. That's it. Next time he's gone!"

Kelly intervened. "She knows better than to trust a charmer like you. Where do you live?"

"I have a winter place in Colorado, near Aspen. I love skiing."

"I love skiing too," Nora said.

Dick took another sip of wine.

"And in summer?"

"Oh, here and there. Mostly out and about, working."

"How long have you been doing locums work?" Kayla asked.

"Almost seven years."

"It's got to be hard to have no home to go to at night, no kitchen, no pets," Nora said.

Umber shrugged. "It's good money. It gives you an opportunity to meet new people." He turned toward Kayla and raised his glass. "And pretty girls like you!"

Nora stood up so fast that her chair fell backward. "Good night, everybody. I have to go."

That was abrupt. Is she one of the names Dick crossed off his list, upset now that he's flirting with Kayla?

"I hope she's OK," Kayla said.

They started talking again, but the easy banter was gone.

Emma turned to Sal, quietly sipping his beer. "What's new with you?"

"Not much." His voice went down a notch. "That kid. The code the other day, the one who needed all that Narcan…"

"Yes?"

"I checked his medical history. The meds bottle wasn't his; it was his girl-friend's. She got four opiate prescriptions last month."

"Any of them fentanyl?"

"None. That's what makes it so interesting. Whatever was in the bottle wasn't what had been prescribed. Must be something they got on the street."

Emma nodded. She turned to Dick. "You still don't think that code you had last week was an overdose?"

"Which one? You can't swing a dead cat without hitting a code these days. Who knows what they're injecting."

"Mine wasn't injected, it was pills."

Dick shrugged. "Pills, popping, smoking, whatever. One way or another they'll find a way to get high, and it'll get them in trouble."

He doesn't care.

She remembered Taylor's dead friend Mike, and Taylor herself who may or may not be using. Her heart sank.

"I'm wondering if it's fentanyl," Sal said.

Dick gave him a side glance. "Fentanyl? Why fentanyl?"

"It's one of the few drugs potent enough to be almost Narcan resistant. Morphine, heroin, hydrocodone, oxycodone—they all should respond to Narcan. Even methadone."

"To various degrees," Dick agreed, "but carfentanyl and remyfentanyl don't."

"They're both so rare that we don't even have them in the pharmacy yet. And I haven't heard about either of them on the street!"

Dick shrugged. "It's just a matter of time. They're on their way, I bet. The druggies will find a way to get them. They'd do anything for a good high. That keeps us all in business, eh? Job security." He smiled, finished his drink, and turned to Kayla. "Would you like a ride?"

"Kelly'll take me."

Good for her.

12

———————

The talk with Taylor didn't go well.

Nestled between the sofa cushions, her dark hair with new green ends falling across her face, she kept her eyes glued to her phone.

"Put the phone down, Taylor," Emma said.

Taylor ignored her.

"We're trying to speak to you, sweetheart," Victor said, "please."

"What?" Taylor glanced at Victor.

He opened his mouth to speak. No sound came out. He looked at Emma for help.

"We heard about Mike," Emma said, "I'm so sorry. Was he a good friend to you?"

"What did you hear?"

"He overdosed."

"What's it to you? Why do you care?"

Emma bit her lip. "Of course, I care. I'm your mother. I love you. I'm worried about you!"

"Whatever." Taylor went back to her phone.

"What's that supposed to mean?"

Emma dug her nails into her palms to refrain from grabbing Taylor's phone and smashing it against the wall.

"You don't have time for me. You're never home. Shifts, meetings, conferences, always something. You say you love me, but you don't care where I am and you don't know what I do. Your career is more important than me. Your patients are more important than me. You pay the bills and stock the fridge. That's all the attention I get. You don't even know who my friends are. And you expect me to believe that you care about Mike? Please!" Taylor rolled her eyes.

Emma swallowed the lump in her throat. *I never thought she wanted me around. She always acts like she wants to be left alone.*

Victor cleared his voice. "Taylor, we both love you. We care about you. We're worried about you."

"Well, don't be. I'm doing just fine."

"No, you're not. You're skipping school, you're failing subjects, and you have friends using drugs. That's anything but fine," Emma said.

"That's all you care about. School. You don't care about what I want, how I feel, how unhappy I am. You care about nothing but my grades."

"Bullshit! I care about everything. I care about your feelings, but school is important. It's the only way you can succeed in life and have a career."

"I don't want a career. Look at yourself. You have a career. What good does it do you?"

"Well, for one, it helps pay your bills. It pays for that phone that you can't put down and for your clothes and for your vacations!"

"Money, that's all you care about."

"No, it's not. And you don't seem to despise money quite that much when you use it, do you?"

Emma knew better than to taunt her, but she just couldn't help herself. Her blood was boiling; her breath was coming out in short angry bursts. Even worse, she was feeling guilty, because deep inside she knew that Taylor was right.

In Emma's life, everything had always played second fiddle to her career—her marriage, her pregnancy, Taylor herself. She had scheduled everything around her work. Yes, Taylor was important to her and she loved her—*I have to, I'm her mother—but my career, that's really important.* Not only for the money, but to silence the voice inside her that told her that she wasn't worth much, and she'd never amount to anything.

Unless I'm successful, I'm disposable. "Nobody's gonna care about you if you don't succeed," her mother said. "People only care about you if you're young and pretty, or you're rich. When you get old, they'll forget you even exist."

Emma grew up hearing that. In that deepest corner of her heart, she knew that she was disposable. *That's what happened with Victor when Amber came along. He left without looking back. As for Taylor, I could die and be buried before she'd care. To her, I'm nothing but an inconvenience.* Still, it was painfully true that she had dedicated herself to her career. In Emma's struggle to become successful, Taylor got ignored.

Victor intervened. "Taylor, what happened to Mike?"

Taylor shrugged. "He died."

"How?"

"You know how."

"What was he using?"

"What difference does it make?"

"I am… we're worried about you. Are you using?"

Taylor looked him in the eye. "So that's the problem? You're worried that I'm an addict and that I'll OD too?" She turned to her mother. "And you? You'd be happy to get rid of me, wouldn't you!"

Emma wanted to slap her, hard.

She took a deep breath instead and stuck her fists in the pockets of her faded scrubs. "You are my child. You are my responsibility. I'll do whatever I can to protect you."

"Except for putting me ahead of your precious career, of course."

"My career is rewarding to me. It gets me money, respect, gratitude, and even love. What do I get from you besides impertinence, dirty dishes, and humiliating meetings with counselors? What do you contribute to this relationship?"

Victor intervened. "Stop that, both of you!" He turned to Taylor. "Taylor, we love you. We're worried about you. We want to help!"

Taylor shrugged. "Well, if you really want to know, Mike's overdose was not an accident. He got bullied in school. He was gay. His mother was an intolerant religious bitch. His stepfather abused him. He couldn't take it anymore. He took his mother's pain pills and went to sleep."

The silence fell, heavy.

"How come you know all that? Victor asked.

"He texted me to ask for help. I didn't get the text until it was too late. Thanks to you," she said, turning around to face Emma, her eyes daggers. "Remember that day last week you grounded me and took away my phone? He'd be alive if it weren't for you!"

Now that's my fault too! Is there anything that's not my fault? Ever?

"You know damn well why you were grounded. You didn't show up until past midnight, though your curfew was ten. You didn't even bother to call and tell me you'd be late. I spent hours sick with worry about you."

"Tell that to Mike. Is there anything else, or are we finished here?"

Helpless, Emma and Victor looked at each other.

"What do you want, Taylor? What is it that you're looking for?" Victor asked.

"I want to move out."

"Out where?"

"I don't want to live here anymore. I want to feel like a person, like I matter and somebody cares about me."

"We both care about you," Emma said, shrinking with the pain of rejection. She knew that Taylor didn't like her, but that hate? That was news.

Taylor's stare would have wilted a cactus.

"Where would you live if not here? Who'd do your laundry and your shopping and..."

"And wipe my ass," Taylor sniggered. "I can do my own shopping and my own damn laundry!"

"Really? You haven't yet shown any signs of that!"

"Emma, that's not helpful!" Victor said.

"I could go live with Katie. Her mother said it would be OK."

Katie had been Taylor's best friend since kindergarten. She lived with her mother in a trailer park south of town. Rumor had it that men would stop by every now and then, and stay for a night or for a week.

"Absolutely not," Emma said, "you aren't going to live in a trailer."

"Really? And how exactly are you going to stop me?"

Victor intervened. "How about coming to live with us?" he asked.

Taylor gave him a long, searching look. "What will Amber say?"

"She'll say, 'Welcome, Taylor.' The girls would love to have you."

The girls, Opal and Iris, loved their big sister.

"Shouldn't you talk to Amber first?"

Emma wasn't happy, but she didn't have a better plan. After all, Victor was Taylor's father, and Amber was OK. *It may do her good to live in a real family.*

"I will," Victor said. "Gather your stuff; I'll be here to pick you up tomorrow.

Taylor grinned, and Emma realized that she'd played them. Again. *That's been her plan all along, to move in with Victor. She's borderline, brilliant, and a pain in the ass. Let Victor have a taste of living with her. It serves him right.*

Deep inside, her heart was crying.

SPIDER

I'm here. It's almost nine. It's cold. Snowing. The snow's covering me. It's soft, white, and quiet.

Like a shroud.

I wait.

I wait some more.

A man comes out. Looks like him. He walks to the far parking lot, checking his phone. Fool!

Take whatever, as long as he's dead, he said.

I want the phone; maybe a laptop, his bag's heavy enough to make him slump. That would pay good.

I've got his picture, but I don't need it. I know what he looks like, but for the hood. He gets close to the car. I check the number. It's the right car, a Mercedes, the right plate.

He opens the driver's door. I'm right behind him now, but he doesn't know. He's on the phone.

"On my way, dear, I'll be home in half an hour."

No, you won't.

I grab the knife.

The handle feels warm.

Warm and smooth.

I know what to do.

"Bring your right arm up, blade horizontal, to neck height. Grab his hair with your left and pull it sideways, the head with it. Slide the blade across his neck like the bow on a violin, waiting for the sound. It sounds like a wisp of wind inside a storm," he

said, "no louder. There'll be no screaming. There's no air to go to the mouth and make sounds; after you cut the windpipe, it's all over. Soft and quiet like the wind in a forest."

"Don't leave anything behind; they'll find you if you do. Don't touch anything but him."

I'm half a step behind him as he puts his phone away to open the door.

I cough. His head whips back.

"I've got a message." The knife hangs along my thigh, out of sight. My left hand is ready.

He looks me up and down. Doesn't know me.

"What message?"

I smile and show him my empty left hand. "This," I say. He cranes his head to see.

I grab a handful of white hair and pull it back to straighten his neck. I move behind him and lift the knife to play the death song across his neck. It slides through skin and flesh like butter. His knees soften. He grows heavy.

The whisper of a scream comes out, then there's nothing but wind. Wind and blood, warm and salty in my mouth and in my eyes and all over me. I haven't been this warm in weeks!

I let him melt into the ground, softly. What if I take the car? It's a nice car, better than any I've ever had!

I know better. I pull him up. He's breathing red bubbles through the hole in his neck. His wide eyes are asking why. I don't answer. He's dead already; he shouldn't care now, should he? Dead people don't care. I lift him into the car. He's heavy. I push his feet inside and bend his knees to close the door. I slam it shut with the hip.

They'll find him, but it's gonna be a while, maybe days, before they wonder what that car is doing sitting here. The snow is falling, soft and thick and white, covering the blood, the car, now his coffin, covering me. His blood, all over me, has gotten cold. I grab his bag—mine now, and leave, walking slowly. Ten steps later I think: I should have checked for a wallet. Maybe it's in the bag. I can't go back. But maybe... No. I can't go back. I walk slowly, whistling "We Are the Champions" to myself. I'm alone in the dark. I'm done. He's done.

We did good.

13

―――――

Emma checked for her phone, her glasses, her ID. All there. Her bag was empty but for her always-there gear: scalpel, flashlight, gloves, tourniquet, stethoscope. No lunch. There'd been no time for that.

The phone rang as she helped Taylor pack. As usual, Taylor wasn't talking. Emma was glad. *The only thing I'd like to tell her is this: Please, please, don't become your grandmother. And that, I can't.*

Emma was eight when she realized that she hated her mother. The woman had been mentally ill, sadistic and evil. Mother —never Mom—had spent months and months in hospitals. She was depressed, anxious, constipated. She couldn't sleep. She was always in pain. She needed constant attention, love, and reassurance. She needed more than eight-year-old Emma could provide. When denied, she started with the shaming: "One day I'll kill myself and you'll be sorry. You'll see how life is without me." The beatings came later. They were well planned and thorough. Mother would get her naked, then beat her with a stick, avoiding her hands and face, until she kneeled, asking for forgiveness, or peed herself. Preferably both. *No wonder I'm a lousy mother. I never learned better. Taylor is just like her. Manipulative, moody, self-centered. She's Mother in a younger package. Mothers are supposed to love their children unconditionally. I love Taylor, I have to, but as for liking her...*

The phone rang. The COO needed her.

"Now."

64

"Now?"

"Now."

This can't be good. She brushed her teeth, threw on some clean scrubs, and got her work bag. She said good-bye to Taylor and tried to hug her, but she got the "don't touch me" look.

Half an hour later she walked into the conference room, still wondering. *What the hell is this about? A patient complaint? That's Ken's job. A legal issue? A bomb threat? Are they firing me? Whatever it is, I wish they'd waited until three when my shift starts, so I could get some lunch. This is going to be a hell of a long day on an empty stomach. Unless they fire me. Then I could go have a nice dinner.* She stepped in the conference room. It was packed.

Mr. Lockhart, the CEO, sat at one end of the long oval table. His face, sharp and unsmiling, and the artificial lights reflecting off his bald scalp made him look like a mannequin in a men's store. A dejected Kurt was sitting at the other end. His sharp suit looked slept in, his face was no better. He glared at Emma with bloodshot eyes, then went back to watching his fingers. Between them were the hospital lawyer, the risk manager, and a couple of suits she didn't know. The tension in the room was thick enough to cut with a knife.

Emma found an empty seat and braced herself.

"Thank you for joining us, Dr. Steele. We've been waiting for you."

She heard the implied reprimand. She almost apologized. Almost.

Asshole. It took me less than an hour to get here. I dropped everything. I left Taylor to look after herself. Again. He can stuff it if he doesn't like it.

"I'm afraid I have bad news for you," Mr. Lockhart said.

No kidding. I thought you called me here just to thank me for my outstanding work. What am I going to do if they fire me? First, go have a nice dinner. Then think about where I'd like to live. There are plenty of jobs for ER docs everywhere. I could go to Colorado or Alaska. Or Australia. Or Guam. I wonder what the weather is like in Guam. And the food. Spicy, I hope.

"Dr. Leep died last night."

"Who?"

"Dr. Leep. Ken. He died last night."

Ken died. Her friend. Her mentor. Her Dumbledore. "How?"

"He was found in his car with his throat cut. Police are investigating. A suicide has not been discounted."

"Suicide? Ken, cutting his throat in his car? You must be kidding!"

Lockhart shrugged. "Police are working on it."

"When did it happen?"

"He was found yesterday. Sorry, honey, I know he was your friend. He was a good doctor and a good man. Our hospital will never be the same without him."

Emma looked at Kurt. He'd been even closer to Ken than she was. "I'm so sorry, Kurt."

Kurt didn't look up.

"We'll get in touch with his wife and try to help." Mr. Lockhart continued, "However, the reason we needed to talk to you today is another but related matter. Since Dr. Leep is no longer with us, we need to establish a new ED leadership. That department needs a strong leader." He started pacing with slow, important steps. "Our community hospital has been struggling. We've been having financial difficulties. We've been in the red for the last three years. The ER is a part of the problem. I tried to address this issue with Dr. Leep multiple times. Unfortunately, we were unable to find a solution. We were forced to look at other alternatives."

Emma looked at him with narrowed eyes. *You were going to get rid of him, and he knew it. When Ken offered me the assistant director position, he knew he was on his way out. Still, he planned to retire and enjoy life. Now he's dead. What a cruel irony!*

"Since we couldn't find a solution, we looked into outsourcing our ED services. We approached EMSA, Emergency Medicine Services Association. We'd agreed to start in April, but Dr. Leep's death has brought a new urgency to this matter. EMSA has graciously agreed to start next month. This is Dr. Drom from EMSA," Mr. Lockhart said, pointing to a slim man smiling like a hungry rattlesnake on the prowl. "Are you familiar with EMSA?"

Emma shook her head.

"We are a contract group providing emergency medicine services," Dr. Drom said, smiling again as if his lunch was passing by, and it finally clicked. *We're getting fired.*

Like all the others, she'd always been a hospital employee, but the healthcare industry was changing. Hospitals started outsourcing their ERs to contract groups. That simplified their operations and helped their bottom line. Great news for the hospitals, but a disaster for the emergency docs. They lost their jobs overnight. *Hard to believe that this can happen here, in the middle of nowhere, but it just did.*

"EMSA has offered to employ all our existing physicians. They're hoping to continue the excellence of care we are known for," Mr. Lockhart said.

Kurt's jaw twitched. The engorged vein appeared like a blue worm on his left temple, looking ready to pop.

Dr. Drom smiled again. Emma wished he'd refrain. *He looks like a snake greeting a rabbit. Delighted and hungry.*

"We're happy to be here," he said. "We've heard good things about the care you folks provide to your little community. We're dedicated to continue good care, albeit in a more efficient and cost-effective manner. We hope to start a successful cooperation. We can work together toward our common goals."

"Such an excellent opportunity to revamp our care," Mr. Lockhart said. "Together we can provide the safest and most cost-effective care for the good of our community."

Emma looked from one to the other, listening to their well-practiced, cardboard speeches and wondered why she was here. *Ken is dead; Kurt was his assistant, but me? I'm just one of the ER docs.*

"We've heard about you, Dr. Steele," Dr. Drom said, looking in her general direction though not exactly in her eyes. *The little patch of hair below his lower lip looks like a hungry leech.* "You came highly recommended by some of my friends. I was really impressed with your CV."

"Thank you," she said. Kurt looked at her as if he were ready to cut her throat.

"We'd like to offer you the position of chief of the Emergency Department."

Really? They're going to ditch Kurt, like Ken said. They want me to take over. Why?

"We've already discussed that with Dr. Crump. He agrees that you will make an excellent director."

Kurt turned dark red. He swallowed. He didn't choke.

"You're too kind. Since you've seen my CV, you must know that I have no administrative experience."

"That's a positive. We'll train you. We'll get you all the help you need."

"What exactly would the job entail?"

"We will talk about that. In a moment."

Mr. Lockhart stood. The meeting was over. "We're heartbroken about Dr. Leep's demise. We'll find an appropriate way to recognize his service. Dr. Crump, thank you for your dedication and for the many years you spent caring for our patients. Tomorrow, we'll send out a memo to the ER staff outlining the things we discussed. The EMSA representatives will be available in the ED to talk to the physicians. We're happy to share the wonderful news. Nobody will lose their job!"

Kurt glared at Emma once more. He left, crumpled and hunched, a shadow of his carefully tended self.

Emma sat waiting for Dr. Drom to speak.

He didn't. He shuffled his papers and looked at her, smiling again.

She couldn't take it any more.

"Why me?"

Dr. Drom had trouble swallowing. The leech moved.

Straight talk's not his thing.

"You're young, dynamic, and unrelated to the previous administration. You were recommended to me by people I trust. You're smart enough to appreciate this extraordinary opportunity. You're a woman. Women are more flexible. They adjust better. They're also more relationship-oriented. I find that essential to making our cooperation a success." He shuffled his papers again. "We'd like to keep the doctors, all of them,"

"Dr. Crump?"

"Him too. It would be easier for you if he left, though. He won't take kindly to your leadership."

"What are my responsibilities?"

"80 percent clinical; 20 percent administrative. Quality control, staff scheduling, new process implementation, training, recruiting, ongoing evaluation for the staff, interactive meetings with other departments…"

Emma's head was spinning.

"We'll discuss the details. We'll provide you with all the tools you need. Your success is our success."

Her brain spinning, she walked to the ED, torn between feeling heartbroken about Ken's death and being excited about the job offer. Ken had advised her against it. But Ken was dead. Very dead.

What a horrendous death! Suicide? That's ridiculous! Who would want to hurt Ken, the nicest, kindest doctor I've ever met? It makes no sense!

She punched the ED code, and she remembered Taylor. *She must have left by now. Too late to call her. Room 3 is screaming in pain. The blood-covered woman in Hallway 4 looks like she's been waiting for hours. The whole place is a zoo. I'll call her later.*

She went straight to Room 3. The lanky teenager on the stretcher was still wearing his dirty blue football jersey. Lying on his side, his half-bent left leg resting on a pillow, he was screaming, staring at the lump outside his knee. His wide-eyed teammates stared in horror, standing as far away as they could.

"What happened?" Emma asked.

He ignored her.

"He was playing football and his knee got hit. He won't let me put in an IV," George said.

"No need." Emma looked the kid in the eye. "I'm sorry, this is going to hurt, but it will get better in a moment." She cupped his left heel in her left hand. She pulled the foot down, straightening the knee. Her right thumb pushed the dislocated kneecap back on top of the knee, where it belonged, almost too fast to see.

The patella fell back into place with a soft thunk. The kid stopped screaming.

"Love you, Dr. Steele," George said, smiling, the gold tooth he'd gotten in Vietnam sparkling under his brushy mustache.

"Love you too, George."

Fixing people is fun! Better than an orgasm! Maybe? It's been too long to be sure.

14

Taylor was ready to have a conniption fit. Except with nobody watching, what's the point? Her mother had left. Her father was late. Taylor was drowning in belongings. She had already filled three suitcases, but more stuff was streaming out of every drawer, closet, and shelf.

It's like the aftermath of a tornado. Clothes, books, makeup. So much stuff! What do I do with it? I didn't know there'd be so much! Her shoulders slumped. She looked at her beloved aqua seascape with seahorses and starfish. Her eyes stung. She'd opened her eyes to them every morning for years. She was deserting them now. The orange seagrass lamp was a souvenir from the Red Sea snorkeling trip when they were still a family.

That had been their last vacation together. She'd loved every moment of it. She petted the curious striped fish taking bread from her hands. She learned the new exotic tastes of tabouleh and tahini. She inhaled the scent of coffee and the heavy sweet perfumes as she walked through the souk, holding hands with her father. She tasted the sweet mint tea served in tiny tumblers. She had never been happier.

They told her the morning after they came back. *I'll never forget, if I live to be a hundred. Cheerios will forever smell like heartbreak.*

"Taylor, I want you to know that we love you very much," Victor said.

Taylor smiled, eating Cheerios from her peacock blue bowl.

"That will never change, even though your mother and I are getting divorced."

Taylor's throat tightened, and she could no longer swallow. She knew what that meant. Her friend Katie's parents had gotten divorced last year. Katie's father had left home. Katie hadn't seen him since.

Cheerios taste like ashes.

"Why?" Taylor asked, tears burning down her cheeks. "Why are you leaving?"

Her dad had looked at his hands as if they had the answer. He said nothing.

"We don't get along anymore. Our lives are different. We no longer belong together," her mother said.

"It's your fault! What did you do to him?" Taylor threw herself in Victor's arms. "Please don't leave, Daddy, please don't leave me; I can't be without you," she cried.

He held her. He kissed the top of her head. "We're going to love you just as much. We're still going to be a family," he said. Stupid lies.

She didn't blame him. She knew it was her mother's fault. She must have done something to make him leave. That's when she started hating Emma.

It took years before she understood about Amber. That didn't change anything. She blamed her mother even more, since she felt guilty. She constructed a scenario in which Emma had forced Victor into a relationship with Amber and then thrown him out. Nothing could ever change her mind.

Right now, though, she wished her mother had been there to help. She'd deal with the mountains of stuff in her easy, competent, and annoying way. *Why does she always have to be right?* As usual, her mother was busy. Her career always came first.

The doorbell rang. It was her dad. *He looks like he hasn't slept in a week!* His eyes were bloodshot behind the steel-rimmed glasses and his hair was a mess, as usual, but his hug was like coming home.

"Are you ready?"

"Not really. I don't know what to do with all this," Taylor said, pointing to the stuff.

"Don't worry about it; we'll come back and get it later. It won't fit in the car anyhow. It's going to be safe here."

He picked up the two heavy suitcases and dragged them to the door. The faulty wheel thumped with every twist, like a broken heartbeat. He opened the back of the station wagon. He strained to lift the suitcases in.

Taylor brought out the last one. She looked back at the house. Dark red and angry, the house looked back. That was the only home she could remember, and they'd never gotten along. She slammed the door shut. She locked it. She considered throwing away the key; then she remembered all her stuff. She slipped the key in her pocket. She dragged the last bag down the steps.

Her father drove the same blue Subaru he had been driving when he left them, nine years ago. The same but for the new dent in the passenger door.

"You need a new car. Nobody believes that you're a cardiologist when they see your ride," Taylor said.

"So what?"

"You aren't cool."

He shrugged. He didn't care. He squeezed the third suitcase in with the first two, then slammed the door shut. "Hop in."

"Other kids have cool parents," Taylor said, putting on her seat belt. She examined his old muddy boots and his padded green jacket. The right sleeve was still missing the piece Thelma had eaten last year when he'd left her in the car.

"Lucky them." He started the car and looked at her. "Got everything that matters? School books, gym equipment, cell phone, purse?"

Taylor shrugged.

He shrugged back and started. His home was a good hour's drive from Emma's, on the other side of town. They worked at the same hospital, commuting from opposite directions. He skipped the downtown to take the side roads. The traffic was light. The roads were dry and white with salt. Taylor watched the patches of bright snow left on the tree branches, the hairy horses dressed in winter coats, the smoke coming out of chimneys. She wondered what dinner was going to be. Amber's cooking…

Her father cleared his voice. "Taylor, I need you to be nice to Amber."

"I'm always nice to Amber."

"Yes, but that's when you're visiting. Now that you'll live with us, the rules are about to change. Amber has a lot on her hands, with the house, the girls, and her job. I need you to be polite and help her. You shouldn't expect her to do things for you like your mother does. Did."

"Why, she started bitching already?" Taylor blurted.

Her father gave her a wilting look.

"Be respectful and polite."

Taylor swallowed her next remark.

"It would be nice if you'd help with things around the house. Cleaning the kitchen, taking the dogs out, cleaning the cat box. That would go a long way to make you appreciated." His voice was strained.

Has Amber given him a hard time?

She used to like Amber. Way more than she ever liked her mother. Amber was young and fun when they met. She was still dating Victor. Amber loved doing the girly things that Emma never did, like doing their nails and their hair. Going shopping. Their first vacation was New York City. They had a blast, eating out, shopping, going to shows. Amber was so much fun!

Then the girls came, first Opal, then Iris. Amber lost her spunk. She no longer had time to just "be girls" with Taylor. *Is this what happens when you have kids? You get to be boring and dull? I don't want kids! Ever!*

They drove up Victor's driveway, lined with Christmas trees of all different sizes—Amber was into the green stuff. They got a live Christmas tree every year, and they planted it afterward. That was nice, but their trees were always small—the roots had to fit in a container. Taylor remembered the fried tofu Christmas dinners. The morning yoga.

I wonder if leaving home was such a great idea.

The red door opened. The girls ran out to meet them. They jumped on Taylor, who picked them both up, hugging them tight. Amber, her ripped skinny jeans topped by a soft rose cashmere sweater like the one on the cover of *Vogue*, stepped out to meet them. She looked at Victor carrying the suitcases. She saw Taylor holding hands with the girls. She smiled. Her makeup was perfect, and her blonde hair fell to her shoulders like golden silk, but her smile didn't reach her eyes.

"Come in, everybody. It's cold outside."

15

———————

Kurt was holding pressure. His gloved finger had been stuck inside the bleeding gash for ten minutes now. The patient was covered in blood. So was he. Room 5 looked like the massacre scene from a cheap horror movie.

Kurt couldn't get the bleeding to stop. The thick, sticky blood had pooled in the depth of the wound. It was impossible to find the bleeder and cauterize it. He lifted his finger from the pumper, trying to see what he was doing. Warm blood, not his own, splattered his glasses, his mask, and everything else in the room.

He's got to be on something else besides Coumadin, the old rat-poison crap. It's got to be something more. Aspirin or Plavix or some freaking NOAC, the goddamn new blood thinners advertised all over TV! What the hell's happening in his brain if his scalp looks like this? He should have gone to the CT already, but he's bleeding like stink. I could throw in a couple of staples. That would stop it in a pinch, but the metal would cause so much artifact that the radiologist wouldn't be able to read the damn scan! Clinical correlation is advised! Bite me!

"Get me some Afrin spray and some gauze," he told Judy.

"Afrin?" Afrin, a nasal spray, was used for colds and runny noses, not for scalp lacerations.

She had a point, but he didn't have time to explain. "Afrin, on the quick."

Her lipless mouth told him that he was going to pay for this. The back of her navy T-shirt said it all: "Be nice to your nurses. We stop your doctors from accidentally killing you." *Damn ER nurses, they have no respect for doctors. It's always been like that, but it's gotten worse since Ken's death! The whole ER's gotten twitchy! Everybody is anxious, irritable, and ready to blow up. They miss Ken—God knows I miss him too—but they're also afraid that somebody's going to cut their throat. Police don't seem to give a shit! What the hell are they doing?*

He bent over the old man. The white hair was now a red helmet, dripping with blood from the four-inch gash. That's where his head had hit the nightstand.

"How did you fall? Did you pass out?"

No answer.

He doesn't have his hearing aids, of course! They never do. He shouted: "Did you pass out?"

"No."

"So how did you fall?"

"I don't know. I tripped, maybe?"

That's not good enough; I'll have to do a full syncopal workup with EKG and enzymes and the whole nine yards. We'll find nothing, as usual. That's how we practice medicine these days, thanks to the freakin' ambulance chasers. We spend money and resources to cover our asses since we're so afraid of getting sued. Common sense is no longer common.

Judy returned with the Afrin.

"Open it for me, will you?" he asked, his left hand still holding pressure inside the wound.

She did.

"Spray some in here. Even better, get some gauze and spray the Afrin on it. Soak it."

He nestled the gauze inside the wound, right on top of the bleeder.

"Get me a pressure dressing."

They bandaged the wound with an elastic dressing tight around the head and chin. They secured it with tape.

The bleeding stopped. The patient looked like a bloody mummy. Kurt didn't care. Neither did his patient.

"Let's get him into the scanner ASAP."

Kurt took off his bloody gloves, his blood-stained face mask, and his safety glasses. He put the glasses under the tap to wash them rather than smear the blood all over them. He took off his blue protective plastic coat. He was sweaty and dirty. He headed to the staff restroom to clean up.

Dick was leaning on Kayla's desk.

"Not today," she said. He smiled and touched her face. Kurt's blood boiled.

"Tomorrow, then?"

"Maybe." She smiled, taking in his strong frame and clear blue eyes.

Just like "The Most Interesting Man in the World" commercial, Kurt thought, feeling dirty, small, and very angry. He stopped in front of them.

"What are you doing here? Not working, are you?"

"I stopped by to talk to the EMSA folks. Did you talk to them yet?"

"Nope. Not yet." Kurt tightened his fists. His head was about to explode. He'd forgotten about EMSA, like he forgot about everything when he was working. The ED was an alternate world. It absorbed him and made him forget everything else. "What did they say?"

"We talked contracts. They don't offer malpractice."

"Really? I've never heard about any employer not offering malpractice."

Malpractice insurance was essential. Nobody'd ever dream of working without it. In the litigious medical environment when everybody could sue anybody for any reason, good malpractice coverage was a must.

"They'll help arrange for individual malpractice. We pay for it."

"No pension either, I guess."

"Yep. No pension, no malpractice, no health insurance, no nothing. You're on your own, baby."

"Are you going to sign up?"

"I don't think so. Even though there are attractions." Dick smiled at Kayla, and she smiled back. "I'm a rolling stone. I don't like to be tied to one place. I love new places and new people. Want to travel together, baby?" he asked Kayla, as if Kurt wasn't there. "There's a beautiful world out there."

Kayla smiled but didn't answer.

Kurt's urge to punch Dick choked him. He clenched his teeth, pushed his fists further down in his pockets, and turned away. He had nothing to say. He was married. He had nothing to offer Kayla. He could even lose his job if their relationship became public knowledge. *Fuck the "Me Too" movement and the overblown feminism. I can't afford to lose my job. But then, I can't afford to lose Kayla.*

Room 5 was empty; the patient had gone to the CT scanner.

Thank God for little mercies. Kurt went to the bathroom. The cold water soothed his face and his burning eyes. To humor himself, he started fantasizing about killing Dick.

An insulin injection, maybe? Too tame. Sux? That would have him awake and hearing, but he'd be paralyzed, so that he couldn't breathe and he'd know he's dying. Maybe. I'd love to see the color of his blood though. Scalpel?

16

———————

 *nother long shift without the light of day.*

It had been dark when she'd come in at seven. It was even darker now.

Emma hurried to her car, cursing the wind cutting through her flimsy scrubs. She scrutinized the shadows, thinking about Ken.

This stuff about suicide is crap. Doctors don't kill themselves like this. We know better ways. We have drugs and scalpels, and we know how to use them. We even know exactly where to shoot ourselves.

She'd often thought about that. She'd wondered how to do it. She didn't want to die, but she wanted to be in control of whatever happened to her when the time came.

Ken didn't cut his own throat. Somebody else did. That somebody may be here, now, in the shadow, waiting. Waiting for what? Why did Ken die? A personal vendetta? A crazy family member? A patient? One of the seekers that Ken had cut off from their candy? Something personal, like Kurt being demoted? Nah, that's not Kurt's style. Who then?

She wondered if she was at risk, walking alone through the dark parking lot. She shivered, the cold going deep inside her heart. She checked her pockets for her short, heavy stethoscope. It was her weapon. She'd been practicing using it like a nunchaku. *I wish I had a gun, or at least a scalpel. That, I'm good*

78

with. Pepper spray! I'll get some tomorrow. She shivered again and looked around once more before opening the car door.

Once inside, she took a deep, relieved breath, started the car, and drove home. Her neck ached, her scrubs felt tight, and her hands were hurting with cold. *I'm ready for this day to be over.*

The last straw had been the drug seeker who'd called her a cunt. Security had escorted him out, but her anger made her blood boil even now, hours later.

It had been his third visit this week. A broken tooth today, belly pain two days ago, back pain the day before. Each time he got an opioid prescription that he didn't need. *He'll either abuse it or sell it on the streets. It's surely easier to give in and give him what he wants, but it's just not the right thing to do.*

Hot with anger, she'd gone to confront Umber, who'd signed his last script.

He wanted none of it.

"You practice your way; I practice mine. You're not my boss. You don't tell me what to do."

"But he's been here three times this week looking for a fix. We can't keep giving him opiates. That's not good practice."

"The Joint Commission says, "If they say they have pain, they have pain.""

"But go look at the Prescription Drug Monitoring database. See how many opiates scripts he's gotten over the last few months for a plethora of complaints. He's not here for pain. He's here for a fix."

"I have to look after patients and deal with a freaking endless amount of paperwork. I don't have time to check the freaking PDM."

"You're indulging his addiction instead of helping him!"

"Once again: I'm practicing the way I see fit. You have no business telling me what to do."

"But it's morally wrong to feed their addiction!"

"They are adults; they do what they choose to do. I'm not their guardian!"

"But you shouldn't be their drug peddler, either! You're a doctor!"

He looked like he was about to hit her.

"Get a life." He left.

She wanted to hit him. She took a deep breath instead and went back to her patients. Now that this damn shift was finally over, she needed to vent. She called Victor.

He was busy, getting the girls ready for bed.

"No, not that one, Opal. The pink one, your mother said." He sighed. "Sorry, Emma, what were you saying?"

"I had a miserable day. I hate the ED. I'm going to take Ken's advice and turn down the job."

"Ken's always been afraid of his own shadow. He never took any risks. You're not Ken."

"I thought you liked him!"

"Sure I did, everybody did, but he couldn't make up his mind to save his life."

"Still, he was right. He also said that I should spend more time with Taylor. I shouldn't take on a job being on call 24/7."

"Taylor's seventeen. She has no time for you. She'll be on her own soon. She's out of your house already. Why on earth would you turn down a career opportunity you may never get again? You don't have to do it forever if it's not your thing."

"But I have no experience!"

"You won't get any unless you take the job."

"What if I fail miserably?"

"You won't. If you fail, you'll fail gloriously, like you always do. You'll get up and move on. It may even be good for Taylor to see you take chances and reach beyond your level of comfort," he said.

"No, not there, Iris, the other drawer. The left. The other left. Sorry about that, Emma. That ED needs some changes. I know you guys are all bent out of shape that EMSA is taking over, but that place is out of control. Everybody does whatever the hell they want. It's an absolute mess. It's high time that somebody with balls got it together, and you've got more balls than anyone I've ever met."

Emma felt warm inside. His vote of confidence was exactly what she needed. She remembered Umber: "You're not my boss; you don't tell me what to do."

"What if they backstab me?"

"They will. They backstab each other all the time; they'll backstab you even more. So what? You'll just do your job. Pay no attention to the naysayers. They'll get over it, or they'll get out."

Victor's right. I should give it a try. I can make the ED better for the patients and even the staff. I'd get to tell Umber and Crump what to do. Wouldn't that be fun!

"Thank you, Victor. I'll do it."

"Atta girl. Go get them," he said, and she could hear the smile in his voice.

17

———

E mma's phone rang. They needed her back. Already.

She'd been the ED director for almost an hour, and her new job was starting off with a bang. One of her nurses was in a coma. Police were on their way.

On her way back, she thought about Ken. It had been a week. There was no progress. None that the ED folks knew of, at least. The whole place was quivering with anxiety. The staff were afraid to walk to their cars. They asked Security to chaperone them after dark. During daylight, they'd wait for each other and leave in pairs rather than risk walking alone through the parking lot. *And now this. Whatever this is.*

It was George. They'd found him unconscious in the shower room.

Police gave her a heavy stare and checked her ID before letting her in.

"You know him well?" the heavyset policewoman asked her.

"Very well."

"How long has he worked here?"

"Longer than I have. Now, if you'll excuse me…" Emma tried to walk past her into Trauma 3.

"What was he using?"

"Excuse me?"

82

"What drugs was he using?"

"What makes you think that he was using any?"

"Didn't they tell you?"

"Tell me what?"

"They found him with a needle in his arm."

Emma bit her tongue. She blinked. She'd thought that George had slipped in the showers, then fallen and hit his head. Or that he'd been attacked. *Apparently not.*

"I see. Who found him?"

"A nurse coming in for his shift."

"I see."

She took in the ED. *What a mess! George is in a coma after using drugs at work. Carlos, who found him, is talking to the police instead of taking care of patients. We're starting two nurses down. Everyone else is either in shock or gossiping in the corners. Nobody's looking after patients. Police everywhere, inside and out. We may as well be in shutdown.*

"Excuse me. I need to go."

The policeman guarding Trauma 3 tried to stop her, but she flashed her new ED DIRECTOR badge and pushed through.

George was lying on the stretcher. His head looked twice its size, wrapped in bloody compression bandages. A stiff C-collar stabilized his neck. He was intubated. The plastic tube connecting him to the ventilator was stuck to his face with tape crossing over his mustache. *That's going to be a bitch to remove.* She checked his vitals: Blood pressure 157/98, HR 86, O2 sat 100 percent, temperature 98.6. Judy, his nurse, was working on a third IV. Nora was doing an EKG.

"How is he?"

Judy shrugged without making eye contact. The red flash in the catheter told her that she got into the vein. She slid the needle all the way in with a smooth move and secured the IV. Safe now, she glanced at Emma.

"We're just back from CT. They said it's a brain bleed. He hasn't been conscious since we found him."

"Who's his doctor?"

"Umber."

"Has he called his family yet?"

"No. The police want to secure his home first."

Emma walked to the head of the stretcher. She squeezed George's shoulder. "I'm here, George, my friend. We'll take care of you."

He didn't move.

She went to look for Umber. She had to circle the ED twice before she found him. For once, Umber didn't look his usual cool self.

Wrinkled white coat; messed up hair; stained scrubs. Blood? Coffee? Worse?

He looked at her with bloodshot eyes.

"How is he?" she asked.

"Bad." He logged in the computer and opened George's head CT. The brain, a gray walnut inside its skull, was marred on the right by a blinding white patch. *Blood.* He was bleeding in his brain; the pressure of the blood inside the inflexible skull was squishing the soft, jelly-like brain, crushing it. The midline had left the middle, expanding, curving around the fresh blood. The right half intruded into the left by almost an inch.

Midline shift. This is the beginning of the end. The increased pressure will start pushing the brain down toward the spine, extruding it into the spinal canal.

That's the end of the end. "Awful. Just awful."

Emma imagined George's brain squeezing out of his skull with everything that made George be George. His knowledge, his sense of humor, his personality, all gone. She envisioned his dead brain liquifying, his body kept alive by the machines.

She shivered.

"I've ordered mannitol from Pharmacy to lower intracranial pressure. I talked to the neurosurgeon across the lake. I'll send him out as soon as I can get an ambulance."

"How about hypertonic saline, while you're waiting for the mannitol? We have it here."

"Yep. Any other ideas?"

"Head up at forty-five degrees. Paralyze him. Maybe even hyperventilate a little?"

"He's paralyzed already. The head up is a good idea. I'll wait to hyperventilate. I hope to get him out of here first."

Keeping the intracranial pressure low to prevent herniation was essential, but hyperventilation was risky. It reduced the blood volume, but it caused vasospasm, shrinking the blood vessels to almost nothing and cutting the oxygen supply to the brain.

That's a Hail Mary pass. What George really needs is somebody to drill a hole in his skull and drain the blood to reduce the pressure. That may give him a chance. He needs a transfer.

"Did you send a drug screen?"

"Yep. Drug screen, alcohol level, blood gas, lactate, the whole nine yards."

"How was he when they found him?"

"Agitated. He was breathing on his own, but I had to intubate and paralyze him to get him in the scanner. I pan-scanned him just in case, but I don't expect to find much. It's all in the head."

"Is it true that he had a needle in his vein when they found him?"

"Yes."

"Anything else?"

"A vial of propofol. Empty. Police took it."

"Ours?"

"Don't know."

Propofol, the drug famous for killing Michael Jackson, lovingly nicknamed "Milk of Amnesia" by its fans, was a white liquid sedative frequently used for procedures. *It's a wonderful drug to put patients to sleep and make them forget. Until they get too much of it and stop breathing.*

"I can't fathom why people use propofol," Emma said.

"Neither can I, but I've seen it before."

"At work?"

"Yes. A while ago, a nurse in Concord, New Hampshire. They found her blue. She'd given herself too much."

"Did she make it?"

"No."

"The crew's here," Judy said.

"Thank God. Let's get this show on the road," Umber said.

"The police don't want to let him go before they finish processing him."

"Are you kidding me? He has to go. Now." He headed to Trauma 3 where one officer was fingerprinting George while another one was inventorying the contents of his pockets. "He needs to go," Umber said.

The officer in charge stopped counting George's change. "Another thirty minutes or so and we're ready."

"He needs to go now. He doesn't have another thirty minutes."

"He's under my charge. We'll finish as fast as we can, then he can go."

"He's under my care. He goes now." Red-faced and angry, Umber leaned over the officer, ready to grab him by the throat.

Emma intervened. "One of you officers can go with him in the ambulance and continue processing him, while we are getting him the care he needs." Dick gave her a killer look. The officer glanced at her, looked apprehensively at Dick, and then nodded.

18

The ambulance left. The weariness remained. This was about to be the second death in less than a week in their department, a place where they were so close that they passed around the clothes their kids had grown out of and they recycled spouses. The mood got even darker when George's wife, Mary, arrived, shrunk with pain, her wrinkled face a mask of grief.

Emma hugged her, holding her tiny frail body close, trying to squeeze away her pain.

"Where is he?"

"He's gone to the trauma center. He'll need surgery. We sent him off as fast as we could."

"They said he was doing drugs," Mary said, blowing her nose, "but that's a lie. He hasn't done any drugs since Vietnam except for pot."

"Are you sure?"

"Of course, I'm sure. I've been with him for twenty-three years. He drinks, he smokes, he does pot, and he's a pain in the ass, but he don't do no drugs."

"What if he does them but he didn't tell you?"

"He doesn't need to tell me. I know it when he's had one glass too many; wouldn't I know it when he's high?"

They had found him in the act. Unless it was a setup... But why? And who? Is she trying to protect him? But he's so sick, why would she bother to lie? "Did you tell the police?"

"Sure I did. They don't believe me. They've made up their mind. They're at home now, ripping the place apart, looking for God knows what. I told them there's nothing to find, but they wouldn't listen."

"Mary, if he's been doing drugs, who would know?"

"He isn't."

"If he was, who would know?"

"Listen to me, he isn't. He doesn't have money for cigarettes unless I give it to him. We can't afford to fill the tank; we only get twenty dollars' worth of gas at a time. Where do you think he'd get money for drugs? Santa?"

"What if he stole drugs from here? He could get them for free. It's easy. If the doctor ordered a dose of Dilaudid, George could just use it himself and give the patient some saline. He'd come back and say that the patient needed more. The doctor would order another dose. It would be even easier if the drug was ordered PRN—as needed. He could give it as often as the patient complained of pain. One for the patient, one for himself—nobody would ever know."

"I don't believe it."

"What do you think then?"

"Somebody tried to get rid of him."

"Who? And why?"

"I don't know. But what I do know is that my George doesn't do drugs. Now I'm going to see how he is."

"Let me get somebody to drive you."

"I'll drive her," the policewoman said. Her knowing eyes looked at Mary with pity.

SPIDER

I'm back.
I got my fix, but it's over. I'm out again.
I sold the phone. Finished that money too.
I need more.
He's got it.
He's gonna give me some more.
He's one of the white coats. I just don't know which one.
I know his voice. "If you cut all the way through the windpipe, he won't scream," he said.
I'll find him.
I sit and wait.
They won't know me. I got rid of my old coat.
This one's pink, but it's got a hood and it's warm.
I wait. A white coat comes out.
"Got a cigarette?"
He says, "No."
Not him.
I try the next one.
And the next one.

19

It was past midnight when Emma finally made it home. She pushed the deadbolt, dropped her bag, and picked up a bottle of red. A Chilean Carménère tonight, an in-your-face wine with much body and little subtlety, so dark one couldn't see the light pass through, unlike those weakling pinots from Washington State, so soft-spoken they looked watered down.

This wine reminded her of Dick Umber. No subtlety about him, no compromise, no softness. As she took her first sip, filling her mouth with the dry, tannin-laden strength, chewing it to bring its flavor under the tongue and behind the teeth to strike every taste bud, she wondered if she liked Dick. She wasn't sure. He was a good doctor, but he was too macho and too much of a showoff.

He could be charming when he chose to be, like with Kayla. That side of him was reserved for pretty girls and important people. She took another sip and remembered that she was the new Ken, therefore important in Dick's world. In the ED world, in fact. Ken was right; everything that happened was her problem. And there was a lot.

Ken's death, to start with. The police had finally concluded that it wasn't a suicide, but there was no further progress.

His death and the attack on George must be related; it's too much of a coincidence to have them both happen here in less than a week.

She had started going around asking questions. She got some answers. Judy remembered a funny little homeless man asking about Ken one night when she was working in triage. He had a gift for Ken, he said. He wanted to thank him for taking care of his son. *That's unusual. Grateful patients may bring some cookies or donuts, but gifts are rare, especially from somebody who looks like he can't afford a cup of coffee.*

"What was he like?" Emma asked.

"Homeless. Disheveled. Bad teeth."

"Anything else?"

"He had a long gray coat with a badge. Like a military something. He dragged his left leg."

Judy's face lit up as she remembered: "He had a spider tattoo on his right hand. Like the whole hand was a spider and the fingers were its legs. Gross!"

This is something. Maybe. I'll talk to the other triage nurses and the security people tomorrow.

She drank down her wine and headed to Taylor's room to check on her. The room was a mess, as usual. It took her a moment to remember that Taylor was gone, and she was half ashamed and half relieved. She thought about Victor. He had Taylor and Amber, both. Lucky him! She poured herself another glass, wondering how Taylor was doing.

She sat on her crumpled bed looking at the family picture on the dresser. *How young we were! Taylor was just a baby. We were still in love.* Victor, dressed in faded scrubs, was smiling, his hair a riot of dark curls falling over his glasses. Taylor, her eye color still undefined, was sitting on his shoulders squinting at the camera. Emma, thin and pretty in her flowery dress, sporting huge dark circles around her eyes from lack of sleep, leaned into him.

Life was good.

Taylor's moods got worse when Victor left for his fellowship. *She's missing her daddy*, they thought. *It will get better soon.*

It got worse. A psychiatrist diagnosed her as bipolar. He started her on mood stabilizers. They stabilized nothing, neither her flash mood changes, nor her angry outbursts or her violent rages. She became the evil genie of the house and Emma's albatross.

Emma poured another glass of wine. She remembered Mary. And George.

All the staff is getting tested regularly. George must have been clean; otherwise he'd be gone. A setup? Why?

The phone rang. It was Ann. She was pissed. As usual. She was talking so fast that Emma could barely follow.

"What happened?"

"I need you to come in right now!"

"Why?"

"I'm tired of fighting with the hospitalists! They don't call back for hours, and then they ask for all sorts of shit before they bother to come see the patient! This has to stop!"

"What exactly happened?"

"Come here and I'll tell you!"

"Why don't you tell me first?" *I've been there the whole day; I've got another shift tomorrow—no, today now. This is just Ann being Ann—she can be a charmer, but she'd rather be a raging bitch. You never know which Ann you'll get; it depends on her meds. She needs to up her dosage.*

"I have this 69-year-old with AMS." AMS, altered mental status, could be anything from not remembering where you left your keys to being unresponsive. It made it hard to get the story, so there was a lot of work to do to rule out badness.

"The hospitalist doesn't even want to see her. 'Admit her to psychiatry,' he said.

"Does she have a psychiatric history?"

"Not that we know of."

"Is she coming from home or a nursing home?"

"She lives alone."

"What's the matter with her?"

"She's confused."

"Anything on the workup"

"Nope. Labs are OK, head CT is OK, vitals are stable. I'm waiting for the drug screen and alcohol level. She's not septic or hypercapnic."

"Does she need an LP?"

"No fever, no white count, no neck rigidity. If they really want a spinal tap, they can do it themselves."

"No neuro deficits?"

"None new."

"Who did you speak to? And what did they say?"

"I spoke to Gandhi. He said there's nothing medically wrong with her, send her home or admit her to psychiatry."

"Did he see her?"

"No. He says he's five behind and he doesn't have time for this crap."

Gandhi, the night hospitalist, was busy. Five behind, that meant five patients waiting for orders and for hospital beds, five families snapping at the nurses, and five ER beds boarding admitted patients. That was bad all around.

"He needs to see her. He has no room to talk before he's seen her."

"Yes, Director. I wish I was smart enough to think of that."

Ann's being a bitch. That's Ann's superpower. She could bitch at Gandhi and have him come see the patient, but no, she calls me instead. In twelve years I'd called Ken only once, when a bus caught on fire and we had a mass casualty incident. Calling me for this?

Still, Emma's first instinct was to help Ann and make friends. Fortunately, she knew better. *Ann doesn't need friends. She needs servants. Giving in to her would only teach her to do it again.*

"I agree. He can't refuse to admit her without seeing her and leaving a note in the chart."

"What are you going to do?"

"Me? Nothing. Ann, I know you can manage this. I have faith in you."

She hung up, smiling.

It's good to be king.

20

———————

Kayla was late again.

Eden was playing on the floor with Lego blocks while Clarissa was cleaning up. He looked up when he heard the door slamming. *He's been crying,* Kayla thought.

"I'm so sorry, sweetheart!" she said, kneeling on the floor next to him, forgetting the nylons and the pencil skirt riding up her thigh. She hugged him, looking over his head to Clarissa, her eyes apologizing. "I'm sorry, Clarissa, I didn't mean to..."

"You never mean to," Eden said. "You never mean to, but then you do." He stopped crying and started putting Legos away. "You forgot again?"

"No, I didn't." She stood up looking regretfully at the nylons. *Gone.* "Something came up."

"What?"

"What did you do today? Were you a good boy?"

"*He's* always good," Clarissa said.

But I'm not. Kayla wished she were a better mom. *I should get it together, but it's so hard to be a single mom, and work, and go to school. It would be nice to have a little time off once in a while and have some fun!* After all, she was only twenty-four! Except that last time had been no fun. Kurt had been in a bad mood. He didn't like Dick's interest in her. He wanted to know if she'd gone out with him, if she liked him, if she was planning to see him. As if he had a right to know!

She got pissed. "Do I ask you what you do with your wife?"

"But Kayla, you know how much I care about you!"

"I care about you too, but that's not the point. You have your life, and I have mine. We need to respect each other's privacy. I never ask what you do with Sheila. I don't see how it's any of your business what I do."

"But Sheila is my wife!"

"So?"

"You barely know Dick! He's nothing to you!"

"And that's your business how?"

"But you and I, we have a relationship! I care about you!"

"I care about you too, but my relationship with others is none of your business."

"So you do have a relationship with Dick." His shoulders slumped, the fight going out of him.

She felt sorry. She wanted to tell him no. She barely knew Dick. They'd gone out for dinner once. That was it. There was something about him... *He's slippery. He looks at every girl. They say he spent some time in a closet with the new CNA. I don't trust him.* She'd seen pictures of his boat and his vineyard, but his Facebook page was blank.

Still, none of this was Kurt's business.

He looked so crushed that she almost broke down to tell him the truth. Almost. *He wants to have his cake and eat it too; he goes back home to his wife every night.* The only weekend they'd ever spent together had been a conference in Florida, that time when Sheila couldn't make it. Kurt had taken her instead, but whenever they were in public, he'd acted as if he didn't know her. It had been humiliating. *I'm only temporary in his life. It's high time to stop waiting for him and get a life. Dick is charming, generous, and single.*

"Sorry, Kurt, that's the way it is." She had left swallowing tears, but she hadn't looked back.

Eden shook her hand.

"What?"

"Can we go to McDonald's?"

That wasn't the healthiest dinner, but she was feeling guilty… and he was so skinny… and he had been so good… and there was nothing to eat at home… "Sure, let's go."

"Wahoo!"

Kayla smiled. Happiness is easy when you're five.

Clarissa shook her head. "You're going to spoil him rotten one of these days!"

"You'll make sure it doesn't happen." Kayla hugged her. "Thank you, Clarissa, and I'm so sorry."

"S'ok. How did the exam go?"

"It went well, I think. I was done almost an hour early."

"When do you get the results?"

"Next week. If I pass, I move on."

Kayla was working on her college degree. She had two years left. She'd dropped out when she had Eden, since she couldn't juggle work and school and motherhood. Now that he'd gotten older, she had gone back. She'd already passed four of the third-year exams. Only one left. *Next year should be easier, with Eden old enough to go to school.* The one thing that got her was the lack of sleep. The other day she'd fallen asleep at her desk. Dr. Steele had woken her up gently but firmly and had brought her coffee. She'd been embarrassed and apologized, but Dr. Steele had just ruffled her hair and said, "It's OK, nobody died, kid. Just try to get more rest." *She gave me a look. I wonder if she knows about Kurt. We've been discreet, but then there was that one time in the parking lot…*

It's not easy to be working full-time and study while being a single mom, but I wouldn't change it for the world.

She unlocked the door of her new Nissan and helped Eden in.

"McDonald's it is."

21

The woman on the hallway stretcher looked more dead than alive. Her conjunctivae, the white of her eyes, was too white, her skin ash gray.

Emma glanced at her as she was passing by, then went to look her up. The chief complaint was rectal bleeding. Emma went back to speak to her. *She's having trouble answering questions. No monitor. No IV access. No good.* Emma went to Brenda, the triage nurse.

"This patient needs a room."

"There are no rooms." Brenda turned around and left.

Brenda knows better. She must be busy.

"Kayla, who's in charge?"

"Judy. Should I get her?"

"Please." *Who can come out to make room for this GI bleeder? Room 6 is waiting for her psychiatric evaluation. Being in the hallway in her blue paper scrubs isn't going to do her any good, but more importantly, Room 6 isn't monitored. Trauma 2 is empty. That should work.*

"Yes?"

"Judy, we need this patient in a room. She needs an IV and monitoring."

"What's wrong with her?"

"Rectal bleed."

"Is she actively bleeding?"

"Let's get her in a room and find out, shall we? Can't do it in the hallway."

"We don't have any rooms at the moment."

"Yes, we do. Room 2 is empty."

"Yes, but it hasn't been cleaned, and it's waiting for an ambulance bringing in a transfer."

"No, it's not. We have a sick patient in the hallway. She needs the room. We can't have that room sitting empty for whenever somebody shows up."

Judy shrugged, told Kayla to send the cleaning crew to Trauma 2, and left.

I'm getting a lot of that lately. My old friends don't like me anymore. The other day she'd asked Alex to have a look at a rash. "I've got my own patients," he huffed. Brenda and Judy were behaving like spoiled children. Ann had asked to try on Emma's new white coat. "You're obviously not counting your calories," she smirked, and her nurses laughed. Emma laughed too—what else was there to do?—but she felt hurt. *Thank God for Sal, who's still my friend.* The doctors from all the other departments—hospitalists, surgeons, radiologists—had been supportive. Even former foes had cut her some slack. *All but my own. They're trying to bring me down.*

"It's because you're a woman," Minerva said later that day when they met at the gym. "Nobody likes a powerful woman, neither the women nor the men."

"Why?"

"The men, because it's not manly to have a woman lead. The women, because it's you and not them." She wiped her sweat off, pointing to the skinny blonde on the cycle. "See her?"

"Yes."

"I'm so envious of her body that I hope she'll sprout a hernia. I'd give her one if I could. Same with your people; they are envious of your power. They'd like to see you fail, like I'd like to see that girl fat and ugly just to feel better about myself, to see myself as less old and inadequate."

"You're neither old nor inadequate!"

"Whether I am or not is irrelevant. What's relevant is how I feel. She doesn't make me feel good about myself, just like you don't make them feel good about themselves."

"What can I do?"

"Hang in there. Do your thing. Be a good doctor; be a good leader. They'll get over it."

Minerva, the eternal optimist. I hope she's right. Ken warned me. I don't know how long I can do this. There's only so much wine my liver can take.

SPIDER

I found him.

Two days I sat on the bench, asking for a light from every man with a white coat.

Security came. "What are you doing here?"

"Waiting for my girlfriend."

"Who's your girlfriend?"

I showed them a picture of Jess. Naked.

They looked away.

"She works in the kitchen. She left me. I want her back."

"You can't sit here on the bench every day."

I left.

I drove back in a motorized shopping cart I got from Walmart. It had just enough juice to get here; then it died.

They didn't say nothing. Can't bother a cripple.

This morning I found him.

"You have a light?"

He looked at me with eyes the color of water. "No."

"A cigarette?"

"Why do you need a light if you don't have a cigarette?" he laughed.

That laugh made me cold inside.

It was him.

"I don't need a light; I need a fix, boss."

He looked at me sharply.

"The fish-knife. It worked. I need another fix."

"I don't know what you're talking about."

"Sure you don't. We never met, you and me. I need a fix. Soon. Like today."
He looks at me.
"No hurry. Tonight's good. I'll be back at ten. I'll look under the bench for my fix.
Maybe it's there. Maybe not. Maybe I know you. Maybe I don't."
"You sure about that?"
"No, not sure. But I kept the knife. The box. The photo. And the instructions. I'll leave
them under the bench if I find my fix. If not, maybe police wants them."
"Maybe," he says.
I get off the cart to shake out the numbness. I'll be back.

22

———————

"What do you mean you don't know where she is?" Emma blurted into her phone.

Judy turned to stare at her.

I'm too loud. She walked to the abandoned X-ray reading room and pulled the door shut to get some privacy.

"She didn't come home last night," Victor said. "I was on call and I never got home, but Amber says she hasn't seen her since yesterday. The girls haven't seen her either. I don't think she ever came home from school."

"Did you call her?"

"Five times. I texted her, too. No answer, but she could still be asleep."

Almost ten. She could be, she sleeps every Saturday till noon. But where is she?

"Did you try Katie's house?"

"I didn't. Can you?"

"I'm at work, damn it. I can't leave here till four. I'll call her, but how about if you drive over to Katie's and call me back?"

"I was supposed to take the girls skiing. Amber is going out for lunch with her friends."

"I'm sorry, but I can't leave here right now," Emma said, stepping out into the fully lit chaos outside. "Code 66, Emergency Department. Dr. Steele to Room 3."

"I have to go." She hung up and headed to Trauma 3. The paramedics were moving a wiggling, half-naked man covered in vomit onto the ER stretcher. *He's breathing.* She counted the "motherfuckers" while donning plastic gloves. She got to three. *Breathing well.*

"What's up?" she asked, grabbing his dirty boots to help move him.

"We found him unresponsive in the McDonald's parking lot," Lou said.

"On the ground?"

"No, in a truck."

"Parked?"

Lou nodded.

"Alone?"

"Yes. Driver's seat, safety belt on."

"And?"

"He had a pulse, but he was barely breathing, eight to ten a minute. His oxygen sats were in the 80s."

"Blood pressure?"

"Was OK."

"Then?"

"We gave him Narcan."

"How?"

"Intranasally."

"How much?"

"Two mg."

"Once?"

"Yes. He came to and started swearing."

That's what they do. You get them out of a high and throw them into withdrawal. That hurts. That's why it's worth being stingy with the Narcan. You want to give them just enough to get them breathing, but not enough to wake them up; otherwise, you get this. If they arrest or stop breathing though, then it's full steam ahead no matter what. They wake up, and they want to leave. Narcan wears off fast. They look OK, they take off, and then they drop dead. Bad plan.

"Where's my phone, you motherfuckers? I wanna call my lawyer! I'll sue your asses, every one of you!"

Funny how all my patients have a lawyer on speed dial. "Restraints, and security, please."

"I'm Doctor Steele; I'm glad to meet you." The patient, held down by the paramedics, made eye contact and spat at her. The phlegm came down to land on his own cheek. Emma wiped away the few drops that had reached her. "What is your name?"

"You motherfucker!" Somebody laughed.

"I doubt that. How are you feeling?" She checked his pulse, palpated his abdomen, and considered listening to his lungs. *Nope. That's getting too close.* "Let's get him a mask, and get those restraints. This week please, rather than the next."

"Let me go, you assholes. You can't keep me here. I know my rights."

"We'll let you go as soon as we know you're safe."

He exploded into another string of obscenities.

Emma was glad to see that he was breathing well, wasn't slurring his curses, and looked intact. She returned to her desk to place orders, when she remembered: Taylor was missing. She checked her phone. Two missed calls: one from Victor, one from Amber.

She stepped back in the dark reading room to call Victor.

No answer.

Tried again.

Still nothing.

She couldn't bring herself to call Amber. She didn't want to hear how Taylor was creating havoc in Amber's home and setting a bad example for her daughters. *I can't deal with that right now. How on earth can I take off to look for Taylor? The place is a zoo.*

"Kayla, can you find somebody to take over my shift?"

"This shift?"

"Yes, there's a problem with my daughter. I need to go."

Kayla picked up the phone. *Slim chance. Who'd come in on a beautiful Saturday on a minute's notice to pick up half a shift?*

Her phone rang. Amber. Emma sighed.

"Hi, Amber."

"Emma, I'm so sorry."

"Yeah, me too."

"She had breakfast with us yesterday. She looked fine. She took the bus to school, and I haven't heard from her since."

"Did she go to school yesterday?"

"I don't know. When she didn't come home yesterday afternoon, I thought she was out with her friends. We didn't worry until she didn't show up this morning. She wasn't in her room. I don't think she's been here since yesterday morning, but I'm not sure."

"Is her stuff still there?"

"There're piles of stuff everywhere, I don't know what's missing."

"Her computer?"

"She took it to school."

"Did Victor get to speak to Katie?"

"He's there now."

"Amber, do you have contact information for any of her friends besides Katie?"

"I don't."

"Can you check in her room and see if you find anything? I'm so sorry to impose on you, but I'm at work and I can't leave now."

"Sure. I'll call you back."

"Thanks."

23

―――――――

She went back to running the board. The kid in Room 6 looked better after fluids and Motrin. His heart rate was down; he was slobbering happily, chewing on his mother's phone. *It's probably just a virus.* "Let's PO challenge him and send him home," she told Carlos. That was ED jargon for "Give the kid something to drink."

"Popsicle?"

"Whatever he'll take."

The woman with suicidal ideation in Room 7 was still drunk. At least that's what her numbers said. She needed at least another hour before being legally sober for her psychiatric evaluation. She'd been awfully drunk last night when the police brought her in. She was angry at her significant other, so she told him that she was going to jump from a bridge. He called 911.

I've heard that a thousand times, even when there's no bridge within a hundred miles. When they sober up, they deny they ever said it. They swear they'd never, ever hurt themselves because of their love for God, for their children, or for their dog, but somehow it all goes out the window after the second drink.

She ordered a repeat alcohol level, also a Tylenol and aspirin level to make sure that the woman hadn't ingested anything else.

"Dr. Steele!" Kayla called. "I found one."

Found one what?

"Dr. Alex. He's coming to take over for you. He said, 'Don't see any new patients, just clean up what you can.' He should be here in half an hour."

"Really!" Emma's eyes filled with tears, and she hugged Kayla.

"I hope she's OK."

"Me too."

When Alex arrived she was ready. "Thank you!"

"No problem. What have you got?"

"The kiddo in 6 can go if he keeps his Popsicle down. The woman in 7 needs a crisis eval."

"Can she go or does she have to stay?"

"She can go, I think. Just give her a once-over first."

"OK."

"The guy in 3, his discharge is in the chart. He can go if he's still awake in an hour. Got Narcan about an hour ago."

"No trauma?"

"Not that we know of, but walk him first."

"Anything else?"

"No. Thank you, Alex."

"No problem. Remember when you came in for me last year when I ran over my dog?"

"No."

"Well, I do."

Emma drove to Victor's house. She rang the doorbell. Thelma and Louise started barking. They'd been hers, once. When they divorced, Victor took them. Emma got Taylor. *Lucky me!*

The door opened to an avalanche of kids and dogs jumping on her and hugging her waist and legs. She hugged them all back, kissed the girls, scratched the dogs, and then turned to see Amber.

"Go play, everybody."

They took off as one.

Taylor's room looked like the aftermath of a hurricane, but the bathroom was almost empty. A white piece of plastic was sitting on the counter.

A pregnancy test.

Positive.

24

Emma was walking so fast down the Administration hallway that the stethoscope was banging on her chest with every hurried step. She tried to stuff it in her white coat pocket, but with the scalpel, hemocult developer, rectal testing cards, and tongue depressors, her pockets were already full.

I really don't have time for this crap now. What on earth is so urgent that it can't wait until the end of my shift? Administrators are important people; they don't like to wait.

She shrugged as she remembered that she was now one of them, as her ER folks told her daily. Everything that didn't work right, from slow radiology reads to the Internet interruptions or the lack of Dilaudid, was her fault—or at least her problem. *This isn't half as much fun as it used to be. And of course, they're all here already, waiting. Déjà vu.*

She nodded to the sour-looking COO and sat in the only empty chair. The plump risk manager was there, so was the anorexic hospital lawyer, sitting next to a wiry man with short gray hair that she hadn't met. The policeman who'd been investigating George's case and had a pissing match with Umber was there too.

George had made little progress; he was still in the ICU, intubated. He'd had an emergency craniotomy. They removed part of his skull to allow his brain to swell without getting crushed. His prognosis was still uncertain.

Mr. Lockhart, the COO, pointed to the steel-haired man. "You already know Officer Boulos. This is Detective Zagarian. He has news for us. He requested your presence."

Why me? Taylor? It can't be; none of these people has anything to do with her. Then what?

"We received the victim's lab results," Zagarian said.

Victim? Oh, George! She'd never thought about him as a victim, not even when she'd seen him intubated.

"He had propofol in his system. A lot. We don't know how much he actually got, since we aren't sure when it was injected. There were no other drugs in his system except for cannabis."

Mary was right. He wasn't using anything but pot.

"His head injury matches the corner of the shower. What bothers me though is that he was found fallen forward, while his injury was at the back, in the occipital area."

"Maybe he turned around after he fell?" Emma asked. "Or maybe the person who found him moved him to see if he was breathing?"

"That's possible," Zagarian acquiesced, "but there's one more problem." He looked at each of them in turn as if he expected someone to confess. "He had a neck injury."

"That's not so unusual," Emma said, "depending on the way he fell he may have fractured..." She remembered: *I've seen the neck CT. There was no fracture.*

"The injury was to the front of his neck. Bruising around his Adam's apple, suggesting strangulation."

The silence in the room grew heavier.

"How old was that injury?" Emma asked. *Could he have been in another fight before?*

"Fresh. The bruising was absent in the first set of pictures, but it became obvious after the transfer, in the second set of pictures."

"So you're thinking that somebody strangled him in the shower, hit his head against the concrete corner, and then injected him with propofol?"

"Exactly. It could also be the other way 'round—someone strangled him until he passed out, then injected him with propofol, and then hit his head against the concrete. Interestingly, the propofol vial found at the scene didn't come from your pharmacy. It came from somewhere else."

"From where?" the COO asked.

"We don't know. Yet." He looked at each of them and said, "The reason I called you here today is to make it clear that we are now investigating this case as an attempted murder. We'll interview the staff. We expect you to cooperate to the extent that you can. We'll make arrangements to talk to each of you."

Lucky us. Emma stood and headed out the door before anybody could stop her, but Zagarian caught up with her. "I'll walk with you.

"We spoke to his wife. She said she has no idea why or who would want to kill him."

"I agree. I can't imagine anybody hating him that much."

"That much? Did he have enemies?"

"He liked to laugh and make fun of people. He could be a little rough."

"How did he get along with his wife?"

"Mary? As well as any couple who've been together for decades. They bickered a lot about money—money was always tight for them, especially after Mary lost her job last year—and about smoking. They both smoked, then blamed each other for not quitting. Mary was devastated when this happened, and I have absolutely no reason to suspect her."

"Could it all have happened by chance? What if George walked into the shower, found someone injecting, and they tried to silence him?"

"I guess that's possible… But you know, this isn't really the kind of place where nurses inject themselves in the shower on a daily basis."

"Well, maybe it wasn't a nurse, and it doesn't have to be daily."

Emma shrugged.

"We also considered blackmail. George's finances weren't as bad as you think. There's $10,000 in his personal checking account. Where do you think that money is coming from?"

"I have no idea." *They weren't well off, Mary and George. That money could have made a big difference, but where on earth was it coming from?*

"I have to go now, detective," Emma said, punching in the code to open the ER doors. She'd been gone for half an hour, which in ER time is an eternity—anything could have happened in that time, and it usually did.

"Thank you for your help. Remember that this is confidential; please don't discuss it with the staff."

"Really? I was just getting ready to post it on Facebook," she said, turning to leave.

He caught her elbow. She looked back. His gray eyes were smiling.

"Wanna be Facebook friends?"

Is he kidding?

"Or maybe just go for a coffee one of these days."

Is this professional or personal? He was attractive and she was single—way too single—but he was a cop.

I don't like cops.

"Maybe I'm just trying to pick your brain," he said, as if he could read her thoughts, "or maybe not. You won't know until you try, will you?"

He said until, not unless.

"Dr. Steele to Room 2," the speakers called. She was grateful for the interruption.

She left without another word.

SPIDER

I'm back.
It's half past ten. I gave him extra time.
I sit on the bench.
I bend over to tie my boot and look under.
There's a blue plastic bag. Small.
I pick it up.
A brown paper bag inside.
I open it.
A zipper bag, snack size. White powder. Like salt but lighter.
I open it. I smell it.
I taste it.
It's my fix. Good.
I close it. I put it in my pocket.
A photo. Car number on the back.
I know this one.
Keep the knife, he says.
Good.
This one's easy.
Fun too.

25

The gray-haired woman in Room 2 gasped for air. Her bony chest, wrapped in the flimsy hospital gown, heaved with every hard-fought breath. Attached to the monitors via multiple wires, she sat upright with her face jutting forward as if she was sniffing. She held herself upright, skinny arms supporting her torso, hands clutching her knees.

Textbook tripoding. She's struggling to move air even though her oxygen sat is 100 percent. That's weird. Bad asthmatics and old smokers with bad lungs would tripod to get more oxygen, but, by the numbers, she had all the oxygen her blood could carry.

Emma went to introduce herself.

"Hi, Emma."

It took a moment.

Sheila, Kurt's wife.

They hadn't met in ages, since she and Kurt didn't socialize. She'd never seen Sheila in the pathetic disguise of a hospital gown. Still, she hadn't aged well.

"Sheila?! What happened?"

"I'm having… a hard time… breathing."

"Since when?"

"This morning… or last night…"

"Anything else? Fever, chest pain, cough?"

"No."

"Are you a smoker?"

"No."

"Any medical problems?"

"Depression… Anxiety… two miscarriages."

Emma had heard about the miscarriages; people said they had ruined the marriage.

Why on earth would people want to have children? They're nothing but trouble! She hadn't slept in days, looking for Taylor who was still MIA.

"Any allergies?"

"No."

"Have you ever had anything like this before?"

"No."

"Any rash, any tightness in your throat? Any vomiting or diarrhea?" Emma asked, wondering if this could be an allergic reaction.

"No."

Sheila was tiring out. Her oxygen sat was still 100 percent, but she was breathing fast at 40—instead of the normal 16. Her heart rate, 132, was way too high.

She's sitting still, but her body behaves like she's running a marathon.

Emma listened to the lungs—clear as a bell—and to her heart—fast, but regular with no murmurs. She checked the EKG, unremarkable except for the tachycardia, the fast heart rate. The skin was clear, blood pressure was OK, no voice change to indicate an airway problem.

"Did you try any new foods, any new medications, any new detergents or lotions or soap, anything that your body may not be used to and might react to?"

Sheila shook her head no, but averted her eyes.

"Any alcohol or drugs?"

"No."

What on earth is going on? She looks fine, but she's breathing so hard! A PE? She has no risk factors for blood clots, and her sats are 100 percent. Anxiety? A panic attack?

"Any ringing in your ears?"

"Yes… my ears started ringing… this morning… how did you know?"

Emma turned to Faith, Sheila's nurse. "Let's give her a breathing treatment and ten milligrams of Decadron, just in case. Have you sent a blood gas?"

Faith was new. She had just moved in from New Hampshire and was still learning the ropes.

"No. It wasn't part of the protocol."

"Let's send it, please, also send Tylenol, aspirin and alcohol levels, and a urine and a drug screen. And let's get a chest X-ray, today if possible, and we'll get respiratory with bipap to give her some rest."

Faith shrugged and left.

"Sheila, did you overdose on aspirin?"

Sheila looked down. "Yes."

"How much and when?"

"Last night… I don't know, a handful… I didn't count."

"Did you take anything else?"

"No."

"Tylenol?"

"No."

"Are you sure?" Emma asked, holding her eyes, her hand on Sheila's shoulder.

"Yes."

Sheila's tears started streaming down her cheeks.

Emma hugged her. "I'm so sorry. We'll make you better."

Sheila hugged her back.

"Why aspirin?"

"They said it doesn't hurt."

It may not hurt, but it doesn't feel good either. Her body is trying to get rid of the acid in the aspirin by breathing it out. Aspirin is a killer. She may need dialysis to remove it. That requires planning and much better IV access than she's got. I'd better call them early. She's going to need a psych eval, but that can wait. Keeping her alive comes first.

"Does Kurt know?"

"He didn't... come home... last night."

"Would you like to call him?"

Sheila shook her head no.

"Would you like us to?"

Sheila started crying harder.

"Yes, please."

"Anybody else you want us to call?"

Sheila started crying even harder. "There's nobody else."

How awful, to be sick and alone. At least I'm not sick. As for alone...

She went to put in orders and checked her phone again. Still nothing from Taylor, and nothing from the police. It was getting old.

26

———

Emma and Victor had looked everywhere. They asked Katie. She said she didn't know. *She's lying. She's not worried about Taylor, and that's not like her. She knows.*

"Please, Katie, help us find her!"

Katie shrugged. Her old green sweater and ripped jeans made her look fragile and much younger than Taylor, but she was steady as a rock.

"You know where she is!"

Katie stayed silent.

"What if she's not safe? What if somebody's holding her against her will? We need to help her!"

No answer.

Katie's mother tried, too.

"Katie, if you know where she is, you must tell them! If you disappeared and I didn't know where to find you, I'd be sick with worry!"

They'd gone to her school. Nobody knew anything. She'd been to all her classes but the last. She didn't take the school bus home. The school counselor didn't know anything either, but she was going to ask her friends. *Her friends? I don't even know who they are, except for Katie!*

"Do you know any of her friends?" she'd asked Victor. "Other than Katie?"

118

"Tom."

"That's old news."

Victor shrugged. "It's all I've got."

"We didn't watch her well enough. I had tried so hard to not be like my mother, who wanted to know everything. She used to open my letters and interrogate my friends. I wanted to give Taylor more freedom. I wanted to trust her." Emma was talking to Victor, but even more, she was trying to persuade herself. *Yeah, maybe so. But, really, I was relieved when Taylor minded her own business so that I could focus on my career. I'm a lousy mother.*

"That's all water under the bridge. What do we do now?"

They went to the police.

"How long has she been missing?" the elderly detective asked.

"Since yesterday at one," Emma said.

"That's barely twenty-four hours. She may have spent the night with a friend."

"She never did that before without letting us know! We've been trying to contact her by email and text and phone. No answer."

"Maybe she doesn't want to speak to you. Did you have a fight before she left?"

"No," said Victor.

Emma shrugged. She hadn't seen her since she moved to Victor's.

"Have you tried her friends and her school?"

"Of course. Nothing."

"How about grandparents, cousins, extended family?"

Emma's parents were both dead, but Victor's mother, Margret, a lovely old lady who spent her days gardening, lived in Georgia. She was Taylor's favorite person.

"There's only my mother; we didn't want to alarm her."

"Well, you can file a missing person and we'll see what we can find. Still, you should get in touch with everybody who may have some information."

"She might be pregnant," Emma blurted; then she wished she hadn't. She hadn't had a chance to tell Victor yet.

"What?" Victor looked ready to strangle her.

"Amber found a pregnancy test in Taylor's room. It was positive."

Victor's face turned gray, and the pain in his eyes hurt to watch.

I wish I had found a kinder way to tell him. No matter what, Victor still thinks that Taylor is a little angel. This has got to hurt him even more than it hurts me!

"I'm sorry, Victor. Let's call your mother."

"I wish we didn't have to."

"It's better if you call her than if we do. What do you really think happened to her?" the policeman asked.

"No idea," Victor said.

"I'm thinking she found out that she was pregnant. She thought about what to do next." Emma was thinking out loud. "We both work at the hospital; she didn't want to go there. She was afraid we'd find out. She went elsewhere."

"How? Does she have a car?"

"No."

"How then?"

"A friend's car. A train. Greyhound. Plane."

"Where would she go?"

"Planned Parenthood. Closest ED."

"Why?"

"To confirm the pregnancy. To get rid of it."

"Where else?"

"Her grandmother? A friend? A trip?"

"A trip where?"

"Anywhere. She loves traveling. But what if she didn't choose to leave? What if something happened to her? What if she was kidnapped or even worse? What if the father decided to get rid of her?"

"Do you have any reason to suspect that?"

Victor shrugged. Emma knew better.

Life's always there to screw you.

27

———

L *ife's always there to screw you.*

"Dr. Steele to Room 2."

Emma sighed and returned to here and now. *Taylor will have to wait.*

Sheila wasn't looking good. Her skin was ashen; her oxygen sats were dropping.

She's tiring out. I have to do something. Like now. Twelve more patients waiting, two of whom I haven't seen. I hope they're breathing. They'll call me if they die. If they notice.

She paged the ICU and the renal attending for Sheila, then went looking for Sal. She walked into Judy, who was charge nurse today.

"Can you call Dr. Crump and tell him that his wife is in the ED? She'd like to see him."

Judy looked put out.

She thinks that I should call him myself. She's right. I should; I just can't. Not right now.

She sighed and walked away. Faith had called the Poison Control Center and they had recommended activated charcoal, even though the ingestion was hours old.

It's late for that, but aspirin overdoses are dangerous. Tablets stick together in clumps, and they get stuck in the stomach for hours. The activated charcoal helps eliminate them. It may not help her, but it can't hurt.

"How can I help?" Sal asked.

"We need a bicarb drip for Room 2."

"Renal failure?"

"Aspirin overdose."

"I haven't seen one of those in ages. Acute or chronic?"

Most aspirin overdoses were chronic. Elderly folks who forgot they took their pills, so they took them again. And again. They got weak and dizzy, like every other patient, every single shift. Easy to miss. Not this one.

"Acute, intentional."

"Wow. Do we know how much and when?"

"Last night. She took a handful, whatever that means."

"Did she take anything else?"

"Not that we know of."

"OK, I'll get the bicarb. That will help alkalinize her urine and enhance elimination. By the way, Dr. Steele, did you hear yesterday's case?"

That's never good news.

"Not yet. What was it?"

"Another Narcan-resistant overdose. They gave him four doses before he responded."

"Did he make it?"

"He made it to the ICU."

"Have you heard any more from your Poison Control Center friend?

"I'm meeting her tonight. You want to come?"

"Not tonight. Thanks, Sal. Please keep me posted. And let's get that drip going, shall we?"

"It's on its way."

She started Sheila on bipap, a plastic mask covering her mouth and nose, pushing air into her lungs to give her breathing muscles some rest. *She's looking better.*

Still no Kurt.

"No answer. I left a message. Should I try Kayla?" Judy asked.

So that's public knowledge. Is that why Sheila overdosed?

The speakers saved her again.

"Dr. Steele to Room 3."

The man in Room 3 had "the look." Pale, ashen, clutching his chest with calloused hands, wide eyes staring into death. *The poster child for a heart attack.*

"How long have you had this pain?"

The man groaned.

Confused?

Sweat poured out of him. They tried to wipe him off, but the EKG leads still wouldn't stick. The CNA tried holding them down with tape. No good. Brenda got IV access. They gave him aspirin and nitroglycerin.

That helped with the pain. He started talking.

The pain started last night as he was cutting wood—bad news. It's been waxing and waning through the night. He's short of breath—more bad news. He's fifty and a smoker; his father had his first heart attack at thirty-eight. More and more bad news.

The EKG was nondiagnostic. Not normal, but not a STEMI either.

"Let's send a cardiac panel. Please get another EKG in ten minutes."

The second EKG hadn't changed much. She signed it, timed it, and asked for another in ten minutes.

"Why? What's wrong with this one?" Aisha, the CNA, frowned.

"There's nothing wrong with it, but I need to see if anything changes. We need to know if he gets worse."

It did.

She paged cardiology. It was Victor.

"I have something for you," she said.

"So do I. We found Taylor."

Emma's breath caught in her chest.

Alive or dead?

Her throat was too tight to speak.

"She's safe."

28

"Where is she?"

"With Mother, in Atlanta."

"Margret said she wasn't there."

"She lied. Amber made her promise, and she didn't want to break her trust."

"How is she?"

"Pregnant. Otherwise fine."

"How pregnant?"

"Don't know. Early, Mother says."

"How did you find out?"

"Mother talked her into calling me. She wants to get an abortion."

"An abortion?!" Emma was not religious, not in the least, but she was a doctor. She was committed to saving lives. She'd thought about Taylor's pregnancy, but mainly she'd worried about her safety. She had nightmares about her lying dead in a ditch.

"An abortion," Victor said.

That was not an option as far as Victor was concerned; he was a practicing Catholic. For him, there was no bigger sin. Nine years ago, when he left

Emma to marry Amber, it had been because of Amber's unplanned pregnancy.

Unplanned, my ass, Amber knew damn well what she was doing when she forgot to take that pill.

"Who's the father?"

"She wouldn't tell me." Victor choked. "She can't have an abortion, Emma, she'll never forgive herself."

Emma wasn't so sure.

"She's just seventeen. What will happen to her future? To her college?"

"She'll manage somehow. Many girls do! You and I will help."

"Oh no, not me!" Emma shuddered. "One child was more than enough for me; I can't even think about having another baby in the house."

"She's your daughter! She needs your help, Emma! You can't abandon her!"

"I know. I can't abandon her, but I can tell you right now that I can't bring up her child. Not me. Maybe Amber?"

"Amber??!"

"Or you?"

The silence at the other end was long and ominous.

"We'll cross that bridge when we get to it," he finally said. "We need to get her home."

"Why? She's better off with your mother."

Margret, Victor's mother, was a real southern lady. Perfectly groomed and infallibly polite, she was a nice person and a great cook. She lived alone in a large house in the suburbs of Atlanta. Emma thought she looked like the aging version of Melanie Wilkes from *Gone with the Wind*—beautiful, dignified, kind.

"She likes your mother. Margret will be kind to her. It will allow her to think things through better than if she were here."

"Are you trying to pawn her off?"

"I didn't send her there. She chose to go. She may be happier there."

"We need to talk to her at least!"

"That we do. Tomorrow I only have one meeting. I can cancel it. Should we fly there?"

"OK. I'll get tickets."

"I'll get something for your mother."

Taylor couldn't find a better place to be. Maybe some of Margret's class and kindness will rub off on her.

Fat chance!

29

———————

Emma wrapped her extra shirt around Margret's present—a blown glass vase. It looked like a Greek museum artifact, with its stunted shape and irregular haziness.

She should get something for Taylor, too, she thought, but she couldn't come up with anything. Moreover, she had few good feelings about Taylor right now. Now that she was safe, she could go back to remembering what a pain in the ass she was.

She'd been a difficult baby, then grew into a stubborn toddler in a perpetual temper tantrum. She was a pain. Other mothers seemed to get along with their children. They even seemed to like them. Emma didn't like Taylor.

She loved her, of course—not like she had a choice, she had to love her, motherly love and all that crap—but she preferred dogs. Even cats. They may be ungrateful, but at least they weren't evil.

She added her *Neurological Emergencies* book to her pack for a little light reading and poured herself a glass of Medoc, a Chateau Greysac 2012, not too expensive but with the distinctive lingering tannins all Bordeaux share. She'd earned it.

The day had been rough. Still, she hadn't killed anyone. That she knew of. Victor had taken the chest pain to the cath lab. He needed stents, and he needed them now.

"Good catch," he said.

He wasn't kidding. That one she'd earned her money on.

Sheila had been another matter.

Kurt arrived hours later. He wasn't happy. He was mad at Emma and the nurses. He was mad at Sheila. Most of all he was mad at himself.

"What did you do for her?" he barked.

Sheila had given her permission to tell him.

"Charcoal…"

"Charcoal won't help. It's too late!"

"The Poison Control Center recommended it."

"What else?"

"I put her on bipap. She was having trouble breathing. I gave her fluids. I started a bicarb drip. I called the intensivist and renal."

"Are they coming?"

"They've been here already. She doesn't need dialysis, not yet."

"Who's admitting her?"

"The ICU."

He clenched his teeth so tight that his jaw muscles twitched. He left without another word and went to sit with Sheila. He accompanied her to the ICU.

An hour later Emma found him sitting in her chair.

I hope he isn't going to blow up again, right here, in the middle of the ED.

He looked awful. His face flushed, his hair a mess, he looked like he'd been crying.

"How is she?" Emma asked.

"She seems OK."

"Dialysis?"

"Not yet."

"Good."

They won't have to shove that damn dialysis hose into her. That'll save her from bleeding like stink after that boatload of aspirin killed all her platelets.

Kurt stood in front of her, checking out his hands. They were shaking. He looked her in the eye. His bloodshot eyes were hurting. His attitude was gone.

"Thank you, Emma. Thank you for everything you did for Sheila. I couldn't have done better."

"It was my pleasure. I'm happy that she's doing well."

"Thanks to you." He turned around and left.

Is that an olive branch? Truce, maybe?

Wouldn't that be good!

Back to the present, she got back to her packing. Motrin, Tylenol, instant coffee, chocolate. Books.

Taylor's room was still a mess. She couldn't bring herself to clean up. Who cared? She'd closed the door and pretended that it didn't exist. Unmade bed. Books. DVDs. Mismatched shoes all over the floor. *Harry Potter and the Chamber of Secrets*, Taylor's favorite book, sat on the bedcover. Emma took it.

She'll love it.

30

The taxi stopped at Margret's door. Emma inhaled the smell of moist earth and spring. Margret's well-loved garden was waking up. The green tips of daffodils broke through the dirt. Birds called love messages. Branches shimmered green. Emma loved spring. A time for hope and joy. The wonder of new beginnings. Then she remembered Taylor's pregnancy and she shuddered.

Margret smelled like cookies and oolong tea. Her hug felt like home. She was perfect from head to toe, as usual, her well-tamed white hair framing her narrow face, her sea-green dress hugging her delicate frame, her lipstick a magnolia shade of pink.

"How was the flight?" she asked, pouring the tea they had both declined in thin porcelain cups.

"OK. How are you, Mother?" Victor asked.

He loved her dearly, but he never called her Mom. Their relationship was warm but formal. Emma wondered sometimes if she was closer to Margret than Victor was.

"I'm well. It's been a pleasure to have Taylor here."

Really?

"I'm glad to hear. How is she?"

"Better. She was a little stressed out when she arrived. She was tired, too. She hitchhiked most of the way."

"She what?" Victor choked on his tea.

Margret gave him a Mona Lisa smile.

"Hitchhiked. Your daughter has an adventurous spirit. I wonder who she takes after."

"Not me," Victor said.

"Why did she hitchhike instead of flying or taking a train?" Emma asked.

"To make it harder for you to find her. She wasn't ready to talk to you."

Margret poured another cup of tea.

"I had a hard time persuading her to call you," she told Victor. She turned to Emma. "She refused to call you. Please be kind to her, both of you. She needs some love."

What she needs is a good spanking. She's needed that for a long time.

"Of course," said Victor. "Can we see her?"

Margret called upstairs. "Taylor, your parents would like to speak to you."

She sat back drinking her tea with small ladylike sips. Her job was done.

Taylor came down two cups later.

Her long dark hair falling over her face and the oversized checkered shirt made her look childish and fragile. So did her bare feet. She sat next to Margret, crossing her legs under her without acknowledging her parents.

Pain in the ass.

Victor got up and hugged her. After a moment she hugged him back.

Emma watched.

"How are you, sweetheart?" Victor asked.

"I'm OK," she said, playing with a rip in her jeans.

Victor looked at her, at his mother, at Emma.

"We love you, you know. We're here to help."

The silence hurt.

Emma couldn't take it anymore.

"How pregnant are you?"

"Emma!" Victor was shocked.

Taylor wasn't.

"I don't know," she said. "Two months, maybe more."

"Did you see a doctor?"

"No."

"We made an appointment for this afternoon," Margret intervened. "I thought you'd like to be with her."

Victor shrank.

"Of course," Emma lied. She couldn't pawn that off on Margret. "If Taylor wants us."

Taylor shrugged.

"Who's the father?" Emma asked.

Taylor looked her in the eye. Margret sipped on her tea.

Nobody spoke.

"I want an abortion."

"Taylor, you don't know what you're talking about. You can't have an abortion!" Victor said.

"Why not?"

"That's a baby growing inside you! You can't kill him!"

"Why not? It's not a baby; it's just an embryo. It's not alive. It's just a few hundred cells."

"It's about to become a baby, like you were! You can't kill it!"

"Yes, I can. I wish you'd killed me when I was like this!" she blurted, looking at Emma.

Emma's heart shrank. She had wished it too, many times. Now, looking at her beautiful, difficult, and unhappy daughter, she knew that her thoughts were a sin.

"Taylor, think about Opal and Iris! This baby's going to be just like them! You can't kill him," Victor said.

That gave Taylor a moment of pause. She loved Iris and Opal; she'd been there when Amber was pregnant with them, and she'd held them when they were just a day old, no larger than a cat, innocent, vulnerable, and with a future of endless possibilities.

"This is not a baby; it's an embryo. It's not yet alive. And it won't be if I can help it. I don't need a baby. I can't even take care of myself," she said bitterly, with an insight Emma didn't know she had.

"You could give it up for adoption," Margret said. "Many families are desperately looking for a baby to love and care for."

They all stared at her. They hadn't thought of that.

"No." Taylor shook her head. "I don't wanna be pregnant and waddle around, like Amber did. I don't want to be sick all the time. I don't want people gossiping behind my back."

"You could stay here with me. Your friends would never know unless you chose to tell them."

So kind of Margret to offer.

Taylor had never been easy to live with. Her pregnancy wasn't going to make it any easier.

"No. I want an abortion."

"How about the father?" Emma asked. "Does he know? Does he agree? After all, it's his baby too."

Taylor gave her a dark look.

Victor brightened. "Yes, it's his baby too. How do you think I would have felt if Amber had gone to get an abortion without telling me?"

"First, if she didn't tell you, you wouldn't have known. You wouldn't have felt anything. Second, you'd still be home with me and Mom instead of abandoning us like you did. I see it as a plus."

Wow!

Victor was silenced. Margret fidgeted with her cup.

Vintage Taylor. After years of blaming me for Victor's desertion, she admits that he abandoned us. All this time, she knew. She blamed me anyhow.

"I want an abortion. Whether you help me or not, I'll get it." She turned to Emma. "You know what it's like to have a child that you don't want and have your whole life ruined because of it. You need to help me."

Margret intervened. "Taylor, you are mistaken. Your mother loves you, whether you understand it or not. You haven't ruined her life."

"Not yet. One way or another, I'll get an abortion; I don't care if I bleed to death. I'll still get it. You won't look so good if your daughter dies because of poor medical care, Dr. Steele, will you?" she asked, her eyes dark with hate.

"Your reputation will be over, your career may be over, and you won't feel too good about yourself, either."

Suddenly, the harpy melted and she started crying, her childish body shaking with sobs.

"You must help me, Mother."

Emma's heart broke.

<h1 style="text-align:center">31</h1>

They didn't talk much on the way back. There wasn't much left to say. Taylor was about six weeks pregnant. That gave her a little time to get an abortion. She needed parental consent. Victor wasn't going to give it. He thought this was all a childish folly. Taylor would fall in love with her baby as soon as she saw it.

Emma knew better. It was on her now.

She could help Taylor get an abortion. That may open the door for a lifetime of regrets and guilt. She could refuse, and risk Taylor getting a backdoor abortion.

She'd risk an infection, sterility, even death. Even if it goes well, she's going to think that I wasn't there for her when she needed me most. There's no good way out.

Victor drove her to her car.

"You can't do that, Emma. She'll never recover from it. One day she'll accuse you of killing her baby!"

"Of course she will! It's all my fault, bringing her to life, you deserting her nine years ago, Mike's death. No matter what goes wrong in Taylor's world, it's always my fault."

"But Emma, this is a baby! This is you, and me, and Taylor, all together! You can't help kill it!"

136

"I don't plan to. I don't do abortions. She's old enough to make her own decisions and live with the consequences. Her pregnancy is not my problem. She is. I'm trying to keep her alive."

Victor wasn't happy. He stopped next to Emma's car, alone in the hospital parking lot. It was past midnight.

"I hope you'll reconsider. I think you're making a mistake."

"I'm sorry. I'll think about it. Thanks for the ride." She opened the door and pushed the button on her key.

Her Hyundai lit up like a Christmas tree.

She stepped toward the door.

A shadow moved.

She opened the door and dashed in. She slammed it closed and locked it.

It was cold.

Victor waited.

She wondered if he'd noticed the shadow.

It was limping.

It looked familiar.

She drove home and bolted the door.

SPIDER

I'm cold.
The car sat there the whole day.
Is she ever going home?
I'm frozen. I have to go.
A car.
I move into the shade and wait.
She comes out.
I grab the knife.
She looks at me.
The other car's still there.
Waiting.
I fade into the darkness.
I'll be back.

32

____

Emma spent the night tossing and turning and woke up haggard. She downed two double espressos to unclump enough to figure out her day.

She had a staff meeting, then a shift. A long day coming. No sleep in sight. Coffee would have to do.

She brushed her teeth twice to get rid of last night's stale wine taste. She put on scrubs. Better than looking for something that fit.

She'd gained weight. The junk food in the break room, the lack of sleep and exercise, the wine, her most important food group lately—*it counts as five daily servings of fruit*—none of that helped. The pounds had been piling on.

The worn-out woman in the mirror looked nothing like she used to. She didn't like her. She didn't love her, either.

She didn't think much about herself. Not unless she did something really special, like saving a life or making a challenging diagnosis. *You're only as good as the last thing you've done. I haven't done much lately. Struggling to barely stay afloat.*

She topped the scrubs with a fresh white coat to cover the bulges. She put on her "Chocolate Dream" red lipstick for a little boost of confidence. She added a touch of red to her cheeks, trying to look less dead. She grabbed her bag with the never-without gadgets and headed out.

The car was cold. She pulled on her mittens and gathered her rust-colored parka around her. She turned on the sound system to a lecture on pediatric trauma and drove off.

Something felt wrong.

The cold? The hunger?

The lack of sleep.

Maybe.

Just jittery from too much coffee.

The staff meeting with her former friends?

No.

Something was wrong.

The window.

She'd been driving the wet, salty roads for weeks now. The car was covered in dirt. All of it. The wipers had cleared just enough windshield to let her drive.

The driver's window had a clear patch.

Right there, to her left.

Somebody had cleaned the window just enough to look inside.

She shrugged.

There's nothing worth stealing, not even the car.

Still…

Her gut told her that something was wrong.

Her gut never lied.

Last night's shadow…

She shivered.

33

____

S he was late. The staff meeting was about to start. Mike, the ED nursing director, gave her a meaningful look. She took an empty chair near Brenda, who ignored her.

"Thank you all for coming," Mike opened. "I have good news. George is better."

Cheers erupted. George was well loved. He'd been a mentor to many, and a friend to all.

"He has become more responsive. He's now alert when they lighten his sedation. They hope to extubate him in a day or two. That's the best news we've had since his accident."

Accident?! That's a misnomer. Everybody knows it was attempted murder; police have been here daily looking into everything, asking questions, collecting fingerprints and whatever else they collect.

"Jennie is collecting money for his family. Whoever wants to donate, please see her. Every little bit helps, even if it's just gas money."

Noise increased as people reached for their money. Mike raised his voice.

"Our second issue today is Narcan. We've been using more Narcan in the first two months of this year than throughout half of last year. We're running out. We tried to contact new vendors and see if the Health Department can help us, but for now we have to conserve it. Please don't use it unless you have to."

The room exploded into indignant vociferations.

"You've got to be kidding!" Suzy said. "How would we know if we need it unless we see if it works or not?"

"Yeah, really! Are you serious? You want to ration the Narcan now?" Carlos, who never spoke, now did. He'd come from New Hampshire, the epicenter of the opioid epidemic. They practically lived on Narcan.

"This is madness," Kurt said. "Narcan's not only a treatment, it's a diagnostic tool. Narcan is part of the ACLS protocol. We won't know if we really need it until we see if it works or not."

"We need to get more," Brenda said. She turned to Sal, who was trying to blend into the background. As the ED pharmacist, he was the go-to person for Narcan.

"Cool down, everybody," Mike said. "I didn't say you shouldn't use it. I just said use it more judiciously. There've been a number of cases—six, to be precise—of patients receiving more than two doses of Narcan. That's not part of the ACLS protocol nor is it standard of care."

"Really? More than two doses?" Kurt asked.

He'd aged. Emma hadn't seen him since the day Sheila overdosed. She had wondered how she was doing. She wanted to check, but she was afraid to antagonize Kurt again.

He looks just as miserable as I feel.

"Yes, three doses in three cases, four in two more, and in one case the patient received six doses of Narcan. That's not in any guidelines."

"That's true," Kurt agreed. "Who gave that and why?"

"I did," said Emma. "The patient was a healthy young man with a presentation typical for an overdose, so I gave him some more. He didn't respond, so I gave him even more."

"Six doses?"

"Yes."

"Did it work?"

"Yes. The patient had return of spontaneous circulation and went to the ICU."

"That's nice, but then what? Restarting the heart is no good if the brain doesn't make it. Putting brain-dead patients in the ICU is only draining our meager resources. The only thing that really matters is a good neurologic outcome. Did he make it to discharge?"

I wish I knew. With Taylor and everything else, I forgot to check on the kid. He was down for so long that even if he's alive he's probably neurologically devastated.

"He was discharged yesterday," Sal said. "He walked out. He was completely normal."

"Really!" Kurt said. "How much Narcan did you say you gave him?

"Six doses, I think."

"Why?"

"It just looked like it should work. Young, healthy, looked like an OD." Emma hesitated, then continued, "I thought it may be fentanyl. I think we have somebody selling fentanyl in our community."

A heavy silence fell. Fentanyl was potent and dangerous. Fentanyl on the street was bad news.

"Was he positive for fentanyl?" Kurt asked.

"Yes."

"Why that much Narcan, though?" Brenda asked.

Sal answered: "Because of its affinity to the opioid receptors. It binds much tighter. You need to overflow it with Narcan to dislodge it and reverse its effects. The only good news is that it wears off fast, so you usually don't need to repeat the dose."

"You mean after the first six?" Brenda asked, and they all laughed.

*Life in the ED is rough. People suffer; people die. Bad news and tragedies are a dime a dozen; the only way to make it through is to grow a thick skin and have a sick sense of humor. We laugh at things that nobody else finds funny; otherwise, we'd cry. It's like being at war. There are no guns, but it's just like M*A*S*H: suffering, death, and weirdos.*

"This is bad news," Kurt said. "Bad for our community and bad for us."

"Is it confirmed?" Mike asked.

"Not yet," Sal said, "I'm waiting for an answer from the Poison Control Center. We sent them some samples from our cases."

"Well then," Mike said, "we'll have to wait for an answer first."

"Better get some more Narcan in the meantime," Kurt said. "You've been fore-warned. If somebody dies for lack of Narcan, it will fall on you."

He still remembers our old fight. They had disagreed about triaging ambulances. A patient died. Kurt got blamed. He blamed Emma. That led to years of bad blood between them. *Is the armistice over?*

Kurt made a strong enemy. That, she could do without. She had nothing but enemies in the ED lately; even old friends like Alex, Brenda, and Judy had been avoiding her.

She headed to the door. Kurt's clear metallic voice cut through the noise.

"Dr. Steele."

I hope he's not going to embarrass both of us.

"Thank you for telling us. I'll be happy to work with you to make our ED even better."

Emma blushed. Her eyes welled with tears. She had expected anything but that. This was not an armistice, it was a full capitulation. Sal smiled. Her old friend Brenda, who had ignored her throughout the meeting, hugged her.

"I'm so proud of you!"

The cease-fire was on.

For now.

SPIDER

She's coming.
She's in the doorway, soaking the light.
I'm outside, in the dark.
She can't see me. I'm the shadow of a shadow.
She steps out.
Fish-knife in hand, I'm ready.
She looks at me.
She can't see me.
I hold my breath.
She sniffs the air.
What's she smelling? The snow?
She looks at me. She knows.
She steps back.
I shiver.
She knows I'm here.
She can't.
I wait.
She's back.
She just forgot something.
I'm ready.
She steps out.
I move closer.
Behind her, the security guards. Flashlights break the darkness, chasing me. I drop to the ground. I roll. Behind one car, then another, then another.

Basic training. Thanks, Vietnam.
She leads them to where I was.
I'm not there anymore.
She sniffs the air and looks straight at me.
She can't see me. I'm darker than dark.
She knows I'm here.
How?
I run.
I'm not going after her again.
She's a witch.

34

Kayla put away the mascara. She took a last look in the mirror, then pulled on her furry Cossack hat. It made her look like a ginger cat. She laughed and looked out the window.

Eden was ready, playing in the snow. With his red hat and flushed cheeks, he looked happy and healthy. She was happy that Dick had asked her to bring him along. They never had enough time together, but today was Sunday, she had the day off, and they were going ice fishing.

They'd never done it before. They had seen the fishermen sitting on their upturned buckets for hours. They held their poles and looked mesmerized at a hole in the ice, waiting for the fish to bite. She'd always wondered what was so exciting about it. It couldn't be the fish; they were smaller than Eden's hand.

So what? The weather was spectacular; the frozen lake shone like scattered diamonds in the morning. Being outdoors made her feel alive!

She started the car and noticed the pile of discarded tissues on the floor. They were left over from Friday, when Kurt had broken up with her.

He'd been avoiding her. He barely ever spoke to her, even at work. She'd tried to be understanding. She knew that his wife was sick. She respected the fact that he chose to spend time with her, but she missed him.

Eventually, she'd asked him out. He had agreed with the enthusiasm one would only reserve for a root canal.

147

They met for drinks at the inn across the lake, where nobody knew them.

She'd ordered coffee. She was half done with it by the time he arrived. He looked handsome and determined, just like he had on their first date, two years ago. Then, his smile lit the room. Now, his face was solemn and dark. Just like that, Kayla knew it was over.

He smiled but didn't kiss her. He sat and drank down his water to soften his throat. He looked inside his glass, staring at the half-melted ice cubes as if he were reading someone's fortune.

Mine.

He looked at her, his eyes windows into pain.

"It's over, Kayla."

"Why?"

"I can no longer do this to my wife. I love you very much; you've been the light of my life over these last two years. I just can't do this anymore. It's destroying her. That's destroying me."

"It took you a while to figure that out."

"I'm sorry to hurt your feelings."

"How about behaving like a man? How about talking to me rather than avoiding me, pretending that I don't exist?" People at the next table turned to stare, and Kurt shrunk in his seat.

Like all my men, he's a coward. He'd wiggle a wand and make me disappear in a puff of smoke if he could.

"I'm really sorry. I wish I had acted differently. I was infatuated with you—I still am. For whatever it's worth, I love you. You are fresh and beautiful and full of life. I love you to the point that I neglected, I almost destroyed, my wife of twenty years. She was so desperate that she tried to kill herself. She almost died." He choked.

"I've decided to make it up to her. I'll try to be a decent husband, like I haven't been for years. I don't know if our marriage can be fixed, but I'll do my best."

"How about me? Aren't you worried about me?"

"Oh, Kayla, if you only knew how much I worry about you! I'm sick with jealousy, but there's nothing I can do. I know you'll find somebody else. I hope it will be somebody who deserves you and cares for you. I hope he'll make you happy."

He stopped for a moment, making up his mind what to say next. The words came out by themselves. He could no longer hold them in.

"Please don't date Umber."

Kayla's jaw dropped. The audacity of telling her what to do and who to date after all this! Her blood boiled.

"Really? Why not? He's rich, he's handsome, he's single. What more can a girl hope for?"

"He's not for you, Kayla. You're bright and kind and innocent. He's a snake-oil salesman, a shrewd two-faced womanizer. He'll chew you up and spit you out. You deserve better."

"Unlike you, you mean? I don't think I need dating advice from you, thank you very much."

"Please listen, Kayla. Don't date Umber. There is something wrong with that man; I know it in my bones. It will be bad for you."

"Thank you for all your time and the lovely advice," Kayla said, gathering her bag and leaving a ten-dollar bill on the table—she didn't want to owe him anything, not even a coffee.

She didn't cry until the car. She cried her heart out then, a box of tissues worth.

Now, two days later, head held up proudly, she was going on a date. With Dick Umber.

She wouldn't have if it weren't for Kurt.

I hope he finds out and suffers!

SPIDER

I told him.
"Yep. She's a witch," he said.
"Sorry."
"No worries. You did well. Check under the picnic table behind the ambulance bay."
I find it.
Welcome, heaven!

35

Dick was waiting. Kayla introduced him to Eden. Always the gentleman, Eden offered a gloved hand. Dick shook it, and they started talking shop, discussing the thickness of the ice, how cold the water was, and whether perch preferred worms to grubs.

They drilled holes with the auger. They marveled at the one-foot-thick, translucent ice. It had pretty air bubbles caught inside. They hooked the bait and dropped the line. They waited.

Eden was too excited to sit. "How did you learn to ice fish?"

"My friend Joe taught me. He has a camp on Bow Lake. He took me ice fishing."

"Where's that?"

"In New Hampshire."

"Did you catch a fish?"

"I caught a small-mouth bass and a perch."

"Two?!"

Kayla listened in, enjoying the sun. Eden needed a male role model, and ice fishing was just one of the manly things she couldn't teach him. She was grateful that Dick did.

She took off her hat and let her hair fall over her shoulders. Dick smiled and touched it, his fingers caressing a silky curl, picking it up…

"A fish! A fish!" Eden screamed, holding on with both hands to his quivering pole.

Five minutes later they had recovered the fish, a scrawny silver wiggler, smaller than Eden's hand, but it was his first fish, and he was in awe. They let it swim in the water bucket. Eden watched him, trying to pet him. After he got bored, he wandered off counting holes in the ice, checking with a stick to see whether they had frozen through.

"You are beautiful, Kayla."

That's what Kurt said.

"How long are you here for?"

"I have four more shifts. I'm leaving on Friday."

"Where to?"

"Colorado, for some skiing. Want to come?"

"I can't. I have Eden."

"Bring him too."

"I have work, and he has school."

"When is he on vacation?"

"Beginning of March, I think."

"That's close enough. March skiing is the best."

That's a little fast.

"When are you coming back?"

"March, I think, then I'm going to Mexico to check on the boat. Have you ever been to Mexico?"

"Never," she said, wishing she was young and free to see the world, taste new foods, and have fun rather than go to work, take classes, and do laundry.

"Mexico is… "

The scream came from the left, where the wind was coming from. Eden was lying on the ice, screaming.

Kayla sprinted. Dick got there first. Eden was lying on his back on a patch of snow, his left leg gone.

Kayla bit her lip and watched Dick kneeling next to Eden. "It's all right, buddy, you're OK. What happened?"

"I can't get up!"

Eden was laying on his back. His right leg was bent. His left leg looked like it ended at the knee. Dick pushed the snow away with his gloved hands to uncover the crevasse. It went all the way through to the water. It wasn't much more than a couple inches wide, but it had been wide enough to let Eden's foot fall through and get stuck. He was trapped.

"Are you hurt?" Dick asked.

"Yes… no… I don't know! I can't get up."

"We'll fix that," Dick said. He laid on his stomach, sliding his hand along Eden's left leg as far as he could, palpating as he went.

"Good job, buddy. It all looks good; the knee seems OK, the bone is in one piece, and the foot…" He pulled his arm out.

"The foot looks OK, but I can't reach it. It won't come back out the way it went in. Kayla, go get me the ice auger and call 911."

"What's 911?" Eden asked.

"The emergency number we call when people get hurt. It brings help. You'll see."

He took the auger and started drilling carefully around the leg to enlarge the crevasse.

"We'll get you out of here in no time, and you'll have the best story to tell your friends. Want to know where the hole came from?"

Eden nodded.

"Ice expands and contracts when the temperature changes. When it gets too big, it breaks. Then, as it contracts again, it leaves a hole."

"I'm cold," Eden sobbed.

"Sure you are. I'm cold, too." The icy water dripping from his drenched sleeve was already freezing. "We'll be home soon, and we'll have some hot chocolate. You like hot chocolate?"

"I like ice cream better."

"Me too, but I think hot chocolate works better today."

He looked at the holes he'd drilled around Eden's leg. He put the auger aside and got his arm back in, now reaching deep enough to untie Eden's boot.

Eden was out when the ambulance arrived. His foot was blue with cold, but he was smiling, holding on to his new best friend. Kayla remembered Kurt's words: "He'll hurt you!"

She fell asleep dreaming of Mexico.

SPIDER

Snow.
Falling softly inside.
Through my eyes.
Through my mouth.
Through my soul.
I'm white inside.
It's been the highest high.
Can't move.
Can't breathe.
Can't cry.
Just the white sky.
Lying ice-colored eye.
Get him, witch.
I count on you.
I love you, Jessy.
I'm the snow.
I fly.

36

Emma was wrapping up to go home when they called the code. Her shift was over, but she went to help.

"Found in the snow. No known downtime. No pulse."

"Any history?" Ann asked, as they unloaded.

"None. We couldn't get an IV; he's got track marks everywhere. We got an IO in the left tibia. We gave three doses of epi. No response."

"How long ago was he found?"

"Thirty minutes. No bystander CPR. We got him eighteen minutes ago."

"Cardiac activity?"

"PEA, pulseless electric activity, only."

"Get a rectal temp," Sue ordered.

The angry monitors rang like chime-bells in a hurricane with the 120 beats/second of the CPR. The body lay quietly. His face was blue and gaunt, his eyes open, his huge pupils unreactive.

He's dead. But it's not my call. He's Ann's patient. She'll call it when she's ready.

Emma grabbed her trauma shears and cut through his right sleeve to expose the arm. His coat, once pink, was filled with down. Stirred by the air movement, white feathers swirled softly, falling slowly and quietly like fresh snow.

She cut through the wet navy sweater underneath to the skin. His bony hand was blue with cold, but the blue spider tattoo stretching its legs over the dirty fingers was hard to miss.

The Spider.

37

Emma signed out to Alex one hour late.

"How's Taylor?"

"She's OK; she's spending some time with her grandmother."

"Teenagers are tough. You look like you could use some sleep," he said, looking in her eyes as if he knew.

He can't, can he? She remembered that his daughter Karen was Amber's best friend.

"Let me know if I can help."

"I will, thank you." She turned to leave and walked straight into Detective Zagarian.

He looked overdressed in his well-cut gray suit, light gray shirt, and burgundy tie with gold flecks. His inscrutable eyes were also gray.

The gray man. Unobtrusive. Dangerous.

"I've been waiting for you. They said you'd be done at four."

It was ten past five. She'd had to stay over to clean up. She'd finally admitted the demented patient whose family refused to take him home. She had found a pediatrician for the wheezing toddler whose mother had no insurance. She had discharged the woman with chronic pain she just couldn't sign out.

"I had to tie up some loose ends. What can I do for you?"

"Do you have time to go for a coffee or a drink?"

"Why?"

It had been another rough shift after a rough night after a rough day. She was looking forward to some peace and quiet. And wine.

"To chat."

He smiled; his eyes smiled, too, and told her she was pretty. They lied. She hadn't been pretty in the morning when she'd put on makeup and lipstick; that had been many patients ago. *I hate to think about how I must smell.*

"Is this personal or professional?"

"A little bit of both."

She looked at her scrubs. *That's no cocktail attire. If I don't talk to him now, he'll be back. May as well get this out of the way.*

Half an hour later they sat at a table for two at Luigi's, looking over the frozen lake. Emma held her steaming coffee with both hands to warm her fingers. It was cold in the ED, so cold that her fingers hurt and she could barely type. She was frozen to the core.

"What can I do for you?"

She kept her jacket on to hide her scrubs. She felt out of place amongst the loud, well-dressed crowd. *They had too much wine. I wish I'd said no and gone home. I'd be drinking wine too.*

"I wondered if you remembered anything. Any ideas about who wanted to kill the nurse? Or about the source of that money?"

"No, I didn't." Between Taylor and her patients, she'd had plenty to worry about.

"Any ideas of where that propofol could have come from?"

Emma shook her head no.

"It was part of a batch that was shipped to five hospitals in New Hampshire, six months ago. Also a couple of places in California. We're trying to pin down exactly where this particular bottle went. Does that ring a bell?"

"Nope."

"Well, let that sink in. Maybe something will come to you." He took a sip of coffee and grimaced. "This'll put you to sleep rather than wake you up."

"That's good, since it's almost bedtime."

"Oh, it's a little early for that. Are you married?"

"No. Are you?"

"Not lately. My ex-wife and I get along better now than when we were married."

"It happens."

"Yes, it's always easier when you don't have skin in the game."

"Kids?"

"Two. Twenty and twenty-two. Both in college. You?"

"One daughter, seventeen."

"Lives with you?"

"She's with her grandmother for the moment."

"That's a difficult age."

If one more person tells me that teenagers suck, I'm going to blow up.

"I couldn't help but notice."

He took the hint.

"Tell me about propofol."

"It's a wonderful drug. For procedural sedation, mostly. They call it "Milk of Amnesia" because it's milk-white and makes patients amnestic. Once you give it, they don't remember anything else. They wake up after the procedure, asking when we're going to start. It takes about a minute to start working, and it wears off in eight minutes or so—except for kids, they burn through it like crazy. It puts the patients to sleep, so you can relocate their hips or put in a chest tube or intubate them. It's a fantastic drug, but if you give too much, they stop breathing. That's what happened to Michael Jackson. It also drops their blood pressure. That's why you need to watch them like a hawk."

"How long would the nurse have been out for?"

"His name is George."

"How long would George have been out for?"

"It depends on how much he got. Eight, ten minutes maybe? If he stopped breathing, he could be gone for good."

"Let's talk this through. Whoever did this, they had to get in an IV.

Emma nodded.

"After that, they had to push the drug. Then it takes another minute to work?"

"Yes."

"How long would it all take?"

"Depends on the veins and the skill level. Three minutes or so?"

"Could that happen if he was conscious?"

"No. He'd fight, he'd scream…"

"Yes, but who would hear? Plus, the showers are locked. They couldn't get in without the code."

"They could call security."

"Unless they thought it was just another lunatic screaming in the ED."

"We call them patients, you know."

"Another patient screaming in the ED. Do women use the same shower?"

"Of course not."

"Is the code the same?"

Emma shrugged. "Probably not, but we can find out."

"I already did; it's not. So it must have been a man."

So why ask me?

"What was George doing in the shower? Was his shift over?"

"No, but if you get sprayed with blood or other body fluids, you need to get changed. It happens."

"Fair enough. I spoke to the nurses who worked with him that day. Nobody noticed anything like that happening. If he went to take a shower or get changed, he'd have told somebody he was off the floor, wouldn't he?"

"Probably. His partner and the charge nurse. Somebody would have had to keep an eye on his patients."

"He didn't. So he went there for some other reason. He didn't expect to be gone long. My theory is that he went there to meet the guy we're looking for. They wanted privacy. To exchange money. Maybe drugs. The other person got close enough to grab him by the throat and choke him—how long does it take to become unconscious when you're choked?"

"Seconds, if they press on your carotids to shut down the blood flow to the brain."

"He then smashed George's head on the concrete corner to keep him unconscious. He put in an IV and then pushed the propofol in—a big enough dose to stop his breathing. He left the needle there to make it look like the nurse... like George had shot it himself. Now it's just an accidental overdose. Does this make sense from a medical point of view?"

"It does, except... I don't think George was blackmailing anybody. It's not like him."

"People never cease to surprise me. It's hard to tell what somebody will do if they have a good reason."

"Did you find any material evidence?"

"We found all sorts of material evidence—hairs, fibers, blood—like you would find in a shower that fifty people use every day. We don't know which is relevant to our case."

"Anything to suggest that George put up a fight?"

Zagarian took another sip of coffee and asked, "Wanna have some dinner?"

She was about to say no, when her stomach reminded her that she hadn't eaten since breakfast. *There's no food at home. I'm finally warm, sitting in my favorite restaurant, and I'm going home hungry?*

"Why not?" She loosened her jacket and her scrubs peeked through. "Sorry for my outfit."

"You'll dress up next time." He signaled the waiter.

Next time? "The Shrimp a la Luigi is great. So is the chicken."

"Shrimp then. How about some wine?"

"They have a nice crisp Marlborough sauvignon blanc by the glass."

"You're not up for a bottle?"

"Not before driving home in the snow."

They ate and drank in pleasant companionship. The flavors of bacon, garlic, and charred meat streaming from the kitchen made her mouth water. The sauvignon blanc, a yellow so pale it was almost clear, was citrusy and light, its dry crispness a palate cleanser after the creamy richness of the shrimp. They talked about work and about their love for travel and food, avoiding personal things like exes and kids. *He's attractive and funny.* She relaxed and made the wine last. Suddenly he came back to business.

"Why would George blackmail somebody? What could be important enough to make him forget his principles?

"Mary and the kids. If they were in trouble, George would do anything to get them out."

"Are they in trouble?"

"Not that I know of. Just the ordinary struggles to pay the bills, but they've been like that for years."

"Could he have a lover?"

Emma shrugged. "Who knows?"

The waiter brought the bill, and Emma tried to pay her share but he declined.

"I'll expense this," he said, making it clear that it had been just business.

Oh well. Emma drove home thinking about George.

38

———————

She called Mary as soon as she got home.

"How are you, Mary?"

"I'm OK. You?"

"I'm good. How's George?"

"A little better every day. They're talking about extubating him. Now he's awake when they turn down the sedation. He can't talk with that tube in his throat, but he writes notes asking about the hockey games. He must be better!"

"That's George all right! Did he tell you what happened?"

"He can't remember anything."

Of course he wouldn't, with all that propofol.

"I'm glad he's doing better. Mary, are you all right?"

"As good as I can be with all this shit hitting the fan. Better now that it looks like he's gonna make it. Can't imagine what I'd do without him."

Emma wished she'd driven to Mary rather than calling her. It would have been easier to talk, but it was late, and she was tired, and she hadn't.

"Mary, is there anything going on that would worry George? Like really, really needing money? To the point of doing something illegal?"

"George is a good man! Whoever says he stole anything is lying!"

"I know George is a good man, Mary. He's a wonderful man and I care for him very much, but… Is there some reason he could have gotten in trouble to get money?"

Long pause, then heartbreaking sobs. Emma sat quietly, waiting.

"I have lung cancer," Mary said. "They found it in November. They said I needed surgery and chemo. Maybe radiation, they weren't sure." She started crying harder, her raw grief piercing Emma's heart.

"I have no insurance. Neither does George, but he's a vet; he gets medical care at the VA. We couldn't afford it, you know. We have no way to pay for the treatment." Her voice became a little steadier. "George said, 'Don't worry, I'll get the money.' 'How?' I asked. 'Don't worry,' he said, 'I'll find it.'"

So that's that. George found a way to get money; he blackmailed somebody who tried to kill him. But who? And why? "I'm so sorry, Mary. You're a strong woman, and you'll pull through. So will George. You are both wonderful, strong people."

"Thank you, Emma. Love you too. Stop by, will you?"

"I'll be over soon." She poured herself a glass of wine to dull the pain and help herself to sleep. She was sad enough and warm enough to open a summer wine, a Kim Crawford Marlborough sauvignon blanc from New Zealand. The pale, light yellow soon faded under the frosting of the glass. Crisp and dry, with hints of passion fruit and fresh-cut grass, it brought memories of long sunny days and hope. *Gone now. Life sucks.*

She went to bed thinking about Mary and George, about Zagarian and Victor, about Taylor and her decision to abort. *What should I do?*

The thought came to her as she was falling asleep. *Whoever George was blackmailing, how come they had propofol in their pocket? Not even ours, but from California or New Hampshire!*

New Hampshire, where they had all those fentanyl deaths! Now we have all these Narcan-resistant overdoses! There must be a connection.

Whoever was selling fentanyl in New Hampshire came here to open shop. George found out something and blackmailed them, so they decided to kill him.

This has got to be it! I'll call Zagarian in the morning!

39

She didn't. The phone rang at 4:45, waking her up from a restless sleep populated by nightmares in which Taylor and Zagarian were fighting for a syringe loaded with fentanyl. She stumbled to answer.

"Mom, you need to come."

"Taylor?"

"Yes. You need to come."

"Come where?"

"Here, at Grandma's."

Emma looked at the clock—not quite 5:00 a.m.

"What happened?"

"Grandma."

"Yes?"

"She fell down the stairs."

"Is she hurt?"

"She doesn't answer me."

"OK, hang up and call 911. Tell them…"

"I already did. Do you think I'm stupid? They're on their way."

"OK. Did you call your father?"

"No. I called you."

That's a first.

"Are you near her? Is she breathing?"

"Yes. She also has a pulse. 58."

That's my girl. "Does she look hurt?"

"No, she looks asleep, but she can't be."

"Don't move her." Emma tried to think quickly.

"Go to her bedroom and find her medication list. The EMTs will want it. Take a picture of it with your cell phone before you give it to them so there's a copy in case it gets lost. Make sure you give them your phone number so they can call you. Better yet, write it on the medication list. Ask them what hospital they're taking her to so we can find her. Unlock the door, open it, and turn on the lights outside so they can find the house easier. Is she still breathing?"

"I don't know. I'm looking for her medication list. I found it… They're here." She hung up.

Emma shook her head to clear it. She washed her face with ice-cold water. That helped. She poured herself a mug of the coffee she'd cold-brewed the night before. She called Victor. She called the ED to let them know she was gone for the day.

She remembered about calling Zagarian on the flight to Atlanta. *I'll do it after I land.*

She forgot.

They took a taxi to the ER. Taylor was standing in the doorway. Sobbing, she rushed into Victor's arms.

He paled, his knees weak. "Is she dead?"

"No." She blew her nose. "They said she had a heart attack."

"Anything else?"

She shook her head no and sobbed, holding on to him. Emma went to the triage nurse, a tired woman whose watchful eyes saw beyond the skin.

"I'm Dr. Emma Steele."

"What can I do for you?"

"We're here for a family member, Mrs. Margret Storm."

The nurse checked the board. "Room 17," she said, letting them in.

Margret, serene and beautiful as ever, not one hair out of place, was lying in the hospital bed that they'd gotten for her instead of the backbreaking ER stretcher. She smiled and greeted them as if they were in her living room. *The only thing missing is the tea.*

"So sorry to have bothered you both. All three in fact," she said, looking at Taylor. Emma kissed Margret's cheek and made room for Victor.

"What happened, Mother?" Victor asked.

"They said I had a heart attack. I got up and I was going to make coffee; then I woke up in the ambulance."

"Are you hurt?" Emma asked, looking at her face, checking out her neck, and fighting the urge to palpate her cervical spine. *I'm not her doctor. I hope they checked her neck... and hips...*

"A few bruises here and there, not bad."

"Did they scan your head?

Margret smiled. "Sure they did, dear; they said it looks alright."

"How about the neck?"

"The neck doesn't hurt."

"Do you have any chest pain?" Victor asked. "Are you short of breath?"

"I'm OK. Both of you stop fussing; you're making me uncomfortable." She turned to Taylor. "I wish you hadn't called them."

"I'm glad she did," Victor said. "May I have your permission to speak to your doctor?"

"Go ahead; I can't stop you. You girls, you look like you need some rest." She looked from Taylor's messy hair to Emma's wrinkled travel outfit. "I do too. Go home and catch a nap. I'll see you later."

The taxi trip was short. They sat quietly at the kitchen table, looking in their coffee cups. Taylor, who knew her way around Margret's kitchen, had made coffee. *It's awful, way too weak, but it's the first coffee Taylor's ever made for me. She's pale and thin. Morning sickness?*

"How are you?"

Taylor took a long time to respond.

"Better now that you guys are here." She took a sip of coffee and grimaced. "That's awful!"

"I've made worse," Emma said, taking another sip. "Did I ever tell you about the first time I cooked for your father?"

"No."

"He came for dinner. I found some baccalà, dried salted cod. It was easy to cook. I got basil and lemongrass and garlic and chilies. I washed it really well, and I tasted it. It tasted good."

Taylor was smiling, waiting for the punch line, and Emma, who hadn't seen her smile in a long time, wondered again at how breathtakingly beautiful she was, and how fragile.

"I baked it with the herbs and wine. It smelled heavenly. It looked good, too, with fresh herbs and lemon slices. Your father brought me roses. I served the fish on a nice white platter."

"And?"

"He tasted it and spit it back on the plate. It was so salty that we couldn't eat it. I had to throw it away. I threw it in the back yard in the compost pile."

"What did you eat, then?"

"I don't remember, but that's not the worst part. I had this one-eyed cat. Her name was Cleopatra. She loved fish.

"She found the baccalà and started eating it, salt and all. We couldn't understand why she was thirsty all the time. She'd always used to climb on the sink to get a drink, but now she was basically living in the sink. She got so heavy that I could barely pick her up. She was swollen, you see, from all the water she'd been drinking because the fish was so salty."

"Did she die?"

"Eventually, but not because of that."

They laughed and sat quietly until Taylor asked, "Are you going to help me?"

Emma didn't know.

"I wish I knew what's best for you, Taylor. I want nothing more than to help you; I'm just trying to figure out how to do that."

"I need an abortion. That's what's best for me."

"That's what you think today, and you may be right. Or not. You may come to be very sorry one day that you gave up the opportunity to have this child."

"No, I won't."

"You don't know that. You just think you do.

"I know it."

I wish I was as half as sure of anything as Taylor always is. I'm always afraid that I'm wrong. This was both a blessing and a curse—it made her a better doctor, since she always kept an open mind, but it was nerve-wracking to always wonder if you were sending somebody home to die. *Taylor has answers to everything. Some day she'll know better, and it's going to hurt.*

"Taylor, things change. People change. Look at your father and me; we never thought we'd end up divorced. Some day you may be sorry you didn't have this child. Look at the woman who helped legalize abortions in the U.S., the famous case of Roe vs. Wade; she's now fighting to overturn the law she helped create."

"I won't change my mind. I need an abortion."

"How do you know?"

Taylor stood up and poured her coffee down the drain.

"You said you wanted to know who the father was."

The silence smelled like doom.

Who could it be to matter? One of Taylor's friends, or Tom, or... Victor? She shivered and was ashamed of herself. *Things like that have happened before... But no, not Victor. That can't be.*

Her voice thin as a thread, looking down with her shoulders hunched, Taylor said: "I don't know who the father is."

What does that mean? Was there more than one guy? Did she have sex with a stranger?

"I was raped. I was at Bill's birthday party; we'd had a few drinks and then one of his friends said, 'Let's try these pills,' and we did, all eight of us, and then I don't know what happened, but the next morning I woke up in Bill's basement covered in blood down below, alone. I had never had sex before. I don't know what they did to me. I felt dirty and disgusting, I still do. And then there's this...this thing growing inside me. I can't have a child like that. I can't. I don't care if I never ever have children. I want it out."

She turned to face Emma, her tears running down her beautiful face like crystal rivers.

"Will you help me?"

Emma stood up and hugged her like she was never going to let go. Their tears ran down together.

"I'll do anything. Anything I can."

40

Emma handed Mary the box of chocolates she got at the hospital gift store. George lay on the sofa, watching the game. He was tired and gaunt, but he hadn't lost the twinkle in his eye.

"Hello, stranger," he said.

"You have room to talk!" She hugged him and assessed him from head to the blanket covering his feet as if he were a patient. *He's tired. Not ill, like he's about to crash and burn, but exhausted.* She missed him.

More importantly, she needed to find out what happened. One way or another, she was going to find the drug peddler. *George knows something. I'll get him to tell me things he wouldn't tell police.*

She didn't like drug seekers. Disingenuous, demanding, and manipulative, they were nothing but trouble. *If you believe they're in pain and give them a script, you get blamed for the opioid epidemic. If you don't, you may be sending them home to die. If you don't give them their fix, they become aggressive; if you do, you're a licensed drug peddler. There's no middle ground.*

She had never thought about drug peddlers until this slew of overdoses. That had hit her hard. So many young lives destroyed! So many pointless deaths!

Taylor's story had been the last straw.

I'm going to destroy this drug peddler if it kills me. I need George to help me.

She pointed at the glass ashtray on the side table.

"When are you gonna quit?"

"I have. I just keep it here for company," he said, breaking into the irritating dry cough of quitters.

"Good for you. How are you?"

"Never better." His rogue smile uncovered his golden tooth—a souvenir from Vietnam—gleaming under his mustache. "How are you?"

"Surviving. The ED is not the same without you."

"That's good. It wasn't that great before."

"Well, it's no better now. We miss you."

"Good. I'll be back in no time."

"No, you won't," Mary said, bringing coffee. "Not if I have anything to say about it."

"But you don't, *agapi mou*," he teased her, using half of his Greek vocabulary. The rest of it was Ouzo and Retsina.

"Do you remember what happened?"

"No. I only remember the damn ICU nurses flashing lights in my eyes."

"What's the last thing you remember?"

"Walking to the showers. Checking my pocket for my cigarettes. I thought I'd catch a quick one."

"Did you ever get that cigarette?"

George shrugged.

"Why did you go to the showers?"

"To shower, I guess."

"Why?"

George looked her in the eye. "To get clean?"

"Were you dirty?"

His eyes looked through her, into his own brain, searching.

She saw the exact moment when he remembered. He looked away. He smiled. He lied.

"I don't remember. Was I?"

"You took off without telling anyone in the middle of your shift. They found you with a needle in your arm and blood in your brain. What happened?

"No idea. Bad luck, I guess." He smiled, his eyes guarded.

"That's more than bad luck. Was somebody trying to get rid of you?"

"They all do. I'm a pain in the arse."

"Having you killed is a bit extreme."

"Maybe they just tried to get me fired. Who knows?"

He's not going to tell me.

"George, this is no good. You could save lives if you spoke up."

"Who? The seekers? You wanna know what I think about them?"

"They are people, too. They have parents and husbands and families who are suffering."

"That's their problem. Their people can worry about them. I have my own to worry about." His eyes slid over to Mary.

"I'll do everything I can for Mary," Emma said.

"I know you would. But she's not yours to take care of. She's mine."

"What if next time you don't wake up? What's going to happen to Mary and the kids?"

"You have a point," he nodded. "I can take care of myself, but I'll leave you a message, just in case it turns bad."

"How?"

"I don't know, Emma. I'll figure it out. I'm sorry. We all have our crosses to bear."

41

H*e's right*, Emma thought on her drive home. *We all have our crosses to bear.*

Taylor had stayed in Atlanta.

"I love it here. Grandma needs me. I'll stay."

Emma knew better than to believe her.

That's bullshit. She's never sacrificed herself for anyone. She's got a plan.

Even worse, she'd asked Emma to tell Victor.

"Can you tell him? I just can't do this again."

Emma waited until the flight.

"Taylor doesn't know who the father is."

"How come?"

"She was at a party. She woke up to find out that she'd been raped."

Victor's wounded sob was the most painful sound Emma could remember. Head bent, eyes closed, he cradled his grief.

"So?" he asked.

"I promised I'd get her an abortion."

He sobbed again.

"She needs testing—HIV, hepatitis, syphilis, gonorrhea—God knows what else."

"God doesn't know. Or he doesn't care," Victor said. "No God would allow this to happen. It's all bullshit."

Emma's eyes stung.

I hoped his faith would give him solace. He lost his religion instead. No parent deserves this much pain.

In her career, she'd given bad news to so many parents. Too many to count.

The first time was a chubby toddler. He'd been tired for a week. He looked good. His labs didn't.

"Leukemia," her attending said. "That white count is too high for a random infection."

"Are we sure?"

"We're in the ER. We're never sure. Of anything. Unless they're dead. Not even then."

"How come?"

"I ran a code on the floor. After half an hour, I called it. I declared him dead. An hour later he came back to life. That made me popular. Now, they all want me to code them if they die. They think they'll live forever." His eyes bore into hers. "Emma, in emergency medicine we're never sure. We're in the business of managing risk. What are the odds that this heartburn is a heart attack? What's the chance that this fever is meningitis? Can this numbness be a stroke? We calculate probabilities. We assume risks. Can you handle this? If not, the ER is not for you."

Emma nodded.

"You have to learn to give bad news. You'll want to run away. You can't. Open yourself to the pain. Embrace it. That's the only way to help your patients."

Emma had told the parents. She sat with them. She listened to them. She hugged them. They were heartbroken and grateful.

Afterward, she went to the bathroom to cry.

That had been long ago, before her life had hardened her.

She took Victor's hand.

I'll cry later.

Time to call Zagarian, Emma thought. George won't talk. It's only a matter of time until the next disaster—another overdose, another rape, another attempt to silence George. Next time he may not be so lucky. She was both angry and in awe of his dedication to Mary. *I wish I had somebody to love me like that.*

Zagarian answered on the third ring. "Let's meet. Are you at home?"

"On my way."

"I'll be there in half an hour." He hung up before she could suggest another place. *No big deal. This isn't personal.* She started coffee and changed into a pink sweater. It covered her curves and gave her a nice glow. She brushed her hair. She put on lipstick. She grabbed her perfume, then felt silly and put it back.

As usual, Zagarian looked as if he'd dropped out of a magazine. She tried to hide her tired purple crocs; then, annoyed at herself, she stuck her feet out in defiance.

"Nice place," he said. He took in the deep green leather sofa, the gas fireplace giving the room a cozy glow, and her paintings—abstract splashes of bright color, bringing life to the room. "Have you lived here long?"

"Ten years or so."

"What's new?"

"A couple of things. First a question: Did you find out where the propofol came from?"

"A critical care access hospital in New Hampshire. The batch got delivered last May, recorded as being used in July."

"By whom?"

"By a nurse in the local ED."

"Did you speak to her?"

"She's dead."

"How?"

"Overdose."

Emma let that sink in for a moment. "Propofol?"

"Fentanyl."

Fentanyl again.

"Self-inflicted?"

"Apparently. She had been using for a while. She was caught diverting drugs. She got fired. They found her dead. There was no reason to suspect foul play. It may have been accidental—or not. She had lost custody of her children, and she took it badly." He finished his coffee. "What's your news?"

"There was a slew of overdoses in New Hampshire. They had 481 opioid deaths last year—the highest rate of fentanyl overdoses in the country. We are seeing something similar here. Then the propofol vial. I think there's a connection."

"How so?"

"Say the New Hampshire dealer moved his business here. George found out. He needed money. He started blackmailing Mr. Overdose. Mr. OD didn't care for the blackmail, so he decided to silence George. He injected George with the propofol he had brought from New Hampshire and nearly killed him." Emma sighed. "Too bad that the nurse is dead!"

"Especially for her." Zagarian took another sip of coffee. "How does one get fentanyl?"

"Melting used patches. You can make it from scratch—the lab equipment is easy to get. The easiest is buying it online. Once you've established your credentials with the supplier, you're all set. There are hundreds of suppliers all over the world. They sell high-purity, uncut fentanyl powder. The dealer cuts it himself."

"Cuts it?"

"Dilutes it. Pure fentanyl is too potent to use. A pinch of it can kill you. You have to dilute it to get a manageable volume for a dose. If you don't do it correctly, some doses will have more fentanyl than others. The users may get more than they can handle. They'll fall asleep. Forever."

"So maybe Mr. OD got the fentanyl online. He cut it and divided it into individual doses, but didn't do it right?"

"Maybe."

"So you're thinking that Mr. OD came from New Hampshire and is somehow connected to the dead nurse."

"Yes."

"So why the propofol? Why not use fentanyl to kill George?"

"Fentanyl takes too long. George would have woken up from the head injury and fought or screamed for help."

"So your Mr. OD has medical knowledge, medical connections, and can access the ED showers. Mr. OD may be working in your ED."

"He might."

"Any ideas?"

"None. I can't believe any of my people would do this."

"Anybody with New Hampshire connections?"

"Carlos and Faith, two of our nurses, came from New Hampshire a few months ago."

"Anybody else?"

"Roy, one of the EMTs, had a cousin there. She died from an OD last summer. Ken, our director, had a cabin in New Hampshire. He vacationed there every summer. Everybody has been to New Hampshire one time or another. By the way, what's happening with Ken's inquest? Any progress?"

"We have no reason to believe that the two are related, at this time."

"Really?"

"Listen, Emma. George was assaulted in the ED during his shift. You are a doctor and the ED director. I have reasons to discuss this case with you. The other one is different. I can't discuss it with you."

"Isn't it too much of a coincidence? Two unrelated deaths happening one week apart on hospital premises?"

"What I suspect and what I can prove are two different things. I'm working on it. That's all I've got for now." He took another sip from his empty coffee cup.

Emma crossed her arms, pretending not to notice.

"Any other New Hampshire connections?" he asked, setting the cup on the side table.

"Ann, one of our docs, does some locums work; she did a stint there last summer."

"That's it?"

Emma shrugged. "I don't know everybody's personal life. Try Jennie, the secretary. She knows everybody and everything."

"Anything else?"

Lips tight, she shook her head no.

"How well do you know Dr. Crump?"

"He's a colleague. We've worked together for years. We don't socialize outside work."

"Did you know that Dr. Crump and George had a big fight the day before George got attacked? Dr. Crump stormed out of the med room so fast that he almost knocked down one of the nurses."

"Who told you?"

Zagarian shrugged.

"That fight may have nothing to do with the assault."

"Dr. Crump said George had made a medication error. He couldn't remember the patient or the details."

"Who'd remember a patient's name a week later? I wouldn't."

"I asked George. He couldn't remember."

"No wonder, after the head injury and all that propofol."

"The propofol was the next day. How far back do people get retrograde amnesia?"

"A few minutes, maybe? But the head injury is another matter altogether."

"I asked him again. He changed his tune. Dr. Crump had apparently gotten mad about a delay in a critical EKG. I say they're both lying."

"I don't think so. Dr. Crump is a decent man," Emma said.

"Does he like money?"

"Who doesn't?" She remembered Kurt's new Audi A7, his gleaming Italian shoes, and his trips to Vegas. *Maybe he likes money more than most.*

"He was in New Hampshire last summer."

"He visited Ken. They were good friends."

"He has a pretty lady friend. She just bought a new car that she can't afford."

Kayla.

Ken was going to demote Kurt...

No. It can't be.

But...

43

———

Emma tied the blue plastic apron tight around her, getting ready for the incoming trauma. Her gloves ripped as she tried to pull them on. She sighed. It was going to be one of those days.

Mondays were always a curse, with way more patients than any other day. Today was also the tail end of a snowstorm. People were coming in like crazy —car accidents, heart attacks from shoveling snow, broken legs from falling off the roof, broken hips after slipping on the ice, kids sleighing into trees, hands filleted by snowblowers.

During the storm, like during the Super Bowl or Thanksgiving dinner, things weren't bad, but the storm was over now.

The team in Trauma 3 looked like a flock of blue Martians in their full protective garb—gloves, hat, booties. They wore tags to recognize each other.

"Pedestrian hit by a car," EMS said. "A hit-and-run."

That was never good. Emma looked at Brenda, who was in charge.

"Any news?"

"A woman. She was hit by a truck. She was unresponsive at the scene, vomited twice, agonal breathing. They are bagging. Probable right femur fracture."

The femur, the largest bone in the body, connecting the hip to the knee, is the hardest to break. That meant high impact, and probably more bad injuries.

"Vitals?"

"OK, they said, except for the tachycardia."

Emma tried to build a mental picture of the patient. *Unresponsive and vomiting! Head injury? Increased intracranial pressure? The broken femur is bad enough by itself, but the kind of force that would break her femur may cause internal injuries and other fractures. Pelvis? Maybe the neck? That could mean paralysis, even death, if the break is high enough to paralyze the diaphragm. The agonal breathing doesn't sound good. This gal is fixing to die. I hate it when they do that!*

"ETA?"

"Five minutes," Brenda said, just as they heard the sirens.

The sirens approached. Emma went to meet them. The two minutes that she stole this way, listening to the EMTs before they landed in the noisy trauma room, gave her a better chance to understand the situation. She won an extra minute to think through her decisions.

Every one of her orders could be a life-or-death sentence for the patient. If she got it wrong, it could be the end of her career.

Every single time, she had to choose the right procedure and order the right medication in the correct dosage for people she'd never seen, before even learning what was wrong with them.

Like now. So many of my friends cracked under pressure and quit. They retired, they moved to urgent care, they became drug reps. I may be the next.

She punched the silver plate to open the door, forgetting everything else but this patient.

Brent, the EMT, opened the door and smiled, recognizing her under the blue garb.

"Hi, Dr. Steele, fifty-two-year-old female hit by a truck. She was unresponsive at the scene; now she's more agitated. She's breathing on her own. Vitals are OK except for tachycardia. She has a right femur deformity. We collared and boarded her, but she started agitating on the way. She vomited twice."

"Did she aspirate?" Boarded and collared was standard procedure for traumas, immobilizing the patient to prevent further injuries. They lay on their back, unable to move or even turn their head. Vomiting was bad. The stomach contents could choke them to death, or at least give them a nasty pneumonia.

"We lifted the board on its side."

Emma nodded.

"Vitals?"

"Blood pressure 95/63, heart rate 123, oxygen sats low 90s."

The heart rate is higher than the blood pressure. That's bad. Plus that blood pressure is too low anyhow. She's bleeding somewhere, probably inside. That broken femur will lose a lot of blood but not enough to make her unstable. I hope she's not bleeding in her brain too; that would explain her agitation. At least she's breathing on her own. For now.

They moved her to the ER stretcher.

"Airway patent. Breathing. Vitals you can read on your own," Emma dictated.

The recorder noted in the trauma sheet.

Emma looked at the bloody face covered in dirt. Left forehead hematoma. A split lip, bleeding. Eyes closed. She tried to pry them open, but the patient resisted. *Good.*

They unbuckled the straps attaching her to the rigid board. The trauma shears came out of many pockets, shredding her wet dirty jacket and pants, then the sweater underneath to expose her.

Emma considered intubating.

Looking iffy. C-collar. She'll need in-line stabilization. Her cheeks are sinking in. No teeth. We'll have a hard time getting a good seal if she needs bagging. Marginal blood pressure. Not just yet.

The left leg looked OK. The right one was in traction, pulled away from her body in a Hare splint. *Looks like a medieval torture device. Must feel like one too.* Her chest was raising symmetrically with every breath. The abdomen looked distended. Emma grabbed the pelvic bones, pushing them together. They didn't move. *No instability.* She pinched her toenails, then her thumbs, checking for sensation and strength. She pulled away. *Good.* She opened her C-collar to inspect the neck, then closed it back, protecting the spine. She listened to the lungs, then palpated her abdomen. The woman gave a blood-curdling scream.

Emma looked up. Kayla, in the door, was waiting for orders.

"Hold the scanner and get me the surgeon."

"What are you scanning?"

"Everything. Head, neck, chest, abdomen, and pelvis. Something bad's happening, and she's too out of it to show us what. I need her history, allergies, and meds. Is she on any blood thinners?"

"I'm on it," Brenda said.

"What does she have for IV access?"

"An 18 in the left AC and a 20 in the right by EMT," Judy said.

"She'll need blood. Can you get in a 16?" The smaller the number, the larger the needle in the IV world; larger needles meant faster treatment, faster fluids, and blood—all essential for someone on the edge to stay alive.

Judy nodded.

"Blood pressure dropping."

Emma glanced at the monitor.

Dropping indeed. 87/65. Heart rate climbing to compensate. Thank God she's breathing on her own; if I had to intubate her right now, I'd kill her. "IV fluids under pressure, please. Two liters. Has the blood arrived?"

"O negative here," said the blood-bank kid. He was standing in the corner with his cooler, keeping out of the way. He looked ready for a picnic, but this was no picnic. *This is death knocking. Not on my watch.*

"Let's give two units. We sent blood for type and cross and the rest of the trauma panel, yes?"

"Yes," three voices answered.

She rechecked the lungs. *Still OK.* They log-rolled her to her left, checking her spine. Emma walked her gloved fingers over each vertebra, looking for step-ups or pain, indicative of a fracture. There was none. She considered doing a rectal exam, then decided against it. *It won't change the management; she's off to the scanner no matter what. There's no time to waste.* She was ready to roll her back when something blue on the left scapula caught her attention. She brushed the dirt away.

Though marred by dry blood, the intricate blue shape was clear.

A blue spider.

44

——————

"CT scan is ready," Kayla said.

The blood pressure is above 90; the pulse is better. She's going in the right direction. She's breathing. Getting blood. She calmed down. The surgeon is on his way; he'll want the CT scan before taking her to the OR. She's as good as she's going to get. I'd better scan her before she crashes.

"Let's go."

If she crashes in the CT scan, I'm screwed. That's a sucky place to run a code—no space, no equipment, not enough staff. If I don't send her and she gets worse, as I know she will, I've missed the opportunity to scan her before opening her on the OR table. Damned if you do, damned if you don't. Emma shrugged and joined the CT procession. *I'd better be there if things turn bad. The others look like they'll stay alive for now.*

The surgeon on call, Dr. Brody, a thick man of few nice words, met them at the scanner.

She told him the story. He didn't look pleased.

"Did you give her blood?"

"She's getting her second unit."

"Did you do a rectal?"

"No. I didn't think she needed one."

Dr. Brody frowned. "Didn't they teach you in medical school, if you ever went to medical school, that the only two reasons to not perform a rectal in a trauma victim are the patient not having a rectum or the surgeon not having a finger?"

"Well, I'm not a surgeon. You are. Feel free to do the rectal."

He frowned deeper. "You're sure she didn't need a chest tube before sticking her in the scanner?

"As sure as I get."

"Is she on any blood thinners?"

"Not that we know of."

"You don't know much about her, do you?"

"I know more than you do. She's been here for all of 20 minutes. We got access, we resuscitated her, and we got her in the scanner. Oh, and we gave her TXA."

"TXA? Tranexamic acid? Why?"

"So that she doesn't bleed out before you take her to the OR." Emma had had enough of being treated like she didn't know what she was doing. "Read the literature. It's recommended immediately in trauma with serious blood loss."

"Who said I'm taking her to the OR?"

"I did. Let me know if you don't."

"Hmm."

"Can you take it from here? There's no point for both of us staying with her in the scanner."

"Yep."

"Thank you."

After the CT, the patient went straight to the OR. Emma wondered how she did. She wanted to call and find out, but she got busy and forgot. When the surgeon called her, four hours later, it felt like it had happened weeks ago.

"She's doing OK. She'll pull through."

"Wonderful. Thank you so much for coming!"

"Not like I had a choice."

What a charmer! "Thank you anyhow."

As she was ready to hang up, he said, "You're welcome. You did a good job down there. Half an hour longer and she'd have bled to death. She had a liver laceration and a tear in the vena cava. Barely made it."

"Thanks again." Emma hung up, fighting to hold her tears. Dealing with kindness was not her thing. She wasn't used to it. Pressure and insults—that, she was used to.

"She made it." Her nurses stared at her, not understanding. It had been many patients ago.

"Our trauma this morning. The hit-and-run. Dr. Brody said she'll pull through."

They smiled. Things like this made up for being harassed, peed on, sworn at, and abused every shift.

"Good job, team! I'm proud of you!"

"We're proud of you, Dr. Steele. She was lucky to have you."

45

—————

That's no good. The toddler in Room 4 was sitting upright on the stretcher. He looked like the bucolic angels on chocolate boxes, with his curly hair and blue eyes, but he was in trouble.

His chest moved way too fast at sixty breaths a minute. His nostrils flared like a bunny's, and his little potbelly pulled in with every breath. *Subcostal retractions; he's struggling to breathe. His oxygen saturation's OK, but then it always is, until they crash. There are almost no breath sounds; he isn't moving much air.*

"Has he done this before?"

The young mother—way too young—was holding another baby in her arms. Her eyes were wide with fear. She nodded, "But never this bad."

"Did they tell you he has asthma?"

"They said something like reductive…"

"Reactive airway disease." The mother nodded again. That was the code word for asthma in young kids.

"Do you have a nebulizer machine at home?"

"Yes, but I ran out of the vials yesterday."

"So, no treatments today?"

The woman shook her head.

Good. A few treatments and some steroids, and he might turn around. Faith, his nurse, brought in the nebulizer—a clear plastic pipe connected to oxygen, releasing a white mist of medicine. She handed it to Mom, who tried to direct the mist toward the toddler while holding her baby.

Not even close.

No good.

"Faith, please administer the Duoneb yourself; then get me a new set of vitals."

She left the room to find the vice president of medical affairs waiting for her.

"You have a moment?"

"Sure."

They walked into the nearest empty room.

"How are you?"

"I'm OK. What's up?"

"We have a complaint."

"About me?"

"About the ED. We were cited for an EMTALA violation."

Horrific. EMTALA, the Emergency Medical Treatment and Labor Act, mandated hospitals and doctors to care for sick patients regardless of their ability to pay, making it illegal to transfer patients before stabilizing them. Being found guilty of an EMTALA could cut off the hospital from Medicaid and Medicare. That meant bankruptcy.

"How so?"

"That sick kid you transferred the other night?"

"Yes."

"He died yesterday. I looked at your documentation. I didn't find much."

"I was taking care of him; I didn't have time to document."

"You need to flesh out your documentation. If they find us in violation, we're toast."

"I understand."

That case broke her heart. She'd been wondering day and night if there was anything more she could have done. She had run the case through her mind a hundred times. Still, she hadn't found anything that she wished she could change, but that didn't make her feel any better. The kid was dead. She had failed to save him. And now this EMTALA crap. *My job is on the line. If they find me guilty, I can get a $100,000 fine, and fines aren't covered by my malpractice. I don't have the money. If I lose my job, I have no way to get it. I'm screwed.*

She shrugged. This could wait. She went back to Room 4. The kid looked better, his breathing now improved. He was still retracting, but he paid more attention to the world around him and wheezed like a locomotive. *Great—he's moving some air. Another couple of treatments and he may be going home.* Mom, her eyelids heavy now that the danger seemed past, smiled.

Emma stepped out to find Dr. Umber waiting.

"Just letting you know that I can't work next month."

"How come?"

"A family emergency."

"A family emergency next month, and you know about it now?"

"Look, I'm trying to be polite about it. I thought I'd let you know ahead of time."

He's supposed to work in a couple of weeks, a string of three nights. That'll be a bitch to cover. Nobody wants to work nights. Still, better to know about it now than get called when he doesn't show up for his shift.

I wonder what's up.

46

Kayla put on the last touch of lipstick and checked her watch. *It's time.* She grabbed her overnight bag, looked around to make sure she hadn't forgotten anything, and opened the door. Dick was waiting.

He had invited her for a weekend of skiing, wine, and adult conversation. She'd felt guilty about leaving Eden, but his friend Jake had invited him for a sleepover. He'd been ecstatic.

Dick stepped out to open the car door for her. He kissed her softly and helped her in, making her feel like a princess.

The old inn was enchanting. White candles standing in silver candlesticks played lights and shadows over the melt-in-your-mouth broiled scallops and gleaming sweet lobster. Crystal glasses fractured the light into rainbows. Soft guitar music set the romantic mood.

They ate the luxurious food, drank too much buttery French wine, and talked.

"Is Eden's father involved in his life?"

"He's deployed, so he's seldom here. He sends him Christmas gifts. They only meet a couple times a year."

"It must be hard to be a single mother."

"It's gotten easier as he's gotten older. He's a good kid."

"He is. He's handsome and smart."

"You have kids?"

"Two."

"How old?"

"Seven. Twins."

"Boys or girls?"

"One of each."

"Do you spend time with them?"

"Not much, with my crazy schedule. They live with their mother. We Skype. In January I took them skiing in Colorado. We had a great time. Soon enough they'll ditch me for their friends."

Kayla laughed.

"I love your laugh." He caressed the edge of her hand with his finger. "It's like a light coming on inside you."

She laughed again.

"I love everything about you, Kayla," he said, looking deep in her eyes.

Kayla blushed and took another sip of wine. "Nice wine," she said.

"It's a grand cru. I love white burgundy. It's smooth and buttery like nothing else. Except..." he said, and kissed her. "It tastes even better from you."

She laughed again, half embarrassed, half flattered, drunk all the way with wine and romance.

Dessert came covered by a silver cloche. It wasn't food. It was a tiny golden box tied with a silver ribbon. The diamond inside sparkled and flashed with fiery lights, putting the candles to shame. Kayla's heart melted.

He put it on her finger.

"It's beautiful!"

"Not as beautiful as you," he said, kissing her. He took her hand and led her upstairs to the room under the eaves. There was no number, just a plaque: "The Princess Suite." He picked her up and carried her in. Kayla felt like a princess. He laid her on the bearskin in front of the fireplace.

The burning logs crackled and hissed as he undressed her, kissing every inch of her. He kissed her mouth. His tongue tasted like pepper and honey and wine. He kissed her left eye, then slid to her left temple. He gently bit her earlobe; then his lips slid down the side of her neck to her breasts, and down to her navel, and lower still. He reached the place between her legs, which was waiting for him. He kissed it and blew on it. She shivered. His tongue found it. She remembered no more.

Ages later, they lay embraced on the bearskin, watching the fire. He caressed her, his nimble fingers playing havoc with her senses.

"Let's go to Mexico. You, me, and Eden," he said.

"And just leave everything behind?"

"Why not? Life's too short to miss the good times. We'll surf, we'll lie on the beach drinking margaritas, and we'll ride horses in the ocean."

"I don't know how to ride a horse."

"You'll learn, my dear. You'll learn that, and many other things."

She wondered what that meant, but he started kissing her again, and she forgot.

By the time she remembered, it was too late to ask. She was back home, looking at the selfie she'd taken of them both on the bearskin.

47

Spider man stayed dead. Just another homeless person found dead in the snow. His damaged body told about a rough life. His scarred veins witnessed a long love affair with drugs. He was going to be a coroner's case, but the chances of finding anything were slim.

Emma talked to the policeman who'd come to the ED to investigate. She told him about the man with the spider tattoo who'd been looking for Ken.

He didn't care.

He's not gonna look into it.

I will.

She got spider man's name, address, and phone number from the records. She called. No answer. A robot asked her to leave a message. She hung up.

She drove to his place downtown. The decrepit house was one step away from being boarded up. Silent and dark. Snow piled on the doorstep, untouched after the last storm. She knocked. No answer. She tried the door. It was locked, but the hinges were falling out of the rotten wood. One good shove would get it open. *I shouldn't go in. I should call Zagarian.*

She remembered the last time they met. She'd been so angry that she'd almost thrown him out. She clenched her teeth and got out her phone. Dead battery.

She headed to her car.

It's the reasonable thing to do. There's nothing urgent about this. The guy's chilling at the morgue. Not going anywhere. I'll charge my phone. I'll call Zagarian.

She took two steps and froze.

What if somebody finds out he's dead and comes to check his place and remove any evidence? What if they know already? What if they're on their way? By the time police arrive, with their mandate and paperwork—IF they do—everything will be long gone.

She went back. She shivered.

What if they're already here, waiting? That's stupid; nobody knows I'm here. Nobody opened that door since yesterday, at least. But the windows...

She kicked the door, hard. It cracked open like a gunshot, letting out darkness.

Emma slid in. She looked for the light switch. She found it.

No light.

She took out her flashlight. The shard of light split the darkness. Scattered glimmers reflected on the snowflakes following her in. The room was almost empty. A mattress. A table. Two chairs. A woodstove. A door.

She pulled the door closed behind her. The room got darker.

It was cold.

She opened the other door. A bathroom. Filthy. Empty but for a stack of syringes and needles in a metal box.

The lonely life of a drug addict.

The tears came out of nowhere. Tears for the lonely, miserable life of this man who must have been somebody's son, somebody's lover. *He's nobody now. Nothing.*

Why was he looking for Ken? Who was he? Did he really have a son?

She searched the place.

I shouldn't be here. If they come, I'll tell them I'm looking for some info on his family so that we can contact them about his death.

She was fast and quiet. She held the flashlight in her mouth to keep her hands free. *Nothing. Nothing in the table drawer, nothing under the mattress, nothing in between the old clothes that served as sheets.*

She heard crepitus as she grabbed the pillow. She palpated it gently, like she would a baby's belly. Nothing. She was about to put it back when she saw the sliver of paper coming out of a hole. She pulled it out. Feathers fell gently on the dirty floor. The yellow piece of paper, ripped from a notebook, was wrinkled. The writing was large, irregular, and childish.

The words were not.

SPIDER

My last will
I leave everything I own to my ex-wife Jessy.
I'm sorry I died without saying I'm sorry.
I was no good. You were right to ditch me.
Love you still and always.
Look inside the oak tree.
Love you.
Spy."

48

Taylor was about to lose it. Her eyes were burning, and she was choking on the knot in her throat. *Three days now and not a single call. Why? Where is he?*

Sick with worry, she bit her fingernails to the quick. She had called a hundred times. No answer. She had left messages.

She was reading *The Chamber of Secrets* for the fourth time as the phone rang. Her heart burst.

It's him.

"Hello, baby. How did it go?" His low, soothing voice was a caress.

"It went great. You were right. She swallowed it like candy."

"She's going to do it?"

"She said she would."

"Good girl!"

Taylor felt proud. She thought it wasn't going to be easy to fool her mother, but he was right. She had swallowed the rape story, hook, line, and sinker. It was a good story too; she had found it on the Internet. It worked like a charm, except that her mother had been hell-bent on reporting the rape. Taylor acted despondent. She cried, pleaded, threw herself on the floor. "It would kill me to go through the details once more, Mother."

Emma had relented, but Taylor wondered if she'd report it anyhow. *Hopefully not. She promised. She's always gung-ho about keeping her word. Either way, she's going to help with the abortion.*

"When?" he asked.

"Next week. I'll fly back on Monday."

"I miss you," he said.

Her heart softened. She had never loved anybody like she loved him.

"I miss you too. I miss your hands. The scent of your skin. The taste of your kiss."

They had met a few months ago at the ER Halloween party. Her mother had dragged her along. She didn't want to go, but Katie told her that the ER Halloween party was the best in town. DJ, the best costumes, prize drawings.

She got bored to death. All the kids were younger. There was nobody to talk to.

She walked outside. The garden was empty but for a lone smoker. She bummed a cigarette. They talked. He was handsome and funny. He liked her.

He offered her a pill.

"Put it under your tongue."

"Will it make me crazy?"

"No. It will make you feel good, really good."

It did. The sun was shining inside her. Her thoughts became pink and blue. Her weightless body flew at warp speed through a twisting rainbow of colors. She'd never felt better. She cried when she landed.

He kissed her and asked for her phone number.

She asked for his.

He smiled. He'd just lost his phone and needed to get a new one.

He gave her some wonder pills.

"Make sure you're alone for at least an hour before you take them. Never take more than one!"

He'd called a few days later. She had run out of pills. They went to a cozy inn. They drank wine and took pills. His mouth made love to her. That was even better than the pills.

The time after that he made love to her. It hurt so good! She decided that she loved him and she was going to keep him.

He gave her some extra pills for her friends. She wanted to keep them for herself.

"Don't worry, we have plenty more," he said. "Be nice to your friends."

She gave them to her friends, then gave them a few more.

Next time they wanted some, the pills were no longer free. "Ten dollars each," he said. Hers were free. He loved her. He wanted her to feel good.

He was so proud of her when she brought the money.

The pregnancy was a surprise. They had always used condoms, unless they were having oral sex. She started feeling funny. She bought a test. It was positive.

He wasn't pleased.

She wanted to keep the baby. She loved him—she loved his baby.

He disagreed. "The kid's going to be a monster, after all those drugs," he said. "It's going to have two heads, or hands growing out of its shoulders."

He showed her pictures. She cried. She vomited. Heartbroken, she finally agreed to abort, but she needed parental consent.

"I'll take you to your Grandma for a few days," he said. "We'll let your parents stew a little. When they find you, they'll be so happy that they'll do anything you ask. Plus, you won't have to go to school!"

"But I'll miss you!"

"I'll miss you too, baby, but it's only for a few days."

Driving to Georgia was fun. They spent the night at a hotel on the way. They drank champagne, took pills, and made love like never before. He dropped her off at Grandma's door.

A few days later she called Victor. He was so happy that she felt guilty. She got over it.

They didn't even scold her. Still, they didn't want her to get an abortion. They wanted to know who the father was. She couldn't come up with a name. She told Emma the rape story. That worked.

Only a few days now.

Her heart sang.

49

———

It was Tuesday, "The Day," as Taylor called it. Emma had cold feet.

Biting her lower lip to focus better, Taylor was putting on mascara. *Why does she need mascara to have an abortion? For confidence maybe. Like I put on lipstick before a trauma code. Whatever it is, I hope it helps.*

Emma checked her phone for work emergencies. None. She finished her third coffee. She looked at Taylor. She was pale, fragile, and unafraid.

"Are you sure you want to go through with this?"

"*Yes.* I've told you a hundred times."

"You could stay with Margret; then you could give the baby up for adoption. You could keep in touch with her, if you wanted. You could see her grow."

"See her grow?" Taylor turned, her eyes shooting arrows at Emma. "I don't wanna see her grow. And how do you know it's a girl?"

"Well, see him grow then. The baby, whatever it is."

"It's not gonna be a baby; it's gonna be a monster after the drugs I took. It won't have arms or legs. It will be a giant toad. I've seen the pictures."

"What pictures?"

"The pictures of the monsters born to druggie mothers."

"Well, it depends on the drugs and how much and how often and…"

"No!" Taylor stormed out, slamming the door.

I wish I could have wine rather than coffee.

She didn't much care about her hypothetical grandchild—she'd been a lousy mother, she wasn't going to be any better as a grandmother—but she was worried about Taylor.

One day she'll realize that she expunged her child. She'll never forgive herself. Abortion has no recourse. Adoption would give her time to think things through.

They drove to the ferry where Victor was waiting and moved into his car.

"Taylor, are you sure?" Victor asked.

"Don't start!" Taylor spitted out. "Don't even go there!"

"But if the baby…"

"I told you, don't go there. I've already had a lecture this morning, thank you very much, not to mention all those I've had over the last few weeks! I've made my decision." She turned her attention to her cell phone. She was done.

Victor sighed.

What the hell did we do to deserve this? We loved her, we cared for her, we bought her the best of everything. True, I never had time for her. Same with Victor. He got her the best bike, the newest phone—but he left her for his new family. We both failed her.

At the hospital, Victor and Emma sat in the waiting room after a nurse took Taylor. Victor read an old magazine. He held it upside down, but he didn't seem to notice.

"Have you been praying?" Emma asked.

"Yes, out of habit. I no longer know what I believe in."

"What have you been praying for?"

"I've prayed for her future and for her to get enlightenment to make the right decision, but mostly I've been asking for forgiveness."

"For what?"

"For what I did to her when I left. For what I did to you."

"You did what you had to do. Amber was pregnant. You felt that it was your responsibility to care for her and your child."

"Yes. I also knew that you'd take care of yourself and Taylor while Amber… She's not strong like you; she needs a man."

"I needed you."

"No, you didn't. That was part of the problem. You didn't need me. You didn't really need anyone. You still don't." He took off his glasses and started cleaning them with his shirt. "I think that's why I got involved with Amber. She was vulnerable. She needed somebody to take care of her. I needed to have somebody to care for, somebody to need me."

Emma wanted to tell him that Taylor needed him and that she did too, but what was the point? He was miserable enough. They waited in silence for what seemed like years.

A nurse wheeled Taylor in. She was pale and tight-lipped.

"Let's go."

"How do you feel?"

"Better."

They drove back in silence. Emma felt better too. *It's over. No more "what if" and "how" and "maybe." We can finally move on.*

50

———————

Sitting in her office, Emma was drowning in papers. It was reappointment time. She had to review all the personnel files. Kurt's file looked good. She put it away and got Umber's. He looked good on paper. He even looked good in person. His second reference was from a small hospital in New Hampshire. Something about it bothered her. She Googled it. Winston, New Hampshire, fifty miles from Concord. Coincidence? She called the director, Dr. Slim. He didn't say much.

"He was fine. Competent, fast, a bit of a showoff. No professional issues."

"Anything with the patients or the staff?"

"No," he eventually said.

He's lying. He's afraid of being sued. The darn lawyers make us all paranoid.

"Please tell me! I need to know. This is just between the two of us."

"Well, if anything, he was too friendly."

"The girls?"

"Yes, there were issues with the nurses. Two of them got into a fight. I had to fire one."

Emma remembered the nurse who'd been fired and then died.

"I thought that was for drugs," she said, throwing a dart in the dark.

"Well, yes, that was part of it too. Joy had some issues."

"What happened to her?"

"She died of a drug overdose. I think she couldn't stand the thought that they had taken away her kids."

"Was she involved with Dr. Umber?"

"She was. There were others. Umber's a good doctor, but he just can't keep it zipped. I've never had more trouble with any locum."

Emma thanked him and hung up. She sat at her desk, thinking. *It's Umber. Everything is falling into place; it must be him.*

She called Zagarian. His phone sent her directly to his voice mail.

Umber must have brought the propofol from New Hampshire. He'd been involved with the nurse who signed it out. He attacked George. He was working a shift that day. He left his area for a few minutes to meet George in the shower room. George wanted more money. Umber assaulted him, injected him with propofol, and then left him there to die. He went back to his patients like nothing happened. Somebody found George. They brought him to the ED and gave him to Umber! No wonder Umber was rattled!

But why didn't he let him die?

He couldn't! All eyes were on them. Every member of the staff was watching George like a hawk. Police came. Umber couldn't take the risk. He pretended to save George's life to shake any possible suspicion. He could do nothing else. He thought George would die anyhow.

How about Ken? Did he kill Ken? Why?

Umber wouldn't cut Ken's throat. He'd find a more elegant way. Like getting the Spider to do his dirty work.

Emma had wanted to give Zagarian the Spider's will, but she couldn't explain how she got it. She couldn't tell him she broke into his house. Still, she wasn't sorry. She was sure he was connected to Ken's death. She'd tried to find Spider's ex-wife. She was listed in his chart as his next of kin, but the phone was disconnected and there was no address. *Dead end.*

She called Zagarian.

"There's this homeless guy with a spider tattoo who was looking for Ken. He ended up dead in the snow a few days later. He's a coroner's case. His ex-wife is his next of kin. She may have some information about Ken's death if we could find her."

"Why should she?"

Emma had hemmed and hawed. "I can't tell you. But I know she's got some of his stuff. In an oak tree." *How stupid does that sound?!*

"We'll look for her. Emma, do me a favor?"

"Yes?"

"Stay out of trouble. Whatever you did, don't do it again. Whatever you found, put it back. Whoever you spoke to, don't do it again. There's a killer on the loose, and you're no match for him. He's gonna chew you up and spit you out before you can say Merry Christmas. Keep out of it, please!"

Emma hung up.

She hadn't heard from him since.

I know it's Umber.

51

─────────

She picked up her white coat. *Boy, is it heavy! I have to throw away some of the crap in the pockets. No wonder my shoulders hurt!*

She put it on over her street clothes and walked down to the ED. The place was its usual shade of crazy, one step short of frantic. Umber was in Trauma 2, dressed in full sterile garb—coat, hat, shield, booties—putting in a central line. He looked like he was having trouble finding the subclavian. He asked the nurse to reposition the patient and started over.

He's gonna be at it at least another ten minutes. She looked at her watch, then speed-walked to the doctor's lounge. She punched in the code, walked in, and closed the door behind her.

His bag, an expensive Italian burgundy leather affair, looked out of place on the cheap green vinyl sofa. It was heavy.

She opened it: a brand new little EMRA guide to antibiotics, a heavy *Emergency Medicine Procedures* book that had seen better days, a *Rolling Stone* magazine, a deodorant, a toothbrush, a tube of Sensodyne, a pair of socks.

What the hell am I even looking for? Two brown medicine bottles, unlabeled, half full. She opened them. One had twenty-two white oblong tablets. The other had twenty-seven round pink pills.

What are they? I should take them with me. Shit, I left my fingerprints all over them. I should have worn gloves, darn it! Too late now.

She took two tablets out of each bottle, dropped them in her chest pocket, wiped the bottles with the tails of her white coat, and placed them back in the bag. *If I wiped away my prints I also wiped his, so they're no longer on the bottles. More likely I left mine everywhere. Stupid! Too late to worry about that now.*

She checked her watch. *Eight minutes. I need to get the hell out of here.* She looked around. His red ski jacket was hanging in the corner.

She looked through the pockets. *Wallet. Credit cards in his name. Healthcare ID. Cash: a couple of hundreds, a few twenties, a lot of tens. Passport.* She opened it to check it—*in his name, has his picture, it looks valid.* She put it back. *Cell phone, tissues, coins, condoms, a power bar, matches, a brown envelope.* She opened it. *Pictures.*

She went through them: *snow-capped mountains, ski slopes, a boat, a vineyard— it's twelve minutes now—more trees covered in snow, a naked girl, a car... The girl!*

She went back.

Taylor, naked, smiled at her from the picture.

The door opened.

52

———————

Umber stepped in and closed the door.

"I knew I shouldn't have taken that with me," he said, sitting in the desk chair and rolling it in front of the door. "Taylor insisted. She said she wanted me to remember her by it."

Emma stood frozen, looking at him.

"So, what are you going to do?"

She was angry. She was so angry that her brain was on fire and she couldn't think straight. She wanted to cry and she wanted to scream, and more than anything she wanted to hurt him. Bad.

Thankfully, a lifetime with the crazy had taught her that letting your anger take hold of you made you a loser. She took a deep breath and closed her fury in a small dark corner of her brain. She'd get it out later.

"About what?"

"About that." He nodded to the picture.

"Nothing, I think. Too late to do anything now. I hope you gave her a good experience. The first time is important, especially for a girl. I want her to like sex. It's a joyful thing."

"Really?"

No, not really, but she wasn't going to tell him that.

"I will tell the police about your drug dealing though, Mr. OD. That should put you away for a while."

He laughed. "No, you won't."

"Why not?"

"I have your Taylor. In every way."

"How so?"

"Who do you think did the selling for me? Who do you think got her friends hooked and collected the money?"

"Who?" She smiled, feeling her sweat freezing on her back. *That can't be true. Yes, it can.*

"Taylor. If I fall, she falls. She was the dealer, really; I just procured the merchandise for her. How do you think she'll fare in jail?" Umber asked.

"She'll have a rough time, I guess. No mascara, no cell phone..."

Emma took the other seat and sat, facing him. She crossed her legs casually and put her hands in her pockets. The scalpel was there, in the right pocket, where it belonged. In the ED, one never knows when there's something needing cutting.

She checked her other pocket. Her eye drops were there. So was the bottle of hemocult developer, the concentrated alcohol drops used to test for rectal bleeding. She'd learned the hard way that you should never confuse the two. One night she'd dripped one drop of hemocult in her eye. She couldn't open it for a week. *It's pure alcohol; you'd be better off drinking it then putting it in your eye.*

She rearranged her stethoscope, a Littmann Master Cardiology III, around her neck. It was good and heavy. It made a good weapon. Since Ken's death she'd been practicing in her basement. She'd learned to swing it like a pro. She could hit something six feet away with a good flick of her wrist.

She leaned back, uncrossed her feet, and smiled politely. "On the other hand, she could finish high school without skipping classes. She'd get an actual education."

"Really? Would you really do that to your daughter?"

"Me? Absolutely not. I would never do anything bad to my daughter. You did. By the way, is the baby yours?"

"What did she tell you?"

"You know what she told me; you taught her." Emma smiled. "So. Is the baby yours?"

"Probably."

"Very nice. With you and Taylor as parents, it should be handsome and smart."

"You told her you'll help her get an abortion."

"Sure I did. That was then. This is now. I can deal with a drug dealer as a son-in-law. I can even care for the baby as long as you're both in jail, or I can hire somebody to do it. Would you prefer a little girl or a little boy?"

His face got white and narrow as the business end of an axe.

"You're bluffing. You'd never ever do this to your daughter."

She smiled.

"You have no proof."

"Oh, but I do. The bottles in your bag. Taylor's statements. Oh, and that nurse in New Hampshire? Joy? She left a letter."

"No she didn't. You're full of shit. There was no letter."

"You checked then?"

He turned dark and stood just as the speakers blurted: "Dr. Umber to Room 3."

He leaped toward her.

It was time. She let her anger out of its dark corner. It gave her wings.

His first punch knocked over her chair, but she'd already jumped on her feet. She stepped sideways. His weight took him past her into the wall. She grabbed the stethoscope and spun it above her head. He charged again, his fists ready to pummel her. The stethoscope got him just below his left eye. The zygomatic bone cracked.

He screamed. He stumbled but didn't fall. He was too close for the stethoscope now. She dropped it. She grabbed her scalpel with her right hand. She opened it with her thumb as she was falling backward under his weight. They fell, him on top. The speakers screamed again: "Dr. Umber to Room 3." *He won't make it.*

His weight pinned her pelvis to the ground. His right hand reached for her throat. She lifted the scalpel to open his carotids. *That will make a bloody mess. I really want him in jail.* She went for his right hand instead. She sliced cleanly through the wrist. He roared. *I got him. Good.*

She dropped the scalpel, now slippery with blood. He grabbed her throat with his other hand. He squeezed. He choked her. She twisted under him. Her left hand grabbed the hemocult bottle she'd uncapped as they were talking. She squeezed it in his eyes. She missed.

"Dr. Umber to Room 3," the speakers pleaded, desperate now. *I hope some-body'll take care of Room 3.*

She squeezed the bottle again. His bloodcurdling scream told her she got him. She felt a sting in her right thigh as she pushed him off. She squeezed out from under him. She stood and opened the door. Covered in blood, he was rubbing his eyes with his good hand. She stepped out and closed the door.

The world went dark.

53

───────────

Emma opened her eyes. Suspended ceiling. The recessed lights were off. She tried to sit up. She couldn't. Her right arm didn't move. Neither did the left.

A stroke?

She tried the legs. They worked. She turned her head right. A wall. She turned it left. A door. Closed. Light outside. Noise. ED noise. She opened and closed her fists—both working. Shoulders too. Wrists hurt.

Not a stroke. Then what?

She lifted her head and looked at herself. She was lying on a stretcher, dressed in blue paper scrubs, the uniform of the mental health patients. Her wrists and her ankles were in soft restraints. She could see the corner of the nursing desk, so she knew that she was in Room 6, one of the three rooms for mental health patients.

She was tied down in her own ED.

I'm a mental health patient?!

The door opened. Umber came in.

"How are you doing?"

"Excellent. Resting. You?"

"Great." *He's lying.* He had a bump the size of a goose egg over his left ear. His eyes were too swollen to tell the color. His right hand was splinted and bandaged, sitting in a sling. *I did a good job.* Then she remembered that she was cuffed to the stretcher and felt less sure.

"Police were here. I told them that you had a psychotic break when you found out that I was dating your daughter. You attacked me and tried to kill me. Fortunately, I happened to have a sedative with me. That saved my life."

"Nicely done," she nodded. *So that's what that sharp pain was. I should have thought about it. I didn't. Umber one, Emma zero.*

"Ketamine?"

Umber smiled and nodded. "You really are smart, for a woman. I like that. I have a deal for you. I'll say that you were so mad with grief for your daughter that you attacked me, but I won't press charges as long as you don't mention the drugs. You can't prove it anyhow.

"How about the two bottles in your bag? And how about Taylor?"

"The bottles are now in the pockets of your white coat. They have your fingerprints all over them. Only yours. I always handle them with gloves. For all that I know, you may be the drug dealer, Dr. Steele. As for Taylor, who do you think she's gonna support?"

Emma had lost hope for her relationship with Taylor long ago. Taylor's latest lies were further proof that she'd be a fool to trust her. *Taylor will never support me against Dick. He won.*

He'd won her daughter. He'd soiled her reputation. He had destroyed just about everything she cared about. She despised him.

"You are smart. Very smart in fact. You are smooth, charming, and attractive. You play people. You turn the heads of innocent girls. You get them addicted and make them your slaves. Does that make you feel good?"

"It does. I've never felt better in my entire life."

He pulled the chair closer to the head of the bed. He sat crossing his right leg over his left knee to rest his splinted arm on top of it. His face would have made Picasso proud, but his mood was elated. His words were coming out fast and furious.

"I hate you. I hate people like you, who think they are better than me. You called me a licensed drug peddler, remember? Told me that I should act like a doctor. Well, let me tell you something, doctor. My mother was an addict. I never knew my father. I grew up in the streets. I never knew when my next meal was coming.

"At nine, I knew how to buy and sell. She'd send me out to get her fix. I got to see things no child should see and withstand things no child should ever withstand. I had to do anything—*anything*—to get her fix. Once she got it, she was grateful and loving. I was her lovely little boy. Until the next morning. She'd wake up shivering and crazy. She'd send me out for more.

"Day after day after day, that's what my childhood was, selling myself to help my mother. One day she didn't wake up. She was cold when I tried to wake her up. They took her to the morgue, and they put me in foster care. That was fun too, house after house of lowlifes using me as free labor and as an opportunity to vent their bile against those smarter than them, literate and hard-working.

"I went through high school, college, and medical school using the skills I'd learned as a child. It felt good to stick it to those who'd enjoyed hurting me.

"Now I'm rich, strong, and free. I can get anything and anyone I want. That makes me feel good, really good. It pleases me to no end to have you down, tied down like a nutcase in your own department. No matter what happens, you'll be too embarrassed to ever set foot in here again. I made that happen.

"Yes, I'm very pleased. I got you down, and I'll destroy you. In fact, you'll destroy yourself; you are well on the way to doing that. I couldn't do as good a job as you have in a hundred years."

"How about statutory rape?"

"You should read the law, Doctor. That's not an issue at Taylor's age. Moreover, who'll complain? You, who tried to kill me and barely failed? Let me be!" he said, laughing. "You're toast, Dr. Steele. You daughter hates you, your career is finished, you may even go to jail for drug trafficking. Wouldn't that be fun!

"I'll take care of Taylor, you know. She'll go into the business and learn. She's really good at it. Education doesn't mean crap to her; she doesn't care about it. But selling? She loves it! You'll be proud of her when you get out of jail—what will they give you for assault and attempted murder? Ten years? Twenty? You'll lose your license and any friends you've got left. You could work at McDonald's—if they take convicts. Do you know how to flip a burger?"

"Not really. I'd rather cook inside. You?"

"Well, you'll get to practice during your jail days. I heard they teach inmates all sorts of skills."

He turned to the door.

"Why did you kill Ken?"

"I didn't."

"You got your Spider to do it."

"Smart girl."

"Why?"

"He ditched me. I'd just built a network to replace New Hampshire; now I had to move again. Bad for business, you know."

"Did you kill the Spider too?"

"Not me. He overdosed. I just gave him the fentanyl. Pure fentanyl."

"Why?"

"He outlived his usefulness. He was a liability."

"And George?"

"He was too greedy."

"You are the essence of evil!"

"What a compliment. Thank you!"

54

Emma hated him. She hated him more than she'd ever hated anyone. He was the worst human being she'd ever seen. She was going to destroy him.

Somehow.

What if I go to jail?

It can't be any worse than this, for fuck's sake. I've wasted my whole life. I've been playing a part, trying to be the person the others wanted me to be instead of who I really am.

First, Mother. I tried to be the perfect daughter to please her. But there was no pleasing her. She could give Marquis de Sade a run for his money.

Then Victor. I tried to be the woman he wanted, to make him love me and keep me. Then Amber came, and I was history.

Then Taylor. I was her mother. She had to love me and need me. Hah! If I drowned in the back yard, she'd be pissed that I fouled the pool.

I've never been essential to anybody.

Nobody gave a shit about her. Not even herself.

She lay alone in the dark, listening to the noises. Speakers, alarms, stretchers rolling along the hallways. The hushed voices of the nurses, her friends, only feet away.

Nobody came.

Her own people, her work family, closer than her real one, ignored her.

She was alone.

There was only one person left to care for.

Not Taylor, the bane of her existence since the day she was born; nor Victor, who'd left her; nor her mother, who screwed up her brain into the mess she was.

It was her, Emma.

She did her best. She failed.

The world could take care of itself.

It was time to put Emma first.

Tied to the stretcher, accused of a crime she didn't commit, she was in peace. The weight of the world fell off her shoulders—tomorrow's shift, Umber, Taylor, EMTALA. Defeated, tied down, humiliated in front of her beloved ED, she was finally free.

She fell asleep.

Umber couldn't believe it when he came back. He came closer.

Breathing softly, she was asleep.

He checked her pulse. Nice, regular.

A good vein, right there. An easy shot for a pro.

He grabbed the syringe in his pocket.

He felt eyes, watching him.

He looked around. Nothing.

The syringe.

Eyes, burning him.

His skin crawled.

He stepped out.

Later.

55

———————

G eorge woke up.

Something was wrong.

He sat up listening to the death rattle. He knew it. The sound of his friend choking on his own blood. *Vietnam. I won't forget it till the day I die. Maybe today.*

He saw the old rocking chair with Mary's knitting. *I'm not in Vietnam. Just a nightmare.* He relaxed.

The rattle came back, coarser now. He stood up on shaky legs—that head injury had screwed up his balance. Heart racing, he wobbled to the bedroom. Mary's bedroom.

He turned on the lights.

Mary, leaning over the side of the bed, was throwing up blood.

She's not throwing up. It's spurting out of her like the water out of a cracked hose. Blood dripping down from the mirror, the kids' soccer trophies, Mary's picture of her first communion. Eleven year-old Mary, solemnly dressed in bridal white, now covered by blood splatter like Dracula's bride.

It was a massacre scene like he hadn't yet seen. Not even in Vietnam. Mary's eyes were pleading for help, but she couldn't speak. Her breath was a blood fountain. His knees gave. He dropped on the bed next to her. He grabbed the phone and dialed 911.

Her blood was spraying him, warm, alive, dying.

He put a pillow behind her to prop her up. He held her hand.

"Dickson, Hunter Street, number 13. Exit 29. Yes, she's alive and breathing. Awake and alert. She's bleeding from her mouth and nose. Yes, both. No, no blood thinners. No, no trauma. She has lung cancer. Yes, I'm holding her up. She can't talk. How long? Ten minutes," he told Mary.

Her eyes were looking into death. Her gaze softened. Her eyes closed. Her rigid body grew heavy.

She was slipping away.

"I love you, baby. I'll take care of you."

Her head dropped on his shoulder. She coughed. A blood clot the size of a child's fist landed in his lap.

The army taught him to deal with bleeding—apply pressure, they said. A single finger if possible. If that doesn't do it, try a tourniquet. Tie it tight enough to stop the bleeding. Release every twenty minutes to allow some oxygen to the tissue downstream. Place it upstream of the bleeding, they said.

That would be around her neck.

He couldn't put a tourniquet there. Pressure wouldn't do it either. Unless he closed her mouth and her nose. She would suffocate.

An eternity later, when the sirens arrived, she was no longer awake.

The EMTs, his old friends Roy and Frank, looked scared. They wanted to stop and put in an IV and start fluids. George said no. They listened, though they shouldn't have. He was not their boss, but he was an old friend and an ER nurse. They lay her on the stretcher and ran with her.

His old shaky hands got in the IV as they were flying to the hospital with lights and sirens. He drew bloods, most importantly the pink tube, the type and cross for a blood transfusion.

She was still alive when they got there. Barely.

Brenda was waiting in the ambulance bay.

"Who's on?" George asked.

Covered in blood from head to toes, like the killer in a cheap movie, he walked with the stretcher, holding Mary's hand.

"Dr. Umber and Dr. Crump."

"Call Kurt please."

"It's Umber's turn to get the new patient…"

"Call Kurt."

She directed the stretcher to Room 3.

"Dr. Crump to Room 3," the speaker coughed.

Kurt did all he could. He gave her blood and TXA. He called the pulmonary specialist.

"She's bleeding from her lung. The tumor must have eroded into a blood vessel. I can't fix that. They can."

He'd selectively intubated the lung that wasn't bleeding, to give her oxygen while keeping the blood from drowning her, but she wasn't doing well. Her blood pressure dropped. The bleeding restarted.

She bled and bled.

Her heart stopped.

The bleeding stopped too.

"Defibrillator!" Kurt said, his fists tight in his pockets, biting his lower lip to keep from crying.

"Charge the defibrillator."

"Don't," George sobbed. "She deserves better."

"Does she have a DNR form?"

"We talked about it. She knew the end was close. She was OK with it. I wasn't. We never told the kids. They'd have enough time to suffer later."

"You have a power of attorney?"

"Yes."

"I'm sorry, George. Let me know if I can help."

"Thank you."

George sat holding Mary's hand. Her body got cold. She stiffened. He thought about their good days. And the bad. *I wish I was a better husband. How am I going to tell the kids? What will I do?*

When Brenda returned, he had decided. He had done what he could for Mary. Time to deal with the rest.

"Is Dr. Steele here today?"

Brenda gave him an odd look.

"No."

"Tomorrow?"

"No. You haven't heard?'

"Heard what?"

Brenda looked around, making sure nobody could hear. "She was arrested yesterday."

"Arrested? Dr. Steele? Why?"

"She apparently lost her shit and attacked Umber. They said she cut him open. She'd have killed him if the police hadn't intervened. They sedated her and put her in handcuffs."

"Dr. Steele? Are you sure?"

"Yes. Hard to believe, in ten years I've never seen her lose it."

"Why?"

"Something about her daughter. I'm not sure. I wasn't here yesterday; that's just what I heard."

"Thanks, Brenda."

"Sure. I think it's bullshit."

"Yep."

Time to see Zagarian.

56

Emma poured herself a glass of wine. She hadn't eaten since yesterday. She took a sip of the heavy, dry, demanding red, its intense aromas of black currant and vanilla softening its tannins. It was a 2011 Pauillac, a Chateau La Tour L'Aspic.

She had decided to celebrate today. She had opened her most expensive wine. *I could toast myself...but that would be silly.* She toasted the bottle instead, touching her glass to the gray tower on the label, and leaned back to rest her neck.

She watched a rerun of *Chopped*, her favorite show. The appetizer round was over. The fleshy blonde with her breasts spilling out got chopped. *Good. This show isn't about breasts. Unless it's chicken. Or duck.*

She'd tried to reach Zagarian. No luck. After a night at the hospital, she'd spent the morning at the police department.

"Why did you attack Dr. Umber?"

"I didn't. He attacked me."

"Why would he attack you?"

"There's been a slew of overdoses. He's the drug dealer."

"Dr. Umber?"

"Yes. I found two pill bottles in his bag and…"

"What were you doing in his bag?"

"I was looking for proof that he's been selling drugs…"

"Did you find it?"

"I found the pill bottles and…"

"You handled them?"

"Yes."

"How do you think we can use them as proof now?"

Emma shrugged.

"He says you attacked him and almost killed him because he's dating your daughter."

"Yes, but…"

"Dr. Steele, I strongly suggest that you get a lawyer," the detective said.

She had refused a lawyer. She didn't have one.

She'd asked about Zagarian. He wasn't available. She broke down and called Victor. He got her a lawyer whose sharp teeth and unruly white hair made him look like a shark with a Hemingway wig.

The shark got her out on bail, but she had to surrender her passport. She was not to get within half a mile of Umber. The ED was off limits. She took another sip of wine.

My job is over. My career too. What am I going to do? I can cook. Maybe I can work as a chef.

She poured the last of the bottle. Her shoulders had softened. Her pain had dulled. The facts hadn't changed, but her mood had. Good enough.

It feels good to not give a shit!

The doorbell rang. She ignored it. She wasn't in the mood for visitors. It rang again. She broke down and opened the door.

It was Zagarian.

"How are you?"

"Better now," she said, lifting her glass. "You?"

"I'm sorry I wasn't there this morning."

"I'm sorry I was."

"What happened?"

She told him. She told him about Taylor. She told him Umber would let her off the hook if she kept mum about the drugs. She didn't tell him that Taylor was going to sink her to help her lover, nor that life, as she knew it, was over.

"Why did you attack him?"

"I didn't. He attacked me."

"They say you almost killed him."

"Sadly, that's not true."

"That's a silly thing to say. There's no recovery from that. You career would be over."

"It's over already."

He shook his head. "I wish you hadn't done it. I especially wish you hadn't gone through his bag, leaving your prints. Now we have no proof. We don't even have a reason to search his place. No judge would give us a warrant based on the evidence we have. I'll have to speak to your daughter. Will you be there?"

"Nope. Ask her father. She's better behaved around him."

Zagarian nodded.

"I do have some good news though. We found Spider's ex-wife.

Spider's ex-wife?

"Jessy. You know her."

I do?

"You saved her life the other night. The pedestrian hit by a truck in a hit-and-run."

The woman with the spider tattoo.

"Did she say anything useful?"

"Maybe. I don't know where you got this oak tree—and I don't want to—but the knife inside it had blood stains. We're working on the DNA. We found the Spider's journal. He knew he was playing a risky game, so he left a trail."

After he left, Emma spent the night wondering whether to go to culinary school or look into becoming a drug rep.

I shouldn't waste all the years I spent in medicine. They cost me my youth and my marriage.

Thanks to Umber, I may start selling drugs too!

57

Taylor's headache made her sick. *I wish I had some Tylenol. It can't be long now. We've been here for hours.*

She'd held strong, like Dick told her to.

"Admit that we're together—they already know. Deny anything having to do with drugs. You had a headache. I gave you Tylenol. You felt better. That's it. Don't say anything more."

"Of course." His hands made love to her. She moved closer to taste his chest.

"You won't break down under pressure? You won't feel sorry for your mom and sink me?"

"I hate her." She kissed his shoulder, then moved lower. "I'd sink her just for the fun of it."

"I love you."

"I love you."

Taylor smiled, remembering the rest of the night. *It was epic.* Somebody coughed. She snapped back to the present.

Detective Z, the good-looking one with short gray hair, looked at her like she was filth.

He's not that good looking, and he's old.

"What did you do with the pills?"

"I took them. They were Tylenol."

"What about those you gave to your friends?"

"I gave them some Tylenol too, when they had a headache. It made them feel better." *They know I'm lying, but they can't prove it. I'm getting tired. I need a lawyer.* She turned to Victor. "Daddy, can you get me a lawyer?"

Victor shrugged. "I'll try. I'm running out of lawyers here. I gave my last one to your mother."

He'd tried to talk her into helping her mother.

She'd held strong, like Umber had told her, but she'd had enough.

"I want a lawyer."

"Sure," Z. said. "We'll wait for the lawyer. In the meantime, let me introduce you to somebody. She's got some interesting things to tell you."

He pushed a button. The door opened.

Kayla came in, resplendent in her golden high heels and wine-colored leather jacket. She smiled. Taylor smiled back. She knew Kayla. She had been her babysitter. She was cool. Taylor wished she had a mother like that.

Detective Z. pulled out a chair. Kayla sat. "Would you tell Taylor about Dr. Umber?"

"Of course. Taylor, Dick and I, we are in a relationship."

Taylor didn't understand. She replayed that statement in her head. Again. She got it.

That's their bullshit. They want me to spill the beans. They got Kayla to play their dirty game. She always liked Mother. She's lying.

"Really?" She hated Kayla.

"Yes. We got engaged the day before yesterday."

Taylor looked at the ring. Her eyes hurt. Her heart did, too. It was a gaudy affair, sparkling even in the grimness of the police room.

"I don't believe you."

"You should. I have never lied to you."

"I don't."

"Well, then…" Kayla opened her designer bag and took out a pile of papers. "These are our flight reservations. We're flying to Mexico in two weeks."

She showed them to Taylor, who didn't even glance at them. Kayla shrugged and handed them to Zagarian. She took out her iPhone and came close to Taylor.

I want to hit her. Her heavy sweet perfume makes me sick.

"There're Dick and Eden, ice fishing. There we are having dinner at the Cricket. There we are…"

Taylor didn't need an explanation for that one. It was a selfie; they were lying on a bearskin in front of the fireplace.

She recognized the mounted deer head above the fireplace. It was missing the third point of its right antler. She'd spent a night with Dick in that very room, on that bearskin.

Less than a month ago. That's when I got grounded and lost my phone. Mike called, but I didn't answer. Then Mike died.

"How long has this being going on?" Her throat was so dry that she could hardly swallow. Her heart hurt.

"A few weeks."

"Are you really engaged to him?"

"Yes, I am."

Taylor started crying. She cried for the love that proved to be a hoax. She cried for betraying her mother. More than anything, she cried because her mother had been right. *Again. I hate her. Oh, how I hate her!* She'd never felt so empty, useless, and stupid.

The one person she hated more than she hated her mother was Umber. He'd lied to her, he'd used her, he'd taken advantage of her in every way. She hated him so much, she could hardly breathe.

I'll destroy him. Even if that gets Mother off the hook. Even if it destroys me.

Victor tried to put his arms around her, but she shook him off. She turned to Zagarian.

"I'll tell you whatever you want to know. Just ask."

58

Kayla walked out of the police department smiling. She looked beautiful and serene, but deep inside her heart ached. For the pain she'd inflicted on Taylor. For the hate in Taylor's eyes.

I didn't have a choice. I had to help Emma. And I had to screw Dick. Both.

She had to tell Taylor the truth. It hurt. She had been there only yesterday.

Last night Kurt had rung her doorbell.

She didn't want him there. It was over. She was wearing Dick's ring.

He waited and waited.

She broke down and opened the door.

His eyes were loving and sad.

He's sorry for me.

"I need to speak to you."

"Go ahead."

"Kayla, we need to talk."

Reluctantly, she let him in.

"It's about Umber."

"That subject is over."

"Kayla, he's married."

"I don't believe you."

"He's married. He has two young children. Look!" He took out his cell phone. He started shuffling through pictures. An attractive woman in her thirties. Two kids about Eden's age. They looked like twins. Dick. Lounging near a pool, getting in a minivan, carrying shopping bags into a house. They looked like a happy family.

They couldn't be. That was Dick, her fiancé. He'd just given her a diamond ring.

"This is Mrs. Patricia Umber, with Dodie and Kitty. You know Dick."

"I don't believe you."

"There's her phone number. Call her."

Kayla didn't want to. She looked at the pictures again. *They're a family. Divorced, maybe? He told me that he's been married and has kids. Maybe he's just visiting? I need to know.*

She called. A woman answered.

"The Umber residence."

"May I speak to Dr. Umber?" Kayla asked, swallowing the knot that choked her.

"He's not available right now. Can I help you? I'm his wife, Patricia."

Kayla tried to breathe through the pain. It was suffocating.

"No, thank you. I'll call back."

She hung up. She looked at Kurt. "Are you happy now?"

Kurt looked anything but happy.

"No, Kayla, I'm not happy. Your pain hurts me. I'm here to help a friend. Emma needs your help."

He told her.

She'd had no choice but to break Taylor's heart. She'd done it. *Time to go home and cry.*

59

───────

Zagarian said it clearly, but Emma had trouble believing it.

"I'm off the hook? How come?"

"Thank your friends. George first. When Mary died, he came to see me. He'd been blackmailing Umber. He risked getting indicted in order to help you."

"What did he have on Umber?"

"Umber gave away opiate scripts like candy. He had patients asking for him by name. George thought it was odd, until he saw him accidentally drop a pack of fentanyl powder. Then he understood. He asked for money. It worked. You know what happened when he went back for more."

Emma nodded.

"Then Kurt. He was so mad that he hired a detective to sink Umber. He found out he was married, and he told Kayla, who talked Taylor into telling the truth. Heartbroken, Taylor decided to support you."

"More likely she decided to destroy Umber."

"That's semantics. All in all, you're clear."

"What next?"

"He'll go to jail for drug dealing and attempted murder of George. More if we can prove his role in Ken's death. We're also investigating his possible involvement with the hit-and-run attack on the Spider's ex-wife.

"By the way, the knife in the oak tree has Ken's blood and the Spider's prints. Umber's medical license is history."

"Too bad. He was a good doctor."

"He's a criminal."

"He was still a good doctor."

Zagarian shook his head. "I'll need you to give a written statement."

"Another one?"

"Yep, another one. I'll call."

"OK."

"And maybe we can do dinner."

The half-smile in his eyes reminded her of early spring.

"Maybe we can."

She sat, looking at the TV. She didn't see it. She thought about the people who had come to help her. She thought about Taylor. Taylor had helped her too, not out of love but out of hate. She had forever struggled with her feelings about Taylor.

I've spent years fretting about Taylor. For better or for worse, our relationship will never be the same. She's still my daughter, but she's no longer a child. She'll have to live with the choices she's made. Her future is hers to decide.

She still wished that she had been a better mother, like she wished that she was slimmer or smarter, but had to accept that she wasn't and was never going to be.

Motherhood is not my thing.

60

———————

Taylor couldn't sleep. She was tired and heartbroken. She was out of pills.

She pulled on her jeans; put on her green jacket; and slowly, carefully, opened the door. The gun.

It was locked in the safe. She'd seen it when her father opened the safe the other day as she was hiding, playing hide-and-seek with the girls. She saw the code—it was her mother's birthday. The Walther PPK/S was the same one he'd taught her how to shoot and clean when she was ten. That was one of the special things they did together, just the two of them.

She punched in the code to open the safe. She put the gun in her right pocket, the ammo in her left. Victor's car started at one touch. She took off, leaving the door open. Hands shaking, eyes blurred with tears, she drove to Dick's place.

She rang the doorbell.

Nothing.

She rang again. Dick opened the door wearing red shorts and a short arm cast. His mangled face was a symphony in blues and greens. His eyes were slits.

"What are you doing here?"

"I missed you. I came to see you."

"At 2 a.m.?"

She pushed past him, her grief choking her. "Is it true?"

"What?"

"About Kayla. Is it true?"

"What about her?"

"That you love her and you're going to marry her."

"Of course not. I love you. Where did you get such a stupid idea?"

"She said so."

He grew darker. He smiled.

"She lied." He came close, putting his good arm around her. "Taylor, I love you. You are tired. Would you like a pill?"

"Yes, please."

She wanted to forget. She wanted to pretend that none of this had happened, that Kayla didn't exist, that he loved her, like he said.

She took the pill. He took one too.

He held her close. She caressed his chest, his back, his groin. He took off her green jacket and her jeans. He laid her on the bed. He kissed her. He made love to her.

Afterward, when she went to the bathroom and found Kayla's perfume, she didn't get upset. She'd known it all along, but she chose to put it out of her mind to enjoy his lovemaking one more time. She showered, dried herself with the snow-white towel, and then sprayed herself with Kayla's perfume all over. Twice between her legs.

He'd fallen asleep. She picked up her jacket off the floor and took out the gun. She loaded it.

His eyes opened, wide. His fear trembled in them like a cannibal lizard. She lifted the gun with her right arm straight, pointing it between his eyes. Just above the nose.

"Don't," he choked. "Taylor, don't."

"Why not?"

"I love you, Taylor. You know I love you."

"I know you do. I love you too." She aimed at the little scar below his left eyebrow, the one she knew so well. She'd kissed it a thousand times. Her finger turned white as she pressed the trigger. Gently...

"Taylor, don't!" He jumped out of bed as the door crashed open. Emma flew in.

61

———————

"Taylor, don't," Emma said.

Taylor's eyes didn't move. Her gun followed Umber without fail. The green dot of a laser would have painted his scar.

"Why not?"

"It will destroy your life. You'll go to jail for years! You'll be an old woman by the time you come out."

"My life is already destroyed."

"Not yet. It just feels like it."

"He's destroyed me already. He didn't do you any favors, either. Why not kill him?

"Because you'll get caught! You'll go to jail."

"Not necessarily. Don't move!" she barked, as Umber tried to sneak to the door.

"Sit," she said, pointing with her chin, her arm following him. "We could kill him and hide the body. They'll think he ran away."

"Your father knows you came here with his gun. He called me."

"He won't tell. He doesn't like him either."

"Taylor, please. He'll go to jail, and they'll destroy him there. Please don't do this to yourself."

"I can't. I can't let him go. I need to see him dead."

"Ok, then, let me kill him instead," Emma said.

"You?"

"Why not? I hate him just as much as you do. I'd rather go to jail than see you go."

"How are we gonna get rid of the body?"

"We can't. If we kill him, we'll have to pay."

"OK." Taylor handed her the gun. Dick dashed through the open door.

Outside, Zagarian was waiting. The cuffs clicked.

Emma put the safety on the gun.

"It's over."

Taylor sobbed.

Emma picked up the jacket and helped her into it, then opened her arms.

Taylor sank into them.

"It's over baby."

62

Emma looked in the mirror. She'd pulled out all the stops: new haircut, lipstick, foundation, *and* mascara. New white coat.

This is as good as I get.

She'd taken time off after the Umber fiasco. She debated whether to stay or move on. The night in Room 6 haunted her.

They had abandoned her. She had never felt more alone. She'd been heartbroken. She wanted to leave, but her pride had kept her here. She couldn't run away. She had to look them in the eye and see them blush.

Back straight, head held up high, she walked to her desk.

A flower arrangement as big as a Christmas tree.

A banner stretched across the ED. "Welcome back, Dr. Steele! We love you, Emma!"

The steel in her back melted. Hug after hug—Brenda, Kelly, Judy, Alex, and Kurt— were all happy to see her.

It was a homecoming like she'd never hoped for.

But…why? If they care for me, why? Why did they abandon me?

"They didn't want to humiliate you," Sal said. "They respected your dignity. They thought it was more important to you than compassion. If you needed something, you'd let them know."

OVERDOSE

What I thought was indifference was a sign of respect.

Fuck communication!

241

63

The doorbell rang.

Taylor was in no mood for visitors, but they insisted.

Pretty flowers. He's not too shabby, either.

"I'm looking for Dr. Steele."

"She isn't home right now. Can I help you?"

His eyes swept over her, taking in her swollen breasts and slim waist, and then came back to hers. He blushed.

"I want to thank her."

"Come in then."

He sat awkwardly, his flowers on his lap.

"I'm Taylor, her daughter. What did you want to thank her for?"

"I'm Eric. Eric Weiss. She saved my life. My doctors said that I wouldn't be alive, but for her."

"What happened to you?

"I accidentally overdosed."

Taylor nodded.

They talked about the weather, about his work, about her school. He recommended nursing.

They planned for a movie next week.

It shouldn't show yet.

The day she went for her abortion, she had made up her mind.

Then, a young mother holding a tiny infant passed by, glowing like Boticelli's Madonna. She didn't notice Taylor or the people staring at her, not even the proud waiting father. She was absorbed in the scrunched little face of her infant, and the love in her eyes had no end.

Taylor's heart skipped a beat.

She wanted that. She wanted to love like that. She wanted to look at somebody the way this mother looked at her ugly baby.

This love was growing inside her, and she was about to pull it out like a bad tooth.

They wheeled her to the OR. The doctor came in.

"I changed my mind. I don't want an abortion. I want to go home."

They wheeled her back out.

She didn't tell anyone. Not even Umber. It was her secret.

She kept it to herself until that day when Emma didn't shoot Umber.

That day she told her.

64

The shadows were growing long, and the air was getting crisp as Emma dropped Taylor off. It wasn't close to home, but it was the best rehab for hundreds of miles.

"Mom, I've been thinking. Did you bring the police there that night?

"No. Your father did."

"Did you know they were there?"

"No. But I thought they'd be coming."

"Were you really going to kill him?"

"Sure, why not?"

"But you were going to go to jail!"

"Well, I could use some rest. I wanted to be a good mother and keep you out of jail. And I wanted to kill him. I still do."

"They'll take care of him in jail."

"Yes."

Taylor nodded. Emma started the engine.

Taylor wasn't showing yet, except for the glow. *Victor was right. She already loves this baby. No matter what.*

"Mom!"

"Yes?"

"I love you, Mom."

Emma didn't cry—she never cried.

"I love you too, baby."

Things were never going to be the same between them.

Emma was never going to be the same.

I may not be the world's best mother, nor the best doctor, but I'm the best that I can be.

I'm Dr. Emma Steele, and Taylor's mom. As best I can.

I'm OK.

MERCY

AN ER THRILLER

1

Death: A friend, that alone can bring the peace his treasures cannot purchase, and remove the pain his physicians cannot cure.

Mortimer Collins

Sitting in front of the huge mahogany desk, Dr. Emma Steele hoped her boss would get to the point. This week. She'd been listening to him for ten minutes. An eternity, in ER time. He wasted her time while her patients waited. To distract herself, she imagined him as a worm. She didn't mind being a robin, but eating him? Disgusting. Maybe deep-fried and crusted in Montreal seasoning? With a spicy dip?

"Emma, you know how much I appreciate you," he said, moving the tchotchkes on his desk to avoid her eyes.

She smiled, waiting for "But..." *Nothing before "But..." really matters. It's just lube, helping slide in the message. Like the KY in rectal exams.*

"But your metrics aren't good. The ER costs are going through the roof. The board grumbles. I can't hold them off much longer."

It's not them. It's you, Emma thought. *You'll throw me under the bus, just to say you're doing something. The metrics can't get better overnight. You know it, but you'll step over me to hold on to your job.*

"I understand."

"You have a month. If your ER's metrics don't improve significantly in a month, I'll have to let you go. I had to pull a lot of strings to give you that, you know. That's all I can do."

"Thanks, Gus."

Dr. Gus Gravelle, vice president of medical affairs of Venice Hospital, nodded without meeting her eyes.

On her way back, Emma checked her watch. *Eight more hours. Today is Vincent's birthday. He'd be nine.* She remembered his red hair, spiking out like a hedgehog. His scent of spoiled milk and baby powder. Her throat tightened. She bit her lip to stop her tears and rushed back to the ER.

2

ANGEL

I hate Mondays. They suck. The noise is deafening. Monitors alarming, phones ringing, drunks cursing. Still, I hear her moaning as I pass by her room. I glance in. She's alone. Screaming.

"Help! Help! Help!"

"What do you need?"

"Help! Help!"

White eyes that used to be green. Thin, greasy hair stuck to her skull. She stinks.

"What can I do?"

"Help! Please! Help!"

"What's your name?"

"Gladys."

"OK, Gladys. How I can help you?"

"Help me!"

She sobs. Tears run down through her deep wrinkles. Her lizard-like hands reach for me.

I step back.

She struggles to sit up. She falls back, screaming.

I grab a pair of gloves to help her up.

She shrieks, burying her dirty nails in me.

I pull away and check my hands. Red crescent marks. That's what I get for helping her.

"Help me."

"I'll be back."

"Don't go, please, don't go."

She wails.

I wash my hands twice. I sign into the EMR, the electronic medical record, looking for her.

There she is. Room 5. Gladys Vaughn, 86. Hip fracture.

I'd like to look inside her record, but I don't dare. Thanks to HIPPA, the patient information protection act, if they catch me I'm screwed.

The computer behind me is on. Whoever used it last didn't log out. Good.

I find her record. She's a wreck. Nursing home. Dementia. Atrial fibrillation. Coumadin.

She's screwed. Her expected mortality is 50 percent per year. She only has a few months. Maybe. Bad ones. She'll hurt when they change her diapers. The flesh of her back will grow holes from lying, rotting in her own urine. It sucks to be her.

I check her orders. A whiff of morphine. Toradol, Tylenol. They won't help much.

I look around. They're all busy, dealing with their own shit.

I go to the break room to get my special vial. I draw it, all five hundred micrograms, in a syringe. It's crystal clear and full. It's happiness in a vial.

I head back. She stares like she never saw me.

"Who are you?"

I smile. "I'm here to help you." I attach the syringe to her IV and push the plunger.

"How's it going, Gladys? Good?"

Her anguish softens. She smiles. Gums only, no teeth. She's happy.

"I know you. You're the Angel."

Me? The Angel? Then it dawns on me.

I'm the Angel of Mercy. I'm the Angel of Death.

I'm the angel.

Her eyes glow.

Then they close.

3

———————

Emma punched in the code to get back in the ER. It was cold. Air conditioners working overtime, as usual. The light, blue and ruthless, was cold too. Emma checked her phone, looking for an answer from Taylor. She hadn't heard from her in two days. That was bad news. *I wonder what she's up to. It's never good.*

She wanted to call her, but she didn't have time. Full stretchers lined the hallways. *Every room must be full.* Monitors beeped, patients moaned, phones rang. It smelled like chlorine and blood. Emma waved her ID over the reader to log into the computer system.

A blood-curdling scream split the heavy background noise. Then another. The circus had started.

Judy, the charge nurse, touched her shoulder.

"Dr. Steele, can you go to Room 1?"

Emma didn't ask why. She threw her stethoscope over her shoulder and headed to Room 1.

Monitors screaming. An old woman. Very old. Cyanotic. Eyes closed. Sharp cheekbones pushing parchment skin. She hasn't had a steak in a while, Emma thought.

She stepped in.

Faith, the nurse, a big, beautiful girl, looked up from placing an IV. The other nurse, Brenda, tiny and brown, killed the alarms.

Emma's nemesis, Dr. Ann Usher, stood at the foot of the bed, watching the resident intubate. She saw Emma and her gray eyes darkened.

The resident, a new one, was bent over the patient. He pushed the laryngoscope blade in the half-opened mouth, moving the tongue out of the way to make room for the endotracheal tube.

The blade is bloody. He's already tried and failed. Maybe more than once.

The RT, respiratory therapist, held the ET tube for him. The alarms screamed. Emma glanced at the vitals. *The blood pressure's low. The oxygen sat is in the 80s. Too low to intubate.*

She moved closer. The RT saw her. His face brightened.

Emma cleared her voice. "You guys need help?"

The resident looked up. The few remaining teeth clicked as they clamped on the blade.

"We're fine, thanks. Let's go!" Ann said, turning her back to Emma.

The alarm got shriller, calling danger.

Oxygen sat 73.

Emma smiled politely. "You may be. The patient is not."

"I can handle this," Ann snarled.

"Of course you can. Can she, though? What's the story?" Emma asked.

Ann crossed her arms. Her lips tightened.

"Nursing home patient. 98. Demented. They sent her here for low oxygen and fever. She had an old DNR, but it wasn't signed," Brenda answered.

Emma looked at Ann. "You think she needs intubation?"

"She'll die without it, doctor!"

"She'll die anyhow. She deserves to die in peace."

"The resident needs to learn. This is a good opportunity. No family, no DNR. It's an excellent case."

Emma's smile vanished.

"She's not a case. She's a person. She deserves comfort and kindness. The resident can learn on other patients."

"She has no DNR. We need to do everything, anyhow. We may as well get something out of it."

"She's 98, demented, and dying. She's not here for our convenience. You have a case for futility. You don't need to do anything but be kind."

Ann's voice rose. "Have you gotten soft? Have you lost your spark? IF you ever had it? I knew they were wrong the day they put you in charge!"

Emma's eyes narrowed, but her voice stayed soft. "She's your patient. It's up to you. I'll review the case. There's nothing that says patients should suffer so that doctors can learn. She'll die, no matter what. Soon. The one thing you can do for her is to give her a good death. Put the patient first. That's the whole point of being a doctor, isn't it?"

Ann grimaced as if she'd stepped in a pile of dog poop. "And you call yourself an emergency physician! You may as well be a psychiatrist."

"What I call myself is not your problem. What you do is."

Her bright red cheeks marring her white face, Ann turned to the resident.

"Thanks to Dr. Emma Steele, our ED director here, we'll just let this patient die. That's how she chooses to practice medicine. I hope you'll do better."

Hands shaking, the resident sat down the laryngoscope. His face flushed, he glanced at the door.

"She needs comfort. Did you give her anything for pain? For sedation?" Emma asked.

He shook his head.

"Try fentanyl. One hundred micrograms to start. Ativan too, if she's still uncomfortable. We don't do things just because we can. When we can't forsake death, we must at least alleviate suffering. That's why we're doctors. We always put the patient first. You understand?"

He nodded.

Poor kid. He'd like a hole to crawl in. There's none. I checked.

Emma left the room. Ann's shrill voice followed her.

"She's totally lost it. She's never been great, but now she's gone out of control. Soon enough she'll start killing them, like Dr. Kevorkian. Stop their suffering, my ass! I can't wait until they get rid of her."

"You'll make a great director, Dr. Usher."

Ann laughed.

Vintage Ann. She must be low on her meds again.

4

____

Her heart pounding, her throat tight with anger, Emma locked herself in the bathroom to catch a breather. She washed her hands. She looked in the mirror. *What a sight! My face is burning; my heart's racing and my head's about to explode. I want to crush Ann. I want to see her splattered, like a bug on the windshield.*

She took a deep breath. She splashed cold water over her face. Again. Her pulse came down. Her throat softened, and she managed to swallow.

Thank God for bathrooms. That's the only place I can catch a moment to reset. This is nothing but Ann being Ann. She's a good doctor, but what a bitch! She has seniority, so she thinks she deserves to be director. She may even be right. Still, I can't let this go, or I'll lose the respect of the staff. I can't afford that.

Back at her desk, she looked up the patient in Room 1. Ninety-eight. Nursing home. Alone.

I hope I die before I have nothing left to live for. Poor woman. I hope they made her comfortable and let her go.

She went back to running the board, a computer screen lit in every color, displaying the long list of patients, their rooms, their complaints, the staff's comments, the things they waited for. The ultrasound for Room 9 was still pending, but the urine was back on Room 15. *I need to discharge her.*

She finished, just as the speakers coughed their scratchy command: "Code 99, Emergency Department, Room 5."

Emma headed to Room 5. The scrubs parted to let her in.

Room 5, barely big enough for the stretcher and a chair, choked with staff. The rebreathed air was thick with human smells. Dr. Alex Greene ran the code, giving orders. Rudy, the tech, performed CPR. *Good chest compressions. Good recoil, allowing blood return to the heart.*

Like a well-oiled machine, they coordinated without talking. Ben, the nurse assistant director, got a second IV. Sal, the pharmacist, got the drugs. Dr. Greene gave the orders. *They're doing good, but this room is too small.*

"How about moving to a front room?" Emma asked.

"Good idea."

"Room 2's available," Judy said.

Emma nodded.

The doors clanged, opening wide. The stretcher, hidden under the cluster of scrubs like the queen under a clump of migrating bees, rolled to Room 2. Faith bagged. Amy carried the monitor box. Emma and Alex followed.

"What happened?" Emma asked.

"No idea."

"What was she here for?"

"A broken hip. She fell. She looked fine. I called Ortho to admit her. Then, when the nurse went in to check on her, she found her pulseless."

"Who's her nurse?"

"Brenda."

Brenda's good. So's Alex. If there was anything to see, they would have seen it.

The code ran, and ran. Nothing helped. Half an hour later she was still dead. Alex called the code.

Head down, shoulders slumped in dejection, he went to tell the family. He returned looking worse.

"They weren't happy. They don't understand what happened."

"Neither do I," Emma said.

"It makes no sense."

"Heart attack? Stroke? Bleed? Alex, did you scan her head?"

"Come on, Emma. What do you think I am? An intern?"

"Sorry. I'm just trying to understand."

"Me too."

"What did you give her?"

"Not much. A little morphine. Toradol. That's it."

"It didn't look like anaphylaxis."

"No."

"We'll see what the coroner says."

"Don't hold your breath," Alex said.

"I know. I've been here for fourteen years. I'm still waiting for him to offer us something useful." Emma patted Alex's shoulder and returned to her desk.

Between the VPM, Ann's case, and the code, she was behind. Her patients were restless.

She tried to hustle, but something about this case bothered her.

This is the ER. People die all the time. For all sorts of reasons. Some obvious, some not. But this? Going from looking fine to dead, in minutes? That's weird.

She shook her head and went back to work.

It took her a couple of hours to catch up. She took a deep breath and straightened her back. She sipped on her cold coffee. She shuddered.

She checked her phone. Two missed calls. One unknown number. The other one was Victor.

"Call me."

5

———

Emma bristled. *That's all you have to say? Seriously?*

Heart pounding again, she walked to the abandoned radiology reading room. A broom closet really, and just as glamorous. But it was the only place in the ER, besides the bathrooms, where she had privacy. She pulled the accordion doors behind her.

Victor, her ex-husband, was a cardiologist upstairs. He was just as busy as she was, and he wouldn't call without a good reason. The only reason Emma could think about was their daughter, Taylor. And she was never good news.

He answered on the first ring.

"Emma?"

"No, Pope Francis. What's up?"

"Are you at work?"

"Like I'm ever anywhere else."

"Taylor."

"What?"

"She's gone."

"Again?"

"Yes. They haven't seen her since yesterday. They think she left last night."

Emma's heart sank. Taylor was in rehab. *No more.*

"She only had a couple of weeks left. She chose to go there. Why would she do this?"

"She changed her mind?"

"I'm getting tired of this," Emma said.

"Me too."

"Did you try Margret?"

Margret, Victor's mother, was Taylor's favorite person. A modern Southern lady, she drank both tea and bourbon, whenever she saw fit. She looked like a porcelain doll but was as tough as an old saddle.

"I don't want to bother her. She's barely recovered from her heart attack."

"Do you have a choice?"

Victor sighed. "Any other ideas?"

"I'll try Eric." Eric, Taylor's latest acquisition, was a nurse in the ICU.

"If only she was with him," Victor said. "He's a good influence on her."

"He would be, if anyone could influence her worth a damn."

Emma had coped with Taylor, mostly by herself, after Victor left. Taylor had been a difficult child, then a worse teenager. *I thought she was getting it together. Silly me.*

"Emma, don't talk like that. She's doing the best she can."

"She's doing the best she can to drive us crazy, like she's always done." *As usual, Victor is cutting her slack.* Emma's cheeks burned. She wanted to scream. She didn't. *There's no point in us fighting. Not now.*

"I have to go. Why don't you call Margret? I'll find Eric."

6

———

ANGEL

That was too easy.

They'll never think of me. She wasn't my patient.

I helped the old girl. She'll never suffer again. But I'm running low on fentanyl.

I have to find something else. Quick, painless, untraceable.

Potassium? That burns.

Morphine? That's a controlled substance. It's hard to get.

Insulin? That's easy!

How about a good old pillow? It's quiet. It's free. The old folks won't put up much of a fight. It would be over in a minute. But I need to silence the monitors first. Nobody ever checks, we're all too busy, but you never know.

That's a plan!

Way to go, Angel!

7

It was dark by the time Emma got home and dropped her work Crocs at the door. Her bag, heavy with her always-there stuff—scalpel, flashlight, tourniquet, Magill forceps, drugs—went on Victor's old chair, as usual. She bolted the door.

Her wine and the hot bath were the best part of her day. They cleaned her from the dirt and suffering that came with her job. And now that she'd gone off her food to lose weight, they were her only indulgence. She picked her wine carefully. Wine was her solace and her pleasure. It was also half of her daily calories.

Time to celebrate Vincent's 9th.

She settled for an old favorite, Tres Picos 2016, a Spanish Borsao Garnacha. *Most Spanish wines are sharp and full of dark corners, like Goya's paintings. This one is smooth as silk.*

The cork popped, liberating the wine. She poured it in a long-stemmed glass, unfit for the bathtub. She looked through it.

Garnet. Dark enough to appear black, but for the edges. Like venous blood.

She shook her head. *This job's messing with my brain.*

She read the label. "Concentrated flavors of blackberries, strawberries with nuances of leather, vanilla and plums." *Leather? What's leather doing in my wine? Oak is bad enough, but leather? What if I was a vegetarian?*

She sniffed it, then swirled it for the second nose. She took a sip. She chewed on it, bathing all the taste buds. The ones at the back of the tongue, specialized in the bitter taste, and the ones on the sides and underneath. She allowed every single one to revel in the taste, then she swallowed it. It warmed her heart.

She sat on the deep green leather sofa in her scrubs, too tired to take them off. She'd skipped lunch to go see Eric in the ICU. She found him at his post, watching his patients and taking notes. His tired eyes and the five o'clock shadow made him look older than twenty-four. Emma smiled. *Handsome kid! He sure looks better than the first time I saw him, pulseless on that stretcher. I'm so glad I didn't call that code!*

"Hi, Eric."

His face softened when he saw her.

"Dr. Steele! Nice to see you. How can I help you?"

"Have you heard from Taylor lately?"

His eyes widened.

"I visited her just the other day. She was doing great! We had lunch, we walked, we talked."

"Did you have a fight?"

"Fight? Not at all. In fact..." he glanced at his patients, then sighed. He looked back at Emma. "I asked Taylor to marry me. I know she's only seventeen, but she'll be eighteen soon. I really love her. I never felt the way I feel about her. She's the girl of my dreams. I hope you don't mind that I didn't talk to you first, Dr. Steele. I wasn't planning on it. She was so beautiful...and so kind. I couldn't stop."

"What did she say?"

"She cried."

"And then?"

"I told her how much I loved her. I'll wait for her to be ready, no matter how long it takes. There's nobody else for me."

"And?"

"She cried even harder. I gave her my bandanna to blow her nose."

Emma laughed.

"We sat on the grass. We ate ice cream. I told her about the wonderful life we'll build together. I told her that I want her to be the mother of my children. Then she started crying again. I said: 'It's all right. If you don't want children, we'll just get a dog.' I thought she liked dogs. But she cried even harder. Then she ran back in. I think it was the surprise."

"She's pretty young to think about children."

"I know. But she'll get older. I will too."

"Things change. People change. You may not feel the same way next year."

"I will. There is nothing stronger than love."

"How about hate?"

"Hate is love too. Just misguided. Hate is love in disguise."

Emma smiled. "Maybe. Thank you, Eric."

"Why? What happened?"

"Taylor disappeared last night. We don't know where she is. I thought maybe you did."

"Disappeared?"

"Yes. She wasn't in her room this morning."

"But…why?"

"That's what I wondered. Why?" *Now I know.*

8

ANGEL

This poor girl has got to have cancer. She's bald as a billiard ball, gaunt and yellow. That's chemo. And she's not that old. Forty? Fifty? I look at her patient bracelet. Thirty-three. She got a raw deal. She's holding on to the edge of the stretcher, retching.

I push the second dose of Zofran for her nausea. "How are you doing?"

"Awful. I wish I was dead." She bends over to retch again. "Chemo sucks. And it only buys me a few months anyhow. I wish I hadn't started it. What's the point of living like this? If you can call this life!"

"Why did you do it, then?"

"My parents insisted. I couldn't say no. I didn't know it would be this bad. I'd rather die. It's awful for all of us. They're suffering, watching me die a little every day."

I get it. I'd wish the same if I was her. I need to help her. I have just enough fentanyl left.

On my break, I get the vial from my locker and I head back. Then it dawns on me.

I can't go back. Not yet. Nobody goes back early from their break. I go to the cafeteria. The stench of grease cuts my breath. I get a cauliflower-cheese soup. It's sickening. I want to puke.

I throw it away, and I go back.

She's gone!

Gone? Did they move her? I check the board. No. She's gone. She got a bed. They took her upstairs. It usually takes hours.

I'm livid. I was going to help her.

I do my circular breathing to calm down. Again. And again. My pulse goes down, and I start thinking straight. I was about to make a huge mistake. She was my patient. If she died, they'd look at me closely. I don't need them looking at me, closely or otherwise.

That was a close call. I was lucky.

Careful, Angel.

9

Walking in from the ER parking lot that morning, Emma relished the breeze cooling her temples. She'd spent the night wondering about Taylor. Where she was. How she was. At the crack of dawn, she had no answers, but her head throbbed with a massive migraine, complete with nausea and blurred vision. *I hope it starts slow today. I can't even see well enough to suture.*

She punched in the code to open the ER door. The door banged open. The noise hurt her brain.

"Code 66, Emergency Department."

A blue shadow wheezed past. A posse of six followed, all running like the Olympics were on.

Emma followed.

They caught him in the hallway. They grabbed him by the blue paper scrubs. They ripped, exposing abundant pink flesh. Quivering like a hooked fish, he shook them off. He bolted.

They grabbed him again. Carlos pulled on his leg, sending the whole cluster crashing down.

"Let me be, let me be, let me be! You're crushing me. Let me go, let me gooooo!"

Limbs entangled on the concrete floor. Hands grabbed on to body parts. In the wriggling mass of scrubs and bare human flesh, nobody knew who held whom.

"Stay still, damn it!" "Don't bite!" "Ugh, I got his crotch." "Let go, that's my hand!"

"Let me go…let me go…let me go…"

An elderly woman shuffling by on her walker stopped dead, watching. A young mother froze in place, her eyes glued to the fight. Kids screamed. Security came, holding on to their Tasers. The cluster scrambled.

"What a circus," Faith said, watching over Emma's shoulder, her pupils swallowing her eyes.

"Yes. Get me a five-and-two, please. And a stretcher."

The five-and-two, the classic "agitation cocktail" of Haldol and Ativan, was a shot given in the muscle, through clothes if necessary, to sedate dangerous patients.

"Sure."

The fugitive rolled. The hallway melee collapsed again.

"He bit me."

A thump. A scream.

"He broke my nose."

Blood spurted red.

The old lady wavered. A security guard helped her to a chair.

The runaway cried. Strangled, childlike sobs, strange in a man that size. A dozen hands lifted him on the stretcher, holding him there. The fight was over.

"Where's the five-and-two?" Emma asked.

"Here."

Faith grabbed the patient's thigh. She pinched a fold of flesh and cleaned it. In one smooth move, she pulled out the syringe from her pocket, uncapped the two-inch needle with her teeth, plunged it in all the way and pushed the plunger. She pulled it out and recapped the syringe.

Emma shuddered. *What a silly thing to do. A needle stick means weeks, maybe months of testing, prophylaxis, and worry. I need to speak to her.*

"Soft restraints," Emma said.

Judy slid the padded soft cuffs around the patient's ankles and wrists, and tied them to the bed. The man banged his head, crying, but his sobs got softer and softer. Minutes later he was asleep.

The fight was over, but the casualties were heavy. Roy was dizzy and nauseous after hitting his head. Alex's glasses had carved deep gashes into his face before falling apart. Carlos bled from his broken nose. Ben got bitten. His swollen right hand had red tooth marks. The skin wasn't broken, but he was white with anger.

"You! You let go of his leg! That's why he bit me!" He scowled at Carlos.

Carlos wanted none of it.

"Really? He broke my nose because you let go of his hand!"

"I wouldn't have, if you hadn't brought us all down when you pulled on his leg, you stupid spic!"

Carlos turned dark. He charged, ready to punch Ben.

Emma stepped between them.

"That's enough!"

Carlos glared at her. He opened his mouth to speak. He changed his mind. He turned around and left. Ben's narrowed eyes followed him.

Men can't resist a good chase and a fight. You'd think that Alex, at least, would know better than to run after elopers. That's what security is for. Nope. Now I have four extra patients instead of staff. She sent them all to register to get seen, and went to check on Alex's patients, hers now.

Two hours later she came back to find her colleague, Dr. Crump, sitting in her chair. Her heart skipped a beat, then she remembered. *We're friends now. Maybe.* Their long cold war had ended.

"Hi, Emma. I stopped by to finish some charts and I heard you're having trouble. Should I sign in to help for a couple of hours?"

"Really?"

"Why not? I'll just have to be home by five for our anniversary dinner."

"Thanks, Kurt. How's Sheila?"

"She's great. She has gotten younger since we're looking at adopting. It's given her a new lease on life."

"Wonderful. Good luck." Emma smiled.

Why on earth do people want children? Like life isn't hard enough without them. I should lend them Taylor. They'd get over it real fast.

10

———————

Hours later, when her shift was almost over, Emma went to recheck the chest pain in Room 14. She turned the corner and walked into Faith. *I need to speak to her about that needle. I may as well do it now.*

"Faith, you have a moment?"

"Sure…"

"Let's go for a walk."

They walked out through the EMS entrance in the back. After the raw electric lights in the ER, the sun was a loving caress. The air was soft, the shadows long, the light golden. The scrawny bushes in the parking lot glowed, unfurling raw green leaves. Spring had finally come.

Emma inhaled the scent of moist, rich earth. Outdoors, she felt free. She looked at Faith and smiled. Faith looked away. *She's worried. She must be busy, and I'm slowing her down. Or maybe she thinks she's in trouble.*

"Thanks for your help with that patient. I know he wasn't yours."

"Of course. We're a team. I'm glad to help."

"You did. There's something I need to tell you though."

Faith stepped away.

"I'm concerned about you recapping that needle. Please don't do that. If you get stuck, you can get HIV, hepatitis, God knows what other diseases that we don't even know about yet. I don't want you to get hurt."

Faith sobbed. Emma felt like she'd hit a puppy.

"I'm sorry, Faith. I didn't mean to upset you. I just want you to be safe."

Tears started down Faith's cheeks. Emma touched her shoulder. "Faith, are you OK?"

"Yes."

"Something's troubling you?"

Faith shook her head, and her silky golden hair surrounded her like an aura.

"What's going on, Faith?"

"I've been emotional lately. Ever since I lost my father."

"I'm sorry. I heard about that. It must be hard for you."

"I was away for a month, taking care of him. It wasn't a good death. He had cancer."

"That must have been awful."

"It was. He was in excruciating pain all the time. Day and night. The cancer metastasized to his ribs. They broke. The pain was so bad that he screamed every time he took a breath."

"That's horrific. How come he didn't get better pain control?"

"He refused. He didn't want to die addicted. He said God was trying him before taking him to heaven. He wanted to be worthy."

"I'm sorry." Emma touched Faith's shoulder.

"Mother and I, we got to watch him suffer. It was hard for her!"

"It must have been hard for you, too."

"It was. It took him weeks to die."

"How are you doing?"

"I'm getting by," Faith sobbed.

Emma looked around for a quiet spot. She remembered the family room, the small private space dedicated to families waiting for news about their critically ill loved ones. She took Faith there. They sat side by side on the cheap vinyl sofa. Emma took Faith's hand.

"What's going on, Faith? You miss your father?"

Faith laughed.

"Oh, no. I don't miss him. Just the opposite. He was a horrible man. He beat me for everything, ever since I was barely old enough to walk. He was not a good man."

Emma patted Faith's arm. *What do I say now? I'm glad he's dead?*

"I'm so sorry."

"It's not about my father. It's about Carlos."

"Carlos?"

"Yes. My fiancé."

Of course. Faith and Carlos are an item. They came together from New Hampshire a few months ago. I forgot.

"Don't worry, his nose will heal in no time! The new ENT is excellent! He'll make Carlos even more handsome than before!"

Faith shook her head. "It's not that. He left me."

"Carlos left you?"

"Yes. He moved out. After my father died, I came back to an empty place."

"That's awful!" Emma hugged her.

Faith clung to her, hugging her so tight that she could hardly breathe.

"He must be stupid to leave you. You're so beautiful, and so talented. Maybe he just needs time to sort himself out. I bet he'll be back."

Faith let go. She blew her nose.

"He won't be back."

"Why not?"

"I have…I have done things that he can't forgive."

"You never know."

Faith shook her head.

"If he came back, would you take him?'

Faith looked at her with unblinking blue eyes.

"I don't know. But he won't come back." She headed to the door. "Thank you, Dr. Steele."

Emma wished she could help.

"Faith? How about meeting somewhere for a coffee and a chat?"

Faith's face lit up. "When?"

Too late, Emma wished she'd kept her mouth shut. *I need socializing like I need a hole in my head. Shit. I just couldn't see this nice girl suffer without trying to help.*

"Thursday?"

Faith nodded. She left smiling.

Emma sighed. *I'm just selfish and lazy. Who knows? It may even be fun!*

11

Taylor had walked for hours. The rehab building had to be miles behind. She looked back. Nothing. No trace of humanity. Nothing but trees, birds, and bees. All having a good time. All, but her. She shrugged under the weight of her backpack. Her shoulders hurt. She rolled them, but it didn't help. She was tired, but she didn't dare come out yet.

I'm too close. They must be looking for me. If they find me, they'll drag me back.

She drank a little water and tightened her waist strap, loading more of the weight on her hips. It was a bright spring morning; warm enough to make her jacket feel like extra weight rather than comfort. She unzipped it to let the breeze in. *I'll walk through the woods for another hour, and then I'll head to the road.*

She was tired and she hurt. More than anything, she was pissed. Really pissed. Her mother was right. Again.

"You can't do that, Taylor. You have to tell him."

"Why?"

"He'll find out. He'll feel betrayed and lose trust in you. You can't build a relationship on lies. It doesn't work!"

"Like you know a lot about relationships!"

Emma took in that quick sharp breath that told Taylor she'd hit the mark. Touched her right where it hurt. Then she smiled.

"I know more than you do. I know how to make them, and I know how to break them. But this isn't about me, it's about you. You need to tell him."

"Maybe. Maybe not. If I tell him now, he'll run away. He may never come back. If I wait, he may care enough to want me, no matter what. Plus, I may never need to tell him. Shit happens. He may be nowhere close by the time I start showing."

"He's a decent person, Taylor. I don't think he'll go away. If he does, he does. That's life. You can't pretend to be somebody you're not. Not for long. He'll find out, and it will be worse."

"I can tell him it's his."

"That's silly. First of all, he'll know. He's a nurse. You're almost four months pregnant. How are you going to explain a full-term baby born at six months? He'll know. So will everybody else. Second, the idea itself is appalling. You can't lie to him like that! Third, the real father knows. What if he comes back?"

"He won't come out for a long, long time. I'll cross that bridge when I get to it."

"What if the baby isn't normal?"

"Eric knows I'm going into rehab. He knows the risks of doing drugs while you're pregnant."

Emma gave up. There was no convincing Taylor. She had made up her mind.

Until the other night. Eric was so sweet! He looked at her as if she hung the moon. He'd do anything for her. She could tell him the baby was his, and he'd believe her. She could tell him the truth. He may run away. He may not. Not because of the baby. Because of the lie, like her mother said.

She had looked in his eyes. She'd wanted to tell him: "I'm pregnant. We've already started a family."

She couldn't. She ran away instead, looking for a hole to hide in. So she planned her escape.

She spent a day getting ready. She could either carry some weight, or she could walk far. Not both. She left most of her stuff behind. She took her computer, her jacket and a flashlight, plus water, cookies, and all the dry fruit she could find.

She left before daybreak. She tiptoed out, then walked to the back fence. She climbed up the leaning oak tree she'd scoped the day before. She dropped her pack over the fence and looked down. The ground was far away.

She remembered something she had read about African women.

They abort by jumping off trees. Gravity pulls the placenta away from the uterus, killing the fetus. If I lose this pregnancy, I'd never have to tell him. Then I could have his child instead.

She looked up. Another branch, six feet higher. *That should do it.* She started climbing.

I can't do this. I just can't.

She climbed back down to the lowest branch. She grabbed it, dangling as low as she could. She let go softly, breaking her fall on bent knees. She rolled over to dissipate the energy, like she'd seen in movies.

She stood up. Her shoulder hurt. She'd caught a rock. She pushed on her belly with her hands. It didn't hurt. She put on her pack, then she walked, and walked. To where? She wasn't sure.

I'd like to go to Grandma. She'll be happy to have me. But that's the first place they'll look. I could go to New York City. They'll never find me there. But I don't have much money. Only enough for a few days. Then what? I'll go to Katie. She won't tell. I'll be safe there while I get it together.

Her back hurt. Her belly started hurting too. A cramp scrunched her over. She stopped to catch her breath. She started again.

Another one. Longer. She checked her watch.

I need to walk for another half an hour.

A third cramp took her breath away.

She didn't have another half an hour. She needed a ride. Now.

To where?

She sat, hugging her knees. She took slow, even breaths.

Something's wrong with the baby. It looks like I'm losing it, after all. Where should I go?

The pain in her heart hurt more than the cramps in her belly. She took out her phone and checked the map. The road was half a mile to her left. She took another sip of water and headed there.

A cramp cut her at the knees. She lay down in the young green grass, moist with dew.

I'll totally ruin my jacket. Another cramp. She gathered her knees to her chest and lay on her side in the fetal position. She waited. The cramps stopped.

She got her pack and headed to the road, crushed by the weight, the pain, and her guilt.

12

B ack in the ER for another shift, Emma was reading Room 5's EKG when Kurt stopped by.

"Emma, you have a moment?"

Resplendent, as always, in his dark suit and tie, he made her feel shabby. Her bleached scrubs were too tight. And dirty. *They were clean this morning,* she thought, hoping the brown spots on her thigh were coffee rather than somebody's body fluids. "Sure."

"Can you look at a rash?"

"I'm lousy with rashes, but I'll do my best."

"Room 20. Failure to thrive. She doesn't look well, and she's got blisters in her mouth. I'm worried about Stevens-Johnson syndrome."

"I haven't seen that in ages. I hope you're wrong," Emma said. Stevens-Johnson, one of the few dermatological emergencies, started with a rash and ended with the skin peeling off in sheets.

The woman in Room 20 was hard to look at. She was small and frail. Her cracked lips were bloody, her eyes glued shut.

Emma turned on her flashlight. *Blisters. On her neck, on the palate, on the tongue. Herpes?* "Does it hurt?"

"Not much," the woman slurred.

"Maybe it's not herpes then. That sucker hurts like a son of a gun! Kurt, I'd call Infectious Diseases. I'd treat her for sepsis. Fluids, antibiotics, bring her in."

"Thanks, Emma."

"I hope you feel better soon," Emma said. She glanced at the old man sitting by the door leaning on his cane. "We'll do our best to help her."

"Thank you." He smiled, looking behind Emma's shoulder.

Her heart sank. *He's blind. How will he manage without her? There's nothing worse than losing one's life partner. Except for losing a child.*

She touched his shoulder, wishing she could help, and went back to her patients. Back pain in Room 12.1. Depression in Room 7. Sepsis in Room 10.

She was just telling the back pain that she can't give him Percocet if he's allergic to Tylenol, when the speakers croaked: "Code 99, Emergency Department, Room 20."

She went to help. The room was already full. Gail performed CPR. Carlos bagged. Dozens of busy hands placed IVs, attached monitors, pushed meds. Kurt was ready to intubate.

Emma prepared his tube. She glanced at the patient to choose a tube size. She recognized the bloody dry lips. *That's the patient Kurt had me see. She wasn't that bad. What happened?*

Kurt ran the code like the pro he was. It made no difference. The patient stayed dead.

Half an hour later, Kurt called the code. Everybody went back to their work. Everybody, but the blind elderly husband. He sat by the bed holding the blue hand.

Emma's heart cried for him. She looked for Kurt.

"What happened?"

He shrugged. "I don't know. I gave her fluids and antibiotics. She looked better. When I went back to check on her, I found her dead."

"Weird!"

Kurt nodded, his lips a tight line.

"A heart attack maybe? A stroke?"

"I don't know."

"Anaphylactic reaction to antibiotics?"

"It didn't look like it. No hives, no swelling, she was bagging all right...It makes no sense," Kurt said.

"That's odd."

"It sure is. It will be a coroner's case."

"Don't hold your breath."

Emma didn't understand what happened, and that drove her crazy. *Things don't happen without a reason. She died out of the blue, only a couple of hours after I saw her. She looked all right. Then Bam! She's dead. Why? Even worse, she's not the first one. The first one was the hip fracture in Room 5. Just like this one. OK now, dead an hour later. For no reason. Something isn't right... But what? A bad batch of medications? The oxygen? Some weird communicable disease we don't recognize?*

Emma hated things she didn't understand. She lived to fix people. That was her only skill. *I'm a lousy mother, I failed as a wife, I can't sing or draw or play sports. The one thing I'm good at is being a doctor. Now I'm failing at that too. I'd better figure it out soon.*

Before it strikes again.

13

ANGEL

That was easy.

Poor woman! The rash! Those bloody lips!

I left to get my fentanyl, when I saw the insulin sitting on the counter. I grabbed it.

"What is it?" she asked.

"Something to make you feel better."

"Thank you. Can I have some water?"

I brought her water. I brought some for her husband too.

"What's your name?" she asked.

"Angel."

"You are an angel," he said.

The poor man is blind. He can't take care of her. She must be taking care of him. What will he do without her? I hate to separate them, but she needs relief. I wish I could send them together, but I can't. Two deaths in one room? That's overkill. Except for carbon monoxide. That would kill them both. I'd have to close the door. But there are detectors. And how do I get carbon monoxide? Not like I can get a car in here.

Cyanide? Mushrooms? I need to think.

Next time.

14

———

Emma signed out her last patient and headed upstairs. Her rotten shift was finally over. She couldn't wait to go home. She had to find Taylor. She needed wine. And a hot bath.

Instead of that, she went to meet Carlos, like the VPM had asked her to. Carlos wanted Ben fired. He threatened to sue the hospital. Emma was supposed to talk him out of it. *Fat chance.*

She stepped in the windowless conference room. Carlos waited, alone but for the dismembered intubating mannequins piled in a corner. Bald heads attached to limbless torsos. Rubber faces with toothless gaping mouths. Glazed eyes staring into nothing.

But for his arms and legs, Carlos could be one of them.

Death awaits.

The thought came out of nowhere. Foreboding poisoned the air. Emma shuddered. She needed to get out.

"Let's go to my office."

Carlos followed. He sat across her desk, staring at his hands.

"What's happening, Carlos?"

He shifted in his chair, his bruised eyes avoiding her.

"What's up, Carlos? You started so well. Everybody loved working with you. Always patient, smiling, ready to help. Then you changed. People complain that you've been short lately. What's going on?"

"You were there, Dr. Steele. You heard him."

"Carlos, there's more to it than that. You've been struggling for a while."

Carlos shivered.

"Are you sick?"

"I need to grab a candy bar. I skipped lunch. My sugar must be running low."

Emma handed him her power bar. Her mouth watered. *I don't need it anyhow. I'm heading home.*

"You're diabetic?"

"Since I was twelve." He unwrapped it and took a bite. He struggled to chew. His face was bruised, his thick nose crooked. He finished, rolled the wrapper into a ball and put it in his pocket.

"Thank you." His eyes, black holes, met Emma's. She shivered.

"Carlos, is this about Faith?

"How do you know?"

"She told me. I'm sorry for both of you. It must be hard."

"It is. I had nowhere to go. I slept in my car, until George took me in."

"He's a good man. I'm glad he's your friend."

"Me too."

"You think it's all over with Faith?"

"Yes. Faith did things I can't forgive. I said things she can't forget. It's over."

"It must be hard to work together."

"They don't put us on the same team."

"Let me know if I can help."

Carlos nodded, his hunched shoulders spelling defeat.

It's sad, but he'll get over it. He's young, he's smart, he's handsome. She will too. It just takes an awful long time. Even after love dies, it still hurts.

"About Ben."

Carlos turned red. "Fucking Jew!"

"Come on, Carlos! How is this better than what he called you?"

"He's not here to hear it. And he started it."

"Carlos, we're not in kindergarten. We're grown-ups. We work together like professionals. We respect each other."

"Is this how he behaved? Grown up?"

"No. That's why he got demoted. He lost his position as assistant director. He got a warning. He'll have to go through sensitivity training."

"And you think that's enough? Dr. Steele, do you have any idea what it took for me to get here?"

"No, Carlos, I don't. Tell me."

"I was a street kid from Puerto Rico. My father? I don't even know his name. My mother worked three jobs to feed my brother and me. She was never home. I was twelve when I joined the gang. I was fourteen when I went to juvie. Do you have any idea how hard it was to get myself together? To get my GED? To go to college? I got my degree working nights as a janitor. I walked dogs. I went hungry. For eight fucking years. I did whatever it took to pull myself together and never go back. And now this fuck calls me an incompetent spic?"

"You just called him a fucking Jew. What do you know about his life?"

Carlos glowered. "I know plenty. He's got an ugly past. I know. I was there for some of it. I heard about the rest. One of these days…One of these days I'm going to talk, no matter what. It's worth it, just to see him fall apart."

"Carlos, you need to stop. You won't throw away all your hard work just because he called you names? You're smarter than that, Carlos. I hope you are."

Carlos shook his head. He stood up and headed to the door.

"Good night, Dr. Steele."

Driving home, Emma wondered what that meant. *It's none of your business, leave me alone? Or is it: I'll think about it?*

She pulled in the garage. She dropped her Crocs, walked in the kitchen, and dropped her bag.

I need wine to warm me up inside. 19 Crimes, 2017 Shiraz, South Eastern Australia. "British rogues, guilty of one of nineteen crimes, were sentenced to transportation. This wine celebrates the rules they broke and the culture they built." The wine reminded her of Carlos. She opened the bottle and poured the dark ruby wine in a tall glass. She inhaled. *Almost black. Rich aroma. Dark fruit. A hint of honey.* Her mouth watered. She lifted the glass.

She heard a sound in the house. She froze. She put down the glass. Head up, chin forward, she listened. Nothing. *The pipes? The heat? A burglar?*

She crept to her bag and grabbed the scalpel. *It won't do much against a gun, but that's the best I've got.* She slid toward the living room.

The noise again.

She blew the door open. Taylor froze.

"Taylor?"

"Mother?" Taylor laughed.

Emma saw herself through Taylor's eyes. *A scared, overweight, middle-aged woman in dirty scrubs threatening the world with a scalpel. Move over, Hitchcock!*

"Welcome home, Taylor."

15

———————

Emma was late on Thursday for her date with Faith. They planned to hike Silver Lake Mountain, and Emma couldn't find a pair of hiking pants that fit. She ended up with a pair of maternity pants she hadn't worn since Vincent. She pulled her red Hyundai next to Faith's black Chevy pickup, wondering about her taste in cars. She knew some girls loved tractors, but a truck?

They headed up the path, Faith first. Emma scrambled behind her trying to keep up. She hadn't hiked in years. Ever since she'd chaperoned Taylor's class in seventh grade. It hadn't been much fun.

The other parents bragged about their kids' soccer goals, violin concertos, and volunteering. Emma wasn't into bragging. She didn't have much to brag about, either. "Taylor's doing great. She hasn't killed anyone yet. That we know of." Fortunately, nobody asked her anything. They only talked about themselves and their kids. As usual, she listened.

Faith's orange leggings moved swiftly, sidestepping boulders and puddles. She made it look easy. Emma scrambled behind her, watching her feet. The trail was uneven and muddy. She had already slipped twice.

She'd never talked to Faith outside work. Not much at work, either. *There's no time to chat in the ER. And if you ever do, it's at 4 a.m., after the evening rush dies down. For an hour or so. By six, the heart attacks start coming. By seven, the nursing homes find those who died overnight. By eight, the hangovers stop by for work notes, and by nine you're back in business.*

She was hungry for air. She stopped to catch her breath, pretending her boots needed tightening.

I wish we had gone for a pedicure instead. Too late now. It's a small hike. Less than a mile. How bad can it be?

Faith waited.

"You have kids?" Emma asked, making conversation.

Faith shook her head. A tear ran down her cheek.

Do I know how to break the ice or what? Her parents are another minefield. So is Carlos.

"They're seriously overrated. You can have mine if you want her."

Faith's periwinkle eyes widened. She laughed. "What's wrong with her?"

"I'd tell you, but we don't have the whole day. You want kids?"

"I always wanted kids. Carlos didn't. And…the other men in my life didn't either." Faith shrugged. "Too bad. I know I would be a good mother. I didn't want to have a kid whose father didn't want him. My own childhood was bad enough."

"I'm sorry about that. Mine wasn't that great either."

"Was it your father?"

"No, he died when I was a baby. My mother was mentally ill."

"Lucky you!" Faith said.

Emma laughed. Faith blushed.

"I meant you're lucky that your father wasn't mean to you. That came out awful."

"Funny though. What was wrong with your father?"

"He was a religious nut. Everything had to be done by the Bible. I couldn't start the microwave without praying first."

"I didn't know they mentioned microwaves in the Bible!"

"They did, in my father's. That's why they named me Faith. It was either that or Genesis."

"You were lucky."

"I guess."

The stony path got steeper and steeper. The trail became an irregular rock stairway heading straight up toward the sky. Emma had trouble putting one foot in front of the other. Her heart pounded fasted and faster. She ran out of air. She felt faint.

She stopped to rest. She drank water. Faith waited.

Emma looked up. A stairway to heaven. She looked down. Between the branches, she caught a glimpse of blue water, far below.

"We'll have a beautiful view when we get there," Faith said.

If we get there.

"How much further, you think?"

"We're about halfway, but it gets steeper toward the end."

"Doesn't it always?" Emma spat.

Faith laughed. "Just like the night is darkest just before dawn."

"Have you been here before?"

"Last winter. Carlos loves the outdoors. We used to hike, bike, and kayak together in New Hampshire. Here too, until..."

"I've heard New Hampshire is beautiful. I've never hiked there," Emma said, trying to change the subject.

"Do you really think Carlos will come back?"

Emma stopped to breathe. She could hike, or she could talk. Not both. *She chats like she's window shopping, while I'm dying. But she's ten years younger, and in amazing shape. Not me.*

"I do. People need time to understand themselves. They come, they go, they wiggle. It's hard to get together. It's hard to break apart. But the question is: should you take him back?"

"It's hard to be alone."

"I know. Were you happy with him?"

"Not when he drank. He got angry."

"He's a mean drunk?"

"Aren't they all?" A shadow passed through Faith's limpid eyes. "Why do I always get involved with nasty men?"

"Faith, you're so young. You're beautiful and vibrant! You'll find a man who deserves you. You have time to have children, if that's what you need."

"I loved Carlos."

"You still do?"

"I don't know. He's comfortable. He's safe. He's home." Faith slowed down as she climbed the last dozen rough steps. "Change is hard," she said softly.

Emma nodded, too winded to talk.

"But it's necessary. Like iron forged in fire, we all have to go through the events that will shape us into the people we need to become," she declared.

Too tired to care, Emma followed her to the top. Far, far below, Silver Lake glimmered in the morning sun. Covered in pine trees, the mountains were dark blue but for the white snowcaps. The blue sky stretched forever. The beauty filled Emma's heart with joy.

She grabbed her phone to take pictures and stepped forward to avoid a tree branch.

A rock rolled under her foot. She slipped. The other foot followed. She slid, feet first. She reached for the tree branch. She missed. She hit the ground, sliding down. Nothing ahead but the lake. A mile away.

The void smiled.

She wished she'd been a better mother. A better doctor. A better person.

The void called.

She tried to grab the ground. The rocks rolled with her.

The void sucked her in.

She stopped.

Faith had grabbed her. Holding her hood with one hand, a tree branch with the other, she dragged her back.

They fell back on the trail.

The lake sparkled. The sun bathed the mountains as if nothing had happened.

Nothing had.

"Thank you, Faith."

Faith smiled, her eyes bluer than the sky above.

"Of course. That's what friends do."

Emma's eyes burned.

It's good to have friends.

16

———————

arlos needed his stuff. Faith was at the hospital. He'd just grab his stuff and go.

He climbed the old sloping staircase and unlocked the door. The spotless kitchen felt foreign. *She must be pleased I'm no longer here to leave a mess. I'll get in and out before she gets back.* He propped the door open with a boot. He got her those boots. *That was before...*

He shook his head to banish the thought. His boxes were in the spare room. He grabbed two and took them to the car. Three trips later, the car was full.

I'll come back for the rest.

He took a last look around. Faith's faded pink robe hanging on the door. Her ER Pearls book, open on the coffee table. Her slippers, shaped like her feet. Nothing of his, but the picture of the day he proposed. Him, kissing her. Faith, smiling, looking at his ring.

I wonder if she still has it.

He headed to the door just as Faith stepped in. Her beauty took his breath away, as always. Her golden hair, alive with movement. Her indigo eyes sparkling against her flushed cheeks. She smiled.

She's not surprised.

"I was expecting you, but I thought you'd call first."

"I didn't want to bother you."

"How considerate! I never get to see you, these days. Sit."

"I need to go."

"Why the big rush?"

Faith stood in the door, blocking it. Carlos sighed.

"Is this how you treat old friends? You come in like a burglar and leave without saying good-bye? What's wrong with you, Carlos?"

"You know damn well, Faith. There's nothing wrong with me."

"You think there's something wrong with me?"

"Come on, Faith. There's no point in opening old wounds!"

"Oh, but there is, my friend. I miss you."

"I don't miss you. And you're lying. You don't miss me. You miss him!"

"I miss him too. But he's gone. You're here!"

Carlos shook his head. He tried to get past her.

She grabbed him. She held him close, lifting her beautiful rose mouth to his. Her perfume, honey, jasmine and moist earth, enveloped him. His knees weakened.

He tried to disengage. She clung to him. His knees gave.

They fell on the floor. Her lips found his. Her tongue tasted him.

He forgot to resist. She slowly, lovingly, opened his buttons. She kissed his face, sucked on his earlobe, breathed short hot breaths under his chin. She stroked the place between his legs where his brain had melted.

He forgot everything: Dick, the car in the driveway, George waiting for him with a beer. He forgot everything but Faith. Her scent, imprinted in his soul. Her moist mouth, hot in the open zipper of his jeans. He hurt in the beauty of the feeling. Nothing else mattered. He was whole.

17

Emma punched the ER silver door opener and flew in through the door. She'd been upstairs, in the hospital, assisting with a code. *Like I don't have enough to do in the ER. I've been away from my patients for half an hour. That's insane. Any doctor should be able to manage that.* She huffed, rushing to her desk.

Kurt was waiting in her chair.

"You care for a walk?"

Like I care for an STD.

She checked the board. Five new patients waiting to be seen. Plus all the others.

"Now?"

He nodded.

They walked out through the ambulance door. Walking from there to the main entrance gave them three minutes of privacy. Five, if they stopped to tie their shoes. Eyes and cameras were everywhere, watching, but they couldn't hear.

"That death, the other day…"

"Yes."

"It was hypoglycemia."

Low blood sugar? "How low?"

"Her blood glucose was 12."

Twelve? How can that be? Normal is 90 or so. At 60 they get weird. Lower, they seize and behave like a stroke. How could Kurt miss that?

"Was she a diabetic?"

"No. And before you even ask: we had already checked her glucose. It was normal!"

"How did you find out?"

"I have friends."

The coroner's office.

"How could that happen?"

"I'm wondering if she got insulin. The next-door patient, Room 21, was a diabetic with a glucose in the 500s. I ordered 30 units of insulin for him. What if she got it instead?"

"That would be a huge mistake. "

"Shit happens. With all the interruptions, I'm surprised we don't make more mistakes."

"You checked your orders?"

"I did. They were correct. Still, the nurse may have given it to the wrong patient."

"But they have to check the patient's ID first."

"They would. Unless they got distracted. I don't know what happened, but I thought I'd warn you. This is going to come out, and we won't look pretty."

"Nope. Can you think about any other scenario?"

"I can't. It's got to be the insulin."

Damn. That's exactly what I needed.

Emma's job hung from a thread. The ER metrics had been bad for years. To fix them, the hospital had fired all the docs and hired a contract group. Fortunately, the group took them on. Emma became director. They told her to improve the metrics and lower the costs. Soon. Or else. She hadn't.

I'm screwed. Even if it's a nursing error, and the nurses are Mike's responsibility, not mine, Gus will drop me faster than a hot potato. Ann is waiting in the wings to take my job. Oh well. It was good while it lasted.

The heck it was. This job sucks. Being director is not doctoring. It's politics. Filthy business. It sucks to fail. But it would be awesome to no longer be on call. And tell them all to fuck themselves. I get five job offers a day. In places more exciting than this. I could go to Australia, where they have kangaroos. Or to New Zealand. They have penguins. I love penguins!

Back at her desk, smiling wide, she logged into the system. Ann stared as she passed by. Emma waved.

I can't wait to see you on call 24/7. Fucked from above and from below. It's all worth it, right there.

Ann frowned.

Emma laughed. *I wish they could transplant a sense of humor. It would do Ann a world of good.*

18

———

By the time she got home that evening, Emma was "hangry". So hungry, she was angry. She had nothing but coffee all day. After February, she decided to do something for herself. She was going to lose those extra pounds. Easier said than done. Her schedule sucked. The break room overflowed with junk food. Only one way to do it: stop eating at work. No doughnuts, no cake, no junk.

This way I can enjoy my wine without worrying about calories.

Her hands were shaky and her fuse was short, as she dropped her bag on the chair. Taylor was obviously better. The sink was full of dirty dishes.

Why does she need a new dish every time she takes a bite? Because she doesn't do the dishes, that's why!

Emma hated dirty dishes. In her private list of least favorite things, dirty dishes were #2. After rats, and before stepping in dog poop. Snot was #4, but that came with the job. Dishes didn't. It took all she had to control her OCD and ignore the sink.

Hip-hop music thundered from Taylor's room, jarring Emma's empty stomach. Taylor lay in bed, reading the second Harry Potter. The book was falling apart.

She's been crying again. That smudged mascara makes her look like a raccoon.

"How are you?" Emma asked.

"OK. You?"

"Better now that I'm home. How are you feeling?"

"Same, same."

"Any bleeding?"

"Not yet." Tears streamed down her thin face.

Emma's soul hurt. She wanted to hug her, but she knew better. *She's like a cat. She only wants to be touched when she's ready. Not now.*

"How's the pain?"

"Same. Cramps every fifteen minutes."

"You want to go get checked?"

Her softness vanished.

"I told you no! Five times!"

"I thought you changed your mind."

"I never change my mind!"

Emma laughed. *Not more than every five minutes, you don't.* Taylor understood and broke in a rare smile.

"Not that often. I'll find out soon enough anyway."

"But…"

"You said there's no way to prevent a miscarriage. If I get worse, you'll take me there."

"Don't you want to know?"

"I'm afraid to find out. I don't want to know. Well, I do, but only if it's good news."

"What's good news for you?"

Taylor frowned.

"What do you mean? I see. If I miscarry, I don't need to tell Eric." She cupped her growing belly between her hands. "Good news would be to see the baby alive. I can't wait to hold him. But I don't know how to tell Eric."

"You'll have to make a decision."

"Not now. I have enough on my plate.

Not really. You lie in bed, wallowing in self-pity. You read Harry Potter. You wonder what's happening but don't want to know.

"Your father and Eric are sick with worry. You need to tell them you're OK."

"I will, eventually."

"When?"

"When I'm ready."

"When are you going to be ready?"

Taylor sat up. Dark hair streamed around her narrow face like hissing snakes.

The harpy woke up.

"I'll let you know. Now, if you don't mind…"

"I mind. You need to tell them."

"It's my business. I'll tell them when I'm ready!"

"It's my business too. This is my house. You chose to come here."

"I needed help. I trusted you!"

"I let you be long enough. You tell them or I will. By tomorrow."

"Are you serious?" Taylor's pale cheeks flushed with anger.

"Damn serious. Get out of the hole you dug for yourself. You shouldn't have lied to Eric…"

"I didn't lie to Eric! I never said a lie!"

"You lied by omission. You know what you did. I told you then that it was a bad idea. You didn't listen. You never do. If you don't tell them, I will. It's up to you."

"Mother!" Taylor sobbed. "Please, you can't do that…"

Miss Bipolar is working on me. She'll do whatever it takes! If anger didn't do it, pity will. No, baby, we've already played this game too many times. I'm not your father, who always lets you have your way. Nor poor Eric.

"Taylor, I'm helping you become a responsible adult. You have until tomorrow. If you don't call Eric and your father, I will."

19

Carlos woke up in Faith's bed. She was warm and soft, and she smelled like chocolate, pepper, and sex. He luxuriated in her scent. Until the memories exploded in his brain.

She enticed him. He surrendered.

She broke down his defenses. Again. He forgot that she cheated on him, betrayed him and uprooted his life. Once again, he fell for her. As soon as she touched him, he melted into a haze of lust. He was her toy. She called, and he dropped everything. He had left his life possessions in the street.

He saw red. He was angry at her, but even angrier at himself. She had wrapped him around her finger. Again.

He struggled to control his breath. He slid out of the bed with less noise than a falling feather. He crept to the kitchen. His clothes were on the floor. No underwear. He pulled on his pants and T-shirt, grabbed his jacket, and snuck out like a thief.

Get out before she ensnares you again.

The last two boxes sat by the door, where he'd dropped them. He wanted to take them, but couldn't take the risk. He slipped through the door, leaving it open. He took the steps as if he stepped on hot nails.

The trunk was empty. So was the car. Every single box was gone. His tools and his bag too.

He spat his anger to the ground and took off without closing the trunk. Anything to not wake her up. He deserved to lose his stuff. He'd been stupid.

Never again.

I won't come back.

20

____

Sitting across the desk in Mike's office, Emma struggled to keep her cool. She had stopped by to talk to him on her way to the ER, but he didn't want her there. He didn't say it, but his eyes avoiding hers and his sullen expression were loud enough.

Too bad. We need to talk.

The coroner's report was out. Hypoglycemia.

"Why would she be hypoglycemic? She wasn't diabetic. She wasn't ordered insulin. She wasn't even septic."

"We'll do a root cause analysis," Mike said.

"Could it be a medication error? We need to test for C-peptide. That will tell us if she received any insulin."

Mike cleared his throat.

"We're still waiting for some of the results."

"Did we test for C-peptide?"

Mike looked at his watch.

"I don't see how that makes a difference."

"There was no insulin order for her. If she received any, that would make it a nursing error."

"There could be a verbal order," Mike said.

"Why? She wasn't hyperglycemic. There was no reason to give her insulin!"

"Her potassium was high. Maybe they gave it for high potassium."

"5.2 isn't that high. If they gave insulin for that, they should give glucose too. And there's still no order."

"As I said, we'll do a root cause analysis. We'll talk to pharmacy and risk management."

"I think it's a nursing error."

"Everything is possible. Don't you worry about this, Dr. Steele. You have plenty to worry about. Your metrics. The door-to-doc time. The patient complaints. Those are your responsibilities," Mike declared. "At this time, this does not appear to be an MD problem. As such, it's not your responsibility. I'll let you know if something changes."

He stood up. The conversation was over.

Mike was new. As ED director, he was responsible for the operations and the ED staff, all but the doctors. Emma, as medical director, was only in charge of the doctors. But issues were never isolated. They were complicated and multifactorial, involving everything and everybody. But Mike didn't want Emma's help. He needed to prove himself. Plus, Mike was a male nurse. Emma was a female doctor, bending the traditional gender roles where doctors were male, and nurses female. Mike chaffed.

Emma shrugged. *Technically, this isn't a doc problem. Not yet.*

"Let me know if you need my help."

She went to her patients, but deep inside she was weary. She knew something bad was going on. She just didn't know what.

21

Taylor woke up with a heavy heart. Then she remembered why. She had to call Eric.

She didn't want to. She'd rather not speak to Eric. But she didn't have a choice. Her mother would do as she promised. She always did.

She sighed and dialed his number.

"Taylor!"

"Yes."

"Where are you? I've been worried sick about you! How are you?"

"I'm OK."

"Where are you?"

She didn't want to tell him. She didn't want him coming to harass her. Though, once she told him... Maybe she could go with the rape story... No, that wouldn't fly. She'd just prove herself untrustworthy again.

"Let's meet."

"Where?"

"The library?"

"I'll be there in half an hour."

Taylor splashed cold water over her eyes to bring down the swelling. She put on mascara. Lots of it. She brushed her hair, for the first time in days. She put on dark sunglasses. She added a baseball cap, trying to hide.

Looking handsome but tired, Eric was waiting. His rapt smile made her heart ache. *This may be the end.*

He hugged her like he'd never let go.

"I missed you! What happened?"

Taylor sighed. She glanced around, looking for courage. No courage anywhere, just kids playing hopscotch on the sidewalk. Their smiling mothers, watching. Trees, sprouting fresh green leaves. Even the wind smelled moist and rich, heavy with the promise of growth, as it caressed her face.

The loss crushed her.

She had hoped to be like these parents. Loving, smiling, secretly proud that their kid was the best. The tallest, the smartest, the most successful.

That wasn't happening.

First, her kid was not their kid. Second, her kid was likely to be different. Between drinking and drugs, she had seen to that.

"Let's walk," she said, avoiding his eyes.

Hand in hand, they walked along the quiet street.

"Eric, I lied to you."

His hand gripped her tighter. She waited for the question, but it didn't come.

"I didn't really lie to you. I just omitted telling you some stuff."

"Like what?"

"I didn't tell you…I couldn't tell you…I…I just couldn't…"

Eric stopped. He took off her sunglasses. His luminous blue eyes melted her soul.

"It doesn't matter, Taylor. You don't need to tell me. The past is the past. I don't care. I love you."

Taylor's heart swelled. Then it shattered.

So much joy. So much pain.

She wanted to let it go. The past was the past.

But the past was not the past. The past was here. Growing into the future, right inside her. He'll notice, any day now. The past, the present, and the future, all here, right now. She had to deal with it.

"I wish it was so."

"It is. The past doesn't matter. What matters is now. What matters is the future. Our future."

She couldn't take it anymore.

"Eric, I'm pregnant."

His eyes lost focus. Then his face lit up.

Taylor understood. She didn't have to lie. He thought the baby was his. She could just let it go.

"That's wonderful! I…"

"It's not yours."

He frowned.

"The baby is not yours."

Scorched.

The light died. The ashes remained. Like the silent torment in Munch's scream, his face became a mask of pain.

He let go of her hand. His arms fell sideways like dead branches. His head hung.

"I'm sorry, Eric."

He nodded. Taylor felt as if she'd hit him.

"I'm sorry," she murmured.

"I see. I have to go now."

He left.

He didn't walk. He ran as if wolves were nipping at his heels. Taylor watched.

Her eyes followed him, hoping he'd stop, turn around, and come back. She could explain.

He didn't.

What do I do?

Her soul drowned in darkness. She felt empty inside. Painfully empty. Like a black hole.

She remembered the gun in her father's safe.

She knew the combination. She'd find a peaceful place. She wouldn't have to suffer any more. No more shame. No more pain. No more nightmares and sleepless nights, wondering if the baby was going to be normal or an abhorrent mistake of nature.

She wouldn't have to face her father, who had always loved and trusted her. She wouldn't have to see his disappointment.

She wouldn't have to face her mother either. She wouldn't say: "I told you so," but she didn't need to. If she'd listened, things would be better now. They could hardly be worse.

She made a beeline to her father's house. It was still early. Amber should be at work, the girls in school. There shouldn't be anyone home but the dogs. They won't ask questions.

She was right. Thelma and Louise jumped on her, yapping their love. She hugged them, scratched them and said good-bye.

The office was dark behind the heavy curtains. The safe combination hadn't changed. It was still her mother's birthday. She took the gun and the ammo. She put them in her pockets. She took a last look around. Nothing new but a frame on his desk. The picture of Amber with Opal and Iris had moved to the side. The new one was a snapshot of herself and her mother. Victor took it the day she went to rehab. She smiled, glowing with happiness, her dark hair ravaged by the wind. Emma, behind her, looked into the camera. Her coffee-colored eyes were smiling, tender and knowing. Her mother's eyes looked straight into her soul, as if she knew she was up to something. Again.

Taylor turned the picture face down and left.

Some parents are too much to bear.

22

———————

ANGEL

"*Mommy! Mommy!*"

I look inside Room 14. She's crying, hugging a teddy bear.

She's not a kid. Not in forever. Her green eyes faded to white. Her skin is so thin it's transparent.

I step in.

"Are you my mother?"

"No." God forbid.

"Where's my mother?"

Her mother must be dead. She should be dead too, if the Almighty was kind. She's not.

"Can you call my mother?"

I check her ID. Ella. She's ninety.

"What do you need, Ella?"

She smiles.

"Can I have a cookie?"

"I'll get you a cookie."

By God's mercy, there are chocolate chip cookies in the break room.

"There you are, Ella."

"Thank you, Mommy. Where's my milk?"

Milk. I get her milk.

She gums the cookie. She chokes.

I take away her cookie.

"My cookie! My cookie!"

I check her chart. Dysphagia diet. Thickened fluids only.

She's screaming. I give back her cookie. She chokes again.

She's ninety, she wants her mother, and she can't even eat a cookie. She drops the cookie and starts screaming.

All right, Ella. How can I help you?

I'm running short on fentanyl. I don't have insulin handy. A pillow won't work for this one. She's too loud.

I spot the hypertonic saline on the counter. It's a concentrated salt solution that helps shrink swollen brains. They ordered it for the brain injury, but the patient that needed it is gone. Pharmacy's so slow, you'd think they made it from scratch.

I don't know if it works. And, if it does, it won't be fast. So what? What's the big rush? She's waited for ninety years!

I give her another cookie. I attach the hypertonic bag to her IV and squeeze it in as fast as I can.

My heart's pounding. I have no business being here. If they catch me, I'm toast. I'm not her nurse, Ben is. What if he comes in? I need to get out of here. I squeeze harder. I'm afraid I'll blow her IV.

The door opens. I hide the bag under the sheets and pretend I'm checking the IV.

It's X-ray. I smile.

"Come back in ten, please."

She leaves. I almost peed myself.

The bag's almost done. She's still gumming her cookie. This was iffy. Stupid too.

I wonder what will happen? Will her brain shrink? Or swell? Shrink, I think. Maybe. It doesn't matter. I'm not doing that again.

I'll get some potassium pills. Crushed and injected, they should work.

But it's not sterile.

So what? They'll die before they get septic.

23

———————

B y the time her next shift came, Emma forgot about Mike and her uneasy feeling that something eerie was going on. She finished draining the swollen knee in Room 9. A full 30 cc syringe. The thick, straw-colored fluid was clear enough to read through. *Great. The knee's ugly, but the fluid looks good. It's not septic. Gout maybe?* She went back to her desk to find Alex waiting. As always, his thick round glasses enlarged his eyes, making him look puzzled.

"Can I run something by you?"

"Please."

"I had this nursing home patient yesterday. She had a urinary tract infection. She was a little confused, but she looked OK. I gave her fluids and antibiotics, and I sent her back."

"Yes."

"She's back today, and now she's completely altered. Her urine looks better, but her other labs are off. Yesterday her sodium was 135, her baseline. Today it's 160.

"Is she dehydrated?"

"Why should she be? She was fine yesterday. She's not vomiting, no diarrhea, she's drinking OK. Why would she be dehydrated?"

"Is she on Lasix?"

"They all are. They must put it in the water at the nursing home. But she's been on it forever."

"Anything else weird?"

"Nothing yet. I re-sent the labs to recheck."

"What are you thinking?"

"I'm wondering about a med error. What if somebody gave her hypertonic saline yesterday?"

"That's weird. Why would they? How could they? We don't even have that in the pixies. We have to order it from pharmacy. Who was her nurse?"

"Ben."

"Ben wouldn't make a mistake like that!"

"Of course not."

"What are you saying, Alex?"

"We've had strange things happening lately. A stable patient found dead. A non-diabetic with a glucose of 12. Now this. I'm wondering if there's a unifying explanation for all this."

Emma knew what he meant. She'd been wondering about that too. She couldn't believe it. But she couldn't ignore it, either.

"Give me her name. I'll look."

"Thanks. Let me know."

24

————

Halfway through her shift, Emma sat alone at the corner table in the cafeteria drinking tea. She was taking a rare break. She didn't want tea. She wanted wine. She wanted to go home. She needed sleep. But she still had hours to go, and she needed to speak to Victor.

The lunch hour hustle was long gone. Just a few scrubs reading segments of the same newspaper at different tables, looking lonely and bored. *I wish they served wine here. The staff would be happier. Patients and families too. French have wine with lunch and they are more productive than we are. Italians give their kids a splash of wine in their water as soon as they can drink from a glass. It removes the mystique. It makes it normal and ordinary, instead of hidden and attractive. That's why they have no binge drinking like we do. Never heard of college students dying from alcohol poisoning in Italy!*

She took another sip of tea, trying to ignore the conversation behind her. Out of all places, they had to talk right there. She recognized Carlos's soft Hispanic accent. The female was familiar too. Judy. She tried to hide, but she didn't need to. They were too busy to notice her.

"He sent that urine sample. Without gloves. Then stopped by the break room and dug into the pizza, without washing his hands."

"Really?" Carlos said. "Disgusting. What a piece of shit."

"Be careful, Carlos. He has a lot of friends."

"I don't care."

315

"Hi, Emma." Victor hugged her and kissed her cheek. With his curly gray hair covering his ears, his John Lennon glasses magnifying his eyes, and his jeans instead of a suit, he looked like an aging hippie rather than a cardiologist. He sat, smiled, and took her hand in his.

"What's up, Em? I hope it's not bad news."

"Nope. Taylor is back." Emma took back her hand and rested it on her knee.

Victor sighed. His shoulders softened.

"Thank God. Where is she? What happened?"

"She left the rehab and hitchhiked home."

"Why?"

"How much time do you have?"

"Not much. I've got the pager."

"Eric proposed to her."

"Proposed to her? She's only seventeen."

"For another month or so."

"Still, she's far too young…"

Emma shrugged. "Either way. He proposed to her. She took off because she had lied to him. She didn't tell him."

"Tell him what?"

"Well…she's pregnant."

"Again?"

"Still."

"Still?"

"Yep. That day she went for an abortion, she didn't get one. She changed her mind. Then, when they started dating, she didn't tell him she was pregnant. Now that she started showing, she had to tell him. She ran away instead."

Victor sighed. "Is she OK?"

"She looks OK. She doesn't want to see a doctor."

Victor smiled.

"I mean an OBGYN. I'm not her doctor, I'm her mother!"

"You're still a doctor."

"Well, you know how we ER folks are about family…"

"I do. Remember when you sent her to school for a week before you got an X-ray to find her broken wrist?"

"It was just a buckle fracture. There was nothing to do about it anyhow."

Victor laughed. "That's so you!"

"That's so ER."

"Is she OK?"

"Not bad. She's upset. She didn't call Eric. I told her that if she didn't, I would."

"Have you called him?"

"Not yet."

"Emma, let her be. Give her time."

"I did. She's been back for three days."

"Yes, but…"

"No but. She needs to grow up. She is responsible for her relationships. She needs to get straight with him. He deserves that."

"But Emma, she's just a kid…"

"She's about to be a mother. She needs to grow up. Fast."

"You're always so hard on her!"

"And you're always so soft! No wonder she's spoiled rotten!"

"She's your kid, Emma! Be kind!"

"You're kind enough for both of us! Someone needs to hold her responsible!"

"I guess you're right. I am too soft with her." Victor took off his glasses and started wiping them with the bottom of his shirt, like he always did when he was thinking. "Now what?"

"It's up to her."

"I'll stop by to see her later. Or tomorrow. No, not tomorrow. Amber's going out with her friends. I need to get home early to watch the kids."

Emma smiled. Ten years ago, it had been heartbreaking seeing Amber take her place. Now it was fun to watch.

Victor cleared his voice. "You know, Emma… I…"

Trouble in paradise?

"I miss you."

What?

"I never thought things would turn out like they did. I missed you as soon as I left. I still do. I wish I didn't do what I did, ten years ago. I wish things were different."

What are you saying?

"I never loved anybody the way I loved you."

Yep. That's what you're saying. Seriously? Has Amber dropped you? Or you've gotten tired of working your ass off to pay the bills?

"I wish we could go back," he said, his voice almost a whisper.

Oh no, we're not going there. Never again. Emma smiled her best smile.

"Wouldn't that be nice? But we can't. Life is what it is. Going back is not an option. Don't worry about me, I'm OK. And you have Amber. You have your two beautiful girls. And Thelma and Louise. You have a full, beautiful life."

Victor's blue eyes embraced her.

"I'm not worried about you…"

"Great. I have to go now." Emma stood.

Victor caught her hand. "Emma, I…"

His pager rang.

Thank God!

"Bye, Victor. I'll tell Taylor you're coming."

She took off so fast that the napkins followed in her wake, and she didn't look back.

I'll be damned!

25

Taylor didn't know where to go. She walked and walked. Her right hand, in her pocket, held the gun. She looked for the place. A good place. A quiet place.

No such place downtown. Everybody was out, having a good time. Everybody but her.

She walked, her shoulders carrying her life burden. She didn't care for the breeze caressing her face. She didn't feel the sun warming her. She didn't even need to pee.

She only felt the rough, firm grip of the gun. The gun, heavier than the ammunition in her left pocket, unbalanced her gait, but she didn't notice. She was too busy looking for a good place to die.

She left the town behind. The forest started. The old pines shielded her in silence. Incense-like resin cleansed the air. Her feet sunk into the soft carpet of pine needles. The quietude embraced her. No birds, no flowers, no grass. Just peace. And dusky green light, one hour before sunset.

This was it. She walked into it like she'd walk into her shroud. She looked for the right spot. She found it. A fallen tree covered in moss, surrounded by saplings. She stopped to listen to the silence.

Inside her head, the voices started.

"I've never loved anybody like I love you. Nothing you can do will make me love you less."

"You need to tell him. He may leave. Or not. You must tell him. He'll find out anyhow. He'll leave. Not because of the baby. Because of the lie."

"You're my lovely little angel. You can do no wrong."

"Maybe if I wait, he's going to love me enough to not care that I'm pregnant."

"You can't build your life on a lie. You need to tell him!"

The voices taunted her. Lied to her. Tortured her.

She took out the gun and set it on the trunk. She loaded it carefully, like her father had taught her. They used to shoot together, just the two of them. Before Amber came. Then Iris. Then Opal.

She rolled her jacket and made it into a pillow. She laid the loaded gun on her chest and rested her hands on the moss-covered bark. She thought about her good days. Not many. Shooting with her father. Laughing with Eric. Her mother dropping her at the rehab.

Father will miss me. But he's got Opal and Iris to love instead. And Amber. Funny, I've never been jealous of Amber like I am of Mother. I've always felt the need to compete with Mother. That's a nonstarter. She's always right. She knows everything. She sees through people.

Taylor didn't like that. Inside her, it wasn't pretty. She was selfish and manipulative. She would do anything to have her way. Nobody knew it. Not Father, nor Eric, not even her, most of the time. Nobody but her mother. *We don't love people who make us feel small.*

Eric said he'd love her no matter what. He abandoned her, only minutes later. He'd be sorry.

She envisioned her funeral. *Mother, dressed in black, her eyes dry. Father, crying, wiping his glasses with his shirt. Eric, sobbing and throwing himself over the casket, covering my hands with kisses. I'll be cold and beautiful in my blue dress. Like a Madonna. They'll be sorry.*

But will Mother know which dress? And how to do my hair? She wished she'd left instructions. She took out her cell phone and started an email. "Blue dress. Mascara. Sapphire earrings. Peacock feathers bag."

She sent it to herself, knowing they'd find it. She laid back. The moss was moist and soft, vegetal velvet smelling like the forest. She listened to a rustle in the branches, wondering what it was. *What if something eats me before they find me? What if there's no cold white hand for Eric to cry on, and no eyelashes for mascara? Even ears for the earrings?*

She shuddered and sat up. *There are no wild animals here. But what if I rot before they find me? What if the birds eat my eyes?* A wave of nausea. She bent over to retch. She took a deep breath, then another. *Who cares? I'll be dead. I won't see it anyhow. So what if they do a closed casket? Eric can cry over my picture. I bet he will.*

She rearranged her jacket and lay back. She took a few cleansing breaths. She picked up the gun. She placed the barrel against her right temple. It was cold.

It's going to blow up my face. There'll be no Madonna to look at.

She thought about putting the barrel in her mouth, to blow off the back of her head instead. That wouldn't show as she laid on her back in the casket. The smell of the gun made her nauseous. *There's nothing like puking as you try to shoot yourself.*

She moved the gun to her heart. The angle was awkward. Her wrist wouldn't flex that far. She'd have to pull the trigger with her thumb. She found the space between her second and third left ribs. She sat the barrel right there, perpendicular to the chest. Her right hand shook. She steadied it with her left. She took a deep breath.

Something moved. She froze. It moved again.

Deep inside her, the baby was moving. *I can't believe it.*

She put down the gun and cupped her swollen belly with her palms. Like a butterfly fluttering his wings, he waved again.

"I'm here, remember?"

She choked. She covered her face with her hands and cried. She cried until she ran out of tears.

She unloaded the gun. She put it in her pocket and headed home. She was somebody's home. She had no right to die.

26

ANGEL

isgusting. He called me disgusting. Me!

That piece of shit impotent jerk called me disgusting.

I want to crush him. I want to break his neck. I want to set him on fire. I want to destroy him.

How?

Killing him would be easy. But it doesn't hurt enough.

I'll make him lose what matters most to him. I'll destroy him little by little. I'll take away everything he's built. He'll be sorry he was ever born. His friends will despise him and his parents will wish they never fucked.

Better than breaking his neck. I'll break his spirit.

They say revenge is better served cold. I'll start cooking.

You'll be sorry you were ever born, motherfucker!

Where do I start?

Then it comes to me.

Life is good.

Death is better.

27

───────────

Her shift almost over, Emma finished examining the back pain in Room 5. Her back was hurting too. She looked forward to going home to lie down and think through the events of her day, from her talk with Alex to the funny meeting with Victor.

The patient looked fine. Good strength, no numbness, no red flags. *It's just a strained back. What is it with these people that they can't resist moving refrigerators?*

She put in orders and told Carlos, "Let's give the guy in Room 5 some Toradol and Valium. I wrote for some morphine too, but please don't give it with the Valium. He may never wake up."

Carlos grumbled.

Emma shrugged. *He's mad that I told him something he already knows. Too bad. It's better than killing somebody.* She went back to running the board. There was a new chest pain in Room 4. Emma went to see her.

The room was a screaming cacophony of alarms. Monitors beeped at a pulse of 160. The blood pressure was low. Gray and shriveled, her eyes closed, the woman gasped for air. By her side, a man held her hand, his eyes wide with fright.

She's fixing to die.

"I need a nurse. Now," Emma called.

Carlos rushed in.

"Let's move her to a front room. IV. Pacer. EKG. The whole nine yards."

The scrubs poured in. They pushed the stretcher down the hallway to Room 2. Carlos stuck on the pacer pads, front and back. Judy looked for IV access. Amy struggled to make the monitor leads stick to the skin, but they wouldn't. The skin was slick with sweat.

She's diaphoretic. Her heart is way too fast. And irregular. She's in atrial fibrillation. The blood pressure's soft. She looks like crap. I'm afraid to give her anything and drop her blood pressure even more. We may need to shock her out of it, and that rarely works in A-fib.

"What do we have for IV access?" Emma asked.

"I got an 18 in," Judy said. "I'm working on a second."

"You're a champ. Let's start fluids."

Emma listened to the lungs, making sure they weren't already drowning. "I need an old EKG. And a cardiologist."

"EKG coming," Amy said.

"Blood pressure?"

"It's too low to measure. I'm getting a manual. 68/42."

Crap.

"Get ready to cardiovert. Get Sal. We need push pressors." *They should increase her blood pressure enough to let me use some drugs.*

Sal materialized as if she'd summoned him.

"Push pressors."

"Which one?"

"Phenylephrine. That should increase her blood pressure without messing up the pulse even more."

Sal produced a 10cc syringe out of his pocket. "How much?"

"2 cc every three to five minutes."

"The code cart's here," Carlos said. "You want to intubate?"

"I can't. I'd drop her blood pressure. That would kill her. I have to wait. Let's try 25 of fentanyl."

"Twenty-five of fentanyl given," Judy said.

That's abysmal, but it will help a little with the pain. I don't have enough pressure to sedate her.

"Let's try 100 volts."

Carlos charged the defibrillator. "All clear?"

They stepped back. He pushed the button.

The current went from pad to pad, across the skin, through the chest to get to the heart and shock it out of its crazy rhythm. The power of the current lifted her off the stretcher. She screamed. She fell back.

The rhythm didn't change.

I hate A-fib. Nasty, stubborn SOB. At least the pressors helped the blood pressure. A little.

"Let's do another 25 of fentanyl. Charge at 150 this time." *What the heck? Why cook her slowly? May as well do the best we can, right now. While she's still alive.*

"Let's do 200."

Carlos moved the button to 200.

"Everybody clear?"

The scream splintered the air. The woman levitated above the stretcher, then fell back, limp.

Silence. The heart had stopped.

Emma stared at the monitor. She waited a few seconds. Nothing. *The monitor line's flat as a pancake. She's in asystole. Damn!*

"Start CPR."

Carlos took a deep breath and clasped his hands together to start CPR. He leaned over the stretcher, just as the monitor beeped again. The heart restarted at 120 beats per minute.

That was close. "Blood pressure?"

"95/60."

Joy flooded the room. They breathed. They celebrated. They had saved her.

Emma smiled and touched the old man's shoulder. "She's OK."

Slow tears ran down his sunbaked wrinkles. He touched her hand.

Emma took it. She hugged him. She held him tight to give him strength.

"Good work, team."

They smiled. That's what they lived for.

Emma went back to her desk to check the board. An eerie feeling fluttered inside her, chasing away the joy. Something, somewhere, was wrong.

The back pain in Room 5? She went to check on him.

He was no longer hurting.

28

It was almost tomorrow by the time Carlos got home. The death of Room 5 produced a shitstorm like nothing he'd seen before. They interviewed him for hours, asking him countless stupid questions. All of them. Mike, Risk Management, the lawyer, some other suits he didn't even know.

None of them ever touched a patient. They didn't know what it was like to live in the trenches. To wear shit-stained scrubs. To wonder if you'd make it to the bathroom. To get abused every single shift. The suits inhabited a different world.

He parked his Subaru behind George's Ford and rested his forehead on the steering wheel. George was home. He could use a drink and a friend. But the lawyer had warned him: "Keep mum. No talking. Anything you say can be used against you. All communications, except those with your lawyer, are discoverable."

This death was likely to go to court. His patient, a healthy man, had died for no reason. They had worked on him for an hour. Nothing helped. Nobody understood what happened.

"Heart attack? Stroke? Dissection?" Dr. Greene asked.

"I don't know," Dr. Steele said. "Nothing makes any sense. He was fine an hour ago. His back pain was purely mechanical. He had strained his back, moving furniture. Unless I'm wrong. I hope the autopsy helps us understand."

Dr. Usher was passing by. She laughed.

"That's how you diagnose your patients, Emma? Via autopsy? What's wrong with a good old CT scan? If you figure it out before they die, you may even save them, you know?"

Dr. Steele smiled. Not a nice smile. Carlos hoped she'd never smile at him like that. Like a barn cat seeing a mouse on crutches.

"Thanks, Ann. I'll keep that in mind. Carlos, when did you see him last?"

"Before you called me for the arrhythmia. I was about to give him the meds you ordered."

"Did you give them?"

"No. But I got them out of the locked med room."

"Where are they?"

"I left them on the desk, but they're gone. Maybe somebody gave them as we worked on the A-fib patient?"

"What does the computer say?" Dr. Steele asked.

The computer said nothing. Nurses helped each other with meds, IVs, or labs, when it got busy. But this time nobody had offered to help.

"We'll have a root case analysis," Mike said. "We'll find out who's responsible."

Somebody was going to face the music. Either Dr. Steele for missing the diagnosis, or him, for losing track of the meds. Carlos hoped it wasn't him.

He sighed, got out of his truck, and opened the door. George was in the living room, watching a game.

"Grab a beer and come here," he shouted.

Grateful, Carlos grabbed a Bud Light, George's go-to beer: "It's good for the kidneys. Keeps them afloat. Good exercise too. Every ten minutes, it gets you off the sofa to the bathroom."

Carlos sat in Mary's old rocking chair. He took a swig. *Piss-like. But cold.*

George glanced at him. "Bad day?"

"Yeah."

"Want to talk about it?"

"I can't."

"Legal?"

"Yeah."

"Want to talk about the game then?"

Carlos sighed. George was a decent man and a good friend. He'd taken him in without asking questions. He never pried. He was always there.

"I don't know much about the game," Carlos said, looking at the score of well-fed men stumbling over each other.

"Neither do they. It's not worth watching, but it's company."

"You must be lonely since Mary died."

"Yep. She was my high-school sweetheart. I've never cared about another woman. I never will."

"You're lucky."

"I guess I am. You?"

Carlos shrugged "I found out that Faith was seeing someone else. She had us move here so she could be with him. Now it's too late to go back."

"Is she still with him?"

"No."

"If she dragged you here, she cared about you. Maybe she still does. Did you speak to her?"

"I'm not interested."

"Why not? If you love her…"

"I can't."

He remembered the morning after. Faith approached him at work. She took his hand. He pulled away.

"Don't touch me."

"Why not? That's not what you said last night…"

"You make me sick."

Faith paled. Her indigo blue eyes swallowed her face, making her look like an alien. "Really!"

"Really. Don't ever touch me again."

She smiled.

"You might change your mind."

"Never."

"Never is a long time."

"Not long enough."

He left. Her eyes burned his back like embers. He shivered and took another sip of beer.

"Never again."

29

___

Taylor walked back home from the forest. It took hours. Her feet hurt and her throat was scorched with thirst, but her baby was alive. She laid down in her bed, thinking about Eric and the things she should have told him. She waited for the baby to move again.

The doorbell rang. She ignored it.

It rang again. Taylor pulled the pillow over her head.

Her phone vibrated. She huffed. *What's wrong with people? Why can't they leave me alone?*

But what if it's Eric? Calling to tell me that I'm still the love of his life?!"

She threw the pillow and grabbed her phone. *Dad.*

She loved him, but she wanted nothing to do with him right now. She went back to bed.

The doorbell rang again.

What if it's Eric at the door?

She went to the mirror. Her swollen eyes looked like overripe plums, her hair like a snake nest. *I can't see him like this! But what if he leaves? I won't even know if it's him!* She splashed cold water over her face and rubbed her skin till it burned. She looked in the mirror again. Her burning cheeks made her eyes look OK. She opened the door.

331

It was her father. It was April and mellow, but he looked like a man in a snow-storm. His eyes were no better than hers: wet, muddled, sorrowful. He sobbed. He pressed her to his heart. He let go. He held her at arms' length, looking her up and down.

"Where is it?"

"Where is what?"

"My gun. You took it. Where is it?"

"How do you know it was me? Maybe…"

"Cut the crap, Taylor. You're the only one who knows the code. If I had any sense, I'd have changed it last time. You were gone, so I thought it was safe. I was wrong, and I was lazy. Where is it?"

Taylor shrugged. "What do you need it for?"

"I don't. I need you not to have it. Where is it? Who were you going to shoot this time?"

Taylor felt hurt. *It's not like I walk around shooting people on a regular basis. I never shot anyone yet. The one time I was close, I had good reasons. Just like Father to overreact!*

"It's in my room."

Secretly, she was relieved. She had been close. She didn't want to go back. She couldn't afford to. She had a responsibility. She had to go on until her baby was born. Afterwards, she could give it up for adoption. Or she could bring it up on her own. She had hoped it was going to be with Eric. No more. Either way, she was going to stay alive long enough to give the kid a chance to live. *Five more months. After that, I'm free. Mother will do her best for the kid, if I'm not here.*

Victor headed toward her room like he still lived there. He went straight to the wardrobe and opened the lowest left drawer. He pushed the button unlocking the secret compartment and grabbed the gun and the ammo. He removed the magazine, checked there was no bullet in the chamber, and stuffed everything in his pockets.

He went back to the living room and sat in his old green armchair. He took off his round glasses and wiped them with the bottom of his shirt. He put them back and looked her in the eye.

"What's this about?"

This wasn't her father. Her father was always kind and patient. He never blamed her for anything. When she messed up, he hugged her, telling her she'd do better next time. *Now this.*

"What do you mean?"

"You know damn well what I mean. Why did you elope? Why didn't you tell me? And why did you steal my gun?"

His words held no softness. He was straight and matter-of-fact. Like her mother, for fuck's sake! She looked in his eyes, forcing out a tear.

He frowned. "Get to it, Taylor! I'm on call. My beeper's about to go off. Unless I'm sure you're safe, I can't leave you alone. I'll have to call 911. I'll tell them that you stole my gun and you're suicidal. They'll come and they'll take you to the ER. Your mother may or may not be working. I don't know which is worse. Get to it, and get to it now!"

This side of him she'd never seen. She told him about the failed abortion. About Eric. About her mother's advice. She told him that Eric ditched her. She told him how she wanted to end her life but couldn't.

He listened.

"You love Eric?"

She sobbed.

"Are you sure?"

She came undone over that one. She cried and cried. He held her to comfort her. His hold was love and safety. But it wasn't Eric.

"Listen, Taylor. I'll tell you something you can never tell anyone."

Taylor nodded.

"If you do, a lot of people will get hurt. Including me."

"OK."

"I still love your mother."

Taylor's jaw fell. *Are you kidding?*

He wasn't.

"Ten years ago, I was infatuated with Amber. She was young, pretty, submissive. She was everything your mother wasn't. We had an affair. She got pregnant. I thought I was being honorable when I left you and your mother to marry Amber. We had Opal. Then Iris. I never worried about you. I knew your mother was going to look after you. I loved you, I wanted you to be happy, but I never worried about you."

Taylor nodded.

"I never worried about your mother either. She's the strongest person I know. She survived Vincent's death alone. She didn't need me. That's hard to take, for a man who wants to be a man. She was who she was. I was who I was. We broke apart."

Taylor nodded.

"It took me a couple of years to realize that I didn't really love Amber. She was pretty. Men envied me. But she wasn't your mother. Nobody is like your mother."

That, Taylor knew.

He took off his glasses and started wiping them again.

"Your mother…"

The beeper went off.

"I need to go."

He hugged her.

"I love you. I'm glad you're alive. I'll change the code on that damn safe. Maybe even get rid of the damn gun.""

"Father…"

"Yes?" He climbed in his old Subaru.

"What are you saying?"

"I'm saying that there is no end to love. If Eric loves you, he'll be back. If you love him, you'll take him back. I'd take your mother back in a heartbeat."

"Would she?"

"She won't, baby. She's smarter than that."

Taylor had never thought about her mother as an object of love. *She's old and always tired. Her hair's a mess. And her clothes! And still, she's attractive and desirable. Or so Father thinks.*

More than Amber.

Really?

30

————————

ours after her shift, Emma was still in her office. Her back hurt and her stomach grumbled as she combed through chart after chart. Something bad was happening. Her patients were dying. She had to figure out what it was and stop it.

She didn't care what Mike, Gus, or the Risk Management people had to say. This last death, her back pain patient, forced her to get involved. No matter what, she had to stop the deaths.

Her stomach burned with hunger. *Another half hour.* She took another sip of water, pulled her jacket closer, and returned to her charts.

Four cases. What did they have in common?

The first one was the rash. Kurt's patient. She combed through the EMR. Vitals. Triage note. Nurse's note. Repeat vitals. Orders. There was nothing wrong. The glucose was fine. No insulin order.

Still, she died. Her last glucose was abysmal. Somehow, she got insulin. But how? Insulin is locked in the med room. You need the code, then two IDs: one for the patient, one for the nurse. It's a tight system. Nobody but nurses and pharmacists can remove meds.

But insulin is easy to get. Many have it at home. Including Carlos. And George, his roommate.

Kurt had ordered insulin for the patient next door. What happened to it? She went through chart after chart looking for a hyperglycemic male in Room 21. She found him. Bob Sexton. Blood glucose 550. Normal is 100. An order for 30 units of insulin. His glucose was unchanged an hour later.

She had to speak to Sal to find out who gave it. She took a screen shot, though she knew she was violating HIPPA. *If they catch me, I'm toast. People got fired for less. So? I'm the medical director. Patient safety is my responsibility, no matter what Mike says.*

She looked for the second case. *Oops! This was the second case! The first case was Alex's hip fracture.* Finding the chart was easy. The only hip fracture who died that day. She combed through it. She found the autopsy report. *Broken hip, arteriosclerosis, aging brain, yada yada. The tox report isn't back.*

The vitals bothered her. The initial pulse and blood pressure were high. Then, the last set of vitals were normal. *It looks like she's getting better, then, half an hour later, she's dead. Why?*

She took another snapshot. She started a list.

This is patient #1.

Patient #2 is the hypoglycemia.

Patient #3 is Alex's dehydration with altered mental status. She didn't die, but she was close. The chart looked fine.

Patient # 4 is my back pain. Normal vitals. No labs, no radiology. The autopsy will take a while. This one was neither old nor sick. Just a run-of-the-mill back pain. Carlos said he left the drugs on the counter. They disappeared. Where? Did somebody give them? Did I miss some pathology that killed him? A dissection? An aneurysm?

She went back looking for similarities.

Three different doctors: Alex in the first case, Kurt in the second, Alex again in the third. The last case was hers.

Three nurses: Brenda. Carlos. Ben. Carlos again.

Four patients: #1: Female, 86, nursing home. #2: Female, 88, married. #3: Female, 90, nursing home. #4: male, 50s, healthy.

That back pain doesn't fit. Is there a pattern? Or just bad luck? A string of unrelated things? People die in the ER all the time. They come because they think they're dying. They're often right.

Her stomach grumbled again, loud enough to hear it from the parking lot. The water bottle was empty. It was late. She had another shift tomorrow. Taylor was home alone.

She grabbed her bag and headed home, leaving the door unlocked for the cleaning crew.

31

ANGEL

That was perfect. I couldn't do any better. Too bad he had to die. Well, at least he's no longer drug-seeking.

Poor Emma. She wonders if she missed something. I wish I could tell her.

Getting away from the pattern was good. It keeps them on their toes.

Did you like that, Carlos, you stupid spic? You shouldn't leave your meds on the counter! I had to give him a little extra, of course. There wasn't enough there to kill him.

As I head out to lunch, I see the guy in Room 3. He's on a bipap mask. The ventilator's breathing for him as he sleeps. He's Carlos's patient. I take his mask off.

Actually, I can do better. I put the mask back on his face but I detach it from the vent.

I watch the oxygen saturation plummet. 90. 85. 79.

He's turning a nice shade of purple.

74.

I'd better leave before they find me here.

68.

32

As she came in for her evening shift, Emma found Faith playing with the baby in Room 4. She smiled. Beautiful and vibrant in her ironed green scrubs, Faith looked like a light had turned on inside her. No more sadness, misery, and tears. Happy Faith was back.

"How are you, Faith?"

"I'm great, Dr. Steele. You?"

"Good. Thanks again for the other day. I wouldn't be here if it wasn't for you."

"Yes, you would. I took you on that mountaintop. The least I could do was to get you back."

Emma laughed. "If you put it that way…"

"Are you…are you up to doing something again?"

"Absolutely. If you'll keep an eye on me."

"I always do, Dr. Steele! You're my hero!"

Emma blushed.

"Just tell me when and where." *I can use the exercise. And a friend.*

"Dr. Steele to Room 1."

The patient in Room 1 wasn't having a good day. Neither were Judy and Suzy, trying to get her from the wheelchair to the stretcher. Her purple left foot

339

hung by the skin. She wailed as they tried to move her. Emma went to help. She bent over to hold the foot as Judy and Suzy grabbed her arms. On a count of three, they got her on the stretcher. The foot flipped sideways, flat on the bed. The woman hollered in agony.

Emma cupped the heel, pulling the foot away towards its normal position. She held it there.

"Splinting materials. An IV. Morphine. Ortho."

Judy took off.

"A chair for the gentleman."

The man holding on to the sink was white as a sheet. Suzy pushed a chair under him and he crumbled.

Emma watched as she held on to the foot, maintaining its proper alignment. The sobs faded. The foot faded too, first to white, then to pink. The blood flow was back.

"I'm sorry about this. Your ankle's broken. I had to reposition it to restore its blood flow. We'll give you something for pain."

"It already feels better."

"What happened?"

"My horse spooked. I fell off and he stepped on my ankle."

Emma cringed. "Does anything else hurt?"

"No. That's it."

That ankle's shot. The orthopod won't like it.

He didn't. He treated her like she was a moron, as usual, but he took the patient to the OR. Emma went back to her desk to find Alex waiting.

"You have a minute?"

"Of course," she lied, looking at the full board.

He glanced around. People, everywhere. Room 5 was empty. They went in and closed the door.

"Emma, something's happening in our ER. Have you heard about my case, yesterday?"

"Not yet."

"A demented nursing home patient. Old smoker, short of breath, oxygen dependent. I threw the kitchen sink at him: breathing treatments, steroids, antibiotics. Magnesium. Bipap. He's fighting it, but he's improving. I go see another patient. I come back. He's blue. I had to intubate."

"That happens. They're confused. They don't like the mask. They pull it off. Then Bam! Their oxygen's down, their CO_2 is up, and they're altered."

"He wasn't that bad. He wasn't even blue! And he was improving. What's worse, though, his mask wasn't pulled off. It was detached from the vent."

"That's weird."

"Did you notice that people are dying like flies here? All old and demented."

"Except for my back pain."

"Yes…that one doesn't fit. But all the others…"

"Alex, they are sick. They're old. Their prognosis is bad to start with. Some die!"

Alex rolled his eyes. "Emma, you know better…"

"But there's been a lot of weird stuff. Are you thinking what I'm thinking?"

Alex nodded. "I think we have a mercy killer."

"What about the back pain? Where's the mercy in that?"

Alex shrugged. "That one is an outlier. Maybe it's not in this string."

"Or maybe it's the key. One death that is not like the others. Why?"

Alex shrugged.

"I saw this movie. The killer murdered a bunch of people just to cover the one crime he intended."

"What if it's the other way around? What if the back pain is the only one he didn't mean to kill?"

"Why kill him, then?"

"Exactly. Why kill him? That may be the answer we're looking for."

33

Emma's shift ended at midnight. The hospital appeared empty as she walked out through the quiet hallways. Her car sat alone in the dark parking lot. Emma remembered February's bloodbath and she shivered. *That debacle is over. Get over it.*

What if I called Zagarian?

They hadn't spoken in weeks. Ever since she blocked his calls.

But now when she needed somebody to run things by, Zagarian was it. He was smart, funny, and good-looking. He was a detective and he knew how to keep his mouth shut.

Except that she didn't want to speak to him. She didn't want to see him either.

They had dated for a few weeks. Sort of. They ate, drank, and laughed together. And at each other. It was fun. Until he wanted more.

Emma's sex life was as extinct as the dinosaurs. There had been a couple of men after Victor. None worth remembering. Then, as she got older, Taylor grew into a full-time job. She consumed all the time and energy Emma had left after work, so she stopped dating.

She didn't miss it. Not that much. *Sex is overrated. Wine is better, and it doesn't judge you.*

She was busy. So busy, that taking care of herself fell by the wayside. She gained weight. She was uncomfortable getting naked.

It didn't matter, as long as she was strong enough to relocate hips, intubate obese people, and run around the department without getting out of breath. Summer was short in the North Country. Parkas got way more use than bathing suits. Her social life was nil. So, who cared?

Zagarian did. That night he drove her home, he came in for a nightcap. She couldn't say no. They drank Grand Marnier and watched the fire. They talked about art, travel, and wine. They laughed.

He got close. He touched her cheek. He caressed her neck. Warmth spread throughout her body, awakening it. Her heart pounded. Her insides tingled.

His hand slid to her breast. She panicked. She jumped off the sofa, pretending to feed the fire. She didn't go back. The conversation died.

He waited. She couldn't think of anything to say.

"Why, Emma?"

"I...I work tomorrow. I need to sleep. I'm sorry."

He nodded and saw himself out.

She spent the night twisting and turning.

Why?

Because I'm fat. I'm embarrassed to be naked. I don't want anyone to see my rolls, my wrinkles, my legs. I don't want anyone to see me.

That was true. She didn't want him to see her. But there was more. She wasn't good enough. She wasn't worthy. Her mother taught her early that nobody would ever love her for herself. They'd love what she had to offer: money, comfort, status, sex. Then they'd get rid of her. Victor and Taylor proved it.

I'm not worth loving.

She couldn't handle any more rejection. She was fine by herself. She did her best as a doctor, as a mother, as a human, to maintain her self-respect. Love? She didn't need it. She couldn't open herself and be vulnerable. And get hurt again. *It's not worth it.*

She hadn't seen Zagarian after that night. He emailed. She didn't answer. He called. She didn't return his calls. He came to see her at work. She escaped through the ambulance door.

He stopped calling. But now...she had a problem. She needed help. This was professional, not personal. Maybe they could go back to their professional relationship. To being friends, without the physical stuff she didn't want to think about.

She called him.

"Please leave a message."

She hung up.

That evening, she opened one of her better wines. Stratus, a rich, smooth Canadian Red from Niagara on the Lake. Ripe with dark cherry and berry, generous, voluptuous, and smooth. It gave her solace and made her warm inside.

Not as warm as Zagarian.

Warm enough.

34

ANGEL

That was close. I went back to Room 3 to reconnect the vent, so they wouldn't notice. But they were already in there. I pretended I came to help with the intubation.

Carlos stared.

Careful, Angel. You're making mistakes.

You have all the time in the world!

The slower you cook him, the more he'll hurt!

Take it easy!

35

———————

Sitting behind the flimsy curtain in Room 12.1, Carlos was having trouble getting blood. He had tried twice already with no luck. The woman had lived a rough life. Thanks to a long love affair with drugs, her veins were shot. *Track marks everywhere. An egg-sized abscess by her left elbow. That must be a recent injection. She looks ill. She'll need the whole nine yards. Thank God that her blood pressure's OK. For now.*

The woman shivered, gathering the flimsy cotton blanket around her.

"How are you feeling?"

"Like crap," she answered, her teeth chattering.

Carlos looked again for IV access. *I could get a tiny twenty-two in her thumb, but that won't be enough. I need a bigger vein, but she's mangled them all.*

A stretcher clanged behind the curtain to Room 12.2.

An old voice. Shaky. "What are you doing? Stop it! Stop it! I'll tell Mother."

"It's all right," Faith said, her voice soft as velvet. "We'll take care of you, Edna. Just relax."

"Mother? Is that you?"

"You're OK. I just need to check your blood pressure."

"She won't let you get blood," another voice said.

Ben.

"Mother, are you my mother?"

"You're OK, Edna. I'll take care of you. We just need to get some blood. A tiny prick…"

"Mother, where were you? They were mean to me."

"I'm sorry, Edna. Please let go of my hand."

Her soft voice warmed Carlos's heart. He took his time looking for that vein.

"Hold her hand. I'll get the IV," Ben said.

"Thanks, Ben. Just a little prick, OK, Edna?"

"Yes, Mother."

"What a good girl."

"Aaargh!"

"All done. Relax. It's over. Would you like some juice?"

"Grape?"

"You got it. Thanks, Ben."

"No problem. I'm always glad to help you."

"Thanks."

"Faith…I have two tickets for the Mellowship. On Friday. Would you like to come?"

"I…have to check my schedule."

"At seven. A cover for The Avengers. We could have dinner on the way."

"That would be nice."

"Great. I'll pick you up at four."

"I live in the…"

"I know where you live."

"Really? How come?"

"I know a lot of things about you, Faith." He laughed a low, dirty laugh.

"Like what?"

"I've been watching you…"

"Really? And?"

"I'll tell you on Friday."

Hands shaking, Carlos blew through the vein.

His patient screamed.

"Sorry," Carlos mumbled, low enough to not be heard next door.

He sat, holding pressure on the vein he'd blown.

"There's your grape juice, Edna."

"Thanks, Mommy. Can I have a cookie?"

<h1 style="text-align:center">36</h1>

The modern new gym was all blinding lights and mirrors. No place to hide. Emma stopped to catch her breath. She wiped the sweat off her face with her towel and sat on a weight bench, watching Faith give the instructor a run for his money. Faith had invited her to try an MMA class. Emma thought that would be fun. Now she knew better.

Thankfully, it was just them and the instructor. Emma didn't need any more audience. She looked like a fighting hippopotamus. She'd sprained her hip. She was spent. Now, past trying to keep up, she struggled to keep breathing. Fortunately the instructor, a handsome brown man moving like a hungry tiger, was nice to her and pretended not to notice she had stopped..

Emma had been kickboxing in her basement for months. both for exercise and self-defense, and she thought she was doing all right. But this class was something else. It kicked her butt. Not Faith's, though. Faith was a natural. Her feet kicking above her head, her strong body glowing with sweat, she smiled with delight. Emma was glad she wasn't her opponent.

Waiting for Faith to be done, she read the orange poster with the MMA rules. She liked "Rule #8: No fingers in the opponent's orifices." Putting fingers in orifices—she did that for a living. It wasn't that much fun.

After the class, they strolled along the river, enjoying the afternoon sun. They sat on a bench, sipping ice tea, watching the mesmerizing Hudson River heading home, and listening to the birds chirping in secret codes.

"You're good! You're sure you haven't done this before?" Emma asked.

Faith laughed. "Not this. But I did other things. Everything you try teaches you something. Life is learning."

After all she's been through, she's still optimistic and full of joy. I wish it was contagious!

"How are you doing, Faith?"

"I'm doing great. Ben just asked me out."

"Really?" *Last time we met, she was heartbroken about Carlos. That was what? Last week?*

"Ben? Our Ben?"

"Yes. He invited me to a concert."

"But...I thought he was married?"

"Yes, but they don't get along. They've been talking about separation."

"But didn't they recently have twins?

"A few months ago."

"You think it's a good idea to date him?"

"I'm not serious about him. I don't think he's serious about me either. He asked me out just to spite Carlos."

"How do you feel about that?"

"I'm thrilled. I'd be glad to see Carlos mad."

"Why does he hate Carlos so much? Because of that elopement incident?"

"It's a long story. They knew each other long ago. When we came from New Hampshire, they became fast friends. They were always together. Then something happened. I don't know what, but I think it had to do with Dr. Umber. Ben was his friend. Carlos hated him. They started hating each other. That fight was just a carry-over."

Umber again. Will that man ever stop destroying people's lives?

"Ben's been around a lot lately. Being nice, helping, bringing me coffee. You know, the usual."

Emma didn't. For her, there was no usual. She only drank coffee if she made it. She got help when she asked for it, but she'd never had to wonder if someone was trying to get into her pants.

"Of course," she said. "But doesn't it bother you that he's married? And has young kids?"

Faith shrugged.

"They are his problem. I have enough problems of my own. And I'd love to hurt Carlos."

Emma got that. She'd wished all sorts of badness upon Amber—acne, alopecia, scabies, every ugly disease, from A to Z. Still, she wouldn't date a married man for that.

"Plus, it's nice to feel wanted. Even if it's just to give Carlos a hissy fit."

"You think he cares? Even though he left you?"

"Oh, he cares all right. Just won't admit to it. Seeing me with Ben will do a number on his liver. How about you, Emma? Is there anybody you're interested in?"

Emma laughed. "I'm married to my job. That's the one thing that interests me."

"That's why you're so good. I've never met a better doctor. But it won't keep you warm at night."

"That's OK. I have a goose-down comforter." *And wine.*

Faith's luminous blue eyes bathed her in warmth. She put her hand on Emma's knee.

"You can do better."

Emma shrunk. She struggled to smile. *I'm just not used to people being nice to me. I don't know how to handle it.* She took Faith's hand to free her knee, then she dropped it, pretending to arrange her hair.

Friendship is hard!

37

Two days later, Emma's whole body was still hurting from the MMA class. It hurt to sit, it hurt to stand, it hurt to cough. Fortunately, the ER was busy enough to take her mind off her aches and pains. She had no time to worry about anything else but her patients. Like the woman in Room 15. She clearly hadn't been well in a while. The flesh had melted off her hollow temples, leaving just parchment skin stretched over bones. She grunted, struggling to breathe. She couldn't speak.

Emma checked the nursing-home paperwork to get her story. "Two days of fever and low oxygen. Seldom oriented. Needs help with all her activities of daily living."

What a sad existence. She can't walk, can't use the bathroom, can't feed herself. She sighed and looked for a MOLST, a document that would convey her wishes about her care. No luck. Only a power of attorney for somebody in Florida.

"I'll call them. George, let's go with the sepsis workup. Don't forget the lactate and the cultures. I'll ask Sal to start antibiotics."

"You want a gas?"

"Yep. I'll get respiratory with bipap. I'll write for steroids and breathing treatments."

"That's not going to do much," George said. "She's too far gone. She'll need intubation."

"It may buy us time to find her family. They may agree to comfort care."

"Good plan. She's suffered enough," he said, his voice cracking.

He's thinking about Mary. Her death changed him. He's still a great nurse, but he's lost the drive to just do anything to keep them alive.

"I'll do my best."

She called. No answer. She left a message and went to see her other patients. When she came back to Room 15, a large blonde woman was sitting by the bed. A heavy, sweet perfume choked the room. Emma's stomach churned.

"I'm Dr. Steele. You are…?"

"I'm her daughter. How is she?"

"I'm afraid that your mother is very sick."

"But you'll make her better. Please, do whatever you need to do to save her," the woman sobbed.

There goes comfort care.

"She's very ill. I don't know that anything we can do will make a difference."

"Are you saying she's dying?"

"She's old and sick. She hasn't been well in a long time."

"She was fine last time I saw her!"

"When was that?"

The woman took out a tissue. She wiped her eyes.

"This year? Last year?"

"It doesn't matter. You must save her! I need to speak to her! I don't care what you have to do, just do it! I need to tell her it wasn't my fault!" Her sobs turned into wails. Staff looked in, ready to help. Emma closed the door.

"She has trouble breathing. To help her, we'd have to put a plastic tube down her throat to connect her to a breathing machine. We'd have to place a large needle in her neck to give her medications. It will hurt."

"Will it save her?"

"Save her? No. It may keep her alive a little longer. It may not. She will never be well. Most likely she'll get worse. Alternatively, we could do all we can to keep her comfortable."

"Will she live?"

"Not for long. But she'd be comfortable. She would die with dignity, and without pain. You could sit and talk to her."

"Will she answer?"

"Probably not."

"I need her to talk to me. She must forgive me."

"She won't do that," George said. "She can't speak."

"You must keep her alive. Do everything! I have the power of attorney. I'll sign for it! Where do I sign?"

"You think she would like that? To be kept alive by machines? Is that what she wanted?" George asked.

Her eyes burning, her fists clenched, the woman turned to George.

"I'll tell you what you need to do. Everything. You'll do everything to keep her alive!"

George shrugged.

"Is there anybody else we could talk to? Your siblings? Any other family?"

"I'll speak to them. I'll speak to whoever I want to! And you, you'll do your job. You'll keep her alive! That's all you need to worry about."

Emma sighed.

"Let's see how she responds to treatment."

She's not ready. There's no point in pushing it.

38

An hour later George went on break. Carlos covered for him. On his way to checking on Room 15, he stopped by the break room to grab a coffee. He had so much trouble sleeping lately that he could barely stay awake during the day.

The note near the coffee maker read: "Fresh at 9:30." He checked his watch. 12:15. He shrugged and poured himself a cup. He was almost done when the door opened and Brenda came in. She smiled.

"How're you doing, Carlos?"

"Good. You?"

"I heard you and Faith no longer…"

"No."

"She's seeing Ben, I heard."

"You've heard a lot of things."

"One can't help it. Gossip travels in the ER like wildfire."

Carlos finished his coffee.

"Carlos?"

He stopped, his hand on the doorknob.

"How about drinks after work?"

"Sorry. I have errands to run."

"Tomorrow?"

"I have a doctor's appointment."

"Next week?"

Carlos took a deep breath. He didn't need this. He didn't want to hurt her feelings, but he had no choice. He wasn't interested in Brenda. He wasn't interested in any woman. But Faith. And his interest in Faith was a disease.

"Sorry, Brenda, I'm not ready to date. Not yet."

Brenda's smile melted.

"I'm not your type?"

"You're a very attractive woman," Carlos said, looking at his shoes.

"But not your type. You like them white, do you?"

Carlos heard his blood boil in his brain He clenched his fists but spoke softly.

"Sorry, Brenda. My personal life is personal."

"You're brown too, you know. Even if you act like you're white."

She slammed the door behind her.

He saw red. *Where the hell's that coming from? What's she talking about?*

By the time his pulse had slowed enough to let him go back, he heard: "Dr. Steele to Room 15, STAT."

That's where I was going.

He was too late.

39

———————

After the conversation with Room 15's daughter, Emma went to see the chest pain in Room 4. He looked OK. The dog bite in Room 11 was easy. No sutures. Just cleaning and antibiotics. *And education: Don't let your child pinch the dog while she's eating. It's not rocket science!*

She stopped by Room 15. The daughter wasn't there. The patient looked much better. Good news all around. Her fingers were so cold that she couldn't get the oxygen sats. She left a note asking George to get a forehead probe. She ordered a repeat blood gas and paged the hospitalist, then moved on to her next patient.

Room 5. Three-year-old fall. The triage comment was "The family demands a head CT scan."

She went to Room 5. A crying woman sat on the stretcher holding a screaming toddler with a bruise on his forehead. A man in a white wife-beater paced the room.

Emma smiled and introduced herself. Nobody smiled back.

"Where did he fall from?"

"The shopping cart," the man said.

They feel guilty. That's why they're angry.

"Did he cry immediately?"

357

"Yes," the woman sobbed.

"Any vomiting?"

"No."

The kid looked great but for the frontal hematoma. Emma sang to him as she checked him out inch by inch.

"Now we try the ankle—and the knee—and the hip."

The kid laughed.

"And the belly—it doesn't hurt—it doesn't hurt—but it's ticklish…"

They all started laughing. *That's my singing voice. I'd better not quit my day job.*

They agreed to watch the kid. No CT. *We'll save a couple of grand on the workup, and save the kid a bunch of radiation.*

As she left the room, the speakers croaked: "Dr. Steele to Room 15."

She ran. George was performing CPR. The daughter got in Emma's face, howling.

"You killed her! You killed her!"

Emma stepped around her to get to the patient. She checked for a pulse. None.

"What happened?"

George, still doing CPR, answered in spurts:

"I don't know… I gave the meds to Room 6… then I went on break…when I came back…she was unresponsive."

"You killed her, you motherfuckers! She's dead!"

She's right on one account.

"I'll sue you! I'll get you fired! I'll put you in jail! You'll never see the light of day! Murderers."

They needed security to escort her out.

Epinephrine, CPR, intubation—nothing helped.

She stayed dead.

40

Emma wished she had a chance to stop and think. To understand what happened. Another elderly patient dying unexpectedly. This was case #5. How? Why? She didn't know. The one thing she knew was that she was toast. This was the fifth sudden death. The daughter's anger and threats were likely to be the last straw. She was done as medical director. Fortunately, she didn't have time to feel sorry for herself. She had an ER to run.

She went to run the board, checking on the new patients.

Room 14. Thirty-eight. Altered mental status.

On her way to the room, she ran through the differential diagnosis. *There has to be a reason. The elderly? Anything gets them altered. A touch of pneumonia, a urinary tract infection, forgetting their meds—or taking them twice. A 38-year-old is something else. Alcohol? Drugs? Seizure? Encephalitis? He'll need a workup.*

He didn't. She diagnosed him from the door. A textbook case for liver cirrhosis. Yellow, distended abdomen, spider veins. *Metabolic encephalopathy.*

She smiled and introduced herself. They shook hands.

"What happened?"

"I'm getting confused. My ammonia must be up."

Emma laughed. "I wish all my confused patients told me what's wrong with them. We'd save time and tons of money."

"I know. I've been here before. Your people scanned the bejesus out of me. They made me into a pincushion. They even wanted to do a spinal tap. I almost signed out against medical advice."

"You can't sign out AMA if you're altered."

"I know."

"Have you been drinking?"

"Not in six months. Ever since they told me I had cirrhosis."

"Good for you. But what makes you say you are confused?"

"Not why. Who." He nodded to the plump elderly lady coming through the door. "Dr. Steele, meet my aunt. She's the one telling me I'm losing it."

"Hi. I'm Dr. Vera Tolpeghin."

"Glad to meet you. What specialty?"

"Oh, I'm not your kind of doctor. I have a PhD in biology."

"Interesting," Emma lied.

"I can see you're fascinated."

Emma laughed.

"Never mind. He has trouble, especially in the evenings. Sundowning maybe? He gets distracted and has trouble finishing his sentences. He's fine in the morning, but the evenings are no good. I hope it's not another GI bleed."

"We'll check."

She headed out. Dr. Tolpeghin stopped her.

"We couldn't help but hear what happened next door. That woman was awful."

"She was upset," Emma said.

"She was a bitch. A raging bitch."

Emma opened her mouth. She closed it. Her nephew laughed.

"That's Vera for you. No sugarcoating, no political correctness, no nothing. You can't tell it by her accent, but she's Russian. They're not PC."

"Get over it, Boris. You're just as Russian as I am. And just as politically incorrect." She turned to Emma. "My being Russian is irrelevant. What's relevant is that I'm on the hospital board of directors. Remember that, if you ever need help. Like maybe with this bitch."

That was a first for Emma. Whenever people told her who they were, they either wanted VIP care, or tried to threaten her. Nobody had ever offered to help.

"Thank you, Dr. Tolpeghin. I appreciate it."

"Vera. And I mean it." She handed Emma her card. "You, ER folks, work so hard. You deserve more appreciation."

"Thank you…Vera."

"Enough sweet talk. Am I getting checked or what?" Boris asked.

She checked him.

"Everything looks good," Emma said, when she went to discharge him.

"Thank you."

"My pleasure."

"Are you single?" he asked. With his yellow face split by a wide smile, he looked like a jack-o'-lantern.

Emma laughed. "I don't think that's relevant."

"Why not?"

"I don't date patients."

"Once I leave the ER, I'm no longer your patient."

"I don't think so."

"Too bad. I'll be in touch. You never know. You may change your mind."

That was the best moment of her day. Even though it reminded her of the dangers of alcohol. Her diet was mostly wine-based these days. Even now, she was looking forward to her wine. Like he must have been, just months ago.

It's too late for him. His liver is gone, and his future with it.

Am I next?

41

ANGEL

This one's for you, Emma. You wanted her dead. She wanted to be dead. Even her daughter wanted her dead.

After she got absolution. No matter what it cost. What a bitch!

I know you wanted to help her across the rainbow bridge.

You can't. They'd take your license. They'd shame you. They'd put you away.

I can. I'm here for you.

For my old friend Carlos, too. Like Hannibal Lecter, I'm having an old friend for dinner.

He's already cooking.

He just doesn't know it yet.

42

———————

That evening something had changed. Emma knew it as soon as she set foot in the house. The place was clean. No dirty dishes. Nothing on the counter. The old kitchen sparkled. That hadn't happened since Taylor came back. That hardly ever happened before that.

It can't be good. Last time I came home to a clean kitchen was when Victor left us. What the hell is it now?

It had been another bad day. Another dead patient. One could hear the daughter's screams across the lake. She threatened to sue them. Risk Management wasn't pleased. Neither was Gus. Her time was running out.

She needed wine. She grabbed a bottle. Heartland 2012. Australian Shiraz. Screw cap, like most New World wines. *Good. I don't need to look for the corkscrew.*

The bottle opened with a crack. Emma poured a good third into a long-stemmed glass. She looked through it. Dark red, opaque, earthy. She sniffed it. *Dark fruit and pepper.* Her mood lightened. She took a long sip, letting the smooth heat of the wine tickle her tongue, bathing her taste buds. She swallowed. She took a second sip. She refilled the glass. She was ready.

No music, no typing, no sobbing. She's either asleep or gone.

Taylor's door was cracked open. Emma knocked.

"Hi Mom." Taylor, beautiful and calm, sat up in bed.

Careful not to spill her wine, Emma dropped in the orange rocking chair in the corner. Rocking soothed her. She loved it, even though it was a trap. Getting out of it was a job for Houdini.

"How are you?" Emma asked.

"I've been better."

"Me too."

"What happened?"

"I lost a patient."

"Don't you lose some every day?"

"Not quite."

"You still care, after all these years?"

"Of course I care. I couldn't do my job otherwise. At least I shouldn't. If you don't care, you don't belong there. People deserve better."

"Yep, but to get upset every time they die…"

"Not every time. Sometimes it's a blessing. When it's their time to die."

"Today it wasn't?"

"I think it was."

"Then why are you upset?"

"Her daughter took it badly. And I don't understand why she died."

"Why does it matter? Who cares?"

"The hospital cares. My malpractice insurance cares. I care. I need to understand what happens to my patients. It's my job."

"Do you always worry about your job?"

"I always worry about my responsibilities. My job is one. You're another. How are you?"

"I'm better now. I thought."

"That helps." Emma sipped on the wine. She rocked. It felt good on her back.

"I thought about myself."

How unusual.

"And?"

"I spoke to Eric. He didn't take it well."

"What did he say?"

"He left."

"He must have been surprised. He needs time."

"He ran away."

"I'm sorry, Taylor."

"You told me."

For once, Taylor wasn't having a crisis, though she was due. She didn't even blame Emma. *Growing up, maybe?*

"I spoke to Dad."

"What did he say?"

"He said that true love never dies. If Eric loves me, he'll come back."

Emma swallowed her remark about Victor and true love with another sip of wine.

"Would you take him back?"

"Of course. If you love him. He needs time to get used to the idea."

"No. Not Eric. Would you take Dad back?"

Shit.

"Taylor, he left ten years ago. He's married. He has kids. There's nothing to take back."

"If he came and asked, would you take him back?"

Not in a thousand years.

"I don't think that's something to worry about."

"I'm not worried. I'm hopeful!"

"Taylor, don't you have enough to think about? You, the baby, Eric? Victor's got Amber, the kids, and the dogs. He's all set."

"How about you? Who do you have?"

"I have you. And I have my work."

"Your work has you. The ER owns you. You need to get a life. You need some-body. I have my own life. I'm going to be gone soon. As soon as I figure out what to do with myself."

"Thanks, Taylor, but don't worry about me. Let's think about you."

"I need a job. I need to make myself useful, instead of laying here, feeling sorry for myself."

Wow. "How about college?

"In a year or two. Maybe. After the baby's born. And I grow up a little."

"What job are you thinking about?"

"I want to work in the hospital."

"Why?"

"You're a doctor. Dad's a doctor. Eric is a nurse. Everybody close to me is into medicine, one way or another. I want to see if that's my thing."

"That makes sense." Emma said, hoping she'd change her mind. Taylor in the hospital? What a disaster! She didn't like taking orders. *And that's what we all do there. Everyone, from the environmental workers to the CEO. We take stupid orders. Patients, consultants, insurance companies, lawyers, the government. They're all riding us.*

"What are you going to do?" Taylor asked.

"Me?"

"Yes. What are you going to do about your life?" Taylor's gaze bore into her.

She's taken me on as a project! God forbid she decides I need to take Victor back!

"I'll get a dog."

The thought came out of nowhere. Her heart sang. She smiled.

I'll get a dog. That's exactly what I need. Better than men, healthier than wine.

<h1 style="text-align:center">43</h1>

Carlos couldn't find a working IV pump. He tried Room 23, then 25. Nothing. He went to 26. He heard moans. Somebody in pain? He opened the door. The IV pump was there.

So was Ben. Lying sideways across the stretcher, his scrub bottoms around his ankles. His coarse face was tight, his jaw clenched. Impaling herself on top of him, Faith smiled, her indigo eyes hazed with pleasure.

Carlos felt sick.

He bolted out, slamming the door. He barely made it to the bathroom across the hall. He retched again and again until he was empty. He felt weak. He splashed cold water over his face. His teeth chattering, he sat on the toilet to recover. He heard the door.

"What if he talks?" Ben asked.

"He won't. Why would he?"

"To sink us. If they find out, we're toast. Our jobs are over. My marriage's down the drain."

"Your marriage was down the drain already."

"Common, Faith! What was I supposed to tell you? My wife's busy with the twins and I feel horny? I want a bit on the side? You know better!"

"So, your marriage…"

"It's fine. As long as he doesn't talk."

Faith laughed. A chill ran down Carlos's spine.

"Make sure he doesn't talk, then."

"How?"

"Find a way."

"I will. One way or another, I will." Their voices faded.

Weak again, Carlos lay on the floor.

Faith. And Ben.

Together. Against him.

44

Emma forgot her wine. *Breed: Any. Size: Any. Area: Northeast. Age: Any. Color: Color?! What's wrong with people? What does color have to do with anything? It's not a wig.*

Taylor isn't excited about the dog. Too bad.

Emma loved dogs. From the mutt she'd had as a kid, to Thelma and Louise, the two Bichons. Victor took them when he left and left her Taylor.

What a deal.

She was getting a dog. Her own. Somebody to share her life with. *I'd like somebody to miss me. It's selfish, I know. Still, it would be nice to have somebody missing me, for once. Somebody to miss me, not the things I can do for them.*

She found puppies. Her heart swelled.

I should get a dog from the pound. They sit there like second-hand merchandise, hoping for someone to take them home. They need a second chance. Don't we all?

But...... she'd always wanted a German Shepherd. They were the kings of dogs. Smart, loyal, strong, beautiful. She loved that in a dog. She'd love that in a man too, but they didn't have those at the pound. Nor anywhere else, apparently.

How about rescuing a German Shepherd? She typed in "GSD rescue."

Puppies. Heart-melting, thick-legged, floppy-eared, black and tan German Shepherd puppies.

She had no time for a puppy. She barely had time to brush her teeth. *A puppy needs time, love, and commitment. Two out of three isn't good enough.* She typed "shepherd rescue."

Amber eyes looked at her from a Facebook post. Long face. Long hair. Dark. *"Her owner died. She needs a home without other dogs. No cats. No young children. She needs a knowledgeable owner, a fenced yard, and a commitment to training."*

The post was three months old. The dog was hundreds of miles away. A beautiful dog in a wire cage. The pictures were taken through the wire. Long dark coat. Ferocious white teeth. Haunting eyes.

Not a happy dog.

Emma called.

"Yes, she's still available." The voice was bored. They'd been through this before. "You'll have to sign that you take responsibility for any damages, injuries, or deaths."

Deaths?

They didn't want money or references. She was four. Her owner left some money for her care. It was running out. They'd been looking for months now. They may have to put her down. Yes, tomorrow morning was OK.

Emma had a day off. If she left now, she'd get there in the morning, and be back tomorrow for dinner. She opened the fridge. Empty. Taylor had eaten it. She tried the freezer. Bread. Frozen broccoli. Spaghetti sauce, heavy on the garlic. Nothing else. *It will have to do.*

She drove for hours in the rain. The glare burned her eyes. She missed a turn. That added another hour. By the time she got there, the sky was blushing pink. She pulled on the side of the road and curled up in the back seat.

She woke up late. She guzzled her cold coffee. She needed to pee. She wanted to brush her teeth. No time, no place.

Oh well. Fuck them if they can't take a joke!

She grabbed the spaghetti sauce and scrambled out of the car. She tried to unbend. Slow going. *I'm too old for this. If only I had some Motrin.*

She straightened up all the way and rang the doorbell.

"You're late," the fat man said. His small pig eyes matched his pink Hawaiian shirt.

"Sorry. I fell asleep."

He appraised her. "You know dogs?"

"Somewhat."

"Police dogs?"

"No."

"This is no ordinary dog."

"How so?"

"She's a police dog. She took a bullet in a drug raid. In the lung. She never got back to normal. They say she has PTSD. They retired her."

"How did you end up with her?"

"My brother wanted a protection dog. He got her when the police got rid of her."

"What happened to him?"

"He died."

"How?"

"A business partner shot him."

"She couldn't protect him?"

"She's fast, but bullets are faster. But the guy will never walk again."

Emma shuddered.

"You still want to see her?"

"Yes."

He pointed to the door at the end of the hallway. "In there."

"What's her name?"

"Guinness."

Emma looked at the closed door. She'd driven the whole night to get here. She could just turn around and go home, or she could open the door. *The absence of fear is not courage. That's stupidity. Courage is feeling the fear and doing it anyhow. Or maybe that's stupidity.* She opened the door. The morning sun poured in her eyes, making the room dark. She shielded her eyes with her hand.

"Guinness?"

Unblinking yellow eyes in the far corner.

"Hi, Guinness."

Emma stepped in. She sat on the stool by the door. The eyes watched.

"How're you doing?"

Nothing.

She doesn't feel like chatting.

Emma looked for something to say. Nothing came. She was stiff and hungry. She needed to pee. She had driven forever to get here, and she had to drive back. The dog didn't seem to care.

"Life sucks." Emma rested her back on the wall. "I have a long drive back. I'd better find a toilet and something to eat first."

Curled up, her dark nose resting on bronze paws, the dog listened. *She gets it.*

"I'm sorry your life sucks. Mine sucks too, you know. My daughter hates my guts. My ex-husband got bored with his pretty wife. I think somebody's killing my patients. You think you have it rough?" Emma looked at her watch.

"I have another shift tomorrow. My daughter is more trouble than any puppy." She looked the dog in the eye.

"Ever had puppies, Guinness?"

The dog didn't blink. Emma shrugged.

"You didn't miss much. They're a pain in the ass. Once you have them, life's never the same. Trust me."

The dog seemed doubtful.

"You're right. Why should you trust me? I'm just a stranger. You must miss your human. Your owner, they said. Like you can own somebody! You don't even own your kids. There's this joke. A woman gets fed up with her kids and decides to sell them on eBay. She tells her friend. He laughs. 'eBay? Are you crazy? You made them yourself! Sell them on Etsy!'"

The dog didn't laugh.

She's got a German sense of humor.

Emma crossed her legs. *I need a bathroom.* She could ask pig man, but she didn't want to use his bathroom.

It's getting late. The dog isn't interested. She doesn't even have a sense of humor.

Emma stood up. She rolled her shoulders.

"I'll go now… Sorry it didn't work out. You'll be all right. They won't put you to sleep, you have money … unless pig man gets to keep it… that sucks."

The yellow eyes didn't blink.

She's beautiful. All dark but for the tan legs. Wise, golden eyes.

"I'm sorry. I wish I could help." She picked up her bag. It was heavy. She remembered the Bolognese.

"You like Italian? It has lots of basil and garlic. Garlic is a vermicide, you know. It kills worms. Not saying you have them, just telling you what it's good for."

She moved closer. The dog watched. Emma opened the Bolognese and sat it by the water dish.

"Good luck, old girl."

Emma wanted to pet the dog, but the dog didn't look like she wanted petting. Emma respected that. She walked out without looking back. She climbed in her car. Her eyes burned. *So much for gut feelings. Crying is for sissies, Mother said.* She set the navigator to "Home," then remembered she needed a toilet. She changed it to the nearest McDonald's.

She glanced back.

The dog. Staring at her, one inch from the window.

She opened the back door. The dog jumped in. She curled up in the back seat. She sighed. She wiggled to make herself comfortable. She sighed again. She looked at Emma. Her tail thumped.

"What are we waiting for?"

"Really?"

Guinness wagged her tail.

"McDonald's?"

Guinness smiled.

"OK."

45

———————

Back in the ER for her next shift, Emma struggled to keep up. It was not a good day. Five psychiatric patients on hold, waiting for a place to go. No beds upstairs, so the ER had to hold admitted patients. Two nurses called in sick, making them short-staffed. The shit was pouring like rain. Emma hoped it wouldn't drown her.

Then Mike called her for a meeting.

"What's it about?"

"Quality."

She was in the middle of a crisis. The drunk in Room 6 had pushed the stretcher across the door, taking himself hostage. There was no ambulance to transfer the brain bleed to neurosurgery.

Now this. Whatever it is, it's not good news. He's not calling to congratulate me. It's got to be about the woman in 15 whose daughter complained. I still don't know what happened.

She talked to the charge nurse about getting a helicopter to fly out the brain bleed, hoped the drunk would fall asleep, and went to the conference room. She found them waiting. Mike, Sal, the Risk Manager, the Quality Control director, George, Carlos, the lawyer, and Gus.

"Thank you for joining us, Dr. Steele," Mike said.

You'd be late too if you had to work with patients. All of you, in fact. Sitting in your office all day makes you feel superior. You're complacent and out of touch.

"We met to discuss a few issues that occurred in our ED lately. Over the last few weeks, our mortality has increased. We have also encountered a number of sentinel events."

The quality director, a thin man with a skimpy white beard, started a Power-Point presentation. He lusted over graphs and pie charts. Patients seen in the last thirty days. Left without being seen. AMA. Deaths. Near-deaths.

I wonder if I ordered the labs for Room 10.

"Emma!" They stared at her. "What's your take on this?"

"We have a number of separate incidents. They involve unrelated patients. The patients were here for different reasons. All, with one exception, were old and impaired. These incidents happened on different days, in different rooms, on different shifts. The patients had different doctors and nurses. We have no clear explanation of why these people died."

"And?" Gus asked.

"I thought the first one was a medication error, but there've been too many. There's only one possible explanation. I think we have a mercy killer."

If she was looking to impress them, she succeeded. They started talking all over each other.

"Preposterous idea! This couldn't happen in this hospital. This is a nice place. A quiet place, with good people. Saying something like that was an insult. She's lost her mind. Inconceivable."

Emma waited for the ruckus to calm down. She looked them in the eye, one by one. "Remember February?"

Silence. Only months before, a slew of deaths had hit their community and their hospital. The culprit had been a shocker.

"Lightning doesn't strike twice in the same place," Mike said.

"Maybe it's the same lightning."

"He's in jail," Gus said. "He'll be there for a long time."

"Maybe he has friends. Or maybe we're just unlucky."

"You may have a point." George shuddered. February had been rough on him.

"Impossible," Mike said. "We need to look at our practices. We need to stop giving verbal orders. We need to improve monitoring. We should round on the patients more often—in every case the patient appeared stable. They were left unattended, and then found dead. If we monitored them correctly, we may be able to detect changes before it's too late."

"We need to improve the pharmacy security," Sal said. "Right now, it's easy for anybody to take meds arriving by tube for somebody else. They can just grab and use them. People can even take medications out of the locked drawers without signing for them."

"Who can do that?" the quality director asked.

"Anyone passing by the tube system," Sal said. "Especially the nurses. They can get into the med room. The pharmacists too. The pharmacy techs, who refill the meds."

"So, then what happens to the meds? They get given to the wrong patients or in the wrong amount. You're getting back to the idea of a killer," Carlos said.

"That's impossible. Nobody in my ED would do something of the kind." Mike turned red, his jaw muscle twitching.

He's about to blow up. Why is he so angry? Because it's his ED. His ED has to be perfect. Nothing bad can happen in it.

"What do we do?" Gus, the VPM, asked.

"How about speaking to the police?" the quality director said.

"NO!" Mike, Gus, and the lawyer chorused.

"Absolutely not!" the lawyer said. "That would be a disaster. Everybody who ever died here would sue us. Their families, I mean. Our reputation would be destroyed. People would be afraid to come here. They'd say we're crawling with serial killers. We'd go bankrupt!"

Gus agreed.

"We'll investigate. We'll create a special committee to research these cases and evaluate the systems. It has to be somebody who's not involved with any of the cases, of course. That excludes you, Emma; also Sal, George, and Carlos. Mike, Lola, and I will look at it."

"Who's Lola?" Emma asked.

"I am." The lawyer's mouth was a thin line. She didn't look pleased.

She doesn't know how anything works. She knows nothing about medicine. That's going to be a hit.

Emma shrugged. Not like she needed any more work, but she was going to investigate herself. She had already started. She hadn't found much, except that both Carlos and George were involved with two of the cases. A coincidence, but they were both a little off, lately. George mourned Mary and Carlos missed Faith. Still… she had to start somewhere. She'd check the schedule to see if they were working during any of the other cases. It would be nice to rule them out. And then? She had no idea. She'd make it up, as usual. The good news: her month was almost over.

One way or another, I'll be done soon.

46

———————

Taylor woke up early that morning. Something felt odd. *Somebody's watching me.* She looked around. Nothing. Just her old bedroom, with the grass lamp, the starfish comforter, and the orange rocker in the corner. She rolled on her other side and went back to sleep.

Somebody's watching me.

She was in her room, alone. She was losing it. She sat up and rubbed her eyes, looking for her Crocs with her feet.

Something touched her. She jumped. A dog. A big dark dog. Staring at her.

Really?

Yep. Really. He lay there at the foot of the bed, staring at her. She stared back.

The dog didn't blink. This was a serious dog. A police dog? How did it get in the house? What was it doing there?

Mother said she was getting a dog. She did.

She'd been gone the whole day. She had a shift today—she kept a copy of her godforsaken schedule on the fridge. Somehow, in between, she had acquired this animal. Then she'd gone to work and left the dog for Taylor to deal with.

Taylor loved Thelma and Louise. She'd grown up with them. They were cute and cuddly, even though they yapped a lot. But this dog was different. It acted like a person.

Oh well. It's Mother's problem.

Taylor found her Crocs. She went to get something to eat. Now that her morning sickness was over, she was always starved. Thankfully, she was slim and burned calories like crazy. Still, she felt like a hippopotamus. She was getting slower and thicker, but she was still always hungry.

She opened the fridge. Mustard, ketchup, mayo, milk. *Like really? Not even eggs? How's a growing woman supposed to handle this?*

She found a box of Cheerios. That would have to do. Lunch looked like a losing proposition unless she got her ass out to do some shopping.

Where's the new you? The new you who'll get a job, grow up, and become responsible?

Taylor flipped the bird to that thought. She grabbed the Cheerios and a box of Oreos. She poured Cheerios, lots of sugar, and milk in a bowl and grabbed a spoon. She dropped on the sofa and turned on the TV.

The dog sat in front of her, staring. His head obstructed the screen.

"What?" Taylor said.

The dog gurgled. It wasn't a bark and it wasn't a growl.

"What do you want?"

The dog gurgled again, staring at her bowl.

He's hungry. We have no dog food. We have no food, period. Thanks, Mom!

"We have no dog food," she informed him. She took a spoon of Cheerios.

The dog gurgled again. Staring her in the face, the dog clearly demanded to eat.

"Don't you get it? We have no..." The dog looked at her bowl like Taylor would look at a fudge Sunday.

He wants my Cheerios. Dogs don't eat people food!

She lifted the spoon to her mouth. The dog drooled, watching its progression like it was the Olympics. Taylor opened her mouth. She closed it.

"Fine. Be that way. They got soggy anyhow!" She put the bowl on the floor next to the sofa. "You happy now?"

The dog stared at her.

"What?"

The dog stared.

"What are you staring at me for? Eat it!"

The dog gave a short happy bark and cleaned the bowl in a blink. He sat in front of it and gave a quick bark. He looked at Taylor and wagged his tail. Once.

"Thanks." He went to lie down by the door.

Taylor scratched her head.

She got herself another bowl of cereal and watched for the dog to come back. He didn't.

She finished her cereal and went to clean up. Brushed her teeth, took a shower, got dressed.

The dog waited by the door.

He needs to go out.

There was no leash—they hadn't had a dog in years. Taylor found a soft belt. She walked slowly toward the dog. She wasn't sure he cared to be touched.

"Want to go out?"

The dog wagged his tail.

She slipped the loop of the belt over his head. She tightened it. He didn't seem to mind. She opened the door. The dog waited. For what?

"Let's go," Taylor said. The dog leapt out. He smelled the bushes, the stones, and the grass. He squatted at the gate.

"You're a girl!"

The dog looked at her and smiled. They took a long walk. Taylor hadn't done that ever since she'd tried to kill herself. She was surprised to see it was still spring. It felt like ages ago.

Back home, Taylor removed the belt. The dog looked at her. She scratched her behind the ears. The dog smiled again.

Back in the bedroom, her phone rang. She had forgotten her phone. Unbelievable. She never forgot her phone. Five missed calls. One was Mother, one was Father, three were Eric.

"Call me."

47

GUINNESS

They're screwed up, these people. There's something wrong with their lives. The Shaman needs help. That's why I came with her. Her spaghetti sauce? Pulleaze! You'd better rub it on against vampires and mosquitoes than eat it! But she's OK.

Why Shaman? She smells like healing and dark magic. She knows things others don't.

On the way home we stopped at McDonald's. She ran out of the car as if she chased someone. I got ready to help her. But no, she just needed to pee. That's the problem with humans. Women, especially. Men—they'd go for a nice bush, but women? They're crazy about toilet paper. Can't imagine why. I tried it. It's not good. It tastes just like cardboard.

She came back more together. She brought a couple of Big Macs and an order of fries. Not my favorite, I'd rather go for a Bacon Quarter Pounder, but she tried. I licked her hands to show my appreciation. Greasy and salty. They tasted good.

It took us forever to get to her den. It smells like her. And the girl. The girl is trouble. I know trouble when I smell it. And she's not even in heat.

A few man smells. Not many. A coward, I think. Then another one, a while ago. Both running away. But I digress. There was no dog bed, so I slept in the armchair.

This morning Shaman microwaved some frozen waffles. She poured butter over them. Never had waffles before. Not bad, especially if you haven't eaten in a week. I didn't feel like it.

OK, OK, I was worried they'd poison me. Yes, I could smell it, but still. How would you eat if you were on death row?

She left me a bowl of water and told me to be quiet. I looked for the girl. I found her. She looked at me as if I wasn't real.

Oh, girl, I'm real, all right. Your stuff isn't real. All those things you ruminate about. We eat, we love, we shit, we die. That's all there is to it.

She came around a little, but she needs a lot of work. They both do. What's wrong with people? As long as you're together, you're OK. Stop thinking about all these maybes and maybe not and such nonsense. I'm glad I'm not people.

The doorbell. I jump off the sofa, where we're watching TV as she's scratching my ears. I rush to the door.

"Back off!"

The girl grabs my collar and opens the door. A man. Shocked. He stares at me. Stares at her belly. Stares at me. She jumps in his arms, crying.

I growl. She turns around and tells me he's OK.

"Then why are you crying?"

She cries some more. They hold each other and kiss. It's gross. They sit on MY sofa! Humans! I watch them.

"This is Eric," *she says, amongst tears.*

I give him a paw to shake. They stare at me. They laugh. Eric shakes.

"Hello…What's his name?"

"She's a girl."

"Oh. What's her name?"

She looks at me. She doesn't know. She texts her mother.

"Guinness. Her name is Guinness. Hi, Guinness!"

I give her my paw again. She shakes it. They laugh. What's so funny?

Whatever. It beats crying!

48

After squaring away the brain bleed and the drunk and the other challenges of another lousy shift, Emma sat in her office.

She finally got to think about the quality meeting. Her jaw clenched, she started fuming. They told her to mind her own business! As her patients died in her ER. Inconceivable.

She logged in the computer to have another look at the charts. She had perused them so many times that her eyes started glazing over them. To focus, she started a list, looking for similarities.

Death #1. Monday, April 9. Room 5.

Patient: Old nursing home patient with hip fracture.

Doctor: Alex. Nurse: Brenda.

Mechanism: Unknown. *Opiate overdose, maybe? The woman's vitals got better just before she died. Opiates would give her pain relief and normalize her vitals. At first. Then they'd put her to sleep. For good.*

Coroner's report: Pulmonary edema. The toxicology report was still pending. *She got morphine, so she's going to be positive for opiates no matter what. Carlos worked that day. George didn't. That doesn't mean much. He could stop by, for one reason or another. We all do. For a meeting, to return a book, whatever.*

Death #2. Wednesday, April 11. Room 20.

Patient: Old woman with dehydration and rash.

Doctor: Kurt. Nurse: Carlos.

Mechanism: Hypoglycemia. *Insulin? Maybe that ordered for another patient?* She wrote herself a note: Who took out that insulin? Who gave it? When? Ask Sal.

Coroner's report: Nothing. Tox report is pending. *This one may help. An abnormal C-peptide will confirm that she received insulin she had no business getting.*

Case # 3. Saturday, April 14. Unknown room. *This one didn't die.*

Patient: Old woman with a urinary tract infection. Discharged back to the nursing home. Returned next day with severe unexplained dehydration.

Mechanism: *Lasix overdose? That would make her pee a lot. That would get her dehydrated. Would anyone notice at the nursing home? The urinary tract infection made her pee a lot anyhow. Hypertonic saline? That would scar the vein. But whoever gave it didn't give a damn. Dead people don't need veins.*

Doctor: Alex. Nurse: Ben.

Coroner's report: None yet.

Death #4. Sunday, April 15. Room 5.

Patient: Middle-aged man with back pain.

Doctor: Me. Nurse: Carlos.

Coroner's report: Not yet.

Mechanism: *Who knows? Maybe I missed a dissection or an aneurysm. I almost hope it's that, rather than someone killing a healthy patient. My patient! But if they did, how? The meds I wrote for him were removed from the pixies. Carlos says he left them on the counter. Did anyone give them? But they weren't enough to kill him anyhow.*

A knock at the door. Emma threw her notes in the drawer and minimized her computer screen. She'd been told to mind her own business. She didn't want to get caught detecting. Not before she found the answers.

"Come in."

Faith came in, glowing and full of life, filling her scrubs in all the right places. Her warm indigo blue eyes embraced Emma.

"You're still here?"

"Catching up on some work. How are you, Faith?"

"I'm good. You?"

"Hanging in there. This work is beating me lately."

"I bet. All these deaths."

Emma cleared her voice. "What's up, Faith? What can I do for you?"

"I wondered if you'd like to go for a hike on Tuesday? Or maybe to a spa?"

"I'd love to, but I can't, Faith. Not until I catch up a little."

"Who do you think is killing all these people?"

"I don't know. I don't think anybody does."

"Well, they are dying!"

"Is there anything I can do for you, Faith?"

Faith's smile faded. "I'll let you be. I can see you're busy. Let me know if you have some time and want to do something."

The door slammed shut. *I must have hurt her feelings. I'm sorry. I'll talk to her tomorrow.*

Death #5: Thursday, April 18. Room 15.

Patient: *That was the demented patient with pneumonia whose daughter wanted everything done. She looked better after treatment, then she coded. What a mess that was.*

Doctor: *Me again.* Nurse: George. Relieved by Carlos.

Mechanism: *Who the hell knows?*

Autopsy: Pending.

Case #6?

No Case #6. Not yet. *The way things are going, there'll be one soon.* Five cases in less than a month. She had no proof that they were related. Some may have been unrelated. Natural deaths. Accidents.

Still, four died. Two of them were hers. The back pain and the pneumonia. That was weird. Different nurses, different rooms, different meds.

What did they all have in common?

1. They were all old, impaired, demented nursing-home patients. Except for the back pain.
2. They all seemed to be medication related. There were no stabbings,

no shootings… But…she remembered Alex's case, the old smoker on bipap he had had to intubate. He got detached from the vent. *Shit. That's six. Case six already happened. I need to find out more.*

3. None of them was anywhere close to dying.
4. There was no family present, except for the blind husband of the hypoglycemia and the irate daughter of her pneumonia patient.
5. None screamed, or asked for help. In fact, they all looked better just before getting dead.

That's it. I don't know where to go from here. If there's anything they have in common, it's me. I had two of them, and I was there for two more. What the hell does that mean? And the back pain? That one doesn't fit. Maybe that's where the answer is.

She made a list.

1. Get data about Alex's bipap case.
2. The insulin.
3. Who gave the meds to the back pain?
4. The back pain is an outlier. What if he's the only target and the others just obfuscate? Did he have an enemy in the ER? An ex-wife? A rival? A competitor?

Her head was spinning. She was ravenous. She had to check on Taylor. She grabbed her coat.

Shit! I have a dog! I hope Taylor let her out! And gave her something to eat! I was going to text Taylor. I forgot!

She flew out the door.

49

———————

Carlos watched the patient in Room 2 like a hawk. Bad things kept happening to his patients. He wasn't going to let this one go bad on him.

The old man had smoked his last cigarette. His bony chest heaving, he sat up propped on his arms to get more air. He fought hard, but he wasn't winning. He was on continuous nebs, he'd already received steroids, magnesium—the whole kit and caboodle, but he wasn't going anywhere good.

His oxygen sats dropped. Carlos turned the oxygen all the way up.

"Let's prepare to intubate," Dr. Crump said, chewing on his lip.

He didn't want to intubate. The man was already hypoxic. His CO_2 was through the roof. The few seconds he had to be without ventilation could be enough to stop his heart. But they didn't have a choice.

The respiratory therapist took over the mask. Carlos went to the locked medication room to get the RSI kit, the sealed bag of intubation drugs. He opened it and waited for orders.

"Thirty of etomidate, then ten of vecuronium," Dr. Crump said. He turned to the RT: "Let's have the nasal canula at 15 liters for apneic oxygenation."

Carlos pushed the drugs. One minute later, the patient stopped breathing. Smooth as silk, Dr. Crump slid the tube in. The oxygen saturation stayed unchanged. The RT started bagging. The sats went up.

Carlos sighed. *Thank God. Maybe the evil spirits following me got the day off today.*

He'd been having a rough time lately. First, the back-pain guy. He took out the meds but never gave them. Then the guy died and the meds disappeared. That bugged him ever since. That, and the feeling that someone was watching him. It was unsettling. Dr. Steele watched him too. She double-checked his meds. She followed him in patients' rooms. Even George was getting weird. He went to bed early. No more sitting and chatting. It was like a heavy cloud hung over him. Always waiting for something bad to happen. *Not today.*

He grabbed the blood vials to send them to the lab. He stopped by the pixies to get another breathing treatment for his patient. He came back and rechecked the vitals. Everything looked OK, except for the RSI kit.

The RSI kit was gone.

50

—————

That morning Emma woke up to Guinness staring at her. One tail thump.

"Good morning."

"Good morning. We have the day off."

Guinness thumped her tail again.

"What would you like to do?"

Guinness smiled.

"After breakfast."

She smiled wider.

I've never seen a dog smile before. Her eyes shine, her mouth's wide open, her pink tongue's reaching her knees. And those teeth. I'm glad I'm not her dental tech.

Emma went to the fridge. The dog followed.

Empty. So much for breakfast! No dog food either.

"McDonald's?"

Tail thump. Emma opened the car door. The dog stared.

"OK."

Guinness jumped in. Emma closed the door and climbed in to find Guinness in the front seat. *There now, as the surgeons say instead of Oops! I guess she's not a back-seat person.*

Emma put on her seat belt. Guinness stared at her.

"What?"

One bark.

"You want the seat belt?

Bark.

Emma shrugged. She bent over to click her seat belt. It didn't fit well.

"I'll get you a leash, a bed, and a seat belt. And dog food. You can't live on fast food forever."

"Why not?" Guinness cocked her head.

They shared the Egg McMuffins, but Guinness declined the coffee. They went to the pet store. Guinness chose a black collar with shiny metal spikes and a six-foot long, heavy leash.

"I didn't know you were into Goth."

Guinness pretended not to hear. She inspected the dog food and settled for a hypoallergenic rice and lamb formula.

Their shopping done, they drove to the park. An overgrown old farm criss-crossed by trails between rocky lakeshores, the park was a joy to explore. Guinness checked the doggie mail. She squatted over rocks. She spotted squirrels in the trees and chipmunks under logs. She ran away. She came back. She ran again.

"You love your freedom."

Emma did too. She felt lighter than she had in a long time. She forgot the ER, the deaths, Taylor, Victor. She forgot everything but the blooming trees, the breeze singing through the branches, the heavy scent of moist earth and spring. Emma delighted in the beauty of nature and in Guinness's unde-manding company. The dog understood things without being told and had no expectations—beyond breakfast. They played frisbee. Guinness went swim-ming, then shook, giving Emma a shower. They laughed.

The phone rang.

They needed her in the ER. A mass casualty incident. A school bus hit a truck, then rolled over in the river. Two died. The rest were on their way.

51

Back in Room 2, Carlos had to hold on to the counter to stay upright. He felt faint and sick to his stomach. His heart pounded in his head like a hammer.

The RSI kit was gone. He left it on the counter and went to send the labs. *Five minutes ago. Now it's gone.*

He checked the patient. He was alive. He repeated his vitals. They were OK. But the kit was gone. Full of everything, but the vecuronium and the etomidate they had used for intubation. Sedatives, putting people to sleep. Opiates. Ketamine. Paralytics, paralyzing every muscle in the body but the heart. Every one of them dangerous. Every one of them lethal.

A single dose of succinylcholine is enough to paralyze you. You wouldn't be able to move. You couldn't breathe. You couldn't scream for help. You'd watch yourself die. Same with the rocuronium. All in all, there's enough stuff there to kill half a dozen people.

He had taken the kit out under his ID and he had signed for it. Now he had lost it. He was already in trouble after losing the meds for the back pain. This was bad news.

If they find out. What if they don't? I can just sign that I discarded them. Nobody knows.

But what if whoever took the kit uses the meds to kill someone?

391

They won't. They only took them to get high. They'll just use the fentanyl, the keta-mine, and the propofol. They'll throw away the rest. What else could they do with them?

Carlos snuck to the med room. Nobody there. He hesitated. *I shouldn't do this. But I have no choice. I can't tell them that I lost the kit.* He charted the meds as discarded. The paralytics, the ketamine, the propofol, the lot. He logged out and sighed with relief. He was done. He went to the bathroom to splash cold water over his face, and looked in the mirror. He looked terrible.

Then he remembered the cameras in the med room and broke into a cold sweat.

52

From the park, Emma drove straight to the ER. She locked Guinness in her office and went to work. The ER was in overdrive. They had lined the hallways with the existing patients to make room for the traumas. That gave them more empty rooms, but it set the visitors free to wander in the hallways and get in everybody's way.

The wounded arrived every which way: by ambulance, by private car, on foot. Scared parents came looking for their children. Volunteers came to help. The waiting room was clogged. Harried staff moved from one patient to the next, checking pulses, holding pressure on bleeding wounds, giving reassurance.

Triage had moved to the ambulance bay. *Good. Triage is not a place, it's a process.*

Ann and Kurt rocked. They glanced at patients, treating the sick, sending the others to waiting areas. The first case was already in the OR. Two more were waiting.

The whole hospital came to help. Environmental workers cleaned the rooms. Father Murphy comforted families in the waiting room. The residents looked for something to do. The place roared like a Boeing 747 on takeoff, fueled by the adrenaline rush.

Judy and Ben triaged, calling the docs for emergencies. Emma assigned them two residents to help. *The kids are awesome, but they don't have fifty years of ER experience like those two have between them. They'll learn a lot today.*

She went to check on the old patients. Ann and Kurt were too busy with the traumas to get a chance to reassess them. She tried to clear the hallways, inviting the visitors to the waiting room. They stared at her and resisted. *It's the jeans and the hoodie. I wish I had my white coat! As always, the clothes are more important than the person.* She called Security to escort a particularly reluctant couple. She moved from stretcher to stretcher, checking vitals, handing out water, making sure they stayed alive.

She stopped by Room 3. An intubated patient. A kid, whiter than his sheets. Monitors alarmed like a pinball machine. She couldn't get his blood pressure or his oxygen sat. She tried to listen to his lungs, but the disposable bedside stethoscope didn't work. *What a piece of shit! Taylor had better stethoscopes in her toddler's doctor kit.*

The beeping stopped just as she bent over him to check for a pulse. The crazy zig-zag on the monitor gave way to a straight line. The heart had stopped. *He's in asystole.* Emma hit the code button to call for help. She looked at him, trying to figure out what happened. She knew nothing about him, except that he was intubated. And young. And dead.

Out of nowhere, her frozen brain replayed the voice of Ghazala, her mentor. That pediatric airway lecture, she'd listened to it a dozen times.

"People say: If an intubated patient arrests, think DOPE: Displaced tube, Oxygen, Pneumothorax, Equipment. I disagree. DOPE isn't cool. The families don't like it either. You standing there, looking at their loved one, mumbling DOPE, DOPE. You look like a dope. Think POET. That's a nice mnemonic. Better than DOPE."

POET. Pneumothorax, Oxygen, Equipment, Tube. Let's see.

The tube looked OK. The oxygen was on. She detached the tube from the ventilator to check it. The vent worked. She laid her hands on his chest, pressing with all her weight to force out the trapped air. Nothing.

The room filled with help.

She untied the endotracheal tube, deflated the balloon, then pulled it out of the airway. The tube looked patent. Judy took over the airway and started bagging. Amy got ready for CPR.

The trachea may be a little to the left. A tension pneumothorax? Air outside the lungs, creating so much pressure that the blood can't return to the heart. That's deadly, unless you decompress it fast.

I hope he's lucky.

"Scalpel."

Emma uncovered the right chest. She pulled on sterile gloves. A scalpel landed in her right hand.

Somebody splashed iodine on the chest, baking the white skin to brown.

Emma bent over, looking for the right spot.

"What do you think you're doing?"

Ann.

Emma didn't look up. She didn't have time.

"This is my patient!" Ann shrieked.

Emma found the space. *Anterior axillary line, just lateral to the nipple.* With her left index she found the soft space between the ribs.

"Let go of him!"

Emma opened the scalpel. She took a deep breath and cut into the chest. The silver blade went through skin like butter. She made a long cut. *An inch and a half. This isn't the time for pretty. This is the time for fast.*

Blood oozed. Fat glistened yellow, exposing dark red muscle. *I need a clamp.*

No time. Her finger punctured the flesh between the ribs to break the pleura and release the air. The flesh resisted. Emma pushed harder.

The pleura, the thin membrane lining the chest, broke with a pop. *Like a champagne cork.*

Air burst out around her finger. She pulled her finger out. Warm blood sprayed her face.

The chest was decompressed. The heart restarted.

Emma straightened. Ann's eyes, dark embers in a ghostly face, burned into hers.

She'll never forgive me for this.

"Your patient."

53

Taylor woke up smiling that morning. She felt happy for no reason. Then she remembered that Eric was back, and the day got even brighter.

They had talked about everything and nothing. About the past, the present, and the future. They learned new things about each other.

"I'll be a better lover. You need to tell me what makes you happy," he said.

"What are you talking about?"

"I'll try to be enough for you."

Then it dawned on her. He thought she had been with other men while dating him. She didn't know whether to laugh or to cry. She did both.

"I love you, Eric. You. Nobody else. This happened way before we met. I didn't tell you, since I didn't want to lose you. That was wrong. I'm sorry."

He held her like he was never going to let go.

"I don't need anyone else but you. I love you. But I'm pregnant. I'm responsible for this child who didn't ask to be born. I did drugs. I don't know what that did to the kid. But it doesn't matter. Whether he's normal or not, this is my kid. At least until I bring it into the world."

"And then?"

"I don't know. I struggle with that. Keep it? Give it up for adoption? I don't know."

"I love you."

That was all she needed.

"I need to grow up and get my life together. I'll get a job. Maybe in the hospital."

"That's where you grow up fast."

"I'll speak to my father."

"Your father?"

"Yes. He works there. He's a cardiologist."

Eric laughed. "I know. But if you want to grow up fast, speak to your mother. You'll grow up faster in the ER."

"My mother may not want me there."

"Of course not. Her plate is full. I've never seen anyone busier. But if you're serious, and if you want to make a difference, that's where you should go."

"Why aren't you there, then?"

"I'm not good enough yet. I'll go when I get better. I can't wait to work with your mother. There's nobody like her."

Taylor grimaced. "I never thought I'd date my mother's fan."

Eric laughed. "You'll be OK. She'll take good care of you."

54

————

The next day Emma and Sal were working through charts in Emma's office. Her coffee got cold, Sal's Coke got warm, but they still weren't getting anywhere.

"The broken hip looks legit. Nothing weird there," Emma said. "Let's move on to the second case."

"The hypoglycemia?"

"Yes. The labs are back. The C-peptide is low."

"Yep. That means she received insulin. There's no order for it," Sal said.

"How about the order for the patient next door?"

Sal checked. "Thirty units of regular insulin. Dr. Crump's order."

"Who took it out? And when?"

"George did. At 11:55."

"Did he administer it?"

"Yes. He gave it at 12:48."

"George did?"

"Yes."

"It's a long time from 11:55 to 12:48."

"It sure is. What did he do with that vial for almost an hour? Carried it in his pocket? Left it on the counter? Why?" Sal wondered.

"Something happened. He got sucked into something else."

"That's why his glucose was unchanged an hour later. He had just received the insulin; it didn't have time to work." Sal went back to the computer.

"What are you looking at?"

"I'm checking who wasted the rest of it. He took out a 100 units vial. He gave 30 units. He's supposed to discard the rest. With a witness." He went through screen after screen, his nimble fingers falling over the keyboard like hail. "I can't find documentation of it being discarded."

"Seventy units of insulin just disappeared?"

"It looks like it."

"Strange."

"Yes. When did the woman die?"

Emma checked. "The code was terminated at 2:03."

"That fits. If she got the insulin IV, she'd get hypoglycemic in minutes."

Emma wrote herself a note. *Ask George.*

"Next case is my back pain. Carlos got the meds for him."

Sal checked. "He did. At 2:31."

"Were they even given? By whom?"

"He gave them at 2:45."

"He said he left them on the counter."

Sal shrugged. "That's not what the computer says."

"What identifier do they use to record giving meds?"

"They can use their ID card and a PIN. Or a fingerprint."

"Same with discarding meds?"

"Yes."

Weird. Carlos said he didn't give the meds. And he couldn't have. At 2:45 we were working on the arrhythmia in Room 2.

"I'll have to speak to Carlos."

"You have a lot of talking to do." Sal looked at his watch.

"Something still bugs me about the first case," Emma said. "Can you have another look?"

Sal looked at the orders. He confirmed the meds.

"It looks OK. Brenda got her meds at 3:35. She gave her the Toradol and the morphine at 3:47…"

"Morphine?"

"Yes. Morphine, 4 milligrams. As prescribed."

"But…" Emma went back to the chart. "The tox report says she was positive for fentanyl."

"Fentanyl?"

They looked at each other. They remembered February.

The time of many deaths. The time of fentanyl.

55

———

That evening, Emma drove home thinking about February. That had been the worst month of her life. She hoped the fentanyl was just a coincidence.

She got home. Guinness was waiting.

"How was your day?" Emma dropped her bag on Victor's chair.

One tail thump.

"OK? Just OK?"

"What did you expect? I was locked in the house the whole day. How was your day?"

"It sucked. But I made a little progress. I figured out the insulin. I also know that Carlos couldn't give those meds..."

Guinness left.

"That's rude. You don't just leave in the middle of a conversation!"

She went to choose a wine. The best part of her day was about to begin.

The Rioja? A little sharp on an empty stomach. The Californian Oaked Chardonnay? She hated oak. She didn't think much about Chardonnays either.

That's got to be a gift from a beer lover.

She found a new St. Emilion. Chateay Puy Blanquet St. Emilion Grand Cru 2012. *That should be interesting.* She pulled out the cork with a satisfying pop and filled a crystal glass. *Everything tastes better in crystal. Even water. It gives you a feeling of luxury and decadence.* She lifted the glass, looking through it into the light. A little transparent for a Bordeaux. Glowing red. Like a pinot noir. She sniffed it. Hints of fennel and black raspberry. It smelled tart. She tasted it. Quite an edge for a Bordeaux. Not smooth. Her mouth puckered. *It's sour. Decadent, my ass.*

Guinness dropped the leash at Emma's feet and stared, thumping her tail.

"What are you saying?"

"Let's go for a walk."

"Seriously! Now?"

"Yep. Right now." Guinness barked twice and headed to the door.

"I guess it's urgent." Emma sat down the glass. "Let me get changed at least!"

"Not necessary." Guinness said, dancing in front of the door.

I wanted a dog. It's almost as bad as being married! Not quite as bad as having children, though. She glanced at Taylor's closed door.

"Let me have a glass of wine at least."

Guinness disagreed.

The phone rang.

Amber?

Victor's wife was no longer a rival. She wasn't exactly a friend, but she was Taylor's stepmother. And, deep in her heart, Emma felt sorry for her.

"Hi Amber."

"I'm sorry to bother you."

"No bother. What's up?"

Long pause. "You got a minute?"

"Sure. I'm just walking the dog."

"Can we meet?"

"Now?"

"If possible."

It's late, it's dark, and I have a dog that needs walking. The marina down the road has a terrace and margaritas. And they love dogs.

"Dizzy Alligator?"

"I'll be there in fifteen."

56

ANGEL

I *love kids.*

Pretty kids. Nice kids. Normal kids.

Not this. This is not a kid.

This is thirty pounds of human flesh kept alive by devices. Peg tube, tracheostomy, ventilator. He's got contractures everywhere. He's so folded he'd fit in my carry on. Not that I'd want to take him anywhere.

I check his chart. Evan. He's twelve. He can't see, he can't talk, he can't eat, he can't breathe.

What's the point of being alive? If you call this alive. He doesn't know he's alive. He can't think.

Can he feel? Let's find out.

I stick a #18 needle in his heel.

He pulls away and tries to scream. He can't. He snorts.

He feels pain. That sucks. I wouldn't have my dog live like this! Any dog! And he's human, if only in name.

I look around. They're all busy.

I turn off the alarms and I detach his tracheostomy from the vent. I cover it with my palm, pretending I'm cleaning it. I wait for the heart to stop.

It takes forever.

I reconnect the vent and leave.

Bye-bye, Evan. If they ask, tell them Carlos sent you!

57

Emma threw a jacket over her scrubs and headed to the Dizzy Alligator to meet Amber. Guinness stopped by the hydrants to check her mail.

What the hell is this about? It's got to be about Victor. I hope it's not bad. He may be a pain, but he's my best friend.

Emma sat at the corner table. Guinness lay at her feet. Emma watched the couple next door gazing at the moon shimmering across the water. Guinness watched them eat their nachos.

It's a full moon. It's going to be another fun night in the ED.

The waiter, old and shriveled under his red baseball cap, stopped by to take their order.

"Two margaritas and a water dish."

Guinness barked.

"What?"

Guinness stared at the neighbor's nachos. Her dinner was late. Emma shrugged. "And an order of nachos."

Emma's margarita vanished almost as fast as Guinness's nachos. She grabbed the second glass.

"Hi, Emma."

She sat the glass down.

"Thanks for coming."

"Of course." Emma signaled the waiter for another drink. *Make it two. It looks like a long night.*

"I couldn't think of anybody else," Amber sighed.

Emma smiled. Thinking had never been Amber's strong point.

"It's about Victor. Things aren't going well at home. He works all the time. He barely sees the kids. They spend more time with the babysitter than they do with him."

Emma nodded.

"He's so distant. We used to do foolish little things, like dancing in the kitchen after the kids went to sleep. Not anymore. Now, it's just work, sleep, and more work."

"I'm sorry," Emma lied. *You stole my husband. Now you're stuck with him.*

"Thank you. You're generous."

Not really.

"You must be wondering why I'm telling you this." Amber wiped her dry eyes. "You know him. You're his friend. He'll listen to you. Something is happening. He's in trouble. Financially? Professionally? I've even wondered if he's doing drugs."

Emma shivered.

"Or if he found somebody else."

That day in the cafeteria, he hinted at getting back together. I'd rather have a root canal.

"That's awful, Amber. Maybe he's just overwhelmed. Did you talk to him?"

"I tried. I prepared a nice dinner. I got wine and candles. Even some nice lingerie—you know what I mean… He didn't come home that night. He said he had to switch call with a colleague."

My ex-husband's wife complaining to me that he's not interested in her. You can't make this shit up.

"Have you thought about counseling? Lots of couples swear by it."

"Maybe… He's so remote… I wondered…" She gave Emma a speculative look. "Would you talk to him?"

"Me?"

"He respects you. He cares about your opinion."

Not so much. He left me for you, remember? But what's the point? That was long ago.

"What would you like me to tell him, Amber?"

"Tell him how hard it is for a woman to be excluded from her man's life. I need him. The girls need him. He needs to reorder his priorities."

"I don't know, Amber. This is very personal. He'll think that I'm intruding. And he would be right. You need to talk to him."

Tears shimmered down Amber's moonlit face. "Please, Emma! You have to help me! There's nobody else I can ask."

Emma wished she could say no. But she couldn't. *I asked for her help last time Taylor disappeared. It's my turn now.* She drained the melted margarita and grimaced. It had plenty of sugar but not much alcohol. She sighed.

"I'll see what I can do."

Amber's face lit up. "Thank you, Emma. I knew I could count on you."

Shoulders slumped, head down, Emma walked home. She felt trapped. She hated doing this, but she had promised.

"Crap."

Guinness cocked her head.

"She conned you into this? I thought you were the smart one."

"Don't even go there!" Emma said.

Guinness wagged her tail.

"Hey, get over it! At least he's her problem now."

58

____

It was Taylor's first day on the job. Her heart was pumping and she was sick to her stomach. She wished she hadn't been so adamant about getting a job. *In the ER, of all places. What was I thinking?* She had to choose between nursing assistant and environmental worker. Cleaning was so not her thing! She went for nursing assistant. She couldn't figure out how to tell her mother, so she didn't. And today was the day.

She said good-bye to Guinness and climbed into Eric's car. He dropped her off at the ER entrance. She snuck in, hoping to miss her mother.

They paired her with Amy for orientation. Amy had worked there for years, so she knew the ropes. She taught Taylor how to check vital signs. She told her which thermometer went in the mouth, and which at the other end. She showed her how to stock cupboards and how to draw blood. By noon, Taylor's head was spinning.

By far the hardest thing was dealing with patients and families. They always had questions.

"You need to speak to the doctor," Amy said.

"When is he coming?"

"In a few minutes."

"We've been here for an hour."

"He'll come soon. It's busy today. The sicker patients get seen first."

"Never say anything else, even if you know the doctor won't see them for hours," Amy told her afterwards. "And always listen to your nurses. If you have their back, they'll have yours. Try to do what's needed before they even ask. Get a urine. Check vitals. You'll make a lot of friends. Don't worry about the doctors. Your go-to is your nurse."

"I thought the doctors run the show."

"Nah, the nurses just let them think so. The nurses run the show. The doctors come and go. Don't worry about them. Except for Dr. Steele. Be careful with her."

"Why?"

"She's the ED director. She makes things happen when nobody else can."

"How come?"

"She's a witch."

Taylor laughed.

"Really. She reads minds. It's like a seventh sense."

"Sixth," Taylor said.

"Whatever. Don't lie. If you forgot something, just tell her. If you lie, she'll know it. It's not worth it."

You got that one right. It's not worth it.

A handsome doctor in a navy suits stopped by.

"Amy, I need help with a pelvic."

"Yes, Dr. Crump. This is Taylor. She'll be working with us."

"Welcome, Taylor. The ER is a fun place to work. When it doesn't suck."

"Good to know."

He glanced at her belly. "Pregnant?"

"Yes."

"How far?"

"Twenty weeks."

"Congratulations. Amy will show you the ropes. She'll teach you well."

"Yes, Dr. Crump. What room?"

"Room 14."

Setting up the pelvic was the complicated process of transforming the room into a torture chamber complete with stirrups, lights, and tubes. Taylor shivered. She still hadn't seen an OB.

No wonder the patient is distraught.

"I'm sorry, but you may lose this pregnancy. It's too early to tell."

The young woman burst into sobs. Dr. Crump touched her shoulder.

"Is this your first pregnancy?"

"My second."

"You have a baby at home?"

The woman sobbed harder. "I lost that pregnancy at six months."

"I'm sorry."

Taylor was too. She felt the woman's pain as if it was her own.

"We'll know more after the ultrasound," Dr. Crump said.

He opened the door for her. They walked into Emma.

"Taylor?"

Taylor blushed.

"You've already met?" Dr. Crump asked.

"A while ago. Taylor is my daughter."

Dr. Crump looked from one to the other. He glanced at Taylor's belly. "Really?"

"Sometimes I wonder too. But that's what her father told me."

Taylor smiled.

I learned that from Mother. Smile whenever things turn to shit. You'll feel better. Plus, nobody needs to know you're hurting, or they'll hit you even harder.

59

The following morning Emma found a white envelope in her work mailbox. She hoped it wasn't a complaint, or another nastygram from Quality, bashing her performance on the sepsis protocol. She took out the golden-edged invitation.

"North Country University has the pleasure… Dr. Tolpeghin's retirement party… Keynote speaker 5p.m. Cocktails on the lawn 5:30 to 7. Heavy appetizers."

Who?

She read it again. She shrugged and dropped it in the wastebasket. It had to be a mistake. Then she remembered.

It's the Russian. The board member. She said she's a professor! But why invite me? We barely met. I won't know anybody there. I'm probably working anyhow.

She wasn't. That evening was hers to waste as she chose, so she chose to waste it there. She had nothing better to do, after walking Guinness. She put on a forgiving cayenne pepper red dress, matching lipstick, and a pair of non-croc shoes. She glanced in the mirror. The mirror smiled.

She was late, but not late enough. The keynote speech was slow.

"We were incredibly blessed to have Dr. Tolpeghin in our midst. She created an interest in biology that was duly received by our students whose hearts were opened to the miracles of the natural world thanks to her…"

Where do these people learn how to speak? And, more importantly, why?

She looked for the exit. *Back through the crowd, toward the toilets, then I swerve to the parking lot.*

She apologized, slithering back through the crowd, when a hand caught her arm.

"I'm so glad I found you! I looked everywhere!"

Boris?

Looking nothing like a jack-o'-lantern, Boris stole the show in his charcoal suit. His unruly silver blond hair set off his tan; his laughing blue eyes caressed her. In a strange Russian greeting, he kissed her cheeks three times. His skin smelled green and expensive, like French cologne spilled in a deep wood.

"Vera will be delighted to see you," he said, taking her hand and dragging her through the crowd.

Sitting on the podium in a red hat that would put Queen Elizabeth to shame, Vera yawned. Boris waved. Vera saw them and smiled. She winked, signaling them to wait.

The keynote speaker handed her the microphone. Applause spread through the crowd like wildfire.

"Thank you all for being here. It was a privilege to work with you. Let's fight climate change and save the environment. It's the only one we have."

She stepped off the podium to a thunderous ovation.

"That's it?" Boris asked.

"That's all I had to say. I don't need half an hour to say it."

Emma laughed. Vera hugged her.

"Welcome. I'm glad you came. I didn't think you would, but Boris said it was worth a try."

"It's always worth a try for something you care about, Vera. Isn't that what you taught me?"

"Thank you for inviting me," Emma said.

"My pleasure," Boris answered. "Don't worry, Vera, I'll take care of her. You go deal with your boring crap."

"Be good," Vera said.

"Where's the fun in that?" Boris asked.

"Then at least be smart," she laughed.

"Come. I'll take you to the cocktails," Boris said.

Emma hesitated. "Are you sure…"

He laughed. "It's OK, Dr. Steele. Relax. I'm no longer your patient. You're not responsible for me. How about having fun for a change?"

Fun? I guess… She wished she could remember how.

Boris did. He ordered for her. In tune with Vera's speech, they had cocktails she'd never heard of, like "Penguin Melter" and "Polar Heatwave" and "Antarctic Beach." He drank club soda with lime, enjoying her pleasure. He made her laugh, he made her think, and he made her feel like a woman worth looking at. Emma was bewitched.

He's the most exciting man I ever met since Victor. Scratch that. He's the most exciting man I've ever met.

The evening was magical and short.

"I'll drive you home," Boris said.

"Thanks, but I drove here."

"That was before the cocktails. I'll drive you home. I'll bring you back to get your car tomorrow morning."

"I work at seven."

"I get up at five."

Emma hesitated.

"Emma, I'll call you a taxi if you want. I'm not looking for sex. Maybe later. Right now, I'm looking for friendship, companionship, and a good laugh. More than anything, I'm looking to keep you safe. You matter to me."

He drove her home. They talked. She told him about her job, about her life, about how poorly she was doing at everything. He listened. He told her about sleeping on tatami mats in Japan, about centenary turtles having sex in the Galapagos, about the Folex—fake Rolex—he had bought in Alexandria.

Guinness came to meet them at the door. She stared at him with her amber eyes, sniffing every inch of his pants. He laughed and talked to her in Russian. Guinness smiled.

"What did you tell her?" Emma asked.

"A secret," he said, scratching the dog behind her ears. "She'll tell you if she wants to."

They sat on the green leather sofa. They talked. He was an artist, working in mixed media. Never married. He hadn't found the right girl until now. His aunt was his godmother and his only family. He played chess.

He asked about her. She told him she had a daughter. And an ex-husband. And a job.

"And? Tell me more about you."

"That's it," she said.

He hugged her. "Let's go to bed."

She blushed. He laughed. "Don't worry. I'll just hold you."

She took him to her bed. He held her. He told her she was wonderful. She laughed.

He didn't. "The one thing I'd like to do is to show you how beautiful you are. You're smart. You're funny. You're wonderful."

Emma laughed.

"I'm serious. Beauty is in the soul, not in the fashion magazines. Look at the most beautiful women ever. Rubens's. Rembrandt's. Renoir's. Look at the freaking Mona Lisa. Not a single one of them is less than a size 12. You need to put on a few pounds to fit in."

Emma chuckled, but she stopped worrying about her body.

They slept embraced. For the first time, she felt at peace with who she was. She wasn't young, she wasn't thin, but she was OK.

It's not only what you do. It's also who you are. And I'm not so bad!

She couldn't wait for their date next week.

60

Next day in the ER, Taylor was having a bad shift. She wasn't feeling well. Her eyes burned with tears. She'd already stuck the patient in Room 10, again and again. No luck. The patient, a lovely old lady, didn't complain, but her family was giving her rotten looks. She told Faith. Faith sent her back to try again.

Taylor gathered her tubes but couldn't bring herself to go in. She stared at the door, tears streaming down her cheeks. Carlos touched her shoulder.

"What's up?" he asked.

"I can't get the labs."

"Go tell your nurse."

"I did. She told me to try again. 'It's the only way to learn,' she said. But I tried three times already."

"Why don't you send this urine for me, then? I'll get the blood for you. Nobody needs to know."

"Thank you, Carlos."

Taylor sent the urine. She returned just as Carlos brought out the labs.

"Thanks, Carlos!" Taylor hugged him.

"Isn't that cute!" Faith said.

Carlos frowned and left without a word. Faith stared at Taylor's belly.

"Is it his?"

"What?" Taylor asked

Faith's chin pointed to her pregnant belly.

"Of course not," Taylor said.

"Whose is it then?"

Taylor's blood rose to her cheeks.

"None of your business. These are your labs." She walked away to chill. Fortunately, it was time for her lunch.

Eric was right. In the ER you grow up fast.

She was learning to control her temper. She couldn't help but notice that some tragedies were worse than her smeared mascara or somebody's snide remark. She was learning about real life. It wasn't always fun, but it was enlightening.

By the end of her break she had chilled. She walked back just as the speakers sputtered: "Code 99, ER, Room 10."

That's my room. The patient that I couldn't get blood from. She rushed to Room 10, now awash with scrubs, and squeezed in.

Faith was performing CPR. Dr. Crump was running the code. The family stared in horror. The lovely smiling lady was now dead.

Nothing helped. Dr. Crump called the code. Taylor didn't understand.

"What happened?" she asked Faith.

Faith's limpid blue eyes didn't blink.

"She died."

"Why?"

"Her day has come." Faith smiled. "Why don't you ask your friend Carlos?"

I'll ask Mother.

That evening she waited for her mother to came home. She watched her drop her bag and pet Guinness. She watched her pour her wine. Her hands, cracked from too much washing, shook from too much coffee. Her bloodshot eyes, dried by the air-conditioning, had deep dark circles.

For the first time ever, Taylor felt sorry for her mother. *She's so tired she's gray. She's vulnerable. She's actually mortal.* She wished she hadn't seen that. It made her feel responsible for her mother, and she didn't need that. It was hard enough to be responsible for herself.

She told her the story.

"Faith told me to ask Carlos."

"How long had it been since Carlos was in the room?"

"Half an hour maybe?"

"Did he give her anything?"

"No. He just got the bloods."

"How did he get them?"

"From the vein?"

"Did she have an IV?"

"Yes. But I can't use that. I had to stick her again to get the blood."

"You can't, but nurses can. They get blood from the IV, then they flush it, so that it doesn't clot. Was the family there?"

"Yes."

"Even when Carlos went in?"

"I don't know."

Emma sipped on her wine.

"What do you think?" Taylor asks.

"I think Carlos is in major trouble."

"Why?"

"That's exactly the question. Why? Why is somebody trying to sink Carlos? And who?"

"It's Ben," Taylor said.

"Why Ben?"

"I heard him talk to Mike the other day."

"What did he say?"

"He said Carlos is back with his old friends. He thinks he's stealing drugs."

"What did Mike say?"

"He asked for proof."

"And?"

"Ben said he'll get it. Soon."

61

———

Emma lay awake that night, thinking about it. Could Taylor be right? Was Ben behind the string of deaths, trying to sink Carlos? Hard to believe. She ran the day's events through her head once more.

Emma was in her office when they called the code. She was struggling to make sense of the latest death. A kid. Vent-dependent, brought in for a fever, looking stable. Carlos's patient. Chest X-ray looked like pneumonia. Vitals were fine. Then he just died. Before the X-ray got read.

Why? No idea. This has got to be another one in that string. Except for the age, everything else fits. Looking OK, dead half an hour later for no reason.

"Code 99, Emergency Department, Room 10."

Emma had grabbed her stethoscope and ran. Room 10 was a sea of scrubs, working feverishly. Kurt ran the code. Emma met his haggard eyes.

"Can I help?"

"Another epi please. Continue CPR." He turned to Emma. "Can you look at the heart?"

Emma brought in the ultrasound machine. The translucent algae-green gel splashed on the probe with a liquid sound. She held up the probe, waiting for a break.

"Check for a pulse," Kurt said. In a smooth move, Faith stepped back from doing CPR, making room for Amy to step forward. Kurt felt the neck for a pulse. All eyes were on the ultrasound screen. Emma placed the probe to the left of the sternum, between the second and third ribs. She pushed it down hard, to make contact. The heart, a pear-shaped dark shadow, materialized on the screen. No movement but the valves, waving, carried by the blood. No contraction.

"We'll call this code," Kurt said, wiping his face with his sleeve. He looked at Emma. "This is ridiculous."

Emma nodded.

She returned to her office to check the chart. Somebody knocked at the half open door.

"Come in."

Sal came in.

"Have a seat. Problem?"

"I found this in Room 10," he said, showing her a vial.

Emma reached for it. He pulled it back.

"Gloves."

She gloved. "Propofol. 200 mg. Empty."

"Yes. I was wasting the meds in the RSI kit when I found this on the counter. It wasn't in the kit. That one was still there. Untouched."

"Dr. Crump didn't order anything for this patient."

"Correct."

"Could it be left in the room from the previous patient?"

"Unlikely. The room had just been through a terminal clean after an infectious patient."

"Weird."

"It gets worse. The serial number identifies this vial as part of an RSI kit Carlos took out last week. He recorded wasting it."

Carlos.

"That's enough to kill that tiny old woman."

"If she got it."

"Yes, if she got it."

"The labs will tell. Either way, Carlos is in trouble."

"Major trouble."

"What next?"

"I'll tell Mike and the pharmacy director. They'll take it from there. I just thought you'd want to know."

"Thanks, Sal."

Carlos? Killing all these people? Not likely.

She went back to her cases.

The door opened wide. Kurt stepped in looking like he'd slept in his clothes, his usual spunk gone. Emma offered him a chair and chocolate.

"I wish it was wine."

"Me too. Who the hell is doing this? Why? And how?"

"Kurt, you're sure you didn't give her anything?"

"Come on, Emma!"

"Sorry, I have to ask."

"Not even Tylenol."

"Sal found an empty vial of propofol in the room."

"I didn't order propofol. I didn't order anything, for fuck's sake!"

"OK. I guess we'll find out."

"Sorry, Emma. I'm just tired and frustrated. I'm sure you are too." He cleared his voice.

"Your daughter…I didn't know she was pregnant."

"Yep. The joys of parenthood."

"How old is she?"

"Eighteen."

"Is she…what is she going to do with the baby?"

"Good question. I don't think she knows. It's been a rocky ride."

Kurt stood. "I'd better head home; I'm late already. Sheila won't like it." He stopped with his hand on the doorknob. "You know, Emma…" He shifted his weight from one leg to the other. "Sheila and I, we're looking at adopting. In case…if Taylor is considering it, we'd welcome not only the baby but Taylor too. Sheila would be overjoyed."

"I'll tell Taylor. I'll tell her to speak to you if she thinks that's something she may consider."

"Thanks, Emma."

Should I tell him that the baby's father is… No. That's up to Taylor.

62

Mike's office was packed the next morning. They held an emergency meeting. Nobody was happy. The voices were high, the tempers short, and the oxygen mostly gone. Emma squeezed a seat between Sal and Brenda.

"The latest event was yesterday. Another patient, MR 0897654454, here for a syncope, waiting for her workup to be completed, arrested suddenly and with no explanation and was unable to be resuscitated." Mike glanced around to make sure they were all paying attention.

Emma uncrossed her legs and crossed them the other way. *I hate medicalese! Why can't we speak like normal people? "Wasn't able to be resuscitated." We weren't able to resuscitate her. That's just like "the patient failed the treatment" bullshit. It's the treatment that failed the patient.*

"This has to stop. We have lost more patients in the last few weeks than in a whole quarter of last year. The Quality team started an investigation. The state will come after us, sooner rather than later, to look into this increased mortality. We can't afford to wait and see what happens. We have to be proactive. We have to stop this."

Proactive my ass! Proactive meant stopping it before it started. If anything, this is post-active.

"I agree," Gus said. "We should have done something long ago."

"What are you saying, Mike?" Judy asked.

"I think we should put Carlos on a leave of absence while we're looking into things."

"Carlos? Why Carlos?"

"Carlos was involved with a bunch of these deaths. He was the primary nurse of four of them. He was also involved with the care of a few of the others," Mike said.

"That in itself doesn't mean anything," Emma said. "So was I. So was Sal."

Sal frowned.

"Come on, Sal, you know what I mean. There's no evidence against Carlos."

"Actually, there is. He was the one who gave the meds to that back-pain patient of yours who died. Then he said he didn't. But it's in the computer. He signed for them."

"That's exactly what worries me. I know he didn't. He was with me in another room. We were working on an arrhythmia. He couldn't be in two places at the same time."

Mike shrugged. "It only takes a minute to leave the room and give the meds. Nobody would even notice."

"And log into the computer to sign that you did? Then deny it? It makes no sense."

"It may not make sense to you, but it's going to make a lot of sense to the police. Then there's the RSI kit."

"What RSI kit?" Gus asked.

"Sal, can you explain?"

"One of Carlos's patients got intubated a few days ago. Carlos took out an RSI kit. They used a couple of meds, not all of them. Carlos recorded discarding the rest. There was no witness. Then, yesterday, a patient coded. The empty vial of propofol found at her bedside belonged to that discarded RSI kit."

"That's bad," Gus said. "That's awful."

"Still, it doesn't explain everything. Some of the incidents didn't involve Carlos."

"That we know of," Mike said. "Not yet. By the way, remember that patient with the agitated daughter, the pneumonia in Room 15? Your patient?"

"Yes."

"George was your nurse."

"Yes."

"George went on break. Carlos covered for him. When George came back, she was dead."

"George and Carlos room together," Judy said.

"What are you saying?" Emma asked.

"Nothing. Just thinking out loud."

"Then this last patient. The one with the propofol vial. It was Faith's patient, but Carlos went to draw blood. When Faith went back, she was dead."

"Death seems to be following Carlos," Gus said. "If he's not guilty, he sure is unlucky."

"What if somebody is framing Carlos?" Emma asked. "Some cases he's not involved with. Some things make no sense. First, why would he do this?"

"Why would anybody do this?" Judy asked.

"Because they're nuts," Mike answered.

"But why sign that you gave meds to a patient you're trying to kill? Shouldn't he pretend he never did? That makes no sense."

"Maybe he forgot and did it by reflex," Mike said.

"This is complicated. It doesn't look like we can clarify it today," Gus said, "We'll work on it. But in the meantime, we have to do everything we can to protect our patients. I say Carlos is out."

"What if it's not him? What if this continues?" Emma said.

Gus glowered at her.

"What do you want to do, Emma?"

"We should call the police. Have them look into things."

"Absolutely not! If somebody leaks the news, we're cooked! Nobody will come here any longer for fear of being killed! We'll go bankrupt. We have to clarify this first."

"We'll be even more cooked if we watch people dying and don't do anything," Emma said.

"That's precisely why we are putting Carlos on a leave of absence," Gus said.

"What if it's not him? What if it's somebody framing him? And they're still here?"

Mike shrugged. "If they're framing him and he's gone, maybe they'll stop the killings."

Emma's jaw fell. "Really? Is this the best we can do?"

"I'm afraid so. In the circumstances," Gus said. He stood. "I'm sorry, but I have another meeting. We'll put Carlos on a leave of absence and we'll see how this goes."

Emma opened her mouth to say something, but Sal touched her elbow.

"They've made up their minds," he whispered. "There's no point in pushing it. You'll just make enemies."

He's right. I guess I'll have to continue to work on it myself. At least now I know what I'm looking for.

Emma ran into Faith on her way to her car. Faith smiled. Emma wanted to stop, but she couldn't. Something inside her said no. She felt Faith's eyes burning into her back. Something stirred in the pit of her stomach. She shivered.

63

ANGEL

t worked. I can't believe it! It was less than twelve bucks on Amazon. It doesn't look like much. A piece of green plastic, looking like a luggage scale. It fits in my scrubs pocket.

I wait until she goes to sew a laceration. She always leaves her coat on the chair, so she doesn't get blood on it. Her ID hangs from the chest pocket.

I snatch it as I pass by, and I head to the bathroom.

I get my RFID reader, and aim it at her ID. I press READ.

It beeps.

I get a blank card and aim the RFID reader at it. I press WRITE.

It beeps. It worked.

That's it!

I return her ID. She'll never know I took it.

I wave my new card over the sign-in reader to make sure it works.

It asks for the PIN.

I have it. I got it last week. She was too preoccupied with that sick patient to see me staring at her hands.

I type it in. It works.

I'm Dr. Steele now. I can look up charts, put in orders, document, whatever. Under her signature.

Dr. Angel Steele. Sounds good!

64

When she got home that evening, Emma checked out the wine rack. She looked for something to warm her inside, to clean her from the day's misery, sadness, and fear. Something unusual caught her eye: Renmano Chairman Selection Shiraz 2017. The bottle was dark green, the label white with a galloping golden horse. That gave her pause. *What does the horse have to do with anything? I hope it's not the flavor! I thought oak and leather were bad.* She shrugged, opened it, poured a glass, and sat on the sofa.

Dark as ink, the wine had a nose of blackberries and plum, with a touch of honey and a hint of pepper. No horse. She took a sip. The wine was full bodied, "corposo" as Italians say, and sensual. She felt its warmth spreading through her. She sighed.

Guinness laid her head on Emma's knees. She rolled belly up, demanding to be scratched.

"I thought you Germans were aloof and dignified." Emma set down her glass to scratch her armpit. Guinness moaned with pleasure.

"What do you think about all this? I think somebody is framing Carlos. He isn't stupid. He wouldn't leave that kind of trail. Somebody's trying to sink him. But why?"

Guinness rolled, offering the other armpit.

"The obvious answer is Faith. They were together, they fell apart, she hates him. But she's a great girl. I'm biased, of course. How could I not be? She saved my life. But she really is patient and caring, especially to the elderly. She'd never do something like this! Carlos has other enemies. Ben got demoted because of Carlos. He almost got fired. Faith said that's just the tail end of the story. There's a lot of bad blood between them. Ben said Carlos is stealing drugs. Was that the propofol vial Sal found? Is there more coming? And what happened to the rest of the RSI kit that vial came from?"

Guinness had no suggestions. She rolled back on her other side.

Emma shook her head. "I'm getting nowhere. I need to speak to him. Let's go."

The red car swallowed the empty roads. George's windows glowed orange in the night.

Emma rang the doorbell. George opened the door, holding a beer.

"Long time no see, stranger. Come in. Beer?"

"No, thanks." Emma shivered looking at the can in his hand. "I'm a wine person."

"Sorry, but I don't..."

"Good. I'm driving anyhow. Is Carlos home?"

"Nope. He came back from work and said they put him on leave. He drove out like a bat out of hell. Said he's going back to New Hampshire to clear his head."

"I see."

"They think he's got something to do with all these deaths, but I don't think so. He's not a killer."

"I agree. But then who is?" Emma asked.

"His girlfriend?"

"I don't think so. She's a nice girl."

"She's not nice. She's disturbed. There's something seriously wrong with her."

"What makes you say that?"

"I've seen her. She's dark inside. Those glass-blue eyes are creepy. They give me the chills."

"I don't think so, George. Just because Carlos is your friend..."

"Listen, Emma. You know me better than that. That girl is trouble."

Emma shrugged. "I'll go now."

"Emma, watch your back. I have a bad feeling."

"What feeling?"

"Something's about to happen."

"Bad things happened already. Too many."

"I know. I have a feeling something bad is going to happen to you."

Emma shuddered. She turned up the heat in the car. She was still shivering when she got home.

Boris was waiting in the driveway.

"I couldn't wait until next week."

Her heart sang.

65

Carlos drove for hours and hours that night. He put mile after mile of dark wet road behind him. His shoulders hurt and his neck was stiff from leaning forward, trying to see beyond his lights. His tired eyes burned from the glare. He was far enough to stop and take a break, but there was nothing. Nothing but the never-ending wet road, the rain, and the forest.

Drunk with rage, he had left on a whim. He couldn't think about anything else to do. He was humiliated and angry.

And guilty.

They called him for an urgent meeting in Mike's office. They were all there: Mike, the VPM, the union representative, the hospital lawyer. They ganged up on him.

They asked about the meds for the back pain.

"I left them on the counter."

"You gave them. There's your signature," Mike said.

"I didn't."

"You signed that you did."

"I didn't."

They didn't believe him.

They asked about the woman in Room 15.

"You covered George's break. How was she?"

That's when Brenda came to me. I never made it there.

"She was fine," he lied.

They asked about Taylor's patient in Room 10.

"Yes, I got the blood."

"What did you give her?"

"Nothing. She wasn't my patient."

"Then why did you get the blood?"

"Taylor needed help."

"How about the propofol?" Mike asked.

What?

"You left the empty vial in the room."

"I didn't leave any vial in the room."

"You did. We checked. It's the propofol from the intubation kit you charted as discarded."

Carlos heard his blood boil, and his brain darkened with fury. Mike was Ben's friend. *That's why he hates me. That's why he blames me.*

But Carlos had indeed charted that stolen RSI kit as discarded. He'd hoped it was gone for good. It wasn't. The propofol had come back to haunt him. *I'm fucked.*

"Don't answer any questions you're not sure about," the union rep intervened. "Even better, don't answer any more questions at all. You need a lawyer."

"I'm here," the hospital lawyer said.

"You're not his lawyer. He needs his own."

Carlos agreed. He didn't need to dig himself any deeper. Security escorted him out, just as Ben was coming in to work. Ben grinned like he'd won the lottery. Carlos ached to punch him in the face. It took all his self-control to refrain.

The smirk on his face! He couldn't wait to go and tell them. As if the whole ER didn't already know.

A burning flash of lightning split the sky. A deafening roll of thunder followed a second later, bringing him back to the present. The rain, falling like a wall of water. The car, skidding on the slick road. A truck's high beams blinded him. He slowed down.

I wish I hadn't left.

Faith and Ben were going to laugh at him. All the others—Brenda, Mike, even Dr. Steele—they'd think he was guilty. And he was. He was guilty of one thing. He had lied about discarding the kit. He had nothing else to be ashamed of. He didn't kill people. He didn't steal drugs. He only tried to do his job and save lives.

Now he was on the run. Ben was laughing. With Faith. His anger made him sick. He opened the window to spit his bile. The rain caressed him with cool fingers. It soothed his forehead and relieved the burn in his eyes.

He couldn't let that happen. He couldn't run away and let them laugh. He had struggled his whole life to become somebody. He couldn't let them steal that. He turned around. *I'm going back. I'll show them. I'll put things right. I'll prove that I'm innocent.*

He drove and drove and drove.

Hours later, he was getting close but he was hurting. He was running out of gas. Another hour or so to go. He rubbed his burning eyes. He saw the lights on the left side of the road. *I almost missed it.*

He turned left.

He didn't see the truck. The road was wet. The night was dark. He wasn't thinking straight.

He slammed the brakes and turned the wheel. The brakes screeched like a dying wild bird. The car swerved, then slid on the slick asphalt. A pole came toward him. He pulled the wheel right, swerved, and slid toward the culvert. He hit it, then flew over it. The car twisted in the air like an Olympic diver. Caught in the blinding headlights, a ghost-like white aspen rushed toward him, upside down. Up again. Upside down.

His head exploded into darkness.

66

____

Taylor's shift was almost over. She dropped the vials in the transport tube and sighed. She was glad to be done. Her feet hurt. Her back too. She was so hungry she could cry.

Working in the ER wasn't what she expected. She'd learned a lot. Some technical skills, like finger-sticks—sticking needles in people's fingers to check their blood glucose—and measuring vital signs. She learned where to find weird things like the anoscope, for looking into people's nether side, and the Magill forceps, for removing foreign bodies from tight places. She learned about the ER culture. ER people were not like the others. Something about working here made them into a team. Some were nice, some less so, but they were all intense, dedicated, and funny.

Getting exposed to the never-ending human tragedy and the occasional comedy had helped shift her focus beyond herself. An only child, then a deserted child when her father left, she got too much attention. She figured out she was the center of the universe.

Nope. She wasn't sure the universe had a center, but if it did, she wasn't it. Maybe her mother. People orbited around her mother like planets on a gravitational pull. Taylor's feelings about her mother had changed after she started working in the ER. Her mother had a peculiar way of interacting with people. They were attracted to her like cats to a sun patch. It was like wherever she was, it was warmer.

Taylor got her bag and headed out. The door opened and she walked into Dr. Crump. She apologized. He smiled.

"Hi Taylor."

"Hello."

"Done for the day?"

"Yes, thank God."

He laughed. "That's what we all say."

They walked out the door. The sky had broken into sheets of rain. Taylor stopped under the awning to get her phone.

"You need a ride?"

"I...I was calling Eric, my boyfriend, to pick me up."

"I'll take you. No bother, I live that way anyhow. You're living with your mother, right?"

"Yes."

"Let's go. Even better, wait here. I'll get the car."

Taylor felt uncomfortable. Why would he give her a ride? She was just a nursing assistant. He was a doctor. And married. Was it...No, he didn't give off that sort of vibe. He was handsome and all, but she was over older men. She had Eric.

His blue Audi arrived and she climbed in. Next to his beautiful dark suit, her scrubs looked out-of-place. She wished she'd waited another five minutes so she wouldn't have to ride with him. She sat up straight, her bag on her knees, trying to cover her bulging belly.

"How's it going? How do you like the ER?"

"It's like no other place. It's fascinating, scary, and exhilarating, all at the same time. Awful and disgusting, at times."

He laughed. "I couldn't say it better myself. The fact that your mother works there must make it harder."

"I haven't worked with her. Not yet."

"You probably won't. She'll try to avoid that."

Taylor nodded.

"How are you feeling?" He took a quick glance at her belly.

Taylor blushed. "I'm all right."

"Do you know if it's a boy or a girl?"

"No."

"You like surprises?"

I hate surprises. I can't remember ever having a good surprise. From Dad leaving home to this pregnancy, plus everything about Dick, every surprise I had was a blow across the head. I hate them with a passion. And I hope there won't be any surprises about this kid, though it would be a surprise if there were no surprises.

"Not so much."

He nodded as if he understood.

"When is the baby due?"

"September."

"That's a good month. The weather is still nice, but the heat of the summer is over."

Not like I planned it this way.

"Have you thought about what you'll do?"

Taylor bristled. *That's none of your business.*

"I know it's none of my business." He drove slowly, looking straight ahead. "But I'd like to tell you a story."

May as well. I hope we get home soon.

"My wife, Sheila, and I, we've been married for twenty-three years. We hoped for children. Sheila did. For me, it wasn't that important. We tried everything. No luck. We went to in vitro fertilization. Sheila became pregnant. Unfortunately, she lost the pregnancy. We tried again. She carried that one to twenty-two weeks, then lost it. She was devastated. She became depressed and withdrawn. We tried all sorts of treatments. Nothing worked. Our marriage... our marriage went through some rough patches. I almost lost her." He choked.

"I'm sorry," Taylor mumbled.

"She's better now. We are better now. We're talking adoption."

Taylor looked out the window. *Five more minutes.*

"I saw you're pregnant. You're so young. You have your whole life ahead of you. I don't know if giving up your child for adoption is something you've considered, but I'd love you to meet Sheila. She's wonderful. She'll be a great mother. We'd welcome your baby. We'd welcome you too. You could spend as much time with him as you wanted. We'd be happy to have you both."

"That's… very generous of you."

"Not at all. It would be generous of you."

"I haven't decided what to do. I'm still trying to find my bearings."

"I understand. I just wanted to put it out there. And I'd love it if you could meet Sheila either way. She's a lovely person and an artist."

"What type of art?"

"Pottery. She has a studio in the back yard."

"I've always had an interest in pottery," Taylor said.

"Why don't you stop by, one of these days," he said, pulling in Emma's driveway.

"I just might. Thank you." She climbed out awkwardly, her thickened belly in the way. He gave it a longing look.

"My pleasure. Good luck, Taylor. Stay in touch."

Taylor smiled and nodded.

Behind the window, a shadow moved.

Guinness was watching.

67

―――――――

Back in the ER for another shift, Emma finished discharging Room 6. Her phone vibrated. A message from Boris. She smiled. Boris was fun to be with and had the best stories. But, more importantly, he made her feel good about herself. *I can use that.*

"Trauma code, Emergency Department, Room 1." The metallic voice cut through the ER noise, stirring a new urgency in everyone but the patients. The scrubs' chaotic movement gathered into a stream flowing to Room 1. Emma grabbed her stethoscope, straightened her achy back, and followed.

"Mine?" she asked Judy.

"Yes."

"What is it?"

"MVA. Male."

"Anything about his injuries?"

"Head and torso. They're still extricating."

"ETA?"

"Fifteen minutes. Longer if they're having trouble."

Time for the full trauma garb—gown, mask, hat, and booties. She suited in a hurry. Two minutes later, the room was crammed with masked blue people she could barely recognize. *We look like a den of Martians! Thank God for the yellow labels.* She attached the one labeled "ER Doctor" to her gown. She pulled on her gloves as the sirens started.

She checked her equipment: video laryngoscope, #8 endotracheal tube ready, with the hyper-curved metal stylet inside and the air-filled 10cc syringe attached, oxygen ports ready, suction, warm IV fluids, difficult airway cart.

The sirens got louder. Their wails intertwined like those of lovesick cats. Emma went to the ambulance door to meet them and gain an extra minute to listen to the EMTs.

She punched the silver plate door opener with the back of her fist. She stepped in the ambulance bay. The sirens died. The silence fell heavy on her ears, still buzzing with the ruckus.

The ambulance door opened. Roy, the EMT, held a mask over the patient's face, pumping air into his lungs with his blue AMBU bag. Brandon, his partner, performed CPR. The deep chest compressions squeezed blood out of the heart, pushing it to the essential organs. His strained face shone with sweat. He saw her, and his tension softened. His work was almost done. *They're off the hook. Now it's us.*

"Hello, Dr. Steele. MVA. Thirty-five-year-old male. We have a 20 in the right AC. He was tachycardic and hypotensive when we got him. We just lost the pulse. We gave two rounds of epi. No return of spontaneous circulation. He's been in PEA for the last five minutes."

PEA. Pulseless electric activity. It can be anything. Shock? Tension pneumothorax? Cardiac tamponade?

The helping crew came to help take out the stretcher. The long, articulated metal legs dropped to the ground with a clunk. The stretcher rolled to Room 1, Roy and Brandon glued to it like limpets. Emma joined them. She looked at the patient, trying to assess his injuries. It wasn't easy, since he was covered in blood. *No beard. Thin moustache. No movement, other than the two-inch chest wall rise when Brandon lets it recoil. C-collar stabilizing the neck. The gash above his ear isn't bleeding. Of course not. There's no blood pressure. All bleeding stops. Eventually.*

Brenda stabilized his neck. On her count, they moved him to the ER stretcher. The respiratory therapist took over the airway. The mask made obscene farting noises with every squeeze. *It's leaking air. The bagging's no good.*

"No breathing, no pulse," Emma dictated. "Let's expose him and hook him up to our monitors. Continue CPR."

Trauma shears came out of pockets. Bloody clothes vanished, exposing a bruised, fit body. *Abrasions everywhere; a palm-sized bruise over his left chest. That chest is moving funny.*

Leaning over the head of the bed, Emma pried open the eyes. "Pupils 4 mm, equal and reactive to light. Ten-inch laceration to the left parietal region, oozing blood." *Something about him looks familiar.* She wiped the blood off his face.

Carlos.

She took in a sharp breath. She opened her mouth to tell them. She closed it back. *They don't need that added stress. It won't help.*

"Dr. Steele!"

Kayla, the ER clerk, stood in the doorway, her face whiter than snow.

"The police are here. We have an ID."

"Yes. Get me the allergies and medical history please."

"It's…"

"I know." Emma tried to stop her.

"Carlos!"

The room gasped. They stepped forward to see him better.

"Back, everybody! We have a patient to save." Emma's voice cracked like a whip over the room. They stepped back. All but Faith. Faith moved in.

Her blue eyes swallowed her face. She sobbed. She screamed.

"Carlos! What did you do? Why did you do this?" Hands shaking, she touched him, exploring him as if she couldn't see. She bent over him close enough to kiss him.

Emma caught Judy's eye. She nodded to the door. Judy put her arm around Faith's shoulders, guiding her out.

"We need a surgeon," Emma said.

"I paged him. He didn't call back," Kayla answered.

"Page him again. Hold the scanner."

She turned back to Brenda: "What do we have for IV access? Labs?"

"Got a 20 from EMS. Working on a second," Brenda said.

"Good. Getting it would be even better. We need a second line and labs. I need a type and cross. He'll need a transfusion." *If he makes it.*

"Amy, get me the IO drill. How's he bagging?"

"Poorly" the RT said, pulling the face into the mask to improve the seal.

"Try an oral airway and reposition the jaw." She turned to Chris. "Start transfusing."

Still no second line.

"The IO?"

Judy handed it to her.

Emma glanced at Carlos. *Almost six feet, maybe 70 kilos.* She chose the two-inch yellow intraosseous needle and screwed it in the business end of the drill. She cleaned the skin below the knee joint and placed the needle tip at a right angle to the shin. She pushed her weight into the drill, then pulled the trigger.

The drill bit into bone. The bone cracked as the needle broke through.

Emma checked the placement. *Solid.* She took out the stylet, attached a syringe to the IO needle, and sucked in the murky red fluid. *Bone marrow. I'm in.* She flushed it and handed it to Chris.

Amy stepped back. Gina took her place, continuing CPR.

Still nothing. He's as good as dead, but maybe... The chest injury—maybe a tension pneumo? Or cardiac tamponade? Either of those could stop his heart. Worth a try. He can't get any deader. She splashed green phosphorescent gel on the ultrasound probe.

"Stop CPR."

She placed the probe on the chest. Left of the sternum, between the second and the third ribs. She glanced at the screen. A thick black stripe between the probe and the quivering heart. *Tamponade. That black stripe is blood around the heart, squeezing it shut. The only way to save him is to stick a needle in it and drain it. But the surgeon isn't here and the only pericardiocentesis I ever did was on a pig, in the simulation lab. The pig didn't make it. I guess I get to do a real one today. I hope it works out better.*

She cleaned the area below the probe with disinfectant. She donned sterile gloves and took the catheter from Judy. It was a 14, as big as a knitting needle, only meaner. Just looking at it made her sick. Her hands shook. She took a slow, deep breath to steady them. She rested the back of her right hand on his chest. Her left pressed the probe into the skin. The needle went in. Its tip, a bright dot of light, appeared on the screen above the dark stripe. She advanced the needle, watching the white tip progress toward the dark stripe. One more centimeter. She got in.

Like the only star in a dark night sky.

Dark blood flashed in the needle. Emma dropped the probe. She held the catheter in with one hand and pulled out the monster needle with the other.

His blood, dark red and warm, splattered her, covering her glasses. She grabbed the large syringe with her bloody gloved hand. It was so slippery she almost dropped it. She struggled to attach it without displacing the catheter. Blood spurted everywhere, blinding her. By feel alone, she got the syringe attached. It instantly filled.

That's the pressure keeping the heart hostage. They say 25 cc is enough to...

The monitor beeped, dancing with joy. The heart was back.

The room gasped. Emma felt faint.

"We have a pulse. Blood pressure?"

"Checking it."

"Labs?"

"I have them. Sending them now."

"IV access?"

"18 in the left AC, and a 20 in the right AC."

"Surgeon?"

"On his way."

It's a darn long trip. Emma wiped the sweat off her forehead with a bloody sleeve.

"Blood pressure 106/93. Oxygen sat 90%."

"Let's start another unit of blood. Recheck vitals in 3. Sal, let's give TXA."

"He's breathing on his own," the RT said.

Should I intubate? If I do, I get control of the airway but I may drop his blood pressure. I may even give him a tension pneumothorax.

"Blood pressure 110/90."

It's holding.

"Quick chest X-ray, please. And pelvis. A finger-stick. Let's get ready to intubate."

"What do you want for intubation?" Sal asked.

"Ketamine and Sux, please. Fentanyl first. He's going to need a drip to keep him down when the RSI wears off.

"Propofol?"

"No. That'll drop his blood pressure. Let's do ketamine while we're figuring things out. Then we can switch."

"OK."

She slid the ultrasound probe along his right abdomen, looking for blood. *Big-time black stripe between the liver and the right kidney. He's got blood in his belly.*

"Blood pressure dropping. 85/62."

Damn it. I can't send him to the scanner, and I can't intubate. I don't even know if it's his tamponade reaccumulating or he's bleeding in his belly. Probably both.

"Where's that damn surgeon?"

"The damn surgeon's right here," a tall white coat said, stepping gingerly to avoid the blood pooled on the floor.

"I'm Dr. Roth."

"Hi, Dr. Roth. I'm Emma Steele, and I've never been happier to see a surgeon."

68

———————

Carlos went to the OR. Emma stole a moment to get herself together. She went to the bathroom to clean up. She washed her hands. She rinsed her face with cold water. She breathed. *What a roller coaster. First the trauma code. Then finding out it was Carlos. Dead. Bringing him back, just to see him fall apart again.*

She looked in the mirror. A pale, tired woman looked back. She put on lipstick to improve her morale. It didn't help. She went back to her desk. Judy was waiting.

"Will you speak to Faith? She's the closest thing he's got to family."

Emma wished she could say no. It was too personal. She was close to them both. Besides that, George's suspicion made her weary. She knew Carlos hadn't killed all those people. Somebody else had. *Faith? It can't be. But then who?*

"Sure."

Faith sat alone in the grim family room. Her hands in her lap, tears streaming from her clear blue eyes, she looked like Botticelli's Madonna. Her golden hair warmed the dingy room heavy with people's misery.

"I'm sorry, Faith."

"It's OK. We were no longer together anyhow."

"Still, it must be hard for you."

"It is. But after he killed all those people…"

Emma gasped. The suspicions hanging over Carlos weren't public knowledge. How did Faith know? What did she know?

"Which people?"

"The patients."

"What makes you think he killed patients?"

"Who else, if not him?"

Emma shrugged.

"It must be him. He was involved with all of them, one way or another. He killed them, one by one. Then he could no longer stand the remorse. Or maybe got afraid of getting caught. That's why he tried to commit suicide. That's what that accident was about."

Emma's jaw fell. She didn't think Carlos had killed the patients. There was no reason to believe that the accident was a suicide attempt. *But then, I barely know him. Faith does. They lived together for years. She knows him better than anybody.*

And she hates him.

"I don't know, Faith. It doesn't sound like the Carlos I know. I think he's a decent man."

In a flash, Faith turned dark. Eyes spitting fire, she stood up to pace.

"You're right. You don't know. I do. Did you know he was only twelve when he joined a gang? He was fourteen the first time he got arrested? He's a criminal. He's always been a criminal. That's who he is."

Fists tight, head forward, Faith paced the small room. Back and forth, back and forth. Like a caged animal.

"He puts on a good face. He pretends to be nice. He acts like he cares about you. But he'll throw you under the bus if it suits him. That's what he did to me. He threw me away. Me!"

Eyes wild, black painted nails digging into her palms, Faith choked with rage.

Filled with unease, Emma leaned back. *She has nothing good to say about him, even as he's dying. No tears, no regrets. Nothing but hate.*

She waited and waited for Faith's anger to die down. It didn't.

"Faith, would you like me to call somebody for you? A friend? A priest? How about getting you something to help you relax?"

Suddenly, Faith's fury vanished. She smiled like nothing had ever happened. She took Emma's hand.

"Oh, no. Thank you, Dr. Steele, I'll be all right. I was just surprised. You're right, Carlos is a good man. I'm heartbroken that this happened to him! He couldn't have killed all those people. Thank you for talking to me."

"Of course." Emma forced herself to hug her, then rushed out. Touching Faith made her skin crawl. She went back to work. She saw the dog bite in Room 4, the drunk in 7 and the broken ankle in 12.1. She forgot about Carlos and Faith, until the phone call.

"I thought you'd like to know how he is," Dr. Roth said.

"Of course."

"He's made it this far. We had to do a pericardial window. It was good that you didn't intubate, he had a pneumothorax too. His spleen was shattered. He made it by the skin of his teeth. For now."

"How about his head?"

"Not much on the CT. No fracture, no bleed. We'll see if he wakes up. We'll lighten up the sedation tomorrow. If he makes it that far."

"Thanks for calling, Dr. Roth. I appreciate it."

"My pleasure. I hope I'll see you around."

Emma smiled and hung up. She ordered antibiotics for the pneumonia in Room 14 and signed out.

69

I t was still early when Emma's phone woke her up the next morning. They needed her at the hospital. She brushed her teeth, threw on a set of clean scrubs, and left.

Mike, Gus, and Sal were waiting in Mike's office.

"What's up?"

"Your patient? Room 14? Yesterday?

The pneumonia I admitted before I left.

"Yes?"

"He died."

"Really? He wasn't that sick! How come?"

"He died from a morphine overdose."

"Morphine? Who gave him morphine?"

"You did."

"I did not. He was not in pain."

Mike's eyes were hard as rocks as he looked at her. He turned the computer screen to show her the chart. Clear as daylight: 50 mg of morphine. Her order.

That's impossible.

She looked again. Yep. Her order.

"I didn't order this."

They stared at her.

"Mike, I didn't order this. This is insane! Why should I order 50 mg of morphine? I never, in my life, gave more than 10 at any one time! And this patient wasn't even in pain!"

"This is your patient. This is the order. This is your electronic signature."

"I did not order this."

Gus stared like he'd never seen her before. Mike frowned. And Sal…Sal's eyes didn't meet hers.

"That's not what the computer says," Gus said.

"What time was it?"

"3:45," Sal said.

Just before the end of my shift. I was still in the ER. Except that I didn't do it.

"Who gave it?" Emma asked. *No nurse in her right mind would give such a monstrous order.*

Sal shrugged. "It's not marked."

"Who was his nurse?" Mike asked.

"George," Emma said.

I didn't put in that order. And George would never give it.

"We'll speak to him. Can I have a moment with Dr. Steele?" Gus asked.

Mike and Sal left, closing the door behind them.

"Emma, how much do you drink?"

Emma's stomach fluttered. A wave of nausea hit her.

"Nothing, ever, when I work."

"Still, how much do you drink?"

"I don't see how that's any of your business."

"Actually, it is. I wonder how much your drinking interferes with your work. As ED director, you're practically always on call. Even in your off hours. As such, you're actually drinking on call."

Emma's anger blew through her like a dark wind. Her throat tightened.

"I know you have a lot of stress. The job is stressful. Your personal life hasn't been easy. Ken's death. Victor. Taylor. All that takes its toll." He paused, waiting for an answer.

One-two-three. One-two-three. Emma counted her breaths in an effort to slow her heart rate. She crossed her arms tightly on her chest, to prevent herself from punching him.

"However, we cannot allow your personal problems to interfere with the care and the safety of our patients. You are becoming a liability for the department. You need to put your life in order."

Emma's teeth clenched so hard she could hear them crack.

"I'll give you one week. Sort out your personal life. Consider detox. There are many upscale, discreet facilities. You could turn your life around."

Emma knew a lot about detox facilities. She had researched them for Taylor, who'd eloped from one only weeks ago. She didn't need detox. Her drinking was *her* problem. Nobody else's. She hadn't ordered that morphine. She never drank on the job. She'd never drink and drive. Somebody was sinking her. She remembered George: *"I have a feeling something bad is about to happen to you, Emma."*

He was right.

70

———

The house was quiet when Emma got home that evening. She walked from the kitchen to Taylor's room, then to her own bedroom, where Guinness slept on her bed when she thought nobody knew. Nobody home. She went to the wine rack.

"If you drink, you are drinking on call."

So what?

She was always on call. She'd been on call for months. Ever since the blasted day they made her director. Her drinking never interfered with her work. If anything, it helped. Thinking of her wine had sustained her through many nasty encounters with patients, consultants, and staff. Instead of blowing up, she'd smile and nod, thinking: *Stupid motherfucker. You're not worth getting in trouble for. I'll reward myself with a better wine tonight for keeping calm as I talk to you. Like now.*

It feels like a night to celebrate. What? I'm not sure. Being alive? Figuring out who the killer is? Having a quiet moment? Between the ER, Taylor, and Guinness, that's as rare as hen's teeth.

She chose a 2004 Brunello de Montalcino. A very special Italian wine. She'd fallen in love with it by mistake. She and Victor were in Rome for their honeymoon. Thanks to Margret, they stayed at an exclusive hotel near the Pantheon, so posh that the doorman intimidated them.

They made love. They slept, embraced. They woke up at midnight, hungry. Rome was asleep. They had to make do with the stale sandwiches in the room and the bottle of expensive Brunello they'd bought for Margret.

"We'll buy her another," Victor said.

They sat together on the windowsill, their thighs touching. They watched the moon pour gold over the Pantheon. They ate stale salami sandwiches and drank Brunello from each other's lips. They talked. They made love. They watched the darkness swallow Rome when the moon hid behind the buildings. Brunello had tasted like love, magic, and Rome ever since.

Emma opened the bottle. It surrendered with a wet "pop." She poured the blood of the grapes in a long-stemmed glass. She sat on the green leather sofa, put her feet up, and sniffed the wine. *Cherry, strawberry, and walnut.*

Walnut? She took a second nose. *Walnut. Enough foreplay.* She took a healthy sip. She closed her mouth around the wine, allowing it to bathe her tongue, the inside of her cheeks, her palate. She chewed on it, driving it into the farthest corners of her mouth, imbibing every taste bud. She swallowed. She focused on the lingering finish pleasuring her mouth even after the wine was gone. Like the glow of the sunset, still there after the sun is gone.

She sat alone staring at the dark TV screen, thinking. About Rome. About Victor. About how marriages fail and love dies. About Vincent.

That's when our marriage died. It died the morning when Vincent didn't wake up.

He woke her up every night, then every morning before dawn, asking to feed. Except that night. Her full, heavy breasts woke her up that morning. He'd never slept through the night. He hadn't this time either. He had been dead for hours. His eyes were open, his face purple, his tiny body stiff as a board. Emma did mouth to mouth. Victor called the ambulance and took Taylor away. Nothing helped. Vincent was dead, and their marriage died with him. For a while, they pretended it was still alive. They were still together, but they each grieved alone. Almost.

Emma turned to wine. Victor turned to Amber.

Amber's pregnancy sealed the deal. She was going to give Victor his son back.

Emma was empty.

Amber had a girl.

Emma had nothing. Nothing, but hundreds of nights waking up in a cold sweat to check that Taylor was still breathing. It took her a year to come alive again. Not fully alive—a piece of her got buried with Vincent. More alive than not.

That was long ago. Too long to remember how it used to feel being a whole person. She survived Vincent's death thanks to wine. Emma knew she was an alcoholic. She drank every day. She never drank before work. She never drank and drove. But she loved wine. Wine was always there when she needed it. He never failed to soothe her, warm her, release her inhibitions, dull her pain. Wine made her feel relaxed, smart, and funny. Wine silenced her mother's voice, that voice inside her telling her that she was never good enough, smart enough, successful enough. She never worked hard enough.

Wine allowed the real her—the carefree, funny, life-loving person inside her —to come out. Life would be untenable without it. At work, she was the straight-laced, never-give-up doctor that she was, thanks to coffee. She always did the best she could. At home, she got to be herself. She ditched the bitchy conscience her mother had beaten into her. She felt less empty, less alone, less of a failure. She couldn't let go of her wine. She'd rather let go of her job.

Wine was her lifeline. She shivered thinking about how her life would be without wine. She didn't want to know. She poured the last of the bottle thinking about Boris. Handsome, charming, futureless Boris, who had stopped drinking.

She drank to his health.

71

"**D**r. Steele to Room 3."

Emma was happy to leave Room 7. He didn't want to wait for his results. He wanted a sandwich and a taxi voucher, and he wanted them now. Emma shrugged. *I'll send the caseworker. I hope she can deal with him.*

Her stomach turned as she stepped in Room 3. Nausea became dizziness. She had to lean on the sink to let it pass. She took a deep breath. *Seriously? I knew that life's always there to kick you in the ass, but I didn't know it had such impeccable timing!*

The patient in Room 3 was Boris. Boris, chalk-white, still smiling.

"Hello, Emma. I couldn't stay away."

"I guess not. What happened?"

He smiled. The dried blood around his mouth made him look like Dracula's cousin. "This happened." He pointed at his blood-covered shirt.

"When did this start?" Emma asked, her thoughts racing furiously. She shouldn't be involved with his case. It was too personal. She should ask somebody else to care for him. But the other doctors were busy. And she couldn't leave him. Not now, when he needed her. Not ever.

"Last night. I hoped it would stop. It didn't."

Emma wanted to slap him and hug him, all at the same time.

"What do we have for IV access?"

"An eighteen in the right AC," Judy said. "Working on a second."

"Thanks. I'll put in orders."

She smiled and left the room, biting her lip to keep from crying. She ordered labs, she ordered blood, she paged GI. She went back.

So pale he looked transparent, his blond hair stiff with blood, he smiled when he saw her.

"There's something about you, Emma. It's like the sun comes up when you enter the room. I'm glad I got to tell you this. Don't ever forget it. You are the light."

Emma's throat tightened. She was about to burst out crying. She wondered what the nurses thought. Then his expression changed. His eyes closed, he bent over the side of the bed. A fountain of blood came out of him. Then another.

He leaned back and smiled again.

"I wish we had more time. I wish we met years ago, when I was a man and a lover, not this grotesque caricature of myself, waiting to die. I wish I could be with you then, now, and forever. Would you have married me?"

"Why don't you wait and ask me later?" Emma laughed, her heart in shreds. "I'll have to think about it. I'm a little busy now. I have a patient to care for."

He smiled again, but the light in his eyes was fading.

"There is no later, Emma. This is it. I know it. You know it too."

His eyes closed for a moment, his blood-splattered face calm, too calm. Dead calm.

He opened his eyes and caught Emma's hand.

"I'm glad I met you anyhow. Even now. My life was brighter because of you, Emma, my light."

He let go and bent over again. He bled, and bled, and bled.

I didn't know one human can have so much blood. Five liters? It feels like five hundred.

Years later, when the GI arrived, he glanced at Boris. He frowned.

"What did you give him?"

"Everything. Blood, Protonix, TXA, octreotide. I tubed him for airway protection. I started the massive transfusion protocol."

He shook his head, his mouth a thin line.

Blood spurted out around the tube. Thick and opaque, blood covered the camera, hiding the bleeder. There was no way to find it. There was no way to stop it. They gave units after units of red cells, plasma, and platelets to replace the puddles on the floor. That kept him alive a little longer. But the only way to save him was to stop the bleeding.

They couldn't do it.

Intervention radiology would help, but there was none in-house.

Surgery would help, but the surgeon was in a complicated trauma case.

The second surgeon came. Too late.

Boris died. With him, another piece of Emma's heart. She'd fallen for this brilliant, charming, terminal Russian like she hadn't fallen in a long time.

Her heart heavy, her eyes burning, she called Vera. She didn't want to tell her.

She didn't have to. Vera knew.

She arrived minutes later. She hugged Emma, her eyes bright with tears.

"I'm sorry, Vera. I couldn't save him. I tried."

"I know. There was no saving him, Emma. His chances died when he drank away his liver, years ago. It just took him a while to catch up."

She didn't know how she went through the rest of her shift.

Back home, that night, Emma looked at her wine with fear and longing.

Am I really killing myself?

She didn't know. Even worse, she didn't care. *Who cares if I die? Nobody, really. Vincent is gone. Taylor is pretty much on her own. Victor has Amber. Boris died today.*

She shrugged. *If I kill myself, may as well do it in style.* She picked her most expensive wine: A bottle of 2012 Domaine des Comtes Lafon Meursault 1er Cru 'Les Perrieres... mineral notes that need some encouragement... citrus peel, walnut, and smoke with a long peacock's tail on the finish that reasserts its position as the most propitious premier cru'. *Propitious? I can use that. Today more than ever. Encouragement too. These wine people have a way with words!*

She sniffed it. She lifted the glass to her lips.

Guinness barked. Sitting facing her, staring in her eyes, she barked again.

She lay her head in Emma's lap.

Tears burned Emma's eyes. "You're right. You care."

She poured the wine back, recorked it, and went to bed.

72

ANGEL

I'm disappointed, Emma. I thought we were friends.

For you, I did things I never did for anybody else. I did things nobody else did for you.

I deserve gratitude, but you gave me the cold shoulder instead.

People don't give me the cold shoulder. Not for long!

That morphine was just a little warning. I hope you got the message.

I'll give you another chance. One more.

You should take it. Or you'll be sorry.

Look at Carlos. Don't you think he's sorry?

If he isn't, he should be. And it's not over. His fun is just about to begin.

Take care, Emma! Make good choices!

I'd hate to lose you!

73

That night, Emma spent hours awake in her bed. Without wine to dull her senses and help her through her misery, her heart felt like a huge hole. A void, sucking her. She was the center of pain. Inside her there was nothing but loss.

She felt foolish to be so distraught about losing somebody she had only met a few times. She barely knew Boris. He wasn't really part of her life. But he taught her hope. He told her that she was worthy and beautiful just the way she was. She felt worthy and beautiful with him. Now that he was gone, she was back to feeling useless and empty. She hadn't been able to save him. She did her best to be a good doctor, a good mother, a decent human being. She failed, more often than not.

She got up to pour herself a glass of milk. Guinness followed, so she poured her one too. They sat on the green sofa, looking at the black windows. She needed to refocus. Give her brain a task. Feeling sorry for herself wasn't getting her anywhere. May as well think about something useful.

She thought about Carlos. She remembered Faith saying that he killed those patients, then, driven by remorse, tried to kill himself.

"That's bullshit. That girl is crazy. Batshit crazy. Is she the one who's framing Carlos? She has a motive. She's mad that he ditched her. Let's say it was her. How would she do it?"

Guinness cocked her head, listening with rapt attention.

"Getting his ID and PIN is a piece of cake. They lived together for years. She knows everything about him. She got in the system under his ID and used his PIN to sign that he gave those meds. Still, those meds weren't enough to kill his patient. So she gave him more, then signed as Carlos."

Guinness laid her head back on her paws, her ears up. She kept listening, waiting for her favorite words — walk, ball, frisbee, eat, bacon. Not coming.

"Giving fentanyl to the woman with the broken hip was a piece of cake. Same with the morphine for the patient in Room 15. She looked so peaceful and relaxed when I went to see her. I thought she was doing better. Instead, she was dying, overdosed on morphine. Taylor's patient? That was the easiest. It was Faith's patient too. She knew Carlos had just been there. She pretended to flush her IV, but she pushed the propofol instead. But how did she get the vial?"

Guinness had no idea, and didn't care. By now she was asleep.

"She stole the kit. She waited until Carlos left the room, then stepped in and grabbed it. But Carlos had signed that he discarded it. What if it wasn't Carlos? It was Faith, signed in as Carlos."

It all makes sense. She could do every one of these things. But that doesn't mean that she did. I have no proof. What if I'm wrong? What if I accuse an innocent person, a friend who saved my life, of something so horrific?

In her heart, Emma knew she was right. That had to be the truth, even if she couldn't prove it.

How can I prove it? Follow her. Where? That's silly. I don't know how to do that. Check her house? There may be something there. Drugs, or Carlos's ID. But how do I get in? And what if I get caught? I'll speak to Carlos. He's got to know something.

I could try to catch her in the act. Who would she go for next? Carlos. She hates him. He knows things about her. She already said that Carlos tried to kill himself. He's in the hospital, sick. He's an easy target.

Carlos may be next.

74

A few hours into her shift, and many more left to go, Taylor didn't feel well. She needed a break, but they were busy. She couldn't leave Faith to deal with everything by herself. She was going to push through.

Something to eat, or at least something to drink, would help, but they weren't allowed food or drinks at the desk. The administrators, bless their hearts, didn't like it. What if JCAHO, the hospital accreditation committee, came for an unannounced visit? They could get cited for irregularities. Maybe even fined. Better keep the staff hungry and thirsty.

Taylor got the urine specimen from Room 6. *Urine is always hard to get. You'd think you were asking for gold.* She sent it to the lab, then went to draw blood in Room 5. She got dizzy. She held on to the corner of the desk. She waited a moment, then headed to Room 5.

The next thing she knew, she lay on a stretcher. Worried faces looked down at her.

"Are you OK?" Faith asked.

"Yes, thanks." Taylor tried to get up.

They held her down.

"Stay right there. We need to check you out," Dr. Crump said.

"I'm OK, really. I just got up late and missed breakfast. Then I didn't drink enough."

"Does your neck hurt?"

"No."

"How about your head?"

"It's fine."

They checked her out. Everything looked good.

"You need some fluids," Dr. Crump said. "Faith, let's get an IV and give her a liter."

"No, thanks, I'm OK, I can drink." Taylor hated needles.

"Will you drink a liter?"

"I will."

She did.

An hour later, Dr. Crump stopped by to see her. Eric had dropped in. He ran back to the ICU to his patients.

"Nice young man," Dr. Crump said. "Is he..." He looked at her belly.

Taylor blushed.

"He's my fiancé."

Dr. Crump smiled.

Taylor felt that she owed him more.

"Dr. Crump, regarding our conversation the other day..."

"Yes."

"There's something you need to know." She took a deep breath, forcing herself to say it. "When I became pregnant, my boyfriend at the time and I, we were doing drugs. A lot of drugs."

"I see," Dr. Crump said, his face darkening.

"I haven't done any in months, but I don't know how this has affected the baby. He may not be normal. I thought you should know."

"I know. Still, thanks for telling me, Taylor."

"It wasn't Eric."

Faith came to get her vitals. She attached the blood pressure cuff to her arm.

"What do you mean?" he asked.

"The baby's father. It's not Eric."

"I know," he said. "It's Dr. Umber."

The IV cart crashed with a bang.

75

Carlos opened his eyes. He didn't recognize the place. He couldn't remember how he got there. He looked around. Suspended ceiling. White walls. A window, framing an aspen. That reminded him of something. Something scary.

He tried to sit up. He couldn't.

There was something in his mouth. He tried to take it out.

His right hand didn't move. He tried the left. That didn't move either.

Where am I? he screamed, but no sound came out.

Things beeped. Alarms rang. Somebody came.

A young man. Blond. In scrubs.

"Carlos? I'm Eric, your nurse. You're in the ICU."

Carlos's eyes shouted a question. Eric heard it.

"You were in a car accident. Do you remember?"

Night. Rain. Long road. Running away. Trying to escape. Changing my mind. Coming back. Then the left turn. The aspen.

He blinked yes.

"Good. You're doing much better. You hit your head. You were in a coma for days. You also had chest injuries. You had to have a pericardial window and a chest tube. They took out your spleen because you were bleeding inside. You understand?"

Carlos blinked.

"I'll tell Dr. Roth you're awake. He'll be happy to hear. Now that you're awake, they'll look into extubating you. I'm sure you'd rather have this tube out of your throat."

You don't know how much.

"You've had a lot of visitors," Eric said, showing him a pile of "Get Well Soon" cards. "George, Brenda, Dr. Steele, Taylor, Faith. They all asked me to call them if there's any change."

Carlos frowned and shook his head no.

"You don't want me to call them?"

He shook his head again.

"None of them?"

Carlos blinked.

"Which one? George? Faith? Dr. Steele?"

Blink.

"OK. I'll call her. She was here only this morning."

She came an hour later, dressed in her faded scrubs as usual. The scrubs looked tired. She did too, her hair in a messy knot, her lipstick gone, her eyes bloodshot. She smiled when she saw him awake.

"Carlos! I'm so happy to see you! We were worried we lost you!"

Who's we?

She heard the unspoken question. "The ED folks. George, Brenda, Taylor, me, many others. How are you?"

He shrugged.

"I have something for you."

She took out a notebook and a pen. She sat them on his chest. His hands were loosely tied to stop him from pulling out his ET tube. She untied them.

"There. You can talk now."

He laughed. He heard a gurgle inside his throat. The alarms went crazy. She laughed.

"I guess laughing is alarming, here in the ICU. I'll keep that in mind."

Carlos took the pen. He bent his knees to support the notebook. His stiff, unsteady fingers, scribbled huge drunk letters. Four words covering the whole sheet.

"I didn't do it."

"Do what?"

"Kill them."

"I know. I never thought you did."

Peace spread inside him. There was at least one person who knew he was innocent. He thought they were all against him.

"The question is: Who did? Do you know?"

Carlos closed his eyes, thinking. He opened them and shook his head.

"You don't?"

No.

"Are you sure?"

No.

"You don't really want to know."

Carlos said nothing.

"I think I do. I have a theory, but I have no proof," Emma said. "I need your help."

What?

"Say, just for the sake of the argument, that Faith had something really important to hide. Something that nobody should ever find. Where would she put it?"

Carlos frowned.

"You don't think it's her?"

Tears streamed down his cheeks leaving a shiny path. They dropped, darkening his pillow.

"You don't want it to be her?"

Carlos closed his eyes. He was tired. He didn't want to hear what she had to say. He didn't want to think what she suggested. He was heartbroken.

But she was right. He opened his eyes again, grabbed the notebook, and scribbled: "My stuff."

"Your stuff."

He nodded. If Faith wanted to hide something that nobody would find, and even if they found it, it wouldn't incriminate her, she'd put it in with his stuff. The boxes he failed to recover were still in her spare room. It was a no-brainer to put it there, whatever "it" was. If anyone found it, she'd say he left it there. Faith was a smart girl. She knew damn well how to play her cards.

She'd played him pretty well.

76

———

The following morning Emma went back to work after another sleepless night. She worried about Carlos. She wondered how to keep him safe.

She had asked Eric to keep an eye on him. He stared at her as if she'd lost it.

"Of course. I keep both eyes on him, every shift, all the time."

She had dropped it. *What else can I say? Watch out for his ex? She's an ER nurse. Nice girl. She may try to kill him.*

Back from seeing Room 4, Emma found Faith waiting. She had brought coffee and stopped for a chat. She smiled, friendly as always, but Emma had trouble looking her in the eye.

"How about a spa day tomorrow? I have some coupons."

"Sorry, Faith, I can't do tomorrow."

"The day after tomorrow?"

"No, sorry, I can't. I'm working," she said. She remembered that the schedule was posted in the office.

Faith will see I'm not on it. She'll think I lied. She won't know that I have administrative work. Oh well. It was time to cool it down anyhow.

Faith hugged her and left. Emma shuddered, threw away the coffee she had brought and went back to work. She rechecked her orders once more. She'd

469

gotten paranoid since that monstrous morphine order. She hadn't done it—but maybe a typo? She mis-clicked? She'd tried to order 50 mg of Benadryl or metoprolol and she somehow clicked the wrong box?

Deep inside she knew she hadn't, but her old self-doubt was back. There was no explanation for it. It had to be her fault.

She'd been thinking about Carlos. She replayed their "conversation" in her head over and over. *He still cares about Faith. He's not sure she's the killer.*

Emma wasn't sure either, but she was getting close. She had no better explanation. In the meantime, she watched her back.

She rechecked her orders again: steroids, nebs, Zithromax. Nothing there to kill anyone. She signed them. She logged off and went to see the shoulder pain in Room 9.

He was riding a motorbike when he slipped and ran into a ditch. He fell off and dislocated his shoulder. The deformity was obvious. The left shoulder was muscular and rounded, the right sharply squared. His other hand immobilized his hurt arm. His eyes widened as Emma got close.

He doesn't want me anywhere near that shoulder.

She sat by his side, keeping her hands to herself. He got back to breathing.

"Does anything else hurt? Your neck? Your back?"

"No."

"Did you hit your head? Did you pass out?"

"No."

"Can you move your fingers?"

Still watchful, he did. He looked good other than the shoulder. Emma ordered an X-ray. He looked relieved that she kept her word and didn't touch him. *Good. I need him to work with me to put that shoulder back. If not, I'll have to sedate him. That takes time and resources. Plus, with all this shit going on, I'm afraid to do it.*

"I'll get you something for pain. It will help with the X-ray too." She ordered Toradol, then reluctantly added 50 micrograms of fentanyl. *They'll take the edge off but they can't hurt him.* She checked the order, then rechecked it. She signed it.

She rounded on her patients once more. She checked on them often, since she was always afraid to find them dead. *They're all breathing.* The chest pain with the wonky EKG in Room 5 looked OK. Room 4 was breathing better after nebs.

"Dr. Steele to Room 9."

Her heart quickened. She dashed to Room 9.

The kid was blue. George was bagging, Amy was doing CPR, Judy brought in the code cart.

"What happened?'

The X-ray tech, , a nice brown woman with gray hair, could hardly speak. "I came to take him to X-ray. He didn't look right. He wasn't breathing. I called for help."

"Did he have a pulse?"

She shrugged.

"No pulse," George said, "at least none that I could feel."

Emma wanted to cry. She wanted to scream. She wanted to throw a massive temper tantrum. She didn't.

"Epi. And Narcan," she said.

"How much?"

"Two."

They gave it. Nothing happened.

"Two more."

Nothing.

After the third dose, the pulse came back. His face turned pink. He started breathing.

Emma grabbed his right arm, bent his elbow for leverage and pulled the arm away. She rotated it outwards, extending it above his head. The shoulder fell back into its socket with a thunk. He opened his eyes.

"That was cool," George said.

"Yes!" Amy nodded.

"Yep, but what the hell happened?" Judy asked.

Emma shrugged. She didn't know what happened. The one thing she knew was that she was toast. Another patient who coded for no reason. Her patient. There was no explaining this away. She was already on notice. This was it.

She signed in to check his chart. Her orders stared her in the face: X-ray, Toradol, fentanyl. Just like she wrote them. Except the fentanyl. She had ordered 50 micrograms of fentanyl. She had rechecked it twice. Now, it was 500 micrograms. Ten times the dose she had ordered. Her signature.

How the hell did that happen? Have I really lost it? Am I going crazy?

That evening she took her stuff with her. She didn't think she'd be back for tomorrow's shift.

She was right. The VPM called her that evening.

"What happened?"

She told him.

"Your order?"

"Yes."

"Sorry, Emma. There's nothing I can do. Time for you to take a breather."

She was put on leave while they investigated. They'd let her know.

"I think I've lost it," Emma said. "I really checked that order. I thought I did."

Guinness understood. She was ready to help. She went to the kitchen and came back with the leash.

"How's that supposed to help?" Emma asked.

Guinness went to the door.

"I know what it's for. I'm asking you how do you think it's helpful?"

Guinness barked.

"A little exercise will do you good. Come on! I need to check my email. And I need to pee."

"Oh well. We may as well. I need the exercise, and it helps me think. And I think it's high time I did some thinking." Emma laughed.

Guinness cocked her head.

"You've lost it."

77

———————

In the ICU, Carlos opened his eyes and looked at the window. He could barely make up the aspen, but the fading sky told him that sunrise was just minutes away. It was his last day there. They were going to extubate him today, and move him to a regular floor.

He remembered everything, and a tear ticked his left cheek. He tried to wipe it away, but his hands were still tied. The ties were long enough to let him write on the notebook in his lap, without letting him reach his tube.

The door opened.

Faith smiled. She bent over and kissed his forehead, then pulled a chair and sat.

"How are you doing, honey? I missed you."

Her finger traced the line of his jaw, the curve of his ear, the hollow in his throat.

I must be dreaming,

He turned his head. Door to the left. Window to the right. Machines beeping everywhere. The tube in his throat.

I'm not dreaming. God can't be so cruel as to make me dream my ICU imprisonment. And Faith. This is real.

He wished he could ask. He remembered his notebook.

"Why?" he scribbled.

"I missed you. I came to say good-bye. Remember our good old days? We were in love, you and I. You were the only one in the world for me. I was the only one in the world for you. Nobody else mattered." Her smile melted. Her eyes became ice shards.

"You had to spoil it all by obsessing about Dick."

Me? I spoiled it? By obsessing about Dick?

"Yes. Everything would have been fine if you didn't act out."

Carlos stared.

"Then, when father got sick, you didn't support me. You were so wrapped up in your jealousy that you didn't even hear me ask for help. Remember when I told you I couldn't bear it anymore?"

Her eyes left his face. She stared at her ring, twisting it around her finger.

My ring. She's still wearing it.

"It was horrendous. All that screaming. Day and night. Screaming. No sleep, no food, no peace, nothing but screaming. All the time. It drove me crazy. It inhabited my dreams. It woke me up from sleep. It got my food stuck in my throat. I couldn't bear it anymore."

She pushed her silky golden hair behind her ears and leaned back in her chair. She crossed her legs, showing off the sharp line of her ironed green scrubs. He'd never seen anyone ironing scrubs before Faith.

"I had to do something!"

She stared at him, her eyes open so wide the white showed all around the blue. Carlos shivered.

"His doctor prescribed morphine. He refused it. He wanted to show God he was worthy. I tasted it. It was sweet. I thought about baking him a cake. 'He won't eat enough of it,' I thought. Ice cream? I don't know how to make ice cream. I made Jell-O. Morphine Jell-O. Ever had morphine Jell-O?" She laughed.

"Me neither. I flavored it with almond extract. It smelled like cyanide, but it wasn't. It was morphine. He loved it. I gave him more. He fell asleep. I poured the rest of the morphine down his throat. He choked, but he was too zonked to care."

She smiled.

"He stopped screaming."

Carlos shivered.

"I tried to tell you, but you wouldn't listen. You kept on about Dick. About me dragging you here. Like it mattered! All that mattered was that I stopped the screaming. I helped the nasty old bastard! What a shit he was! With his God, his crappy death, and his nasty attitude toward life. The son of a bitch ruined my life, my mother's life, and his own life, the stupid, bigoted piece of shit. Did you listen? No. You left me."

She sobbed.

"I tried to be understanding. You were upset. Your manliness was threatened. I gave you time."

Carlos broke into a cold sweat.

"Something had changed in me when I came back. All those old people suffering. It hurt. It made me relive the nightmare with Father. I couldn't stand it. Then it dawned on me. I could help. I had some fentanyl left over from Dick. I gave it to her. I freed her from her pain. She was grateful to die. She called me an angel. I had made a difference."

Her eyes returned to him.

"I was happy. I was so happy I gave you a second chance. I took you back in my life. Back in my bed. And you? You ran away. That was stupid."

Her eyes darkened with anger.

"You said I'm disgusting. I disgust you, you, dirty little spic! I had to punish you. I killed your patient. The back pain. Yes, it was me."

"They came after you. I let you take the fall. It would be fun to see you in jail, I thought. What if they put you in with Dick? You two have a lot in common. But then you ran away again, you bastard. You ran away again!"

Faith smiled.

"You didn't make it far. It's good to see you again, honey."

She caressed his cheek and straightened his hair. "You've always had nice hair. You need a shower though. Don't worry, they'll wash you afterwards."

She leaned over to kiss his forehead. Her perfume, chocolate, jasmine, and honey, got through to him, in spite of the tube in his throat.

Sweet and intoxicating.

"It was nice talking to you, but I have to go. I just wanted to say good-bye."

He stared at her, his eyes wide. She understood.

"Oh, I don't know. I'll figure it out. Wherever the wind takes me. But I have to take my baby first."

She opened her red bag.

I gave it to her for Christmas. It was a month's salary, but it was worth it. She loved it.

She took out a syringe. Carlos' heart skipped a beat.

"It won't hurt. It's going to be all right. You won't feel anything, I think."

"Why?"

He couldn't scream. He couldn't run. He couldn't move.

She knew.

She laughed.

"Are you kidding? You didn't think I was going to let you live after telling you? I wouldn't anyhow. But look at the bright side: You got to understand what happened. I bet you racked your brains trying to figure it out. Now you know. You can die happy."

She attached the syringe to his IV. She pulled the plunger to check the line. It flashed red. It worked. She looked him in the eye. She smiled and pushed the plunger in the whole way. She detached the syringe and dropped it in her bag.

Sick with fear, Carlos stared.

"What is it? Surprise."

She waved, then left closing the door.

Carlos waited. Nobody came.

The terror filled him like darkness. He was dying. He knew he was dying. He didn't even get to clear his name. She was going to get away with it, like she did with all the other murders.

I need to tell them I didn't do it. She did it. The notebook.

His heart fluttered. His eyes got blurry, as if he was under water. He blinked to clear them. It didn't work. The world became a blur.

He scribbled blindly on the notepad.

His heart fluttered again, like a bird locked in his chest, trying to fly out.

His brain fogged. He forgot what he was writing.

He forgot he was writing.

He forgot he was…

78

———

Down in the ER, Taylor checked her watch. The end of her shift was getting close. She straightened her back. It hurt. So did her feet, especially at the end of a twelve-hour shift. But, all in all, she was doing better. She hardly ever got sick any more. Just the opposite. She lived thinking about food. She started drooling, imagining a succulent burger. Biting into it with her mouth fully open. Juices running down her chin. She swallowed her saliva. Two more hours. Then she was going to Burger King. She'd get a Double Whopper. With cheese. No. Two. She started drooling again. She took a sip of water, wishing it was a smoothie. She got back to work.

Today she worked with Faith. Faith was nice. Since she'd heard that Umber was her baby's father, she'd been even nicer.

The day Taylor passed out, Faith sat with her.

"It must be hard for you. So young, pregnant and alone."

"I'm not alone."

"But he's…he's not here."

"I have Eric."

"Yes, but it's not the same thing. He's not your baby's father."

"No, but he's a good man and a good friend."

"You're so brave! Do you miss him?"

"Umber?"

"Yes," Faith said.

Taylor didn't miss him. *I hope he rots in hell. I hope his jail mates cut off his dick and make him eat it.* He had lied to her. He had betrayed her. He was the scum of the earth. A newt classified higher than Dr. Dick Umber in Taylor's book.

"No."

"Not even a little bit?"

"No."

Faith smiled and nodded. She didn't believe her, but she was exceptionally kind to Taylor, and Taylor was grateful.

She took another sip of water and went to triage to get the new patient, a large girl with purple hair and a nose-ring. She got grounded after stealing her mother's car, then threatened to kill herself when they took away her phone. Her friend called 911, so Police brought her in for an emergency mental health evaluation.

A few months ago, this could have been me. I'm no longer who I was in February, thank God. Or thank the ED. I look at this girl and I think there, but for the grace of God...

"She needs to change," Faith said.

To stop them from hurting themselves or the staff, mental health patients got changed into blue paper scrubs. Their belongings got inspected down to the last used condom, then locked away.

"I'll get the blues," Taylor said.

The clean utility room was in the back end of the department. She punched in the code, opening the heavy metal door to the cave-like, dim room. Heavy metal shelves sagged under the heavy bundles of blankets, pillows, and scrubs.

She found a large bundle of XXL blues on the bottom shelf. As she bent over to free a top, she heard the door behind her. She managed to get a top, then she struggled to break free a bottom. It wouldn't come. She pulled harder.

She felt a sting in her hip. A hand grabbed her neck and pushed her down.

She fell on top of the scrubs, her arms protecting her belly.

Hands pushed her to the ground. The weight on her back forced her into the floor. She tried to resist. She couldn't.

She rolled.

Faith, her face distorted by hate. Unblinking blue eyes, staring into hers. Feral teeth, gleaming white under rolled lips. Faith, rabid, ready to bite off her throat.

"You, miserable little bitch. You took my man. You took him and threw him away. You bitch." Her voice, low and cracked, held nothing human.

Taylor gasped. Her heart raced. Her brain too. *She lost her mind. What's she talking about? I've never been near Carlos.*

"No, Faith, I've never had anything to do with Carlos, I swear! He just helped me get those labs…"

Faith's rictus reminded her of tetanus. She'd seen pictures. *What did they call it? Risus sardonicus. It wasn't funny.*

Her arms got heavy. Her whole body did.

"You took my man, you lying slut. You took him, but you aren't going to take my baby."

Her baby?

Taylor shuddered. Her whole body went into a spasm. Then again. And again.

She couldn't move.

Faith let her go.

Taylor tried to get up, but she couldn't. Her body was too heavy.

Faith's hand reached for her pocket. She took out a scalpel.

"I'll take my baby now."

She's crazy. Totally crazy.

The scalpel descended toward Taylor's belly.

She's going to cut me to take him out! This is insane. She wanted to tell her that it was too early. The baby couldn't live out of the womb. Not yet.

It's too early. He needs at least another couple of months inside!

She couldn't speak. Her tongue was lead. Her face was heavy. Her arms weighed tons.

She couldn't move. She lay there, watching.

Faith undid the tie of Taylor's scrubs. She pulled up the top. Set free, the pink belly glowed, lighting the dark room. *Grotesque.* She took a bottle of iodine from her pocket. She opened it and splashed it over Taylor's belly, painting the skin brown.

The chemical fumes burned Taylor's eyes, but she couldn't blink. She watched the scalpel come closer. And closer.

Faith smiled. She pushed the scalpel blade open with her thumb.

Taylor's brain sank in darkness. The black engulfed her. Everything was dark, but the blade. The blade caught the meager light, reflecting it. It glistened closer and closer to her skin.

To her womb.

To her baby.

79

That morning, Emma had to force herself to return to the hospital. She hated being there. Now, that she was on leave, there was no place she'd be happier to avoid. Well, maybe the ER. But she had to see Carlos again. She needed his help. Nobody but him could help her expose Faith.

She opened the door to the ICU. The place was in chaos. Carlos's room was a cacophony of alarms, screams, and people rushing. Emma couldn't believe it. *It can't be Carlos. He was doing so well last time I saw him. We worked so hard to keep him alive.*

It was him. Dead.

A sweaty nurse moved aside from doing CPR to make room for another.

"What happened?" Emma asked.

"He coded."

Thanks, Nurse Obvious. What the hell happened?

She waited, hoping they'd bring him back.

They didn't. The intensivist called the code.

"What happened?"

He shrugged. "No idea."

Emma sighed.

There's no talking to Carlos. He can't help me anymore. Unless...

She went back to the room. They were cleaning the room, preparing it for the family.

There's no family. But Faith.

She sat in the chair by the bedside, looking at him. Dead, he looked serene. Emma remembered him alive. His passion. His troubled life. His struggles. His sorrow. His work as a nurse. The patients they saved together.

He had told her that he didn't kill their patients. As if she didn't know. *The notebook...*

"Was there a notebook?" Emma asked his nurse. "I lent it to him. I need it back."

The nurse checked the bag with his belongings: keys, belt, phone, the notebook. He handed the notebook to Emma. She grabbed it and left. She wanted the keys too, but couldn't think of a good excuse to ask for them.

I'll think of something and I'll come back

Shoulders slumped, heart heavy, she dragged herself to the cafeteria. She sat at the remote corner table, sipping on cold burned coffee. She turned the pages. Not many.

His unsteady writing on the first page: "I didn't do it."

Page two: "Kill those people."

She felt sick. *It must be the coffee.* She pushed it aside.

Communications with the nurses: "Too cold." "Turn me." "Chest hurts."

The last page said "Why?"

Emma wondered what that was about. Nurses telling him they were going to keep the tube another day? The doctor was going to be late?

Lower down, on the same page, two thin, shaky, hard-to-see letters.

"Fa..."

That could be anything. He was Catholic. He may have asked for Father O'Meara. Maybe he asked them to call his father. No, he said he never knew his father.

Fa for Faith?

Faith what?

"Faith killed me".

I'm getting ahead of myself here. But it makes sense.

I wish he'd completed that sentence.

80

─────────

Deep in thought, Emma walked slowly to her car. She didn't want to meet anyone, so she had parked far away, in the night lot parking. She didn't want people staring at her, wondering what she did to earn her disgrace. She didn't want them asking questions.

She opened the door but couldn't get in.

Something was pulling her back.

I have to go to the ER.

She slammed the door and headed back, mad at herself.

I have no business going there. I'm on leave. Everybody knows it.

Her cheeks burned with humiliation. She wanted to go home and get drunk. Very drunk. This was not about wine appreciation. This was about numbness and pain relief and forgetting that she was incompetent and useless, like Mother said.

I knew Carlos was in danger. I wanted to protect him. What a good job I did!

Deep inside her head, Mother laughed. *"It's your fault that he died. You fucked up again."*

She wanted to go home and drink. She wanted to forget how she'd fucked up her life. *That's the one good thing about Alzheimer's. You forget a lot of crap. I wish I could forget Mother.*

485

She didn't want to go to the ER but she had to. She didn't know why, but her gut told her to. And her gut never lied.

She punched in the code. The door opened. She wandered in, not knowing where to go. She didn't know what she was there for. People saw her and smiled. She bristled. *They're laughing at me, damn it.*

She went to the desk. Kayla was watching the cameras. a frown on her face. They covered the hallways, the med room and the mental health rooms. Kayla saw Emma and her face lit up.

"Go to the clean utility room."

Emma didn't ask why. She sprinted there and punched the code. The door opened to the gloom inside. Taylor, laying on the floor, staring at the ceiling. Faith, bent over her, holding a scalpel.

That's not how you hold a scalpel. That's how you hold a kitchen knife.

The scalpel descended toward Taylor's chest.

Not the chest. The belly.

Emma leaped forward. Faith turned.

Emma's right foot front-kicked toward the scalpel. She missed.

She got Faith's ribs instead. Faith slumped, but she didn't fall.

Emma's foot hurt. *This is different. Workouts never hurt. But of course, you hit nothing but air. Here, you need to connect.*

Eyes glued to the scalpel, she threw a right hook to Faith's cheek. She connected. A loud crack. Searing pain. *A boxer's fracture? That's going to screw up my work. Fortunately I wasn't working anyhow.*

She prepared for a left hook. She glanced at Taylor.

Why isn't she moving?

She lost sight of the scalpel. Faith slashed her arm. The deep, burning pain scorched her arm to the tip of her fingers, then back. Blood gushed.

My left has never been much good anyhow. I wish I had a weapon. A scalpel, or at least my stethoscope.

She remembered the leash. Guinness had brought it as she left. She thought they were going for a walk. Emma sent her back, rolled the heavy leash and put it in her pocket.

She pulled it out in one smooth move. The heavy metal clip flew like a bird. The air hissed. Faith's face cracked. She dropped the scalpel.

Her hand covering her face, she pivoted. Her right foot side-kicked Emma's knee from under her. The knee gave. Emma fell to the ground.

Faith bent over, picked up the scalpel, and went back to Taylor.

Emma rolled toward them. Faith ignored her. Bent over Taylor, eyes glued to her belly, she brought the scalpel to the skin. Her hand shook. She steadied it with the other.

The scalpel touched Taylor's navel.

Emma grabbed the metal linen shelf above them, and pulled on it with all her strength.

The shelf leaned, shedding heavy bundles of blankets. One fell on Faith's shoulder. She dropped the scalpel. She picked it up again.

Emma pulled harder. The shelf groaned, teetered, then crashed over Faith's back. Faith screamed.

The door opened. George, his face darker than the night. Faith saw him.

She glanced at Taylor, lying on the ground. She dropped her scalpel and ran out past him.

George's eyes followed her. He looked at Emma, kneeling, covered in blood. Three feet away, Taylor, blue and motionless, lying on the floor.

He let Faith go.

81

———————

Emma crawled toward Taylor.

"Taylor," she heaved.

"She isn't breathing," George said.

"Pulse?"

"Yes."

Emma bent over Taylor and started mouth to mouth. George called the code.

I never kissed her on the mouth. Not even when she was a child.

She kneeled by Taylor's head and extended her neck to straighten her airway. *The only one I kissed that way was Vincent. But he was stiff.*

Taylor's body was flaccid, her blue face relaxed. Her open green eyes stared into nowhere. *Succinylcholine. Or vecuronium. Or roc. The bitch paralyzed her, and let her die.* Emma breathed another breath into Taylor's chest. She didn't have time to be angry. Not yet.

She needs oxygen. She's pregnant. They desaturate like crazy. Then the heart stops.

Another breath. *The baby. If she's not breathing, he's got no oxygen either.*

I won't think about this. Not now. Breath in, breath out, breath in...

"I got her, Emma," George said.

He had the mask with the blue bag attached.

Emma grabbed the mask and placed it on Taylor's face.

George started bagging.

The stretcher came. The people too.

A dozen hands lifted Taylor on the stretcher. George kept on bagging. Brenda pushed the stretcher to Room 3.

Emma tried to stand up. She couldn't. Her left knee gave.

Somebody pulled her up.

Ann.

"We got her, Emma."

Emma limped behind the stretcher to Room 3. She leaned against the sink, staying out of the way, watching.

"She has no muscle tone. She must have given her a paralytic," Emma said.

Ann nodded. "Let's intubate."

George lifted the mask. Ann grabbed the laryngoscope.

The monitor stopped beeping.

The heart had stopped.

Ann froze.

"Start CPR." Ann, her face heavy as lead, stared at the swollen belly.

She's thinking about a perimortem C-section. You have four minutes to cut a baby out of a dying mother. If she does it, they may die. If she doesn't, they may die.

Ann's eyes found Emma's, burning the question into her.

"Don't. It's too early. The baby isn't viable yet. Ventilate her. That's what she needs."

Ann nodded. She put the laryngoscope aside. They ventilated.

One hundred percent oxygen.

Epi.

Fifteen seconds or an eternity later, the beeping restarted.

She's back.

The baby? Who knows?

At least she's alive.

82

A lifetime later, Emma made it home. She struggled to open the door. Her left arm hurt. Her right hand too.

Everything hurts. But it's good to be home. It's good to be alive.

Her right hand was broken. A boxer's fracture. The 5th metacarpal, the tiny bone connecting her wrist to her pinky, was gone. Her cast went from her fingers to below her elbow. The 5-inch gash on her left arm needed 12 staples. Kurt wanted to put in stitches, but she didn't have the patience. She'd been away from home for too long, while Guinness was locked in the house.

And she needed wine.

Taylor was doing well. Physically. The paralytic wore off. She was breathing on her own. They extubated her. Her psyche? That was a different matter.

This day will haunt her forever. Paralyzed, watching an unhinged killer cutting your baby out of you? That's the stuff of horror movies.

Emma shivered. She hated horror movies. Life was horror enough.

Victor came to check on Taylor. Eric sat with her. The OB came to check on the baby. He looked all right. They kept her overnight to monitor them. Eric stayed with her.

Emma had a rough time making it to her car, with a cast on one arm, staples in the other, and a mangled knee. Victor offered to help, but she declined. She didn't need another complication. The drive home was a nightmare, but she made it. She closed the garage door and went inside. Guinness was waiting.

She'll jump out of her skin. She's been locked in for hours.

She didn't. She was polite and cautious. She sniffed every inch of her as if she read a small print newspaper.

What's she making of all these smells? Of the way I look? A cast on my right hand, a bandage on my left arm. I'm covered in blood. Mostly my own. Who am I kidding? It's all my own. I'm lucky if I gave her a bruise.

Emma let her out. She gave her water. She fed her dinner.

Guinness didn't want it. She lay by the door, pretending to be asleep, but her ears were up and the hair on her neck wasn't sleeping.

She's waiting for something? Taylor! That's what she's waiting for.

"She's not coming home tonight. She'll stay at the hospital, with Eric."

Guinness thumped her tail once. "OK." She went back to waiting.

"You understand, Guinness? She's not coming tonight."

She doesn't. She's just a dog, for God's sake. German, to boot. How would she understand? She's worried about Taylor. Nothing I can do. Unless...

Emma went to Taylor's room and got her sleep T-shirt. XXL, black, a red jaguar on the chest. She offered it to Guinness.

Guinness glanced at it, then went back to the door. Her long black nose on her paws, she was waiting.

"Sorry, Guinness. I can't walk you tonight. I ran out of hands. Tomorrow maybe, after Motrin."

Emma checked the wine rack. She hadn't had a glass since Boris died. That felt like a lifetime ago.

She needed wine tonight.

She needed it to clean her inside. To escape the horror, dirt, and suffering she'd been through today. In a life of daily horrors, this day took the cake.

Carlos died. He was a good man. He deserved better. He died because of this psychotic bitch.

Taylor's heart stopped in front of Emma's eyes. As for her baby? Nobody knew.

I should have destroyed Faith long ago. I knew it was her. She was behind those patient deaths. I knew it for a while. She sabotaged my career, killed half a dozen people, and almost killed Taylor, while I sat and watched. And I did nothing. Why? Because I wasn't sure.

Emma learned early that she was incompetent and useless. So, in spite of common sense, logic, and evidence, she doubted her own judgment. She couldn't have been smarter than all the others. Mike, the VPM, even Carlos—all said she was wrong.

I thought they knew better.

Instead of doing something, she'd looked for more proof. Now she had it.

It was too late. Carlos was dead, Taylor had been close. Faith had escaped. And Emma was damaged. Seriously damaged.

Wine would help her through this. Just one bottle. She needed it today.

She examined bottle after bottle, prolonging the foreplay. She found what she was looking for.

Carménère. Not subtle, like a punch in the gut isn't subtle. Dark, dry, and intense with edges you'll never find in an Australian Shiraz or a Californian pinot noir. *Pinot Noir! What an inaptly named, watered-down excuse for a red wine.*

She took a sip. She rinsed her mouth with it, exorcising the evil she'd breathed in through the day. She swallowed. She took another. The warmth entered her. It spread through her body, loving her. The wine took away the pain. It blunted the remorse. It blurred the worry.

Before too long, the bottle was empty, and the pain was gone.

I'll deal with everything tomorrow.

She called Guinness. The dog didn't come. She glanced at Emma, then thumped her tail against the floor. She went back to watching the door.

A little miffed, Emma shrugged and closed the door. *You want to sleep in the kitchen, there you go. Have at it.*

She went to her bedroom. She lay down.

Her back was grateful.

She fell asleep.

83

She woke up bathed in cold sweat. She sat up, her heart racing, and stared into the darkness. *It's nothing. A nightmare. No wonder, with the day I had. Plus the wine.*

The house was dark and quiet. But there was something. She shivered.

Something evil.

A noise, almost too soft to hear. In Taylor's bedroom.

Mice?

She stood up. With soundless soft steps, she tiptoed to Taylor's room. The door was cracked open.

She wished she had a weapon. Anything. She had nothing. Her stethoscope was in her bag, on Victor's chair. Same with her scalpel. And her pepper spray.

That's silly. It's probably nothing. I'm just paranoid.

She stepped softly inside the darkness to Taylor's room.

The curtains fluttered in the night breeze.

Taylor left the windows open. That's it. The breeze moved the curtains and the windows. There I am, all bent out of shape for nothing.

She went to close the window.

An arm closed around her throat, choking her.

She bent forward to escape.

The arm's owner bent with her, laughing softly in her ear. That laughter froze her heart.

She wanted to scream. She couldn't. She could barely breathe. She thumped her bare foot to make noise. It hurt. The carpet hushed the sound.

"Where is she?" a soft voice asked in her right ear.

Emma couldn't answer if she wanted to. Not enough air through her vocal cords to speak. She didn't know what this was all about.

That's bullshit. Of course I know. It's Faith. She's come for Taylor's baby.

Police had come to the ED. They took statements from everybody. Kayla, who watched the cameras and saw Taylor heading to the utility room, then Faith following her. Emma, who'd fought her. George, who was there when she ran away.

Faith had attacked Taylor, but she was gone. They couldn't find her.

Emma had.

I wish I hadn't.

With all her strength, she pushed the arm away. She took a gulp of air. She screamed.

Guinness heard. She barked, clawing at the kitchen door.

I locked her in.

Someone may hear. Maybe.

The arm tightened again and cut her breath. It choked her scream. It made her dizzy.

Something sharp pierced Emma's throat below her right ear.

A knife. If it was a scalpel, it would be through the carotid by now. Even so, if I move, that knife will go through. She stilled.

"Where is she, I asked?"

No point in lying. She'll figure it out by herself.

"At the hospital."

"Why?"

"They're making sure your baby is OK."

A sigh warmed Emma's ear. The arm around her throat softened.

"When's she coming out?"

"Tomorrow, if the baby's OK."

"My baby."

"Tomorrow, if your baby is OK."

"I'll call him Dick."

Good name. It fits right in.

"What if it's a girl?"

The knife went in a little deeper.

"It's not a girl. My baby is a boy. You get it?"

Emma did.

"You're not a bad woman, Emma. You're even a good doctor. I learned a lot from you. Remember how you told us: Don't give insulin without glucose if they're euglycemic, or you'll kill them? Don't give opiates and benzos at the same time? Never give hypertonic saline unless they're actively seizing or in a coma?"

Emma nodded.

The arm around her neck softened.

"That's how I learned. They don't teach you how to kill people in nursing school. You learn that from the doctors. I learned from you."

How ironic.

Guinness's whining faded. *She went back to bed. I shouldn't have closed that kitchen door.*

"You were kind to me, when I was in trouble. I appreciate that. I'll be kind to you."

Kind to me?

Faith's weight drained Emma's strength. She could barely stand under their combined weight.

"I'll even let you say good-bye. Sit in that rocking chair."

Faith led her to Taylor's orange rocking chair and pushed her.

Emma fell in. She took a deep breath.

Good news: I can breathe. I can even scream. Bad news: Nobody will hear me. Escaping that chair is a challenge on a good day. Today isn't one of those.

She started circular breathing to slow down her heart. *One in—one hold—one out. Repeat.*

To escape the rocker, she had to push herself up on both hands. She didn't have two working hands. Not even one. Faith would cut her before she got up.

That's not going to happen.

Faith grabbed Taylor's leather-bound journal from the nightstand and threw it in Emma's lap. She stepped back.

She's out of reach. She has a knife.

Emma looked at the open window.

Too far.

Faith leaned against the opposite wall.

Too far.

Emma picked up Taylor's purple pen and started writing. A few seconds later she stopped and looked up.

"Did you kill Carlos?"

"Of course."

"Why?"

"He was suffering. He was a liability. I'm here to help people. I didn't want him to suffer. I didn't want him to tell anyone about me, either."

"What was there to tell?"

"Oh, you're so smart, Emma, aren't you? Trying to keep me talking. Hoping to find a way out. Not today. You have five minutes to finish. Five. That's five more than I gave Carlos. He didn't deserve them. He betrayed me. Time and time again. You were good to me. That's why I'm nice to you."

I hate to think how this would go if I wasn't.

"If I was nice to you, why kill me, Faith?"

"I'm not Faith. I'm the Angel. The Angel of Death. I'm here to help you."

"How does that help me, Angel?"

"It ends your suffering. You're old. You're fat. Your husband left you. Your daughter hates you. You're all alone. Who wants to live like that? What do you have to live for? Work? They hate you there too. I'm only trying to help you out."

This is déjà vu, all over again. Just like Mother. The worst is that it's true. She forgot that I'm an alcoholic. That would round it up nicely.

"That's generous of you, Angel. Don't you think you should ask me what I want, though?"

"No. People don't know what's good for them. They're too stupid."

Emma nodded. She'd often thought the same. She didn't take over though, like Faith was. Angel, that is.

"You have one minute left," Angel said, shifting her weight from one foot to the other. Leaning against the opposite wall, she was too far for Emma to reach.

"Then what?" Emma asked.

"I'm going to help you pass. I'll open the rainbow bridge for you. You'll be with those you love."

I'm not so sure. All those I love, except for Vincent, are still alive.

"It's time."

Faith stepped forward. Her knife, a sleek eight-inch blade, thin enough to fillet fish, was ready.

"Nice knife."

"Yes, isn't it? I love it. It's sharp, light, and smooth."

"I'd love it for cooking. Do you cook?"

"Not really, except for toast and eggs. Ready?"

"I don't know. How should I get ready?"

Angel got angry. "You've had your time. I was generous. It's over."

"Then what?" asked Emma.

Angel came closer, bending over to pick up the journal, her knife ready.

Emma rocked back and lifted her legs. She kicked as hard as she could, just under Angel's knees. Angel fell forward over Emma, knife first. Emma lifted her right arm to protect her throat. The knife came forward, all of Angel's weight behind it, piercing Emma's arm. Emma twisted. Loud as a gunshot, the knife broke, stuck in Emma's cast.

Emma rolled left with the rocker. She fell on the floor. She rolled again.

Angel rolled toward her, lifting the broken knife.

Emma tried to sit up.

Her left arm gave. She fell back.

Angel fell over her.

"I told you to be good. I was nice to you. You had to be the smart one. Again. It could have been easy for us both. One stab and done. Now it's going to hurt. It's your fault." She lifted her right arm with the broken knife and lowered it onto Emma's chest.

Blood spurted. The pain blinded her. The knife stopped in the ribs.

Emma tried to push her away. She couldn't.

She twisted and rolled over to her left, catching Angel under her.

She placed her cast over Angel's throat and pressed. Hard. With all her weight.

Angel's beautiful face turned purple.

The broken knife hit Emma's back. Searing pain took her breath away.

She kept the pressure on Angel's throat. Angel groaned.

The knife twisted between Emma's ribs, the broken tip aiming for her lungs.

She knew exactly when it got there. The pain exploded inside her chest like fireworks, blinding her. Her breath failed. Her strength vanished. Like a butterfly somebody stepped on, she shrunk, coiling into herself.

She was done. She wished she'd been better. A better person, a better doctor, a better mother. Too late. She felt sorry for all the things she failed to do. *Broken glass. Far away.*

Angel rolled over her, smiling.

"You had to make it hard, didn't you! You always make it hard for yourself. What's the good in that?" She lifted the broken knife once more. She lowered it into Emma's chest.

The ribs stopped it from reaching the heart.

She threw it down. She grabbed Emma's throat. Her thumbs pressed on the carotids.

Emma's brain darkened.

This is it. I'm gone.

The pain faded into darkness just as the window crashed open.

The pressure on her throat released. She inhaled. Her brain cleared.

Angel screamed.

Emma opened her eyes.

Guinness, dragging Angel off her by her throat.

Limp as a rag doll, Angel made no sound.

Neither did Guinness.

"Let her go! Let her go!" Emma managed, her voice so strangled she couldn't understand herself.

Guinness did.

She dropped Angel at Emma's feet like she dropped the frisbee.

Guinness looked into Emma's eyes. She licked her face.

"I told you something was wrong. You shouldn't have closed the kitchen door."

Emma's tears ran down her cheeks.

Guinness took care of them.

84

The ambulance got there first. The EMTs took in the scene. The first one went to Angel, lying motionless on the floor. The tall one grabbed his radio to ask for reinforcements.

He kneeled in front of Emma. He frowned.

"Dr. Steele?"

"Hi, Joe," she said, her voice like a coffee grinder.

His partner, Roy, was checking Angel. He heard and turned around. He recognized her. He gasped.

Their horrified faces made her laugh. That hurt.

I must look a sight. Bloody, cut, barely breathing. Nothing like the Dr. Steele they know. I can't look human, in fact. I don't feel human, either. But I'm alive. Thanks to you, my friend. She put her good hand on Guinness's head, lying on her thigh. The dog hadn't moved since she'd dropped Angel. Emma scratched behind her ears.

Angel had gone to the angels.

Don't think so. She was playing for the other team, poor soul.

Police arrived. The first policeman, a heavyset man she'd never met, had questions. Emma had trouble answering. She had trouble speaking, in fact. Her

501

lungs were not behaving. Everything hurt, from the top of her head to her toes. She could hardly breathe.

"She needs to go to the hospital. Now," Joe said.

The policeman hesitated.

The door flew open. Victor burst in.

"I thought it was a mistake! They said they dispatched an ambulance to this address. I was sure it was a mistake!" He kneeled in front of her, arms open to hug her. He looked at her battered body and didn't dare hold her. He stroked her cheek.

"Emma!" he sobbed.

"She needs to go, Dr. Storm," Joe said.

Victor stepped back.

The door opened. Zagarian burst in.

"Emma! Are you all right? I heard the radio. They said it was a crime scene! I knew it was a mistake!"

She hadn't seen him in weeks. Months ago, they were getting close; then Emma got cold feet and stopped returning his calls. He stopped calling.

Now there he was, impeccable as ever. His perfect gray suit made Victor look shabby in his jeans and dog-chewed jacket.

"I'm fine, thank you," Emma said, even though she was anything but.

"Really?"

She shrugged. The pain in her back made her groan.

"I see." He walked to Angel. He kneeled and felt her neck for a pulse. None.

"An unwelcome visitor, I take it?"

"It's a long story."

Joe was losing his patience.

"We need to take her to the hospital. Now."

"We'll block the door when we're done," the policeman said. "This is a crime scene, we need to work it up."

Emma nodded. The EMTs lifted her on the stretcher. Guinness stood, ready to follow.

"You can't come, sweetheart. I'm sorry. Taylor will be back tomorrow."

"I'll take care of her," Victor said, bending over to kiss Emma's forehead as he patted Guinness's head.

"Thanks."

The officer came closer. "The dog comes with us."

Victor turned, facing him. "Don't touch the dog."

"This dog has killed a person. He's going with us."

"Don't touch the dog. She saved my wife's life."

Moving casually, Zagarian came closer.

"She's not your wife. Not anymore."

Victor looked at him. They'd known each other since February. They worked together to put away a killer, letting Emma off the hook. They stared at each other.

Victor stepped back.

"I'll take the dog."

Zagarian nodded.

"Her name is Guinness," Emma said, as they wheeled her out.

85

Two days later, when she made it home, Taylor looked around in disbelief. Her bedroom looked like a war zone.

Why?

She came for the baby.

That crazy woman came to take her baby. She failed to cut it out of her in the utility room, so she came back looking for her.

Taylor shivered. Eric put his arm around her shoulders, pulling her closer. His touch gave her strength.

That was the worst day of my life.

She had thought that many times before—when her dad left, when she decided to abort, when she found out that Dick had betrayed her, when Eric left.

Nothing like this.

Lying down, unable to move, watching that woman bring a scalpel to her baby.

Nothing. The terror of those moments would follow her to her grave and beyond.

Knowing she was dying wasn't fun. Seeing her baby getting killed was beyond any badness she could imagine.

The last thing she saw, before her mind faded to black, was her mother. Her mother was there. She was going to put it right.

As always, she had.

She woke up thinking about the baby. Was it alive? She welcomed the OB with her ultrasound machine. They looked at the baby together. The heart was beating. The baby moved.

It was alive.

"Does it look normal?" Taylor asked.

The OB doc took a long time. "Two arms. Two legs. Hands. Feet. Spine. Brain. To the best that I can say right now, it looks OK. We should test for genetic anomalies. We'll have another look in a week. For now, I don't see anything bad."

Taylor cried and cried. The OB couldn't understand why.

Eric cried with her.

It was good to be home. With Emma in the hospital, Taylor had the house to herself. The mess that the house was. She had to get it together. Somehow.

What would Mother do?

"OK. Let's get it together. Eric, you go shopping. We need something to eat. I'll clean."

"I don't want to leave you alone."

Guinness barked.

"Alone? What are you talking about? I'm right here!"

86

———————

The hospital drove Emma crazy. She drove everybody crazy too. She climbed out of bed to fix the back support.

A missing screw. She replaced it with a paper clip.

The door opened.

"If you were a dog, you'd be a border collie," Victor said, helping her out from under the bed and handing her an armful of flowers. "You always need something to run after."

Emma smiled.

"If you were a dog, you'd be a Labrador. You haven't met a sofa you didn't like."

Victor laughed and sat in the chair by the bed.

"Touché. We should talk to the administrators about the furniture. I could do with a sofa right here. How are you?"

"I'm OK. They say they'll let me go tomorrow."

"They must be exhausted after caring for you."

"They are. Like all doctors, I make an awful patient. How are you?"

"I'm OK. Taylor's good too. She told me to tell you: 'Don't worry, everything is under control.'"

Emma shuddered.

"I know. I looked around; it looked OK though."

"Guinness?"

"She took her back. I wanted to keep her, but she said absolutely not."

"For someone who didn't want a dog, she surely changed her mind."

Victor laughed. "She didn't not want a dog. She wanted you to have more than a dog."

"I know."

Victor gave her a long look. "And?"

Emma smiled. "How's Amber?'

Victor sighed. "She's good. Busy as usual with the girls and work and her friends and…"

"She thinks you're too busy to spend time with her."

"Really? What makes you think so?"

"She told me. She'd like more time with you. You're always busy. She worries there may be something else happening. Somebody else."

Victor gave her a speculative look.

Emma recognized it, even though she hadn't seen it in ten years. It was the signal for foreplay. She laughed.

"Oh no. Don't even think about it."

He laughed. *Sort of.*

"You sound like my mother."

"That's a compliment!"

"She's sending her love. She said don't forget what you discussed, it still stands."

Emma laughed. "I won't."

"So…"

"No. Give Amber my regards."

Victor bent over to kiss her.

The door opened.

A large bouquet of yellow roses came in, followed by Zagarian.

The men measured each other.

"Come in," Emma said. "Victor was just leaving."

Victor nodded and left. Slowly.

Zagarian took his seat.

"How are you?"

"OK. They're letting me go tomorrow. You?"

"I'm good."

He crossed his legs. He realized he forgot to give her the roses. He lay them on top of her. Emma laughed.

It's good I'm not dead, but if I was, this would make a good start...

He rubbed his chin. "You were right. All the boxes checked. She did murder her father. He was full of morphine. Odd for somebody who refused pain medications. Carlos's potassium was 11. It was normal only that morning. She must have injected him with potassium. His heart stopped. She couldn't use fentanyl, since he was already on the vent. Stopping his breathing wouldn't have done much."

"How about my orders?"

"She logged in the system under your name. For a few bucks, you can buy an RFID copier on Amazon. She copied your ID. That allowed her to document under your signature. Same with Carlos."

Emma shivered.

Zagarian continued: "By the way, we checked New Hampshire. She was involved with Umber. She got into a fight with another nurse, Joy. Joy was fired. Faith followed Umber here. She also dragged Carlos. He found out and ditched her. The rest you know."

Emma nodded.

"What a tortured mind. She said her men refused to have her children. When she found out Taylor's baby 's father was Umber, she lost it. She thought Taylor was having her baby. She decided to take it back."

"That's the most horrific story I've ever heard." Zagarian shuddered. "Thank God you were there."

"Yep," Emma said. She looked at the cast on her right hand, the bandage on her left arm, the bandage over her left chest, where the chest tube used to be. She looked like leftovers.

"Thank God I was there."

She looked him in the eye and asked: "Guinness?"

He smiled. "She's OK. We'll call it 'justifiable use of force in self-defense.'"

Emma sighed. "Thanks!"

"Thank her. Emma, I have two tickets to a jazz concert next Saturday. Want to go?"

"I..."

The door opened. A large bouquet of white roses came in, followed shortly by Dr. Roth.

"May I come in?"

Emma laughed.

I wonder if I'd get that many flowers for my funeral. Probably not. Just as well I'm not dead then.

87

GUINNESS

*S*he's back. She smells awful. Like hospital crap, and disinfectants, and iodine, and sickness. But... there's something.

I check her left pocket. I stick my nose in it.

She laughs. She takes out a strip of bacon.

"There. I thought you'd like that better than flowers."

Not bad for hospital food. Salty and smoky. Not crispy. Got soggy with sitting in the pocket and whatnot. No crunch, but hey—two out of three ain't bad. I inhale it. More?

No more.

The girl comes out of her bedroom. She looks at her. Her eyes start tearing.

I growl.

"She looks like shit, I know, but you don't need to tell her!"

She sobs.

"Come on, girl! She's home! She's alive! She brought bacon!"

She stares at Shaman, her shoulders slumped, her belly sticking out.

Shaman sits up straight. She hurts. I smell it. There's a freeze where tears should be. She doesn't do tears, this one. I won't tell.

"Hi Taylor. How are you?"

"I'm OK. You?"

"I'm good. Thanks."

The girl turns around and leaves the room. Like, really?

Shaman slumps. No more need to save face. Nobody here but me.

She looks at me. I put my head on her thigh. She tries to scratch me with her right hand. It's not working. The cast is in the way. The left is better.

"Thank you, Guinness," *she says.*

I don't know what to say. I just did my job. That's what I do. I lick her hand to tell her it's OK. I look up. Her eyes are suspiciously shiny. Not tears, no, she doesn't do that. I get up and lick them. She laughs. Good noise. I like that.

I lay next to her, enjoying the scratching. She's a good scratcher! No, scratch that! She's a great scratcher. Maybe the best I've ever...

The door opens. The girl's back.

"I got this for you." *She brings a bottle.*

Shaman reads. "Brunello de Montalcino..."

Her face drops. Tears start running down her cheeks. I get up to lick them. It's embarrassing. It's only wine, people! If it's no good, just open another bottle!

The girl opens the bottle. She pours a glass. She hands it to Shaman. The girl lifts the bottle. Shaman lifts her glass. They knock.

Shaman takes a sip. She swishes it around like she's brushing her teeth. She swallows it and smiles.

"That's beautiful, Taylor. Really lovely. Thank you."

"Thank you. I wouldn't be here if it wasn't for you."

Shaman shrugs.

"We already knew that..."

"I'm serious. Thank you for saving my life. Even more, thank you for saving my baby."

"It's my job, Taylor. I'm here for you." *She smiles.* "It was also my pleasure. Well, sort of..."

She takes another sip.

"How did you choose this wine? It's spectacular."

Taylor smiles. "I asked Father to get it for you."

"Oh."

"No worries. He told me. I also spoke to Grandma."

"What did he tell you?"

"He said that we all sleep in our beds the way we made them. He made his wrong, but he'll sleep in it."

"Good."

"What will you do, Mom?

"Frankly, I have no idea. But that's kind of fun for a change. And you? What will you do?"

"The baby seems all right."

"Good."

"Dr. Crump said they'd be happy to have it."

"Yes."

"Eric said it was up to me."

"I see."

"What do you say?"

"I say wait and see. You've grown like crazy over the last few months. There's no hurry to make a decision. Wait and see what feels right when the time comes."

"That's what I was thinking."

"So you 're going to change your mind, since I've said the same thing?"

"Maybe. Have we ever agreed before?"

"Not that I recall."

I bark.

"Enough with this shit. Let's go for a walk."

They stare at me and laugh.

"Well, maybe about this dog," *Taylor says.*

"You didn't want a dog."

"I didn't. But I want this one."

"You can't have her. She's mine."

I bark.

"Get on with it, will you people? I need to shit!"

"She disagrees. As far as she's concerned, we're hers."

POISON

AN ER THRILLER

PROLOGUE

Ben didn't feel right. He hadn't eaten in days. He'd been so sick he'd been living in the bathroom.

A wave of nausea overtook him. He retched in the sink while emptying himself in the toilet. Cold sweat, smelling like fear, poured out of him. The smell made him sick, and he retched again. This time there was nothing but a little blood.

A spear of pain pierced him, taking his breath away. He tried to stand, but his weakness was stronger than he was. He dropped on the bathroom floor, his pants around his ankles. He lay there, panting softly to escape the pain.

If only he could get his phone. He'd left it in the bedroom. He rolled on his belly to crawl there, but the pain exploded in him like a grenade. Something inside him had broken. *That's how the samurai must have felt when they carved into their belly with their sword*, he thought.

He stuck his hands in his pockets, looking for something to throw and break the window. The neighbors may hear and come to his help. Though none of them had spoken to him since Mia had left with the twins. *They were all on her side, the assholes.*

There was nothing in the pockets but his wallet. And a folded piece of hospital stationery. On it, in red capital letters: #1. ASSHOLES BEHAVE.

He didn't know what that was. Nor did he care. Another wave of nausea hit him. He retched, and the pain blew his mind away. He passed out. He never saw the river of dark blood flowing out of him.

Dirty, smelly, and exposed, he died the undignified death he had earned.

1

———————

I t was just another ordinary day in the Venice ER. Under the harsh lights, stretchers lined the hallways, patients waited to be seen, staff hustled, phones rang, monitors beeped, and air conditioners worked overtime. Bleach fumes fought with the smell of blood and body fluids and lost.

Dr. Emma Steele, the ED Medical Director, was too used to it all to take notice. She only noticed the things that were out of the ordinary. Sitting at her desk, she was busy trying to make sense of the certified letter she'd just received. She started reading it for the third time.

"We regret to inform you that pursuant to a complaint to the State of New York Board of Professional Medical Conduct, the New York State Professional Misconduct Enforcement Committee has opened an investigation into your medical practice. The Committee will endeavor to determine whether you committed professional misconduct by practicing medicine with negligence on more than one occasion, gross negligence, and incompetence..." *Are you fucking kidding me?*

She checked the envelope, making sure the letter was addressed to her. It was. She started over again.

The piercing call of the ER speakers broke her concentration.

"Dr. Steele to Triage for a signal 600."

She looked up.

"Me?"

Judy, the charge nurse, nodded. "Yes. It's a kid. A pediatric code."

Emma stood up so fast that her chair rolled back.

"A pediatric code? Seriously? Isn't it great to get advance notice?" Her heart pumping, her throat dry, she rushed to triage.

Judy shrugged. "Sorry, I just found out…"

"What?"

"That your team is getting the code."

Emma looked her in the eye. Judy looked away.

Emma understood. *It wasn't supposed to be mine, but she switched. She gave me the code in exchange for some sprained ankle she gave Burt. She doesn't think he can handle it. What a deal. I hate pediatric codes.*

So did everybody else. For the ED folks, from docs to environmental workers, there was nothing worse. A kid's life depended on one moment's thinking. It only took one mistake. But somebody had to take it, and today was Emma's turn.

The triage was packed. Patients and families clustered on the stretchers like grapes. Emma zipped between chairs, people, and IV carts to grab the heavy black handset of the radio phone. She pushed the TALK button.

"MD 107."

"MD 107, we're heading to your facility with an eleven-month-old boy. No breathing, no pulse. We established an IO in the left tibia, but we were unable to intubate. We gave epi x 2 with no result. Our ETA is 10 minutes. Do you have any orders?"

"You have the mother?"

"Negative. The mother wasn't home. But the father's here."

"Any history?"

"The kid rolled over from the changing table and fell."

"That's it?"

"Yes."

"OK. Please find out whatever else you can. It will save us time when you arrive."

She hung up. Listening in behind her, Judy kept her eyes cast down, looking as guilty as Guinness when she got caught rummaging through the garbage. *She's saddled me with this disaster. And she knows that I know.*

Emma shrugged. There was no point in holding a grudge. As always, Judy had done the best she could for the patient. She sighed and put her arm around Judy's shoulders, walking her back to the ED.

"Sorry, Emma, I…"

"I know, I know. What room?"

"I got Room 3."

Room 3, their best trauma room, was full of scrubs hustling to get ready for the code. Emma took charge.

"Let's get the Broselow tape. We need respiratory and the pediatrician. Get the pediatric code cart open. Call Sal. Tell him it's an eleven-month-old trauma."

Judy nodded and left. Emma checked her watch.

I have time to go to the bathroom. I shouldn't start this on a full bladder. Emma washed her hands, glancing at the ghostlike face in the mirror. She got her "Carmenere kiss" lipstick from her scrubs pocket and put some on for the morale, then walked out without checking it the mirror. She hoped she didn't look like the Joker, but if she did, who cared? Nobody. Not even her. They all only cared about what she was able to do.

Back in Room 3, she rechecked the equipment. The suction worked. She asked the RT, the respiratory therapist, to change the Yankauer, the plastic suction wand, to the pediatric one. She checked to ensure they had a pediatric mask and two oxygen ports ready.

She grabbed the Broselow tape—a long paper ribbon with colored markings at specific lengths. Each color corresponded to the size of a child of a particular age, listing the correct drug dosage to prevent medication errors. Emma stapled the tape to the bed to keep it from moving, then folded it at the eleven months mark. She glanced at the dosages for the essential drugs: epinephrine, fluids, platelets, red cells. She was going to forget them before the child arrived, but it made her feel better. She took a couple of controlled deep breaths to slow down her heart, then assessed her team. *Brenda's great with kids. Judy is standing by to help. Tom, the RT, is getting his stuff organized. He got the right ETT tube. Darn, that thing is small. Barely thicker than a drinking straw. He has an infant bag. Sal's here, looking like he just left his hairdresser. How on earth does he always manage to have his hair perfect? He's flushed. Excited, like everybody else but me. I'm not excited. I'm terrified.*

She pulled on plastic gloves and headed out to the ambulance door, as usual. The sirens wailed louder and louder as she punched the silver door-opener with the back of her hand. They choked just as the door opened, and the silence fell, ominous and heavy. The wind wailed, shaking the trees. Yellow acacia leaves rained over her like tears. *The fall is coming early this year,* she thought, then the ambulance door crashed open to the scene inside and Emma shuddered.

2

----

an, the EMT, was performing CPR. His partner, Roy, was bagging something. Whatever was on the stretcher. Something barely big enough to see.

This can't be an eleven-month-old! They've got to be wrong!

Dan unlocked the stretcher to get it out. The feet dropped to the ground with a clang. He pulled, and the stretcher glided out.

The tiny purple body on the stretcher wore an orange hat. Eyes closed, hands blue, the baby showed no sign of life. Emma sighed and looked in Dan's eyes.

"How old is he?"

"Eleven months…" Dan's eyes widened, and his jaw dropped as he glanced at the patient. "Sorry…eleven weeks old."

That made all the difference in the world.

"Any other history?"

"Healthy. No allergies, no meds. The kid was home with his…his mother's boyfriend. He left the baby on the changing table and went to get a diaper. The kid rolled down. The father found him on the floor and called 911."

"The mother?"

"She's coming."

"Anything else?" Emma asked as they rolled into Room 3, where the team was waiting.

"We have a working IO in the right tibia but no IV. We gave two rounds of epi."

Brenda glanced at the kid and turned white. She looked at Dan.

"Seriously? Is this an eleven…"

"Let's get going here. He's eleven weeks old," Emma interrupted. It was a big mistake, and it screwed them out of everything they had prepared, but Dan didn't mean to do it. Humiliating him in public didn't do any good, and it was a waste of time.

"Let's get an IV. Sal, please figure out the meds."

Dan moved aside. Amy took over the CPR, pressing the tiny chest with two fingers of her right hand.

"Let's get ready to intubate," Emma said. "I need an oxygen forehead probe."

Judy took off to find it.

"Meds?" Sal asked.

"No. He's out already."

Emma moved to the head of the bed, bending over the tiny round head crowned by a golden puff of hair. *He looks just like Taylor! She was a blonde baby too. Then she grew and her hair turned dark to match her temper.* Emma shook her head, forcing herself back into the horror of the moment. No time for memories.

She slid a rolled towel under the baby's upper back to extend his neck, opening the view to his airway. *I should be doing in-line stabilization, but that will make the airway harder to get. I need to get it on the first try. He has no time.* She glanced at the monitor, checking the oxygen saturation. *100%. It's now or never.*

She grabbed a Miller 0, the newborn laryngoscope blade, small enough to fit in her closed fist. She opened the toothless mouth with her left hand, sliding in the laryngoscope blade with her right. She lifted gently. The large tongue filled the tiny mouth. Emma displaced it with the blade, lifting the whole head off the stretcher. The airway straightened. The epiglottis, the floppy tongue of tissue protecting the airway, fell into view. Emma slid the blade underneath and lifted it. The fat white vocal cords gating the airway blinked at her, then disappeared.

She placed her right hand on the throat, pushing until the cords came back into view. She took Tom's hand and put it on the neck, guiding it until the airway came back.

"Hold right here!"

She grasped the soft ETT tube, the stylet inside it a thin wire, and slipped it through the cords. The airway was safe. The second dose of epi went in through the IO.

"I have an IV," Brenda said.

"Labs would be good," Emma said.

Brenda gave her a look.

She's telling me to bug off. She doesn't want to lose the IV by drawing blood. She's right.

"A glucose, at least, please!"

Taylor stuck the tiny right heel with the lancet. She squeezed out a drop of blood, sucking it into the glucometer strip. She straightened, leaning back to balance her heavy belly.

"Fingerstick 65," Taylor said.

It's a heel stick, in fact, but that's not important right now. What's important is that the glucose is normal. "How long have we been doing this?"

The nurse recorder checked his watch. "Fifte..."

"The CO_2 is up!" Tom squeaked, his voice high with excitement.

"'Check for a pulse," Emma said.

Brenda felt for it at the right groin. "We have a pulse."

"Stop CPR."

The monitor beeped like a metronome. The heart rate was 140 and holding. The room breathed. Emma did too. *We may make it. Too early to tell, but...*

The door burst open. A heavy young woman dressed in a green Stewart's uniform erupted in, choking with sobs. Vera, the volunteer, followed, holding her back.

"My baby! My baby! What happened to my baby?!"

"He's here," Emma said. "We just got his heart back."

The woman stared. "You mean..."

"His heart had stopped. It's beating now. We're doing our best to keep it so."

The woman crumpled on the concrete floor and sobbed, hugging the leg of the stretcher.

"Now, now," Vera said. "Let's let them do their job, Lorraine. They're working to keep him alive. They need space. Let's you and I step out. They'll tell us if anything changes, OK? Let's go."

Vera pulled Lorraine off the floor and walked her out the door. There was nobody better than Vera at dealing with angry patients and worried families. She'd started volunteering in the ER when she retired. After losing her godson Boris, Emma's friend, she'd pretty much adopted the ER staff.

Thank God for Vera, Emma thought, rechecking the baby's pulse. The pulse was good, the blood pressure too, but he wasn't waking up.

"Where's the surgeon?" Emma asked. "The pediatrician? Anyone? Are we a one-doctor establishment here?"

"They're on their way," Kayla, the clerk, said. "CT scan is ready."

"Let's go then, before he gets worse."

In the ER, things will often get worse before getting better. And if there was no way for things to get worse, they still found one. The ER lives by Murphy's law.

3

———

The family room, a grim space off the ER waiting room, was eerily quiet as Emma stepped in. Barely furnished with green vinyl furniture, the place had witnessed too much suffering. Here, daughters learned about the death of their fathers, husbands cried for their lost wives, and mothers agonized waiting to hear about their children.

Emma had brought Judy along to help and to witness. A witness was always helpful when speaking to families. It was even more so in a case like this.

Vera sat on the sofa, holding Lorraine. The boyfriend, a handsome specimen, had the loveseat to himself. He leaned back in his sleeveless T-shirt showing off his wide shoulders and the mesmerizing blue full-sleeve tattoo covering his left arm.

"I'm Dr. Steele." Emma extended her hand.

"I'm Andy. She's Lorraine."

"Are you the baby's father?"

"No. She already had a bun in the oven when we hooked up."

Vera stood. "I'll let you guys talk now."

"No." Lorraine grabbed on to Vera's orange volunteer jacket. "Please stay with me."

Vera looked at her, then at Emma.

Emma shrugged. "It's up to you, Lorraine."

"I want her here."

Vera sat back, taking Lorraine's hand. The girl squeezed it, staring at Emma.

"Is he…"

"He's alive," Emma said. "For now."

Lorraine sighed like a doe you pulled out an arrow from, hiding her face in Vera's shoulder.

"There. I told you she'd keep him alive. If anybody can do it, she can," Vera said, patting Lorraine's back.

"What's your baby's name?" Emma asked.

"Tyrion."

"Andy, you were taking care of Tyrion when this happened, correct?"

"Yes."

"Were you alone?"

"Yes."

"Lorraine, was Tyrion OK when you went to work?" Emma asked.

"Yes. He took his bottle. I changed him and put him in his crib, and then I left for work."

"What time did you leave?"

"At six. I start at six thirty."

"What happened next?"

Andy shrugged. "He woke up at eight. I gave him the bottle. He didn't want it, just kept whimpering. I tried again at nine, but he still didn't want it. He kept fussing the whole morning. At noon, I laid him on the table to get him changed. I came back with the diaper, and I found him on the floor. I called 911."

"Where do you keep the diapers?" Emma asked.

"In the drawer, under the changing table," Lorraine said.

"So where did you go, Andy?"

"I'd left one in the kitchen when I went to get the bottle. I went to get it."

"Why? If the diapers were right there in the changing table…"

"I didn't want to leave it in the kitchen." Andy shrugged.

"But you should never leave him on the table! I told you: Don't leave him on the table alone!" Lorraine cried.

"I forgot," Andy said.

"You forgot! And you left my baby on the changing table!"

"Well, if you don't like it, you may as well change him yourself! I'm not your babysitter!"

"But I went to work!"

Andy shrugged.

"If you had a job, I wouldn't have to go to work! I could stay home and take care of the baby! That's the least you could do since I'm going to work to bring in the money!"

"Like it's a lot of money. Nine dollars an hour, you call that money?"

"It's more than you bring in. You haven't worked in months. I had to go back to work. You said you'd take care of the baby."

"I did. It's not my fault the little bastard decided to roll off the table!"

Lorraine jumped to charge Andy. Laughing, he pushed her back with his large hand. She lost her balance and fell to the ground. Instead of getting up, she curled up on the floor, sobbing. Vera pulled her up and held her as she wept.

"Get security," Emma whispered. Judy left.

"I told you to keep your hands to yourself," he said. "Next time, you may not be so lucky."

"Lucky?" Vera sputtered. "You call this lucky?"

"Chill out, old girl. I didn't hit her; she came to me. You saw it. And it's not for the first time. She's got a temper, this one. That kid takes after her. He wouldn't stop crying no matter what I did. Drives a man insane."

The door opened letting in two navy-clad security guards. Judy followed.

"You called the troops?" Andy laughed. "No worries. We'll settle out accounts at home, not here."

"Yes, we will," Lorraine said, her eyes burning with anger and impotent tears.

"Back to the baby..." Emma said. "He's in critical condition. We have to transfer him to the trauma center, across the lake. They have the specialists he needs. We don't."

"What's wrong with him?" Lorraine asked.

"We're not sure yet, but we know he's got a couple of broken ribs and a broken arm. Also, some bleeding in his brain."

"In his brain!"

"Yes. There may be more. We don't have all the radiology readings yet."

"That's from the fall?" Andy asked.

"Maybe," Emma said.

"What else can it be?" Lorraine asked.

"We aren't sure. That's why we'll have to do more testing. We also have to call the police."

"Police?" Lorraine's jaw fell. "Why?"

"Here at the hospital, we all are mandated reporters. When we have kids with unexplained injuries, we must report them. We need to make sure that the child is safe at home."

"But why? You said that the fall could explain the injuries."

"Yes, Lorraine. The fall could explain the injuries. But what explains the fall?"

"He rolled off the changing table and..."

"Lorraine!"

"Yes."

"Eleven-week-old babies don't roll. Babies don't start rolling until they're at least four months old."

Lorraine didn't seem to understand.

"Have you ever seen him roll?"

The understanding hit her. Like a sheet of ice cracking, Lorraine's face broke into the shape of sorrow.

"Eleven-week-old babies don't roll." Her eyes were dark holes as she looked at Andy. Lips tight, fists closed, he dared her to say something. She didn't. She crossed her arms across her chest, hugging her grief, and left. Vera followed.

4

―――――

Back at her desk, Emma signed in to the computer system to run the ER board. The board, a rainbow screen, listed all the patients with their complaints, their location, and their progress. A faithful, moment-to-moment snapshot of the ER, it told her who was where and what they needed, allowing her to prioritize.

"How is he?" Taylor asked, her face swollen, her eyes red.

Taylor never spoke to her mother at work. She didn't want people thinking that being the boss's daughter got her preferential treatment. Today she did.

"We're not sure yet. The brain bleed isn't big, but we don't know how much brain damage he suffered from being deprived of oxygen. We'll have to wait and see."

"Aren't you shipping him out?"

"As fast as I can. The pediatric transport team is on its way."

"If he's going, how will we know how he's doing?"

"We'll call and find out."

Taylor nodded. Tears ran down her cheeks, then down her chin, dropping on her pregnant belly, but, for once, she didn't pitch a fit. *She's growing up. This pregnancy and working in the ER taught her to act older than her eighteen years. Much older than she was only months ago, when she thought she knew it all.*

"You think he'll be all right?" Taylor asked.

"I hope so. Babies' brains are amazingly resilient. If one area gets damaged, another one takes over. Many grow up to be normal, even if they've had some brain damage. We'll see."

"Yes. We'll see," Taylor said, cupping her belly between her hands.

She's thinking about hers. Hoping she'll be all right, after everything she's been through.

"How are you feeling?"

"I'm OK. You?"

Emma laughed. *Six months ago, it wouldn't have crossed Taylor's mind to ask about her.* "I'm good," she said, as Vera came to hug her.

"Excellent work, Emma. Very proud of you, as usual."

"How's Lorraine?"

"She's shaken. She's getting ready to go across the lake with the ambulance, but she doesn't know how she'll get back. I told her I'll go and get her."

"You are so kind."

"I live to please," Vera laughed. "How about him? The boyfriend?"

"Police are speaking to him now."

"Is this what I think it is?"

"Abuse? Absolutely."

"Is there any doubt?"

"I don't think so. He may not have meant to do it—the kid's crying must have driven him nuts. He probably shook him or slapped him to get him to stop. But there's no doubt he did it. They fit the demographics to a T. Teenage mother, child left with the boyfriend who's not the father. That's classic."

"Eric would never do that," Taylor said. "Never."

"Of course not. We weren't talking about Eric, who's a great guy. This is different. Different situation, different people, and terrible luck," Emma said.

"Not Eric," Taylor said again, her words a prayer.

"Not in a hundred years," Vera said. "Come, let's take a breather."

5

Vera took Taylor's arm and dragged her out. Taylor felt guilty, but it was time for her break, and her back was killing her. She was grateful to breathe real air instead of the recirculated germs they got allotted in the air-conditioned ED.

They headed toward the pond. The waterfowl showed off their young, almost grown now. Most couples had only two or three, but one light-gray goose and her big-headed partner had five between them. They glided proudly across the pond from one end to the other, like soccer moms parading their offspring.

"I hate those two," Vera said, waiting for them to disappear before grabbing a handful of bread from her pocket and handing it to Taylor. She took another for herself.

"Why?" Taylor asked.

"They're showing off. Like making children is anything to be proud of!"

She sent a well-directed piece on top of a male. He shook it off. His partner swallowed it.

"You know we're not supposed to do this, right?" Taylor glanced around, hoping nobody would recognize her and turn her in.

"So what? Where's the fun in doing what you're supposed to?"

Vera threw another piece of bread. Two goslings started fighting over it. Vera laughed. That sent her into a coughing fit. She caught her breath, laughed again, and threw another.

She's got to be at least 60, Taylor thought. *She smokes like a chimney and drinks like a sailor. No, drinks like a Russian and curses like a sailor. And look at her. She's younger than me, in body and spirit. How does she do that? I used to be a rebel, and now I'm even afraid to feed the ducks.*

"Have you always been like this, Vera?"

Vera cocked her head to look up at her. Small and plump, she barely reached Taylor's shoulder.

"Like what?"

"Like a spitfire."

"Of course. When I was a kid in Russia, it was OK. Then we came to the States, and I tried to behave so I could fit in and make friends."

"Did it work?"

"For a while, but it wasn't much fun. My friends weren't much fun, either."

"What did you do?"

"I said F.U. By that time, I had learned to swear in English. It's not as good as Russian, though. English profanities are bland, like the cuisine. You know a good language to swear in? Hungarian. They're world-class. They're fighting the Romanians for the World title. I heard Romanians can swear for a full hour without repeating themselves. I wish I could speak it!"

Taylor laughed. The baby kicked, a healthy knee in the liver that took her breath away. She gasped, waiting for the second one. They always came in twos. It came, and she sighed a sigh of relief. She looked up to find Vera's worried eyes watching her.

"Are you OK?"

"Yep. The baby moved. Vera, do you have children?"

"Other than you and Emma? No."

Taylor laughed. "Why did you take us on?"

Vera turned back to the geese She got more bread from her inexhaustible pockets. "Your mother needed a friend. You too."

"Everybody needs a friend! Why her?"

"She's OK. Most people have friends. If they don't, they're assholes. I hate assholes. If there were one thing I'd like to do, I'd like to rid the world of assholes. Like say: "'Evanesco!'" and they're gone."

Taylor laughed. "I love Harry Potter too."

"I know. Are you going to read it to your child, or are you going to wait until he's old enough to read it himself?"

"It's a she." Taylor threw another piece of bread to the ducks. "I don't know if I'll be there."

"Be where?"

"With her, when she's old enough to understand."

"How so?"

"I'm thinking about giving her for adoption. A nice couple wants her."

"And you don't?"

"I don't think I'd be a good mother. Especially if she's disabled."

"Do you love her? Any mother is a good mother when she loves her child."

"No. That's not true."

"How so?'"

"Mother wasn't a good mother. Nor was her mother. It's in our genes."

"That's absolute poppycock! Where the hell did you come out with that?"

"Mother told me."

"I'll have to talk to Emma. For somebody so smart, sometimes she's seriously foolish."

"Are you going to tell her that?"

"Why not?"

"Aren't you afraid of her?"

"Of course not! Why should I be?"

"Everybody is. The staff is. I am. Even Father is."

Vera laughed. "You must all have things you feel guilty about."

Taylor nodded.

"See, I don't. Guilt is for the birds. I don't do guilt. I do fun." She brushed her hands against her apron to get rid of breadcrumbs and caught Taylor's arm. "Let's go grab the cupcakes from my car. I got a brand-new recipe. Chocolate, walnuts, and almonds. Let's take them to the break room. After this morning, everybody needs a little pick-me-up. I also have some ginger tea that I'd like you to try. We'll take some of it to Lorraine, too. She'd be better off with some whiskey, but I don't have any of that with me. Just my vodka. Eh, my water, I mean."

6

———————

By the time Emma made it home, it had been dark for hours. She dropped her heavy bag with her always-there essentials on Victor's corner chair. She still called it Victor's, though he hadn't sat in it for ages. Ever since he'd left her to marry Amber. It had been hard, especially for Taylor, but they managed somehow, and now they were friends again.

Guinness, Emma's German shepherd, greeted her without any dignity. She whined and complained of being locked inside the whole day. Emma would have none of it.

"You're lying worse than a communist newspaper! I happen to know that Vera came to let you out at noon! I bet she brought you cookies! Maybe even a cupcake!"

Caught lying, Guinness looked down. Her black triangular ears flattened. She licked Emma's hand to apologize, then rolled on her back.

"Let's make up. I forgive you for catching me."

Emma scratched her in all the right places, then walked to the wine rack.

"OK. Time for my wine."

Guinness disagreed. She went to the kitchen and came back dragging her black studded leash. She'd chosen it herself, but Emma had to put up with people's nasty looks.

"We go now. Wine later," she barked.

Emma sighed. *It's either that or cleaning the floor.*

"You're worse than Taylor." Emma grabbed the leash and opened the door.

Fluffy white tail raised like a flag, Guinness darted out. She stopped by the mailbox to check her mail, checked in, then headed down the road to the park, a mile away.

"We were just coming for bathroom duty," Emma said. "You said I could have my wine."

"I said no such thing," Guinness mumbled in dog. *"You have too much wine anyhow. A walk will do you good."*

Emma hated to admit it, but she was right. She was in better shape, and she'd lost weight since she got Guinness—more precisely, since Guinness got her. Gone were the long evenings with her best friend, the wine. They went on long daily walks instead. She didn't feel like walking when she came home. She felt like wine. But Guinness didn't care.

Walking was good for her. She slept better, she felt better, she even looked better. The long daily walks forced her to think through her problems rather than numb them with wine. It wasn't easy, but it was healthier in the long run.

Like today. Without Guinness, she'd be through half a bottle of red by now. Tyrion's purple little body and Lorraine's tortured face would have faded from her mind. Without wine, she couldn't escape. She had to remember them and suffer.

They had called the police and CPS, child protective services, who interviewed everybody: the EMTs who brought Tyrion, the nurses, Emma, the family. They left without saying much, but their investigation had just begun.

Speaking about the investigation. What the hell was that? Emma remembered the certified letter she'd received that morning. She had been too busy with the code, police, and everything else to think about it, but now she remembered. What a disaster! A Board investigation meant months of humiliation and misery. Emma could end up losing her license and being unable to practice medicine. What would she be if she wasn't a doctor? Being a doctor was not what she was; it was who she was. Anger filled her brain like black smoke. *An anonymous complaint? They're going to turn my life upside down, and I'm not even entitled to know why?* A wave of nausea hit her. She took a deep breath.

Far ahead, Guinness heard. She stopped, turned around and looked her in the eye. She understood and headed home.

Emma needed wine.

7

———————

As she ran the ER board sitting at her desk two days later, Emma tried to ignore her pounding migraine. No luck. The migraine, well deserved after a bottle of red and a sleepless night, would not be ignored. Emma sighed and took another sip of her extra-strong salted coffee, her migraine remedy of choice. She struggled to keep it down as the metallic voice of the speakers broke through the background noise, hitting her brain like a hammer.

"Code 99, Emergency Care Center, Room 2."

Emma glanced up. She didn't know there was a code coming. She walked to Room 2 with the others to find her colleague, Dr. Kurt Crump, getting ready.

"Yours?" she asked.

"Yep."

"What is it?"

"Twenty-something man. Not breathing. No pulse. Probably an overdose."

Emma nodded. Thanks to the opioid epidemic, they'd had a lot of that. The scourge of fentanyl had blown through the county like a blizzard, leaving behind a trail of death and destruction.

"You need any help?"

Kurt shrugged.

"I don't think so. But stick around if you've got a moment. You never know."

Emma nodded and stepped back, making room for the EMTs pushing the stretcher. Slick with sweat and breathing hard, they looked like they'd been through the wringer. They moved the patient to the ED stretcher and stepped back, letting the ER crew take over.

"We gave three doses of epi and two of Narcan with no result. No return of spontaneous circulation."

"Never got a pulse?"

"No."

"Where did you find him?"

"At his home, downtown. He was in the bathroom, curled down on the floor."

"Who found him?"

"His girlfriend. She says she came home and found him there."

"CPR?"

"Not until we arrived."

"Any history?"

"None."

"Drugs?"

"She said no."

"She may be lying."

"Yep. But he's got good veins. No track marks. But he smells funny."

"Like what?"

"Dunno. Just funny."

"Well, he was in the bathroom."

Trauma shears came out of pockets. The dark flannel clothes fell off. But for the washcloth covering his groin, the body lay exposed under the harsh blue lights like a marble statue. Young and muscled, he was all clean and white but for the full-sleeve arabesque on his left arm.

The door crashed open. A sobbing woman burst in.

"Hello, Lorraine," Emma said.

8

———————

Andy stayed dead.

"Probably an overdose," Kurt said.

"But there's no drug history."

"Not that we know of."

Emma nodded. "You know, I saw him just the other day."

"What for?"

"That pediatric code? He was the caretaker."

"Really! That's interesting! Was it abuse?"

"Yes."

"You're sure?"

"99.5 percent."

"You think this may be intentional?" Kurt asked.

"Suicide, you mean?"

"Yes."

"I don't know. He didn't strike me as the remorseful type."

"You never know."

"True. But he was harsh and nasty with the mother. And she was distraught when she understood."

"That he abused her baby?"

"Yes."

Kurt looked back. Lorraine cried quietly, holding Andy's hand. "Are you thinking…"

"Not really," Emma said. "But you never know. It's just a strange coincidence. The baby, two days ago. Now him."

"I don't like coincidences," Kurt said. "I'll send all the tox labs I can think about. And he's going to be a coroner's case. We'll see what he has to say."

"Yep."

"Thanks for your help, Emma. How's Taylor doing?"

"She's OK. Growing up. Sheila?"

"She's good. I don't know if Taylor told you, but she came to visit a few times. She and Sheila are getting along well."

"Great," Emma said. She didn't know whether to be happy or heartbroken.

Sheila and Kurt hoped to adopt Taylor's baby. Taylor's pregnancy had been eventful. So much so, that having a "normal" child was unlikely. Plus, Taylor was barely eighteen, and the baby's father was not in the picture. Adoption looked like the right way to go.

Emma should have been happy, and she was, but…

She was worried about how Taylor would feel if she failed as a mother. Emma knew exactly how that felt. She wasn't the best mother in the world, but she was the best she could be. Which wasn't much to say—the mothering gene didn't seem to run in their family. She was better with dogs. And speaking of dogs, it was time to go home and take Guinness for a walk.

9

———————

Some days there just isn't enough coffee. Back in the hospital parking lot the next morning, Emma slammed the door to her red Hyundai and headed to her office, hoping the fog in her brain cleared before she killed someone.

She had tried to be good last night. She went to bed early, but then Margret called, as soon as she fell asleep. Her ex-mother-in-law didn't call often, and she never called without reason.

"Hello, Margret."

"Hi, Emma! I'm so glad you're still up!"

Emma coughed.

"I have some wonderful news, and I needed to share it. Two sets, in fact. I couldn't think of anyone better than you."

"How nice."

"I'm coming over in a few days. I'll be looking after the kids while Victor takes Amber on a second honeymoon. Well, it's got to be the other way, since they're going to the Caribbean. Victor wouldn't choose to go there in a hundred years. He'd drag her to some mountaintop, someplace without shoe shops and hairdressers. She must have dragged him."

"That's wonderful!" Emma said. She couldn't wait to see Margret. She was also glad that Victor and Amber were working through their issues. Lately, their marriage had been going through a rough patch. Even worse, Victor had hinted at getting back with Emma. *I'd rather get a root canal.*

"I may even stay until Taylor has her baby! Wouldn't that be wonderful?"

"Fantastic."

"Let's see how it goes. I'm flying over next week."

"I can't wait to see you! What's the other news?"

"The other news?"

"Yes. You said two sets."

"Oh. I've received a proposal."

"A proposal?"

"Yes. A marriage proposal, dear. Nobody would make me an indecent proposal at my age. It's surprising enough to receive a marriage one!"

"Absolutely! I haven't received one in…ever?"

"It's not all it's cracked up to be. And you seem to have married Victor anyhow. Did you propose to him, or did you just inform him you were getting married?"

Emma laughed. "Well…"

"Just as I thought."

"Did you accept it?"

"Not yet. I'm thinking."

"Who is it?"

"My new cardiologist. He's fifteen years younger."

"Does that bother you?"

"Not that much. I think he's mature enough. And at least he doesn't need hearing aids. I hate men with hearing aids. It makes for too exciting a private life. Whenever you get close, the thing starts buzzing like a mosquito. It's bad for the foreplay."

Emma choked with laughter. Margret, a distinguished lady living in Atlanta who spent her life gardening, was Emma's role model in case she ever tried to become classy. No immediate danger of that, but she never failed to amuse and amaze with her attitude and life outlook.

"I have somebody you'll have to meet when you arrive."

"Not another man, dear. At my age, one is plenty."

Emma laughed. "It's not a man. It's a lady. Her name is Vera. She's Russian."

"Does she speak English? I'm afraid my Russian is not one of my better skills. Now French…"

"She's lived here since she was eight. Her parents fled the Russian revolution and came over. She's a volunteer in the ER."

"OK, Emma, if you think…"

"She's fascinating. And she's into gardening, like you. She used to be a biology professor. She's also hilarious, and she drinks tea." Emma wasn't sure about the tea, she suspected that Vera was more into vodka, but she was Russian—they drink tea—Margret loved tea—and whiskey—one more thing they'd have in common.

"OK. Looking forward to meet Vera and seeing you. And Emma?"

"Yes?"

"Don't tell Victor. Not yet. You know how he gets. He's going to go full protective and start questioning me. I don't have time for that. He'd better take care of his own marriage than stick his nose into mine."

Emma laughed and agreed. She hung up to discover she'd missed a call from her old friend George. George was a vet, and an ER nurse. He'd just been promoted to ER director and he didn't like it much.

She called him back.

"Can you come in early tomorrow? We need to talk."

So there she was, bright and early, wondering what was coming. The only thing she knew was that whatever it was, it wasn't good news.

10

———

Bent over his keyboard, typing away with two knotty fingers, George looked like he hadn't slept in a week. The dark bags under his eyes half-covered his sunken cheeks. His dark brushy mustache looked like it hung the wrong way. Still, his face lit up when he saw Emma, and he caught her in a bear hug. He dragged a chair and closed the office door behind her.

"How are you doing?" he asked.

"I'm OK. How are you? You're not looking happy. How do you like your new job?"

"I love it. I just wish they'd use some ointment when they bend me over."

Emma laughed. George hadn't changed, and for her money, he didn't need to. But since political correctness was the rage these days, it was only a matter of time until somebody's hurt sensibilities were going to get him in trouble.

"Yep, some ointment would be nice, but I don't think it's in the budget..."

"Funk the budget! And funk the administrators too."

"Not me, thanks. I love you dearly, but I'm not interested."

George laughed.

"Emma."

"Yep."

"The code yesterday… that child abuser you called police for…"

"Yes."

"Any idea what happened?"

"He died."

"Why?"

Emma shrugged. "Kurt thought overdose, but there's no evidence he was doing drugs. Somebody suggested he committed suicide, overwhelmed by remorse, but, to me, he didn't look like the remorseful type. Maybe we'll get something helpful from the coroner. Why?"

"They found this when they cleaned the room." He grabbed his phone and scrolled through pictures of kids, dogs, and beers until he found the one he wanted. The photo showed a sheet of hospital stationery with: "#2. ASSHOLES, BEHAVE!" written in all caps with a thick red Sharpie.

"That's weird," Emma said.

"Isn't it?"

"Probably nothing, but…"

"Police didn't think so."

"What did they think?"

"They didn't tell me, but from their uptight attitude and crummy behavior, they seem to believe it's a clue."

"That somebody killed him?"

"Police seem to think so."

Emma shrugged. "His girlfriend, Lorraine, was heartbroken about what happened to her kid."

"I could see that. But why #2? Not good enough to be #1?"

"Be careful, George! One of your silly jokes will get you in trouble."

"Yep. I'd better get myself some lube," George said.

11

———————

Emma left George and went back to her office. She opened her computer and looked for Andy's record to review it. Nothing interesting. The toxicology tests were still pending. For whatever reason, all drug tests besides the basic panel took weeks to return, and this case was no exception.

She shrugged and went back to her certified letter, trying to make some sense of it, when Detective Zagarian, her on-again, off-again paramour, stopped by.

"Fancy meeting you here," he said.

Emma blushed. She had avoided him and hadn't returned his calls in weeks. She liked him, but she wasn't ready for a physical relationship. Now he was here. Impeccable as always in his gray suit, he stood in the open door blocking her escape.

"I…"

He laughed. "I know. That's not what I'm here for. I'm here for work. You know Ben?"

"Sure."

Ben had been the ER nursing assistant director until he got into a fight with one of the nurses. His racist remarks got him demoted, and he narrowly avoided being fired. He was big, rough, and testosterone fueled. Emma had

had to put him in his place more than once, since he could only think of one use for women, and that was not being his boss.

"He's dead."

"Dead?"

Zagarian nodded.

"How?"

"That's exactly the question. We found his body in his home. He had been dead for a while."

"That's odd."

"I wonder… You know him. We worked together before. How about coming to have a look at his place? Unofficial, of course. I'd like to see what you think."

Emma couldn't say no. She didn't really want to say no.

She was fascinated with people's homes. She had once worked for the census and spent weeks going from home to home and meeting people. She had discovered that people's homes told the story of their lives. She was particularly interested in Ben since she had been close to his girlfriend. Then, recently, she'd learned about his wife from Taylor.

Just a few days ago, she and Taylor were chilling in the back yard with Vera, when Ben's name came up.

"He's an asshole," Taylor said, taking a bite of Vera's almond brownies.

Guinness came closer to check them out. Taylor laughed and pushed her away.

"How do you know?" Emma asked.

"From Amy. She's Mia's best friend."

"Who's Mia?" Vera sipped on her vodka.

"Ben's wife. Well, soon to be ex-wife."

"What did he do?" Emma asked.

"He cheated on her. When Mia found out, she packed her suitcases, took the twins, and left. She went to live with a friend. Mia is from Laos and has no family here. She came here to study, met Ben, they got married, they had the twins. She has nothing here: no money, no job, not even a green card. She came back to get the kids' stuff, and he told her to leave him the kids and go back to Laos. She tried to sneak in to get the kids' clothes, but he caught her and beat the living daylights out of her. Amy said her eyes were so swollen, she could hardly see."

"I remember now. That bake sale for a homeless mom with infant twins was for her? I made some cupcakes," Vera said.

"They were awesome. The bake sale made a little money, but then Ben found out Amy was helping Mia and filed a fake complaint. Now she's on probation."

"Nice guy, this Ben," Vera said. "Why didn't Mia go to the police?"

"She's afraid they'll take away her kids and send her back. She's not a citizen, but the kids are."

"Sadly, that may happen," Emma said. "She's in a tight spot. We should look for a lawyer for her."

"I don't know if she'll agree. She's afraid of authorities. She thinks they are more likely to protect Ben than her."

"She may be right," Vera said.

"I hate that asshole. I wish he'd drop dead," Taylor said.

That was only last week. It looked like Taylor's wish had been granted. Somehow.

As they drove to Ben's house in silence, Emma glanced at Zagarian. He smiled without meeting her eyes. *It's weird to be with him again. It was good while it lasted, but I wasn't ready. Now it's too late.*

The drive to Ben's house was quiet. And too short.

12

———————

Ben's house was a small white ranch in a cul-de-sac. The grass needed mowing, and the house itself looked like it could do with a little TLC. Police cars blocked the driveway, but the street was empty. Curtains moved behind dark windows as the neighbors watched.

Emma followed Zagarian into a dark, cramped hallway. The first door opened to a bright, clean kitchen. Nothing on the table but an empty Alka-Seltzer container.

He must have had an upset stomach, Emma thought. She looked around. Boxes of cereal, tall glass containers of flour, sugar, rice, and oil stood aligned like soldiers on the shelves. It was as if the woman of the house had just cleaned up. But the woman of the house was gone. Unless there was another.

I wouldn't have thought he'd be so tidy. I imagined that, with all that testosterone, there'd be nothing but chips and beer. I was mistaken. What else was I wrong about?

A door to the left opened to the bathroom where they'd found the body. The odor of decay still lingered. The toilet paper roll was empty. Under the sink there was no other. *He must have had diarrhea,* Emma thought. Blood and vomitus soiled the floor. The smell made her gag, and she stepped out.

She went back to the white kitchen, then through the living room into the bedroom. The room was tidy and smelled like old sweat. Free weights sat under the window. The elliptical machine looked fresh and clean as if he'd just used it. No medications, no books, no clothes hanging. Not much about

551

who Ben had been and his life. The picture of an Asian woman with two smiling infants on the night table. *It's got to be Mia and the kids*, Emma thought. The woman was beautiful but unsmiling. Her heavy lids hid cautious narrow eyes.

"We found this near the body," Zagarian said, showing her the picture of a yellow piece of hospital stationery. On it, written in thick red Sharpie: #1. ASSHOLES BEHAVE.

Emma's mouth fell open. She stared at Zagarian. "This is just like the other one. The one they found in the hospital with the body of the child abuser. Except that one said #2."

Zagarian smiled. "I know. That's why I brought you here. It looks like you got yourself another killer in your ER. I wish you people would content yourselves to those who die naturally."

He was kidding, but there was a kernel of truth to his words. For the third time this year, death was making a home in their rural ER, as if an evil spirit had awakened and wouldn't go back to sleep.

"What do you think?" he asked.

"It's weird. Ben must have had an upset stomach. The Alka-Seltzer, the toilet paper running out, the vomiting in the bathroom. It looks like it happened suddenly. Like he had an upset stomach and diarrhea and then just died. But that's not how it works. Otherwise, every cruise ship with norovirus would return to port with a pile of corpses."

Zagarian nodded.

"I agree. Did you know he called in sick five days ago?"

"I didn't."

"He called in to say that he wasn't feeling well. He didn't give any details. They called him two days later to see how he was doing. He didn't answer. He was probably dead already."

"Who called you?"

"A neighbor walking his dog. He said there was a bad smell coming from the house, and nobody had seen him in days. We came for a well check. The doors were locked. He was lying on the bathroom floor."

"How about that piece of paper?"

"It was on the floor, near him. Like he'd taken it out of his pocket and dropped it."

"Sounds pretty much like the other one."

"Except that one was found sooner," Zagarian said.

"Was there any relationship between them?" Emma asked.

"Not that we know of. You know that Ben used to date one of the nurses. Faith. You remember her."

"I do."

"His wife took the twins and left him when she found out. We're looking for her."

"Why?"

"To tell her he died, of course. And ask her a few questions."

Zagarian looked around one last time.

"Anything else you can think of?"

"Not really. But it doesn't look like a natural death."

"Do tell. I thought you'd never get there."

Emma laughed. "You know something I don't know?"

"I know a lot of things that you don't know."

"Is that so?"

"Yep. One of them is that I'm taking you out for dinner."

"I can't."

"Why not?"

"I have to go home and take Guinness out."

"I thought you drank wine."

Emma laughed. "That's funny. You remember Guinness."

"I do. Your black-and-tan saving angel."

He was right. If it wasn't for her... Emma shuddered.

Zagarian said: "OK. Let's go."

"Where?"

"Home to take Guinness out."

Emma shrugged. *It beats walking home.*

13

———————

Back in the ER the next morning, Emma smiled, remembering the evening. They'd walked with Guinness to the Dizzy Alligator, the restaurant at the marina down the road. They drank watered-down margaritas, ate loaded nachos, and watched the moon pour gold over the water. They talked, laughed, and remembered the good old times. Emma was worried he would get too close, but he hardly paid her any attention. He was more interested in Guinness. He scratched her in all the right places, and she loved it. *Like I wasn't even there! Well, it's better than having to tell him off again.*

Emma shrugged and checked the board. A new fall in Room 15. She went to see her.

The lights were down in Room 15. Even so, the woman on the stretcher looked like a blue period Picasso. Her split lip matched her purple, swollen-shut left eye.

Emma turned up the lights to see her better. "Carrie?"

"Yes?" Carrie covered her eyes with a bruised hand.

"What happened?"

"She fell," the man answered. He sat by the stretcher holding her hand, a toddler asleep in his lap.

"How did you fall, Carrie?"

"She tripped and fell against the guardrail."

"Thank you," Emma said. "I'd rather hear her answer. How did you fall?"

"I tripped and fell against the guardrail."

"What did you trip on?"

Silence.

"She didn't trip. She was drunk," the man said. "She stumbled, and she fell."

"What hurts?"

"Everything."

"What hurts the most?

The woman felt her face, her left breast, her leg. "The eye, I think."

"Can you see with it?"

"I don't know. I can't open it."

"When did this happen?"

"Last night," the man said.

Emma frowned. He glared back.

"Does your neck hurt?"

Carrie moved her head.

"A little."

Emma stepped between them.

"Can I examine her?"

The man stared at her, then dragged his chair back to make room.

Emma examined every inch of Carrie. Her neck was tender, so she stabilized it with a rigid collar, but she couldn't get her to open her left eye. *She needs a CT.*

Emma went back to her desk to put in orders.

"I don't like this," Brenda said.

"Neither do I."

"It looks like..."

Vera came in like a tornado, her raincoat still on. She dropped her bag on an empty chair.

"Hi, girls. I brought coffee and cookies."

"You're an angel," Brenda said. "Thank you. I didn't get breakfast today."

"Like you ever do! They aren't low calorie, but they're worth it. They're mostly butter and nuts. Speaking about nuts. What's new?"

"The woman in 15. I don't like the looks of her. She's got a fishy story and an overbearing man," Emma said.

"I hate those," Vera said.

"Me too. I hate it when they speak for the patient. It drives me crazy."

"Are you thinking about domestic abuse?" Brenda asked.

"Yes. We need to find a way to separate them so that we can speak to her. There's a kid too."

"I'll take her to the bathroom to get a urine, and we'll have a chat," Brenda said.

"Good."

"I'll get the kid some cookies and keep the man distracted," Vera said.

It took Brenda a long time to return.

"You were right. He beats her. She's terrified, but she doesn't want us to say anything. He threatened to kill her if she speaks. He said that if she leaves him, he'll kill the kid. She's desperate."

"How did you get her to speak to you?" Emma asked.

"I told her I knew. I've been there."

"Sorry, Brenda, I didn't know."

"It was long ago. And it's over."

"So, what do we do now?" Vera asked.

"I gave her the phone number for a women's shelter, but she didn't want to take it. 'He'll kill me if he finds it,' she said."

"Can we call the police?" Vera asked.

"Not without her permission," Emma said.

"We can if he abuses the kid," Brenda said.

Emma shook her head. "We have no reason to think that he does."

"Isn't threatening to kill him enough?"

"We have no proof. She'll deny it, and we'll get her in trouble. No, we can't do anything if she says no."

"This is absurd. We can't let that poor woman go back to this monster with her kid. It's inconceivable!" Vera yelled.

"Shush! You don't want him to hear you, for God's sake. It will make things even worse."

"I wish we had a way to at least give her the phone number for the shelter," Brenda said.

"I have an idea," Vera said. She rummaged in her huge orange bag and got out a stuffed yellow puppy. "There. Where's the phone number?"

Brenda handed her the card.

Vera wrote the number on the label sewn into the puppy's belly with a sharpie. It was impossible to see unless you knew it was there.

"How are you going to tell her it's there?"

"I'll tell her when I take her to the CT," Brenda said.

Emma nodded.

"How about admitting her to the hospital?" Brenda asked.

"I can try, but unless she's got something nasty, she won't stay. She won't let him go home with her kid."

Carrie had an orbital fracture, and she needed follow-up but no admission. They left, the perfect little family: the toddler, his yellow puppy under his arm, holding his mother's hand; the man, his arm around Carrie's shoulders.

"I wish there were something we could do," Brenda said.

"Me too. Life sucks," Emma said. She wished she could do something to help Carrie and her kid. It felt so wrong to let them go home with their abuser. Carrie's life must be a nightmare. Emma knew. She remembered her own childhood, and the beatings her mother gave her. *Mother was smarter, though. She only hit covered skin, so she never left a trace. Nobody ever knew. Nobody, but me.*

Her heart heavy, she went back to running the board: A chest pain in Room 5. A headache in Room 11.

She needed a drink. She went to the break room and got a cup of Vera's coffee. She grabbed a cookie too. *Damn, they are good. I love the taste of chocolate with almonds, even if it smells like cyanide.*

14

——————

By the time she got home that evening, Emma was exhausted. That wasn't news. She was exhausted every single damn evening. Working in the ER sucked the living juices out of her every day. Still, today was worse. She felt awful for letting Carrie and her kid go home with the abuser. She had failed. Again. She couldn't find a way to keep Carrie safe with her kid. She didn't know what else she could have done, but what she did— nothing— was no good. She hoped Carrie wasn't going to show up in the ER dead one of these days. Or the kid, God forbid. She hoped, but she was anything but sure.

She parked the car and got out. She ached all over. Her neck, her feet, her back, all ached. But the worst was the pain in her chest. Her eyes burned, and she wanted to cry, but she remembered Mother. Mother didn't like crying unless she'd caused it. *"I'll give you something to cry about,"* she said. She always kept her word. Emma had learned that crying was for losers. She bit her lip and smiled instead. She opened the door, bracing for Guinness's greeting.

Guinness didn't come. That had never happened. Ever since they'd been a pack, Guinness welcomed her every time she came home. Not today. *Where is she? Has she escaped?* To where? Emma checked every room, every window, every door. Nothing. Nothing broken, nothing missing, nothing wrong.

Where is she?

She thought about calling the police, but she felt foolish. *They have important things to deal with. People things. A dog? Not a priority.*

559

She thought about calling Taylor, but she didn't want to worry her. *She's about to have that baby soon. She doesn't need any more excitement. Victor? Victor has Amber, Opal, and Iris to worry about, not to mention the dogs. He's overbooked to the hilt.*

Vera, maybe? She has a key. Nah, I just left her at the hospital.

She went to grab a bottle of wine to help her think. Carmenere. Shiraz. Pinot noir. Nothing looked good. This was an emergency.

She opened the freezer. For the days when wine was not enough—thank God, there weren't many—the Good Lord had created gin. A thick brown bottle of curiously infused Hendrick's Gin lived in the freezer since she didn't want to ruin it by diluting it with ice. She grabbed one of the frozen glasses and poured a healthy dose. *Stiff enough to kill Mother, but Grandmother would approve.* She sniffed it, ready to take a sip.

The front door burst open, and Guinness flew in. She jumped up on Emma, placing her paws on her shoulders and licking her face. The martini glass exploded in shards on the floor. Guinness heard. Overcome by remorse, she lay on the floor in the puddle of gin, her ears glued to her head, the guiltiest German shepherd in the North Country.

"Nice to see you too," Emma said, wiping the gin off her hands on her scrub bottoms. "How are you?"

"Excellent, thank you." Zagarian closed the door and dropped the leash on the sofa. "How about you?"

"What are you doing here?"

"Returning your dog."

"How so?"

"I came by earlier to see you. I rang the doorbell. Guinness welcomed me. She said she needed to go out. The door was unlocked, so I grabbed the leash, and we went for a walk."

Really? I left the door unlocked? Unbelievable. You'd think I'd would have learned something last time. Apparently not.

"Thank you. By the way, what's your first name?"

Zagarian laughed.

"How long have we known each other for?"

"A few months?

"What did you call me, throughout this time when we were sometimes close to dating?"

"I called you 'you.' I couldn't think of anything more appropriate. Names didn't seem important. At work, I often call everyone honey and sweetheart because I don't remember their names. I have more important things to remember. Like the dosage of Precedex or the correct size for pediatric ET tubes. So, what's your name?

"Why don't you call me honey or sweetheart?

Emma shrugged and went to pick a wine.

"Australian Shiraz?"

"If I must," Zagarian laughed.

She opened it. It was easy. Like most Australian wines, it had a twist cap. She poured.

She looked through the wine. Its red was so dark that the light got through only at the edges. She sniffed it.

Zagarian did too. "Dark cherry. Violet. Tobacco," he said.

She swirled it again, then took a second nose. The wine left legs on the glass, streaks trickling down after she swirled it.

"Not bad. But it's not tobacco. It's leather." She sipped.

"Really?"

"Yep."

They sat looking at their glasses, Guinness's head resting on Emma's thigh.

"What did you say your first name was?"

He smiled.

"Why don't you just call me Z, like everybody else?"

Good question.

"Armand. My name is Armand," he said.

Emma nodded.

"It fits you."

"Thanks."

"I'll call you Z."

15

———

Back in the ER for another shift, Emma wished she could get out of Room 12.1. She'd tried again and again to explain to them why a prescription for opiates for a patient with chronic pain was not appropriate, but she couldn't get through. In the meantime, she had three patients waiting to be seen, all getting angry as they waited.

The speakers cracked, coughed, sputtered, and finally spoke. "Code 99, Emergency Department, Room 3. Code 99, Emergency Department, Room 3."

"I'm sorry. I have to go."

She headed to Room 3. The staff stood in the doorway as thick as a forest, but they parted to let her through. Standing at the foot of the stretcher, her colleague, Dr. Alex Greene, ran the code. His thin frame and his thick, round glasses made him look like a wise, oversized insect. Tom, the RT, was bagging the patient. He held the mask over his face with one hand while squeezing oxygen in with the other. Judy kneeled by the stretcher to work on an IV while the EMTs were giving their report.

Emma caught Alex's eye.

"You need me?"

He shook his head no. "He's dead already. We're just going through the motions."

He was right.

The patient was not a small man. His feet clad in steel-toed boots overhung the stretcher, while his barrel chest crushed it under his weight. He looked too big to die, but his mottled skin and blue nails told Emma it was over.

She stepped toward the door just as the curtain opened, letting the woman in. Her purple left eye was fading into green, and the swelling was mostly gone.

Good. *She can see through it*, Emma thought, glancing back at the body on the stretcher. She now knew who he was.

"Hi, Carrie."

Carrie's puzzled eyes wandered from Emma's face to her scrubs.

"Dr. Steele?"

"Yes."

"How's Chip?"

"He's not my patient. Dr. Alex Greene is his doctor. He'll let you know as soon as he figures it out."

"Is he dead?"

"He doesn't look too good for the moment. How about we walk out and talk?"

Carrie nodded. Emma led her down the hallway to the empty family room and sat on the green vinyl sofa.

Carrie paced.

"How's the baby?"

"She's all right. I left her with my mother. That's why it took me so long to get here."

"What happened?"

Carrie sighed and took a seat next to Emma.

"When he got home last night, he said he didn't feel right. He didn't want to eat."

"Yep."

"I fed the baby. I changed her and put her in her crib. He got a beer and turned on the TV. There was some ball game."

"And you?"

"I had a beer too. Then another."

Carrie looked down at her rough, shaky hands.

"And then?"

"I asked him what he wanted for dinner. He said: 'Whatever.' I looked in the fridge. There was nothing."

"Yep."

"I drove to Stewart's. I got another pack of beer and some hot dogs. They were on sale—two for three dollars, plus tax. I got four, two of them Kielbasa, and the fixings. I drove back home."

Emma nodded.

"He was asleep on the sofa. I didn't want to wake him up—you don't want to wake him up when he's asleep. I didn't even touch the TV. I don't like ball games, I like food shows, but I was afraid he'd wake up if I touched anything. You don't want him to wake up."

Emma nodded. "Yep. You don't want to wake them up. Ever."

"I checked on the baby. She was OK. I ate two hot dogs. He was still asleep. I left him there, and I went to bed. I hoped he'd stay asleep through the night."

"Did he?"

"No. He woke up at two. 'I don't feel good,' he said. He went to the bathroom. He puked. I could hear him from the baby's room, even though it's down the hall."

"Then what?"

"It was quiet for a while. I went to find him. He lay curled on his side in the bathroom. He said he wasn't feeling good. I asked if I should call an ambulance."

Carrie started crying. Tears ran out of her yellow-purple eye like a waterfall.

"I was trying to help him. He punched me. He said: 'You bitch. I'll kill you and your piece of shit daughter if you call anyone. A good woman would give her man a son. You cheated on me. That's why you had a girl, you piece of shit.' Sorrow choked her. "But I never did. I never cheated on him. She's his daughter, I swear to God! I never slept with another man since the day we met! He was wrong! Please, Dr. Steele, believe me! He's wrong!"

"I'm sure he is," Emma said, moving closer to Carrie. "I'm sure. I'm so sorry, Carrie!"

Carrie calmed down a little.

"I left him there. I went to the baby. She was OK. I didn't dare take her to our bed. I was afraid he'd wake up and find her there. He'd beat us both. He doesn't like her in our bed. I got my pillow, and I slept on her floor, holding the crib. I was afraid to pick her up, in case he woke up. Last time he kicked me, he hit her by mistake."

Carrie's sorrow was beyond anything Emma could fathom. As an abused child, she'd been powerless and afraid, but she had never worried about anyone else. Well, except for her dog. Carrie's story was worse. A mother who has to sleep on her child's floor, afraid that the father would wake up and hurt the kid—that was something else.

"What happened next?" Emma asked. She held Carrie to give her strength, hoping it wasn't a mistake. *Will somebody see us and take it the wrong way? Am I invading her personal space?*

"When the baby woke me up, it was light already. She wanted her bottle. I fed her. I changed her, and then I put her back in her bed. I went to see how he was. He was not in our bed, nor watching TV. He was still in the bathroom where I'd left him, covered in puke. That wasn't special. It happened many times before when he drank too much. He wasn't right, though. His skin was purple and cool to the touch."

"You called 911?"

Carrie stared at her, her eyes big as saucers. "No. He told me not to. He said he'd kill the baby if I did."

"So, what did you do?"

"I took the baby to my mom's—it's only a couple of miles—then came back. He hadn't moved."

"And then?"

"I walked out and went to Aisha. She's our neighbor. I always go there when I'm in trouble—she's nice. She even helped me take care of the baby when he…when I broke my hand. I told her he looked dead. She came to see. She said: 'Yep. Dead as a doornail. What did you do to him, girl?'"

"Did you do anything?"

"No! I love Chip. He's a good man. It's not his fault that I'm no good, and I never do anything right. It's my fault. I just wish he wouldn't hurt the baby."

Emma nodded. "And then?"

"Aisha called 911. They came and brought him here. I wish I called sooner, but I was afraid."

"I'm so sorry about all this, Carrie. Dr. Greene will come by to speak to you as soon as he has some answers. In the meantime, is there anyone you'd like me to call? Your mother? The priest?"

Carrie shook her head. "My mother's taking care of the baby. There's nothing better she can do. As for the priest, God doesn't think much of me. Otherwise, he'd have helped me long ago. But I'm just not good enough to deserve his love."

"I'm sorry you feel that way, Carrie. You want me to call Aisha?"

Carrie shook her head.

"She has her kids to worry about. She's already spent more time with me than I deserve. No. Can you get Vera?"

"Vera?"

"She's nice. She told me I'd be OK, and to just hang on. Everything will turn out for the best. I'd like her with me."

Emma hugged her and headed out.

Vera?

16

Emma's shift lasted forever. Or at least it felt that way. By the time she signed out, she'd forgotten about Chip and Carrie. Since them, she'd had countless other patients and families to worry about. She only remembered them when George stopped her on her way home. In spite of all the efforts, Chip had stayed dead and was going to be a coroner's case. Another one.

"Hello, stranger. Let's go for a drink," George said.

They stopped at Caron's, the bar across the street from the hospital. That place had seen more drama than the ER itself. People stopped by after their shift to have a drink and chat with their friends, unloading their stress rather than take it home to their families.

"This is ridiculous," George said, taking a thirsty sip out of his white collared Yuengling.

"What is?" Emma asked. She didn't do beer—too many calories, too little flavor. She got a gin and tonic instead, the tonic on the side. She hadn't touched it and didn't plan to.

"These healthy young people, dying for no good reason. It's all déjà vu all over again. Except that we don't have an opioid crisis—not that I know of."

Emma couldn't disagree. They'd had a few strange cases lately. Not like in February, when people dropped like flies. This crisis was strangely and subtly different.

They had all been in the ER recently for one reason or another. They weren't likable people. Not one of them was somebody Emma would want for a friend. There was something about the latest ER codes that didn't hint of lovely people.

The first had been Andy, the child abuser. Emma had no doubt that he had caused Tyrion's trauma. The child was still in the PICU, and nobody knew how he was going to do. Lorraine, his distraught mother, had left her low-paying job to sit with him day and night.

The second one was Ben. Or maybe the first, if the notes found with the bodies meant anything. Ben was an asshole. Emma wondered what happened to Mia and his kids. She'd have to ask Zagarian. Either way, they were probably better off with him dead. They could stop hiding and come back home. Mia could bring up her children without living with the fear that somebody would take them away.

The third one was Chip. Chip was a domestic abuser if she'd ever seen one. Carrie would be better off without him. So would his daughter.

"What are you thinking?" George asked.

"What were you saying?"

"Somebody's killing our assholes. They have no right to do that. It should be us."

Emma nodded. That's the problem with kindred spirits. It's hard to disagree.

"We didn't."

"Sadly."

"Do you think there's any other possible explanation?"

"Yep. I think it's God," George said, taking another swig of beer.

"God?"

"Yes. God is good; God is fair; God is almighty. The Bible says he sent plagues and draughts and locusts. I think God decided to clean up our community and went to work on it."

Emma looked him up and down.

"I didn't know you were so religious."

"Neither did I. But it looks like my grandmother's teaching is catching up with me."

"Are you serious?"

"Of course. Do you have any other ideas?"

"Nope," Emma said.

"Neither have I, but I'll go to church on Sunday, and I'll light a candle. Do you want to do anything?"

"Do anything for what?" Emma asked.

"For what happened."

"What happened?"

They looked in each other's eyes. Emma and George had known each other for a long time, and they seldom disagreed.

"Nothing that I know of," George said. "Do you know of anything?"

"Know what?" Emma asked.

George smiled.

"Another drink?"

Emma nodded.

"We should do this more often," George said, signaling the waiter.

Emma smiled. "Good idea. Let's."

17

I t was a bright fall morning a few days later when Margret's plane landed five minutes early at the tiny airport by the lake. The airport with only one luggage carousel had one of the longest runways in the country since it used to be a B-52 Stratofortress base. Margret recovered her purple roll-ons and dragged them behind her, looking for Victor. He wasn't there.

Margret shrugged and headed to the taxi stand. He must have forgotten. No wonder, with everything he had on his plate, but she could see how Amber would get spitting mad.

"Ms. Storm? Margret?"

She turned around to see a woman about her age—late 60s, she guessed— dressed in a tan trench coat like Colombo's. Short and plump, she had laughing blue eyes, bright red lipstick, and a mop of unruly gray hair.

"Yes?"

"I'm Vera. Vera Tolpeghin, Emma's friend. I'm glad to meet you."

"Glad to meet you too."

"I'm here to pick you up. Victor had to deal with an emergency, and Emma's at work."

"You are too kind, but I hate to bother you. I'll take a taxi."

"No bother. We were going to meet anyhow. Emma told me that we are to be great friends. I'm delighted to have somebody to chat with. As one gets older, it's harder and harder to meet interesting people."

"That's true," Margret said. "We're lucky if we get to keep our old friends."

"Unfortunately, I keep losing mine," Vera said. "Oscar Wilde would call me negligent."

"Maybe you should be more careful then," Margret said, wondering when she had last heard somebody quoting Oscar Wilde.

Vera laughed and grabbed one of the roll-ons.

"You and I, we're going to be great friends. Let's go. We're late for lunch."

"Lunch?"

"Yep. We're having lunch at Tony's; then I'll take you to see my garden."

"Your garden? Emma did mention that. I garden too."

"I know. I'm looking forward to comparing notes. Your garden must be different. You're so much further south. The weather must be softer there."

On their way to Tony's, they chatted soils, humidity, and pests. Margret loved talking to someone who shared her passion for gardening. Victor and Emma tolerated it lovingly, and Victor's father, now deceased, could barely distinguish a plant from the shovel used to plant it.

Tony's was an old wooden house with exposed beams and creaky floors. The walls displayed a rainbow of modern art from local artists, prices attached.

Hot crusty bread, smelling heavenly, arrived wrapped in blinding white napkins with sea-snails of yellow butter on the side. A waiter looking like he inhabited the House of Lords recited the menu, drooling over the specials. They had shrimp and chorizo with linguini in white wine, and a sauvignon blanc to go with it.

"I don't usually drink wine with lunch," Margret said. "I like tea."

"Me too. When I'm out of vodka."

Margret laughed. "Emma said you're Russian."

"I was. That was like sixty years ago. I guess I'm American now. Sort of."

"You miss Russia?"

"Not at all. I don't even remember it. My parents fled it when I was eight. I never went back."

"You speak Russian?"

"Yes, with an awful accent. Fortunately, nobody else here speaks it, so they wouldn't know."

Margret laughed again. She liked Vera, who was the most exciting person she'd met in ages, direct, funny, and very entertaining. She was glad that Victor had been busy.

"What do you grow in your garden?" Vera asked, sipping on her second glass of wine.

"I like flowers. I love watching every season come with a different bloom—the daffodils and the hyacinths, then the peonies—I have them in every color—then the roses and the lilies. I also love shrubs."

"Which ones?"

"The ones that attract butterflies. Honeysuckle and such. What do you like to plant?"

"Why don't I show you?" Vera said.

They drove to Vera's home. The wrought-iron fence was green with climbing vines. The house was small, old, and utterly charming, all covered in vines but the windows.

"This looks like Hansel and Gretel's cottage! I love it!"

"Me too," Vera said. "Let's go inside."

Rough-cut, comfortable stone steps led to an ancient wooden door opening to the living room. Leather armchairs faced a sofa stacked with bright pillows. A tortured Japanese blown-glass vase held hostage a bunch of rainbow-colored wildflowers. The fireplace was only waiting for a match. Tall, narrow, stained-glass windows fractured the light. Books everywhere. Old books, new books, open books, closed books sitting on shelves, laying on coffee tables, spread on the floor. Behind glass doors, old tomes stood in dark cabinets, their leather spines covered in strange writings.

"Cyrillic?"

"Some. Some just fancy Latin and plain English. You wouldn't believe what those old people did with their fonts."

"I've never seen this many books together outside of a library. When on earth do you get time to garden?"

"They're mainly reference books. I've had them for a long time."

"On what?"

"Plants. Biology. Medicine. Divination. Witchcraft." Vera handed her a short, heavy glass half-full of amber fluid smelling like last winter's smoke. *"Za Zdarovje!"*

"Cheers." Margret sniffed it and coughed.

"Laphroaig. I didn't think you'd like vodka."

"As you said, if you ran out of tea…"

The single malt was harsh and peaty like nothing Margret had tried before. It was so heavy it made her skin crawl. She choked, but she kept smiling.

"Phew! That's disgusting!" Vera said, putting the glass down. "I don't know how you people can drink this! Give me a good Stoli any day!"

"I don't drink this! Nobody I know does."

"Glad to hear. It's horrific."

"Why do you drink it then?"

"I don't. I keep it there for annoying guests. It makes them leave sooner," Vera laughed. "Come, let's see the gardens."

The first garden was utilitarian and open—potatoes, tomatoes, peppers, corn, squash—all in perfectly straight rows. The wildflower border gave it color and spunk. A high fence with a forged iron gate surrounded the back garden. Vera opened the lock to allow them in, letting Margret marvel at a profusion of plants like she'd never seen. She recognized a few: graceful oleander bushes blooming pink, dark green shiny ficus, green lacy hemlock, the dark waxy leaves of the rhododendron, the low green ground cover of the lily of the valley.

"You're a genius," Margret said, caressing the long stringy leaves of an oleander.

"Not at all, I'm just interested in plants. And their uses. They're fascinating. Peppermint helps upset stomachs. Chamomile infusion disinfects and soothes. A few eucalyptus leaves thrown in hot water will help with a cough. And if you rub your shoes with chili peppers, the dog will stop chewing on them.

"Fascinating," Margret said.

By the time Victor came to pick her up, they'd made plans for the coming week.

18

———

Victor moved a pile of books, a pair of muddy boots, and a small dog crate to make room for Margret in his car. She smiled, wishing she could wipe the seat without making him feel bad. She sat, hoping the mud was dry enough to not show on her light brown coat.

She waved to Vera as they left.

"What a woman!" Margret said.

"Taylor told me she's a force."

"Taylor is right. How is she?"

"She's OK. Not long before the baby comes now."

"Is she worried?"

"I think so. She never speaks about it, so she must be."

"Has she decided what to do?"

"She changes her mind a few times a day."

"I don't blame her. I don't know how I'd make that decision!"

Victor nodded.

"She needs the father's permission to give the child for adoption, doesn't she?" Margret asked.

"Not if he's not on the birth certificate, I don't think."

"But what if he wants the kid?"

Victor shrugged. "He can't."

"Why not?"

"He's in jail."

"So what? That doesn't end his parental rights. Does he know she's pregnant?"

"Yes."

"Then he must know the baby's coming soon."

"There's no reason for him to be interested in the baby."

"Why not?"

"He has other kids. And he's not the parenting type."

"That's what you think," Margret said.

"I'll have her speak to a lawyer," Victor said. "I just didn't want to bother her with this, now that she's about to give birth."

If not now, then when? And you didn't want to bother yourself either, Margret thought. She loved Victor but had no illusions as far as he was concerned. *If Victor were a verb, he'd be "chill."* No worries.

"He may want to give her trouble just out of spite, after what Emma and Taylor did to him. He may be looking for revenge."

Victor's face darkened. That was something he hadn't considered.

"When are you leaving?" Margret asked.

"Next week. I wish I weren't. I wonder if I could just send Amber and stay home."

"On a second honeymoon? Really?"

"Well, it's more like a vacation. If there's good shopping, she won't even notice I'm not around."

"Why don't you want to go?"

"I'm worried about Taylor. I know she's not due for another month, but she's been through so much. It will be a wonder if she doesn't have the baby early. And I have no interest in lying on the beach. Not my thing."

"Why did you book this vacation then?"

"You know I didn't! I wouldn't in a hundred years. I wonder if I could find a good excuse to stay home. Like an ankle sprain or appendicitis or something."

"Victor."

"Yes."

"You won't get Emma back."

He shrugged. "Maybe not. You never know."

"Seriously!"

He laughed. "I know. I just said that to rile you up."

They turned right into the long driveway lined with uneven spruce trees. Amber was into green living. Every Christmas, she got a live potted tree that she eventually planted along the driveway. The idea was excellent, but the effect less so. Last year's tree looked puny next to the one she'd planted nine years ago.

The car stopped in front of the red door. As Victor helped Margret out, the front door blew open. Thelma and Louise flew out, followed closely by the girls, Iris and Opal. The dogs were a little grayer than when Margret had seen them last, but they hadn't forgotten her. Nor had the girls, so Margret found herself hugged, licked, and stepped on from every angle. She struggled to stay upright.

"How big you are! And how beautiful!"

Like their mother, the girls were both golden blonde. In their pink matching outfits, they looked like angels, but for Victor's mischievous sparkle in their eyes.

The door opened again and Amber came out, looking like a Greek goddess in her gold one-shouldered dress. She was beautiful and smiling, but her smile didn't quite reach her eyes. She leaned over to place a kiss near Margret's cheek.

"How lovely to see you, Mother! I hope you had a good day! I wanted to come and get you, but I had an appointment with the hairdresser that I couldn't..."

"No problem. I know you're busy," Margret said.

"Did you manage OK?"

"I managed better than OK. How are you?"

"Oh, struggling, as usual. The housekeeper was supposed to be here at one, but she was late, so now everything's running behind, including dinner," she said, leading them back to the house. The dogs followed. Then the kids.

Margret's eyes met Victor's. *And you left Emma for this? Really?*

Victor shrugged.

19

———

Back in the ER, Emma logged off her computer and went to see the chest pain in Room 14. Brenda intercepted her at the door.

"Dr. Steele, can you please stop by Room 2?"

"Room 2?"

"You'll see," Brenda said.

Emma shrugged and changed course. Room 2 was packed. She remembered the trauma code they'd announced earlier, a head-on collision that went to Burt. The room was full of people from all over the hospital, most of them gawking. Dr. Burt Funk, looking like an old barn owl with his white hair and oversized glasses, leaned over a belligerent patient. He tried to talk to him while the EMTs held him down.

"You motherfuckers! Let me go, you motherfuckers! I'll call my lawyer if you don't let me go right now," the patient screamed, shaking off one of the people holding his legs.

"We need to make sure that you are OK first," Burt said.

"Fuck youuuu! Fuck youuuu!" the patient howled, thrashing to get off the stretcher. The EMTs groaned, struggling to hold him down. He turned his head to bite them.

Burt leaned in to speak to him.

"Listen, what's your name…"

The patient spat. A blob of thick bloody phlegm landed on Burt's glasses.

"That's not cool," Burt said, taking off his glasses and wiping them on his white coat.

"Fuck youuuu! Fuck youuu!"

At the head of the bed, the RT stood watching, holding the bag and the mask. His eyes lit up as they met Emma's, but she shrugged. It wasn't her case. She couldn't just step in and take over.

The patient bent his knee and kicked Joe, the EMT holding his legs. The dirty boot got him in the jaw. Joe stumbled to the corner of the room, holding his face. A dozen hands grabbed the patient, holding him down. The man wiggled and kicked to free himself. The stretcher became a melee in which nobody knew who held who.

"Grab his head. He's going to bite! Grab his head!"

"That's my arm. Let go of it!"

"Put a mask on him, for God's sake; he's about to spit again!"

Burt put his glasses back on and stared. He was thinking.

"Burt, I think you may want to sedate him," Emma said.

"I'm trying to deescalate the situation verbally."

"I understand, but I don't think that's going to work in this case."

Burt shrugged.

"What do you want me to do?"

Emma looked at Sal, standing by the code cart.

"Ketamine?"

"Here." Sal lifted his hand with the syringe. He was waiting for the order.

"We have an IV?"

"No."

"500 IM then."

Sal handed the syringe to Brenda, who found a spot between the entangled arms and knees holding the patient on the stretcher. She plunged the needle to the hilt and pushed the plunger home.

Emma checked the clock. *The ketamine will take a couple of minutes to work. Maybe more. I hope Brenda got it right.*

"You sure you gave it to him?"

Brenda shrugged. "I think so. But you never know. We'll see who falls," she said.

"No worries. We have more," Sal said, preparing a second syringe.

Emma laughed.

Burt didn't. "This is not a joke. This is a patient, and he deserves respect."

Emma had had it. Burt was slow, inefficient, and the cause of half the patient complaints she had to deal with every week. He was also a pain in the ass, acting like he always knew better than anybody else.

"He deserves respect. He also deserves appropriate care. He deserves to be kept safe. He needs to be prevented from hurting himself or others while he's mentally impaired and we don't even know why. It may be the trauma; it may be drugs or alcohol. Whatever it is, we need to control the situation and the patient and prevent him from harm."

"Suit yourself." Burt said and left the room.

Emma shrugged. That solved one problem. In the meantime, the patient had relaxed. Laying on the stretcher, he breathed evenly while his eyes rolled around in his head as if he was acting in a poorly directed scene from *The Exorcist. Thank God for Ketamine,* Emma thought. *He should be out long enough for us to do our job.*

The melee had disassembled. People checked themselves and the ones around them to see who was hurt.

"Right. Let's get it together here. Brenda, Judy, I need two IVs. Labs. Aisha, monitor, and EKG. Let's expose him and be prepared to intubate if necessary. Tom, please stand by."

The situation was under control.

20

____

A couple of hours later, Kurt stopped by Emma's desk.

"How's he doing?"

"He's OK. The workup was essentially negative except for a clavicle fracture and a couple of broken ribs."

"Did you need to intubate?"

"No. He slept like a baby. If babies snore, cough like an old engine, and drool. And stink of beer."

Kurt nodded. "I wish mine was that lucky."

"Yours?"

"Yep. The car he collided with."

"How is he?"

"She. The driver, a woman in her thirties, has a brain bleed. We'll have to ship her over for neurosurgery."

"I'm so sorry, Kurt!"

"That's the good part. The bad part is that her three-year-old kid, who should have been in the back in a car seat, was sitting in front. He got ejected. He died. They pronounced him at the scene. I haven't told her yet."

A wave of nausea ran through Emma. She took a deep breath and waited for it to pass. She looked at Kurt. His dilated eyes were windows into pain.

"I'm so sorry, Kurt!"

"Yeah, me too."

He sat at the desk, his back bent, holding his forehead in his cupped hands. "I don't even know how to tell her. She keeps asking about him. I told her he's not here yet. But he's not going to be here. They took him directly to the morgue."

Emma touched his shoulder. Vera stopped by and sat a cup of coffee next to him.

"I wish it was vodka."

"Me too," Kurt said. "But it still helps. Thank you, Vera."

"My pleasure. Emma, police are here to speak to you."

A young, tall officer she'd never seen before shook her hand.

"Dr. Steele?"

"Yes."

"You have a moment to talk to us about Mr. Peterson?"

"Who?"

"Mr. Peterson. Your patient in Room 2."

He'd initially arrived as a John Doe. They only merged his records to his previous history after they got an ID, and Emma hadn't seen them yet.

"Yes."

"Are his injuries…"

"He's not going to die. Not today. He'll likely go home in a few hours."

"In a few hours?"

"Yes. His alcohol level was high. I can't let him go before he's sober."

The officer nodded.

"This isn't his first time, you know. He already has a DUI. Last time he was here, he'd been driving a truck, and he hit a pole."

"I didn't know."

"Yes. He's got a bad history. His mother was in the passenger seat. She didn't make it. But that didn't stop him from doing it again."

"This is horrific! He drove drunk and killed his mother, and then you people let him out to kill some more?" Kurt asked.

"No sir, I didn't let him out. That's what the court decided."

Kurt shook his head. "This is disgusting."

Emma agreed. "This is unfortunate. Very sad."

"I'm sorry, ma'am. Will you please make sure somebody calls us before you discharge him? We are going to charge him, so we'll return to take him into custody."

Emma nodded, and the officer left.

"Can I help, Kurt?" Emma asked.

"I don't know how. I'll have to tell her, one way or another."

"Is there any family? Priest? Social worker?"

"I'll check. Thanks, Emma."

"Anytime. I wish I could do more."

"By the way, what happened to Burt?"

"Burt?"

"Yep. I came to see if I could help in Room 2 just as he burst through the door, cursing, and spitting on his glasses."

Emma laughed.

"He got mad at me. He had the code in Room 2, but I had to intervene. The patient trashed the room and hurt the staff. Burt tried to verbally deescalate."

Kurt laughed.

"God bless you, Emma, I didn't think I was going to laugh today. Verbally deescalate a drunk trauma patient? What's wrong with him?"

"I've been wondering too. He hasn't been himself lately."

"He wasn't that fast before, but the last few months he's been losing it. Do you think it's dementia?"

"He's not that old!"

"He's got to be close to seventy. If it's not that, then maybe something else? Drugs? Alcohol? Personal problems?"

"I don't know. I don't even know how to speak to him, now that he's so mad."

"Give him a couple of days to chill. We'll think of something."

"Thanks, Kurt."

He nodded and left to tell his patient that her child died as if he was going to his execution. Emma wished she could help. *Nothing is harder for a doctor than telling somebody their child died. Nothing.*

21

———————

Taylor woke up close to noon that morning. She wasn't working that day, and she loved sleeping in.

She groaned as she got up from Eric's bed. She had moved in with him a few weeks before, after the April disaster. She felt better having him around, and her mother was safe at home with Guinness. *She's never lonely. I think she sometimes locks herself in the bathroom to get some peace, but Guinness doesn't care. She'll follow her there, or anywhere else.*

Taylor looked in the mirror. Not a pretty sight. She could barely recognize herself. She used to be slim and flexible, like an eel, but these days she couldn't even bend to tie her shoes. She hadn't seen her private parts in ages; she got winded climbing a few stairs. She was ready to be done with her pregnancy, no matter what. *No, not no matter what! But I'm ready to be done. Four more weeks.*

She found Eric's note on the kitchen table.

"I love you. Have a good day. Rest and keep your feet up, you know they swell. Remember I got you that biology book on Kindle, in case you feel like studying. Don't wait up for me, I should be done at seven, but you know how it goes. I love you." He ended with a dozen hearts.

He's so sweet. I'm lucky to have him.

She poured herself a cup of coffee. She needed the bathroom. Again. On her way, she glanced in the extra bedroom. It started looking like a nursery. She'd gathered a toy here, a pair of booties there, a cute onesie. They got piled on the extra bed for now, but she needed to make up her mind.

She had been seventeen, high on drugs, and drinking, when she got pregnant. She thought that Dr. Dick Umber was the love of her life. But she was wrong. She'd met Eric, and her life had never been the same.

She went back to the kitchen and sat, sipping on her coffee while checking her email: junk, an invitation from her friend Cathy, pictures of kittens from Iris, more garbage.

Then her heart skipped a beat.

An email from Dr. Umber.

She hadn't seen that email in a long, long time. Six months almost. She'd hoped never to see it again.

The subject was: *"Long time, no see."*

Her hands shook so bad she had trouble opening it.

"Hello, Taylor. Long-time no see.

Remember me? Sure you do, it hasn't been that long.

How are you doing? You look more beautiful than ever. Pregnancy suits you well.

How do I know? I saw you the day before yesterday as you left the hospital. I come to see you. I love the way you do your hair now. Much better than those green tips you used to have.

What I didn't like, though, was seeing you walking hand in hand with that guy. You said you were going to love me forever. It looks like, for you, forever is a short time. Not even six months! That's sad!

On a happier note, I'm glad you decided to keep our baby. It shouldn't be long now. What? A few more weeks?

I'm looking forward to meeting him. And you! I look forward to seeing you again!

How come?

I'm out. A free man. The world is my oyster. Police messed up the evidence, so they had to let me go.

Are you happy?

Of course, you are. How could you not? We're old friends, you and me. We have so many memories together. And a baby.

I can't wait to see you. Give my best regards to your mother. She'll be glad to hear I'm back."

Yours truly,

Dick."

Taylor's heart froze. She couldn't believe it. Maybe a farce? Somebody's idea of a joke?

She rechecked the address. It was correct.

She had indeed left the hospital with Eric, the day before yesterday.

He had seen her.

He was back.

He wanted to meet her.

Even worse, he wanted to see the baby.

Right then and there, she knew she should have killed him. Emma had been wrong. She said they were going to take care of him in jail. They didn't. They let him go, and he was back.

I knew I should have killed him that day. I was close. I wish Mother hadn't stopped me. I could have rid the world of that vermin, and I wouldn't have to deal with him now.

But then I wouldn't be here, in Eric's home, drinking Eric's coffee. I'm alive. I'm happy with my life. I wouldn't want it any other way, except for that fucking asshole. If I killed him, I'd be in jail learning to knit. I'd wonder how long they'd let me keep my baby before sending her away. So yeah, Mother was right. She always is. But it still sucks.

What do I do?

Call Eric? He's at work. He doesn't have time for this. He doesn't even know about Dick, and I don't want him to know. That wouldn't do anybody any good. I bet Dick would love to tell him every detail, the asshole!

Call Mother? She's working. It's not that urgent. There's nothing she can do, anyhow.

I'll call Grandma.

She stood to get her phone. A hot wave of pain struck her, bending her over, taking her breath away. She waited for the pain to fade, then walked to the bedroom to get her phone.

The second cramp hit her as she bent over to pick it up. She let herself fall on the bed and curled around her belly, waiting for the pain to go away.

She grabbed the phone. *Dead.* She forgot to put it on the charger.

Where is the damn charger, anyhow?

The third cramp came, and the pain invaded her like a tsunami, taking her breath away, driving her mind into blackness.

Pain makes you stupid.

She waited for it to pass.

It didn't.

22

Back for another ER shift, Emma got ready to sew the lac in Room 5. She left her coat on the back of her chair, pulled 5cc of lidocaine with epi in the syringe with the large #18 needle, then changed it to a finer #27 to make it hurt less.

The elderly patient in Room 5 had stumbled over his dog. In his fall, he struck the table corner, carving a four-inch gash over his temple. The skin split open into an extensive L-shaped laceration, with a corner hanging loose.

"I'm sorry, but this will hurt," Emma said. "Let me know if we need to stop and take a breather. Please don't move. Otherwise, we both get hurt."

"Don't you worry, I've seen pain like you've never seen before. I'm a vet."

Emma smiled. She'd heard that before, usually from the loudest complainers. She injected the lidocaine slowly, through the broken skin, to hurt less. Or so they said.

She cleaned the wound with saline, then started sewing it with Vycril #5. The old skin was thin and fragile. The work was going slowly. *The ER's going to hell in a hand-basket while I'm stuck here. If it was just two inches higher, I could throw in a few staples. Oh well. There's nothing I can do. They'll have to wait. I may as well relax and enjoy it.*

"What kind of dog do you have?"

"Oh, she's just a mutt."

"What's her name?"

"Mutt."

"That's not very respectful!"

"We didn't plan to keep her. We gave her some scraps. She returned the next day. Then the next. One day she didn't come. We wondered: 'Where's that mutt?'

Then my wife called me: 'Your mutt is here.'

The dog never left, and her name stayed, too. That was ten years ago. My wife died last year, so now it's just the two of us."

"I'm sorry," Emma said.

"That's OK. I'll be joining Ella soon. I know she's waiting for me. But I don't want to go before Mutt. I don't want to leave her. She's gray now, and slow. Nobody wants her."

Emma's eyes teared. *He loved his dog so much that he wanted her to die first so that she didn't get abandoned.*

"How about you? Won't you feel alone?" Emma asked.

He shrugged. "I know I'll be going soon. Mutt doesn't."

She wished she could hug him, but couldn't—sterile gloves, needles, blood.

"I'll take her if it happens."

"You will?"

"Yes. Tell whoever deals with your affairs. Give them my name."

Tears started running through Emma's sterile field, soaking the paper.

"Thank you."

"You're…"

A scream interrupted her.

"Put me down!"

Emma looked out.

"What's that?" he asked.

"They're bringing in a kid."

"Why is he screaming?"

"He doesn't want to be here."

"Put me down. Put me down, you motherfuckers. I'm gonna kill you all. Every one of you. I'm going to stab you in your sleep. Put me down!"

"He doesn't sound happy."

"Not really."

They had tied the kid to the stretcher and cuffed his hands in front of him. The EMTs pushed the gurney while the police officers walked behind, their heads low.

Really? Cuff a kid? What's he? Nine? Ten? That looks like overkill.

Judy came in just as Emma finishing sewing.

"The kid."

"Yes."

"We need to sedate him."

"Will he take a pill?"

"No. He ripped apart the mattress. Now he's hitting his head against the wall."

"Give him 5 of Haldol IM. Make sure he's not allergic."

Judy nodded and left.

The closed door muffled the screams, making them even eerier.

"Let me go, you fuckers. I'm going to kill you all. And your babies. And your mothers. And your cats."

"Wow, even the cats," the old man said. "That's serious. And I don't even like cats."

Emma smiled. She was done.

"You look as good as new. Put some antibiotic ointment on it, come back here or see your doctor if it bothers you at all. Stitches need to come out in five to seven days."

"Thank you, Dr. Steele."

"My pleasure."

"And…were you serious? About Mutt?"

"Of course. There." She took her card and wrote on it: "I'll take Mutt." She signed it and gave it to him.

He read it. His eyes started tearing again.

"Thank you."

"Be well. Stop by and tell me how you're doing, one of these days."

In a gesture of old courtesy, he bent over to kiss Emma's hand. He left, and a piece of her heart went with him.

She went to see the kid. The Haldol hadn't touched him.

"Let's give him another ten minutes and try again."

He peeled the paint off the walls, put it in his mouth, then spit it against the door.

"This young man has issues," Emma said. "What happened at home?"

The police officer, a former EMT, smiled.

"Hello, Dr Steele. His mother called us. He killed the cat."

"He killed the cat?"

"Yes."

"How?"

"He stabbed her with a knife."

"Wow! That's different."

"Not for him. Last week he set the dog on fire. He poured gasoline on him and lit him up."

Emma felt sick.

"The mother called us because he threatened to kill the baby."

The urge to vomit became overwhelming.

"Excuse me." She rushed to the bathroom to splash cold water over her face.

Something was wrong with this kid. No normal kid would set the dog on fire or stab the cat. What the heck do I do with him?

The speakers called her before she could figure it out.

"Dr. Steele to Room 1. Code 99. Code 99 Room 1."

The code in Room 1 looked familiar. She leaned over him to see him better.

"It's yesterday's drunk driver," George said, looking up from the IV he was placing, while Joe continued CPR.

One hour and many procedures later, the patient was still dead.

Police came.

"I thought you took him into custody?" Emma asked.

"We did. They let him out yesterday."

"Why?"

He shrugged. "The judge did. His lawyer got him out on bail."

After he left, George and Emma looked at each other.

George shrugged. "God's work."

"I don't know, George. It's getting hairy. I'm not that religious. It's hard to believe that, suddenly, God decided to fix our community. We need to look into what's happening."

"We're not the police. It's not our job." He glanced around, checking that nobody listened. "Listen, this guy already killed two people—his mother, and the kiddo the other day. Maybe the kid's mother too. We don't even know yet. He was a danger to society. The world is better without him."

Emma couldn't disagree. But she couldn't pretend that nothing had happened.

The screams coming out of Room 6 reminded her.

The kid. He set the dog on fire, stabbed the cat, and threatened to kill the baby.

What if the world was better without him too?

23

T *hank God for wine*, Emma thought, when she finally made it home that evening. She looked for the right wine to pair with another eventful day: Mutt and his owner, the drunk driver, the kid. She chose an Australian red. A Covenant Shiraz 2012 from Claire Valley, the wine had a humble screw cap, but its humility stopped there. It poured garnet, but, in the glass, it was as dark as squid ink.

She sniffed it. Dark fruit. The acidity of dry wines. An unexpected herbal note. She swirled it again. The floral note was gone, replaced by the bitterness of oak. She took a sip. She rinsed her mouth with it, bringing it forward, then back to the remotest taste buds. They sang. The wine was deep and smooth to the palate.

The second sip was deep and thirsty. Relief was on its way. Wine helped cleanse her from the horrors and misery of another day that should never have happened.

She felt torn. She had two reasons to suspect that the string of deaths was not an accident. One, they had no explanation, and healthy people don't die without a reason. Second, she didn't believe in coincidences. Coincidences happened. Occasionally. Once, maybe. But four times in a row? It was not impossible, but it was improbable. And improbable, Emma didn't do.

The crux of being an ER doc was managing risk. She went through every shift calculating probabilities. The probability that four healthy men, all nasty sons of bitches, all having something to do with her ED, died for no good reason was infinitesimally low. The likelihood of it being a coincidence was not worth mentioning. Something—or somebody—tied these deaths together.

They had happened in different places, at different times. They hadn't dined together; they hadn't socialized, they didn't drive the same car, they didn't even live in the same neighborhood. Or did they?

I'm getting ahead of myself here. I don't know that. I know nothing about them. For all that I know, all the dead could belong to the same Masonic Lodge, play Russian Roulette on Friday nights, or date the same psychopathic black widow.

And why do I care? I'm not even sorry they are dead. I should do what George said: mind my own business. But I can't.

There's this kid. In a way, he's even worse than any of the others. He is evil. And a child who kills pets for fun and tries to kill a baby will only get worse. He's going to become a psychopath making Ted Bundy or Jaime Gumb look like little angels. His wires have crossed somewhere, and there's no uncrossing them. It's in his DNA. He's wired wrong. So what if he dies?

But he's just a kid!

He's a killer in training. He's got the heart; he's got the drive. It's only a matter of time. Next time, it's not going to be the cat. How can somebody set a dog on fire?

She glanced at Guinness, who was sleeping on the floor by Emma's feet, dreaming she was chasing something. She bent over to hug her. Guinness woke up with a surprised bark. She tolerated this invasion of her personal space for a moment, then she got up, pretending she heard something at the door. Guinness wasn't much into displays of physical affection. She preferred scratching. She was about to lay down again when the hair on her back suddenly rose.

She growled a deep, threatening growl, looking in the darkness outside, then turned and looked at Emma.

"What?"

She growled again, then yelped.

A chill went through Emma, and she shuddered. Something was happening. Something bad was happening. She set the glass down just as the phone rang. It was Eric.

"Taylor. She's in the hospital."

"Ours?"

"Yes."

"Why?"

"I came home after my shift. She was unconscious. She's bleeding. I called the ambulance. I'm on my way there."

"I'll meet you there."

Emma hung up, put her half-empty glass down, and looked at the bottle.

Half gone. Almost two glasses.

She could drive, or she could call a taxi. That would be another half hour at least.

Unconscious. Bleeding.

She grabbed her keys and left.

Guinness watched.

24

———————

The ER was full, as usual, just a hair off from batshit crazy. Emma had only left an hour ago, but the place looked like they'd been parachuting people in. People everywhere, anxious and angry, demanding to know why nobody was looking after them.

Still in her scrubs, Emma got the brunt of nasty looks as she made a beeline to the clerk's desk. There, Kayla kept a sharp eye on everything without getting too close, like a young witch watching a bubbling cauldron while avoiding the fumes.

"Taylor?" Emma asked.

"Room 3."

"Who's the doctor?"

Kayla looked down. "Dr. Burt."

Emma took a deep breath.

"Did he page OB?"

"Not yet."

"Page them for me, will you please?"

"Sure."

"And get some blood."

"Group?"

"O positive."

Kayla nodded.

Emma zipped to the room. She dreaded what she was about to see. What she found was even worse. Burt was performing a pelvic exam on a half-conscious Taylor while Eric was holding her hand. Blood bubbled out of Taylor like a stream. Mona, the new nurse, assisted, her eyes popping out of her head like a frog's. The monitors were off.

"Hi, Burt. How is she?"

He looked at her above his glasses, scowling to keep them from falling off his nose.

"She's OK."

"What's her blood pressure?" Emma asked casually, approaching the stretcher. *She's white. Clammy. She looks like shit. Hemorrhagic shock, probably.*

Emma felt Taylor's wrist for a pulse but couldn't find it. The systolic was below eighty. Emma moved to the head of the bed looking for the carotid. The pulse was crazy fast. Taylor's heart was beating fast to compensate for the low blood pressure. *She's young and healthy, but she'll sink like a rock when her reserve is gone.*

"Blood pressure?" Burt repeated.

"Yes. Let's recheck it. Mona, will you?"

Mona dropped the bouquet of oversized obstetric Q-tips she was holding and pushed a button to check the blood pressure. It failed. The pressure was too low to register.

"Let's check a manual, shall we?" Emma said. Mona glanced around for the "nurse-on-a-stick," a portable device with a manual blood pressure cuff, but didn't find it.

"I need to finish the pelvic. We'll check vitals afterward," Burt said. "Get me the Q-tips, Mona."

Mona went back to the Q-tips.

"Eric, check the blood pressure and get me the charge nurse. The charge nurse first," Emma said.

She turned around to Burt.

"There may be no vitals left to measure by the time you finish, Burt. She doesn't have a radial pulse now. She's bleeding like crazy. You ordered blood, I assume? And paged OB? By the way, you have no business doing a pelvic on a thirty-six-week bleeding pregnancy. None, whatsoever."

Burt stood up so fast his stool shot backward, crashing to the floor.

"This is my patient. You have no business interfering with my care. You're a control freak. You need to get your OCD treated. You're losing it. My patient is none of your business."

"Blood pressure 75/50," Eric said.

Emma nodded. "Charge nurse?"

"Coming."

"Good. It is my business, Burt. Taylor is my daughter, and I prefer her alive. I know this is a break in protocol, but I can't sit and wait to see if she's still alive when you're done with her. Some things are more important to me than my career. Taylor is one of them."

The door opened. Brenda walked in.

"Dr. Funk asked me to take over. Can you please get the OR ready?"

"Yep."

A tall man in a white coat walked in. The new OB that Emma hadn't met.

"What's up?"

"I think it's a placenta previa," Emma said.

"Previa? And you did a pelvic?"

Emma looked at Burt. Burt shrunk.

"It was a mistake," Emma said.

The OB gave her a look she'd seen often. The "how stupid can you be" look.

He glanced at Taylor.

"She needs the OR."

"The OR is ready," Brenda said. "So is the blood."

"Let's go," he said, avoiding Emma's eyes. He looked at Eric. "Are you the father?"

Eric mumbled.

"OK. You can come."

The door opened. Tired and haggard, Victor walked in.

"What the hell's going on?" he asked.

The OB didn't stop. Nor did the stretcher. Eric followed.

"She's getting a C-section," Emma said.

"Now?"

Emma looked at him.

"I mean, why?"

"She has placenta previa."

Victor frowned. He'd known that before, twenty years ago, in medical school. Not since. He did hearts. Kidneys and lungs occasionally, when they affected the heart, but uterus? No.

"It's when the placenta grows over the birth canal. When labor starts, the placenta is torn and bleeds. Taylor needs a C-section."

"I know that."

"Let's go get some coffee while we're waiting."

"I'm on call."

"Of course. You're always on call."

"What are you saying?"

"Relax. Let's go to the cafeteria."

Victor checked his watch. "It's closed."

"Of course. Come, I'll buy you coffee." She dragged him to the ER break room where the coffee stayed hot, pizza stiffened, and donuts often stopped by.

The sign under the coffeepot said: "Made fresh @4:15." It was nine thirty.

"Let's make a fresh pot," Emma said, looking for something to do to kill time. She found the filters and cleaned the pot.

Fresh coffee smell filled the room. Emma poured coffee in two cups, handed one to Victor, then leaned against the back wall. Victor leaned against the counter. They looked into the steam.

"How are you?" Emma asked.

"Surviving," Victor said. "Your mother-in-law is a challenge."

"She's my ex-mother-in-law. But she's still your mother."

"Why don't you tell her that?" Victor asked. "The way she's acting, you'd think I'm an intruder trying to hit on you."

"She's trying to keep us both safe," Emma said.

Victor nodded.

"How are you?" Victor asked.

"How much time do you have?"

The pager rang.

"None, it seems." He checked the number. It's the damn ER again!"

Emma sighed. "I'll see you upstairs."

25

———————

Emma checked her watch. *Not even half an hour. I've never seen a slower half an hour.* She couldn't sit. She went to the OR waiting room, though she knew it was too early. Worried families sat on cheap plastic chairs, staring at old magazines. Their heads perked up when they saw her, hoping she was looking for them. She was still in scrubs. *They think I'm here to tell them what's going on with their loved ones. They don't know we're all in the same boat.*

She walked back to the ER. Same there, everybody stared, hoping she was there to see them. She walked to her office instead, and turned on her computer, trying to finish her charts, but she couldn't focus. There was no point in even trying. *Whatever I'm doing, I'll have to redo.*

To take her mind off Taylor, she reopened the certified letter about her inquest. She had tried again and again to find out what that was about. No luck. She had even asked some well-connected friends for help, but nobody seemed to know anything. She had nothing else to do but wait. That drove her nuts.

She checked her watch. It was time to return to the OR. She turned off her computer.

A knock at the door.

"Come in," she said. Then she realized that it was past ten. *I must be alone in the building, and I just invited someone in. With my luck, it will be another serial killer.*

602

She looked around for a weapon. Nothing but the triangular wooden award for "The Most Improved Department" that the ER had earned last week. It was well-deserved, but the trophy was just another useless piece of junk gathering dust. She also had a bowl of sweets to soften visitors. *That's a killer, all right, but it works really slowly. It's not going to get me out of whatever I got myself in.*

She checked her pockets. Full of crap, as usual. She found her scalpel. Holding it felt better.

The door opened. Burt came in looking a hundred years old. A long hundred.

"Hi, Emma."

The relief ran through her. *Burt won't kill me unless I'm already sick.*

"Have a seat, Burt. Candy?" She offered him the bowl.

He declined and sat. The chair facing the desk was low, making him look even smaller. With his crazy Einstein white hair, old metal-framed glasses, and watery blue eyes bulging through the thick glass, he looked more like a character than a person.

"No, thanks." He coughed a heavy cough, then wiped his mouth with a blue and white checkered handkerchief. He looked inside it, then put it in his pocket and rested his hands on his knees.

He looked at Emma. "I came to apologize."

That, she didn't expect.

"I'm sorry about your daughter. I didn't know she was your daughter, but I'm sorry, anyhow."

Emma studied him. A tired old man, working in the ER past his expiration date.

"What are you sorry about, Burt?"

"I'm sorry I didn't do better by her. I tried. You're right. I should have gotten the vitals, and the blood, and the consult. I didn't think about it. To me, she was just another young, healthy vaginal bleeder, like we see every day. I forgot she was in the third trimester. That made all the difference in the world. I was sure it wasn't an ectopic, so I thought there was nothing to worry about. I did the regular workup. I didn't see she was in dire straits. I'm sorry. I didn't mean to hurt her."

"I understand."

"How is she?"

"She's in the OR. We don't know yet."

He nodded.

"Will you please let me know when you find out?"

"Of course."

He stood up, leaning right to keep his weight off his left hip. He turned to the door.

"Burt?"

"Yes."

"What's going on?"

"With what?"

"With you. In the last few months, you've been struggling. Am I mistaken?"

Burt coughed again. The handkerchief came out, wiped his mouth, got examined, went back in.

"Probably not. It's been rough."

"Why don't you sit down and tell me?" Emma said, knowing that it was time to go and see Taylor. *She'll be all right. She's got Eric and Victor. There's nothing I can do for her. If they need me, they'll call.*

Burt coughed again, then sat, staring at his hands joined in his lap.

"My wife, Ingrid, died last year. We were together for 46 years. She couldn't see well. A car hit her when she crossed the street. I should have been with her, but I went fishing with my buddies. She said she was going to be all right, so I went. I wanted to believe her. I wanted to spend time with the boys. It made me feel young."

Emma nodded.

"After she died, I didn't know what to do with myself. I'd been retired for a year. I'd never got used to it. Then, without her, there was nothing left: nothing to do, nobody to speak to. I tried golfing and gardening and all that crap. I don't give a shit about it. The kids are gone. They call every week to see if I'm alright, but they're never here. I looked for something to make my life worth living. The only thing I could think about was coming back to work. I thought I was doing OK. It felt good to be needed." He got smaller as he talked, as if he melted, crushed by the tragedy of his lone decay.

"Then we had that case. The drunk driver you took over. I was mad. I thought you were overreaching, and you were just a controlling bitch. Sorry!"

"A lot of people would agree," Emma said.

Burt looked at her with a little sparkle in his eye.

"You're something else."

"Yep. I heard that before."

"Then, today, I took care of that girl. I was doing fine. I knew what to do. Then you barged in. I was furious until I realized that she was dying. I didn't even notice. She'd be dead if it took you another half an hour to arrive."

Emma shivered. *She may be dead anyhow.*

"And it's not because you're so good—even though you are. It's because I'm so bad. I don't belong here anymore. I'm killing people. I need to move on."

"Move on to what?" Emma asked.

Burt shrugged.

"I don't know. But that's not your problem. I just wanted to tell you I am sorry. You were right."

Story of my life. Unfortunately, that never got me any friends.

"Thanks, Burt. That means a lot to me."

He nodded.

"We have some fast-track shifts available, you know. The PAs usually cover them, but it would be wonderful for them to see an old pro at work. We all need to learn. You have so much to offer. You could educate patients, families, and staff. You have a treasure trove of experience that none of us has. Better hours too—you wouldn't have to be up at night."

Burt looked at her incredulously.

"You'd keep me after I almost killed your daughter?"

Let's wait for the almost, shall we?

"You have an extraordinary amount of knowledge and experience. It would be awful to waste it. I want to put that, and you, to good use if you agree."

Burt's eyes started tearing.

"I didn't expect that. I half-expected you'd call the cops on me."

"For what?"

He shrugged.

"Because I'm a loser, I guess?"

"Oh, Burt. You've got nothing on me. Let me look at the schedule, and I'll get in touch in a day or two, OK?"

"Thanks, Emma."

He left, his back bent, but his head a little higher.

"Good for him." Emma looked at her watch.

An hour. It's time.

Her phone rang.

Eric.

26

─────────

L ying quietly in her hospital bed, whiter than the white sheets covering her, Taylor looked dead. But she wasn't. The heart monitor beeped her heart rate. 127. Not bad, considering. Blood ran into her left AC, the large vein in the crook of her elbow; something else in her right. *Pitocin, probably. To contract the uterus and stop the bleeding.* Emma leaned over to check. She was right. The door opened, and the OB doctor came in.

The green faded scrubs hung loose on his tall narrow body. His eyes, the color of smoke, were tired but marked by laugh lines.

He looked her up and down. "You're the ER doc?"

"I'm her mother."

"Her mother? Weren't you down there doing that pelvic?"

"Not quite. It's complicated." She extended her hand. "I'm Emma Steele."

"You?"

"As far as I know. Somebody had to be, and it was my turn."

"Wow. I heard about you. I imagined you differently."

"Like what?"

"More…imposing."

"Fat, you mean?"

The OB laughed.

"I believe you now. I thought you'd be bigger. And harsh."

"It's all in the eyes of the beholder. How is she?"

"She'll be OK."

Emma's relieved sigh could shake the leaves off a tree. She'd been too worried to let herself think about the prognosis. She buried it all inside to examine later. That was now.

Taylor's life was in danger, and she was in critical condition by the time she made it to the OR. Emma worried that Taylor might need a hysterectomy to stop the bleeding. That meant no more children. That tragedy, Emma knew too well.

When Vincent died, the one thing keeping her alive was the hope for another baby. It didn't work out that way. Amber got pregnant first. Victor left. Emma stayed behind with Taylor and her wine.

Amber took away not only Victor, but also Emma's hope to have another child. She hoped that that wouldn't happen to Taylor.

"No hysterectomy?"

"No. I removed the placenta and the bleeding slowed down. She's young and healthy. She should pull through."

Emma didn't cry—she didn't cry out of principle. She looked at Taylor and traced her white, thin face with her index finger to imprint it in her heart.

"Thank you, Dr…"

"Suru."

"That's an unusual name."

"I'm an unusual guy. You want to hear about the baby?"

The baby. Sure. The baby. More chances for things to go wrong. She'd been so wrapped up in Taylor's situation that she forgot to worry about the baby. Just as well. Worrying had never done her any good.

"Of course. How is she?"

"As good as one can hope for, for a premature baby in her condition. She's three pounds, two ounces, and she's breathing on her own. The pediatrician will tell you more."

"Wonderful. Thank you, Dr. Suru."

"Of course. The baby's father and your husband are with her."

"My husband?"

"Taylor's father."

"Oh, of course. Victor is my ex."

"Oh."

"It's OK. That's nothing compared to some of the things I say."

"Are you married?"

"No."

"Are you single?"

"Almost. I have a dog."

"What sort of dog?"

"German shepherd."

"What's his name?"

"Guinness. Her name is Guinness."

He nodded.

"Can I meet her?"

"Guinness?"

He looked at her as if she was feeble-minded.

"Of course."

Dr. Suru took out his card from the pocket of his ill-fitting scrubs, grabbed a ten-cent pen from his chest pocket, and scribbled something on the back of the card.

"This is my number. Call me when it's a good time to spend some time with her—and you."

Emma put the card in her pocket. She couldn't remember a man hoping to meet her dog. Or giving her his phone number, instead of asking for hers. *He gave me the choice of calling. Most men would rather keep the ball in their court.*

"Thanks. You're that much into dogs?"

"More than into people. I do people, too, when they're worth it."

Emma nodded. "I'll give it some thought. Are you single?"

"Nope," he said. "I have two cats. Paxil and Lucifer."

"That's different."

"They are different."

"But no…fiancée?"

"No. Just the cats. But it shouldn't matter, should it? I just offered to meet the dog."

"I see," Emma said. "I'll consider meeting the cats."

She glanced at Taylor. She was still asleep. Her heart rate had dropped to 115, going in the right direction.

"I'll be back," she said.

He nodded.

"Me too."

27

Emma had never seen a smaller baby. Ever. Except for the fetuses preserved in formalin. This baby was the tiniest live human she'd ever met. Mesmerized, Victor and Eric stared at her through the glass of the cubicle.

"What's wrong with her?" Victor asked.

"What do you mean?"

"Why is she translucent?

Victor had a point. The baby was red and shiny, and her skin was almost transparent. Light shone through her hands, revealing hair-thin blue veins."

"She's a little premature," Emma said. "She'll need some time to grow."

Victor looked unconvinced.

"When was the last time you held a baby?" Emma asked.

"Well, Iris. Eight years ago. She was big and pink. Not like this."

"This one came a little early."

Unconcerned about the fuss around her, wrapped in her pink blanket, the baby slept. A pink hat, the size of a nectarine, framed a triangular face. She wasn't cute, since she had no fat to smooth her angles. Curled up in her glass warmer, she looked like a tiny alien.

Her eyes opened and she looked straight at them. Emma knew she couldn't possibly see them, but the baby stared at them until her smoke-colored eyes, too big for her small triangular face, focused on Emma's.

It was magic. A current passed between them. Emma stared. The baby stared back like nothing else existed in the world. The baby smiled.

Emma knew this was just a reflex. Normal babies only smile around six weeks or so. This one had way longer to go.

"Look, she's smiling!" Eric said.

"That's cute!" Victor replied. "She's weird but cute."

Emma moved aside to let them get closer. The baby's eyes followed her.

That can't be.

Emma moved back. The baby's eyes followed. Her eyes, glued on Emma, wouldn't let go. She smiled again.

Weird!

28

When the boys finally got tired of staring at the baby, they went back to see Taylor. They filed into her room, Victor first, Eric following, Emma a few steps behind.

Taylor was just as pale, but awake now. Her heart rate was 111; she didn't look clammy; she made good eye contact. *She's looking good,* Emma thought, before she realized that she was assessing her daughter as if she were a patient.

Victor kissed Taylor's forehead. "I love you, sweetheart."

"Love you too, Dad."

Victor moved aside to make room for Eric. He hugged her and buried his face in her neck, sobbing.

"I'm so glad you're here. I was worried sick about you. I was afraid I lost you. I'm glad you're doing OK."

"Me too," Taylor said. "I love you, Eric."

"How are you feeling?"

"Drained."

No shit, Emma thought.

"No wonder, after everything you went through! But you're pulling through, and looking like a champion!" Victor said.

"Thanks, Dad."

"You are. You look so much better," Eric chimed in.

"Good to know. How's the baby?"

"She's beautiful," Victor said.

"Really?"

"She's going to look just like you," Eric said.

"Is she OK?" Taylor asked.

"Absolutely," Victor said.

Taylor looked from one to the other, then at Emma, leaning on the opposite wall, watching.

"Mother?"

"Yes."

"How is she?

"She looks all right for a preemie. She's beet red and transparent…"

"Emma!"

"Dr. Steele!"

Their shouts covered her. She shrugged. Her voice had quit long ago, after this twenty-six-hour day.

"Thank you, Dad. Thank you, Eric. I want to speak to Mother."

They looked at each other, then at Emma.

"Love you both. Why don't you get something to eat and maybe a drink? I'll see you tomorrow," Taylor said.

"Really?" Victor bent over to kiss her cheek.

"I can be back in a moment. Just call me," Eric muttered.

"Thank you, guys."

 Like a couple of scolded kids, they left the room one after the other. Emma stayed behind.

"Grab a chair. Your feet must hurt. If there's one thing I learned in the ER, it's that your feet always hurt. You should grab a chair whenever you can."

Emma laughed.

"You learned a lot." She grabbed the only chair and pulled it by the bed. She sat.

"What do you say?"

"You look good. Way better than you did a couple of hours ago. It was a close call, but you look like you made it."

Taylor nodded.

"That's good. The baby?"

"She's a preemie. As you know, she's had a few rough spots on the way."

Taylor nodded.

"She looks way better than I had expected her to. She looks uncannily aware. I know it's unlikely, but it looked like she could see me, and she smiled. She looks like an alien. A bright one. I think she's going to be all right."

Taylor closed her eyes. Tears streamed down her cheeks, soaking her white pillow into a shade darker than her face.

"Thank you, Mother."

Emma touched her hand, and Taylor held it. Not something Emma remembered ever happening before. They sat quietly.

"Mother?"

"Yes."

"Umber is back."

Emma's heart skipped a beat.

"How do you know?"

"He emailed me."

"How so?"

"Apparently, police botched the evidence, and they let him go. Probably for good. He says he wants to see me. And the baby."

This was the worst news Emma had heard for what? Three hours? When Eric called to tell her about Taylor. *Can I get some good news for a change? The baby! That's better news than I could have hoped for. And Taylor's going to make it. I have no right to complain.*

"I see."

"I don't want Eric to know about it."

"I understand."

"What are we going to do about it?"

"I don't know yet. We have to think. We got him once. We'll get him again. We'll have to figure it out."

Taylor squeezed her hand.

"Thank you, Mother. I knew I could trust you. Father and Eric, they're both wonderful, but they're too emotional to make any sense."

Emma choked. Was this Taylor? Her Taylor, saying this? Miss Emotion herself?

"What will you call her?"

"Hope. I'll call her Hope. I hope she'll be able to overcome the shitty odds I gave her, and become a whole, successful, beautiful human being."

"That's a wonderful way to think," Emma said. "And an excellent name."

"Thank you, Mother."

"Any time." Emma laughed.

"No, really. Thank you. I know you'll do the best you can for Hope and me. And your best, that's not too shabby. Thank you for fighting for us."

Emma shrugged. "Of course. That's what I do."

Taylor laughed. "I know. That is what you do. Some people chill. Some people struggle. You fight and overcome. That's what you do."

Emma kissed her forehead and headed home. Taylor praising her? That was weird.

29

Two days later, back in the ER for another shift, Emma was happy to see that the evil kid was still alive. She didn't like him any more than she did last time, when he'd stabbed the cat and threatened to kill the baby, but she was glad he hadn't died—sort of.

Mostly because that blew a hole in her theory that somebody was after the sociopaths. Maybe George was right, and it was God. She couldn't argue with God. She'd only be grateful.

This time the kid was back after stabbing his mother with a steak knife. Fortunately, he didn't get any of her vital organs. The knife only went through the subcutaneous fat layer and the muscle, no further. *That's one advantage of being curvy that nobody promotes. They should add that to the mortality statistics. Overweight people are more likely to survive stab wounds.*

This time, the kid wasn't her patient. His mother was.

"I'm so sorry this happened," Emma said.

"Oh, no, not at all. It's all good. I'm glad he didn't hurt the baby. When I saw him with the knife, I jumped in front of him. He got me, but the baby's all right, praise the Lord."

"Has he always been like that?" Emma asked as she cleaned the wound.

"I don't know. We've only had Jock for a month. I knew he was troubled, but I didn't expect to have to fear for the baby's life."

"You're not Jock's mother?"

"Oh, God, no. I'm his foster mom. We've fostered kids for years. They've had it hard, so most of them are suspicious at first. They don't know who you are. They don't know what to expect from you. But they usually settle, when they see you're not trying to hurt them. Jock is number fourteen for us. Since we couldn't have our own, we tried to help some of those other kids out there. We adopted four, and we're in touch with them all. We love them. We root for all of them. But Jock, he's different."

"How so?"

The woman sighed.

"Am I hurting you?" Emma asked.

"No, no, I'm just trying to put my finger on it. Jock doesn't hear you. He doesn't like chocolate. I've never seen a kid who doesn't like chocolate. He's, like, not human. He doesn't care if he's hurting. He doesn't understand that when people are hurt, that's bad. He set the dog on fire, just to see what he does."

"What did he do?"

"He died."

"I'm sorry."

"Me too. We had Choco since he was a puppy. He was nine." She sobbed. "He'd never hurt a soul. He was old, fat, and lazy, but he was my friend. He just wanted to play. And eat. Jock bribed him with bacon, then poured gasoline on him. Choco didn't understand. Jock lit a match. He always has matches, though we forbid it since he tried to set the house on fire. Jock lit a match, put it to Choco, and watched him burst in flames. He watched him run in circles, ablaze, screaming, and laughed. You wouldn't think dogs can scream, but they do. My husband ran out to catch him and smother the flames, but Choco was too crazed. He couldn't catch him until he collapsed."

Emma felt sick. That was the most horrific story she'd ever heard. She thought about Guinness running ablaze in circles, and that made her even sicker.

"I'm just happy it wasn't the baby," the woman said. "We didn't think we were ever going to have a baby of our own; then I got pregnant. That was the happiest day of my life, when God gave me a gift I didn't deserve. I cherished it. She's only eleven months old, so she cries at night. Jock doesn't like it. He doesn't like that we're paying so much attention to her, either. But she can't do anything for herself, you know. We need to feed her, change her, soothe her. He's mad that she doesn't do chores, while he's supposed to take out the garbage and sweep the porch. He's upset that she doesn't do anything. I told him: "She's a baby. She can't do things. She doesn't know how." He looked at me with his eyes like glass. He said nothing. He hates her and wants her gone."

"What are you going to do?" Emma asked.

"About what?"

"About Jock. And the baby."

"What can I do? I'll watch him closer. I'll make sure he doesn't get near her."

"Are you going to send him back?"

"I can't do that. God sent him to me to care for and cherish. That's what I must do."

"How about the risk to the baby?"

"God gave me the baby too. I'll do my best to protect her, day and night. I'll sleep by her side and never let her out of my sight."

"What if you fail?"

"God will help us. I know he loves us. He'll give Jock a change of heart. He'll let him see the light and understand that hurting people and animals is cruel."

"What if he doesn't?"

"He will."

"And what if he doesn't?"

The woman shrugged. "I don't know. I guess it means that we didn't deserve his love? God gave Jock to us to test our faith. I'm with him."

Emma nodded, placing in the last staple. She took off her gloves and threw them in the trash.

"I'm glad your faith is giving you strength. I wish you all the best, and good luck."

She left the room wishing Jock had died, like the others.

30

───────────

B ack home after the end of her shift, Emma parked the car, grabbed her bag, and headed to the door. She was spent. *Some days aren't worth getting out of bed,* she thought. *I'd be better off if I laid in bed the whole day, staring at the walls. I'm tired, I'm hungry, I'm crabby, and I stink. And, in spite of that, I've done nothing worth remembering.* She sighed, opened the door, and braced herself.

Guinness touched down like the tsunami she should have been named after, launching the carpets behind her in her gallop. She dropped at Emma's feet and flipped over, presenting her belly for scratching.

Emma dropped her bag and obliged.

"How was your day?"

"Awful," Guinness moaned.

"Really? How come?"

"I was all alone the whole day. I lay on the carpet. Then I lay on the sofa. I barked at the neighbor's cats—they stink. Especially the orange one. Then I lay on the sofa. Would you like a day like that?"

"Well, as a matter of fact," Emma said, "I'd rather have your day than mine. Laying on the sofa isn't that bad, you know. I'd even take the carpet if everything else fails."

Guinness gave her a hurt look. *"You wouldn't say that if you knew the cats. Let's go for a walk."*

"How about chilling with some wine instead?"

"Nope. Walk first. I need to pee, and you need the exercise."

Emma shook her head. "That's what I get for having a freaking German shepherd. I could have gotten a French bulldog or an Italian greyhound. They'd be all in with the wine. Even an Irish setter, or an English sheepdog. We could share a beer. But no, I had to get this German character with a German sense of humor and Teutonic attitude. How about a Riesling?"

"Let's go!" Guinness danced in front of the door.

"Ok, taskmaster. Let me at least take a sip to keep me going until we get back."

She went to the wine rack. She considered. *This miserable fucked-up day, this is not one for meek wines. I need something exploding in my mouth to take my mind off the misery. A Carmenere. A Shiraz. Or even one of those attitude-laden Valpolicella from the Veneto. Something that can't be ignored.*

She checked the bottles. Guinness would have none of it.

"Time to go." She barked.

"Really?"

"Yes. Let's go."

Emma gave up. *There's just no talking her into it. I'd better get moving; otherwise, I'll get to clean the floor.* She grabbed the leash and opened the door.

Why did I want a dog?

Guinness flew through the door and went to sniff her email on the mailbox post. Emma followed, her day replaying in her mind. She'd hoped that the talk with the foster mom would be the worst part of her day. She was wrong.

The elderly couple in Room 5 looked like decent people. In their seventies, they weren't well preserved. She walked with a walker; he walked with a cane. They were both white-haired, clean, and well behaved, unlike their daughter. She was a skinny, angry blonde in her thirties, there for pain, the seventeenth time this month. Abdominal pain, back pain, migraine, toothache, knee pain. This young lady's life revolved around her pain. She lay on her stretcher, covering her eyes with her arm. She felt too ill to answer Emma's questions.

"How long have you had this pain?"

Shrug.

"How is it different today?"

Shrug.

"Come on, Annie. Speak to her. She can't help you unless she understands what the problem is," her mother said.

"They won't help anyhow," Annie said. "These motherfuckers don't care to help you!"

Her father shrunk with embarrassment. "Annie, they can't help you if you don't talk to them. Tell them what the problem is," he said.

"You tell her," Annie said, turning her back to Emma and exposing the track marks on her arms.

She's a seeker, Emma thought. *She's not here for pain; she's here for pain meds. She needs comfort, relief, and a high.*

"She's been in pain for a long time," her father said in a shaky, thin voice. "It's been years now. At times, she had to go on the street to buy drugs to get relief. They said she was addicted. But she's suffering. She's always in pain."

"Has she tried Motrin or Tylenol?" Emma asked.

"They don't work, you stupid bitch," Annie said.

"Annie, you can't speak like that to the doctor," her mother said.

"Sorry, please don't take that into account," her father said. "She's in so much pain that she doesn't know what she's saying."

Emma didn't think so. Annie knew very well what she was saying. She was playing her elderly parents to do her bidding and get her the drugs she craved. Denying her the drugs was easy, but saying no to her loving parents was hard. But Emma had no choice.

"I'm sorry, but with her history, I don't think pain medications would help. I think they are more likely to harm her than help her. Addiction is an awful disease; giving her pain medication would only make things worse."

"I understand," the mother said. "I've always wondered. Her pain seems always to be different. That time she stole his gold watch and pawned it to buy drugs..."

Annie's scream splintered the air.

"You stupid fuck! That's what I brought you here for? To screw me? Miserable bitch!"

She stood up, staring at Emma.

"I need Dilaudid, and I need it now, no matter what these fuckers tell you…"

"Now, now. That's not a nice way to talk, Annie," her father said.

"Shut up, you cunt!"

They both sat, looking down like scolded children. The mother looked up at Emma, tears running down her cheeks. "I'm so sorry. I remember when she was a lovely little girl. She picked flowers for me. She kissed me good night. It's hard to believe she's still the same person. She's always angry, and we don't know what else to do. We're running out of money. We're old and sick; we can barely care for ourselves. We can't help her anymore. Can you help her? Can you put her in a detox or something?"

Annie, moments before, too sick to speak, jumped to her feet, her cheeks burning with anger.

"You miserable bitch!" She slapped her mother across her cheek, then turned around and left.

Silence filled the room. They sat quietly, avoiding eye contact.

"I'm sorry," Emma said.

The old man nodded. "Me too. Elvira, there's nothing left for us to do. She needs to hit rock bottom. She'll either sink or swim, but we can no longer help her."

"You're right. We're too old for this. Whatever we did to deserve it, we're too old. I can't do it anymore."

They stood up slowly, helping each other. She, with her walker, he with his cane, they headed out the door.

Emma's heart hurt. *There's no fixing this. There's nothing I can do, but it sucks. People shouldn't live their old age like this.* She wondered if Annie was going to be her next code.

I wouldn't mind.

She realized what she'd just thought and felt guilty. *Annie is just a flawed, hurt patient who needs help. She deserves a second chance. We all do. Isn't that my job? To give people second chances?*

That was the better Emma. The idealistic, publishable, politically correct Emma.

The real Emma took over. *Cut the crap. She's a drain to society and a curse to her aging parents. She's had all the chances in the world, and she squandered them, just like she's going to waste the next one. How about her parents? Aren't they entitled to respect and peace?*

I wish there were something I could do, Emma thought, then she went to see the next patient, then the next one, and the one after that. But now that her shift was over and she had time to think, her sorrow was back. She hadn't helped Annie, she hadn't helped her parents, and there was nothing she could do. She sighed.

Guinness barked.

"What?"

"Get over it, will you? Look, they have sausages at the stand!"

"Well, then. Sausages. I guess we have priorities. Do you know how many calories in a sausage? Not to mention the bun?"

Guinness couldn't care less.

Emma shrugged. She didn't mind a sausage either, especially if they had sauerkraut.

"Can I have your sauerkraut?" she asked Guinness.

"Knock yourself out," Guinness barked, getting in line.

Emma followed.

31

———————

Sitting on the love seat in Victor's living room, Margret shrunk, trying to look smaller. She wished she was elsewhere, but she couldn't get up and leave without making it evident that she was present.

"You've got to be kidding me!" Amber's beautifully made-up blue eyes were shooting daggers. She bit her lips, messing up her lipstick. "You can't be serious! We booked this vacation months ago. We paid for it. It's nonrefundable. And now you want to cancel it?"

"I'm sorry, Amber. Taylor just had her baby a month early. She went through a rough patch. It's still a little touch and go. I have to be here in case she needs me. I can't just pack and go to the other end of the earth while she's in the hospital with a premature baby."

"She's got her mother here. Emma is more than competent to deal with whatever may happen. She's got her boyfriend, Eric. He's with her. Margret is here, caring for the girls. She'll be helping with whatever needs help. What do you think you can do that they can't?"

Victor nodded. "You're right. Maybe there's nothing I can do for her. And Emma can do it all—God knows she always could. But I can't conceive of going and chilling on some faraway beach while my daughter's life is hanging in the balance. My granddaughter's too. I need to be here, whether they need me or not.

"You're insane," Amber spat out.

"Why don't you go without me? Take a girlfriend. Or go alone. I'm sure there'll be plenty of opportunities to make new friends there," Victor said.

"Why not, indeed?" Amber said, storming out.

Victor sighed. "You can appear now, Mother."

"Thanks." Margret stood up and straightened her back. "I'm sorry I was here."

"It wasn't your fault."

"I know. Still, it wasn't a good place to be."

"Sorry, Mother. We had to clear up some things."

"You think you did?"

"Not really. But at least we set the front lines."

"You're not going to go?"

"I can't. I wasn't looking forward to going anyhow, but now I can't. I have to be here in case Taylor needs me. And don't say it please: I know that Emma is more than capable of handling whatever. That's been the story of my life. That does not exonerate me from being a father—and now a grandfather—as unfit as I am. "

Margret nodded. "I understand. I even agree."

She headed to the door.

"I have to go now. I'm meeting Vera at Tony's for dinner."

"That's the best place in town. Enjoy."

"I will. You behave and take care of the girls."

"I will. Amber's going out for drinks with her friends. She'll complain about how awful I am and how hard it is to put up with me. They'll feel sorry for her. Then, she'll pay the bill with my money, and everything will be better tomorrow."

How sad, Margret thought. *A marriage shouldn't be like that. It should be two people who want to be together, who support each other, even love each other. They both deserve better, and the girls too. But it looks like it's too late.*

32

———————

By the time Margret made it to Tony's, Vera was already waiting. Not outside, of course. Vera knew better than anyone how to make the most of every moment. She was sitting at her favorite table, drinking something pink and frosty adorned with a slice of lime. She had secured the little booth for two behind the bar, the most private spot in the house. From there, they could see the restaurant without being seen. The booth was a favorite with illicit couples looking for a discreet night out, but Vera got there first.

"Why here?" Margret asked.

"It's my favorite spot. I love eavesdropping. Listening to people is an art. You'll see."

They sipped on their aperitifs, watching well-dressed people showing off their fashions. Most were old couples or old friends. *Not many young people,* Margret thought, just as a beautiful blonde walked in, turning heads in her wake.

"Look at her!" Vera said.

"Yep. Good-looking girl," Margret said, staring at Amber.

"Nice legs, too." Vera admired the legs in extra-high heels crossed under the barstool.

Amber ordered a glass of white wine.

"Yes, but which white wine?" the man asked. "Not all white wines are the same."

He sat on the stool next to her, bathing her in the warmth of his ocean-blue eyes.

"An Italian dry white, with a hurry to quench your thirst? A yellow French Chardonnay, flowing like oil, smelling like oak, with a Hollywood attitude to match? A New Zealand Marlborough sauvignon blanc, citrusy crisp, so light yellow that it looks white? A German riesling, dreaming it was soda instead of wine? Which white do you want?"

Amber stared at him. The man was worth it. In his late forties, he was tanned and wide-shouldered with short-cropped gray hair and a blinding smile.

"What would you recommend?"

"How about a cocktail to start? It warms you up for the wine and puts you in the mood. It helps you decide. As I said, not all wines are created equal." With a dazzling white smile he called the bartender.

"A "Special Pretty Girl" for the lady. And one for me."

"You're not a pretty girl," Amber said.

"I'm glad you noticed," he said, touching her arm.

Amber giggled. He laughed and leaned toward her, speaking too softly for Margret to hear.

The cocktails came in tall pink frosted glasses with a sprig of green.

"What is it?" Amber asked.

"Gin, rose water, passion fruit juice, and basil."

"It's divine."

"So are you. I'm Dick."

"I'm Amber."

"Glad to meet you, Amber. To good friends."

They knocked glasses. Amber took a long sip, draining her glass.

"I love it."

"I love that you love it." He signaled the waiter for two more. "What do you do, Amber?"

"I work in the local hospital. I'm a nurse. You?"

"I'm an entrepreneur. I live in Colorado; I'm just visiting here. I came to see a family member."

"How nice," Amber nodded. "How is he?"

"It's a she. She's doing all right for the moment."

"Wonderful."

"I can't wait to meet her. You'll meet her too. We have a connection, you know. I'm Dick Umber, Taylor's baby's father."

33

The morning Emma went back for her next shift, Burt was waiting. His worried old eyes enlarged by his thick glasses asked her before he did: "How's Taylor?"

"She's OK, Burt, thank you. How are you?"

He sighed. His tension gone, his shoulders dropped down from his ears, and his face relaxed.

"Thank God. I'm good." He took out a rolled paper from his pocket. "I brought a lesson plan. Here."

He showed her a five-page lesson plan hand-written on a notebook:

1. What are we looking at when we look at the patient?

2. What do we do if our patient looks sick?

3. What do we do if our patient worries us?

4. What if we aren't worried, but his family is?

5. When do we ask for help?

Emma read through it and she was impressed. Burt's draft was the wisest, most thoughtful approach to the ED patient she could remember.

"This is awesome, Burt. I love it."

Burt blushed.

"No, seriously. It's spectacular. I wish I got something like this when I was learning. Actually, I wish I had something like this now!"

"Why, thanks, Emma…"

"Do you have it as an internet presentation?"

"No, I'm not that good with that kind of thing."

"Then, it's time to learn."

"I don't know how."

"Go see Taylor. She's upstairs in OB, running crazy for something to do. She'll help you put it into PowerPoint or web-based or whatever perversion they're using these days."

"But…"

"No but. Just go. If you want to teach, you need to learn how. The web is the way. You need to learn to speak their language if you want to make an impact. Taylor will teach you."

Burt nodded and left. Relieved, Emma sighed. *That's a double whammy. It gives them both something to do, and it gets them out of my hair. Thank goodness, since my hair's getting pretty tangled.*

She had been waiting for Annie to turn up as a code. She didn't. Neither did the dog-burning kid.

After days of waiting, Emma started to wonder if she was paranoid. She'd been told that before. Nothing odd was happening. Maybe all those deaths were just a coincidence. But then what about the notes? The numbered assholes? What was that? Somebody's bad joke? The last two cases had had no notes. Or maybe they existed, but nobody found them?

Just as she decided that she was probably losing it, the code rolled in.

"Code 99, Emergency Department, Room 3. Code 99, Emergency Department, Room 3."

As always, she headed there with the others, waiting for the stretcher to roll in. Eight minutes later, the doors opened, letting in the EMTs. Sweaty and tired, they were still performing CPR.

"We got her in her bedroom downtown. She was in her bed. She's been in asystole all the way. She's got track marks everywhere. We were unable to establish an IV. We started an IO in her left tibia. We gave Epi x 3 and Narcan x 2 with no relief."

"Any history?"

"She was here multiple times last month for pain issues."

"Anything else?"

"Her parents are coming as soon as they get a ride. They don't drive. They say she has a history of chronic pain and drug use—nothing else.

Emma headed to the head of the bed. She already knew what she was about to see. She was right. Annie had finally found respite from her pain and suffering.

Emma lifted her eyelids with a gloved hand. The pupils were widely dilated, at 9mm, and unreactive to light. Annie was dead. Her parents were finally going to get peace. They ran the code, as usual, but nothing changed.

When her parents arrived, Emma tried to find out what had happened, but they knew nothing. Annie had gone to bed. She didn't wake up. They went to check on her, and they found her dead. That was it.

With red, teary eyes, they looked at Annie, at Emma, at each other. They didn't know what to do, now that she was dead. They'd been under her cloud for too long.

But they still had each other. Now, they could make the most of whatever time they still had left, together, instead of struggling to help a daughter who was beyond help.

"What happened to Annie?" they asked.

"An overdose, most likely," Emma said. "We'll see what the coroner has to say."

They were not surprised.

"It's not surprising, with her history." Sal shrugged.

"Maybe." But Emma was unconvinced. Annie's death was the fifth sudden death of an unpleasant person she'd seen in the last few weeks. Were they all related? Maybe. Were they suspicious? Absolutely!

34

Taylor was still in the hospital, but she was doing much better. She'd been bleeding that morning when she went to see Hope, but the OB was not concerned.

"That's OK. Your uterus needs to get rid of all the crap in there. It has to be empty, so it can contract, and heal. The more you walk, the better."

She had walked up and down the corridors, up and down the stairs. She walked and walked, letting the pain in her belly empty her mind of everything: her near death, Umber, the need to decide about the baby. She tried to forget how she'd drugged herself into oblivion, risking her baby's life.

As she got stronger, she yearned to go home. But the baby wasn't ready, and Taylor was afraid to leave her.

"They'll take good care of her," Eric said. "The nurses are wonderful. They all love her."

He was right, but that wasn't the problem, and she couldn't tell him what worried her. *Umber is back. He didn't want the baby; he betrayed me and tried to destroy Mother. He failed, but in the process, he lost his license and his business. Now he's back to destroy us. The easiest way to do it is through the baby. He's her father, and he's entitled to see her, but I know he'll try to hurt her or take her away.*

The thought that Umber could take Hope away filled her with dread. Her heart heavy, she walked down to the NICU. A couple stood by the door, looking in through the window. She recognized them, and her heart skipped a beat. Ignoring the pain in her belly, where her scar was pulling apart, she straightened to her full height. She rushed to the door before they could open it and grabbed the handle.

"Taylor! You look…good," Amber mumbled.

She can't find a word that's both truthful and polite, Taylor thought.

"Thanks, Amber." Taylor blocked the door. "How nice to see you."

Amber had the grace to blush. "I…I…sorry I didn't make it here any sooner, but you know how busy I am, with the girls and everything else…"

"No problem. I didn't expect you. And I especially didn't expect you to bring a guest."

Amber blushed deeper. "I know it's none of my business…"

"Correct."

"But he wanted to see the baby…"

"Hello, Taylor. How lovely to see you again! You look prettier than ever."

"And you're lying just as well as ever. I'm glad to see that nothing changed."

"Oh, but it has. You have. I have. And little baby…"

"Hope. Her name is Hope."

"What a lovely name. I find it hard to believe that I created hope. Isn't life wonderful?"

"Yes. And full of surprises. What makes you think she's yours?"

Umber laughed. "Come on, Taylor. You should find a better story."

"Why? This one's good enough. What makes you think she's yours?"

"You were a virgin. I was your first."

"Maybe. But not my last."

"You said the baby was mine."

"I lied. That makes two of us."

"I don't believe you."

"Good. You're learning."

"This is my baby."

"Nope. It's mine and only mine."

"I can sue for paternity."

"You can. In the meantime, you will have nothing to do with her."

"Come on, Taylor," Amber pleaded. "I know you guys had a misunderstanding. You thought he was unfaithful. He says it was just a mistake. Give him a chance," Amber said.

Taylor measured her, from her perfect bob to her perfect heels.

"Amber, you'd better stick to hairdressers and shoes."

Amber turned red.

"You are disrespectful."

"Bringing a stranger to see my baby without my permission is disrespectful. Don't do that again."

Umber stepped forward, getting in her face.

"Are you sure you want to play it this way, Taylor? You and I, we used to be good friends. We can do that again. It would be so much better than being enemies," he said, his honeyed voice dripping with menace.

"I was a child. You were a doctor. Things changed, didn't they? For both of us. We can't go back."

Umber's face darkened.

"I'll see you in court. We both know that this baby is mine. It will only take a simple DNA test to prove it. What you're doing is futile. It's just a waste of time. What do you hope to get out of it? We'd all be better off if we can compromise. We'll get there anyhow, but it's going to hurt."

Taylor smiled like she didn't care, but she felt her strength leaving her. Blood was pouring out of her, warm moisture flowing down her legs. The pads weren't thick enough. She hoped they couldn't see it.

"Hurting people never bothered you before, Dick. Why change now?"

He shrugged.

"I hoped we could find an amicable solution. Better for you, better for me, better for the baby. But you don't want to be reasonable, just like your mother. Let's go, Amber. Thanks for trying to help. Sorry it didn't work out."

Amber gave Taylor one last hurt look, and they headed to the elevator.

Just in time, since Taylor's strength was gone. Her knees softened.

"Here. Sit." Vera pushed a chair under her.

Taylor crumbled on it.

"Thanks, Vera."

"You're welcome."

Vera handed her a bottle of cold water. Taylor drank it.

"Thank you."

"He's right, no? He's the father."

"Yes."

"Why did you lie to him?"

"He's the scum of the earth. I'd rather kill the baby than let him have her. Well, no. That's not true. But I'd do anything to keep him out of her life. Anything."

"Is he going to win his court case?"

"Yes. If he lives long enough."

Vera nodded.

"How did you know I needed help?"

"You didn't. That's why I didn't intervene."

"But you came with the chair."

"Only when I saw that you were about to faint. Your color disappeared, but only after they left. You did fine on your own. I watched, in case you needed me, but you didn't. You made your mother proud."

A light came on in Taylor's brain. She had felt threatened. Even worse, he had threatened her baby. She didn't know what to do. Then she thought about Emma. What would Mother do? She'd smash them to the ground if it killed her. I did the same.

"Thank you, Vera."

"He'll be back."

"I know."

"What will you do?"

"I don't know. But one way or another, I'll be ready."

35

Instead of going home after her shift, Emma locked herself in her office to stare at patient charts. Annie's death gave her no choice. Like it or not, she had to look into what was happening. All those deaths, they were real. Something, or somebody, caused them. But what? Or who? She had to find out.

She sat at her computer, juggling between the five charts that worried her. What did they all have in common? Besides all the victims being nasty people. She started a list, as always, in her doctor's writing that nobody could read, sometimes not even her. But that didn't matter. It wasn't about the list. It was about slowing down her brain to the speed of her writing, allowing the light to come through.

#1. Ben, the racist, misogynistic nurse who abused his immigrant wife. He died in his home, a few days after calling in sick. There was no sign of violence. The Alka-Seltzer, the lack of toilet paper, and the way they found him in the bathroom, pointed to a gastrointestinal problem. He had been healthy and had no history of drug use. He had lived alone since Mia took the kids and left.

#2. Andy, the child abuser. He died in his home, a couple of days after Emma saw him in the ER with the abused baby. He was found in the bathroom again. No violence, no history of drugs. He just got sick and died.

#3. Chip, the domestic violence perpetrator. He also died in his home, after bouts of vomiting and diarrhea. Not unusual when he drank too much. Like

637

the others, he died in the bathroom, a couple of days after having been in the ER with the woman he abused.

Emma rolled her shoulders to loosen them up and took another sip of water. She wasn't thirsty; she was hungry. She drank to dilute her hunger. No luck. She wished she was smarter, more competent, and better suited to this job. *If Agatha Christie wrote this, she'd call it "The Bathroom Deaths." The killer would have to be the sweetest, kindest, least likely person. Who's the least likely person here? Probably me. Except that I'm neither sweet nor kind, and I happen to know that I didn't kill them.* She shrugged, took another sip of water, then got back to her task.

#4. The drunk driver. He left the ED in police custody. They let him go. He came back dead a couple of days later. She wondered if they found him in the bathroom, like the others. He was incontinent and covered in vomitus, but that wasn't uncommon for drunks.

#5. Annie. She'd also been in the ED, abusing the staff and her elderly parents, only to come back dead a couple of days later. Sal thought she was an overdose. That made sense, considering her history. She had overdosed before. Still, Emma didn't think so. She didn't respond to Narcan, she didn't have pinpoint pupils, and she was the fifth case fitting the same pattern.

There had to be something unifying all these cases. They ware not good people. Worse than that. They had all hurt, even killed, others. Victims who couldn't protect themselves. Old parents. Young babies. Innocent bystanders. Spouses. But there had to be something more.

It's the ER. Their sins came to light here. They got exposed, then they died. Why? George said God had punished them. Emma was skeptical. In her fourteen years in the ER, she'd seen her share of evildoers and psychopaths, but she'd never seen God go beyond the call to clean up crime. She sighed, turned off her computer, and went home to her wine and to Guinness. There would be another day tomorrow.

36

———

Emma tried to run, but her legs were heavy as lead. A hooded figure leaned over her, bringing a beaker half-full of a bright-green bubbly potion to her lips. She tried to push it away, but she couldn't. The liquid was so close that the bubbles sprayed her skin. The smell of bitter almonds choked her.

She screamed and sat up covered in cold sweat.

"I know what it is. It's poison."

Woken up from a sound sleep, just as she was about to catch the neighbor's orange cat, Guinness jumped up and ran to the door, growling. Nobody. She looked around. Nothing. She looked at Emma, her head cocked in a question.

"What?"

"Somebody is poisoning them."

"Why?"

"Because they're assholes. It must be some religious lunatic punishing the sinners to prove his love of God. But that's not the question. The question is how? And with what?"

Guinness yawned and lay back to get some rest. Maybe even get the cat, too. She didn't think she was needed here.

She was wrong. Emma needed to talk through all this, and she needed her advice. She shook Guinness awake.

"What?"

"I know what you're thinking. How about the toxicology report? It's still pending. That's what toxicology reports do. They take forever."

Guinness was thinking no such thing. She didn't give a hoot about the toxicology reports. She turned on the other side, trying to go back to sleep. No luck. Emma was on a roll.

"It will be weeks before they return. By that time, someone could poison half the North Country. And it looks like they are."

Toxicology had never been Emma's strength. Just like Guinness, she thought it boring. No more. She had to learn, but she needed help.

Where would she get it? Sal was good, but his strength was not in poisons. His forte was overdoses and antidotes. The closest Poison Control Center was hundreds of miles away. It took a full day to get there and return, let alone spend time to learn. And Emma didn't have a full day.

She could call, of course, but she wouldn't get a toxicologist. She'd speak to one of the people operating the phones who told parents to take their kids to the ER if they'd swallowed anything but their food, then telling the ER to get an EKG, give charcoal, and watch them for six hours.

And even if she got a toxicologist, what would she say? "Hello? I think somebody is poisoning our assholes. They vomit, and then they die." How would that go? No. She needed to speak to somebody in person. Somebody who knew about poisons and could tell her what to look for.

What if I went to the university? They have scores of PhDs and researchers who love this kind of thing. Maybe they'd talk to me.

But who? Should she try the biology department? Or chemistry? She didn't think they had a poison department. She found the address, put on some clothes instead of her eternal scrubs, and headed out way too early. The doors didn't open until eight.

The receptionist, a blonde girl with green nails and eyeliner to match, unglued her eyes from her cell phone.

"I'm looking for someone good with poisons."

"You have an appointment?"

"No. I don't even know who they are."

"Hey, Greg."

The young man sporting an afro sitting at the other computer raised his head.

"This lady's looking for somebody good with poisons."

Greg studied her.

"What for?"

Emma opened her mouth to tell him that it was none of his business. She closed it back. *That won't help. Telling him that I have somebody killing my ED assholes is no good either.*

"I'm researching a book," she said. "A crime novel."

He nodded.

"You want somebody in the biology department. Or maybe chemistry?"

The green-nailed girl looked at them pensively.

"I saw Dr. T. here earlier today. She must be in the greenhouse."

"Dr. T?"

"Yes. Our old biology department chair. Dr. T. retired a few months ago, but she still comes to check on things and get close and personal with her beloved plants," Greg said. "Great idea. I can't think of anyone better. Come, I'll take you there."

They went through a maze of corridors, all empty.

"The kids are still on vacation," Greg said. "In a week or so, the place will be packed."

The steamed glass door to the greenhouse opened to the hot, humid, and heavy air inside, rich with the scent of decay. Fat dark leaves, dripping with water, filtered the light into a deep green like the bottom of the sea.

"Dr. T?"

"Yes?"

"There's somebody here to see you!"

"Come over. I'm by the ficus."

Greg took a narrow path left. Emma followed.

"Don't step on the plants; she'll get upset".

Emma nodded.

They took a right over a tiny curved red bridge covered in climbing vines, then another left, bending over to pass under a floppy green tree. Emma didn't bend far enough. The tree shook, soaking her.

"There," Gregg said, pointing to a red silhouette kneeling in the dirt.

Emma stepped forward.

Vera stood up, smiling.

"How lovely to see you, Emma. Welcome to my world."

37

———————

Sitting in the hospital, Taylor got more and more antsy. She was tired of reading, she could no longer suffer to watch TV, and walking the hallways drove her crazy. She needed to be outside, to breathe real air, to live on her own time. It was time to go home.

Hope wasn't ready yet, but she was. She needed to be out to be able to think. She had to decide about the baby. And Umber complicated things no end.

If he sues for paternity, he'll win. I can't give Hope for adoption without his consent. And he won't consent. Why should he? His only interest in the baby is to hurt Mother and me. I need to speak to a lawyer.

She packed her things, then, walking bent over, she went to say goodbye to Hope. Her C-section still hurt. She touched Hope's tiny soft hand, the wrist smaller than Taylor's finger, the minuscule fingers relaxed in sleep. She bent over to smell her baby, closing her eyes to take in her scent. *I should make it into a perfume. I'd call it baby Hope. A hint of peppermint, baby shampoo, and the faint tang of spoilt milk of her sweat. I'd market it to new mothers. Better still, to mothers-to-be. New mothers have their own baby to smell.*

Grief seared through her like a knife at the thought of giving her away. She couldn't bear the pain and the sense of loss of never breathing in her scent again. She couldn't imagine life without Hope.

She remembered the Crumps. *They are mature, smart, and well off. They have time, patience, and knowledge—all, things that I don't have. They'd be better parents than I ever would.* But she knew right then that she couldn't give Hope away. She'd rather cut away one of her limbs. It may be illogical and selfish. They said she could spend as much time with Hope as she wanted. But she couldn't do it. Hope was her baby. Hers.

She buried her tears in the soft little belly, breathing her in again and again.

"I'll be back, little one. I love you. I love you more than I knew I could love. I'll be back. Be good."

As she got up to leave, she walked into Dr. Maw, the pediatrician.

"Hi, Taylor. Are you leaving today?"

"Yes. But I'll be back to visit."

"I know." Dr. Maw glanced at Hope. "Taylor, I…I don't know how to tell you this, but we received a court order to test the baby's DNA. Somebody thinks he is her father and wants proof. We have to do it."

That was fast. Taylor had hoped maybe he'd just go away. He didn't. She went back to her room and splashed cold water over her burning eyes. She packed her stuff and got ready.

Eric came to pick her up with a large bouquet of yellow roses and baby's breath, which must have cost a day's salary. His hug gave her strength. He pushed her wheelchair to the front door and parked her there as he went to get the car.

Taylor sat with the roses in her lap, relishing the sun on her skin. After so many days inside, it was delightful to be caressed by the wind.

"Hi, Taylor," Umber said.

He stood in front of her, holding a massive bouquet of red roses that made Eric's gift look humble. Tall and handsome, his tan set off by his blinding white smile, he towered over her. His eyes, the color of deep water, took her in lovingly.

"For you!" he said, depositing the roses in her lap. "I missed you."

And just like that, his soft low voice churned her insides, making her long for the time they were together. Her treasonous heart forgot his betrayal, her sorrow, and everything else. His smile, his voice, his scent of sandalwood and bitter carnations overcame her, sending her back to the naive girl in love she used to be.

"Dick…"

"I'm back," Eric said, scrutinizing Umber.

Umber smiled.

Taylor faltered. She couldn't find her voice. She didn't know what to do with it if she did.

"Nice flowers." Eric looked wistfully at the glorious bouquet. "I'm Eric Weiss," he said, extending a hand to Umber.

"Dick Umber. Taylor and I are old friends."

"I see. Nice meeting you. We should get going, though; the car is in the way." Eric pushed the wheelchair to the car, then helped Taylor in, arranging the flowers in her lap to close the door.

"See you," he nodded.

Umber nodded back.

"You bet. I'll be around. It's good to see you again, Taylor. It's been too long. I'll see you again soon." He stepped back.

They took off.

"Who was that?"

"Someone I used to know," Taylor said, turning away to hide her tears. She didn't know what made her cry, but she couldn't stop her tears like she couldn't stop her blood from flowing through her veins.

"He looks impressive," Eric said. "I wouldn't want him for an enemy."

Taylor nodded.

38

———————

Dripping with sweat, Emma stood in the hot, humid greenhouse. She took a deep breath. The air, heavy with the scent of leaves and the aroma of decay, made her dizzy.

Vera's hug smelled like dirt and cookies. *Of course. Silly me. I should have thought about her.*

"Let me show you around and introduce you to my friends." Vera wiped her dirty hands on her red slacks, then caressed the bark of a tall tree with thick green leaves. "See this ficus? I planted it twenty years ago, from a seed. Did you know that its fruit is the fig? It blooms as an enclosed inflorescence, an urn-like structure lined on the inside with minuscule flowers. Tiny wasps enter it to lay their eggs and BAM! They pollinate it. A really unique pollination style. I didn't think it would make it! And look at it now!" Vera beamed with pride.

Emma looked. It was big, green, and wet, and it smelled like compost.

"Wow," she said.

"And see this rhododendron? I smuggled it from Nepal—it must be ten years ago. It's their national flower. I carried it in my water bottle. Isn't it wonderful?"

The excitement flushed her skin, making her eyes sparkle, and taking twenty years off her age. She rejoiced in showing Emma her favorites like a mother would love showing off her kids.

646

Of course. The plants are her kids. She loves them, and she's proud of them, Emma thought.

"It's wonderful. They are wonderful."

"Then there's…"

"Vera, I need your help."

"Taylor?"

"No, Taylor's OK. I need help with my work."

"OK. Shoot."

What a loaded word, Emma thought.

"Poison. I'm looking for a poison that kills within a day or two. It has digestive manifestations."

"Aren't we picky! Have you changed professions? I thought you were in the business of keeping them alive."

Emma laughed. "I still am."

"Then what do you need it for?"

"I can't tell you."

Vera laughed. "OK. How do you give it?"

"I don't know."

"Well, there aren't that many ways. If you breathe it, if it's lethal, it probably won't take 24 hours. It would likely kill them instantly. Those around them, too. It may smell funny so that people may notice it. Its manifestations would likely be respiratory rather than digestive. Cough, choking, trouble breathing. That kind of thing."

"That makes sense."

"Does that work for you?"

"Probably not."

"You could inject it."

"Yes."

"That would be hard to do without them noticing it unless they have an IV. Then it's easy."

"Say they don't."

"Then it would be injecting it IM or SQ. Are you familiar with ricin?"

"Something about a Russian defector?"

"Bulgarian. In London, in 1978, Georgi Markov was killed by a poison dart filled with ricin. The dart got fired from an umbrella. The reason they figured it out was that the ricin pellet did not dissolve completely."

"What exactly is ricin?"

"It's a poison derived from castor beans, the spotted beans that they make castor oil from. They're so pretty that people use them for toys and rosaries. They aren't dangerous unless you crush them. But if you do, just a little purified powder can kill a whole block. That's why they're looking at ricin as the next WMD."

"Does it have to be injected?"

"No. Ingesting it works, but slower. It gives you vomiting and diarrhea; it kills you in a couple of days."

"Is it detectable?"

"The CDC has a urine test for ricinine, but it's not widely available. So no, not through routine testing."

"Do you have something that works faster?"

"Two days is not fast enough for you? Have you ever heard of abrin?"

"No."

"Abrin is a toxic toxalbumin. It's ricin's faster, stronger cousin. It comes from the seeds of Abrus Precatorius. It's also known as Jequirity Bean or Rosary Pea. It's a pretty red-and-black bean looking like a ladybug. It's used in percussion instruments, or for jewelry. It's not dangerous when it's intact, but chewing only one seed could be fatal. Symptoms are identical to those of ricin, but abrin is almost a hundred times more toxic. The toxic dose in humans is about 0.1 mg for a human. That's infinitesimally small. Three ounces of it could kill a million people. A pound of it would kill the whole population of Alabama. But of course, you can't use the seeds whole. You have to grind them into powder first. And it's not heat-stable. At high temperatures, it deactivates. You can't bake it or make tea out of it. You have to use it raw."

"Anything else?"

"Strychnine."

"Isn't that coming from a nut?"

"Yes. Nux Vomica. They used to use it in all sorts of tonics and laxatives. Some alternative herbal medicines still use it, but nowadays, it's most important use is for poisoning gophers. It increases muscle contraction to the point that the patient looks like he's having a seizure, even though they're awake. It eventually kills them by paralyzing their respiratory muscles."

"Not a pretty death. How long does it take?"

"It starts working in an hour or so. It would probably kill in less than a day."

"How would you get it?"

"Well, you could plant a tree and let it grow. Like this one," Vera said, caressing the rough bark of a short green tree with dark shiny leaves and orange fruit. "I brought it from Thailand. Well, I brought its seed. The seeds contain about 1.5 percent strychnine that you have to extract first." She picked an orange fruit off the ground and opened it, showing Emma the flat, gray seed inside. "Or, if you're lazy, you could buy it on the internet. A pound of Gopher Bait, whose active ingredient is strychnine, is less than $20."

"Anything else?" Emma asked.

"Hundreds of things. Mushrooms. A nice flavorful mushroom soup of Amanita Phalloides can kill a household. They're easy to find in the forest, and you don't need many. I don't have them here, but there's this." Vera led her to another corner of the garden and showed her a beautiful tree with pink blooms and long leathery leaves. "Oleander. A tea made out of its leaves can kill you in a few hours. It works like Digitalis, causing hyperkalemia and heart arrhythmias. Oleander is a popular way to commit suicide in Sri Lanka. Then there's yew. And curare. And foxglove. Or you could use cyanide.

"Cyanide?"

"Yes."

"Doesn't that kill you instantly?

"It depends. If you put it into a slow-dissolving capsule, it will take a few hours."

"And where would you get it?"

"You can extract that from peach, apple, or apricot pits, but you'd need a truck full of them. Or you can buy it on the web. Try Cyanolabs."

"This is scary."

"Isn't it? It's a wonder any of us are still alive."

Emma nodded.

"You know a lot about plants. And about poisons."

"I do. It's my passion. Just like you know a lot about diseases."

"Thank you very much, Vera. I have to think this through."

"Any time. I'm happy to help. Say hi to Taylor. See you next week."

Emma pondered what she'd learned. Vera had been a treasure trove of knowledge, but no help. Emma left more confused than when she had arrived. So many possibilities. So many sources. She wasn't getting anywhere. The poison could be anything, obtained anywhere, given anyhow, by anybody. She wasn't any closer to the answer.

But there was something else. There was something about Vera.

She knew a lot about poisons. More than ordinary biologists would know.

But there was more. Vera hadn't queried Emma about her sudden interest in poisons. She could have asked a few questions out of curiosity. She could have joked about it—like "Who are you planning to kill?" She didn't. It was as if she knew.

How would she know?

She's a smart girl. She's seen them, as I have. She must have put it together, just like I did. But wouldn't she say it? "I know what you're looking for; I've been wondering about it too?" She hadn't. Odd.

39

GUINNESS

Guinness was sitting at the door, waiting for Emma to come home.

Something funny's going on. They're all acting weird.

Shaman wakes up in the middle of the night and talks to herself like they're fighting.

"No, it can't be. But…no, it can't be."

It can't be what?

I brought her leash, and I took her for a walk to take her mind off it. It didn't help.

I showed her how to check her mail at the hydrant. She didn't even pay attention. It's like something's eating her inside, and she can't make up her mind.

The only thing that helped was when I rolled in that dead fish. She forgot all the shit she was thinking about and paid attention. Well, she couldn't help it. That fish was ready. It was awesome. The smell alone could wake up the dead.

Afterward, she bathed me. Don't get me wrong now: I like water. The muddier, the better. It has more flavor. But the shampoo? It takes away all your good smells and makes you all fluffy. You look like a sissy. And, as if that wasn't bad enough, she got the hairdryer? Are you kidding me? I had to draw the line at that.

Still, it got her back to here and now, instead of fighting with the voices.

The girl's acting weird too. She was here yesterday. She laughed, then cried, then repeated. She kept checking her phone like she was waiting for something. Eric? Just

651

call him, for God's sake! But no. She paced around the house as if she was walking on hot coals. She couldn't settle.

I think she's coming into heat.

40

Back in the ER after another shift, Emma was getting ready to go home. Only half an hour to the end of her shift and her evening was hers to enjoy: walking Guinness, hot bath, wine. She and Guinness had settled into a comfortable routine since Taylor had moved in with Eric. The evenings were nice and quiet. Even better, she was off tomorrow. She had the whole day to look through charts and work on the poison problem.

She had researched abrin, Cyanolabs, Sri Lanka suicides, and everything else that Vera had told her. It was all true. But the more she thought about it, the more uneasy she felt. Vera asked too little and knew too much.

Emma shrugged and went to see the spider bite in Room 4. Just like every other presumed spider-bite she'd seen in the last few years, this one wasn't a spider bite. It was an infection with a nasty, drug-resistant bug. As she explained this to the patient, the screams started.

"Let me go, you motherfuckers, let me go, untie me, let me go!"

It was déjà vu all over again. Jock was back. Tied to the stretcher, he kicked, screamed, and spat at the EMTs holding him down in a self-destructive fit of impotent rage. They pulled the gurney in Room 6 and closed the doors, and the sound went down a notch.

"Let me go, you motherfuckers, let me go…"

Emma sighed and headed that way, wondering what happened. The speakers summoned her.

"Trauma code, Dr. Steele to Room 3. Trauma code, Dr. Steele to Room 3."

Emma dashed to Room 3. The room was full of scrubs, but the stretcher looked empty. The screaming infant, covered with a sheet, was small enough to lie sideways. Emma was glad to hear the screams. They meant that the baby was alert, breathing, and had a patent airway. That was all good news.

Dan, the EMT, lit up when he saw her.

"Hi, Dr. Steele, we have a little kiddo here. Eleven months old. Alert, breathing, vitals are OK."

"What happened?"

"She has second-degree burns over most of her body," Dan said.

Emma felt sick. Eleven months old. Burns. Most eleven-month-olds don't walk, so they can't get themselves in trouble. Somebody did this to her, and that somebody was usually the caretaker. Probably abuse. Unless…"

"Her older brother threw a pot of boiling water on her."

Jock. It has to be Jock.

"He was mad that she threw her cereal bowl on the floor. He told her to clean up. She didn't. He took the pot boiling off the stove and threw it at her."

Emma felt sick. Not because she didn't expect this, but because she did. The last time she had seen Jock, he had stabbed his foster mom. He was trying to hurt the baby, but he failed. This time he succeeded.

She lifted the sheet covering the infant. The plump little body and the front of her legs, angry red, were sprinkled with fluid-filled blisters. The belly was the worst. A couple of red spots on her face, but no blisters. The eyes were intact. The hands too.

It wasn't good, but it could have been so much worse.

Brenda, her nurse, waited for orders.

"Let's get her something for the pain," Emma said. "Let's do intranasal fentanyl, two micrograms per kilogram, half in each nara, also full doses of Motrin and Tylenol.

She turned to the mother. "She doesn't have any allergies, does she?"

Standing by the stretcher, the mother cried, afraid to touch her and hurt her more.

"No."

The hot water had hit the front of her body, then had run down her legs. The back was fine. The blisters were ugly, but they would heal, and there were no third-degree burns. Fortunately, it was water, not oil.

"She's hurting, but she's going to be all right. She'll feel better in a few minutes after the drugs take effect," Emma said, touching the mother's shoulder.

"Thank you," the mother sobbed. "It was my fault. I was in the kitchen, feeding her, when my phone rang. I'd left it in the other room. I ran to get it. I thought it was my husband; he was late, and I was worried. When I came back, Jock had thrown the hot water on her. She screamed as if he'd skinned her alive. He was about to bash her head in with the pot, but I stopped him. He bit me, but I managed to take it away from him. Thank God my husband came in through the door and called 911."

Emma smeared lidocaine gel on the fiery red skin to numb it up, then soaked a clean towel in lukewarm water and covered her burns. The screaming slowed down, then stopped. The baby fell asleep. Emma debrided the blisters, stabbing them with a sharp scalpel to drain them as the mother watched in horror.

"The blistered skin is dead. What's underneath hurts, though, and so do the red areas. It looks bad, but it's not a huge burn. The baby's eyes, her hands, feet, and genitals are all fine. She'll be as good as new in a few days."

"Thank God, the Good and Almighty," the mother said.

Emma sighed. *I'd be livid if the good God had let that happen to my kid. And things are only getting worse. Jock's growing. Soon enough, they won't be able to control him. One of these days, this baby won't be this lucky. We'll call CPS again, for whatever that's worth, but what will they do? Nothing. Like they did the last two times.*

Sitting cross-legged on the floor in Room 6, Jock watched cartoons while eating a cupcake. The violet frosting covered the lower half of his face, making him look like a purple Santa Wannabe.

It would be funny if it weren't tragic, Emma thought. *What can I do? I'll admit the baby for the burns. That should buy her a few days. And then?* She shuddered. She didn't know.

41

──────────

Taylor was back at the hospital, visiting Hope. She choked with love. Was this miraculous baby really hers? She traced the translucent pink seashell ear, caressed her soft hair, watched the rosebud mouth sucking in her dreams. Hope was the most beautiful baby she'd ever seen, even though she looked like Umber. Or maybe just because of that? Taylor was confused. She was worse than confused; she was perplexed.

Her brain and her heart collided into a turmoil like she hadn't had… since the last time she'd been with Umber. That was long ago. She was no longer the kid she used to be. But still, he had the same magic, the same power over her. Every time they met, he turned her life upside down. She didn't know what to do.

She needed to talk to someone to clarify her thoughts and her murky feelings. But who?

Not her mother. Her mother didn't do confused. Nor weak. She always knew what to do and did it. For her, it was as simple as that.

Her father was easy to speak to, but he was a man. He'd hug her and encourage her, but he wouldn't understand. Plus, Amber's new friendship with Umber complicated things even more.

Grandma. I can always talk to Grandma. She always listens and never gets mad, Taylor thought.

She called. No answer. She called her father. "She's with Vera," he said.

Taylor walked the two miles to Vera's house and rang the old doorbell, even though the door was cracked open. She heard the bell inside sounding like vespers, but there was no answer. She stepped in. The living room overflowed with books and flowers, as usual, but was otherwise empty. So was the kitchen.

She stepped out in the garden. Something red moved under the dark green canopy. It was Vera, unconscious, lying on the ground. Her open eyes stared left, while her left hand clutched something that wasn't there, and her feet pedaled a nonexistent bike. Vera was seizing.

Heart racing, palms sweaty, Taylor kneeled and turned her on her side, then called 911.

Ten minutes later, Vera was on her way to the ER. Taylor followed as fast as she could.

Half an hour later, she found her comfortably nestled in Room 3. Vera lifted her arms to hug her and smiled, as usual. Taylor took a deep breath. Her shoulders softened with relief, and her pulse slowed down. *No stroke, thank God. But then what?*

"How are you?" Vera asked.

"How am I? How are you?"

"I'm great. A little headache, but otherwise OK."

"What happened?"

"I had a seizure."

"I know. I found you in the garden. You almost gave me a heart attack."

"I'm glad to see you're still alive," Vera laughed.

"Do you have a history of seizures?"

"I had a couple—no big deal. I'm better now. How are you?"

"I'm OK," Taylor lied.

Vera looked at her and saw the lie. Just like her mother's, Vera's eyes could see through her. "No, you're not. What happened? The baby?"

"She's great."

"Eric?"

"He's great too."

"Then what?"

Taylor looked down.

"Come on, Taylor. Nothing you can tell me will shock me. I've seen it all. What's up?"

"Umber is back."

"I know."

"He brought me flowers."

Vera looked at her with pity.

"So?"

"He said that we should be friends."

Vera nodded.

"At first, I thought he was back to torment me, looking for revenge. I thought he was only interested in the baby because she's a way to get to Mother and me. But now I'm not so sure. I'm confused."

"About what?"

"About what to think. About what to do."

"What are you thinking?"

"Maybe he's genuine, and he cares about me. Maybe he cares about the baby, too. She's his daughter, and she's beautiful. He has no reason to hurt her."

"And if so, then what?"

Taylor looked down, unwilling to meet Vera's eyes.

"Maybe…maybe I should give him another chance?"

Vera sighed. "I thought that's where you were going. And Eric?"

Taylor shrunk. She'd forgotten all about him. Eric had been there for her, forgave her lies, tolerated her silliness, and treated her like a princess.

"As open-minded as I am, I don't think you can have them both."

Taylor sighed. "I think you're right."

"You know, Taylor, the past is seductive. So is the future. We can ignore the unpalatable details and focus on the things we choose. The past, like the future, is like a picture. You can choose the composition, the lighting, the filter. You can highlight the things you want and obscure the ones you don't.

But the fact that you don't see them doesn't make them disappear. Is he still married?"

"I don't know."

"That's worth considering. Either way, that doesn't mean he's changed. People seldom change after they grow up. They just become an older version of who they already were."

"I changed."

"You're eighteen. You're still growing. And really, have you changed that much? If you had, do you think we'd be here talking about this?"

"You're right. Maybe I didn't change that much."

"You're older. You're wiser. You're a mom. You need to take all that into account when you make your decision."

Taylor nodded.

Vera didn't tell her what to do. She didn't call her silly or childish, but Taylor understood. Vera thought she was still infatuated with Umber. She'd be stupid to give in to her feelings about him. Again. She had done it once. What good did it do her? It almost put her in jail.

He was scum, and Taylor knew it. Her brain knew it. Her heart didn't.

"Thank you, Vera."

"Any time, sweetheart. Don't hesitate. And don't feel bad. If you just knew all the stupid things I did for love. And I still do."

The door opened, and a somber Dr. Crump came in.

"How are you feeling, Vera?"

"Never better. How about you?"

"I'm fine, thanks. Would you like Taylor to step out while we talk?"

"No need. Taylor is like the granddaughter I never had."

"If you're sure… Your blood results look OK. No electrolyte abnormalities, no reason to suspect an infection."

"Good."

"Your brain CT scan, though…"

"A bleed?"

"Yes. It's a tiny little bleed that irritated an area of the brain and probably caused that seizure."

Vera nodded.

"But the bleed...it looks like there's something that caused it. Maybe a mass. We need to get an MRI to have a better idea."

"OK."

Taylor couldn't keep quiet anymore. "A brain mass? As in cancer?"

Dr. Crump shrugged. "That's why we need the MRI. Have you ever had cancer, Vera?"

Vera nodded.

"Where?"

"Lung. My fifty years of smoking caught up with me. They thought they'd gotten it all out two years ago. Maybe not. Isn't life full of surprises?"

Dr. Crump nodded. "That could be it. I'm sorry."

Taylor sobbed.

Vera smiled and took her in her arms.

"What are you crying about? I've had a wonderful life. I have no regrets. And I plan to make the most of the time I have left. There's nothing to cry for. Nothing."

42

After hours and hours of speaking to Child Protective Services, police, and everybody but the Pope about the burned infant and the awful situation in her home, Emma finally made it home.

The discussions went nowhere. Everybody was horrified. Everybody agreed that the situation was awful, and the child was in danger. Somebody needed to do something before something worse happened. Who? Somebody. Somebody else, of course. Not them.

Emma sighed and went to the wine rack. Guinness walked to the door and thumped her tail. *"Time for a walk."*

"Not this time. You'll wait for your turn, goddamn it. I'll have a glass of wine first."

Guinness glanced at her and understood. She lay in front of the door, waiting.

Emma sniffed the wine—it was a Carmenere type of day. Things had not gone well, and she had a feeling, deep inside her bones, that they were getting worse. She could feel trouble coming like others felt the weather changing in their joints. Something bad was happening.

She took a thirsty sip, relishing in the taste of the wine: a good, deep body, long notes of cherry and oak. She took another sip, looking back on her day.

She was overwhelmed and torn. That baby was in danger. Her God-fearing mother didn't see that one of these times, Jock was going to get her like he got the cat and the dog. The thought made Emma sick.

Jock likes burns. Stabbings, too, but burns are more fun to him. He's got to have anti-social personality disorder, Emma thought.

She took another sip of wine and Googled the prognosis and treatment of young psychopaths. Not good—reward-based treatment and maintenance. No cure, just like she'd thought.

She'd made no progress with those inexplicable deaths either. Looking at poisons hadn't narrowed things down, and she didn't know where else to start. She'd thought about calling Zagarian, but she didn't know what to tell him.

Plus, in her heart of hearts, she half-hoped that whoever was killing the assholes had a little poison to spare for Jock. The thought was horrific, but really, the dogs, the cats, and the babies of the world would be better off without Jock. *It may not be his fault that he is this way, but it's his nature. He is destruction and cruelty personified. He's even worse than Umber. Umber uses things and people for his goals without worrying about what happens to them. Jock enjoys watching suffering. It gives him pleasure. He's not doing it as a means to a purpose; he's doing it for fun.*

She poured herself a second glass of wine.

Guinness lay by the door, her nose on her paws. She had waited patiently, but now she was done. She barked. Emma shrugged.

"OK, OK. I know. I said one glass. Let's go."

She grabbed the leash and her jacket, just as the door blew open and Taylor burst in, stumbling on Guinness. Guinness protested. Taylor swore.

Emma took another sip. *There it is. I knew it was coming.*

"Mother!"

"Yes, Taylor."

"It's horrible!"

Emma nodded. That, she knew, though she didn't know what it was.

"Baby Hope?"

"She's OK."

"Victor? Margret?"

"They're OK too."

"Great. Let's go for a walk."

"I need to talk to you."

"I understand. You need to talk, Guinness needs to walk, I need my wine. The sooner we walk and talk, the sooner I get to my wine. Let's go."

The light was fading as they left. The evening fell, quiet and tender. The softness of the dusk helped calm Taylor down.

They walked together side by side along the empty streets, watching Guinness inspect and mark every tree, every mailbox, every bush.

"I wonder where she gets enough pee for all that! She's worse than you when you were pregnant," Emma said.

Taylor laughed, in spite of her swollen red eyes.

"Tell me."

"Vera."

"Yes?"

"She's got brain cancer."

Emma stumbled. That, she didn't expect. "How do you know?"

"I went to see her. I found her in the garden, seizing. Dr. Crump saw her in the ER and said she has a little bleed, probably because of a brain tumor. She's got a few of them."

"Mets?"

"He thinks so. She had lung cancer a few years ago."

Emma nodded. "How is she?"

"She's good. She seems upbeat."

"Where is she?"

"In the hospital."

Emma nodded. "I'll go to see her tomorrow." She looked Taylor up and down. "What else?"

Taylor blushed. "What makes you think there's anything else?"

"Come on, Taylor. I'm your mother, remember? What else?"

"Umber."

"What about him?"

"He came to the hospital."

"And?"

"He brought me flowers." Taylor looked down, avoiding her mother's eyes.

Emma's heart froze. *Really? And you fell for him, after everything that happened? A bunch of flowers, and you're all upside down? Oh, Taylor, how it sucks to be young!*

"So?"

"He said he missed me."

Emma nodded. Taylor looked anywhere but in her eyes.

"I missed him too."

"I didn't think so," Emma said calmly, helping Guinness disentangle herself from a mailbox she'd circled twice. "I thought you and Eric were happy together."

"We were," Taylor said. "Until Umber came back."

"I see. So, what are you thinking?"

"I don't know. I'm confused. I love Eric, and he's a great guy, but Umber... Umber is exciting and unpredictable and brilliant. And he's Hope's father."

"He is. He's also a killer, a drug dealer, and a liar."

Taylor shrugged. "If you put it that way..."

"He's also married if I remember correctly."

"You don't know that."

"Do you?"

Taylor shrugged.

"He's also the one who told you to abort your baby because she was going to be a monster. Remember that?"

"Oh, mother, why do you have to be that way?" Taylor sobbed. "Why can't you understand the way I feel? That was long ago. Now he's back! He wouldn't be back if he didn't love me!"

"I'm not so sure about that, Taylor. He has reasons to hate you. Nothing drives Umber more than his need for power unless it's the lust for revenge. He's here to catch you again. He'll crush you, and me, and the baby, if he gets a chance. He's back to pay his debt. He couldn't have hoped you'd make it that easy. And you're going to drop Eric? He stood by you through all the misery you put him through. He's a decent human being. You'll dump him for this double-crossing, lying sack of shit? After everything he's done to you? Really?"

Emma knew this wasn't helpful, but she couldn't stop. She was so angry she was sick. She had hoped Taylor was growing up to be a decent human being. Then this? She wanted to slap her. She sunk her fists in her pockets to control herself.

Taylor choked. Her breath came out in raspy gasps around her sobs. She was livid.

"What do you know about love? Who are you to give me advice on something that you don't even begin to understand? I love him, and he loves me. He's the father of my child! Isn't that good enough for you?"

"No, it's not. First, that's not true. Umber doesn't love you. He didn't love you then, and he doesn't love you now. He used you. He's still using you, and you are allowing it. You're letting him destroy you. This is insane. You're risking your relationship with Eric, your child's safety, and your own life for what? Because he brought you flowers? Are you for real?"

"Oh, leave me alone! Leave me alone and go back to your wine! You witch!" Taylor turned and ran, bent over by the pain in her belly. Emma looked behind her and sighed. She'd screwed up. She should have been patient, kind, and supportive. She'd failed. *There's only so much stupidity I can swallow. Taylor went beyond her allotted quota. I know she's only eighteen, but still! She learned nothing from everything that happened to her. Unbelievable. And all this, on top of five unexplained deaths; a kid who likes to burn dogs, stab cats, and wants to hurt his sister; and Vera's brain cancer.* What next? She didn't want to know. She'd had enough insanity for one day.

"Let's go home, Guinness. I hope there's enough wine. It's shaping into a two-bottle night."

43

After an awful night inhabited by nightmares, the morning crashed on Emma like a ton of bricks. Her head was about to explode, and her stomach was queasy. She had maxed on Motrin and Tylenol, but they didn't help much. *I'm in worse shape than most of my patients*, she thought, as she wrote a work note for a nauseous teenager.

She took another sip from the cold coffee she'd found in the break room and shivered.

"You shouldn't drink that. Nobody should drink that. They should use it to kill rats. Here, try this instead," Vera said, putting a steaming mug next to her elbow. "This will grow hair on your chest."

"I hope not," Emma laughed. "That may be the one thing I don't need. How are you? And why are you here?" She hugged Vera.

Vera smelled wonderful. Like cinnamon and eucalyptus and coffee. Good coffee.

"Where do you want me to be?"

"At home, resting. When did they let you go?"

"They didn't. I don't think they even noticed I'm missing. I got bored, so I left. I came to the ER to see what's going on. There's always something happening here. There's not much fun up there, except for the dementia patients. They have their moments. Jerry pooped in his mug—think about the accuracy—

then he dumped the mug on the nursing desk. That got them busy, so I snuck out."

Emma looked at the steaming mug Vera had brought her. She hesitated, then shrugged and took a sip. It was green tea, and it had a delicious, unique flavor.

"What is it?" She buried her nose in the cup to inhale its scent. "I know it's tea, but there's something different about it."

"It's my special recipe for my very special people. It will get you feeling better in a minute."

"Thank you, Vera."

"Anytime. What's new?"

"Not much. Taylor..."

"What?"

"She's struggling. She's confused about her feelings."

"I know. Give her time."

"I have no other choice. What else can I do?'

"Everything will work out. You'll see," Vera said.

"You're such an optimist!"

"Why not? It costs just as much as being a pessimist, but it feels better."

Emma laughed.

"How are you feeling?"

"Great."

"What did they tell you?"

"I'll have to see a neurosurgeon. They're also talking radiation to shrink the tumors."

"How do you feel about that?"

"I'll do the radiation. Not the surgery. I'm close to my expiration date, Emma. I won't waste the little time I've got left in the hospital, hurting, unable to do the things I want to do."

"What do you want to do?"

"Have fun. Drink vodka. Laugh with my friends. Finish my life's work."

"What is your life's work?"

"I'd like to leave this earth a better place than when I found it."

"That's a lofty goal!"

"Sure, it is. That's your goal, too, isn't it?"

"I guess so, though I never thought about it that way."

"That's what we all try to do. In our own way, with our particular skills, we try to make the world better. You heal people; Margret beautifies it with her gardens; artists create art; architects build. Chefs cook. Exterminators destroy vermin. We all try to make the world a better place."

"Not all of us," Emma said, thinking about Umber.

"Not all of us. But most."

Emma nodded.

"I wonder about Taylor."

"She's looking for her place on earth. It may take some time, but she'll find it."

"I hope..."

"Pediatric code 99 in the ED, Room 3. Pediatric code 99 in the ED, Room 3."

Emma jumped off her seat and headed to Room 3. Judy was getting the room ready. A river of scrubs flew in, checking equipment, opening Ambu bags, hanging fluids, unfolding the Broselow tape. The faces were frozen and tense.

"What is it?" Emma asked, remembering the burned baby. *Has Jock finally managed to kill her?*

"I don't know," Judy shrugged. "They lost connection. ETA was fifteen minutes, a few minutes ago.

"Do we know anything else? Age? Mechanism of injury?

"We know nothing. For all that I know, it could be a baby rhino."

One can only hope, Emma thought.

They waited in frozen silence for the ambulance to arrive. An eternity later, the lovesick cat song of the sirens came close.

Unable to wait any longer, Emma stepped out to the ambulance door. The ambulance stopped. The door opened.

"Hello, Dr. Steele," Roy said.

44

———————

itting at Victor's breakfast table, sipping on her second cup of tea, Margret wished she'd never left home. *I'd be working on my garden, listening to the wind, and breathing in the smells of the earth. It would be peaceful, quiet, and relaxing. Not this. It's getting old.*

Victor and Amber were at odds with everything. Now, on top of that, Taylor had returned with a suitcase, reclaiming her old room. With her swollen red eyes, she looked like she'd been in a storm.

"What happened?" Victor asked.

"Nothing. I just need to think."

"Think about what?"

"About life. About my future. About what to do."

"And you couldn't think about all that with Eric?" Amber asked. Her hair was perfect and her makeup flawless, but her eyes were cold.

Instead of answering, Taylor played with the bichons, Thelma and Louise. The three of them had grown up together, and the dogs loved having her back. So did the girls, Opal and Iris, who adored their older sister.

Sipping quietly on her tea, Margret watched, wondering what was going on. Victor and Amber's marriage seemed on the rocks. They barely spoke to each other. Fortunately, the girls, the dogs, and Taylor made enough noise to cover the funk.

669

Taylor looked at Amber, her green eyes warm. "No, not really. I needed some peace. Amber, I want to apologize for the other day. I know you meant well. You may have been right. I'm sorry I was rude to you."

Amber's eyes stayed cold.

"She was right about what?" Victor asked.

"She said I should give Umber a second chance." Taylor poured herself some coffee. "I think she's right."

Victor choked on his coffee. "Give Umber a second chance? Seriously?"

"Why not?"

"Because you know better than anyone what he did and who he is. He hasn't changed."

"How do you know? You speak like Mother!"

"Your mother may be right. She usually is."

Taylor sighed.

"I have to agree," Amber said.

"But it was you who brought him over and said…"

"That doesn't make it true. That's what I thought then. Since then, I've thought more about it. I'm not sure it's a great idea."

"Why not?" Taylor asked.

Amber checked her nails. They were perfect. "You heard your father. He's not trustworthy."

"Amber, you brought him to the hospital to see Hope. You asked me to give him another chance. What changed your mind?"

"I listened to your father. He knows him. I don't," Amber said, getting up to clear the table. "Come on, girls, it's time to get going."

Margret watched her fussing over the girls to change the subject and remembered them having dinner at Tony's a few nights ago. *She's lying, she knows him better than she says,* Margret thought.

Breakfast finally over, they all went about their business. Margret took Taylor for a walk.

"What happened to Eric?"

"Nothing. He's fine."

"What did you tell him when you left?"

"I told him I needed to think about the baby and the future."

"What did he say?"

"He said, OK." Taylor looked down. "He said: 'Take all the time you need. I'll be here.'"

That kid is too nice. He should keep her a little insecure. That would stop her from looking around for more exciting opportunities, Margret thought.

"He may not, you know."

"Why not?"

"He's young; he's handsome; he's a professional. He's a good catch."

"Grandma, nobody speaks like that anymore."

"Maybe they don't. So what? That doesn't make it less true."

"Am I a good catch?"

Margret looked at her tenderly.

"Taylor, you know how much I love you. You're young, beautiful, and bright. You have a great future. But for the time being, you have no education, no money, no job, and you have a kid to take care of. Not to mention that your personality takes some getting used to."

"Well, Umber wants me anyhow."

"You should wonder why. And, more importantly, why would you take him back? What do you expect to happen?"

"We'd be together. We'd be a family. Hope would grow up with her father."

"Together, where? Here, where everybody hates him? In Colorado, with his wife? What are you going to live on? He lost his license. You don't have a job. Are you going to go back to selling drugs?'

Taylor gasped. "How can you speak like that, Grandma?"

"I'm sorry, Taylor. I love you, and I wish you well, but I'm worried about you. I think you've lost your way. You're a mother now; you have responsibilities. Think about Hope!"

"But I'm only eighteen! I still have a life to live!"

"Of course. That's what we're talking about. Don't screw it up."

"You all hate Umber! I don't understand why! He's handsome; he's smart; he's like nobody else I ever met."

"That, he is. He's also a killer."

"They couldn't prove it. That's why they let him out of jail."

"That doesn't make it less true."

"You don't understand!" Taylor screamed and ran into Amber, who was coming through the door.

"What happened?" Amber asked.

"I told her Umber was no good for her."

Amber smiled.

"He's no good for you either, Amber. Be careful."

45

———————

Standing by the stretcher in Room 3, Emma sighed, her heart torn between relief and guilt. She was happy to see that her worry was unfounded. The pediatric code was not Jock's baby sister.

It was Jock.

He lay on the stretcher, quieter than Emma had ever seen him. This time there was no fight, no swearing, no need for sedatives.

They did everything they could, as always. Nothing helped—neither the CPR, nor the fluids, the epi, or the intubation. Nothing made any difference.

Jock's foster mom stood at the foot of the bed, holding her baby, her face frozen in pain, rivers of tears streaming down her cheeks. She wailed like a wounded animal when Emma told her there was nothing left to do. The baby touched her tears with pink little fingers, stared at them, then stuck them in her mouth to taste them.

Her mother didn't notice. She traced Jock's cheek. With a gentle hand, she smoothed his hair, uncovering his face. She bent over to kiss his forehead. The baby cooed, but she didn't hear. She sobbed, consumed by pain.

Emma could hardly believe it. The woman was genuinely heartbroken, instead of feeling relieved that her baby was now safe.

"I'm sorry," Emma said. She was sorry about the woman's grief, the stabbed cat, the burned dog, and about whatever caused Jock to be the way he was.

Emma was sad about the waste of a young life. The one thing she wasn't sorry about was that Jock was dead. He was a monster. The world was a better place without him. Still, she was torn, confused, and heartbroken about this woman's grief.

"Was he sick?"

"No. We were here just yesterday. He had another meltdown, and I couldn't control him. He stole matches from somewhere and tried to set the baby on fire. I took them away, but he wouldn't stop. It was like he was possessed. I had to call the ambulance. When we finally got home, it was too late for dinner. He didn't want to eat anyhow. He said he was sick to his stomach. I gave him some milk, then put him to bed."

"And then?"

"We went to bed too. I checked on him. He was asleep. I locked the door—we always lock his door at night, so he doesn't wake up and come to get the baby. He did it a couple of times."

"And?"

"I went to bed too. I was exhausted. The last few nights, I've been up with the baby—she was in so much pain from the burns. When I went to check on him, I found him curled up on the floor. He wasn't breathing. I called 911, and I did CPR, but he didn't wake up. Then the EMT brought us here."

"What did he eat and drink yesterday?"

"We had cereal for breakfast, with milk. The milk was OK—I tasted it; I always do. For lunch, I took them to McDonald's. He had a Happy Meal. I gave him the baby's fries and her toy. I was afraid she'd swallow it."

The baby started fussing, and the woman rummaged through her pocket and handed her a cracker. The baby munched on it, drooling happily.

"Anything else?"

"Then, when he tried to set her on fire, we came here. He was here for hours until the psychologist got to talk to him. Somebody gave him a cupcake and some Pepsi. I told him Pepsi was no good for him, it makes him wired, but he doesn't care. He laughs when I tell him. He laughed."

"Who gave him the food?"

"I don't know; I was out in the waiting room with the baby, so he was here alone. Somebody from the ED, I think. It wasn't my fault," the woman said. "I had no one to leave the baby with. If I bring her in the room, he gets beside himself that I hold her and not him. But how can I not? She can't walk. There's no crib, no chair for her, no nothing. I couldn't put her on the floor."

"Of course," Emma said. "Did he have a fever?"

"I don't know. He looked a little flushed, but then he had just vomited, and he said he was hot."

"Anything else? Diarrhea? Trouble breathing?"

The woman shook her head no.

"I'm so sorry," Emma said. "Can I call somebody for you? The priest, maybe?"

"That would be good," the woman said. "God understands that I tried my best to keep him safe, but it's always good to have another prayer."

"How about your husband?"

"He's away. He's a truck driver. He's in Georgia today. He should be back tonight."

Emma nodded and headed to the door. The woman called.

"Dr. Steele?"

"Yes."

"What happened?"

Emma took a deep breath. "I don't know. We'll have to do some testing. It may take a while to get the results."

"You think it was the McDonald's? I let him have too much?"

"No, not at all. I think it was a nice thing to do. It made him happy."

"Thank you. I tried to be a good mother to him. God sent him to me to love and care for. I did my best. Sometimes it wasn't easy, but I never tried to hurt him. Never."

"I understand," Emma said.

"I think God took him. He was not happy. He couldn't get enough love. I tried to give him more, but it was never enough. But he's good, now that he's with God. God is love. God has more love than the earth can take. I know he's happy now. I'm happy for him, but I'll miss him."

"Yes," Emma said.

"He's going to be better off there."

"Yes. He's better off there."

Who sent him there, though?

Emma had an idea. More than an idea. She had a theory. But she had no proof.

46

Taylor grinned at the mirror to make sure she had no lipstick on her teeth. She studied herself from the right, then from the left. Looking good. She checked her watch. Another hour. She couldn't wait any longer. She put on her jacket and left. Ten minutes later, she grabbed her phone to reread his email.

"My dear Taylor. I'm so happy you agreed to meet me. I've missed you terribly. I miss you even more now when I see how beautiful you are. Motherhood suits you. If only our daughter grows up to be as beautiful as you, we'll be fortunate parents indeed.

"I look forward to meeting her. I used to think that all babies are the same, but I know that our baby will be special, unique, and particularly gifted.

"Thanks again for agreeing to meet me. I know I've been awful to you in the past. My heart breaks thinking about how horrible I've been toward you, but I want you to know that there's nobody like you for me. I've thought about you every night and every day since the last time I saw you."

Her heart swelling with joy, Taylor sauntered toward the hospital. She knew she was early, but she couldn't slow down. When she got there, she wandered around, looking for something to do. The gift shop was open. She read the baby books and tested the hand creams to kill time. Five minutes later, she stepped out to walk into Eric. His face lit up, and his arms opened.

"Taylor! You came to meet me!"

Taylor opened her mouth. She closed it back.

"Nice to see you, Eric."

He hugged her tight. He kissed her and held her close.

"I've missed you something awful! Oh, Taylor, I'm so glad you're back! It was awful! I can't even sleep without you!"

Taylor struggled to smile. She glanced around, knowing that Umber could arrive at any moment. She didn't know which was worse: Eric speaking to Umber, or Umber talking to Eric.

"I went to see Hope. She got so big and so beautiful. She smiled at me."

That was unlikely. Taylor had been reading books on child development, and she knew that babies don't have a social smile until they're six weeks old. That was far away for Baby Hope, who hadn't even reached her expected birthday. But she didn't have the heart to contradict him. Nor the time. She needed to get him out of there. Quickly.

"Isn't she wonderful? Let's go to…"

"How lovely to see you again, Taylor. And young…"

"Eric," Taylor mumbled, wishing a hole would open to swallow her.

"Mr. Umber," Eric nodded politely.

Taylor opened her mouth to correct him. Dr. Umber, not Mr. Umber. Then she remembered that he'd lost his license to practice medicine, thanks to her and her mother. She wondered if he was still a doctor if he didn't practice anymore, or was his title revoked too?

The men smiled frozen smiles, staring at each other, each willing the other one to leave. Neither one moved.

"Eric, I was just taking Dick to see baby Hope."

"Really? How nice."

"Yes…"

"Let's go then," Eric said, grabbing her hand and heading toward the elevators.

Umber followed.

Baby Hope was asleep. Her red skin had lightened to a rose-petal pink. Her soft puff of chestnut hair gleamed red under the electric lights. She was minute, delicate, and perfect. Taylor's heart swelled with love for her.

"Isn't she beautiful?" Eric said, gazing at her lovingly. "She's just perfect."

"Yes, she is," Umber said. "She's lovely. Almost as beautiful as her mother."

Taylor blushed.

Eric looked at the baby, his eyes shining with love for her.

"Yes, she is, isn't she?"

His finger traced the side of the baby's tiny fist, with pink fingernails smaller than peppercorns. The little hand opened and closed back in a sleepy wave.

"Can I pick her up?" Umber asked, then he bent over the cubicle and slid a hand under her head, another under her back, and he picked her up to see her closer.

"You'll wake her up," Eric said.

"That's OK. She's got nothing else to do the whole day and all night," Umber said. "Eat, poop, sleep, repeat. That's all they do."

That's true, Taylor thought, but she didn't like it.

Neither did Eric.

"She's two weeks old," he said dryly. "What else would you like her to do? Play chess?"

Umber gave him a surprised glance.

"Aren't we being possessive! Don't take it personally, young man; I didn't say anything bad."

Taylor didn't like that either.

Something in Umber's attitude, in the cavalier way that he picked up her baby without waiting for permission, in the fact that he didn't care if she woke up, rubbed her wrong. *He looks at her with amusement. As if he's checking out a product, trying to decide whether to buy it or search for a better one.*

Umber laughed and put the baby back in her cubicle. She opened her eyes. *Mother was right; she still looks like an alien,* Taylor thought.

The baby looked at Umber. Her eyes, too big for her small triangular face, were the color of deep water, just like his. Her eyebrows rose, and her forehead furrowed in wonder.

He smiled.

She screamed a high-pitched, heart-wrenching wail.

"Now, now, little one. Why the fuss? Everything's OK. Daddy's here!"

The baby screamed again as if somebody had stuck her with a needle.

Taylor bent over to pick her up and rocked her, breathing sweet nonsense in her ear. The baby sobbed, then sighed. Taylor turned around.

Eric, pale as death, stared at her with haggard eyes. He glanced at Umber. He took a last look at the baby, and he left.

47

———————

The evening Jock died, Emma couldn't find peace. She got home, walked Guinness, and tried to watch TV but couldn't focus. Her soul was in turmoil, and dark thoughts raced through her mind. She had to do something. Or did she? She paced from the living room to the kitchen and back, stepping over Guinness who blocked the door in the time-honored shepherd tradition. Wet and covered in mud to her elbows after an extra-long walk in the rain, Guinness was the picture of contentment. They had walked for miles and miles as Emma struggled to think things through. Guinness didn't mind. She was always up for an extra mile, and the good thick mud made it even better.

Emma sat on the sofa, staring at the dark TV screen. Guinness watched her with one half-opened eye.

"I don't know what to do," Emma said.

Guinness slapped her muddy tail on the floor. *"Try some wine,"* she suggested.

Good idea. Emma went to the wine rack. She dismissed the whites—this wasn't a white type of night. Those were for light summer days and happy moments. Not tonight. She needed a dark, deep wine to warm her soul, to soften her inhibitions, and get her over her hang-ups, conformism, and fears. She needed to soften enough to think better.

She chose a Canadian wine. While Australia, Chile, and South Africa, the new wine nobility, frowned upon by the snobbish Old World, took over the wine markets, Canadian wines still struggled to make a name. This Stratus Red 2015 was one of them.

The dark, sober bottle with a plain black and white label reminded her of the snow melting over the fields at Niagara-on-the-Lake, the lovely wine country south of Toronto. Their motto was "Minimum handling, maximum patience." Emma got that.

She opened the bottle and poured it in a long-stemmed crystal glass. The wine poured thick and black. Gleams of garnet only showed when she swirled it. The first nose was heady—cherry, licorice, and blackberry, with a touch of oak. The taste was demanding and stringent, driving her salivary glands into overdrive and rewarding her taste buds with the smooth warmth of the blood of noble grapes.

She allowed the wine to warm her insides, opening her to herself.

After the first glass, she started to see. After the second, she knew.

It's Vera. It has to be her. So what do I do? Call the police and tell them? "I think my friend is poisoning people in my ED. She poisoned five already. Maybe six. No, I'm not sure how. No, I'm not sure with what. Why? To make the world a better place. No, I don't have any proof." They'd think I'm crazy. They'd probably be right.

So what?

She looked at Guinness. "What do I do now?"

Guinness thumped her tail.

"Nothing. Let her be. She's doing a great job."

"Seriously? A great job? She killed half a dozen people! Even a child!"

"The kid was a monster. The others were all assholes. The world is a better place without them."

"But that's immoral!"

"No. It's illegal. There's a difference."

"Are you saying that killing people is moral?"

"Killing people happens all the time. In war. In legal executions. In assisted death. What's so different about that?"

"But, that's entirely different."

"Really? How about Angel, then?"

"That was a case of legitimate defense."

Guinness was done. She didn't understand humans and their inhibitions. People lived. People died. That was that. She put her head in Emma's lap to get scratched.

Emma sighed and obliged, wondering what to do next. *I have to speak to Vera.* Emma put down the wine glass and grabbed her keys.

"Let's go."

48

———————

It was late, but the windows still glowed orange at Vera's house. Vera didn't burden herself with conventions. Time included. If she felt like it, she'd stay up the whole night, then sleep the next day. She ate when she was hungry and drank when she felt like it. Her motto was: "It's got to be five o'clock somewhere."

The great forged iron clock in her living room had only one hand. Instead of pointing to numbers, it indicated the place on earth where it happened to be five o'clock. It was Honolulu's time as Emma stepped through the door.

Leaning back in her bentwood recliner, Vera was reading a leather-bound tome. She looked at them above her round metal glasses and smiled.

"Emma! And Guinness! How lovely!"

Guinness leaped forward, put her front paws on Vera's chest, and gave her a deep wet kiss. Vera laughed.

"There now! That'll help my complexion!" She kissed Guinness on her cold black nose and scratched her behind her ears. Guinness stuck her nose in Vera's pockets, looking for a treat. Vera always had the best treats for people and dogs.

"I have these peanut butter chicken biscuits. I baked them yesterday. Let's see where they are," Vera said. Emma's heart skipped a beat.

"There's no need. Guinness had dinner already."

"Then it's time for dessert. I think I put them in the freezer to give them an extra crunch."

"She doesn't need them. She's put on some weight."

"Really? I guess we'll need to walk her more then."

"No, really, please don't," Emma said.

"OK." Vera smiled. "How about a cookie for you then? If you're not into peanut butter chicken, I have this new recipe with walnuts and chocolate."

"No, thank you, Vera. I'm not hungry."

"This isn't about hungry. It's about pleasure! You'll love them!"

"No, really, thank you, I don't want them. I came to talk."

"Taylor?"

"She's…I don't know how she is. I haven't spoken to her in a couple of days. We…We didn't… we don't…"

"See eye to eye."

"Yes. About Umber."

"I know."

"I didn't come to talk about Taylor. I came to talk about the ED."

"OK."

"People have been dying."

"Yes."

"For no good reason."

"That you know of."

"Precisely. We've had a lot of unexpected deaths lately."

Vera nodded, rocking gently. Guinness lay next to her and put her head in her lap, demanding scratching. Vera complied.

"I believe somebody is poisoning people in the ER."

Vera nodded again.

"Somebody with enough knowledge of poisons and enough skill to make it look natural, even if it's not."

Vera nodded.

"I've been wondering who that could be. There's not that many people in the ER with that knowledge and that kind of skill."

Vera listened, looking her in the eye and scratching Guinness's ears. Her blue eyes sparkled behind her round glasses, and her mouth softened in half a smile.

Emma lost her patience.

"Aren't you going to ask me?"

"You'll tell me when you're good and ready. Would you like some tea?"

"No, thanks."

"How about vodka?"

"No, I'm good."

"Wine? I have an excellent Bordeaux. I got it just for you."

"No, thanks, Vera. I'm good."

Vera smiled.

"OK. I'll get some tea for myself then. It looks like we have a while to go, and I'm thirsty."

She left for the kitchen. Guinness followed. Emma wanted to stop her, but she couldn't think of an excuse. Why would Vera kill Guinness? She loved her. There was no reason for her to do it. *Unless she plans to kill me too.* Emma's throat went dry, and she had trouble swallowing her saliva. She needed a drink. *Not here, not now.*

Vera returned with two steaming art mugs. She put Emma's favorite, Van Gogh's *Starry Night*, in front of her. She picked up the one with Monet's waterlilies and sniffed it.

"It's a new recipe. Mint and orange peel, plus something special I've never tried before. Let me know what you think," she said, taking a sip.

"Thank you." Emma pushed the mug away.

"Anytime. You were saying?"

Emma sighed. She wasn't getting anywhere, and she was tired, crabby, and thirsty. She was torn.

"Vera, have you been poisoning people in my ER?"

"Your ER?"

"The ER. Have you been poisoning people?"

"Why on earth would you ask me this, Emma?" Vera asked.

"People have been dying. You know it. There's no explanation for it other than somebody has been poisoning them one by one."

"Better than all of them together, don't you think?"

"I'm not kidding."

"Neither am I," Vera said. "Why do you think they are dying?"

"Because somebody is poisoning them."

"Why?"

"They're not nice people."

"Would that be a good reason?"

"They are worse than not nice people. They are people who have hurt others and might do it again."

"That sounds like a good reason."

"Vera, they are people. They have a right to live. If they did wrong, they are entitled to due process."

Vera nodded. "So are their victims."

"Vera, we are not the law. We can't take justice into our own hands. We can't start killing people right and left because we don't like the way they live their life."

"That, I agree with. But how about defending the innocent?"

"We are a country of laws. We have laws to defend the innocent. We have laws to punish those who hurt them."

Vera laughed. "It's good to hear."

Emma's throat was dry. She was frustrated, exhausted, and feeling foolish. Deep inside, she knew that Vera was right. The laws intended to protect the innocent failed to protect them. Those meant to punish the perpetrators failed to punish them. The babies, the women, the weak, they were not safe. She remembered sending a beaten woman and her child home with her perpetrator. She recalled sending the burned baby back home with his mom, wondering if she was going to see her back dead. While playing by the rules, she had failed to protect her patients. What else could she do? She was a doctor, bound by the Hippocratic oath: First: Do no harm. That was her duty.

"Vera, you can't take justice into your own hands."

"Why not?"

"You'll go to jail."

"Are you going to send me there?"

Emma scrutinized Vera, her best friend. A tiny woman with a mop of white hair and blue eyes shining with intelligence, marked by laughter lines. Her hands were rough from gardening; her nails always darkened by dirt. She smelled like chocolate, cinnamon, and chicken, and she was full of life, in spite of the tumors consuming her brain. She had only months left to live.

Emma's heart ached. *Should I call the police and tell them? Tell them what? That this tiny old lady is a serial killer? I have no proof. There may be no proof.*

"I don't know what to do, Vera. I honestly don't know what to do."

"Here, have some tea," Vera said, pushing the Van Gogh mug closer. "It will make you feel better."

Emma looked at her tea. She wanted it, but she was afraid of it.

She looked in Vera's eyes. Vera smiled.

"I'll have your mug," Emma said.

Vera laughed.

"That's so like you, Emma. I knew you'd say that. I didn't poison your mug. But what if I poisoned mine?"

Emma blushed. She was no match for Vera. Vera was everything that Emma was, without the hang-ups, the guilt, the inhibitions, and the conscience. Vera was the free spirit Emma wished she could be. She wasn't.

"Emma, relax. It's OK. Everything is going to be OK." She handed her the *Starry Night* mug. "There. Drink this."

Emma took a sip. Soothing and refreshing. Very different.

"What is it?"

"My new recipe. Soothing herbs. A touch of violet. I didn't want to add autumn crocus to your tea."

Emma knew that autumn crocus contained digitalis, causing heart arrhythmias, like oleander and yew. Emma took another sip and felt her worries fade. She relaxed for the first time in ages.

"This is good." She drained the mug.

"Excellent. Relax, Emma. It's almost over. Not long now, and you won't have to worry about any of this anymore. I'll take care of everything. It's going to be all right."

Emma's limbs softened. The pain in her neck faded away.

Vera helped her to the sofa. She put a pillow under her neck and covered her with a soft quilt. She turned down the lights and locked the door.

Emma's eyelids got heavy. She felt sleep taking over, making her wonderfully soft and relaxed.

She struggled to open her eyes. Vera gave Guinness a bowl of water. Guinness inhaled it. *She's got to be thirsty,* Emma thought.

Then she thought no more.

49

Taylor's fogged brain signaled something was wrong, but she couldn't remember what. She opened her eyes. The room was a kitschy nightmare: gilded ceiling, busy wallpapered walls, cabbage roses weighing down overstuffed armchairs, heavy velvet curtains cutting out the light.

She didn't know where she was, nor how she got here. The one thing she knew was that she was sick. Every heartbeat pounded in her brain like a broken washing machine. Her stomach revolted, and she rushed to the bathroom. The bright light hit her retinas like spears tearing into her skull. She closed her eyes, allowing them to adjust, then opened them again to more obscene luxury: Clean white marble, snow-white towels, a Jacuzzi big enough to soak a small elephant.

She splashed cold water over her face, then looked in the mirror. She wished she hadn't. That girl that looked back, she hadn't seen her in a while. Blood-shot eyes, blotched skin, messed-up hair. She looked like a secondhand version of herself, suffering from the mother of all hangovers. More cold water cleared the fog and tickled her neurons into waking up.

She sat on the toilet to think.

I took Umber to see the baby, and Eric came along. Umber told Hope that he was her father. Eric left. Then Umber took me out for dinner.

In the fog of her brain, memories surfaced slowly, one by one. Umber said he had separated from his wife. She was nothing but a gold digger. When he lost his income, she found somebody else. She took his children and refused to let him see them. He was stricken with grief.

"That's awful. They are your children! You have a right to see them, just like she does."

"I do, don't I? Unfortunately, that's not how it worked. Once in jail, I became a second-class citizen. Her lawyer argued that I was a danger to the kids. I was a drug dealer, possibly a killer. They were better off without me since a relationship with me would ruin them. They'd become criminals, like me. She took the kids, and I haven't seen them in months. I can't even text them. For all that I know, they may not even be alive."

Taylor understood the heartbreak of losing your kids. There could be nothing worse. And it was her fault—she'd helped Emma put Umber in jail. Her heart sank.

"I'm so sorry, Dick. I never thought something like this would happen."

"Neither did I." He shrugged, pouring more of the lovely, buttery French wine.

Taylor took a sip, then another. The wine was lovely.

She hadn't had wine since her last date with Umber. She was pregnant then, but that didn't matter. She was going to get an abortion anyhow.

Then she didn't.

Afterward, she'd kept clean and sober throughout her pregnancy. She had spent weeks in rehab to get rid of her pill habit. But that was long ago. Now, Dick was back. His laughing eyes, the color of the ocean, held her with love. He'd been her first lover, and losing him had almost destroyed her. He was smart; he was charming; he loved the good life. Being with Dick was fun.

Eric was different. He always did what she asked. He was kind and supportive, but not exciting. Being with Dick was exhilarating. You never knew what was coming. With him, every moment was thrilling. He brought her to this beautiful place, ordered this exceptional dinner, and chose this heavenly wine. Life was better with Dick.

He took her hand and kissed the inside of her wrist.

"Thank you for meeting me, Taylor. I missed you. And I missed our baby." He poured more wine. "You must be so proud of her. She is so beautiful."

"Yes, she is."

"She's even more beautiful than my other babies were," he said, knocking glasses. "But then, how could she not? She's ours. To Hope."

They drank. Taylor was feeling woozy. She'd had enough, but he suggested an ice wine she'd never tried. She couldn't say no.

It was a lovely meal, but she had trouble walking to the car. The sidewalk moved under her feet like the deck of a boat in a storm. She laughed. He helped her to the car, then took her hand and kissed the inside of her palm. His tongue swirled, circling her lifeline, and her insides melted. Heat started between her legs and invaded her, spreading through her body to her brain.

He took her face between his hands and came close. His bitter-green scent made her dizzy. His bright eyes shone light into her soul.

"Taylor, I'll drive you home to Pretty Boy, if that's what you want. But I booked the best room at an exceptional hotel. We could spend more time together and talk about Hope's future. Stay with me, please. For the good old times' sake?"

Taylor sighed and massaged her hurting temples. *By then, I didn't care. Actually, I did. I wanted him. I wanted the past to come back and end better. I wanted to be the love of his life. I wanted him to be my forever after.*

She couldn't remember how they got here. He drove? He had opened the champagne bottle, now empty, sitting in a silver bucket by the bed. The cork exploded into the ceiling, dusting them with white plaster. The bubbly spilled over. They laughed.

He poured champagne into delicate crystal flutes and got a pillbox from his pocket. He shook out two white oblong pills and offered her one. She took it with champagne. She didn't remember anything else, but the scent of wild carnations was still lingering on her skin.

That had been last night.

And this was now.

She shook her head. Her brain felt like a bucket of gravel. It was heavy, and it hurt. She splashed more cold water over her face, then returned to the room and pulled the curtains open. Her jeans and her hoodie lay on the floor by the fireplace.

Blood rose into her face, burning her cheeks. She didn't remember anything, but it wasn't hard to figure it out. She didn't know which was worse: that it happened, or that she couldn't even remember it.

Now what? She looked in her jacket for her phone. Dead. No charger. She glanced out the window. A street she couldn't recognize, bathed in the morning sun. She thought about calling reception. Then what? Tell them: "I don't know where I am. Can you please send me home?" She could walk out and try to find out where she was. It couldn't be that far from home. She could catch a cab. Or walk. She didn't want anybody to know. They wouldn't approve. *They don't know him like I do. But where is he? Why isn't he here? I should wait for him. Maybe he just went out to get coffee. He should be back at any moment.*

She took off her jacket and sat in the oversized cabbage rose armchair, thinking.

He's separated, soon to be divorced. He's longing for his kids; that's why he loves Hope so much. He needs love, and a family. He needs me. That's why he's back. If I take him back, we'll be together, just like we were always meant to be.

She remembered what had happened last time. Umber lied and cheated on her. *He might do it again.* She pushed the thought away. *No more negativity. Life is good: I have a beautiful baby and the world's best lover. I'm lucky.* How was she going to break the news to her mother? And her father? She didn't want to think about that. Not now.

There was plenty of time for that.

A knock at the door.

"Yes?"

Amber came in.

50

Her blonde hair in a perfect bob, her outfit to die for, Amber stared at Taylor as if she'd found a poisonous snake in her bathtub.

"Taylor?"

"Yes."

"What are you doing here?"

"Me?"

Amber blushed.

Taylor's plans crashed down on her like a ton of bricks. She was in Umber's room, and Amber had just waltzed in. That could only mean one thing, and that wasn't a good thing for either of them or for Victor.

"What are you doing here, Amber?'

Amber's blush deepened. She stared at her feet, then back to Taylor. She looked around the room, taking it all in: the champagne bottle, the crumpled bed, Taylor herself. Taylor wished she'd had a chance to brush her teeth.

"I'm…I'm just visiting."

"Me too."

Taylor got up to leave, then remembered she didn't know where she was and she didn't even have a phone. She sat back down.

Amber shifted her weight from one foot to the other. She looked at the messy bed and the empty champagne bottle.

"I thought you wanted nothing to do with him anymore," she said.

"You talked me into it."

"I did?"

"Yes. Umber deserves a second chance, and all that crap, remember?"

Amber's lips tightened into a thin line. She glanced at the door, then back at Taylor. She shrugged. Her back straight, her chin up, she sat in the other armchair.

"What are you going to do now?" she asked.

"Good question. I don't know. How about you?"

"I…Are you going to tell your father?"

"Why not?"

"That would break his heart!"

Taylor laughed. "Bless your heart, Amber, I didn't know you were that funny."

Amber's perfect mouth curved down in displeasure. "I don't find it funny."

"That's what makes it so funny."

The door opened. Umber came in with two cups of coffee. His smile melted like the face of a Dali clock when he saw Amber, but he recovered quickly.

"What a nice surprise. I wish I knew that two of my favorite ladies were here, waiting for me. I'd have brought more coffee. There, Amber, have mine," he said, placing a coffee near her.

Amber stood up. She glared at him, glanced at Taylor, then turned around and left.

The door slammed behind her.

51

——————

Umber shrugged and sat in the empty armchair. He lifted the coffee cup to toast Taylor as if it were wine, then took a sip. His legs crossed, he studied his gleaming Italian leather shoes in silence.

Taylor couldn't take it anymore.

"What's this all about, Dick? What are you here for? What do you want?"

"Now, now, Taylor, it's not like you to speak like this. You're sweet, loving, and innocent, remember? Don't talk like your mother."

Taylor remembered her mother and blushed. She had been right again. *Will this ever end? Being perpetually directed, corrected, and humbled?*

"Let's leave my mother out of this, shall we? What do you want?"

"We can't leave your mother out of it, Taylor. This is about your mother."

"How so?"

"I want my medical license back. Emma will help me get it."

"Are you out of your mind? She made you lose it."

"That's precisely why I need her help. I need her to give me an affidavit that the accusations she made against me were false. She lied and falsified the documents that incriminated me. She will exonerate me, and I will get my license back."

"You know damn well that's not true!"

Umber shrugged. "What does truth have to do with it? I'm talking about my license."

"You must be deranged. Why would Mother do that?"

"You'll talk her into it."

"Me? Not in a thousand years."

"Yes, you will. If you want to keep your baby, you will."

"What does the baby have to do with this?"

"I'll sue to take her away. You're an unfit mother. You were drinking and using drugs when you were pregnant. You ran out of rehab and went back to doing drugs. That's why the baby was premature. I have witnesses to testify that last night, you were too drunk to walk, but you drove here. The receptionist saw you crawling out of the driver's seat. You're also doing drugs. If they test you, you'll test positive for all sorts of interesting things. You left the baby in the hospital to go partying. You have no job and no income to support her. I'm only doing my duty, taking her away from you. You didn't want her anyhow. You planned to give her up for adoption. You already have a couple lined up to take her. I'm her father. I have rights."

His words ripped into Taylor like bullets. She hadn't known such pain existed. She'd been despondent when he betrayed her last time, but this? There were no words to describe that kind of suffering. And she had brought it all on herself.

She stared at him, wishing she had shot him long ago. He smiled.

"That's just the beginning. We'll find more if need be."

"You think my mother would do that?"

"Yes. It will be the end of Emma's career, and it may land her in jail, but if she has to choose between your well-being and her career, she'll choose you."

"I don't think so."

"You don't know her well enough."

"And you do?"

"Of course. She's exactly like me."

"Are you insane? My mother? Like you?"

"Yes. I will do anything, whatever it costs, to get what I want. Nothing but death will stop me. Your mother is the same. She will do anything, whatever it costs, to get what she wants. The only difference is that we don't want the same things."

"What do you want?" Taylor asked.

"I want power. And money. They are interchangeable. One begets the other. And I will have them both. Don't you want to know what your mother wants?"

Taylor's eyes burned with impotent hate.

"You want to kill me. I know. Get over it. It's not going to happen, baby. You missed your chance. But we weren't talking about you; we were talking about your mother. What Emma wants more than anything is to do her job. She can't respect herself otherwise. She thinks she's not worthy if she fails her responsibility. And you are her first responsibility. She'll do whatever it takes to keep you safe, even if it kills her."

"And you think I'll ask her to destroy her career, her reputation, and her freedom? For you?"

"Oh, no! Not for me! She'd never do it for me! But she'll do it for you. And for baby Hope."

"What if she doesn't?"

"She will."

"What if she doesn't?"

"I'll sue for paternity, and I'll take the baby. We both know she's mine. There's at least a fifty/fifty chance that I'll win the suit and take her. Are you willing to take the risk?"

"How are you going to care for her? Every three hours, she needs to eat and get changed. She needs 24/7 care. What are you going to do with her?"

"You're missing the point, Taylor. It's not about what I'll do with her."

He pulled her up, put his hands on her shoulders, and kissed her hair. He looked in her eyes. "It's about what you'll do without her."

He pushed her out the door and closed it behind her.

Taylor walked out in a haze, her eyes burning, her brain numb.

The Indian receptionist smiled as if they shared a secret. *She's got to be the one who saw me drunk last night.* She wanted to tell her that she hadn't been driving, but she wasn't even sure about that. She didn't remember what had happened last night.

She stepped out in the morning sun, shielded her eyes with her hand, and looked down the road, trying to figure out how to get home.

A white BMW convertible pulled near her. It was Amber.

"You want a ride?"

52

———

Emma woke up and opened her eyes to Vera's drinking clock. Last night, she had come to confront Vera with the string of deaths. Vera didn't admit to having caused them but didn't deny it either. Then she'd given her tea, and Emma drank it. She had been worried about poison, but instead, she'd had her first good sleep in weeks, and woke up feeling better than she had in ages.

She got up to look for Guinness, but she was MIA. So was Vera. A pot of heavenly smelling coffee, still hot, called her name. She read the note on the counter:

"Have some coffee. It's not poisoned. Neither are the scones on the table. Guinness and I went for a walk. Go home; I'll bring her later. She'll have a good time with the girls."

What girls?

"Thelma and Louise," the note answered.

Emma drank the coffee, ate the scones, and drove home.

She called Zagarian. No answer. She left a message.

"I need to talk to you."

What if he thinks it's something personal? She called again and left another message.

"It's not personal; it's professional."

She hung up, feeling like a fool. She walked around, looking for something to do. Since Guinness wasn't there to take her for a walk, she felt abandoned. She had chores and shopping to do, but she didn't feel like it. She paced around the house instead, waiting for Zagarian to call back until she couldn't wait anymore. She grabbed her jacket and went to work, even though she had no business being there. She started perusing the charts again, looking for anything she may have missed. A clue. An idea. There was nothing new, except for Andy's tox results. No drugs. Nothing unusual, except for the results of the very special test Emma had sent to the CDC. Andy's blood was positive for anti-abrin antibodies, confirming that he'd been exposed to abrin.

53

———————

The sun was still up, but there was nobody else walking the long sandy beach behind McDonald's. *This McDonald's must have the best views in the country*, Margret thought, contemplating the Green Mountains of Vermont across Lake Champlain. The tall chin of Mount Mansfield had grown a beard of clouds. August was almost over, and the maple leaves had started turning. Margret and Vera walked on the sand, avoiding the dogs who kept entangling their leashes and yapped whenever a wave came close. Guinness shepherded the pack, giving the dogs well-deserved nasty looks.

"She's counting us," Margret said, bending over to disentangle Thelma and Louise, who had braided themselves around her legs.

"There now, girls. Look at Guinness. See how she never gets entangled? She walks so well, even without a leash. You can do that too, you know."

Vera laughed. "I'd be surprised. Guinness is a German shepherd. She lives for her job. Those two live to play."

"Yep. Kind of like Emma and Taylor and Amber. Different breeds."

"How's Taylor?"

"I don't know. She and Amber came home together this morning. I don't know where they were, but they looked weird."

"How so?"

Margret shrugged.

"Conspiratorial. Secretive."

"I didn't know they were such great friends."

"They aren't."

Vera nodded and sat on the wooden bench overlooking the lake. Guinness lay by her feet.

Margret glanced at them, and her heart tightened. Vera had shrunk. She got a little smaller, a little slower, a little grayer every day. They hadn't known each other long, but Margret had fallen in love with Vera's almost brutal directness, her sharp wit, and her killer sense of humor. For Margret, used to the polite hypocrisy of the South, Vera's freedom was as refreshing as a cold beer on a hot summer day. There was nothing fake, no pretense, no ambiguity about Vera. She always said what she meant, and she only did what she wanted—with gusto. But she was fading.

"How are you?" Margret asked.

"Great. How about you?"

"No, really. How are you?"

"I'm as good as I'm ever going to be, Meg," Vera answered. "I'd better make the most of it since I'm running out of time."

"Have you talked to them about your options? Chemo may…"

"May make me so sick I will wish I was dead. No, Meg, I've decided. I only have a little bit left. I'm going to make the most of it. If you had, say, a week left, what would you do with it?"

"A week?!"

"Just for the sake of argument."

"I' d…I'd put my affairs in order. I'd pay my debts. I'd hug the ones I love."

"Sure. What else?"

"I don't know. A week isn't enough time to cruise around the world. Maybe fly to one last place? Do one last thing?"

"Now, you're talking. Where would you fly? And what would you do?"

"I'd fly to Paris. I'd go to the Orsay to see the Van Goghs."

"Atta girl. I've been thinking about stealing one."

"A Van Gogh?"

"Yes."

Margret laughed. "I think they guard them."

"I do too. Sadly. I wonder if I could rent the room and spend my last week there."

"In the museum?"

"Yes. Sleep on a mattress on the floor, drink wine, and watch the Van Goghs in the candlelight. Unfortunately, I can't. I don't have that kind of money. And I have to put my business in order and hug my loved ones. Can you ask Taylor to stop by?"

"Sure. You need help with something?"

"Yes. I need to finish weeding my garden."

"I'd be glad to help you."

"I know, Meggie. Thank you. But, for that particular job, I need Taylor."

<h1 style="text-align:center">54</h1>

Emma was home, drinking her fourth cup of coffee and learning about abrin poisoning symptom onset. She glanced outside again, waiting for Vera to return Guinness when Zagarian returned her call.

"To what do I owe this pleasure? Have you got another serial killer?" he joked.

"As a matter of fact…"

"You're kidding, yes?"

"Well…"

"Sometimes, your sense of humor gets ahead of you, Emma."

"Not today."

"I'm on my way."

Emma looked around. With Taylor gone, the house was mostly tidy. She went to brush her teeth, then grinned in the mirror. They were still gray. *Red wine does a job on your teeth. So does coffee,* she thought. She brushed them once more and put on red lipstick. She changed her coffee-stained robe for a light-green summer dress. She bent over, brushing her hair backward to give it some lift. It looked fake. She ran her fingers through it and messed it up. *Should I serve wine when he's coming to talk about a bunch of murders? Well, whiskey isn't any better, and I had enough coffee to sink a ship. He can always refuse.*

She chose a Bordeaux. A 2015 Saint-Georges Saint-Emilion, Les Abeilles. Three tiny golden bees chased each other on the bland tan label. The wine was dark and opaque, albeit a little thin, as it flew in the glass. The first nose was light with fresh fruit; the second brought oak and darker bitterness. Pleasant on the tongue, with ripe fruit flavors followed by the darkness of the tannins, the signature of Bordeaux. She enjoyed the heat spreading through her body, softening the ache in her shoulders and the emptiness in her soul.

The bell rang.

Emma opened the door to Zagarian, radiant as always, in one of his eternal gray suits. He handed her a bouquet of yellow spider chrysanthemums.

"I happened to be near the flower shop when you called."

Emma smiled. She hadn't received flowers for a long time. The yellow globes with gracious spiky petals were bigger than Emma's hands. Proud and vivid, they brought light to the room. Emma inhaled their fall scent and gave them water, then turned to Zagarian.

"Wine?"

He frowned. "I don't know. Should I?"

"Why not? Wine makes everything better."

"That, I can't argue with."

He took his glass and sniffed it. "Not bad." He took a sip. He nodded.

"What's up?"

"I have a story to tell you."

He sat in the green leather armchair by the fireplace and crossed his legs.

"Say there was a little old lady who wanted to make the world a better place."

"Like the God Fairy?"

"Pretty much."

Zagarian took another sip of wine and smiled. He relaxed, leaning back in the chair.

"She decided to get rid of those who were evil and mean."

"Get rid as in how?"

"Get rid as in kill."

Zagarian sat up. "This is not really a story, is it?"

Emma shook her head.

"Kill them, how?"

"Poison."

"How many?"

"Six."

"Six! Are you sure?"

"No."

Zagarian put the glass down. "Better start at the beginning."

Emma did.

"This is insane. I've never heard about anything like this."

He stood and paced, then took the glass of wine and drained it down. He stopped facing Emma. "Do you have any proof?"

"No."

"Emma, if anybody else would have told me this, I'd say they were delusional. Since it's you, I don't know what to think. I'm at a loss. I don't know what to do, either."

"You could start looking into the case with the abrin. That one, we already know. The other ones will follow. Send Ben's blood to CDC for abrin antibody testing. It will take a while to get the result, but I think it will be positive."

"Maybe."

"Maybe."

"This is the craziest thing I've heard in a long time."

Emma shrugged.

"Stick with me."

He sighed and headed to the door, just as it opened, letting Vera and Guinness in.

"We're back!" Vera said. "We had a great time with the girls."

"Vera, let me introduce you. This is Detective Zagarian. My friend Vera."

Zagarian stared at her as if he'd seen a ghost.

Vera smiled and shook hands.

"Nice to meet you, Detective. You like chocolate?"

"Aah…eeh…"

"I made a special batch of brownies for Emma. I'm sure she won't mind your trying one."

"No, no, thanks. I have to go home for dinner."

"Why don't you take a couple for dessert then? She reached in her shoulder bag and took out a beautifully wrapped golden package. "There. They go great with wine. I made them for Emma; she loves wine."

"Thank you; I wouldn't want to deprive Emma…"

"No worries. I have more." Vera reached into the bag again and brought a second package, this one in silver. She handed them to Emma.

"Thank you, Vera." Emma set them on the counter.

Guinness checked them out.

"They're not for you." Emma moved them to a higher shelf.

"Now Guinness, you know you can't have chocolate. But look what I have for you since you've been such a good girl! She reached back into the bag for a zipper bag of bone-shaped dog cookies. "Peanut butter, chicken, and gravy." She handed the bag to Emma. "These are for later. She's had plenty today."

Zagarian choked.

"Are you OK?" Vera asked.

"I'm good. Thank you. I have to go now." He left.

"Emma!" he called from the car.

"Yes?" She walked out to him.

"Don't eat the brownies," he whispered.

"They're OK," Emma laughed. "She could have poisoned me a hundred times. She didn't. She's not after me. You, though, I'm not so sure."

She went back in to find Vera checking out the golden mums.

"Nice flowers," she said.

Emma blushed.

Vera smiled.

"He looks like a nice man."

"He is."

"You know, Emma, we only live once."

Emma thought that was funny, coming from Vera. Then she remembered that Vera was running out of time.

"You're right. Do you have any regrets?"

"Not really. I did everything I could do; I took every chance I could take; I lived through every day; I enjoyed my time and made the most of it. No, I have no regrets."

I wish I could say the same, Emma thought. *As I look back, I have nothing but regret for all the things I didn't do and those I should have done differently.*

"Vera, I told him."

"Told him what?"

"About the abrin."

Vera frowned. "That's unfortunate. He's going to throw away those perfectly good brownies."

55

Looking straight ahead and keeping quiet, Amber drove as if she didn't care if they made it home. Taylor wished she had walked instead. Her brain splintered and burned with every noise and bright light. Amber's sweet smell made her nauseous, and the tension in the air didn't help any.

"Thanks for the ride," Taylor said.

Amber nodded.

"I'm sorry about this, Taylor. I didn't know you were there."

Well, duh!

"Are you going to tell your father?"

Amber's doll-like face had crumpled in sorrow. Her pretty mouth trembled as if she was about to cry. In spite of her own misery, Taylor felt sorry for her.

"I don't know, Amber. I need to think."

"There's no point in telling him. It will ruin our marriage, and it won't help you any."

"That's not the point, Amber. The point is honesty and truth."

Amber shrugged.

"That's one way to see it. The other way is that you would ruin our marriage and leave your sisters with a broken home."

"Amber, I didn't ruin your marriage. I didn't bring you to that room. You did."

Amber's lips tightened. She spoke without taking her eyes from the road.

"Taylor, if you think that breaking our marriage will bring your parents back together, think again. Emma won't take your father back."

"I know that, Amber. I don't even know that he wants to go back."

"He does. He's been thinking about Emma for years. You think I'm stupid? You think I don't know? In the beginning, I couldn't believe it. He had left her to be with me. But it was obvious. He always talks about her, and his face lights up when he says her name. Emma, this, Emma, that. He loves her. If she'd take him back, she'd drop us, the girls and me, in a minute. Thankfully, she won't."

Listening to Amber's bitter resentment, Taylor didn't know what to say. She was surprised that Amber knew. She had thought Amber was oblivious since she was always obsessed with shopping, hairdressers, and manicures. But, all this time, she knew.

"Can you imagine how humiliating it is to see your husband pining for his first wife? She's more than ten years older than me, too. It's maddening always to play second fiddle. In the beginning, when I met Umber, it was all about you. He wanted to get close to you, and I wanted to make your father jealous. Umber was handsome, charming, and funny. Then he told me he loved me. That was good for my ego, after your father, who'd rather spend time with the dogs than with me. Then I fell for him. Having an affair was exhilarating. Plus, I felt like I was paying back your father for ten years of neglect."

Tears streamed down her cheeks. She wiped them away with the back of her hand.

"I thought: I'm young. I'm pretty. I'm entitled to have fun and enjoy life. I had thought he liked me. Boy, was I mistaken. The one he wanted was you. He only used me to get to you. Second fiddle again. It doesn't feel good."

Taylor shrugged. *If you only knew. He doesn't want me, and he doesn't want the baby. He only wants power and money. He told me. To him, I'm just a tool, like you are. Through the baby and me, he's only trying to get to my mother. We all are nothing but tools to him.*

"If you tell your father, he'll leave me. And the girls. We won't be destitute. I work, and I know he'll provide for them. But like you, they'll grow up without a father. They'll only see him on the weekends and vacations, like you did. I'm sorry I did that to you. I didn't really think that far. He was smart and handsome. He looked at me, and it was like the sun came up. I fell in love with him. I didn't care that he was older; I didn't care that he was married; I didn't even care about his money. I just loved him."

Tears dropped from her chin, making dark wet spots on her rose silk skirt. Her voice was deep and raw. "I still do, you know. I still do. That makes it even more stupid that I fell for Umber. But I did."

How sad, Taylor thought. I didn't realize that their marriage was in trouble. I thought they were happy together. I was wrong. We all want things that we can't have, and people who don't want us. I wanted Umber. Eric wanted me. Father wants Mother. Amber wants Father. We all want whatever's out of our reach. Is this what life is? Wanting one thing and making do with another? Boy, does that suck!

"I'm sorry, Amber. I didn't know any of this. I thought you and Father had a perfect marriage. I'm sorry that all this happened, and that I was there to see you in Umber's room. I don't know what to do. I know that Father would want to know the truth. I would if I were him. I'll think about it, and I'll let you know before I speak to him. OK?"

"Thanks, Taylor."

Taylor nodded, adding another reason to hate Umber to her long list. He had lied, betrayed, and humiliated her again. He had played her to get to her mother. Now, she was supposed to do his bidding, destroy her mother's career, maybe even have her go to jail. All that so that Umber could get his license back and go on wrecking people. Otherwise, he'd take her baby. Not because he wanted her, but because he wanted to destroy Taylor and Emma. Hope was just collateral damage, just like Amber, her father, Iris, and Opal. And Eric.

Her anger choked her.

She had brought that upon herself and the others. If she had listened to her mother, she wouldn't have touched Umber with a ten-foot pole. But she hadn't. She had walked right into his trap, launching her destruction and that of all these people she loved.

They'd all be better off without her. Her mother would keep her job and take care of baby Hope. Amber could work on her marriage, and the girls would grow up with a father, and Eric... He'd find somebody else.

They'd all be better off without her.

56

GUINNESS

T hey've all gone crazy. Like they caught dog madness. That's when dogs who didn't get their shots foam at the mouth and then lose their minds. But they aren't foaming. Not yet.

Shaman is restless. Like she's sitting on hot coals. She can't sit still and hasn't slept a night in forever. She wakes up and paces. It's exhausting. I only get to sleep when she's at work.

The girl has lost it too. She came home yesterday, looking for something. She hugged me, and she cried and cried. I told her I was OK, but she didn't listen. She never listens, that one.

The only one who's still sane is the Cookie Fairy. She's gotten a little smaller, but she's as happy as can be. She stopped by this morning to bring me cookies and take me for a walk.

Good cookies. I love chicken. Chicken liver, too, with gravy. And sour cream. I don't care about garlic, but she insists. "It's good for the worms," Well, then give it to them instead, I thought, but I didn't say it. I ate them anyhow. Not like I have a date tonight, but they make me fart. That's why Shaman always keeps the windows open.

Cookie Fairy hugged me as she left. What's with people and hugging? I don't get it. Scratching, I understand. That's OK; you can even do it from a distance. But hugging? That sucks. I'm too hot already. I didn't want to be rude, especially after the cookies, so I put up with it.

"You're such a good girl, Guinness."

"Of course, I'm a good girl." I wagged my tail. Tails are so useful. They keep away flies, and they help communicate with people. Even dogs. Get one if you have a chance.

"I love you."

I wagged my tail again. "Me too. Especially your cookies."

"Take care of Emma. I know you always do, but she may need a lot of help. She'll have to do some things that break her heart. I'll try to do them for her, but I'm afraid I'll fail. Guinness, you must be there for her if I'm not."

"Of course. Where else would I be?"

She patted me again and left. There was something sad about the way she shuffled. She didn't look back. I watched her until she crossed the street, beyond the street, and I couldn't watch her anymore.

She's sane, the Fairy, but she's leaving. Soon. I'm sorry. I love you, Fairy. I love you even more than I love your cookies.

Until we meet again.

57

The day Taylor went to help Vera with her garden was sunny but cold. In the few days she hadn't seen her, Vera had faded into a smaller, grayer version of herself. She looked fragile and slow, like she'd aged a few years, but her smile was as warm as ever, and her hug smelled like chocolate.

"Taylor, you look terrible, but it's still great to see you. How are you?

Taylor laughed. "You don't want to know."

"Oh, but I do. I really do. I want to know everything."

"Everything?"

"Every little thing. Tell me."

Taylor did. She sat on Vera's sofa, eating brownies and drinking tea. She told her every little thing, like she had asked. It took a long time.

Vera listened. Her eyes didn't leave Taylor's for a second. She sat quietly, inhaling her words without comments, questions, or signs of disapproval.

"I promised Amber that I won't tell Father yet. I'll think about it, and I'll warn her first," Taylor finished.

"What did she say?"

"Thanks."

Vera nodded. "She needs to tell him herself. He needs to know. It's better if she tells him. They have to work through their issues and embrace the truth. Lies are like boils. They rot you from inside. You need to cut them open to heal. There is no other way."

"What if she doesn't?"

"She will. Give her a week. She needs to find the right way."

"Thanks, Vera."

"Of course. You don't know if you had sex that night?"

Taylor blushed. "I don't."

"It's unlikely he'd do it without a condom. And it's probably too early for you to get pregnant again. Still, safer is better. You'll need to take Plan B. Your doctor can get that for you if you don't want to talk to your mother."

Taylor nodded.

"As for your mother, he is right. She will do whatever it takes. She'll die to save you. Let's hope it won't get to that. Do you have a way to contact him?"

"Email. Or call."

"Why don't you email him? Tell him you want to talk. Your grandmother would like to meet him, since he's the father of your baby. Tell him that she hates your mother. She would do whatever she can to bring her down."

"But that's not true! Grandma loves Mother!"

"Of course. And your grandma isn't going to be here. You'll bring him to me."

"Here?"

"Yes."

"Why?"

"To talk. I think I can convince Umber to leave you and your mother alone."

"Really?" Taylor appraised Vera, feeling nothing but doubt. Vera was half her size, more spirit than flesh. Umber was a mountain of muscle and well-honed skills. He was evil, and smarter than anybody Taylor knew.

"Really. It's not about the muscle. It's about the brain. You get him here. The sooner, the better. Tomorrow afternoon, say. I'll be waiting. Be nice. Tell him that you're sorry you hurt his feelings. He has good reasons to be upset. Tell him you tried to speak to your mother, but she wouldn't listen. She got so mad she left you talking and left. You didn't know what to do, so you spoke to your grandmother. She said she could try to help, but she wants to meet him first. He needs to come over."

"Vera, are you sure…"

"I'm sure. Go now. I have things to do. See you tomorrow afternoon. Be here first. I need to talk to you." She hugged her and pushed her out the door.

"Go. Do what I told you: Amber, Plan B, Umber. Kiss Hope for me."

Taylor left.

"Taylor?"

"Yes?"

"Don't tell your mom."

58

For her lunch break, instead of eating, Emma went upstairs to see Hope. She stood in front of her crib, and her heart melted with love. She couldn't believe how much little Hope had grown. She hadn't seen her in three days. Busy with work, unexplained deaths, and the suspicion that her best friend was poisoning people, Emma didn't get a chance to visit.

She looked just like Taylor the first time she'd seen her: small, pink, and beautiful, the most beautiful baby she'd ever seen. Hope was her spitting image.

Emma bent over to inhale her scent. She smelled like baby powder, spoiled milk, and Hope. Emma traced her face with her finger, searing it in her memory. She was in love like she'd fallen in love with Taylor. But with Taylor, that love had been tenuous and stayed that way.

Emma sighed thinking about her daughter.

I hope Taylor finds whatever she's looking for. I don't believe that Umber is the answer. And I'm sorry for Eric, too, but I think that's for the best. Eric is not a match for Taylor. Sooner or later, they'll both realize it. In the meantime, I hope Taylor doesn't destroy her future by betting on Umber, but there's nothing I can do about that.

She shrugged and kissed Hope, ready to return to the ED.

"She's beautiful, isn't she?"

Emma turned around.

Umber, smiling. His short, salt-and-pepper haircut brought out his tan. His white teeth didn't look like they needed brushing twice. He was strong, confident, and handsome, and Emma wished she could obliterate him into dust.

She smiled back.

"That's one thing you did right, Dick. She's beautiful."

"Yes. Wouldn't it be a pity if she grew up without her mother? And grandmother?"

Emma's heart sank. He was back at it.

"It would certainly be sad, though motherhood is overrated. I'm sure you agree."

"Well, if I think about my mother, who sent me out to get her fix, and never asked how I paid for it, I'd have to agree. But you're not like that, Emma. You'll do right by them, won't you?"

"I'll certainly try. How about you? She's your daughter."

Umber laughed.

"She's the byproduct of a good fuck. You should try thinking like a man sometimes, Emma. It would relieve your inhibitions. You'd make a better man than you are a woman. Your brain is your best tool. That's not womanly. They flaunt their stuff to get the boys hooked."

"And what are boys thinking with when that happens?"

Umber shrugged. "Good point. Not me, though. I love girls, but I have different priorities."

Emma nodded. "I know."

"So, are you going to do it?"

"Do what?"

"What Taylor said."

Emma hadn't seen Taylor in days. Umber seemed to think differently. He was probably just fishing, but...what if she was out of the loop?

"I don't know. I have to think about it."

"So you're not saying no."

Emma's heart pounded. Whatever that was, it was so awful that she was supposed to say no. She wished she knew what he was after.

"I'll probably decline. I think it's a lousy idea. I can't imagine how I could ever go there. Like, really? What are you thinking?"

"I want my license back, Emma. You took it away from me; you'll help me get it back. If you want your daughter to keep her daughter."

Emma's heart sunk. There it was: the threat. He wanted something he knew she wouldn't give him, so he was threatening her into it. Whatever it was, she wouldn't like it. Umber wasn't stupid.

"I don't know, Dick. I think I've done enough for Taylor. It's time for her to start doing things for herself and her daughter. We all have to live with the consequences of our actions: you, me, Taylor. I can't spend my life getting Taylor out of tight spaces."

"Really? You'll just let her go? And the baby?"

"There's no reason to believe you won't be a good father, is there? Your wife may welcome a baby. Aren't your kids older now? A baby would breathe new life into the home."

Umber's face darkened like the sky before a storm. "You can't be serious! What about Taylor?"

"That would solve a lot of Taylor's problems. She needs to go to college and has to study. She wants a social life. It won't be easy with a baby. She'll hurt for a while, but she can have plenty of children. She was considering adoption anyhow. It would be better for Hope to be with her real family. Did you speak to your wife? What did she say?"

Umber bit his lip.

He wants to crush me. I know the feeling.

"You're bluffing."

"Am I?" Emma smiled.

"You are. You're not as smart as you think."

"That makes two of us."

Umber glared at her and left, without another glance to the baby.

Emma sighed, hoping she'd never see him again. *Fat chance. There's a story Taylor didn't get around to telling me. It doesn't sound like something I want to hear, but I won't have a choice. It won't be pretty. Nothing ever is, when Umber is involved.*

She touched Hope's cheek one more time and left, her heart torn between love and fear.

59

Taylor glanced in the mirror one last time before heading to Vera's to meet Umber. She looked good. Way better than she deserved, for somebody about to break her father's marriage, destroy her mother's career, and lose her baby to the serial killer who happened to be her father. She sighed and added a touch of mascara. She was ready.

Slim hope that Vera would dissuade Umber. Nothing would. But Taylor had no other choice, besides speaking to her mother, and she'd rather cut off her tongue than do that.

She grabbed her bag and made a discreet exit out the back door. Things were tense in the house. She'd been avoiding her father. Amber too. She'd given her a week to tell him. Amber wasn't pleased. Too bad. That was the best Taylor could do. She avoided her grandmother, also. Between Umber's threat, Amber's betrayal, and Vera's directions, she had so many secrets weighing on her that she couldn't think about anything innocuous to talk about.

Vera's house was only a couple of miles away. She walked, too deep in thought to notice the scorching heat. She arrived ten minutes shy of four and found her waiting.

The house, cool and dark, felt terrific after the August heat. The shades were down, and the clock was at five, as usual. Buenos Aires today.

"Everything OK?" Vera asked.

"Yes. Umber said he was coming."

"Excellent. Here, try this, Vera said, offering her a tall frozen glass."

"What is it?"

"My new concoction. Summer herbs, honey, and lime. What do you think?"

Taylor took a sip, then drained the glass.

"It's phenomenal. Love it. Can I have another?"

Vera seemed doubtful. Then she shrugged.

"Sure. Why not?"

She poured another glass.

Taylor drained that one too.

Vera ogled her through her steel-rimmed round glasses, her regard intense and demanding.

"Taylor?"

"Yes."

"Whatever happens, stay out of it."

"What do you mean?"

"Things will happen that you won't understand. You may feel uncomfortable or worried. You may feel that you need to jump in to rescue someone. Don't. Whatever happens, happens. Stay clear. Think about baby Hope. She needs her mother. The rest of us will manage. Don't intervene, no matter what."

Taylor's heart darkened. She'd thought this encounter was just Vera talking Umber into leaving her mother alone. Not so. Bad things were about to happen, and she was supposed to watch. That was odd. When bad things happened, it was usually her doing. Not today.

"Are you expecting trouble?"

"You never know. Umber may not take kindly to being talked to. That's not your problem. You stay put. Don't talk, don't intervene. And most importantly, you don't eat or drink anything that I haven't specifically offered you. Anything. You got that?"

Taylor was confused. What the hell was happening? She opened her mouth to ask, but the doorbell rang. Umber had arrived.

60

Vera opened the door with a smile and looked up at Umber, who dwarfed her. They shook hands, and he handed her an impressive bouquet. Vera brought it to her nose to breathe it in, but the flowers were store-bought and scentless.

"Thank you. Nice to meet you, Mr. Umber."

"Dr. Umber."

"No more, if I understand correctly." Vera smiled.

Umber didn't.

"It's lovely to meet baby Hope's father. Now that I see you, I understand Taylor's youthful transgression. It's not often that one meets a man of your caliber. She must have been bowled over by your charm."

Umber lightened up. A little.

"I find it sad that Emma doesn't see it that way. But then, that girl always missed the obvious. Can I offer you something? Tea? Brownies? Cookies? Wine?"

"I'll have whatever Taylor is having," he said, glancing at Taylor's empty iced glass.

"Unfortunately, I have none of that left. Taylor was a thirsty girl. But I have something a tad better. Check this out."

723

She brought a frozen carafe. The clear lime-green liquid was thick as it flowed into two glasses, one for Umber, one for Vera. The glasses frosted from the cold.

"How about me?" Taylor asked.

"You've had your share." Vera smiled pleasantly. "There's water in the kitchen." She turned back to Umber. "I understand you need Emma's help to retrieve your license?"

"Yes," Umber said. "She made me lose it. I need her help to get it back."

"I understand." Vera placed a plate of brownies on the table between them. "I love experimenting with recipes. Most people don't know herbs. That's what flavor is all about. Ninety percent of taste is smell. The difference between cocoa and garlic is as substantial as the distance from the earth to the moon. I'm a gardener," she said, picking a brownie and placing it on a tiny plate near Umber. She took one for herself. "I love to try new flavors, new plants, new recipes. That gives me joy."

She picked up the brownie and sniffed it. "Almonds, pistachios, and Kefir lime. Not for the weak, but I don't think you're one of those, Mr. Umber."

Taylor opened her mouth to ask for some, then remembered Vera's stark warning. She sat back, watching.

"And of course, vodka. Everything flows better with vodka. Don't you think so, Mr. Umber?"

"I'm rather partial to wine, myself, but I have nothing against vodka," Umber said.

"Wine has more calories, more attitude, and it's rather snobbish, I think. Vodka gets the job done and doesn't pretend to be there for fun. It's there for the drinking."

Vera took out three glasses from the fridge and a bottle from the freezer. She poured a frosty glass for each of them.

They knocked.

"To a better future," Vera said.

Taylor nodded, but she set her glass on the table. She didn't feel like vodka. She wanted tea.

Umber smiled. "I can drink to that."

They drained their glasses and smiled, their faces glowing. Trust was taking shape.

The second glass helped.

"To your future," Vera said.

Umber nodded.

Taylor sighed. *This is crazy. Vera isn't talking him into anything; they're just chilling and drinking. When is this going to get real?*

"What exactly do you need?" Vera poured a third glass of vodka.

"I need Emma to admit that she lied. She falsified documents to put me in jail. That's how I lost my license."

"Will that be enough?"

"Yes. I have friends. They'll take care of everything else," Umber said.

"Friends are good," Vera said. *"Nasdrovnie!"*

They knocked their glasses and drained them down.

Taylor was getting restless. She had tried to understand what was happening, but it didn't look like much. They were bonding over vodka and bashing her mother, but Vera's progress to persuading him was nil.

"I guess I could speak to Emma," Vera said, pouring another glass.

"I never found talking to Emma to be helpful," Umber said.

"Neither have I. I guess it depends on how you speak to her." She raised her glass again.

"Nasdrovnie."

Her eyes looked glassy and her crisp enunciation had lost some of its spark.

Umber knocked, and they emptied their glasses again.

"How about some food?" Vera asked. "There's only so much vodka I can take on an empty stomach."

Umber smiled.

Vera brought up a plate of caviar loaded on hard-boiled goose eggs and garnished with Wasabi.

"Try this," she said, serving one to each of them. "Beluga sturgeon. The best that Russia has to offer."

The caviar didn't appeal to Taylor, who didn't care for fish.

"No, thanks," she said.

Vera shrugged. "Suit yourself."

Vera poured another vodka. Her manner was getting unsteady, and Umber's matched it well.

"To Baby Hope, she said. Umber nodded. They knocked their glasses, and they drained them.

Taylor was losing hope. They were drinking and getting nowhere while she was cold, tired, and getting hungry.

She eyed Umber's untouched brownie.

"Can I have this?"

He shrugged.

Taylor picked up the brownie.

Vera glared at her.

Taylor brought the brownie to her nose and smelled it.

Vera grabbed it from her hand.

"This is not your thing, Taylor. These are not your flavors. Try this," she said, pushing her plate toward her.

Umber stared.

"How about some tea?" Vera asked, lifting the still frosted green glass.

Umber lifted his. He took a sip.

"Delicious," he said.

Vera nodded.

"Yes, isn't it?"

"Would you like to try it, Taylor?" he asked.

Taylor picked it up and sniffed it. It smelled like mint, pistachio, and bitter almonds. She lifted it to her lips, but Vera knocked it out of her hand.

"So sorry, I got so clumsy lately," she said, standing up to clean the mess.

Taylor shrugged. "I'll just have yours." She reached for Vera's glass, but Vera picked it up before she could grab it.

"Sorry, Taylor. That one's mine," she said.

She looked thoughtfully into the green liquid as if she was reading the future. She lifted the glass and smiled, looking in Taylor's eyes.

"To the future," she said. "To a better future and to those who'll make it happen. I know you're one of them."

She drained the glass and set it on the table; then she collapsed, seizing. Taylor gasped and dropped to the floor to help her. She turned her on the side, protecting her neck, and checked her pulse. Vera's pulse was erratic and barely detectable. Her breathing was labored.

Umber called 911. The ambulance arrived in minutes, taking Vera to the ER. Taylor followed. By the time she made it there, Vera was dead. Stroke? Heart attack? A bleed in her brain because of her cancer? Nobody knew. She lay on the stretcher, pink and peaceful, a mysterious smile on her lips as if she had a secret nobody else knew.

Taylor touched her hand and cried, remembering her laughter, her smell, her deep, throaty voice, the way she'd talked to her only an hour ago. "Most importantly, you don't eat or drink anything that I haven't specifically offered you. Anything. You got that?"

She'd forgotten.

Her heart got dark.

61

Emma's drive to the ER would have made Lewis Hamilton proud. When Taylor called to tell her that Vera had collapsed, Emma dropped everything, locked Guinness in without letting her out, and drove like a bat out of hell in her slippers. She made it without killing anyone, including herself, but it was too late. Vera was dead.

"What happened, Taylor?"

For the first time in her life, Taylor had no words. She shrugged.

Emma had no time for that. Not today.

She grabbed Taylor's shoulders and stared her in her face, tears running down her cheeks.

"What happened, Taylor? What did you do?"

Taylor shrunk.

"I took Umber to her."

"Why?"

"She told me to."

"Why?"

"He...He wanted me to speak to you about recovering his license. He was going to take away baby Hope if you didn't agree. I told Vera."

"Why?"

Taylor looked at her as if she'd lost her mind. "Because she asked me to?" One didn't question Vera. If Vera asked you something, you answered. If she told you to do something, you did it. That was that.

"Then?"

"Vera told me…" Unable to speak, Taylor exploded into uncontrollable sobs. Emma wanted to hug her but didn't. She was worried she might strangle her instead. She waited.

"Vera told me to bring him over. She told me not to eat or drink anything that she hadn't offered me."

"And then?"

"I tried to drink her tea. She took it away from me and drank it. She collapsed."

Emma nodded. She got the picture. Vera had tried her last stint, and, thanks to Taylor, she died.

Emma tried to have no bad feelings for Taylor. *She's young. She didn't know any better. There's no reason to slap her silly and kick her into the ground.* She failed. She wanted to kill her. Right there and then. She looked in Taylor's troubled eyes.

"Do you understand what happened, Taylor?"

Taylor shrugged.

"You know why Vera died?"

Taylor opened her mouth, then closed it back. Shaking like a leaf, she was a wreck. Emma should have been sorry for her, but she wasn't. Taylor had finally gone too far. Her stubbornness, her entitlement, her lack of discipline had led to this. Her inability to follow Vera's instructions had killed Vera and had thwarted her plan to set them free. Vera sacrificed herself for nothing, and she was dead, while Umber was still there. What would happen tomorrow was anybody's guess.

Emma headed to the door. She couldn't stay there for another second without telling Taylor what she thought about her. God knew it was long overdue.

"Mother?"

Emma stopped without looking at Taylor. She wasn't sure she could look at her without hurting her.

"I have this."

Taylor offered her a white rectangular envelope like Emma had never seen before.

"Before…before Umber came, Vera gave me this. She said: 'Give it to your mother if I'm not here tomorrow.' I laughed. I asked, 'Where would you be?' She said: 'There's a world out there, Taylor, that you don't understand. Sadly, you will, someday. Please give this to your mother when nobody's watching. And don't talk to anybody about it.' I put it in my pocket. I thought it was just a crazy old lady talking. I guess not."

Emma took the large sealed envelope made of rough paper. It was off-white, handmade, and expensive. The front, in elegant cursive indigo ink, said: Dr. Emma Steele.

The back said: Vera.

Emma put it in her pocket and went to say goodbye to Vera, her best friend. They'd had a complicated relationship. In her effort to leave the world a better place by ridding it of evil, Vera had killed bad people. Many bad people. Emma had no choice but to tell the police. Instead of being worried, Vera was amused, as if she felt invincible. But she wasn't.

Vera, tiny Vera, brave Vera, stronger-than-steel Vera, was gone, and Emma's soul was raw with pain and loss. She bent the small cold body and hugged it. She tried to stop the tears burning her eyes, but she failed.

She kissed the marble-cold forehead, then turned to the door. The ER people, all of them, stood there, crying. Brenda. Judy. Kurt. Taylor. George. Amy. Vera's friends were presenting their respects to somebody who had done everything for her cause.

Vera's mission was to free the world from evil. She died trying.

Head down to hide her tears, Emma left, looking for privacy to mourn. She stopped at the boat ramp on her way home. The place was deserted now that the sun was going down. She sat under an old ash tree, leaned against its rough trunk, and grabbed the letter. She opened it with her index finger, ripping the envelope apart like she always did. She set the shreds in her lap and opened the sheet of paper inside it.

62

———————

VERA

*M*y dear Emma,

If you're reading this, it means I failed.

Not only did I fail, but I won't get up to try again. I'm sorry.

Meeting you has been one of the highlights of my life, and I've had a good one. You are unique, worthy, and valuable. It's so sad that you don't see it. Your crazy mother managed to screw your brain to the point that you feel worthless if you don't save the earth every day. I have news for you. That's not the way it works. If the planet got saved daily, it would a better place than it is. But I digress.

I'm sorry I failed to keep you, Taylor, and Hope safe. That was the last thing on my to-do list. Remember making the world a better place? I failed.

I know you'll manage, one way or another. You always do. Except that this guy, you need to take him out. For good. Like parasites taking over a garden, he won't quit unless you kill him. There's no shame, no jail, no law, nothing to stop him. You got in the way of his power quest. You prevented him from getting what he wanted. He'll destroy you, Taylor, Hope, and himself before he quits. You have no way out besides killing him.

I know you detest killing. I do, too, you know. I just wish those who get up in arms about killing the killers would stop eating meat and wearing leather. No cow, no pig, and no deer ever caused as much trouble as Umber. Still, they get killed and eaten every day. Those cows are nicer people than any of those I managed to curtail. Not a single cow murdered a baby, burned a dog alive, or abused their elderly parents. Still,

731

they get killed. They aren't human, I know. We seem to place an undue amount of respect on human life. Why? I don't know. Having opposable thumbs and walking on your hind legs shouldn't be more important than honesty, kindness, and truth.

I don't believe in sanctifying life for its own sake. If so, we shouldn't use exterminators, we shouldn't fish with bait, and we shouldn't slap mosquitoes. Life is worthy only when it brings value to the earth. I've never met a dog who didn't bring more value to the planet, in love, loyalty, and kindness, than Mr. Umber.

It breaks my heart to have failed. For your sake, I hope you never get to read this. I'd rather have your Detective Zagarian, the brownie thrower, putting me in jail.

Hah! We both know it won't happen.

I'm close now. My morning headaches and the numbness in my limbs tell me it's time. Fortunately, I can still think, walk, and play the part, even though I had a few more seizures, reminding me to hurry. I'd love to get you off the hook, but I'm afraid I won't. I'm getting weak and slow. I may not be good enough. I won't taint Taylor by telling her what I'm doing. She's been through enough. I'm sorry she has to be there, but I can't think of any other way to make it happen.

I value your friendship and your honesty. I wish I were here a little longer. I'd love to see you get over your hang-ups and become the confident, powerful woman you already are, but you don't know it. I wish I were here to see you bloom.

I know you're worried about Taylor. Don't be. She'll make it, even though she's had a hard trip, for many reasons. One is that she always tried to compete with you and she lost. It's not her fault. She's too young to understand that the world is big enough for all of us. We, the women of the world, don't have to compete with each other. We just have to do our best. She'll learn, and, someday, she'll be your best friend. She'll see Hope grow, and she'll learn what motherhood is all about.

Don't worry about the baby either. She'll be OK. Taylor learned from you, even though she doesn't know it, that we need to do anything to protect our young. She will. Taylor will be a force. Maybe even more than you, because she doesn't have your hang-ups. She feels worthy and entitled. Unlike you, she doesn't feel like a fraud.

That gets me to my last word. Emma, you're not a fraud. You're human, and you make mistakes. We all do. But you haven't gotten here by mistake. You carved your way to where you are by the skin of your teeth, as you Americans say, even though teeth have no skin. You are worthy. You've earned everything you have and many things you don't. I hope you get them someday.

You need to kill him, Emma. I know it's not your thing; you save people. But this one is not people; he's vermin. He's a threat to your people, to your family, to your life. You need to kill him. I tried to do it for you, and I failed. I hope you don't.

I love you. I hope you make it. If you don't, I'll be waiting for you on the other side. We'll drink vodka—OK, OK, Bordeaux—and we'll look down, hoping that Taylor succeeds where we failed.

I'm keeping my fingers crossed, Holubchyk. I'm rooting for you.

Forever your friend,

Vera

PS.

Everything in my fridge is OK. Except for the black tea. I wouldn't drink that, even though it's delicious. It tastes like liquorish and goes well with gin. That's in the freezer. Oh, and the cyanide brownies. I mean almond. I wouldn't eat those either.

Don't forget the clam juice rosemary cookies I made for Guinness. Tell her that I love her.

63

Emma folded the letter and put it in her pocket. She shook the dirt off her jeans, headed to the car, and climbed in, then took the letter out and read it again. She drove home.

Her beautiful black face frowned with worry, Guinness was waiting. Her unblinking golden eyes looked straight into Emma's soul. She put her paws on her shoulders and licked her face.

Emma hugged her. Guinness's kiss freed up the gate holding her pain inside. Sobs choked her. The air grew scarce. She couldn't draw enough air in because of all the sadness that needed to come out. She lay on the floor, holding Guinness. She cried and cried and cried.

Guinness watched.

Eventually, Emma's sobs slowed down. She rinsed her face with cold water and drank some from her hand to soothe her parched throat.

She came back. She sat on the sofa and read Guinness the letter.

Guinness listened to every word. When she heard her name, she cocked her head, like she always did when she heard something exciting.

"I can't do it," Emma said. "I know she's right. He's vermin. The world would be a better place without him. I can't do it. I can't kill a person in cold blood. I don't know what to do."

"Vodka," Guinness said. "To honor Vera. She said it helps with the hang-ups."

"Good point," Emma said. "But I don't know that we have any."

She went to check—nothing on the shelves. In the freezer, between Guinness's marrow bones and Emma's forgotten bone broth, was a bottle of Stolichnaya. Vera had brought it for her birthday.

"I know you prefer wine, my dear, but I don't know enough about wine to choose a good one. But I know vodka. This one is a good all-rounder. It's not Russian like you Americans think, it's from Latvia. When we occupied them, we adopted their vodka. That's how we roll.

"For us, Russians, vodka is our best friend and medication. We drink it when we're happy. We drink it when we're sad. We drink it when we can't sleep. We drink it when our teeth hurt. We drink it when we lose something, when we find something, and anytime in between. Someday you may find that it helps. Keep it in the freezer. You don't want to dilute it with ice. That melts into water and it ruins a perfectly good vodka. That's blasphemy. You don't want to do that."

The bottle frosted as Emma took it out. She poured some in a wine glass and sniffed it. It smelled like rubbing alcohol. She swirled it in the glass for the second nose, but the second nose was no better. She took a sip, and she shuddered.

"This isn't wine," she told Guinness.

Guinness agreed.

Emma took another sip. It tasted better. The liquid was colder than cold, but once inside, the freeze became a soothing heat, melting away the pain. The third sip went in smoothly. So did the fourth. After the second glass, the pain was still there, but it was farther away, like she watched somebody else's suffering instead of feeling her own.

She picked up the letter and reread it. She agreed with everything Vera said, but she couldn't do it. What would she do? She didn't know. She poured another vodka and lifted the glass.

"Love you, Vera. Miss you. Until we meet again."

Vera was right. Wine was pleasure and relief, but vodka was medicine.

64

———————

A few days later, Emma was walking down the quiet hospital hallways after another busy shift. She checked her watch. It was close to midnight, and the place was empty. That last septic patient had kept her hours late, but he made it, and now her shift was finally over. In half an hour, she'd be back home with Guinness and a glass of wine. She only needed to drop her white coat and grab her bag.

A sliver of light outlined her closed office door. *I must have left the light on,* Emma thought. She opened the door.

Umber, sitting in her chair, stared at her.

"You're here!" he said.

"I think that's my line," Emma answered, taking in the open drawers and the files covering the desk. "What are you looking for?"

"My file."

"Police took all that mattered."

"It never hurts to try," he shrugged, rocking in her desk chair.

Emma nodded.

"It doesn't. Until it does. Like if I call security."

"You won't."

736

"Why not?"

"Did you speak to Taylor?"

"More often than I'd like."

"Did she tell you what I want from you?"

"You want me to help you get your license back."

"Exactly. I need you to admit that you lied, you falsified documents, and your boyfriend Zagarian planted evidence to screw me."

Emma smiled and nodded.

"A piece of cake."

"Will you do it?

"No."

"Really?"

"Yes."

"Did Taylor tell you what happens if you don't?"

"You'll try to take Hope away from her."

"I'll take her."

"You won't."

"Yes, I will. Did Taylor tell you what she did?"

Emma's heart skipped a beat. There it was. Whatever that was, it was not good news.

"Why don't you tell me? I'm sure you can't wait."

"She went back to drinking and doing drugs. I have witnesses who can attest that she drove when she was too drunk to walk. She left the baby in the hospital and went to party, and I can prove it. She'll test positive for whatever they test her for. If I sue for the baby, I'll win."

Emma's heart sank. *I can't believe that Taylor is so stupid. Maybe he's just framing her. Either way, this won't look good in court. Even worse, she fucked herself up again, after it took weeks of rehab to get her sober. She looked like she was getting it together. Then Umber came back and it all went up in flames. Eric, the baby, college, all gone. She's back to drugs. After all the effort we all put into getting her clean. She, most of all. Vera was right. He'll destroy us all before he quits.*

"Give me some specifics. What exactly do you want me to do?"

"You'll need to give an affidavit that you lied. You persuaded your boyfriend to plant evidence. Then I expect you to come and testify to the same at the hearing."

"That means my career, my reputation, probably my freedom. Also, Zagarian's career and reputation and our relationship. In exchange for what?"

"I'll let Taylor have Hope." He laughed. "Doesn't that sound funny? I'll let Taylor have hope."

"How do I know you'll keep your word?"

"You'll have to take your chances. But you know I'm a man of my word. I wouldn't lie to you."

Emma laughed.

"As a bonus, I'll drop the complaint I filed against you with the State Board for Professional Medical Conduct. Remember the little matter of that professional conduct investigation? It was me. I arranged it with a friend of mine. I wanted to give you a taste of how it feels to have your license threatened. But I'll make it go away in exchange for your full cooperation."

"How generous of you," Emma said, crossing her arms to refrain from punching him.

"That's me," Umber said. "Always giving. Plus, I won't tell anyone you sent that old hag to kill me. She was pathetic, really, Emma. That wasn't up to your usual standards. Next time you should look for better minions."

Emma's anger went from black to red. His disparagement of Vera, who had died to protect her and Taylor, was more than she could tolerate. But she couldn't afford to lose her calm. She knew that those who lose their cool lose their fight. She pushed her anger in a far corner of her brain. She'd let it out in a minute. For now, she relaxed, smiled, and leaned back against the wall, sticking her hands in the pockets of her white coat.

He rocked in her desk chair, looking up at her above the low writing desk. Her bag, with her Mace spray and her other never-without stuff, was on her desk, behind him. *May as well be on the moon.*

"Well, me, with my old ladies. You, with your young girls. We all have things to be sorry about."

"I have nothing to be sorry about. I'm leaving my life exactly as I choose to."

"Except for your medical license."

"You'll help me with that."

"Tell me, Dick, why do you want your medical license back? Are you desperate to help humanity? Little ladies with broken hips? Old gentlemen with trouble breathing? No. You want your prescription rights, so you can write scripts for people who don't need them, and destroy them to make money. Which are you pining for? Your medical license or your drug-dealers license?

Umber's face darkened.

"I'm a doctor, just like you. I've gone through years of training and hard work for my title. I earned it. It's mine. Giving people pills to make them happy is just an extra. It helps with the Press Ganey. It also helps with the bottom line. Your daughter, and others like her, have expensive tastes. They like posh places, diamonds, escargot and good wines. On the other hand, desperate people need relief. They need somebody to understand their plight and help them. You, and those like you, see them as pests. You call them drug seekers and want nothing to do with them. To you, they're a scourge. They're beneath you. You despise and mistreat them, even though it was you and others like you who got them hooked in the first place. You're just a tease, Emma, while I'm here to help them and give them what they need. In exchange, I get the means to offer your daughter and others like her the sweet life they think they deserve. It's a win-win. Nobody gets hurt. Everybody benefits except for uptight people like you. You don't understand the future, Emma. You're a relic; you should be buried."

Emma smiled and shifted her weight from her right foot to her left, while her fingers explored her pockets. *If only I could get to my bag!*

"You know, Dick, I think I understand. You feel that you are providing a needed service to an underserved market. I get that. That's a businessman's point of view. There's a market out there, and you're ready to serve it and profit. But that has nothing to do with doctoring. Nothing. Doctors don't sell what the market wants. Doctors heal. When they can. You're not a doctor. You're a dealer. You don't need a license to serve the market; you just need to get fentanyl online and distribute it. Your license has nothing to do with it. The only reason you want a license is your self-esteem. Get over it. Admit that you're not a doctor, you're a drug dealer. Accept that, and move on. You'll be happier."

Umber's face froze.

He wants to think about himself as a healer, and a dealer, and the best thing since sliced bread. He can't accept that he's either one or the other. They're mutually exclusive.

He glared at her, choking with fury. "You don't understand. Your conventional, cluttered judgment blinds you. Your problem, not mine. So, are you going to do this?"

"Absolutely not."

"You'll lose Taylor and Hope, you know."

"We all lose things. You'll lose your hope of having your license back. As a matter of fact, I'll call security and police right now. Your fingerprints are all over the place. How do you think that'll play? I hope your wife doesn't mind you going back to jail. She may even be grateful!"

Umber exploded up, and the chair fell back with a clang. He shoved the writing desk toward Emma, throwing it forward. It crashed to the floor just inches from Emma's toes and blocked the door.

Emma jumped left to avoid it.

Umber leaped over it, charging her like a rabid wolf. His ocean-colored eyes were muddy with anger, and his perfect tan blotched as he reached for her throat.

Emma took a step back and hit the wall. There was nowhere else to go. She was trapped. As his hands closed around her throat, she lifted her right leg, kneeing him in the groin with all her strength. He groaned but didn't let go. She punched him in the stomach, then in the side, but to no avail. It was like hitting a brick wall.

"You know nothing about my wife. You know nothing about my life," he said, squeezing harder.

Emma's vision grayed, and her world started closing in as his thumbs pressed on her carotids, preventing the blood from reaching her brain. She struggled to unlock the steel fingers that were circling her throat, but she couldn't. Through the fog enveloping her mind, she saw the "Most Improved" trophy the ED had won. A wooden triangle on a metal base, its sharp peak pointing to the sky, it sat on her shelf, ever useless. She grabbed it with her left hand, then crushed it on top of his head with all her strength.

Something cracked—the trophy, most likely. Umber's skull must be stronger than that. The hands around her throat softened, and he faltered, ready to fall. Emma took a long, delightful breath and stuck her hands in her pockets, looking for a weapon. Nothing but the scalpel. It had been there for ages, just in case. Its time had come.

No. I can't kill him. That's not what I do.

He rallied and came back, groaning. His body crushed Emma against the wall, and something cracked as her head struck the shelf. Her stomach turned, and she got dizzy. She took a deep breath.

A sudden sting burned her left thigh. This time, she knew what it was.

He injected something in me. Again. Ketamine, if I'm lucky. Sux, if I'm not. Either way, I have less than three minutes. In three minutes, I'll be either unconscious or dead. This is it.

Her right hand went back to her pocket and grabbed the scalpel again. Blindly, she removed its cover and pushed the blade open with her thumb. Maybe. She didn't know for sure since she couldn't see it. The only thing she could see was Umber, strangling her. In his muddy eyes, she could see how the light was fading in hers.

I may not have three minutes, after all. It's time.

She had to make sure that the scalpel was open. There was only one way to check. She twisted her wrist inward and stabbed herself in the thigh. The jolt of searing pain spreading through her leg told her that the scalpel was open. She faltered. She'd have fallen if he didn't hold her by her throat. Umber felt her soften. He smiled. Looking in her eyes, he tightened his hands around her throat.

She brought up her right hand. She had to flex it hard to get it between them. A ray of light reflected off the blade. In one clean, smooth, desperate move, she slashed, left to right, through the well-groomed skin of his throat.

The world stood still. Blood splashed her face and air whooshed. Her eyes closed to keep his blood out, and the hands around her throat loosened. As she opened her mouth to breathe, blood gushed in, hot and salty. She realized it wasn't hers, and her stomach churned.

They crushed to the ground together, his weight, like lead, on top of her, cutting her breath. She tried to push him away. Too heavy. She tried again.

Her brain flashed into a swirl of colors. Bright colors were spiraling around her, sucking her in. She spun faster and faster through a tunnel of rainbows, then she soared, becoming the colors. She flew, higher and higher, until she disappeared.

65

Emma opened her eyes, looking into a popcorn ceiling. She lifted her head to see that she was lying on a stretcher in a treatment room.

It was déjà vu all over again. She'd been there before.

She tried to remember what had happened. She went to her office to find Umber there. They talked. She baited him, and he attacked her. They fought. Then what?

She wasn't sure. But from the fact that she was hurting everywhere, she must be alive. How about Umber? She didn't know. Or care.

The door opened, and George came in. He bent over to hug her and patted her on her shoulder.

"Good work, Emma."

"I guess I'm still alive?"

George laughed.

"Very much so. How do you feel?"

She shrugged, and that hurt. "Like I wish I was dead."

"You were close. You know what you did?"

Emma shuddered. That was a loaded question.

"No."

"You killed Umber."

Vera would approve.

"Dead?"

George laughed.

"You never go halfway, Emma. He's as dead as they get."

"I didn't expect that."

"Well. You need to expect more from yourself, you know. You never under-deliver."

Emma nodded.

"Thanks, George. Can I go home now?"

"Half an hour or so, just to make sure you're safe. Then the police want to speak to you."

A wave of nausea hit her. She took a deep breath, and George handed her a blue emesis bag.

"Ketamine?"

"Of course. What else?"

"Sux."

"He didn't want to kill you, Emma. He needed you alive."

Emma nodded. As she fell asleep, she thought about Vera.

"You need to kill him, Emma. There is no other way."

I did.

66

Sitting in her father's living room, Taylor was chatting with Margret when her phone rang. It was the hospital, telling her that Hope was ready to go home. Taylor stood, her heart pounding, her hands shaking.

"These people are crazy. They can't give me the baby! I don't know what to do with her or how to care for her. That's insane!"

"She'll be all right," Margret said. "We all had to learn sometime. You will too."

"But…but she's fragile. And so small! I don't know how to care for a baby!"

Margret laughed. "You'll learn like we did."

Panic flooded Taylor, and she choked with fear.

"I can't! I'm too afraid."

Margret shrugged.

"Then you give her to the Crumps. I'm sure they can deal with her."

Taylor glared at her.

"I can't give away my baby!"

"Then learn to care for her," Margret said, then picked up her book and started reading.

Taylor studied her grandmother, wondering what had happened to her. She had aged. Deep lines marred her delicate face, and her serene smile had all but disappeared. Even worse, she didn't seem to care much about Taylor anymore. Margret had always been kind and loving, but Vera's death changed her. Vera's death changed all of them. Marget had even started talking like Vera, and Taylor didn't like that. Straight talk looked good on Vera, but it was harsh on Margret, and Taylor missed her polite, soft-spoken, Southern lady grandmother.

"Are you mad at me, Grandma?"

Margret glanced at her over her book.

"Maybe. Yes, I think I am."

"Why?"

Margret shrugged.

"I'm not sure. I think it's time for you to act like an adult. We all treated you as if you're still a child. We spoiled you, we covered for you, and we didn't hold you responsible for what you did. That was a mistake. It's high time for you to grow up."

Taylor's jaw fell. She'd never heard her grandmother speak to her like that.

"What happened to Vera, to your mother, to Eric, and even to Umber, is to some degree your fault. It's high time you understood that actions have consequences. Some are good, some are bad. Baby Hope is one of them. Eric's distress is another. You need to take responsibility for your actions. The world is not there to clean up after you."

Taylor's eyes burned. Tears came.

"What do you want me to do, Grandma?"

"Stop complaining. Learn to take care of Hope, or give her away. Apologize to Eric. And more than anything, apologize to your mother."

"Why my mother?"

"She's lost her best friend because of you. She almost died because of you. Again. She had to kill Umber because of you. And you dare ask?"

Margret stood up and left without looking back.

67

August left. September took over, with shorter days, cooler mornings, and a splash of color in the woods. The sun was still up as Taylor rang Eric's doorbell, holding Hope to her chest in her baby carrier. She didn't need to, she still had a key, but she didn't want to ambush him.

"Yes?"

"Taylor."

He buzzed to let them in. Taylor climbed the two flights of creaky stairs she knew so well. Eric was waiting at the door. He looked faded and shrunk like he'd been left in the sun for too long. The separation hadn't done much for him. *Unless it's not the separation, but our relationship,* Taylor thought.

"Hi, Eric," she said, shifting her weight from her right to her left.

"Hi."

Taylor stood, holding the baby. She looked at the sofa.

Eric didn't invite her to sit.

"We just stopped to say hi."

Eric nodded, looking at her with hollow eyes.

"I'm sorry about what happened, Eric. I didn't know it was going to go this way."

"Neither did I."

Taylor took a deep breath. "I love you, Eric. I know it's not the kind of love you want. Sadly, we can't choose who we love. I just stopped by to say thanks. We love you. I thought you'd like to see baby Hope. I know you care about her."

"Thanks, Taylor. I'm sure it wasn't easy."

Eric bent over baby Hope, studying her rounded cheeks and the dark eyelashes shadowing them. He touched her silky red hair.

She opened her eyes. She looked straight into his, and she smiled.

Eric smiled back.

"She's beautiful. I wish you and her all the best."

"Thanks. Keep in touch, will you?"

Eric shrugged.

"Maybe later. Right now, I need to get myself together. I need to remember who I am and why I'm here."

Taylor nodded. She understood.

68

———————

The day was still young as Margret dragged her bag out to the porch. The sun was barely up, gilding the white-capped mountains far away. *Snow already. Winter is coming. Soon. It's going to be a long one,* Margret thought.

She sat in the rocker, drinking her tea and waiting for her taxi.

Amber came out. She was perfectly groomed and beautiful as always, but she too had aged. Her relaxed confidence and entitlement were gone, leaving her looking tired and vulnerable.

"Are you leaving, Margret?"

Margret nodded. "It was time to let you guys be by yourselves."

Amber shrugged. With Taylor and her baby in the house, being by themselves didn't quite happen.

"I have a huge favor to ask," Amber said. "We're…we're thinking about going away for a week. Can you please stay and look after the children?

Margret's eyes widened. Things had been rough in the house lately. Victor and Amber didn't speak to each other unless they had to. Their marriage was on the rocks. Victor was on call every other night. Margret was so tired of the perpetual tension that she'd decided to leave. They had said goodbye last night. Now, this.

"Victor and I talked last night. We agreed to take some time together and try to rebuild our marriage. For the sake of the kids. And…and ourselves."

Margret felt sorry for Amber.

"Of course. I'll be happy to."

Amber smiled. For once, it was a real smile, bringing up the new lines around her eyes.

"Thank you, Margret."

"Where are you going?" *The Caribbean, probably, or Southern France. A place with beaches and shopping, no doubt.*

"Not too far. We're going hiking in the Adirondacks and maybe kayaking too. I booked us a cabin in the mountains. Victor would like to try hiking Marcy and Algonquin again. He hasn't done it in twenty years."

"I didn't know you hiked!"

"I don't. But I can learn."

Amber was doing her best to rebuild their marriage. To do that, they had to find something in common beyond the kids. Margret hoped for the best.

"Good luck, Amber."

69

———————

Apologizing to her mother was even harder than apologizing to Eric. There was so much to apologize for, Taylor didn't even know where to start. Her relationship with her mother had always been challenging. Until Taylor's pregnancy, when she had a change of heart and they could finally relate like two loving adults. Then Umber came back, and Taylor threw it all away. Vera died. And Emma had to rescue her once more. How do you apologize for all that?

She'd brought a bottle of Brunello de Montalcino, a wine that Emma loved but couldn't often afford, and a bouquet of yellow roses.

Emma smiled when she saw the flowers. She smiled even wider when she saw the wine.

She opened the bottle and poured them each a glass. She scrutinized it, then sniffed it, like she always did, then took a sip. She smiled.

"That's lovely. Thank you, Taylor. I haven't had this in months."

Taylor knew precisely how long it had been. She had brought a bottle just like this one the last time her mother had saved her ass.

Guinness lay on the floor, watching them. Taylor played with her soft ears, and Guinness sighed with pleasure.

"I'm sorry," Taylor said.

"I know." Emma took another sip of wine.

Out of words, Taylor looked around for something to say. She noticed a half-packed bag on the bedroom floor.

"What's happening?"

"I'm leaving," Emma said.

"Where?" Taylor asked.

"South America to start. New Zealand. Australia. Then we'll see."

"How long will you be gone?"

"I don't know."

"How about your work?"

"I quit."

"You quit?"

"Yes."

"Why?"

Emma shrugged. "I've been here forever. It's time for a change."

"Are you kidding?"

"No."

"What will you do?"

"I took an assignment as a cruise ship doctor."

"Are you serious?"

"Of course."

Taylor's jaw dropped. She didn't expect this, her mother leaving. She'd dreamed about this for years, hoping Emma would go away, leaving her free of scrutiny, expectations, and judgment. Now she was, and it was unsettling.

"Why?"

"For many reasons. I can't go back to my office, even though they cleaned Umber's blood. That night will stay with me forever. I'm not ready to revisit it yet. You need to grow, and you can't grow while I'm here, watching you. You'll have to find your own conscience."

"How about you?"

"I also need to grow. I need to explore places I've never seen, try things I've never done. You think I'm too old. You may be right. But I'm finally ready to live my life like I never did before. That's something I learned from Vera. She died with no regrets. If I died tomorrow, I would have nothing but regrets. I need to live my life now."

Taylor shook her head.

"I can't believe this!"

Emma shrugged. "You'll get over it. We weren't together much anyhow."

She drained the glass and poured another.

"Taylor, I will leave Guinness with you. She'll take good care of you and Hope. It breaks my heart to leave her behind, but I can't take her with me. I know you'll do your best for her. If you can't care for her, let Margret have her."

Taylor blushed. That hurt, but she knew she deserved it.

She waited for her mother to tell her to give baby Hope to the Crumps if she couldn't care for her, but she didn't. For that, Taylor was thankful.

70

Margret sat on the wooden bench under the oleander, where they had buried Vera's ashes. She had wanted her body to feed her beloved garden. Margret poured frozen Stolichnaya in two crystal glasses.

"*Nasdrovnie,*" she said, knocking them together.

Vera's picture, dressed in red with a yellow lei of marigolds around her neck, her hair messed up by the wind, smiled from the other side of the bench.

The Indian summer had been generous this year, and the evening was soft and golden in Vera's garden. The luxurious plant aromas mingled with the bitter, crisp fragrance of dead leaves.

"I miss you, Vera," Margret said. She drained the glass, and she shuddered. "With drinks like this, no wonder you had no appetite for bullshit."

She placed the empty glass in front of Vera's picture and took the full one.

The lei of marigolds around Vera's neck absorbed the last rays of sun.

"You were right."

Vera's smile got wider.

"Yes, I know you know, but still. How about a little modesty?"

She drained the other glass and shuddered again. She poured more vodka.

"Victor and Amber came back. They're better than they've ever been. She took to hiking and biking with him. He's making an effort to notice her hair and her new dresses. He's so clueless that he compliments her on her old dresses, but she knows he's only trying to please her. They're doing good. So are the girls, all four of them. Thelma and Louise are slowing down a little. They're almost 15, older than me in dog years, but they're still happy and kicking."

She took another sip of vodka.

"Taylor started college. She's going premed; she wants to be a doctor like her father. Sheila helps her look after the baby. Hope is growing like a weed, surrounded by love and well cared for. Taylor went back to Eric, but he said no. Smart boy. I think that did her good. She's learning some limits. She's finding that there's no one to catch her if she falls. You were right. Emma needed to go."

She drained the next glass. Vera's smile was getting blurry.

"I got an email from Emma. She enjoys traveling, even though she's on-call 24/7, and the wine on the ship is not up to her usual standards. The Bordeaux is pathetic, she says, so she has to stick with the Chilean."

The sun went down, and it got chilly. Margret pulled her jacket closer around her and took another sip.

"She says Zagarian is flying to meet her in Tasmania for a few days. That man's going a long way for her. She's worth it. I hope she sees that too, someday. Like you said, we all know it, except for her."

A gust of wind shook the trees, and a rain of acacia leaves fell like tears on Vera's picture.

Margret picked up the picture and headed inside.

She remembered something. She stared at the picture again.

"Thank you for the house and the garden, Vera. I'm happy to be here, near them, and near you. You were right. I didn't want a husband, not even one without hearing aids. I didn't want to be alone. Thanks to you, I'm here, with all those I love. I'll take care of everything the best I can, and leave them to Hope, as you asked. She needs to be independent of Taylor, even though Taylor has come a long way."

Margret went inside and turned on the lights. It was five o'clock in San Francisco.

71

GUINNESS

I *t's dark. The girls are asleep.*

She's not.

I can see her, even though she's far away.

She's alone.

I call her. "Come back, Shaman. I miss you."

She hears me. She smiles at me through the long darkness.

She'll be back.

I know.

She'll be back.

AFTERWORD

Dear Reader,

Thank you for reading OVERDOSE, MERCY and POISON. I hope you enjoyed them. If you did, check out RadaJones.com for updates, freebies, and to connect. I'd love to hear from you.

If you loved Guinness, check out her memoir, BECOMING K-9. It's the story of a feisty puppy becoming a fierce K-9, written in her own words. There's a sample following.

And thanks for giving me, Emma and the gang your precious time. See you soon for their cruising adventures.

Rada

BECOMING K-9: AN EXCERPT

Who knew training humans was so hard? You'd wonder why. They aren't that stupid. It takes them a while, but they eventually learn when you want out, you're hungry or you're thirsty. They can even talk to each other by making noise with their tongue. How weird is that? Even my brother Blue, who's the slowest of us all, knows that the tongue is for lapping water and panting to cool down.

Mom cocked her head and licked my nose.

"That's the best they can do, dear. They have no tails, their ears don't move, and most don't even have enough fur to raise their hackles. No wonder they're confused and need us to guide them. And that's what we do; that's our life's work. But we need to choose them carefully."

Mom was on her sixth litter and very wise. Beautiful, too, with her long muzzle, amber eyes, and smooth, shiny fur, all black but for her golden legs and loving pink tongue.

She glanced at Yellow, who chased his tail instead of paying attention, and growled. He hung his head and sat in line with the rest of us to listen.

It was a lovely summer day as Mom homeschooled us in Jones's front yard. The warm wind tickled my nose. I bit it, but I caught nothing. I tried again, but Mother threw me a side glance, so I closed my mouth and sat still.

"Boys and girls, today's the day. People will come to check you out and choose which one to take home. They don't know it, but it doesn't work that way.

You choose your humans, but choose them wisely. Sniff them all, then pick the ones that smell like food if you want a good life. You may sometimes get bacon, maybe even grapes. Humans say dogs don't eat grapes, but that's poppycock. They just want to keep them for themselves. My grandma was a pure-bred Alsatian, and she loved Riesling. I never had Riesling, but Concord isn't bad."

A shiny strip of drool dripped from Mom's mouth. She licked it off and inspected us. We were seven: three boys and four girls. But that doesn't much matter when you're just ten weeks old. The only difference is how you pee. The boys don't know how to squat so they need something to lift their leg to, like a bush or a mailbox. How stupid!

"Why don't you just lift your leg, if that's what you need to do? What does the bush have to do with anything?"

Mom bristled.

"Leave them alone, Red."

I tried, but it was hard. I was the runt of the litter, so I had to prove myself all the time. Mom said I had a Napoleonic complex.

"What's that?"

"It's when you're the smallest, so you have to be meaner to show them that size doesn't matter."

I told you Mom is brilliant. She came all the way from Germany when she was just a pup. Our human, Jones, has two passions: German shepherds and history. Mom was his first German shepherd, and he spent lots of time teaching her things most dogs never heard about.

He still does, even now that she's old. He sits in his recliner and reads to her as she lays by the fireplace. Sometimes I listen in. There was a story about a dude named Hitler. Not a nice guy, but for loving German shepherds. Another one about that short guy Napoleon who tried to conquer the world while wearing funny hats. And one about some place called Afghanistan.

"That's a bad war, Maddie," Jones said, scratching the four white hairs in his beard. "Those Taliban, they are not nice people."

He calls her Maddie, but her real name is Madeline Rose Kahn Van Jones. He is Jones. The Van is for Van Gogh, some orange dude who got so mad he bit off his own ear. The rest is just for show, since people pay more for dogs with long names; they call that a pedigree. Mom's pedigree is longer than her tail.

As always, Mom was right. People came to see us, and they brought their spouses, their kids, and even their dogs to check us out and choose which one to get. Like, really? Jones said that only one out of twenty German shepherd owners is smarter than his dog. I don't believe it. I bet he fudged the numbers to feel better. You think you own a dog? Who feeds who? Who cleans after who? Who does the work, everything but making decisions? You, human, in case you didn't know it. You don't buy a dog; you hire supervision. But I digress.

My littermates and I wore colored collars so humans could tell us apart. There was no need, really, since we were all different, but humans couldn't see it. What color did I wear? Red, of course. I was small, but I was the queen of the litter, whether the others liked it or not.

A fat man in a Hawaiian shirt stopped to stare at me. He called his female.

"Look at this red one! Isn't he cute?"

She hobbled closer, leaning on her crooked stick. I love sticks, so I tried to take it. She didn't want to let go, but I insisted. They laughed.

"Let's get him."

Jones cleared his throat.

"Red is lovely, indeed, but she's a very active little person who needs a lot of attention. How much time do you plan to work with her every day?"

"Work with her?"

"Yes. Walk her, train her, and play with her."

They stared at him like he'd lost his marbles. He smiled.

"May I recommend Brown here? He's lovely, easygoing, and eager to please. He'll be happy to lay on the sofa watching TV. Or Miss Green? She's a polite little lady who gets along with everyone and never disappoints."

Brown left. So did Green, Yellow, and even White, while I stayed, waiting for my forever home.

"Take it easy, Red dear," Mother said when there were only two of us left—Black and me. "You need to soften up a bit; otherwise, you'll be left without a family. People look for easygoing dogs to fit into their lives, not for somebody to take charge. Though maybe they should, really, but they aren't smart enough to know that."

Her German accent made her words feel harsh. Have you ever listened to Germans? It's like they're constipated while they also have a cold. They keep clearing their throats, so their words come out like bullets from a machine gun. I don't speak German, but I love watching old war movies with Jones.

"What do you mean, Mom? What should I do?"

"Lick their hands, sweetheart. Wrap yourself around their feet and stare at them like they hung the moon."

"Are you serious?"

"Of course."

"But they're stupid!"

"Come on, Red, don't be so judgmental. You're just a pup, and you have so much to learn. A nice family will give you a good life. They'll love you, play with you, and spoil you. Knowing you have a good, safe home will lift a weight off my soul."

You think I listened? You've got to be kidding.

That's how I ended up in the military.